Praise for *My Name Is Resolute*

"A novel that should be absorbed and savored as much for the lovely, tensile line of its prose as for its well-drawn cast of characters."

—Steve Donoghue, *Open Letters Monthly*

"The author convincingly conveys a pivotal time in American history and provides a rewarding reading experience. A fitting story about resiliency, ingenuity, and heroism."

—*Kirkus Reviews*

"Turner has drawn a character whose trials, loves, losses, and achievements Turner fans will happily follow."

—*Tucson Weekly*

"Astonishing, compelling, heartfelt."

—Kathleen Kent, author of *The Heretic's Daughter*

"Fiercely independent, stubborn, and sometimes endearingly naïve, Resolute is one of those magical, insistent characters who lives on in your head and your heart long past the final page. Nancy Turner is one of my favorite storytellers: I'm always hooked from her first sentence and sorry to reach the last. In *My Name Is Resolute,* she brings colonial America to life, endowing Resolute with her signature mix of humor, spunk, courage, common sense, and passion. From pirate attacks and Indian abduction to the shuttling of a loom, Turner is equally marvelous with larger-than-life heroics and the quiet joys of hearth and home. Sarah Prine has a worthy "sister" at last—this book was totally worth the wait!"   —Jennifer Lee Carrell, author of *Interred with Their Bones* and *Haunt Me Still*

Praise for *Sarah's Quilt*

"A sensitive, vibrant story about the strength of love and family . . . Reminiscent of Larry McMurtry's *Lonesome Dove*."   —*The Denver Post*

"Hard times, danger, love, well-defined characters, and a strong sense of place all merge to form the heart of this novel."   —*The Dallas Morning News*

"Action-packed."   —*Tucson Guide*

Praise for *These Is My Words*

"Incredibly vivid and real."

—Rosamunde Pilcher, author of *The Shell Seekers*

"I read it with great delight. . . . says more about America than *Gone with the Wind,* and up there with *To Kill a Mockingbird.* Moving, funny, and rings very true." —Mary Stewart, author of *The Crystal Cave*

"Readers who enjoyed Sandra Dallas's *Diary of Mattie Spenser* are sure to love this one." —*Booklist*

"Readers come to admire Sarah, to share her many losses and rare triumphs. If even half these events are true, she was an amazing woman."

—*Library Journal*

"A compelling portrait of an enduring love, the rough old West, and a memorable pioneer." —*Publishers Weekly*

"A lushly satisfying romance, period-authentic, with true-grit pioneering."

—*Kirkus Reviews*

"Incredibly vivid and real and almost as though everything has been found, complete in a box somewhere." —*The Washington Post*

"Nancy Turner has spun a frontier novel that teeters on the fine edge of truth and fiction." —*The Arizona Republic*

"Belongs on your must-read list. Nancy E. Turner approaches the fine qualities of Larry McMurtry's Pulitzer-winning *Lonesome Dove* . . . unforgettable characters, a grand sweep of history, adventure, love, and emotion so real that you feel it. *These Is My Words* is a book not to miss."

—*Omaha World-Herald*

My Name Is Resolute

My Name Is Resolute

NANCY E. TURNER

THOMAS DUNNE BOOKS
ST. MARTIN'S GRIFFIN
NEW YORK

This is a work of fiction. All of the characters, organizations, and events portrayed in this novel are either products of the author's imagination or are used fictitiously.

THOMAS DUNNE BOOKS.
An imprint of St. Martin's Press.

MY NAME IS RESOLUTE. Copyright © 2014 by Nancy E. Turner. All rights reserved. Printed in the United States of America. For information, address St. Martin's Press, 175 Fifth Avenue, New York, N.Y. 10010.

www.thomasdunnebooks.com
www.stmartins.com

Designed by Omar Chapa

The Library of Congress has cataloged the hardcover edition as follows:

Turner, Nancy E., 1953–
    My name is Resolute : a novel / Nancy E. Turner. — First Edition.
        p. cm.
    ISBN 978-1-250-03659-9 (hardcover)
    ISBN 978-1-250-03658-2 (e-book)
    1. Young women—Fiction.   2. United States—History—Revolution,
1775–1783—Fiction.   I. Title.
    PS3570.U725M9 2014
    813'.54—dc23   2013031729

ISBN 978-1-250-06097-6 (trade paperback)

St. Martin's Griffin books may be purchased for educational, business, or promotional use. For information on bulk purchases, please contact the Macmillan Corporate and Premium Sales Department at 1-800-221-7945, extension 5442, or write to specialmarkets@macmillan.com.

10 9 8 7 6 5 4 3

This book is dedicated to Jackson Bracht,

to Martin Richard, Krystle Campbell, Lu Lingzi, and Officer Sean Collier,
killed in the second Boston Massacre, April 15, 2013,

and to all, whether their acts be great or small, who ever have stood or ever
shall stand fast in the face of tyranny and injustice.

ACKNOWLEDGMENTS

Were it not for the encouragement from, patient rereading by, and good advice of brilliant writers and beautiful friends Bonnie Marson and Jennifer Lee Carrell, I would never have heard Resolute tell me her story as you find it here. My agent, the late John A. Ware, provided helpful feedback along the way, along with a line-by-line check as one of his last acts. My husband, John, went with me through the ups and downs of creating such a lengthy work, supporting every decision along the way, trudging the hills of Boston and the vales of New England, carrying the apple cider doughnuts necessary for intensive research. And, of course, my great thanks and appreciation go to Thomas Dunne of Thomas Dunne Books; my editor, Marcia Markland; her assistant, Kat Brzozowski; and copy editor Ragnhild Hagen for attention to detail above and beyond the call of duty. For the first time ever, I have included a bibliography at the end of a novel. It is not to be taken lightly, for those wonderful authors have recorded in their works much that is both fascinating and largely forgotten, and which should be read and relished as much as any fictional account of the world past.

Proclamation regarding linen and woolen goods . . .
of use to the enemy:

*I am informed there are large quantities of goods . . . which, if in
the possession of the rebels, would enable them to carry on the
war.*

*And, whereas I have given notice to all loyal inhabitants to
remove such goods from hence, and all who do not remove them,
or deliver them to your care,
will be considered abettors of the rebels.*

*You are hereby authorized and required to take into your
possession all such goods as answer this description . . . And, you
are to make inquiry if any such goods be secreted in stores, and
you are to seize all . . .*

—General William Howe, Commander in Chief of the British
   Army in America, March 10, 1776

My Name Is Resolute

CHAPTER 1

Two Crowns Plantation, Jamaica—September 30, 1729,
by the old reckoning

Never step over a lighted candle. If you do, the flame she rise and the Shush-shush come and take you. *Gumboo.* I used to laugh when my favorite person on this earth, Old Poe, furrowed her brow and whispered that like a sing-song rhyme, then put her finger against her lips, saying, "Hush, now, child. Don' tease de devil, now, child." When I heard Ma say it just now across the supper table, all fine and glowing with porcelain and crystal, and me nowhere near a candle other than those high above in the chandelier, it made me run cold, deep in my bones. There were few things in the life of a young girl wearing her first long skirts more treacherous than a candle on the floor. I held a picture I had drawn in India ink on heavy paper. A drip had formed at the bottom edge, pulling the shoe on one of the figures to un-natural length. My eyes went from my drawing to Ma, to Uncle Rafe. He had just invited me to sit upon his knee and show it to him.

My sister Patience had called me to dinner many minutes earlier and I had ignored her summons to put some finishing touches on it that were now ruining the picture. It depicted two little girls, one white, one black, holding hands and running across the white-sand beach. Their faces smiled quite cunningly, I thought. The figure of my dear Allsy in the picture held up an apple, precious fruit shipped here from far away, the last apple we shared, the danger of it so like one of my favorite stories in which a princess sleeps for a thousand years after a single bite. I had drawn crowns over Allsy's and my heads, as if she and I were princesses.

Uncle Rafe slammed his tankard of rum on the table boards, and said, "Aye. A girl's petticoats catch fire soon enough. Tender as tinder." He laughed and winked at Ma, his face all bright and sweating in a way that made me push his cup and plate over into his lap. I stuck out my chin, thinking old Rafe did not know aught about a fiery petticoat. Uncle Rafe roared and hollered, "God's balls!"

I may have been ten years old but I knew Rafe was not my real uncle, and that Pa's voice got thin and Ma's hands trembled when he was in the house. I stood and stuck out my tongue just as Pa came into the dining room, buttoning his vest, with Patience and our brother, August, following him. He looked from Uncle Rafe to Ma and to the mess on Rafe's pants and me standing there with hellfire in my eyes.

I am old, now, wizened, some might say. I will tell you how I came to *this* place from that potent evening so long ago and so far across the oceans. The day after I was born my parents named me Resolute. Pa said it gave me an aspect of solemnity and perseverance, which are pretty things for a child with a sanguine humor. It was a good name for a girl, Ma always added, and there was nothing wrong with a girl being confident and ruddy. A boy could grow to "make a name for himself," but a girl needed a special one from birth.

I knew all about fire. I had been playing with Allsy when we were both but six years old and my family had been on the West Indies island of Jamaica for the same six years. Allsy and I had been hiding in the priest's hole, up the steps behind the fireplace. I brought two cakes and an apple for us to share and she carried a burning candle, placing it on the floor. I jumped over it. As I did, my petticoats made the flame bob and nearly go out. The edge of my skirt got a brown place and we held it between us, curious, as the spot grew and grew. A yellow tongue of flame suddenly burst from it, licked at us and burned my fingers. Allsy slapped her hands upon it and crushed out the flame. She winced, but made no sound; putting her hands over her mouth, she made the sign of the cross as long black shadows of us spun around in the stair tower like ghosts dancing.

We held our breaths. We laughed. Hand in hand, we climbed up to the widow's walk on the highest part of the house, where we could see far and wide across the ocean. In the distance, storms sometimes carried on all day, lightning dancing upon the water against a backdrop of gray roiling clouds like a silent mummer's play, never a stray wind ruffling our hair. We watched, hoping for the rise of a mast that might mean cloth or shoes or more of Ma's precious goblets made of real glass. After we got tired of mocking seagulls squealing at each other, we shared a cake and took turns eating the apple.

I had stepped over a candle and nothing had happened. I thought we were safe. But five days later, I took fever. The sixth day, Allsy did, too. The Shush-shush, Old Poe's name for the devil or death or something that you must not say out loud, something bad and haunted, he came whilst I lay afevered. I retched and I itched, covered with smallpox. I cried and Ma brought cold rags for my head, and after two weeks I got up. Allsy must have been too close to me in that stairway. As I jumped over that lit candle, the old devil reached for me and caught Allsy. While I was too sick to know, Pa and Old Poe wrapped her in white gauze and laid my heart's friend in a grave.

Old Poe caught it and died, too, after two days of sickness. Cost Pa £15 to replace her. That meant nothing to me. Talk of pounds and crowns and sixpence went on all the time in Pa's office at the side of the good parlor. What mattered to me was that Old Poe knew how to make a lap for me to sit upon, knew more stories than I could ever remember—some of them including two fine wee girls just like Allsy and me—and knew how to wrap a sore finger with potash and brown paper and kisses.

I never told Ma or Pa that it was my fault Allsy died. I had escaped Old Scratch's claws. Ma said it is because I have something special to do. What is a girl going to do? Embroidery and arithmetic, that's what I get. I wondered someday if the devil might wake up and see he got the wrong girl, what will happen then?

All my days I had heard things about England where Pa was born. Even more about Scotland, Ma's homeland, the two of them united into one country by that time. I knew about how my brother, August, used to wait with Pa until a dark night and watch the farmers light gorse when the village had a festival. How Patience, my only sister and ten years older than I, had loved the son of a lord, a lord who faithfully waited on Anne the Queen's favor. Anne was a Stuart and a Tory through and through, and our father, being of both Tudor and Plantagenet lines with Radclyffe blood thrown in, made Patience a politically unsuitable bride for his son. So, on recommendation of Sarah, Duchess of Marlborough, Her Highness and His Lordship found that the Crown was in great need of Pa to mind a plantation in the Indies.

This is where I was born and all around us is all I have ever known, fields of sugarcane and coffee, slaves to tend the cane fields, and then, wearing starched white linen, to bring in the roast chicken at dinner, the smell of the sea and the soil and the perfume of flowers. Throughout the night, breezes off the mountains brought the rhythm of drums from the slave quarters. Sometimes if I kept quite still I heard singing. I imagined their happy world filled with music. I wished I could join them.

By day I did my lessons in the schoolroom on the top floor where the window blinds were all that kept a girl from dreaming of a home she had never known beyond the sea, for the wind off the ocean seemed to pine for England, to mourn her like a lost promise, the way Patience weeps at night for her lost love and lost future marriage. I pressed her to tell me how she could have threatened the son of a lord with marriage if she herself had been but ten years old. She told me that the path between our house and his was a common one, but a hedge had grown at a certain shady secluded point where they had used to meet together and play. He was two years older—a vision of manliness, she said—though I pictured a boy of twelve being spindle-legged and having great flopping feet. Such keen friends they had become that they spoke to each other of promises and everlasting love, and when he told his father, that was that. She kept a lock of his hair, near black as pitch, in a box along with a little paper he had written upon with their names entwined by something rather like a crow carrying a twig although Patience says it is a dove holding a ribbon.

For me a land called England was but a magical tale of far away and long ago. My own ma and pa would tell me fancy tales they must have fashioned in their own minds about some kingdom of gold and crowns and cold such as I could never imagine, a land without mountains, without snakes or cane fields. I did not believe in those things. To me, it was make-believe just like the fairy folk, brownies, and selkies. For myself, I believe in God and a few saints and of course duppies, the sprites that live here. Pa would laugh and say treacle ran in my veins.

Uncle Rafe stood, his back to the hearth and hellfire as big as mine in his eyes. Pa looked to Patience and said, "Daughter, fetch Uncle a new plate. Son," he said to August, "bring the tobacco box."

"But, sir," August said, and Pa raised his hand. He sat and opened his hands toward Rafe. Rough, broad hands that knew work. As if that were his only apology for a wayward bairn like me. After that Pa offered Rafe his new pipe and filled it himself with his best tobacco. Pa sent me to bed. As I left the room I made note that Uncle's wig was askew and smelled bad. Pa wore no periwig, just tied his hair in a lock at the back of his neck. Boiling-sugarcane odors clung to Pa like a coat. I had thought I loathed the smell of cane, but any horse in the barn smelled better than Uncle Rafe and I knew I loved the smell of Pa.

"Pa?" I whispered.

Pa made a squint sidelong at me. A string of thought came unspoken from his face, saying, "Try to obey this time," and, "I will explain later," mixed with, "You are two shakes away from getting a well-deserved walloping, girl." So I climbed the stairs to my room and listened from the doorway.

Rafe's voice grew loud as if he meant me to hear, saying, "Cocky little oyster. That'n needs to feel a boot. I'd give her a taste of Rafe MacAlister's hobnails."

"She is not grown. We will discipline her, sir," Ma said.

The air grew tight with silence and their voices lowered so I could not hear as well. I tiptoed down five steps. The sixth one always had a squeak so I stayed five from the top. I heard Rafe laughing and he said, "So, maybe you won't have to. I've waited all I'm about to wait. You've sworn a bargain. Be she ready?"

I stretched one leg as far as I could, stepping over the noisy stair to the one below.

"By no means," Pa's voice said. "Patience is still a child. And she's recently had smallpox and quinsy. You should have sent word you were coming."

"A delicate child," Ma added.

"I sent word before and you'd sent her on an errand to the parish convent. Our deal was your safekeeping on this island in return for a wife. You've no dowry for her, no legacy except for the boy, there. Two wenches who'll be nothing but a drain on Her Majesty's profits for the length of their lives. You've put me off long enough. I'll see her home."

"Mistress Talbot," said Pa, in a voice he used during their most formal balls when something more needed saying, "will you speak to Miss Patience? Explain the situation."

I knew then that more danger was afoot. When slaves had come from Benderidge Plantation, carrying forks and fence posts and wanting food, Pa had said we had a "situation." When two boys waylaid August in Kingston, that was a situation, too, and it took him two weeks to get up from his bed. Ma nearly bumped me over in the stairway, rushing with her hand on Patience's arm, their faces dreadful, their eyes gleaming, even in the darkness of the staircase.

I heard Rafe saying, "I'll take the two of them off your hands. There's room enough for the second one and you'll be freed of both."

"Where is August?" I began, but I said no more. Ma grabbed my shoulder so tightly it hurt, and bustled me along with them. In Patience's room, Ma let go of me and took Patey by both shoulders, frowning.

"Move the armoire," she said. "Help me, lasses." Ma pushed the heavy furniture from its nook. Patience took hold, too.

I started to ask why we were moving it, but the moving cabinet came toward me as if Ma had grown the strength of five men. Instead, I asked, "Ma, why do you let that awful Uncle into our parlor if all he wants is to steal Patey?"

"Sometimes you have to befriend those you do not like, my bairny, to keep away others you like even less. Rafe is a powerful man."

"He hates Pa," I said. "I can see it in his eyes. I think he loves *you*."

"It's not love you see in him, lass, but something else not so grand. Now, help us push. You'll be safe in here."

Patience's room overlooked the bay. From my windows I could see only cane fields. There had been work done in Patience's room, part of fixing the house for a new waterwheel system besides the one that crushed cane all day. We had kept out of the way for nine long weeks as men tore through the wall to add the wheel and its gears, pounding, banging from morning until night. I remember because Patience slept in my bed with me and the nights had passed intolerably crowded. She tossed around, she smelled like a grown-up, and she constantly put my counterpane off the end of the bed though I asked for it. She said girls should not sleep so warm at night but did not tell me why. After they restored her room and Ma put back the bedding there seemed not a speck of difference except that the stones in the niche were a newly cut color and the armoire stood taller.

The armoire rolled on cannonball legs away from the wall where they had bolted the side of it with a door hinge of worked iron. A passageway as narrow as one stone opened behind it. Patience and I looked at each other, astonished that it was there, and I was doubly puzzled that she had not inspected her own room. From the dark opening we heard a soft whistling like a garden bird. "Go," Ma said, and pushed Patience to the opening. "Down the stairs inside, and when you get to the bottom, hide."

To my horror I was next, pressed through the slot in the wall by hands from which I had never felt pain, shoved in like a sack. The armoire swung into place, crushing my protest in the thump of the tight-fitting frame. My hand lay at the corner. If one finger had lain in the spot where the hinge slammed, that finger could have been crushed and Ma would not have known. I whimpered, not from pain but from the possibility of it. "Oh, la, Patience. What are we to do? It is so dark."

"Shush," whispered Patience. "You had n'a cry out now. Reach for my hand. I am below you on the steps." The bird called again. "That is August," Patience said. "My hand is before you. Take it and feel the side for the rope."

A palpable, clinging blackness enveloped me and for a moment it cut out all sounds, too. I found my sister's hand as I touched the walls, wet as if rain had fallen upon them, and felt with my feet for the steep stairs. "If Rafe MacAlister is pretending to be our uncle, why would he want to marry you?"

"He doesn't. Not really. His family fought against our pa though they were but yeomen on our estate back in England. They were devious to the last, stealing, poaching. He thinks Ma and Pa owe him a woman, for his wife died. It was none of our doing, but she died. He pretends to court me, but I'd not have him if I had to hang myself first."

"Patey! But if they were only farmers, why have we aught to do with him now?"

"He sallies with every picaroon in the Carribbean Sea, and keeps them from our door. Stop talking and come this way." The stairway of short, narrow stone took us down into night that grew ever darker with air so damp it pushed against our every movement. A ship's mooring rope, latched to the wall on one side, hung loose in its channel bolts. Slipping off a stair I fell upon Patience. The rope gave with my weight like a loose stitch in a fabric of stone. I hung from it by one hand, flailing for her lost grip until I found her hands. She whispered, "Be caresome, Ressie."

Each step took us closer to the noise of the new waterwheel. At one point the wall opened and there was nothing to hold to but the rope. Patience dropped my hand as we passed the open hub. Though we could not see it, the vibration and the splatter of the waterwheel made a wall of sound where stone had been. Where the stone wall shielded us from the danger of the open gears, I felt the pattern of the steps, the breadth of them being more equal than not. We were lost in a clock ticking; each step, every drop of water adding up to hours. "Patience?" I called softly. I felt I must hold on to her just as a baby creature holds its mother's hair. I called again, this time with a whine, "Patey?"

Her voice came muffled, as if her shadow spoke to me. "The bird you hear is August."

August opened the window on a tin candleholder he carried. The light that came from the little light house seemed not to go beyond his sleeve but I knew his sleeve and the sight of it calmed my heart. "Come with me, lassies," he whispered.

We came to the bottom landing and there was no door, just the open side of the house hidden by drooping vines and a fat, scratchy tree trunk. "Where shall we hide?" I asked. I also wanted to ask why I had not known this place. I loved a good hidey-hole, a place to haunt, for there was little to do and no one to play with in this great stone house since Allsy died. I used to spend hours in the attic amongst the old chests and dusty trunks, pretending I had found treasures from a kingdom far away. Now that we stood at the foot of the steps, they did not seem near so black and menacing. When the sun was up, I wagered it would be a sight to see.

"To the kitchen," August said, and took one of my hands and Patience took the other, to run down the sandy path toward the kitchen, which was separate from the house. The path actually wound past the kitchen and went to the sugar mill. A puckish wind caught my clothes and hair. Only then did I realize how the mist in the passageway had soaked me to the skin. As we reached the coral outcropping where the path widened, he stopped short. He dropped my hand and closed the door on the candle-light. We had little need of it now, for the moon overhead had just risen over the hump of land on the far side of Meager Bay and glimmered across the quiet water.

A galleon under full sheets left a clear wake coming this way. From where I stood the still-golden moon glinted off something on the port bow as the ship swung its side toward us. "Black sails," I said. "She looks a phan-tom a-crossing under the moonlight." No sooner had the words escaped my lips than the top- and mainsails collapsed, rolled by men we could not see. The shine that I had seen before now became clear. Someone watched our shore with a long glass. Six ports on the side opened and the unmistak-able rounds of a cannon's mouth filled each of them. We saw longboats. Three of them already lay aground on the sand and men moved upland toward the house with one left beside each boat.

"Saint Agnes, save us," said Patience. "We have to warn Ma and Pa."

"Five, nine, now sixteen, maybe twenty, or twenty-two men," August said. "And six cannon on the port bow. *I* shall go back to the house. You girls stay in the kitchen."

I pictured myself running up the loft steps to the cribs over the kitchen to hide, and August charging home, when Patience said, "I am coming with you, too. Ressie—you—you run to the well house. Tell Joseph to warn the slaves to hide in the fields. You stay there."

"I cannot," I said. I wanted to hide in the kitchen. "They always turn the pigs out when there is a *situation*." I had seen pigs kill a man little more than a year before. My worst dreams held no suspense, no surprise, just the horror of being eaten alive by pigs.

August was but fifteen and taller than Patience, though his voice had not yet a man's depth. It slipped fully back to boyhood as he stomped and waved his fists in the air. "No arguing! I am the man, here. Both of you go to the fields and I shall tell Pa," he shouted. He pushed the tin light into my hands and took off at a run down the path straight toward the front door. For a moment I marveled at the moonlight, and how I could see his satin coat gleaming as it had not in the passageway.

Patience and I made our way to the well house, the white rock pathway lit by the moon. It was MacPherson's lantern tonight, a full moon so bright and close and gleaming that the notorious highwayman Jamie MacPherson could have had his way with travelers as well as in broad day. The crashing of an ocean wave and soft voices that I knew made the whole scene seem tranquil and for just a moment I felt safe there.

Our man Joseph was supposed to sleep in the well house. Lucy, a kitchen helper, must have come for water after dark. They murmured to each other, low, laughing, not aware of our coming until we stepped through the open door.

"Pirates!" I said, bursting the cushion of night air with the word. Their two faces, one round, one narrow, looked toward me and smiled with puzzlement.

Joseph said, "Missy Talbot? What you doing tonight? What you say?"

Patience said, "Tell everyone they best hide in the fields. We saw a ship in the bay that looks to be—" but her words dropped off the end of the world as a cannon boomed from close by.

The *bum-bum* sounds repeated thrice more. Something splashed in the bay, a larger noise than a dolphin. Joseph's and Lucy's eyes looked the same, bright white and shining in their dark skin. I hoped they would take hold of our hands and help us get to a safe place in the fields, and keep us from the pigs, but they ran away, leaving us in the well house! As they ran their voices rang across the clearing, echoing against the circled wooden shacks, and people poured from every door. Dogs, naked children, partly clothed and even naked full-grown men and women slaves emerged and ran to the cane. The pigs squealed somewhere distant. All of life in the huts vanished into the black and rustling cane fields except two dogs. The dogs danced and barked as if they had been waiting for this night: a full moon and a frolic.

"Let us hide," Patience said. "Come, now."

"I am going home. I am not scared o' Rafe MacAlister," I said.

"Resolute! I said no."

I started toward home. Over my shoulder I shouted, "You had best hide here with Lucy. You are not marrying Rafe and pirates do not want a *little* girl."

Out of the shadows Patience screamed with a shriek of terror and it caught my feet sure as any trap. She stood at the edge of the wagon road cut between two fields. One crop brake stood almost four feet tall, the other over five feet. Slave men stood at the edge of the field, a quivering naked army of plant men waving their great sugarcane knives, threatening to hack anyone who came nearer.

A woman's voice with a strong Dutch-African accent said, "You gone back to the big house and tarry, Missy Talbot. Gone, now. You be safess' dere. Don' be laying out here with us. Summa dese folks don' speak English. Don' knows what could happen."

Patience ran from them and followed me. She cried as we ran, and I wondered if they had hurt her feelings, or did she cry from fear of having Rafe for a husband, or from pirates coming, or from the rocks under our thin parlor shoes? I heard a new cannon report, and this time close enough to hear the concussion of the ball against the stone walls of our house. Another cannonball crashed through part of the roof near one of the fireplaces and a great splintering of glowing cinders shot into the air.

Through a shout of men's voices I heard Ma calling our names, and I saw her silhouetted against fire, standing alone in the front carriageway. "Daughters!" Ma said. "Go! Go, run." For a moment Ma ran toward us then back to the house, then turned around and came at us again as if she could not make out which way portended better. "I thought you were safely away! Come. I will give you something. Come quickly." She pulled us inside, where furniture lay tossed about. The curtains at the far wall waved in flames. Wind blew through the gap where the fireplace had stood. Pa came through the room, his arms loaded with two boxes where he kept the pistols. August followed, holding three swords. Rafe had drawn a sword and carried it aloft, and I saw two pistols pushed through the sash at his waist.

We followed Ma through a hallway to her sleeping room. There she flung open a chest and pulled out two blankets with ties fast at each top. I had seen her a-working at them and asked after them but she had not said what the purpose was, for never would we have needed such heavy covers. She shook one and set it in a ring on the floor. The sound of pistols and a crash of metal on metal seemed far away. Were Pa and August holding off twenty-two men? Might Uncle Rafe be fighting, too? If he were to save my pa, I should have to think on him much more kindly in the future.

Ma pushed Patience's skirts up and said, "Step in this petticoat," pointing. In less than a moment Ma had pulled it up and fixed it by the ties around Patey's waist. "Take everything from this," she said, pulling her fine worked-silver jewelry casket from its shelf. "Put them all in the folds here." She plied the quilted petticoat and, as if by magic, opened pockets and duckets, pushing in rings and brooches, and in one, a string of fine pearls long as an ell, which she lifted from her own neck. In the shortest order I had ever seen, she pushed at the seams and squeezed forth threaded needles at the waiting, whipping the openings closed. She tied on Patey's pocket, a small bag that hung at her waist, and in it put the silver-and-jeweled casket itself. It was no bigger than an egg, and disappeared into the folds.

"There. If they be found, produce that and there remains a gold ring in it. Say your mother gave it ye as a wedding ring that had been her grandmother's and it will buy you freedom. Let no one find any other of these." We heard shouts. "Bar the door, Patience. Resolute, come here."

Ma did the same to me as she had done to my sister, dressing me with a second quilted skirt, procuring yet another casket, smaller still than Patey's, upon which I had never laid eyes ere now. "Quickly, wait still!" she said when I squirmed a bit. Another cannonball landed so closely that dust and rubble fell from the ceiling. "Wear this petticoat and never, never take it off, understand?"

"It is so warm," I said. "Makes me drain sweat."

She did not answer but opened the second casket. Though it was merely wood laid about in gold, it held eight gold rings, eleven silver coins, and a ruby necklace. These she pressed into slits in this new heavy skirt. Then, on her knees, she stitched up the folds and tucked the needle back into the seam. "You take care and you will have a needle. Thread can be found but a needle is a treasure. Keep it close by and oft oiled. If you get a chance to move it to a safer spot, do that, but until then, keep it there."

"I am sorry we did not stay in the kitchen, as you told us," I whispered. "Uncle Rafe—"

Ma's face flushed dark. "There's no fault in ye, bairny," she said as she laid coins into the casket. She put two new pieces of eight and six shillings in it and closed the lid, fastening the hasp. She tied a brand-new pocket to my waist with the wooden casket in it. That was to buy my safety, too, I expect. That last, the name she had called me as a wee child, brought tears to my eyes. "Rafe MacAlister is no' the threat what's comin' up the beach. Your pa'd have talked him doon like he done before. Now girls, go. Up the priest's hole by the fireplace."

Hiding holes and tunnels threaded through our house. Escape was always in our sights. The sounds of battle grew closer, and shouts followed the pistol fire. I heard glass breaking as Patience and I reached the fireplace. We nestled into the shadows. Fallen stones blocked the way up. I turned to see what had happened behind us. The leaded window lay in shards on the floor and from Ma's raised hands a thundering bang deafened me. A man dressed in short breeches and a torn vest fell to the floor without uttering a sound. Ma turned to stone, her eyes locked on the blunderbuss in her hands. At that moment two men who had been kicking at the door with hard boots accomplished their task and the wooden door hung loose on its hinges.

Two more men clambered through the window opening and reached Ma. She had drawn a dagger, one I had seen lying in the shelf of books she kept in this room. One of the men smiled, his mouth a toothless cavern, his long cutlass waving in front of her. I would have screamed had not Patience's hand covered my mouth and nose so that I could hardly breathe. Ma stepped backward, rotating the dagger from pointing at the intruder to pointing it at her own chest. I bellowed into Patey's hand. I fainted, I suppose, for I knew nothing more but Patey crushing me to her bosom.

"Back to the new stairway," she hissed, "behind the waterwheel."

The bedroom seemed empty, and we stood in the open fireplace in perfect silence for the span of several heartbeats. "Where's Ma?" I asked.

"Do not talk. Run." We hid at the doorway until we were certain no one saw, and then pounded up the stairs. At the landing I looked down to see Uncle Rafe, Pa, and August, all fighting beside each other, holding four men back with their swords. Pa had blood on his shirt but he moved so boldly that I was sure it was not his. Patience pulled my arm nearly out of its roots as she forced me away from that spectacle and toward the armoire. Heavy steps came up the stairs behind us. She tugged the great chest forward and put me into the opening first, climbed through, and pulled at it with the handle.

Again, blackness enveloped us. I stood by my sister, motionless. I leaned toward her and whispered, "Where did Ma go?"

"Out the door."

"Did she get away from them, then?"

She let out a tiny sob and said, "Be quiet. Shush."

At first I thought a mouse had whimpered, then I heard the voices, speaking some foreign tongue—I knew not what—and the armoire rattled as its door opened and the drawers were pulled from their frames. Light came through the place where the slats in the back did not meet, and Patience leaned back so far she nearly fell on me. She tapped my shoulder and, when I did not move, tapped again harder. I took three steps down. This was more clumsy and frightful because I was leading. There was no one there to catch me. August was not waiting at the bottom.

When I had gone down a dozen steps or more, the wall opened up to the place that the water splashed in and there I stopped. "Stop," I said aloud, lest she tumble us both to our deaths. I spoke over the water. "If we go down all the way, we shall be in the midst of 'em."

"Let me think. We'll tarry here a while." Patience put her hands on my shoulders, but since I stood two steps below her, when I tried to return the embrace I could only hug her knees. I felt the heavy quilted petticoat she now wore, and the funny lump of the pocket with the casket in it against my face. She held my back and we each held the rope on the wall. We both began to weep.

We had seen pirates before, and thieves or renegade slaves, and all manner of situations. But never with such force. Never with cannon. Another cannonball shook the house, yet though it sounded far from us on the steps, people might be in danger in other homes, too, and that was a powerfully troubling thought. I would not mind a great deal if Uncle Rafe were blown to bits, but I wondered where Pa and August were.

With a mighty crashing, splintering sound, the wall where the waterwheel gears threatened and sprayed us fell away. We screamed with all our might and water gushed across the opening from the pipes, which had fed the wheel and now swayed overhead. I would have fallen through had not Patience clutched my clothes, for I felt as if the gears pulled at me. From somewhere in the dark below us, a three-pronged metal claw on the end of a rope came up like the hand of the devil. It reached for me again, closer, and closer yet the third time. It slashed at my skirt, taking a bit of the hem down, and it flew up a fourth time, arching far above our heads, hanging itself on the wall above us. A man scrambled up that rope as if he were a ship's rat, clutched me around the waist, and tore me from Patey's arms, swinging him and me down into the spray. We landed with a hard bang and hands pushed me about, wrapped me up with rope, and in a few minutes, Patience stood by me, tied the same as I. I stopped crying, too afeared to make noise.

The men about us wore brushy beards and turbans, some no more than a torn rag about their heads; they smelled of filth and fusty old rum and something far nastier than Uncle Rafe's wig. Betwixt these ugly fellows, meant to guard us, we stood long enough that my feet began to burn though I chilled from being soaking wet. The men spoke to each other in their strange tongue. Soon, along came a train of our slaves, tied with their hands bound to the neck of the person in front of them, and still naked. They brought children and adults, all tied. At least Patience and I were not tied in a chain, I thought. At least that.

"Where's Ma?" I asked Patience. I got a cuff across the back of my head for it.

I saw Pa and August and Rafe coming, tied hands to neck just as were the African slaves. Surely, Ma would appear similarly bound. No one dared speak. So, if Ma had been there, mixed in, and tied, and afraid, she could not speak. I told myself she was there. Doing just that. Staying shushed. She would find me in a while.

It seemed as if we waited hours on the beach. I shivered, sometimes almost faint, my teeth chattering. I looked for Ma as much as I dared. At last they allowed us to sit, though the sand wet our skirts through to the skin. Fingers of pale washed-silk green sky moved through the smoke that rose over our plantation. Slivers of light gold reflected in the misty air. They had lit the cane fields and they had burned the house and kitchen and all the slave houses. If I had hid in the cribs in the kitchen loft I might have had no other fate than to roast there like a goose.

Men came from the smoke, blackened with soot and carrying crates and sacks filled with our household goods. I felt the small casket in my pocket and the jewelry sewn into my clothing. Ma always sat with sewing. I never looked at nor cared what she made in recent days, as I was always laboring over my own embroidery stand, wishing for my carefree days before I was expected to learn it. When had Ma done these things? Why had she created such a cloth for me, like nothing I had laid eyes upon? I had never before had such a garment. It was heavy and thick as if I had been clad in mud. I whispered to Patience, "My embroidery. What is to become of it?"

Patience's face reddened and puckered with sorrow and she began to cry.

"I will make another," I said, to comfort her.

"Are you blind?" she asked.

I studied her eyes for a moment then turned my face from her to our burning house. No, I was not blind. I only meant that we had lost all. Down to the smallest things. My things. And here I sat tied like a pig held for slaughter. I had been stolen; we had all been stolen, as if we were gilt furniture or a chest full of linen and purple-dyed cloth. I pulled myself into my clothes, shrinking from her chastisement. I received a shove from a foot behind me, pushing Patience and me as if we were indeed a pile of goods that must be kept aright.

I turned to see who had kicked me. I said, "We are being held by hideous, pitiless gargoyles that are not decent enough to speak the queen's English." The man felt nothing of my reproof, though, and kept on watching over our heads toward the ship in the bay.

CHAPTER 2

October 1, 1729

Tidewater receded and the galleon listed, her foredeck thrust upward in the morning light, masts angled against the sky. Indeed, someone on board may have been surprised by the great uplifting, for even *I* could have told the pilot not to moor her so close. I had seen ships careened before but this one looked in danger of tumbling over. The coral at that place is so near the top that at low tide August goes there with Pa and standing waist deep they fish with gigs for my favorite lovely white-meated fishes.

From the deck, men tossed ropes thick as stumps and climbed down the treacherous rigging, some getting into smaller boats, some just hanging there at the side of the ship. A few stood in the water on the shoal. Soon the sounds of scraping and banging filled the air as barnacles flew off the hull. One man made excited motions with his arms and pointed to the water nearby. Several of them shouted something like "Oh-ho!" just as one of the working men fell into the water. I saw his knife rise in the air. He struggled and fought near the fin of a shark. He had met his fate.

As the tide went out they worked on and on, and the day grew warm. I slept, leaning against Patey, and I dreamed of lying in a hammock full with comfits and warm bread. Eating sausages in cream.

As I began to taste the sweets I awoke. Patience had tears running down her face. She stared into the distance, so I followed her gaze to the ruins of our house. I marveled that there were girls seated nearby, no taller than I whom I had never seen before, but there were always whole groups of people we did not house living in the brush shacks and cane brakes, besides those we did. I supposed I should feel sad. Or afraid. All I felt was hunger gnawing at my insides. Ma might have brought something if she had had a chance, but then we were not here for a picnic. The African slaves next to us seemed almost nonchalant about being held as we were. These brutes saw all of us as nothing more than booty. The image of sausages came back to mind a few minutes later and made my mouth water. I could have eaten sausages, even without a proper dish.

In the bright sun, Patience's skin was sure to freckle. Oh, la, I thought. She had hair of deep auburn, given to waves; she was always brushing and fixing it with combs. Mine was a mix of red hues with yellow, and quite curly, so that when it was clean and brushed into finger curls, it seemed at times like faded pink roses. Sometimes Pa called me his "old rose," and said to me to never forget who I was. I did not know at the time what he meant by it. Then, I only thought my face was already feeling the sun. My lashes and brows were almost invisible, compared to Patey's nice brown ones. Her skin was whiter than milk and when she blushed it seemed wine had infused the milky satin. My skin freckled despite the various bonnets and hats I wore. I rubbed my face with milk and honey each day. My eyes were pale, the color of a shallow pool, so that all my features seemed quite plain and faded in appearance.

The tide turned and the scraping of the hull finished. A man came to us and hoisted Patience to her feet, compelling me to follow, prodding others behind me. He pointed to the shallop, and when I paused at its edge, he lifted me up without so much as a by-your-leave, and dropped me into it. They made me sit in the reeking damp hull. Some other girl wearing rags far inferior to my gown, soiled though it was, sat upon me as if I were a cushion, perched upon my drawn-up knees. She looked down upon me and made a noise, wrinkling her nose. "Ach. Ye be 'ant so fine now, Mistress."

I recognized the accent more than the face. One of the red-haired Irish slaves bought out of the gallows, as Pa would say. Uncle Rafe always added that it proved more merciful to work them to death than to pile their corpses in the lochs. If I could have moved, I would have found that needle under my skirt and poked her right in her so high-and-mighty rump. I jerked my knees and hoped the bones gave her a poor chair.

The tide began to rise. Four men rowed us nearer the ship. As we reached the reef's edge, that hulk righted itself in the bay with a loud creak and a rush of wake that raised our smaller craft by two feet so that the rowers had to fight to keep from circling. I knew that once Pa came by, he would help us find Ma. Patience sat upon a seat at my back, and I said to her, "Can you see Ma from there?"

A man holding a curved blade longer than his own arm shouted something at me. I shrank away from his cutlass and deeper into the muck, and wept. My gown had been blue. It would never be blue again. It had a nice silken flounce with a wee farthingale made just for me. My slippers were almost gone, wet through, and my stockings had fallen down. I wondered if Ma would be upset. Surely she would not find me at fault for the ruination of this gown. Surely she would come soon.

When we reached the side of the galleon my mouth opened. I had never been so close to a ship this size. She looked to be a thousand tons. Maybe more. Rows of openings marked decks loaded with cannon. From far overhead, rope nets slid down her sides, looking for all the world like a gigantic version of Ma's plaited silk hair coif.

They untied our bindings and held us at knifepoint. As if we were rats in a harbor, all the maids in my boat climbed the rigging laid on the sides. I could have gone faster, but a woman above me could barely get up and she seemed not to have balance for the swaying of it. Her bare feet were callused, but they were not used to climbing. I felt the little casket banging against my legs and for a moment entertained the thought that a four-shilling piece in the hands of one of these pox-eaten devils might be all that it took to get us back on land. Of course, I did not have enough shillings for every man, so I kept climbing. On reaching the deck I chided myself for my haste. I have always felt a hurry to get things done. If I must take a medicine, I would gulp it, rather than sip it and prolong the misery. If I must climb a rope scaffold, I would as soon get it climbed.

We had scaled the ship all that way to be led across the deck and down three sets of stairs into the pitch and dark of a hold where they herded us into compartments made of iron. One by one the doors clanged shut. The air smelled of sewage and cattle and rot. The gloom felt so cloying that the dim light of our jailer's lantern did little to break it, and the thought that it shone full morning outside made it seem all the more mysterious.

Patey stood beside me, as we could not have sat without stacking ourselves like so many chairs. When the last iron had been shut and locked, the men filed up the stairs and dropped the hatch over our heads. At that sound many of the women and girls around me began to cry; first whimpering, it turned to angry wailing. Patience joined them, crying aloud, holding my shoulders. "Patience," I whispered, "do not cry. Call Ma. She's full well got to be in one of the other cells."

I felt Patey's hands cross my face, fumbling, feeling, as if she had become blind and was using her fingertips to see me. She slapped my cheek soundly and said, "It's only by grace that we are not all dead. Do not be daft, Ressie." She hugged me to her bosom and I clutched at her. I began to cry, my heart joining the bedlam about us. How long we huddled together and moaned, I could not say. Our cries began to wane when a great banging and shouting came from overhead followed by scuffling, then men's screams.

I heard the distant clanging of iron bars. Over our cries, over our heads, many men, maybe Pa and August, maybe even Rafe, were put into cells gated with iron. A man grunted, loud and hard, and others cried out. I heard swords clanging and more grunts followed by groaning. A woman on our deck screamed and cried out, "It's blood! I be covered in blood from above. The devil Saracens are killing 'em all!"

A wail rose from our deck like a great wave. "Saracens—!" The word sprang from all around, followed by curses and prayers. There was no one my pa feared more than Saracen pirates. Were we now in the hands of minions of

Satan, our fates were sure to be monstrous. I cried out in earnest, calling for Ma, reaching for Patey but not sure I had her; I slipped from one form to the next until the voice in front of me confirmed her presence.

"Pa!" I screamed with all my strength. All the girls and women on this deck began to call for their men and boys above. The noise grew to deafening. Out of the shouts came a steady banging, a drumming that vibrated through the ribs of the ship.

I heard Lucy's voice! She called from a far corner, "Don' you be calling all at a time. Everyone, you be still, now. You be calling out de names one after de other. Starts here. Call out de name if you mens be up above." I felt the ship begin to move, as one by one, some meekly, some heartily, women's voices called names of men and boys. Others repeated the names up and down the length of the deck, so the pattern of it became a ribbon of hope strung from one cell to the next. After a while, the men above began to hear us and rapped on the floor in answer. I wondered how were we to know that a knock meant the man was dead or alive, but I heard a woman call "Bertram? Bertram Willow?" Silence followed. She cried out his name again, and "Bertram Willow" echoed from cell to cell but when no knock answered her, she wept softly.

As I listened to the rhythmic calling, the names became for me a chantey, a sea song, and the ship began to rock with the movement of names round the despicable place. And I realized that at least some of these women knew how to do this. They were no strangers to captivities and bars. The deck rolled and I knew we had left the bay and made for open sea.

They might take us to Kingston. Houses all along the beach had been beset by thieves, far back as I could remember. Indeed, Pa had fought off others, but these he could not prevail against. A striking pain went through me as if I had been stabbed from my shoulders to my knees in one thrust, with the thought that we might not be headed to Kingston but to some far-away island.

I heard Patience call out, "Allan Talbot? August Talbot?" The names echoed from lips down the way. Now it seemed I could make out the length of the place, having grown used to the dark, and the ship turned east so that sun came in through small openings and a single porthole. Patience shouted again, more loudly, "Allan Talbot? August Talbot?"

I held my breath. At last, two raps. "They're alive!" I said, pushing my hands against my face. "Pa!" I shouted. I turned to Patience. "Call for Ma. Your voice is louder than mine."

"She is not here, Resolute."

"She escaped, then!"

Patience sighed but answered not. "Do not make me say it, sister."

Crushing our petticoats to the side, we nestled together and managed to make seats for ourselves as the whole lot of weary women sank to the floor.

The ship rocked with the comfort of a hammock. Weariness took me. Sounds around me, the heat, the stench, nothing could keep me awake.

Patience later told me that the day and the night had passed before I awoke. A man in a dirty turban came with a great tub of cold gruel that he slopped into a trough in each cell. It seemed we were supposed to lap it up like dogs. "Sir? Oh, sir," I called. "A spoon, sir, if you please?" No one seemed to hear me. Some women fought over it, scooping the stuff with their hands into their mouths. I did not get any. Within a few minutes those who had eaten the most began to be sick. I did my best to resist, but with people packed so tightly, I became ill with the rest of them.

The next two days or more were lost to me as I groveled there in the bowels of that ship. The wretchedness cannot be described, so dire became our misery. After two days three women had died and later, upon reflection, I think perhaps our heathen captors either had mercy or began to worry that their cash bounty on our heads might disappear if they did not feed us. They brought in crockery jars of rum and tow sacks full of hardtack. That day they also brought two of the men from above, both prisoners but neither of whom we knew, and showed them how to work the pumps. While the captives pumped, our deck flooded with several inches of freezing seawater, complete with small fish and octopuses and other creatures I could not name. They opened drains and let the spilth run off, then flooded us twice again.

We were sopping and sick, and I, nearly out of my mind with torment. Why would Ma not answer me when I called? Had she escaped and stayed on the plantation? Had she run to the kitchen to hide and there escaped the fire? In anguish, I knelt beside Patey and cried against the iron bars, a deep and terrible sort of sobbing that made me feel helpless as a babe. I could not stop. I cried myself to sleep. I roused when a dark brown hand came through the bars and shook me. The man offered more rum and hardtack. I took the tack from his dirty hands and clutched it close to my chest, drank the fiery rum in one swallow, and passed the cup back to him. I took a small nibble of the hardtack and tucked it into my cheek, putting the rest into a fold in my bodice for later. Not even a plate! Ma and Pa would hear about this roughness, I promised myself.

I dreamed, then, of games of hide-and-seek with Allsy, dashing through the herb garden by the kitchen, filling our noses with the smells of trampled oregano and mint. I proffered my cheek to her for a kiss then pulled it back, and when she laughed I kissed her cheek, instead. We danced jigs on a plank set up for a bench. I gave her my lavender chemise for Hogmanay Day, and since she had just learned to weave basketwork, she gave to me a small, patterned basket. Before she put it in my hands, she said, "Look-a dis, Missy," and interwove our fingers, light and dark. She pointed to the leaves of the weaving, light and dark, as patterned as checked cloth. "Oh, la," I said, "it is you and I!"

I opened my eyes and smiled, for these were not dreams but memories. "Allsy, I miss you," I said in the darkness.

"Pray, did you call me?" Patience's voice came into my room in the darkness, and for a moment I thought I was at home sharing my bed with her.

I asked Patience why we had not yet reached Kingston, and we talked about where we might be going if it were not Kingston. The Tortugas? Or the opposite direction and far worse, Barbados? "As far as Turks and Caicos," one woman declared. I knew nothing of that place. I wanted my own fireside and bed and Ma and Pa and August and Patey. Allsy. Without sunrises and settings, every hour seemed eternal. I ached. My teeth hurt. On and on we sailed. Sometimes people got sick with the pitching, but I did not unless I could not hide my eyes and ears and nose from their seasickness.

Then one time, with night coming on after another day we could measure only by glimmers of light through the single porthole, men came down. Five of them came straight to our cell. Patey slept in a corner, being sick now as many were, with the beginnings of scurvy, but she roused upon hearing the lock clicking and the door open. One pirate held a lantern aloft and looked us over. Like fluttering doves all the women cowered away from his glare. His lips curled around his three off-centered teeth, and he reached straight for me, clutching a large handful of my gown. I screamed with force I hardly believed came from me. Patience wrapped her arms about me and pulled back mightily; I became a rag between two mad dogs.

Patience rolled me to the floor and flattened herself upon me, crushing the breath from my bones. She bellowed, she kicked, and she thrashed, and pulled other women off their feet. Our clamor rose and we writhed together, fighting for our lives, trying to get the hoard of women to hide us. His grizzly hands drew girls apart like baggage. Between the slime on the floor and the lengths of cloths that made up every skirt and petticoat, we made a knot of shrieking females that closed back as soon as he tore us asunder.

Men from the deck overhead began to yell and curse, too, cheering us on. On my feet for a moment, Patey banged me against one of the massive ribs of the hull, and though I did not lose consciousness, my eyes rolled upward. I could neither resist nor stand any longer. Patience grabbed an arm and shoved someone else before us, and the man's claws let go of my clothes.

He dragged the girl from the cell and another closed the lock. It was the Irish girl. I remember the red hair, hanging down his back, with her upended on his shoulders. He pushed her at the ladder, but when she refused, he hoisted her like a sack and darted up the steps as if she weighed nothing at all. Her howling left an echo that hung in the air for a long time. They took one other woman from another cell who did not fight at all but climbed the ladder to her fate.

"Stop!" I cried out.

Patience clapped her filthy hand across my mouth. "Be still. I have saved you."

We slumped to the floor, and others stood above us. A reeking stench came from every square inch of this place, as if the scuffle had awakened sulfurous demons. Someone made dry coughing sounds across the way.

Later, I said, "I hear her crying," to Patience.

"No you do not. They've given her a nice dinner and comfits and sweets of every sort. Pies and puddings. Turtle soup. Ham and sprats and kingfish. She is not crying."

"I hear her crying," I said. "She was no bigger than me. Poor wee Irish mite." Pa used that word for me sometimes. Mousy, mousy, wee mite, he called me. "Why would they give her food and not us?"

"Go to sleep."

"I cannot. My head hurts. Were you trying to knock my brains out?"

"If that was what it took to save you."

"La, Patey. You are hard." I shoved her away from me. How could she hate me so? What had I done to be so abased and abused?

Three times that night we heard great splashes off the side of the ship. I thought and I thought. I knew people who died on a ship got buried in the sea. If they fed that girl and that woman a dinner, had their stomachs exploded and they died? And why were there three splashes? Who else had eaten with them? Maybe the food was poisoned, but I felt so hungry I would gladly eat poisoned food. I would.

Patience slumped against the hull, and though she was breathing she did not wake, as if her last strength had gone to hold me back from the pirates. Some of the women began to cry, but we all knew by then that sadness was useless. The dead do not mourn the dead.

Sometime after that we came to quieter water in a bay of some sort. My mind felt bleary. My head pounded. I dreamed sometimes of a great banquet being laid for us, but that at that banquet table all the food held poison; the meat tasted of iron rust and the drink tasted like spoiled fish. We slept in the exhaustion of sickness. When I awoke, it was always to hunger. There was no food but hardtack and watered rum. Sometimes they brought uncooked rice or wheat grains we sucked on until we could chew them. Another woman died in our cell and two died from across the way. I felt ashamed that my first thought was that at least there was a bit more room. Maybe they would give us more rice to chew with one less to feed. Hunger had pushed away all the human kindness I owned. Patience would not suck on the rice. I feared she would die next. If Ma would but call out to us, we should take heart, I thought, but I dared not tell Patey that, for she tried to slap me again if ever I mentioned Ma or Pa. I suspected she was angry at me for not running to warn them fast enough.

I plotted to ask the next pirate who came by here to take me to the banquet hall. While I thought of that I searched inside my clothing for any scrap of fabric that was not filthy. When at last I came upon my pocket holding Ma's little casket I found it was made of two layers, and keeping the lump hidden between my knees I pulled at it on the inside until I got off a shred of linen cloth about an inch or two long. I put that in my cheek and sucked on it. I chewed it and swallowed it. I pulled a larger piece off, and put that in the opposite cheek. I tore loose a third bit and shook Patience's shoulder but she merely opened her eyes and stared at me. I whispered to her, "Try to eat some of this cloth before you perish. I will ask the next pirate I see, for our sake, to take us to the banquet above."

"No," she said, "for we had rather perish than go above."

"You are mindless for hunger," I said. "My pocket was still clean inside. Let me help you find yours."

At that moment sailors shouted from above and we heard a great trampling of many feet. Then followed shouts, chanting words over and over, yet they were nothing I understood. The imprisoned men overhead raised a clamor. This ship's cannons began firing and the tomb in which we lay filled with a thundering roar. The whole place shuddered with each concussion. At one point the firing grew so constant that I could not draw a breath between one explosion and the next.

A ball came through the side of the ship, not four feet from where I stood. A few women found the strength to scream. Though the cannonball brought with it a great deal of splintered wood, it fell in its path like a dead thing hitting the floor. It rolled the length of this dark cavern, petering down to a crawl. It came to a halt at the end of the corridor. Light poured in through the hole left by the ball. Light and air. The fragrance of clean air lifted my soul from its dungeon and I stood, pressing my face against the bars, gulping at the breeze coming through the new porthole. If I were to die or drown, I swore I would have at least a breath more of that clean air to go with me. I sucked in air and held my breath as long as I could. I let it out with a burst and took in more.

The ship groaned and listed as a full broadside shook us from keel to flag. Men screamed in agony. The water around us churned with splashing and our guns fired again. The sound of small guns followed like plunking stones compared to the cannon. We heard more shouts. First many, then a few, and two men called back and forth, one apparently on this ship and one from the second one.

"We're saved!" someone said. A few women cheered.

Someone else called out, "One master's just another master. Them be privateers' colors I spy. They're not for sinking this bilge bucket. They're for taking her!"

"Yes, but they're English!" another woman said.

"Patey? Wake up," I said, jostling her. "We are saved by the English."

Patience groaned and looked at me through filmy eyes. She had dark circles under them and when she tried to speak her teeth had taken a pink color. "English?"

"We are going home, now," I said, and patted her hand. "Do not try to stand up. Everything will be all right, now."

A wrenching scream—a man's voice—tore the air, and a great splashing with more shouting followed that sound. A deep-voiced man said, "Anyone *else* crave a taste of steel?" The rest of what happened I could narrate only with my ears. The sounds of hard-soled boots clamored overhead. Orders given. Ropes tossed. Saracen pirates were hung, some strangling for several minutes before they died swinging from the yards over the deck. Served them justice, I thought.

Men swung axes at the heavy bars over our heads which held our prison hatch closed. A man stuck his head in and threw up on the ladder. Apparently we were sickening to an English privateer's delicate sensibilities.

In short order, more Englishmen came down the steps and again pumped seawater about our ankles. Eight fellows stood in the row between the cells and opened the gates. Six of them held swords drawn and two had pistols. We were marched up the stairway and made to stand on the deck. We were near land! My mind was already home again. There would be so much work to do, putting our house right once Patey and I got home. We might spend weeks living in a shade tent. What a bother that would be! Then I looked about. This ship was surrounded by three other vessels loaded with men all brandishing cutlasses and pistols. One of them flew a flag I had heard much about but had not seen before, black silk with a white human skull and crossed bones beneath it.

They moved the men captives to another ship. I could see the heads of our desperate fellows, recognizable by their filth and wasted stance. Many women were so weak that they could not climb down the rigging again as we had come up. After two fell to the sea and drowned for they could not be pulled up with the weight of wet clothing, the sailors stopped sending captives over the side.

These sailors were little different from the Saracens in their smell, but they were indeed different in their means of holding prisoners. The English pulled sails down to form tents on deck. They put up cots. They called a physician to see each person. They even procured odd bits of clothing, ragged coats, old trousers, a few gowns and shifts for the women. Imagine, women in trousers! They guarded us day and night with armed and fierce sailors rather than keeping us in animal pens in the hold. They sent ashore for crates of vegetables and they butchered a kid right there on the main deck and made stew. I helped Patience eat from a wooden bowl though they still afforded us not a spoon amongst the bunch.

The men brought up some kind of plant that they pounded into a soapy pulp with a mallet. We washed with it in sea brine, clothes and all. At least we were not as wretched as before. I told Patience I would help her, but she would not let me. Said her clothing was her own affair. As I stood in line for my turn at the wash kettles, one of the women told me to pile all my clothes aside and she said, "You be wearing twice the frocks some has got. You don' gan to wear dem all w'en dere's dem goes naked. Put dem down."

"No. I shan't," I said. I stood as tall as I could make myself, rising up on tiptoe. "My ma made my clothes. You shan't take these. They would not fit you, madam."

"Put dem down, Missy," she said, and stood over my head, as if to frighten me.

I put my fists against my waist and said, "Show me one person here my size who shall gain from my clothing!"

"How now. Stop the squalling!" called one of the English. "Hark ye here. No one's to pinch from another on this ship!" At that many of the men laughed. Then that man—a short but brawny fellow and clad in once fine clothes himself, though I doubted he had done more than purloin them from some real gentleman—walked toward the woman, passed her, and stood squarely in front of me.

"Look here, now, sir," I began. "I am the daughter of Allan Talbot, master of the Talbot plantation and chief director of the Two Crowns sugar mill. It is your duty as an honorable English citizen to return me and my sister to our family and home at once. Now that you have rescued us from the accursed—"

"Rescued you, be it? Duty? As an honorable English citizen?"

"My sister there, Patience, will verify my claim and our brother is on that other boat yonder with Pa. Ma escaped and is still at home. She will be awaiting us and fairly worried." As he made no move at all but to put his fists on his waist similarly to mine, I added, "Take us home, sir, and you shall be paid well for your trouble."

He put one hand toward me as if to take my hand in his, to bow and kiss my fingers, or to shake it as a man would, I knew not which. I began to reach forward, but as I did the cur reached behind me and clutched a great pawful of my gown, hoisting me in the air. I hung from my waistbands, startled and grunting. He strolled to the side of the ship and hung me at his arm's length over the water, well away from reaching any ropes.

He laughed. "That's a muckle grand idee!"

"You cursed vagabond!" I said. "Put me down this instant!"

I felt something spring loose in my clothing and I feared falling into the sea. Wet clothes pulling me down, I would drown and be eaten by a shark before I could hope to reach the shore, although I knew somewhat how to swim.

Another English sailor came toward him, this one wearing a proper officer's hat and coat. He said, "On deck, Mr. Beckham."

"This one 'as asked to be put ashore, Cap'n. Says she'll pay to get 'ome."

The captain looked upon me with such distaste I felt ashamed and my face reddened. He turned his gaze toward another ship closer at hand, and said, "She'll pay in copper and iron like the rest of 'em. Don't spoil the goods, Beckham. Put it down before you catch something." The captain walked away and Beckham swung me to the deck, banging my bones against the planks.

My pocket with Ma's casket came loose and fell between my knees. I tried to stand, holding my legs tight around it. Mr. Beckham watched me and pursed his lips.

I scowled at him. "Privy!" I said, and he turned away, thinking I had need of a water closet. I returned to the line before the iron wash cauldrons, now standing at the tail rather than my place before.

"What," I asked Patience, "if I take one of my bits of eight and show it to him? Perhaps they did not believe we could pay. I could pay one for each of us."

"They would take it and you would pay *all* and we should still be afloat here."

I scuffled under the top skirt for the pocket straps. "See, my pocket has come loose and I cannot tie it without notice by them. So I might as well offer—"

"Do not! Do not even think on that."

"Why would not they take us home?"

"They are not going to take us where we tell them. They are going to do with us as they wish. Keep all that hidden until there be no hope without it. You will know when it must be spent. Ma said it is to save your life someday. Your life be *not* in danger at this moment and producing the coins could change that. They might strip us bare to take what else we're hiding."

She must have meant the needles and the jewelry. "I would give it, to get home."

"Home can be got to by other means. We are not going home, maybe not for a long time. Going there is not saving your life; it be merely going to a place where you are not."

"Any place is better than this place. And you are mean."

"Will you not listen? You always think you know things that you cannot know. The world be a hideous place, Resolute. Full of danger and trouble and pain. You have survived the pox-ridden hold yet the pirates who kidnapped us have in turn been thwarted and captured by other pirates. Did you not see the Jolly Roger?"

"I did."

"Do you hold that this has now become a seagoing play party? That all you must do is say, 'Take me home, sir,' and they will send footmen to bow and scrape to us?"

I said nothing for a bit. What I intended to answer would draw her scorn so I said, "They *did* feed us."

"As you would an animal fit for auction." Patience continued, "How did your pocket come loose?"

"I ate some of the cloth on the inside. A little. Actually, almost all of it. I told you. Do not you remember?"

"Was it not awful?"

"No worse than the other they gave us."

She made a face with half a smile that reminded me of Ma, and said, "Well enough. If I had thought of it I might have fared better. Just be caresome lest any see you about it. And take no more else the whole of it shall come undone and we be found out. Come here and I will help you wash so that no one sees our treasures."

As we finished and dressed in our soggy rags, I leaned toward her ear and whispered, "I hope I am all done eating pockets. I will not mind having more goat stew, I think."

"Less talking here. Keep quiet!" an English sailor shouted at us.

We sunned ourselves, turning up petticoats to dry even as we wore them. I was careful to check all the places where Ma's precious things lay hidden. All remained safe. Fresh air and buoyancy filled my soul as the rest and food worked its task. After a couple of hours on the deck spent thus, they lined us up and marched us below again.

Awaiting my turn I spied August among the men who had all been loaded onto another ship and ran to tell Patey.

Patience called to him, "August Talbot! Where's our father?"

August called back, "Killed. Buried these four days." Patience sank to the deck and frowned, moping. I heard his words repeated as if they existed in an echo or came from a noise in the back of a house. They made a little scratching sound in my head like a mouse raking through a corncob with a tiny clawed hand. I stood, watching him, waiting and hoping for him to say other words that undid what he had said.

I looked over the side of the ship, expecting to see Pa's face in the green churn below. Buried there? Dropped below the waves, eaten by all manner of fish and bones picked clean by lobster and stingray? Washed up on some lost beach by a storm like the bloated remains I once found? I sank beside Patey. She took my hand, and as people moved around us, we listened to each other breathing for a while. Sadness o'erwhelmed me, yet I could not cry. I imagined our horrified mother, weeping inconsolably. I also imagined that without Pa, Uncle Rafe might never again be convinced to leave us alone.

After two more days of calm sea and warm food, many of the women had revived. Our clothes were ruined. Our hair hung matted against our gaunt faces, but we no longer stank of death from the hold.

With that much reviving, it seemed that all the prisoners save Patience and I began to take great heart. The third night they held forth with singing and some even danced jig steps to the songs. They sang and rocked, and stomped their feet. Some drummed on the casks and hogsheads in the aisles. Soon the women around us began to dance in a line. Two of them came to Patience and me, took our hands, and bade us walk with them. Patience walked but with no joy. I lifted my feet, trying to keep time. Around and around we went as the songs got louder. We circled and coiled through the small hold. The sailors heard from up above and did the same. They stamped their feet with thunderous noise, and the shouting became rhythmic. Reels from our island and from theirs blended together. African songs took hold, drowning out the English reel, and the drumming became loud and heavy and insistent as a beating heart. They held my hands and swept me into their rhythm, pounding, pounding my blood through my feet and arms. A smile crept across my face. The movement was earthy and fierce and lively.

Patience had pulled herself from the line and stood by the wall, her hands over her face. I jerked myself free and went to her. "Come and dance!" I called.

"No. I am not a slave that I should be dancing as they."

"It is pleasant. It's, it is diverting!"

"We are prisoners. I will not be diverted."

"I am sorry, Patey." I felt her sadness rolling over me, yet for no reason I could speak, I backed away from her and into the line of singing, dancing women. We coiled like a great snake through the tiny prison, until, sweating and ripe as old fruit left in the sun, the drumming stopped and we all sat where the drums stopped us. I panted against my arm. I knew that, as much as she could not, I *must* dance the sadness out of me, dance and dance. I raised my face from my arm and looked about me at the slaves in this prison. I thought of the nights I had lain awake in my bedroom, steamy nights filled with far-off drumbeats and the songs from the quarters, and I knew now why they danced. It made something in the chains and bars that held us demand our spirits to take flight. I would take that with me, I decided. That knowledge would abide. It made me feel larger than I had before. As if the bars did not, could not, contain me.

That night a quick rain washed the decks and drizzled upon us. I awoke and moved to a place where the water hit at my feet rather than my face, and saw Patience awake, too, her eyes focused on some distant dream. I leaned against her breast, she put her arms around me, and I slept.

After that time, the women talked more to each other. They included us, but just as often spoke as if we were not there. I learned things. I learned about what men and women do. Things I should not have heard, I suppose, yet they meant little to me and were so strange as to seem like tall tales and nothing more.

CHAPTER 3

October 17, 1729

The sailors treated the men on the other ships with the same food and physick that we had gotten. The privateers started dividing up the stolen goods. As I watched I could see that they had also divided up the Saracens. Some who had not been hung had been pressed or volunteered, and now served the privateers.

After loading the ships with food from shore, they lined us up, sorting us by age, I think, but in any case, Patience and I were placed in two different lines. Longboats unloaded a few of the men captives and took women from her line in their places. Patey and I looked from one to the other as Englishmen prodded some reluctant woman toward the railing where other women scaled the rigging down to the longboats which had come from the third sloop. The woman balked and spoke some language not English nor the patois I knew. While they fussed with her I sidled like a crab across the line and stood behind Patience. I felt the wind leave me as a blow I never saw coming pushed me back into the other line.

"Ressie!" Patience cried, rushing to my side. Women gave us wide berth.

"Patience!" I replied. We clung to each other and I buried myself in her skirts.

"Please, sir!" Patience said. "Please let us go together. We're orphaned enough. Let her come with me or me with her!" She spoke to a man whom I had not seen before, one who sported a long, bushy beard and had come from the third sloop. He stood next to the man who had knocked the spine out of me. Patience said, "My brother waits in your ship, sir. I beg you by God's grace. Will you let us go together?"

The two men turned from us and conferred for a few minutes. One left and came back with the man I had heard called "Captain." Finally he said, "All right. Take 'em. But leave the other white ones with me so there's equal."

Then the bearded man whistled as shrill as ever I have heard, and his companion shoved Patience and me toward the railing. I found climbing down the rigging staggeringly more difficult than climbing up had been. With my foot searching and not finding hold, each web of rigging shifted under me and took my strength. Halfway down I began to tremble and my hands grew weak. My knees shook and dark spots welled up behind my eyes. I believed I was going to fall into the sea before I took a last step, but as I did, hands took hold of me and set me into the longboat. I crouched low and put my head on my knees, quivering violently.

Patience held me in her arms as they took us toward a new rig sitting shallow in the water. She climbed behind me, holding me upright as I progressed on shaking legs. The rope rigging took us over gun ports, and it made me shake with greater violence than ever. I put my toe in the mouth of a cannon to steady myself.

On the deck this ship seemed much smaller than our previous prison. Not more than forty or fifty tons. Her masts were leaner but tall as those before though raked at an angle like a shark's fin. Everything I could make out about this vessel was sleek and lean, riding high in the water as if she were built for speed and nothing less. Above the jib the colors she flew were a long square of red and a yellow triangle, foreign to me except for the topmost one. The Jolly Roger.

I could not count the sailors. I saw a dozen but knew that some might have been plundering some other plantation onshore. There were forty-three of us prisoners on this ship. Men bunked before the mainmast, too, so the women's ride in the aft was roughest. August restrained himself from coming to us, but he stood in his line of captives and nodded. I felt foolish, for all I dared to do was nod in return.

I gripped Patience's hand. For a long moment I stared at her skin and mine together. I felt a great longing to hold August's hand. Patey's skin and mine were so alike, same freckles, same lines in the palms, same-shaped fingernails. August had my same tawny hair, almost a shade of red in the sun. It troubled me that I could not remember a sense of his skin. We three were all we had until we could get home somehow.

In short order they herded us belowdecks. As I stood in line for my turn to descend, I looked back at the other ship, so much higher in the water, pocked with cannon holes and missing a mast. None of the prisoners were still on the deck there. I supposed they had returned to that filthy hold already. At least—at *least*—I thought, I was here with Patience and August. A swell of distress filled my eyes with tears at the thought of having been left behind—though I knew where my feet carried me, down into this ship's nether regions—just as I had cried over nearly having my finger crushed. I believed I would have died there. If not from cause, I would have died of loneliness.

"Ressie. Quit crying. You're calling attention to yourself. Hush."

"I will try." That was when I learned to cry inside. Tears welled up and ran down my throat and through my nose, making it run. I gritted my teeth and sniffed hard.

We were prisoners, yet once a day about mid-morning we were marched up the steps and fed real soup. It was three days until I spotted August again. To my surprise he walked straight toward me, unshackled and hearty. He seemed uncommonly cheerful. "Hail, Resolute, old girl," he said. He took my hand and bowed over it as if he were mocking a true gentleman.

"Hail a chicken's hind foot, *old* brother," I said. "I had no idea if they had kept the men and boys. You have new clothes, too."

"We were lying before the mast, in a separate hold. That is until yesterday, when some of us became sailors, too."

"What are you speaking of?"

"I've signed on. They read us the articles and I've signed on. I ain't a prisoner no more. Coxswain second class. Ship's boy. I get double what the prisoners get to eat and a *share* in all the plunder. All I have to do is row the captain around and sometimes climb the rigging—" Besides the crude manner, his voice had taken a lower register as if he had a bad ague of the chest.

"How you speak. Is your voice this low all the time now?"

"Of course. Why would it not be? I am grown, after all."

"La, August. How you go on."

"I fear, Miss Resolute Catherine Eugenia Talbot, that you mistrust my words."

I pouted and stuck out my lower lip while I balled up a fist. "Mistrust? August Talbot, if you have signed on with a ship of pirates, you are bound to hang as a criminal!"

He grabbed my shoulders and inclined our heads together, whispering, "Not pirates, Ressie. *Privateers.* Your feet stand upon the deck of the *Falls Greenway,* as true a sloop as ever sailed, contracted by the Crown to lay waste to them that scuttle her goods and profits. And I shall be rich before long and take back all that was stolen from us and more!" A breeze ruffled August's hair, sticking out like feathers from a knitted Monmouth cap, the type worn by many of the men.

"Well, then. Well. If you are one of the sailors, then, master seagull second class, I wish to go home."

"Nah. We're headed north to the American colonies." As he spoke he looked about himself as if he were now the proud owner of his own rig called *Falls Greenway.* "That ship you left behind was bound for Port Royal. There you'd be sold like any common slave and it's a rum time you'd have of it. The quartermaster is watching for a ship to take. These three and their longboats—I mean, we call them snows—work together, you see, for the common good. We'll surround her—Spanish, I think, more's the gold—and the three will take her. *I* am to truss the tops'l if it's called to me."

"Port Royal! It is the other side of the island. Over the mountain to home! I would escape and get home to Ma." I raced to the side and held fast to one of the pins. "I want to go home!" I cried aloud. The ship rolled. A gull squawked overhead and landed on the railing next to the table where the food sat. The bird dared to take a dash at the soup pot and left a splat of filth on the table, barely missing the open pot.

August cast his eyes around us. "You would drown. Do not even think of escape."

Not think of escape? I pulled the shore closer with my eyes. "How far away are we now from Port Royal?"

August said, "Port Royal? Why, this ain't Jamaica. This be Hispaniola. I told you we're lying in wait. Our scouts have just returned. A Spanish brigantine be bound here before long and they'll surround her. I hope we see some guns firing." A light came from my brother's eyes when he spoke. Sea madness had taken him.

"Like they did to us?"

His face sobered. "Well, and aye."

Tears came then, running down my face and chin. "You've struck your lot with freebooters and picaroons. What about me? What about Patey? How shall we get home?"

"There's nothing left there. Did not Pa always say to make the best of things? Keep it in your cock-hat that we're bound for the northern colonies."

A sailor had approached us unawares and now his shadow engulfed August's form. "Get away from there. Sop's thataway." He jerked his head toward the table.

I recognized the voice. I suppose because of that I hoped for a moment for mercy from the man. My eyes gathered the spectacle of him from his boots to his coat and tricorn hat and my mouth dropped open. His clothes were different, his manner, too, but I knew him. We stood in the shadow of Rafe MacAlister.

"Aye, aye," August said, and he darted away, with that foolish, boyish, duck-footed run he has. A pirate boy is my bonny brother. Well and aye, then. Uncle Rafe might have been looking upon me with disdain, I was not sure. That was one of those things that was hard to measure, for grown people always lie to children about whether they like them. No matter, for my ability to despise Rafe MacAlister had long ago grown to full breadth. Now that I found him here in the company of privateers, I knew I had been right to loathe him, and I kept my eyes away from his as I joined other captives at the soup kettle. Perhaps he had been the one to trick August into signing the ship's articles, too. Not until I had a bowl in my hands and could appear preoccupied did I chance to turn and look at him. But the man was gone. As for August, I promised myself that if I should see him again I would tear out his eyes.

When I finished my soup, I followed the row of women back to our jail. This vessel, the others said, had been built to carry cows and sheep. If the builder had spread the bars one inch wider in any place, I could have slipped between them and made my escape. But to where? Swim to Jamaica? I would swim, I vowed, as no one had swum before. Only when I sat on a knee formed by one of the ship's ribs, leaning my head against the side, did I notice that Patience was not to be found. It never occurred to me where she might be, and I felt I had but to wait for her. After all, she was not a good swimmer.

I picked at a piece of tar squeezed from between the planks near my head and rolled it between my fingers as I thought about home. From a tiny opening where tarred rope connected parts I could not name, I could get one eye to the outside and see that it was still daylight. The Saracens' hideous ship, now run by English pirates, was going to our home, albeit the ship itself was full of holes and might sink on the way. This one, no matter that it was cleaner and there was food and air, was not going home at all! We were already at Hispaniola and this accursed boat was going north.

I whispered against the hull, "I will always live in Jamaica. No one can take me far enough that I shall not find a way to return." I used the piece of tar to scratch a line against the wall. I drew Patey, August, and myself, with sad faces and chains around our feet. I wrote, *"Jamaica, Two Crowns, we are prisoners here."* I drew Pa, lying down with a cross upon his chest.

As I drew, I thought of Ma, pining away there, with no way with which to write us, her children, and now with Pa buried in the ocean—oh, Saint Christopher, do not let him wash up on shore where she finds him—she'll be widowed and no doubt unable to manage the plantation, then put out. She'll need us. And now, August a turncoat and a vagabond privateer! Ma's heart will break upon hearing that news. When I drew Ma, I drew tears falling from her eyes. I vowed then that when I found opportunity to write her, I would not write of his wretched apprenticeship. Patience and I would write of our captivity and deprivations. We would somehow make our way home and together we and Ma would survive, perhaps on Ma's sewing.

"Oh, la," I said aloud, for want of any real words to tell the depths of my aching emptiness. The thought that I had begged to go aboard this ship plagued me above all else. If I had stayed where I was, I would have been put off in Jamaica!

"Let us have a seat, there, girl," a woman said to me. She pointed to a small mat. "You can have my bed there, if you wish. My back pains me so."

At that moment the iron door creaked open and I said, "Here, madam, you may have it," as I saw Patience slip through the opening, clutching a parcel, her head bowed. She flinched when the door closed with a loud clang. I thought she had carried her pocket and I called, "Patey!" At once I felt a thrill that she had procured our passage home, and the same moment a terror that her rings had been traded for naught.

Patience came toward me, eyes on the floor, and reached my side just as men above slid the hatch cover closed and the twilight of this deck enveloped us.

"Where have you been?" I asked.

"Above," she whispered.

"That lady said I could use this mat. Would you sit with me?"

Patience lay upon the mat but turned her body away from me and curled her knees up. Her shoulders shook as she cried.

"Patey?" I whispered. "What is that you're carrying? Well, no matter. Please take heart. We shall find a way to get home." Even as I spoke, I doubted we could. I thought of what August had said about escape. I thought of Ma, looking out to sea from the widow's walk, day after day, waiting for us. I put my arm around Patey's waist to comfort her.

She flung my arm from her as if it had been a snake, hurting my shoulder. "Keep still!"

I pulled back a little. "Where did you go? Why did they not bring you with the rest of us? Tell me what happened. Why are you carrying that?"

"Leave me alone, Resolute. Leave me."

I was not sure if she had not finished her words or if she meant more than a wish for me to keep shushed and meant me to leave away from her side. I said, "You did not have to hurt my arm. I merely reached to pat your side."

"Simply do not touch me."

"Fine, then."

She lay a-weeping then, moaning sometimes, and as it was dark and I was fed, I slept to the sound of her sobbing, an old familiar tune. When the woman asked for her pallet again, Patience sat next to me on the wale. She reached under her skirt and loosened a tie, then pulled off the petticoat Ma had made for her. She raised it over our heads and made for us a little tent. She held my hands, and when I started to make a sound, shook them. She opened the parcel she had brought. Into my hands she placed a boiled turtle egg and half an orange. The need for food was ever awake in me and I crammed the egg into my mouth, whole. The fruit had dried, but once I bit through the hard part, the juice was sweet and tart on my tongue.

"Do not smack," she whispered. "I have one for each of us."

"Oh, this is excellent. How did you get these?"

"Just eat it. Eat all of it, too. Even the rind will keep us from scurvy."

"Someone will smell these." But no one did, or if they did they had no idea whence it came, and so we crouched in our dark corner huddled together and ate. Although I might at one time have been loath to eat an orange rind, my hunger spoke over the bitter tang on my tongue. I stuck the orange rind in my cheek and sucked at it until it dissolved. It left a raw place on my tongue and I rubbed the spot against my teeth.

The next day passed with no sign of August or a Spanish galleon filled with gold. I felt renewed enough to feel both thankful to Patience and irritated at our situation, and I complained to anyone who would listen. That evening before I closed my eyes, I hoped for another stolen morsel from Patience, but she stayed at my side all the time and so was not able to collect anything extra. I believed she would do what she could for both of us, just as Ma would have done. It gave me some peace to know that.

At dawn calls from above awoke us. "Strike colors! Take the whip! At the guns! Man the sweeps!" This was followed by the sounds of hurried action, and from my tiny peephole I saw a set of oars thrust from our ship's sides begin to move in tandem to a chant of "Yo-hope!" We turned sharply; the ship listed hard to one side until it rose upon the surface of the water. Our vessel cut through waves helped by sail and oar alike. Some woman of our group cried, "We're going keel over!" and someone else hushed her.

Cannons bellowed off our port side and shook the ribs of the ship and all mine, too. I screamed and clasped my ears at the unexpected roar of them. They levied a full broadside and all of a sudden everyone on this

deck lurched and fell as the ship turned into the wind, jerking and hauling
with shouts from the oarsmen as it started moving full astern. We swayed
again, falling upon each other, and felt the concussion of another full broadside from our ranks of starboard cannon.

In the midst of it I heard, "Run up the colors! Man the canoe!" I had no
idea what the canoe was, but I knew the colors would either strike terror or
a challenge in the souls of our prey. They would either surrender or begin
a terrible battle in which we prisoners could die more easily than the sailors. If they sank this crock we were doomed.

What followed was eerie calm, a chorus of cheering, then more silence.
The English had taken another ship by means of that wrenching maneuver
that tossed us off our feet. I lost my fear as soon as I had heard the cheers,
since the battle was won. I stood upon the wale and got my eye as close to
the little hole as I could, wishing I were on deck to watch. We floated beside
a great ship, as large as the one that had first taken us. The name on her
aft was *Castellón*. I saw "our" longboat coming alongside the *Castellón* and
men climbing aboard with no shouting nor fighting at all. Sailors from
this vessel threw ropes between the two, stitching them together. I heard a
drum playing and a whistle blew.

I peered right to left trying to see anything more, and was about to step
away from the hole when I heard a pistol shot. Someone on our ship
shouted, "Trap! It's a trap!" and the air filled with the sounds of swords
and axes clashing, men commanding orders, men groaning, dying, things
and people falling overboard. Cannons roared from both ships. After many
long minutes, the firing of cannons ceased, but pistol fire continued as long
as the first battle. What had seemed a peaceful surrender turned to a bloody
slaughter.

The air belowdecks filled with smoke and the women began a chorus
of wailing that we were all to perish. From overhead a short silence broke
with a weary-sounding round of cheer. For several hours the English sailors boarded and returned, taking goods from the *Castellón* to the *Falls
Greenway*. Now and then a call echoed above but I grew tired of watching.
Patience was not curious and cared not at all to do it. She took off her petticoat again and rolled it for something to put her head upon. She lay there
at my feet, staring at the beams overhead whilst I stared out the hole. I
wondered if all this fighting and plundering would take the place of our

morning goat soup, and I pressed against my middle, wishing I had another of those precious stolen oranges.

The day waned and the sailors talked more loudly. Some moaned in pain. Others shouted and called to each other. Hour after hour, the sounds did not change. Then, a surprise came such as I had never imagined. Music! I heard a fiddle and drums, and some kind of high-pitched flute. The fiddler played and played, and stamping feet joined in the beat of the drum. The sounds became more drunken and loud, the music less easy to follow. The hatch above us opened. Rafe MacAlister came down the ladder steps followed by a sailor and stomped straight to the cage that held Patience and me. He motioned the man to open the lock, and took Patience by the arm. She went with him. He stepped through the gate as the sailor looked through the women and chose an African slave. "Know ye English words?" he asked her. "I favor singing and dancin'."

"I come by some," she answered.

"Up top wid ye."

Later, I heard music again. Patience did not come down. I thought about the Irish girl with the long red hair. How she had been taken to the banquet. Maybe Patience was dancing and eating. I thought about the splashes late in the night and I tried not to think about Patience eating until she burst, or of her falling overboard. I tried not to think about the sounds of the laughter and dancing. Foreign, delicious smells wafted through the wooden floor. I imagined them having all my favorite sweets. I vowed to try not to think of them eating but the more I tried the worse my hunger grew, so I closed my eyes. I hummed to the tunes amidst the perfume of turtle soup and roast pork haunch.

I thought about the rules of pudding instead. I do not know who made rules about pudding, but there are rules. Pudding should always be larger than the smallest child's head, was one rule. And if it had fruits it should not have hard sauce, but without fruit it should always have sauce. Sauce, I decided, was better when it was warm. And if it had rum in it and Pa lit it at the table that was always nice. I liked the way it glowed around the edges of the flames, kind of blue-green, as the color of the bay most days. I liked the way it was sweet and hot and left a hot place in the back of my throat after I swallowed it. If Patience was having a banquet with pudding I should like to know what kind of pudding was made by pirates, who might not follow the rules. If they had no pudding, I supposed after a difficult day as this when they had been tricked and fought for their lives, one should understand. A roast leg of pork or mutton would do. Perhaps chicken. A string of drool slipped from my lip and drizzled onto my chin. I wiped it away, angry because I had no pudding.

Without food, the other thing I longed for was sleep. That night it did not come, so empty was the place where Patience should have slept. All the other women around me were asleep when the sound of the jail door opening and shutting cut through the rhythmic breathing of midnight.

Patience tiptoed over sleeping women to what had become our place, again carrying a parcel, and again she laid herself down, curled tight as a snail, away from me. She spoke not a word but soon in her sleep she moaned and whimpered. I lay beside her but did not sleep. After a while, she began to whisper, "No. Please not again. No, no."

I did not touch her, but I wondered if her feet had blistered from too much dancing. Familiar sounds awoke me, the watch changing, the clanking of chains, thumping of hard boots on the deck above, men calling orders. Light came in the hole above the wale. Most of the sailors above slept, their raucous snores a constant hum. Women in my cell sat up and stirred.

When Patience sat up, I looked on her with horror. Her face was blue and one eye swollen, her top lip had blood matted in the corner and it was as round as if she had hidden an egg in it. She put the parcel in my lap and lay back, covering her eyes with her arms. Her gown was nearly gone, worn out and torn; it was all but indecent.

"What you got there, missy girl?" a woman asked.

I peeked into the parcel. It was a cake or loaf of some kind. It smelled fruity and tangy. "It is Patey's," I said. "From the dancing."

Patience laid her hand on my arm. Fresh scabs covered her knuckles. I looked from her hand to the loaf to the woman. The women around us shushed and gathered close. Wretched hunger painted all their faces gray as a tombstone. My eyes rested on Patey's, and she nodded to me.

"It is—to share," I said, too softly. I repeated it louder, feeling my heart sink as I said the words. I could have gobbled the whole thing. I had just been thinking that I did not want to share it, even with Patey, rather steal it for myself and eat the entire cake. And here stood twenty-one other people to take a bite. I stuck my thumb into the loaf and pulled off a chunk about an inch wide. I held it to the closest person. For a moment I wondered if they would come for it and beat me and take the thing, but each one waited, silently. Because they were gentlewoman-like about it, I did my best at making the same-sized pieces. When each person had had a token amount there were about enough crumbs left for three more. I pressed a hunk into Patey's hand.

"I do not want it," she said.

"You eat dat, girl," came a voice. Others chimed in. "Don't spare you'self. You take some!"

I took a bite of my piece. It tasted sweet but strange. "It is not bad," I said. " 'Twould be much helped by rum and hard sauce." Some of them thought that was wondrously funny, and many women laughed.

Then one came to Patience and put her hands comfortingly on Patey's head. "We know, girl, what dat cake cost. You keep t'inking how you save all our lives with it."

I said, "There's one extra piece. Who shall have it?"

The woman who held Patience's head said, "Give it to dis girl, here. Keep her heart strong. When you eat dat, girl, you takes all our hearts in with it. Dat keep you."

I looked at the African woman more closely as Patience dutifully sat up and chewed on the morsel of cake. She was the woman who had gone up the ladder with Patience, but she had not come down with cake, or with bruises. She must not have dared to steal some, too.

After that time, the system of feeding and airing prisoners changed. There were so few sailors left whole from the surprise attack that to man the *Castellón* had left the *Falls Greenway* shorthanded. Both ships moved slowly under half sails. Often they brought us abovedecks and left us for hours at a time. I heard one of the English tell a lady that she would get a larger share of food by some mopping. I think it was not a question but an order, for they put us all to cleaning and scouring. They sent me around with a raveled rag to polish the brightwork.

Much as I rubbed, not much changed, but I cared not the least. What mattered was that I was above and fed and could feel the air on my face. In short order I grew to love the sea spray and the sight of dolphins running alongside us, even the rocking of the ship as she moved through the water. There was a certain front-to-back, side-to-side sway that felt as comforting as a hammock on a summer day. Our friend the African slave woman had told us her name. Her slave name was Cora, but she said her real name was Cantok. She said to call her Cora until she died, to pray for Cantok so the spirits in heaven would know who I meant. She calls me "Miss Resolute" and Patience is "Miss Talbot," instead of "Missy," which is proper. It was convention that made that rule, rather like not scratching yourself in public, for I think she is not as old as Patey, and could be our friend and playmate if we were all back at Two Crowns. Cora can read as well as Patience and she has sworn us not to reveal that, too. It is quite a responsibility keeping someone's life inside my heart and not letting any of it slip out my mouth, so I must think about things I say. Captivity was closing my lips.

CHAPTER 4

October 29, 1729

I had almost forgotten we were sailing north, until one day August approached me again. It had been a fortnight since I had seen him last, and he had changed. His face appeared gaunt and hollows had sunken his eyes. The eyes themselves held no sparkle but were dull and lifeless, withered as if the spirit in him had fled and naught was left but the skin. I turned away from him and worked my rag around the knob on the captain's door.

"You're alive?" he asked.

"I am," I said. "Are you? You look as if the duppies have taken your soul to hell and left it there." I said that because I wanted to hurt him for being a traitor. He had seemed so robust while boasting about signing articles.

"Maybe they did. So many was—butchered. Like swine."

"I heard one of the English say the ship was trapped."

"Bloody—I have never seen so much blood."

"And did you fight?"

He gulped, trying not to gag. "Spaniards."

"With pistol and cutlass? You fought?" I could not imagine August, slight and gangling, brandishing a cutlass and flying from a yard.

"They made me clean up the deck. Sharks, you know, circling for days. Hark, though, I have *my* share of rum, now. As good quantity as any sailor," he said, nodding and forcing himself to smile.

"La, August. Are you really my brother? Maybe a good quantity of rum is the difference between what's called 'fierce' and plain '*fear*.'" He turned and made away, but his steps lacked levity. I called after him, "Someone has beaten Patience and blackened her eye. You tell them to leave her be, Seaman Coxswain Second Class."

A few days later I was still scrubbing brass as the sun began to sink; I filled a bucket with seawater from a tackle apparatus, off the port side. I had grown nimble at the task. While dropping a bucket was simple, hauling one up without spilling its contents was no small thing. So long as I pulled slowly I kept most of the water in. I was after my task as the setting sun turned the moisty air to green and then gold. Through the mist where sea and sky became one brassy cloud, I spied a ribbon of black laid on like a mark from a tarman. Not long after I saw it, a fellow rushed past me, put his dirty paw on that brass doorknob I had just shined, and called out, "Captain? Cay off the port amidships. We're in sight of the outer reef."

"Halloo, good man," I called to the sailor as he returned. "What coast is that?"

The man sneered at me but he said, "Cay Largo."

Panic took me. Where was Cay Largo? Was this the northland we had come to? The end of our travels and the beginning of some new villainy? Although shipboard life was not comfortable, Patience had endured no further beatings, and our food rations had neither been shortened nor improved. I took my bucket of water and returned to the deck as if to mop with it. Looking in before I poured it, I saw a tiny fish had come up in the bucket, a wee striped fellow. I chased him through the water and caught him against the side, lifting him from the water. His fine gills strained for air and his mouth opened and closed as if he were wishing water to flow through him as usual. The working of him was as exquisite as any clockwork toy in my bedroom, and infinitely more delicate.

I put the fish back into the bucket and carried him to the side. "It is not for us, to be in familiar waters, wee fish," I said. "Go to my mother at the big house of Two Crowns on the lee side of Meager Bay, Jamaica. Tell her I am coming. Tell her to pray for us." I lowered the bucket over the side, and said to the fish, "It is a long way. I will pray for you, too."

The cries of seabirds, the freshening smell of tidewaters, and the greening of the sky swelled some longing inside me as I had never known before. I held the rope as long as I dared. I imagined that I could see the fish leaving the wooden coffin in which I had caught him and making for a southerly current. The orange of the horizon deepened. A rush of gold light painted the wood of the ship and a thickening fog softened the world to my eyes. The only thing before me with sharp edges was the bucket in my hands. Across the water I saw not merely the small cay of land but in the distance a heavy cloud perched on the surface of the sea. A foul odor came in whiffs, but the pissdale was not far from where I stood and some sailor stood before it, so I returned with my bucket to my task.

One of the captive men motioned to me. He gestured with the hob of kindling he carried. "See here, girl," he said. "Don't suppose you caught any tatties in that?"

Ach. He was Irish. I decided to pretend I could not tell. "No, good man," I replied. "I am made to clean brass knobbings from morn till dark."

"Well, see ye add some to season the pease, as we got no fresh water left nor any salt other than what crusts the splinter of dried beef at the bottom of the pot."

"You want to make soup of ocean water?"

"Just a nogginful. It helps the taste."

A small iron cauldron hung from a trammel over a brazier in the center of the deck. Patience and Cora knelt beside it. Under the watch of an English sailor, Cora was holding a dagger, cutting calabash in chunks and slipping them in it. A whole pineapple roasted in the coals, giving off a delicious fragrance. I hoped Patience would fare more kindly now, and cooking was a good chore for her, for perhaps she would get a little squash rind or dried beef suet that fell into a folded sleeve. I meant to ask them if they had seen the cay afloat in the mist on the water, but for a moment, I stared at the world in this strange golden light.

The sun was reaching the horizon and had painted the entire ship in shades of amber. The brass fittings appeared to be solid gold. Light flashed off the captain's glass window like liquid fire.

At once from overhead a voice called, "Dogwatch to the deck! Mast on the wind*ward*!" He sang the last word, lengthening it long as all the other words he had said.

We girls shrank against a hogshead and a bale of something wrapped in rough cloth and tarred, as we were surrounded by sailors, all peering this way and that. Finally came the ship's captain with his long glass. He climbed halfway up the mainmast to the wide step built there, and hanging by one arm looked through the glass all about the area. When he returned to the deck, he motioned to several of the crew.

I knew them by now. The captain's name was John Hallcroft. The quartermaster was Percival Dinmitty, and the boatswain went by Aloysius though I never heard whether that was a given name or surname. They circled right next to where we knelt by the fire brazier. Patey, Cora, and I shrank down and did not move, trying to become but shadows upon the deck.

Captain Hallcroft said, "It's a ship of the line. Looks French. We've no one left to man her even if we take her."

"We'll take 'er, Cap'm," said Aloysius. "Our men are stouthearted to the last."

I watched the captain as those bragging words made play upon his face. I could see that the man Aloysius had little thought other than fighting and plundering, while Captain Hallcroft held responsibilities in mind. Even a girl young as I knew that for this ship, just as the ships that came to Meager Bay, there was a master someplace back in England who'd paid for the rights to her cargo. It was a risk to what he now carried to take another ship without adequate defenders. I wondered, would the others take us instead? He pursed his lips and tapped the glass with the fingers of both hands as if he were playing it like a flute. "No. We'll make way. Strike the sails and drop the small anchor."

I was well away from the men who had argued over tossing me overboard on the Saracen ship; indeed, Hallcroft was not one of those. Hearing that, I believed I was fond of Hallcroft. Perhaps he had been one of many kind and gracious captains who discussed cargoes in my pa's study. Then I remembered that *I* was the cargo, and I seethed with hate.

Dinmitty cleared his throat and spat on the deck, narrowly missing Cora's skirt hem. "There's no' a drap o' clear water left. Rations will go to half tomorrow. If we don't move along smart, they'll stay on half for four days, then a quarter."

Hallcroft nodded. "As you say, then. We will make for land in a few days. For now have the men heave to."

"And what, sir, if they don't let *us* pass? Men on short rations—"

"Strike sails, Aloysius."

Aloysius was disappointed, but kept his face pinned so that no one could have claimed he had disagreed with the captain. I caught it, though. How a stern visage could make even a dull person of good use. A great bustling ensued about us as everything aboard this ship, whose purpose in creation was meant for movement through water, was brought to halt. The stoppage was so abrupt that even the towed canoe, the shallop from which they had boarded the *Castellón,* bumped nose first into the aft hull. The *Castellón* languished far to the rear. It had been unable to keep time with the *Falls Greenway* and was not even a concern at the moment.

Night was falling and a French ship of the line was approaching. These were two facts on every tongue, and though they meant little to me, I feared they made all about us so wary that we keened our eyes toward the far horizon, trying to see what fate that could bring us. Perhaps, I thought, this meant a vessel large enough to take down these English rogues. We had gone from the hands of Saracens to these men, and rough though they might be, we were far better off. What would French sailors be like? And would they return us to Jamaica or take us to France? The English struck the colors and shrouded all the sails, sending men to man the guns but wait with the hatches shut.

"Strike that lamp!" someone called, and the single lantern on board was doused.

The Irish prisoner who had asked me for the salt water shoved us aside and poured my bucket of salt water on the brazier, sending a plume of smoke into our faces. Hallcroft himself shouted, "Damned fool! The smoke will be seen!"

"Aye, sir. I should have put a plank on it. My apologies!"

I watched him with open mouth. The man was lying! He had done it for a signal, I would swear on a Bible.

Dinmitty turned to another sailor and said, "Get the prisoners below and lock them up. Take that little one," he said, pointing to me. "One sound from any one of them and cut out her heart and feed it to the sharks."

"Aye, sir," the sailor said. "Move!" he shouted in my ear.

I moved without sound, bare feet on wood planks, to the place he chose for me to stand. I chanced to look beyond the rail to the dark form that approached us out of the rust-colored sky. Everyone held quiet. Even the sea stilled and the wind paused as the hulk came within hailing distance and crossed our bow. I heard a loose sail flap on the ship across the waves.

Captain Hallcroft took his chin in his hand and frowned. "Not a light. Not a sound. She's dead in the water."

A lone seagull begged exception from above. Then, no doubt at the same moment the others saw it, I perceived a swarm of gulls on the deck, circling, quarreling, chasing up and down the rigging. The great, lumbering ship of the line was adrift. A voice just audible above the screeching gulls floated on the wind, saying, *"Ohé, ohé. La peste! Sauvez-vous! La peste!"*

I watched Hallcroft sneer and turn to Dinmitty, whose mouth opened wider than his eyes. "They have the plague, sir. Make sail immediately."

"Ask him how many are alive."

Dinmitty went to the railing and called out, *"Combien en vie?"*

"Aucun," came the answer. *"La peste."*

"None, sir," Dinmitty said. "Even the warning man must be afflicted."

The sailor prodded me in the side and I began the descent into the hold, but I heard Hallcroft say, "Burn it to the waterline."

From my peephole I could not see the death ship but I heard the call for archers to ready their oil pots and bows. I put together the whole story from the springing sound of the arrows' flight, the roiling sound of angry, hungry gulls, the crackling of burning timber, falling rigging, and great exploding powder kegs. I smelled the reek of broiling flesh burned too long. From my wee hole I saw that the sky again turned orange and bright for many minutes before darkness fell around us.

Another call sounded from above. "Rats! Rats!" men shouted. Hundreds of desperate, swimming rats came this way after leaving the death ship.

Cora said, "Rats will bring plague to us all, then," and she rolled over and said no more. I heard hissing, as if gravel fell from the sky, and though it was dark outside, I stood and put my eye to the hole again. I could not make out the calls overhead. I pictured the pelting sound on the water being the feet of hoards of black rodents running across the surface of the sea clambering over each other toward this ship. I kept my face away from the wood itself, afraid the rats might see me and scurry right into the peephole. After more shouting, the crew spread a path of oil and tar around us. I watched an arc of fire go across the sky; sizzling, it vanished into the water. Another dot of fire soared off the top deck and this time it hit something in the water and flames spread across the waves and came to life.

The rats swam into the flames. Their other choice was to drown. I saw a fin. A shark had come to dine. I smiled, wondering how he would enjoy roasted rat instead of raw fish. All that mattered was that the rats did not make it onto the ship. Whether a shark took the plague and died I cared not at all.

The waves kept on, but at length the heavy splashing and the frantic small splattering sound ceased. The flames died at last. Darkness covered the deep, and there was naught to see or hear. I sat, my back against the hull, and stared into the emptiness in my soul. "We shall get home, again," I said. "I know we shall." I curled up next to Patience.

Cora lay on Patey's other side and said a single word and nothing more. It was enough. "Plague."

Full seven hungry days came and went without further events except one. Patience had gone above the night before, then woke me one morning, and asked, "Did you move my shoes?" She called out, "My shoes are gone. Who has taken my shoes? I will tear your hair out and chop you into shark bait."

"Patience," I said, raising my voice to the level of hers, "what a threat to make. Ma would be ashamed." Had she learned such glorious villainy from dancing with the sailors on those nights when she went above? I had never heard such abuse from a female and I enjoyed the power of it. She was filled with venom and I wanted to remember the words for the sheer strength they implied.

"I want my shoes."

No one made a sound. My own slippers were long gone. They would not have fit her anyway, but there was nothing I could offer. "Maybe some-one borrowed the shoes." I turned toward the other women. "Some person has borrowed Miss Talbot's shoes. They should hand them back and no trouble will come to them."

"La. Be shushed, Resolute," Patey said. "No use. There is a thief's heart amongst us and it is colder than stone already."

The ship moved, and I had gotten so used to its sounds, that I knew we made way with great speed. I believed they never struck sail but kept at it day and night. I could not imagine how far north we had come, though the sun no longer climbed straight overhead but rose off the stern and set off the stern. It felt to me as if we were bound to sail off the top of the world and into an abyss the likes of which God alone would fathom. Patience contin-ued to go above about every three or four days, but in all those nights she had not found a way to scavenge us another loaf or even a small egg. Even the sailors were going hungry, and naught to drink but poor rum. I was thankful she had not come back with so many bruises. No one returned her shoes.

After a few more days' hard sailing we lay at anchor two nights, not moving until the third day. During those days they sent the canoe ashore to bring back food. I wondered if August, the ship's venerable new coxswain, had rowed it.

They brought back water and dried beef, casks of oranges for the sail-ors. For the prisoners, though, they put hardtack in the pot and added wa-ter and fish heads. Sometimes our stew was naught but fish heads. Often it had vegetables I knew nothing of, nor would I have sought those save that my stomach was so unaccustomed to being full by then that I would have eaten a bedpost had it been well steamed. Once in a while Hallcroft took a look at the captives' cooking pot, wrinkled his nose, and walked on.

On a day like all the others, I hauled my bucket of water to the deck and sat upon a coil of rope. I began to shake and stared for some moments at my feet, missing both slippers and stockings, covered with a scum of dull black. The nails had grown some and the bottoms had become cal-lused. I feared I had taken ill, but felt no pain, nor did I faint or have any vagary other than a swimming in my brain. It was the scurvy, I feared. I sat for several moments and had just found my feet when I heard a cry from across the deck and rose on tiptoe to see.

One of the Saracen sailors joined another captive in argument with one of the English and without warning he bolted for the side of the ship. He lunged fast and sailed forward in a jump overboard but his foot snagged part of a net. Like a great bass they pulled him aboard, fighting and straining. They clapped hands upon him and dragged him to a post where they made his hands fast with knots. The sailors brought Dinmitty there and the captain came, too. Men gathered around so I could not see, but I heard the men make charges against the Saracen. Dinmitty ordered the man who'd caught him to deliver forty lashes with a cat. A voice I knew as well as my own came through the din, and August's voice said, "Sir, you can hardly blame them," though it stopped short. I thought that August had been murdered, and began to cry over my saltwater bucket, turning my face to the wind.

I was glad I could not see then, for I heard enough. Each fall of the cat snagged through the air like a wind-whipped thorn bush, making me shudder, the sound pricking my skin as if I felt each blow. I could not know who was being lashed but a man roared in agony. Was that the prisoner or my brother's newfound deep voice? After twenty-eight lashes he ceased crying out. At thirty-nine lashes, Dinmitty's voice called a halt and someone said, "Dead, Cap'n."

Naught but silence followed. A few mumbled words I could not make out flitted across the deck like so many dead birds blown to the boards. I gave full way to my tears then, staring hard toward the crowd of sailors. When the men moved away at long last, there was August, standing at attention next to the gory body of the beaten man. He stared over the waves across the beastly remains, glancing neither left nor right, as if pinioned in place. August was not dead, that I knew. I dipped the rag into the bucket. Little by little, keeping my eyes away from the dead man hanging from his pillar, I found brass bits all the way across the deck and rubbed middlingly until I reached his side. "What are you doing, August?" I whispered.

"Toeing a line." He tapped his toe against the deck, and I saw August's boots were on the line of pitch between the beams. He hissed out the words through stiff lips, "Have mercy. Do not speak to me."

I moved on, cleaning, if whisking a wet sop across anything in my path could be called cleaning. I made quick time away from my brother, to make myself appear as if I were carrying out my task. I was hurt that he should think my talk was some offense. Perhaps if he was seen in conversation his punishment could be far worse. There was that hideous corpse in his face to remind him. I rubbed my saltwater rag across nails on the pinnacle. It left shredded thread behind. My throat hurt from the tears running down inside it, though I felt relieved.

In the afternoon, August stood there while we were served our noggins of soup. He stood until the last dogwatch was called. He was still standing there when they herded us below like the oxen whose stalls we had replaced. I lay awake for hours. I might wish to say that dread about my brother's welfare filled my mind; what kept me awake was a lost feeling that rather than them tormenting him to death, he would, by dint of all this rough treatment, become one of them, the tormentors.

And, while Patience had endured beatings, and August was standing stiff under the hot sun, I had suffered nothing more than famine. They *had* threatened to tear out my heart, I reminded myself, but that had not happened nor was there a sign that it was probable at that moment. Surely they would not have carried it out, one part of my mind said, while at once another part argued back that these were men who had thrashed a starving prisoner to death for trying to escape. He would have drowned anyway. Why not let the fool go? I thought, might I also prefer a quiet sleep in the sea with my pa, than to have the skin flayed from me until I bled away? These thoughts stayed fastened in my mind as if they made a pitch line against which I, too, held my dirty toes.

When they called the morning watch and a few of the women went up to start chores, I asked them to inquire for us about August's welfare but no one spoke of him. By noon, they were sent down and I expected that I would be among those called to replace them, but we were kept below and the hatch above pinned fast and locked. The seas had grown during the morning, and hit the ship from the opposite side as it had the days before.

"Patey?" I asked. "What is happening?"

She shrugged lifelessly. "It might be a storm we have sailed into. A hurricane. I pray we shall all drown and they will lose their profits."

"La, Patience. I do not want to die."

The ship rose at a perilous angle then rocked back into place. She said, "I do."

I stared into her eyes and what she said terrified me no less than the death I saw in her already. "I shall pray against you, then," I whispered.

"You pray anything you choose. Pray to the wind, the sky, or the filth in the bilge. No god waits to either hear you or do your bidding. Pray to him or curse him, no matter. No saint arrives to save any girl from violence no matter the number of prayers. The saints are naught but shriveled skins and piles of bone. Fools all. What do I care if you pray? You may as well dance a jig or curse heaven. It does the same good."

"La," was all I could get out. I pulled away from her.

A sound assailed us much like the hundreds of rats swimming across the sea. The wind unleashed the wrath of the ages upon us. Sails whipped about with a great shearing sound; one of them tore asunder. The ship rose and fell across great swells as if it were crossing mountains. Some of the women grew sick from the pitching, though I stayed whole, proud now of my sea legs though I shuddered constantly. Beams all around gave out with great groaning and cracking as if the belly of the ship were coming undone and the *Falls Greenway* were as sick as the people aboard her. The malaise I felt was fear of Patience's words. My sister, cursing God, brought this storm.

Yet, morning came. We crept up the ladder with something near jubilation into fresh air. August was near his post, exhausted and drenched, pale gray and drear as a heap of rope; he had tangled himself in heavy lines to save being washed overboard.

"On your feet, boy!" Aloysius said to him. August struggled but righted himself and stepped from a loop of rigging. I feared that the fool boatswain would deliver my brother a sound cuffing or worse, but all he said was, "That was a right williwaw if I ever seen one. Go below and sleep for the first watch and let that be a lesson. Never speak back to the officers of this ship." As August passed Aloysius, the man slid something into August's hand. It was a carrot-sized slice of dried beef. My throat went dry for the want of that beef, though glad I was that August had food. Had I known the man was capable of that sort of tenderness, I would have taken all his words differently.

On we went, forever it seemed, heading so that the sun rose at my right hand and set at the left as I faced the bow of the ship. As we moved, we found ourselves wont to huddle together at night for warmth. During the day my tattered gown did little to keep me warm, save for the heaviness of Ma's quilted petticoat.

One day we sailed into what looked like a great loss of downy feathers from a flock of geese. Cold and wet, the stuff vanished in my hands. The wonderment of snow caused me to stare without ceasing at the sky. Patience helped me that day to remove my quilted petticoat and wrap it over my shoulders as if it were a cape. What a marvelous thought she had, too, as that made me a great deal warmer.

Even though the English sent parties to shore and brought back fresh food, Patience began to be sick even when the ship was still, or at least when the rocking seemed a melancholic swing caught in a breeze, rather than the high gavotte of the stormy days. Nothing would calm her stomach, and if I tried to comfort her she shrieked at me so that I wondered if she had gone mad. After all those days aboard a ship, being a prisoner seemed inconvenient, rather than a hard punishment or captivity, for though we needed perhaps a doctor and rest and good broth for her, for me boredom had been my chiefest complaint other than hunger. Now it was cold.

These days there were no songs sung belowdecks. The earthy joy of African rhythm had frozen, too. When I was above and one or another of the sailors would take a rest from his work and pick up a flute or squeezebox, I clung to the notes of music as if they nestled in my innermost workings. One evening as an old squeezebox lent "If I Wast a Blackbird" the most elegant melancholia, I found privateers weeping in their cups. I gave myself to learning the tunes though some of the men spoke with the direst accents or mispronounced things entirely. I learned the words, too. Ma would have disapproved. *"A coarse and lusty wench a-riding barebacked on a mare,"* went one song, and another began with a chant of *"Damn your eyes, Bos'n Bandy. Damn your eyes."* I had no idea what the song was about, but the tune was merry and anyone aboard deck might step out a few paces of a jig when they played it.

When I was made to clean, I was often cursed at in language of an art that would have made even my pa faint. I grew used to their words and soon realized there was less threat behind them than there was a natural tendency to venomous hissing, rather like a basketful of snakes afloat on the sea, so to even the reckoning, I began to pilfer. First a bit of thread or a button, sometimes a nail or a bit of rope, once, a hat. I tossed the things overboard soon as I got a chance, placing them on the gunwale and bumping them off with my elbow. It was rare I heard the splash, but I felt satisfied that their things were lost forever. One time I tossed over a belaying pin left loose in its notch. A sailor was cuffed and sent hunting the thing, and I smiled heartily at seeing his blackened eye.

Just when it seemed that the sea was to be my life, that nothing changed nor would it ever change, that dirty men and piteous women were to be my life's companions and cold starvation my lot, the ship changed course and heeled the sails leeward. We began to move with the sun and toward its setting. I watched men furling sails and fitting out the canoe with its small sail and oars and three lanterns. When the sun went down, four men climbed into the boat and began to row for shore. The night closed around them just as I climbed down the ladder. I felt the ship moving in the night, yet, rather than the usual rhythm of calls and chatter above, we sailed in ghostly quiet. Before morning broke the ship had calmed in a way that I knew we had moored in a bay. Nary a lantern gleamed above. No moon cast a shadow, nor did stars prick the heavens. Save for the glow of sea foam, it was black as pitch when they led us to the ladders.

Against the coldest wind I had ever known, the English lined the women up and made us climb down the rigging again. This time they ferried us ten or so at a time, still under guard, to an empty beach of dull buff and stone. As I awaited my turn, I looked hastily for August. I spotted him below in the boat holding an oar, once I had both feet over the side and was about to take a step downward. "Brother!" I called out.

"Get on wi' ye," one of the sailors barked at me. I was afraid he would give me a shove over the side, so I scrambled down the ropes.

"Ho!" August called, and helped me settle my feet into the boat. He reached up for Patience and settled us in. I took a seat beside him. He took up his oar as the other men did, and one called out the strokes.

I asked him, "You will come with us, will you not?"

"Quiet. I am a sailor now, Resolute."

"But August, we'll be alone. You cannot stay. Oh, tell me you shall not stay with—these"—I looked about to see if anyone paid me heed—"men!"

"I must. I signed papers. I will only go around, though, Ressie, and then I will come for you. I promise." An unsteady glow filled the sky, as if the sun hid behind a blanket of dense clouds.

At long last I asked, "How far around? How long will it take?"

"I do not know. But I will come for you. I will."

When we made the land, they put us off into what I found was a circle of Englishmen holding captives at sword's point. The sailors with all haste started to make for the canoe again. I held August's sleeve and looked into his eyes, trying to see what he might feel for us, his sisters, cast ashore on some strange land. There was something there, I vow, though what it was I could not say. Not a tear marked his countenance. Perhaps he had learned to cry on the inside as I had. Or perhaps he was keeping a stern face for those who might watch him. He whispered to me, "I will make my fortune and I will come for you both."

I called out, "I will watch for you, August. Do not forget us, your sisters. Do not forget we are deserted here." There was no time to hear his answer if he gave one, for he had turned his face to the sea.

On the beach we waited and shivered, sitting upon the sand. Cora and I sat on either side of Patience, who said nothing, staring at her feet. I felt an urge to lean to one side or the other, to make up for the swaying of the land. I knew the ground was not moving, yet my constant rolling with the ship had become such a habit that it continued here. I felt ill, so much did the ground seem to swell and sway.

Cora asked, "Feels like you still on the boat, don't it?"

"Yes," I said. Though in truth it was worse, for the ship would come to rights, but this ground moved with some scheme other than an ocean, some devilment of my mind, so that I could not guard against it. I lay upon the sand and stared at the sky, all gray and heavy with clouds. Only then did the earth seem to lie still beneath me. "August is gone, Patey. Gone with the rovers."

"I know," she said.

What a land this was. What a sea. Cold. Bleak. Black. Not a hint of a shimmering blue-green coral reef. Not a leaf hung on any tree. Dead trees stood like gray skeletons forked against a drab sky. I needed no further proof that we were indeed nearing the top edge of the world than the closeness of the sky, for the gray clouds caught and snagged on the tops of the trees. How much farther the edge was, God knew, but I feared we should find it and plummet into the abyss. I whispered to myself, to the sky, repeated it louder, "I hate my brother August. I shall always, always hate him." As I said it, I squinted at the clouds, willing them in my imagination to part, for the sun to appear, for the sand to warm, and the voice of Ma to call me home for dinner. I would eat all my vegetables, this time. I said, "He will come back for us."

Patey turned to me and let out a deep breath. "Yes. Keep watching for him. Watch for him always."

CHAPTER 5

November 20, 1729

The men bade us stand. I watched money change hands, new voices and faces amongst the men who scrutinized us as if we were wild boars that might charge their drawn cutlasses at any moment. And then the walking began. Uncle Rafe came along at the rear of the line as we walked. He was the only one from the trip here that came; all the other pirates went somewhere else, back to the sea, I suspect. May they all drown. God send them the plague. The pox. A fire. A Gypsy ship loaded with Saracens, rats and plague, and blasting kegs and fire.

We walked any number of hours I could not fathom. I had no shoes. My feet ached but yet grew numb; I could not feel the ground I walked upon, yet every pebble made me wince. I began to imagine the drumming of each footfall as a pace in a dance. A chant came from some lost memory, and I began to sing something old that Ma sang when she walked upon the hills, mumming it with my lips.

Everyone stumbled. I began to believe Patience's hand holding mine was the only feeling I had in the world. After a while we could go no other way but single file and so I had to let go of her hand. I got a stitching in my side and it spread to both sides. If I could have found time alone I would have eaten the rest of my pocket.

I stared at the ground in front of each step, wishing that Patience's feet would stay long enough to warm it before I stepped there. I tried to step into her footprints, but of course, that was imaginary, for there was no print on the frozen ground. Her feet were as frozen as mine. I had never known such agony. The numbness and burning and bitter shivering never stopped.

With every step I thought of new ways to hate Rafe MacAlister, whose fault it was we were here. "Patience?" I whispered.

"Yes?"

"Do you think Uncle Rafe was a pirate always? Did he join them as August did?"

"I do not know. Be shushed, Ressie."

"He was fighting the other pirates. I saw him do it. Right alongside Pa."

"Nary the first man with duplicity of heart."

I made her explain that as I stumbled onward another length of time, holding to my sides against the shooting pain that threatened to bend me. "I wish someone would steal us back and take us home again."

"It will not happen."

"August said we have to start over. I just want to go home, that's what I want. Some bloody French pirates could kill Rafe MacAlister and take us on a big man-o'-war or a ship of the line, as they called that one they burned down with the rats and the plague, remember? And then they would take us back to Jamaica. And then we would find Ma and take up sewing. I figure since those Saracens fed us almost not at all, and the English fed us quite a bit better, well, the French do like their victuals, Ma always said, and they would have more food and sail around the other way and take us home if we asked them to and explained how we were stolen. Mostly should someone kill Rafe MacAlister, that's the good start of it. French voyagers, I think—"

A hand jerked me from the line. "Who's going to kill Rafe MacAlister for you, brat? I'm going to tie you to that tree there and leave you for the crows." I looked up into Uncle Rafe's grizzled face, aware that although I began with a whisper my voice had taken strength from my words and I had been talking loudly enough to echo in the woods around us. He held my arm with a grip that felt like he would crush my bones. He pulled a dagger and held it against my lips, sliding it up and down so that I felt a stinging, as he said, "It would be worth the ten pounds I'll get for you, to me, to cut your throat and watch you strangle on your own blood, you little cur.

Maybe I will just cut your tongue out. How would you like that? Maybe I'll cut out your briny tongue and give you a taste of what's been keeping your sister company. Eh?"

My mind raced. My stomach gnawed and growled as he shook me. Had Patience been given extra food? The look in his eyes told me something more, as if I were to know something unknowable. Remembering Patey's bruised and bloody face, I shrank from him and he let go my arm. Soon as we began to move again, I sang Ma's old charm against evil to the rhythm of my steps, my voice meant for Patey's ears. *"Gum-boo cru-ah-he na clock. Gum-boo du-he-he na'n gaul, gum-boo loo-ah-he na lock."*

Patience turned and stared at me, not watching where she walked, and my heart was moved, for she smiled! She turned and took up my song, the first part which I had forgotten, and whispered the song under her voice to the rhythm of our feet. *"Ulk-ah he-en mo-lock; gun gaven-galar gluk-glock."*

I answered back with my part and she sang again, *"Go-intay, go-intay, sailtay, sailtay, see-ock, see-ock, oo-ayr!"* I thought of Rafe MacAlister, and chanted the ancient words under my breath until I laughed aloud. My laughter was not mirth but clinging faith in the words I said, a curse against all who might do us harm. I wished I had thought of the songs while still in the capture of the Saracens. Perhaps they would never have got us as far as the English sailors and Rafe, and we would be home already.

The path widened into a narrow road. Waist-high brambles lined both sides. If a cart had come along we would have had to stand in deep brush to let it pass. They stopped us by a well to rest. The well was below a small rock circle, under a roof so low that anyone taller than me would have to stoop to reach the cracked and useless bucket that had been left by it. We fixed our quilted petticoats as capes. "That is warmer," I said. I thought Patey looked so haggard, so drawn, that I feared for her life.

"Why do you look at me so?" she asked.

"Something is so lost in your eyes. Your face is so terrible you make me afraid."

"'Tis merely that you have not seen me in the light of day in so long."

"We shall go home soon. Mayhap that old charm will work."

"'Tis old foolishment. Ma was naught but a gentlewoman and she would never cast a spell or a charm. 'Twas a song she knew from her granny." Patience brushed her hands along her arms under the petticoat-cape. "I doubt we shall ever see Jamaica again. I doubt I will live to see Christ's Mass Day."

I pressed her arms with my hands then, the same way she was doing, to give more comfort to her. "I am more afraid now than ever I was before. We must go home again. If the charm helps, it is good to remember it."

Cora fiddled through the other women toward us. She said to me, "Little Miss Resolute, what is that shining on your sister's back?"

I saw the shine just as she said it, too, and clasped my hands across my mouth. "Patience, turn quickly." The cloth had worn through and showed a glint of metal with the too obvious shape of a coin printed into the linen. Our treasures!

Patience rolled it in her hand. "I shall turn it inside outside," she said, and worked the cape over her head again.

Cora squinted and asked, "What's you got sewn into that, Missy?"

Patience shrugged and said, "It is nary a thing," but I heard how Cora's voice had changed. Now on land, she had said "missy" the old slave way instead of Patey's name.

I said, "It is nothing but Ma's wee duppy charm. Back of every petticoat."

"Maybe you need to give me a duppy charm," she said. "Maybe you got more charms dan dat. Maybe I keep quiet about 'em shiny golden charms and you could keep de res' if you shared but one. Duppies never harm no one dis far away."

Patience raised her eyes to look at Cora's face and said, "I shared our food when you were starving."

"Share one t'ing more. You Massa's daughter. You live on de backs of my mother and my gran. You ne'er eat a crumb dat someone else didn't hand-make and bring to you. All I got to do is say it loud and mens take it all from you."

Was Cora one of our slaves? I did not know her at all. She must have always worked in the fields or someplace away from the house. She had seemed so decent when we were in the cage together. Yet if she belonged to Pa, she belonged to us now. Patience glared at Cora. I did not dare let down my posture of defense. "How you change so from what you seemed on the ship. I thought you were our friend. Our companion."

"You don' share with a friend?" she asked. "Den you lets me wear dat and be warm for a whiles. I give it back to you in a whiles." She laid her hand on Patey's cape and I saw her fingers wrap themselves into it and hold tight.

"Cantok!" I said. Cora jerked her hand away from Patey's clothing as if there had been a thorn in it.

A voice broke the air among the three of us. "You!" Uncle Rafe said, coming for us. I cringed and held Patey's hand, ready for him to clutch at me again. Yet the arm he jerked was Cora's. "You come this way."

He pulled her down the path. As she went, Cora turned and looked toward us. She grimaced as if she might start to cry and Rafe gave her a shove. Two men, one old, one younger than my pa seemed, stood at a short fence with a horse and a small donkey by them. They gave Uncle Rafe coins that he counted, and when he was finished, he tooth-marked two of them.

I expected the men would ride the horse and put Cora on the donkey. Instead, they tied her hands with coarse rope and bound the other end to the saddle of the horse. The young man got on the horse. The old one swung himself onto the donkey, his feet dragging the ground. Cora walked alongside, her face toward the road. Under her skirt, rotted and torn off at the hem so it was shorter than was decent, I spied Patience's shoes moving along on Cora's feet. She never looked up as they passed us.

I wanted to call out "Farewell!" but I did not. I had known her kindness longer than I had known her greed, and the part of Cora that I would miss was indeed the good part. At least, thank heaven, she did not say anything to give away our secret. The rest I did not try to understand just then, for we were compelled to get into two lines and walk the road.

We walked until the air darkened, for no sun set. Staying off sharp stones, thorns, rough clay, and horse droppings occupied my mind fully. I could sing no more. All my strength went to putting one foot ahead of the last. We stopped at a place that was more of a cave than an inn. After they barred the door they gave us potatoes boiled with milk and herbs. For me it tasted wonderful, but Patience could not keep it down and as we had sat where we stood before, she leaned over on the floor to be sick.

They bade us lie side by side on damp ground, and for coverings against the cold, tossed a few old flea-bitten skins upon the lot. With some tugging and grunting, the skins moved about and covered perhaps half the women. A few of them set up a squabble and exchanged blows for the rights to a filthy old hide. I lay low, ducking the fists swinging over my head, and tried to lie as close to Patey as I could. The men prisoners were across the room. A man from the inn stood to guard us with a musket. One of the older women asked him the name of this place. "It has no name," he said. "It is just a place."

Then one of the men asked him where we had landed, and the man said that we came ashore around the heel of Casco Bay. And where we were now was outside of Harraseeket. A woman on my left side said, "Ain't that jus' like 'em? Won't tell a woman nothing but has all the time in the world for a bloke."

I wondered if more houses stood over the next hill and if there might be someone to whom I could explain our lives and how we had been kidnapped. I would make them understand that Patience and I did not belong to this group. I meant to remember these places. "Casco and Harraseeket, Casco and Harraseeket," I chanted under my breath. I would write a letter to Ma. I would tell her how to find us. I decided I would not tell Ma about Cora being greedy, and perhaps we would find her and buy her from those men and keep Cora with us. I would see she got a whipping for the shoes, though. Things like that cannot go unnoticed with slaves. I thought about telling Patience, or asking if she had seen them, too. At length, however, I decided again to keep the thoughts with me.

In the morning we were fed the same stew of potatoes. It was so cold in the cave my breath formed a cloud such as I had never seen before. After those days aboard ship, the potatoes were quite comforting to me, and Patience did tolerably better with it today, too. Rafe MacAlister blustered into the room and whistled as if we were a pack of dogs. "Get in line. Get in line," he called. "End of the road for most of ye."

A woman from the inn pushed and shoved at us with a heavy stick the way you might work a hesitant sow into a corner. She growled and muttered, threatening us with the stick but none dared affront her. She produced a bucket of water and walked before the women. "Wash yer faces, ye hoors. Get tha' glin off yer. Get to it, now. Ye's'l ne'er be her lady's dresser wi' them foul troll's faces. Any you 'as bleedin' get back and leef t' others first."

"Why, Patey!" I whispered. "How rude."

Patey cautioned me with a raised finger. "Put your petticoat back under your skirt." She snatched it from my shoulders, and with the same brusque motions Ma had used, tied it to my waist.

"But I am cold. And I do not want to be some woman's dresser."

"Check later for holes and patch them. Sew a piece of your gown to it."

"Where shall I get thread? You will have to help me."

"Scrub your face, Ressie," she said, falsely cheerful as the bucket came past us. We dipped in our hands and took water. Cold drizzles of it ran down my arms to my skirt. "Take a thread from someplace that cannot use it anymore. You shall always, from this moment on, have to be clever and make use. Do you hear me?"

"Well, tell me what to do," I said, as she threaded a needle from her petticoat.

"I told you. Be clever. Make everything count. Let me fix your pocket." When she felt satisfied, she put her own back in place.

Rafe strutted about the room and stood upon a small chair. "Line!" he called. From under his coat, he produced a long black whip. He thrashed it over our heads as if in warning, snapping it on both sides of the line. Someone behind me cried out with pain. Once in line, we trudged up the frozen road. I had felt cold inside the cave but the chill outside was bitter. My feet felt as if every step were trod across hot coals, so great did the pain shoot up from the soles. My arms, my nose, everything became numb and yet pained at the same time. I could not speak. My lips froze in place with the cold.

A collection of small wooden shacks, no more than our slave quarters, sat beyond a small hill. In the midst of the little houses, a clearing held a wooden platform that wore a covering of white dust. All the women stepped upon the platform, and Rafe began that shrill whistle again, time after time, until people emerged from the houses. They collected about us, looking upon us as if we were sheep or horses.

I peered in awe at my feet and the pressing of my steps upon the white stuff. "Patey? What is this?" I asked.

"Frost. It got so cold in the night that the wood froze and the dew upon it became ground snow."

"Ground snow?"

"The white thing you thought was feathers falling from the sky. Snow. This kind is on wood or the ground. The kind in the air falls to the earth. Sometimes in great amounts, sometimes mere—"

"Quiet!" Rafe hollered. He stepped upon the platform, too. In ones and twos, he along with our other captors sent the men aboard the platform. People crowded up. Some stayed silent, but many jeered and called out. Some of the buyers seemed stern and some appeared gentle. Pious men in black frocks. Lordly men stepped from carriages and rough men came on foot. Men were sold for coins, for pistols, and one was traded for a horse. Then they came for the women. Rafe took Patience's arm and pulled her to him. "I'll see what you'll bring. If it ain't enough, you be mine."

I made fists with both my hands, but he left her and took up the arm of an African woman and called to the crowd. "Fresh and sturdy stock! Fresh and sturdy stock! Trained. Hardworking. Who'll give me fifteen pound for this one here?"

"Let's see 'er teeth!" a man called from the people gathered.

"Open yer mouth," Rafe said. When the man was satisfied with the captive's teeth, he nodded and she was led away. I thought about that Saracen beaten to death under Captain Hallcroft's orders, and though he had seemed genteel, he had stood there, watching. And August, though he protested, he, too, watched. I shuddered. Why, any sort of man could buy any other man and be kindly or be the devil himself, and the sold person had no voice in his own fate! Black spots swirled before my eyes and I nestled closer to Patience's skirt. Very soon, they came for her.

Patience held her hands toward me in a gesture of pathos as they pulled us apart, more conjoined than if we had been two halves of a cloth rent asunder. I remembered for a long time, the feeling of her hands pulled away from me, the last touch of her upon my arms. She stood as two men bid for her, and a low and hard-looking one came up and offered seventeen pounds and nine. Rafe held out his hands to collect Patience's earnings and dropped one of the coins, having to chase it around the planks before it quit spinning. I was incensed that he had dropped my sister's price on the floor.

When they led her from the step, I followed on her heels. The man who bought my sister pushed me away. "Get back, ye!" he ordered, raising his hand to strike me.

"I am going, too," I said. Without Patey I would die. I would surely die.

"I bought one. Won't feed kin, neither; that's trouble. Get back." He kicked at me as if I were a dog snapping at his feet.

"Please!" I shouted. From behind me an arm wrapped around my middle and carried me like a peck of flour away from Patey's side. I did not cry out again, or sob. I put away more feelings. Put them deep. I would give them no satisfaction with my tears.

Patience did not cry or say a word or even make a sound, but went into a wagon with a short top on it which was closed down the way you'd pack up an animal. They crowded two others in with her and drove it away. I watched her go and felt indignity, not longing or sorrow. How little I had known my own sister, my own skin, before our kidnappings, and how she had changed by the brutality and beatings she had suffered on the ship. The strange way she had of treating me, also, for I had not forgot that she had nearly unbrained me at one instance to keep me out of the hands of the Saracens. I had been orphaned indeed. That notion took hold of me while her cart made its rattly way down the path until my heart seemed as if it lay at the bottom of the sea. All was lost.

An hour later, in the year of our Lord seventeen hundred and twenty-nine, on the twenty-first day of November, I was sold for the first time to a black-frocked farmer and his wife. Both of them wore high-peaked black beaver felt hats such as I had seen in drawings before. Both were so homely and sallow that under those great dreary hats I would never have known the sex of one or the other were it not for madam's frilly mobcap. As they pulled me from the platform and pushed me into a cart, I called for Patience. She was long gone away. As were they all.

Rafe MacAlister walked off with his bags jingling, filled with the solid coin of our skins. I had brought him only five pounds.

I looked like trouble, they said.

CHAPTER 6

November 21, 1729

"Resolute Catherine Eugenia Talbot," I said.

"You'll be Mary."

I stared, somewhat dumbfounded, and in a quite ill-mannered way, at the old woman. "I shall not."

"And what talent have you?" The hag sorted me with her eyes as if I had been a bowl of seeds.

"Talent? I have learnt two songs on the harpsichord."

"I'm talking about your work, you little heathen."

"What do you mean?" Now that I was out of the ship's hold and in a proper lodging, I wanted a bath and a rest, and to have someone get the knots out of my hair.

She poked my arm as if I were contagion itself. "What skills? Are you a laundress? Cook?"

"I have always *had* a laundress," I said. "And there were three cooks. One for meats, one for sweets, one for everything else." I said, "I can do embroidery." I drew myself up, saying, "Quite fine embroidery," though my work was barely passable.

"Well, Mary, you shall carry the chamber pots each morning and fill the scuttles."

"I would never do that. It is filthy. Have one of your slaves do it."

She continued as if she had not heard me. "Then there's milking and washing and any other task Mistress requires of you. You shall be allowed one afternoon each week for school. Work not and you shall know the rod of correction. You are right pinched and meager, quite scunging in your appearance. Have you other raiment?"

"Raiment, madam?"

"Where be your other clothes?"

"Stolen away by the same villain who has taken me from the bosom of my family and delivered me into your hands. Ask Rafe MacAlister. Have someone bring me a bath and a fresh gown immediately."

She stood, grunted, giving me a slight shove, and tromped about the room as if a better answer were hanging on a peg, for there were many pegs, all filled with different hanging fabrics on the walls of this small wooden room. "No, you'll not have a cloak," she repeated twice. Then, "Were you raised Papist?"

"No, mum."

"Is there anything but heresy taught on such an island?"

"As I come from, madam? I do not know what is taught there. I know only that Ma and Pa were both godly and taught us what they knew." I felt afraid to say more. I knew by the way she asked it that she expected an answer that matched her creed. We held that the Virgin was pure and that certain of the martyred saints followed and watched over those who loved them, yet the Talbots as far as I knew were Anglicans and not given to claiming any original sins as did Catholics. All my sins were my own creation and had come by way of my invention, of that I would swear.

"So you've been baptized? I'll not have a foundling heretic under this roof. Speak up. Baptized? How?"

"Yes, madam. Baptized, indeed." I asked myself whether I should say 'twas last spring, or say that I was christened at eight days old—neither of which was true. I hit upon a middle ground. "In the scriptural way, same as you, madam."

She whirled at me, her hands swirling musty-smelling clothing. "Good, Mary. Now, see if this will fit you." She tied a rough cap upon my head. She came at me with a gown, whisking my arms into the sleeves, tying it in back but not taking off my soiled things. She gave me a short and oft-patched coatlike casaque. Over that she laid a pelisse which had once been grand, but which was several inches too long. "Oh, that won't do," she said. "Much too big."

The promised warmth of the clothes after these days of cold had an immediate effect and I clutched my arms across my ribs, holding on to the garment lest she take it back. I said, "Perhaps if I also had some good shoes to wear, I would be taller and it would fit better."

I knew the argument was ridiculous, but the old woman put her gnarled and twisted dog-finger against her lips and pondered it. "No, no," she said. "If one of the girls has a shoe close to the size—"

"Birgitta!" I heard from another room. "Birgitta, I need you upstairs."

"Follow me and keep quiet," Birgitta said. "These people are the Hasken family. Patented and Puritan. You address them as 'Master' and 'Mistress,' understand?"

"Yes, madam."

"You call me 'Birgitta.' I'm the housekeeper but I am Mistress's sister, too, full part of this household. I sleep by the door, so there'll be no running out without my knowing."

"Yes, madam," I repeated, as we trundled up the poorest stack of stairs I had ever seen, more rickets than wood and less foothold than the secret stair by the waterwheel. I began to feel warm under the layered coats, yet my bare feet ached from the cold. At the top of the stair, we entered a low-ceilinged room where three beds crowded together in such tight space that there was no room betwixt them. A fireplace that had gone cold came off the chimney. Beyond, the attic was dark and drafty.

"The misses sleeps here," Birgitta said. "You'll find the honey pots under there. Mistress won't allow the girls to the outdoors in this weather. You take 'em to the outdoor privy and dump 'em in the hole. Wipe 'em good and clean, after."

"Ah, no," I said. "I told you, I could never do that." Birgitta rapped me on the shoulder with the rod she produced from a rope at her waist. I gasped in pain. Even the lowest pirates who stole me never whipped me. I cried out, "Do not hit me with that again!"

"Who!" came a child's voice, from under the beds. "Who is this lady?"

Birgitta patted the bed nearest her. "You hiding again, Lonnie? Come out. This is Mary. She's to dump the pots. You're to find your old shoe for her."

"There's only one. Mother took one to save for the wall on the new house." The girl wiggled from under the bed as she spoke. "It's good luck to put a shoe in the wall of a new house." She stood taller than I, with a stunted left arm and leg as if she were a doll assembled from two different patterns. "I have a long foot and a short one, a long leg and a short one, a big arm and a little. I even have a big titty and a little 'un. You can't have my new shoe!"

"No, of course, I would not—" I began.

Fast as the strike of a snake, the old woman brought the stick down upon my forearm. "Don't talk back to the misses. Best you learn your place quick. Now, Lonnie, give me the old shoe. You, Mary, you say 'yes, mum' to everything."

I was about to insist that Mary was not my name when Lonnie reached under the bed and came out with a squashed and battered wad of leather. I thought it a dead bat and shrank from it in her hand. She shook it at my face and sang, "What are you scared of? Scary Mary! Scary Mary."

Birgitta took the leather thing and tugged at it. It changed not at all under her hands, and she tossed it at my feet. "Well, there's one. We'll find you another."

Lonnie said, "It has been squashed under the bed for a year," as she dove back under. She came up with a worn-out larger shoe. It had a hole in the toe.

By the time the candles were put out that night, I had learned much about these people and none of it endeared them to me. The old woman made me wipe out pots and I vomited with each one, worse than seasickness. I was to sleep in a tiny alcove under the eaves, furnished with a fetid mat and a bearskin. I pulled the mat against the chimney and made myself a tent of the skin. I pilfered a rug I found rolled in a corner behind a chest, adding that to my little tent-house. Master and Mistress and Birgitta slept downstairs.

The Haskens' three daughters ranged in age from twenty-one to fourteen. All of them snored. Lonnie was given to fits where she stuttered and stammered and sometimes fell down, spitting and foaming. Birgitta warned me to keep her from falling in the fireplace and away from all candles and lamps. When she was not taken with fits, she played at braiding and unbraiding Christine's hair while Christine sat knitting. I longed to have my ma work the painful knots from my hair and I would have asked Lonnie to do mine had this been any other place. Lonnie's given name was Livonah, but she could not pronounce it. Lonnie found ways at odd times to pop out of a corner or from under a bed and call out, "Scary Mary!" It kept me so uneasy that I wanted to scratch her face. She slept with Rachael and clutched a doll made of wood and dressed in miniature clothing.

Rachael was the eldest, cross-eyed as a baby bird, and made me most uneasy. She had a way of asking, "That, there! That one, I told you, Mary," without pointing a finger or naming a thing, expecting me to guess which eye she had aimed at something she wanted brought to her. I could not tell what she wanted and I hated the way it made me feel stupid, as if I had left my senses behind on the voyage. I thought of her as a prating, narrow-backed, long-nosed, cross-eyed fool.

Christine was the middle girl, nineteen, plain as her mother and more dull than Birgitta, as if her mind had a hollow place in it which wanted filling. She did nothing throughout a day other than sit and knit stockings. The stockings seemed nice and there were more than enough to go around, so I smiled and remarked to her that they looked ever so nicely made, and that I should enjoy having a pair of the extra stockings to keep my feet warm, as she had a stack of nine or ten pairs in her basket. Christine flew from her chair, squalling, "Mary tried to steal our stockings!" which caused Birgitta to lay me a whipping across the back.

The next day I sneaked up to Christine and hissed into her ear, "You pathetic, defective creature. I would not touch your worm-infested, pox-ridden, goat-shit-filled stockings if I held the devil's pitchfork in my hand."

That got me a whipping by Master himself with a leather strap he tethered next to the fireplace and once a week used to strop his razor. Once he had laid five great whacks across my back and legs, he said to me, "You are not an equal in this house; you are a servant. You will never address this household with insult or familiarity. You will never say the name of the father of all evil aloud within these walls. It is my duty and right to train you until you understand your place. It is also within my right to take you to the deep woods and leave you for the wolves. Is this understood by you?"

I nodded that it was, though I could not speak, for the effort of weeping inside myself had left me mute. That night after hauling wood, water, and slops all day, I was sent to my corner in the upper floor without supper. I did not wake until Lonnie poked me with a broom handle the next morning.

They kept goats in a room of the house. The stench was as wretched as the hold of the Saracen pirate ship. I suppose one might say that that goat room was in its content and purpose a barn, but they had created it by simply building a wall at one end of the house itself. The whole place smelled dismally sharp. Everything I touched and cleaned, even the food I ate, tasted of the tang of goat dung.

The flattened shoe was too tight and gave me blisters. The other one was loose and floundered upon my ankle, causing me to trip. This house where I had been lodged was somewhat bigger than our kitchen, though the whole of it including the fenced yard would have fit into the first-floor ballroom at Two Crowns. I dumped their pots and wiped them with a towel. Not in all my days had I known any such duty, and every time I performed it, I vomited everything I had eaten until at last I fainted and the old woman, Birgitta, dragged me into the house.

Birgitta talked and scolded without stop. Mary, this, Mary, that, until my ears felt as bruised as my arms. I was made to bring in snow and melt it in a pot for cooking and cleaning. Birgitta told me to peel vegetables but hit me for the result, saying I wasted too much. She constantly referred to the single table over which hung two copper kettles and a prong for meat as "the kitchen." I did not dare ask whether there weren't a proper kitchen. No home I knew had a kitchen in the house. Too dangerous and hot with all that cooking. Birgitta bade me to clean the master's boots but beat me for not knowing to rub them with a lamb's wool bob she kept in a wooden safe with tallow and old candle bits.

One morning Birgitta led me to a shed hard against the house which held a stack of logs as tall as the house and several feet thick. She lectured me in her droning, nasal voice about their last house girl who had pulled the pile down upon herself. I watched a mouse pitter around in a corner, thinking that I wished the whole pile to fall upon Birgitta. I imagined Birgitta aboard ship. I would bet my one good shoe that no becalming doldrums existed which she could not break with speeches about scrubbing, tending, sewing, and milking goats, goats, and goats, buckets and stools. What they ate. What they excreted. When to set the ewes and when to butcher the kids. Everything about goats tied itself to Lent and Easter and Passover, Midsummer Day, and the black days of the moon. How to tell if the goat had been possessed by a demon or spirit of Satan, for goats were easy prey to that Villain. If I asked a question I was as likely to get a rod as an answer, so I did not inquire as to the nature of a goat that made it Satan's prey, after, of course, unchaste little girls.

Morning and night I carried pots. After a while, I was able to keep down my food by covering it with the towel first, holding my breath, and closing my eyes. I ate at the foot of the table if anything was left in the trencher after the family gobbled their fill. Sometimes there was little but drippings and a crust. Each night I pulled off the miserable shoes and I tried to rub my frozen toes to keep them from hurting so, but they hurt worse with every passing day. They stung so that I could not sleep at times. Birgitta watched me at every moment, quick to bring that rod down upon my shoulders. I crept into my small hole under the bearskin, more tired from work, more bruised by beatings, until I felt at last I might cry out in my sleep as Patey had done, "Not again!" I wrapped my feet in the bottom of my skirt and put them against the chimney, curled up like a housecat, waking stiff and cold.

By the passing of another week I almost looked forward to the dumping of pots for the chance to emerge from the house, to look for a road or path, some way to leave. My main reason for staying, however, came as Mistress Hasken settled her girls for the night, telling them stories of "the old country," as she called the place. It did not sound anything like the Scotland and England I had heard of, but was wintry as this, full of harsh people and wolves, as well. In one of the stories, a queen saved her three daughters from being eaten by wolves—massive hairy animals with teeth like daggers and a never-ending hunger—by throwing out their worthless servant girl when the wolves clawed at the door. At night, the howl of wolves in the distance made me too afraid to sleep, much less think of running. If only there came a night without wolves, I decided, I would know it was safe. I lay awake, after the stories and their shared kisses and tucking in of wrapped, heated stones from the fire. Every sound triggered my heart to beat faster, my eyes to open wider. An owl called. Something rattled in the thatch. I often slept with my arms over my face so nothing could claw at my eyes.

Master Hasken was a puffed-up booby who fancied himself a scholar and philosopher, prating before a polished copper plate every Sunday morning. In another home equally as dismal as this, a crowd assembled and stood, there being not room for a single chair. I found a corner and crouched so I could rest my sore feet. Master Hasken fumbled the words of a psalm so that it came out that the Israelites had prepared a feast to eat their enemies. I covered my smile.

By the time Meeting was finished, a stormy wind blew and sleet hit the house. They sent me to their house alone to build up the fire so it would be warm for them. I thought of escape, but where and how could I, in such a storm? They must have known I could not run away in such weather. Still, it was blessed to be alone. I pushed the coals with an iron rod, and fed straw into the fireplace. I looked out the door. No one yet, so I ran upstairs, pulled off my shoes and dug into Christine's basket of stockings. I selected two pairs and put them on, one over the other, and got the shoes tied on just as I heard stamping at the doorstep. I nearly fell down the stairs in my rush, but I sat myself upon the floor, flushed and panting. I knelt, holding kindling against a mound of coals and blowing at it by the time they'd removed their wet blankets and cloaks enough to see me. Christine never mentioned that her store of stockings had changed.

A couple of days later, while I melted snow, I watched from the corner of my eye as Mistress sat to spin thread of the goat's wool. She had a round of wood with a spindle on it, and whirled it. Now and then she grunted if the thread broke. The woman was twiddly and had nervous episodes where she paced across the two small rooms, and sometimes up and down the narrow stairway fidgeting with her hands, shaking them as if they were wet and needed drying, or as if something dreadful were stuck to her fingers.

"Are you listening?" Birgitta hissed, shaking the rod at my face. "I'll have a word with Master Hasken about you if you are too simple to learn a thing."

Had she been talking again? I looked first at the tip of the rod, inches from my nose. I had no idea she had been talking and I followed its length with my eyes, up her arm and to her face. As I did I remembered Aloysius, the sailor. "I am listening, madam." I smiled to prove it, though I had no idea what she had said. "Thank you for explaining, Birgitta. I shall not forget." My answer took her off her guard, for she shook her head, blinking long and hard, screwing her eyebrows up. I nodded and stirred the stew bubbling on the hearth. "Would you have me put more kindling by the great fireplace or the lesser?" I asked, reaching for a chunk of wood.

"Go and get more for the great one. Be careful," she said, suddenly gentle, "and remember not to loosen any above and cause it to kill you dead. And get five more buckets of snow. Mistress will want tea for the honorable reverend. Last Meeting was for his and Miss Rachael's Walking Out. To-night's supper is First Courting."

I loaded up the box by the fireplace, my arms as full of wood as I could carry. I collected snow and sat to pluck floating bits of twig and leaf from the pot as the snow melted. I kept my hands in the warm water until it got hot. Mistress and the older girls spent the morning preparing a leg of goat that had been hanging inside the woodshed where it had frozen solid. I marveled at that. Had it hung in a shed at Meager Bay, flies and wasps would have cleaned it to the marrow in half a day. Later in the afternoon as the preparations slowed and bread rose on a board, all the daughters assembled for "school." I sat on a small stool behind them, happy for a change from my endless tasks. I remember having been told I'd be schooled, but this was the first time in two months of living with them that any mention was made of it. As the girls recited addition by rote, I tried to join in, sensing a rhythm to what they were doing. Arithmetic seemed to be a pattern of things, such as three threes made nine. I smelled the goat shank boiling in its pot and roots roasting in the coals. My mouth watered. My stomach made meowing sounds like a hungry cat, and Rachael frowned at me for it.

We were an hour into school when Reverend Johansen arrived with his leather satchel and his Scriptures. Master Hasken answered the knock on the door himself. Birgitta showed him to the single real chair and Master sat upon the family bench. Mistress Hasken intended to give our little schooling an airing before him, for she did not dismiss us from our places. I used my hiding place behind the girls to study this reverend. He had a kind expression, and a sadness about the eyes that was appealing despite his thinness. Perhaps he would save me.

Mistress broke the silence, saying, "Rachael, what is the greatest sin?"

I thought about stealing stockings, while Rachael said, "There are seven major sins. The greatest of these is sloth, because under its cloak abide all the others."

"Good," said Mistress, nodding. "Now, Christine, what are the seven detestable sins?" Christine gave no answer. Lonnie sat without speaking, a string of drool escaping her lips. "Mary," said Mistress, "clean her face."

I waited and watched. Reverend seemed unamused.

"Mary! Clean her face, I said," the woman demanded.

I grew aware after a moment that she meant me. I had been called "Mary" all these days but could not reply to it when caught off guard. I pulled up a bit of my skirt and swiped it across Lonnie's face while turning my eyes to the ceiling. Nothing repelled me more than slaver running from a mouth.

Christine mumbled something and her mother nodded, head inclined toward the girl, as if by that motion she could produce words from Christine's mouth. Mistress said, "She knows them by heart. She—she speaks softest of the girls."

I folded my skirt so I could not see Lonnie's mouth spot on it. The reverend appeared bored. I wanted to jump at him and shout the wrongs done to me. I made a noise, accidentally scooting my stool a bit.

Mistress eyed me and her face changed somewhat. Her smiling lips thinned out and her brows lowered. "Mary? Do you know the detestable sins?"

Pa always said if you wanted a man to befriend you, get him to talk about himself. If I could get the man to feel fondness toward me, to feel pity and perhaps admiration for my ma's teaching, perhaps he would take me home to her. What more would a parson love than to talk about his philosophies? Perhaps he needed asking. Perhaps I should ask him. Ma had never spoken of a list of such things as detestable sin. I said, "I—I am sure that Holy God detests all wickedness."

The reverend raised one brow and nodded.

Mistress said, "Mary, the kettle is hot. I'll serve Parson some tea." She had laid her teapot and tea safe on a kerchief at the table. She seemed uncertain at its preparation. They drank nothing but hard cider usually, as there was naught else to drink. I knew all about tea for I had helped my mother so often. I hurried to the fireplace and pulled the trammel with a crooked rod she used for it. As Mistress tried to whittle the corner off the tea brick, she said, "Of course we never use tea often. We keep frugal." I poured hot water into the old teapot, and with a look on my face and a nod, took the tea brick from her, breaking it as Ma had done, dropping it in, to stir with a fork. Mistress began to smile but stopped herself and turned away from me. "Lonnie?" she went on. "What is the greatest commandment?"

"Honor thy father and mother," Lonnie sang out, clapping her hands. "My father and mother, honor them, honor them, ho-nor them."

When I turned to hang the kettle of hot water back in the fire, a coal popped and a spark flew toward me. I kicked at it, intending to send it back into the bank of coals, but it caught in the hole of my tattered shoe. Pain shot through my toe. I cried out, holding forth the iron kettle. Lonnie came running to me and held her hands under the hot kettle as if I would lay it into them. "No!" I cried. "Lonnie, move your hands!"

"Mary," Birgitta said, coming at me, "you earned three strokes for raising your voice to the misses of this house."

My hands sweating and the handle slipping, I held the kettle with every bit of strength I could find. I cried, "Lonnie! The kettle will hurt you. Get away." At last I could keep it suspended no more and my arms began to fall lower.

Birgitta reached forward and took Lonnie's hands in hers, leading her away. I set the kettle on the floor and shook my shoe. The spark had no more light in it but smoke came from my shoe like a candlewick just snuffed. Tears poured down my face.

"What is all this?" asked Master. "Pick up that kettle, Mary!" It was such a small room to have so many people, he could not see what had happened to my foot. He raised his fist, ready to fetch me a clap on the head.

"I am sorry, Master," I said, ducking my head. In that moment, a picture of Cora, bowing and ducking in Patience's stolen shoes, appeared in my mind. My toe hurt too badly to think more. "I did not want to hurt Miss Lonnie."

Reverend Johansen came to my rescue, saying, "I believe her voice was raised only in warning, Hasken. Let the serving girl have some tea for it."

I did get a cup of their tea but it was just as ordinary as any I had had. The food was better than usual, and plentiful, though I had to wait until everyone had taken their fill before me. My portion of potatoes was one small nub no larger than my thumb, and the bread had fallen into the pot and was sopped by the time it got to me. The women all stayed hushed as the parson and Master went on about the threat of the French fort not far away. They talked of Indians and the parson said he could speak Indian language and gave forth with some stirring words no one could understand, of which, it seemed, he was proud. The evening wore on and the fire burned low. I felt cold, then hot, my eyes burning as if I had been too close to the fireplace.

The Hasken daughters lined up to bid farewell. I felt a trembling take my bones. I had no time left to plead to him to take me home. I could travel with him wherever he went. Despite Patey's warning, I thought, I would gladly pay him two gold rings to take me. I sprang from my place on the floor, hoping to elicit recognition that I had something important to say.

"Mary? Come stand behind the girls," coaxed Master, with a grandiose wave of his arm. "The staff may attend the departure of our guest."

"Our children," said Mistress, "shall bid you farewell with a Scripture verse."

Well and aye, I thought. The girls shall speak to the parson, and I was girl enough for that task. I inched my way into the line of them, standing next to Lonnie. Rachael recited a long and, to me, meaningless verse. The parson corrected her, saying, "The word is 'thine,' my dear, not 'thy.' Thine own."

Rachael bowed and curtsied and replied, "God's blessing on your travels, Reverend Johansen."

I looked back and forth between Rachael's face and the parson's. Betrothed? The parson was older-looking than Rachael's pa. Why, that would be like Patience marrying some old, old man like Rafe MacAlister! I shuddered. Christine and Lonnie recited. I stared at the parson.

Master said, "Fetch the parson his cloak, Mary."

"Yes, Master." I did my best and most gracious curtsy, despite my toe hurting beyond mercy and my clothing smelling of rot. I saw a quiver at the corners of his mouth. He was dampening a smile. I had his sympathy! I ran to the peg and lifted down the cloak to keep it from the dirt floor. "Here, your lordship, reverend sir," I said, holding the cape as high as my arms would reach. It blocked my face from his view so I spoke through the wool, in the moment it took him to slip on the cloak and fasten the frog. I began a verse, saying, "'As the hart—'" My eyes went to Master's face. At his frown I lowered my voice to a whisper and chattered fast as my lips would move, "'As the hart panteth after the books'—I mean brooks—'water-brooks: so panteth my heart after—after—Thee'!" I raised my brows more, trying to sort out whether I could ask him to take me away at that moment. "I should like to hear your philosophy about the Psalms." I shuddered, nearly falling to my knees in a faint, my head swimming as black spots swirled before my eyes.

"The Psalms?" Reverend Johansen asked. He swept the cloak over one shoulder and bent toward me, smiling and patting my head, and said, "Why would you like a sermon on the Psalms?"

My eyes darted back and forth, testing his right eye then his left, trying to discern the answer he wanted most to hear, and without thinking at all, with no reason, I said, "For I want to know when I shall go away, how soon, and for what I am here." Mistress glared at me. Birgitta, too, and she stepped forward as if to snatch me away for my boldness, but stopped, unsure of whether her duty lay in waiting upon the guest's departure to lash out.

The parson said, "When shall you go? You are too young to think of death. I doubt that answer is in the Psalms. The reason you are here is that you are to be a maid-of-all-work. See that you glorify the Lord with every good deed." He turned to the room and said, "God give you good e'en, then. Bless this house and all who reside therein. Amen." He made for the door and pushed it open, letting a rush of icy air into the room.

I dashed after him, clinging to the wide cloak. "Take me with you, please, your lordship. Help me get home to my mother. I am captured, sir, by pirates. This is not my place." A sudden sweat poured from my skin and the frigid gust of air made me shiver. "How shall I get home to my mother? She will surely be terrified at this long absence."

"Mary! Still your tongue!" Mistress hissed at me. "Girls, up to bed, then."

Birgitta's coarse hands wrenched my grip from the parson's cape. "Beg pardon, Parson Johansen. This'n is new and han't learnt manners yet." She closed the door before he could respond, and shook me by the shoulders. "What a foolishness!"

He was gone. "How long must I stay?" I cried.

Mistress came before me, her arms crossed. "Mary? Let this happen again and I'll remember it for sure."

Birgitta said, "If you have done your duty, you'll be granted free in eight years. We have paid your indenture and you are ours. You go to your mother after that. Or you hire out under wages. Until then, you do as you are told."

I sank to the floor. The pain in my toe took my breath away. Eight years. It was more days than stars in the sky. Thousands and thousands of days without Ma and Patey. Without August. Pa dead. In eight years, August would have come back to Casco Bay to find me and I would not be there. I was the daughter of Allan Talbot, not a slave. My eyes filled with visions of dark women wielding arm-length blades against the sugarcane under a heavy sky, dank with approaching hurricane. Their chants filled my ears. I shook from the inside as if my bones had gone cold, already dead. The smell of goat dung overpowered me. My bones turned to water. I woke later on a pallet before the fire. My throat was raw and pained me to swallow. Every bone ached. My head felt pierced by a great pinion chained to the floor. "So thirsty," I said. "Please. A drink."

Birgitta's voice hovered in the air over my head and lifted a cup of warmed cider to my lips. It was difficult to swallow. "Sudden fever. I've seen it before. Possible you've been bewitched. Or taken water-sick. Mistress would have sent you up to bed but 'tis better you keep by the fire."

"Water?" I asked. She fed me the strong cider. Was there not a drop of water in this hellish prison? I slept a deep sleep so that I felt pulled by fairies and duppies through forests and ocean waves, cold as ice and warm with sweat, barely breathing, barely alive. Ma came to me and held me against her breast. She told me I was dying and not to be afraid. When I asked her how she knew, she said she had died, too, and not to trouble about it. "No!" I screamed with all my might. I found myself sitting up in a wretched cave, dressed in rags and watched over by a witch, the kind of raspy bogle's maidy that guarded the captives in any story of fairy folk and duppies, selkies or brownies.

"You little spider! You scared the marrow out o' my bones!" Birgitta's voice said. "Where did you get them stockings?"

"I want my ma," I said, and lay upon the hard floor. I stared into the fire and soon I slept and soon Ma cradled me again in her arms.

"Mary! Get up and empty the pots!" Mistress called, jabbing my bottom with the broom. "Lazy lout. Up with you!" I kept my eyes closed and my body still. My head hurt. Every bone felt every deprivation and bruise, and I wore my agony like a cloak. Indeed, some type of blanket covered me yet I shivered, too, with cold. "I am sick, Mistress."

"What's that? You lazy thing. Up from there!"

Birgitta said, "Best leave her for a time. It could be contagion."

"Well, then," Mistress said. "Then you will empty the pots."

"As you say, Mistress," Birgitta said. With my eyes still closed I heard her mutter, "Yes, sister. You old spider."

CHAPTER 7

December 19, 1729

It was a fortnight, rather than three days, before I could arise from the pallet. When at last a bit of strength returned, I woke to discover that someone had shaved my head, and sank down again, this time to weep in self-pity and self-loathing. Every few moments my hand crept under a wrap to my head, feeling the strange bristling under the kerchief. Shuddering, I cried again. "My hair. Oh, my hair." I slept.

Birgitta's voice awoke me. "There you are, girl. Here, Mary. Have broth."

"What happened to my hair?"

"Hair holds fever. Had to come off. It'll grow."

Tears rained upon my face. "My lovely hair."

"Now, there. It's a known cure for dry-ache fever. You're alive. Think on that."

I took the bowl and spoon from her. "I can feed myself, thank you."

"Well. That's improvement. The misses is all sick, too. Master has a cough and Mistress has misdelivered another babe before its time. Parson Johansen had been at the Mayweather house and they was all afevered, so likely he brought the fevered air here. It took right quick, coming on us all." She looked on me and smiled. "Had a heavy snow, day before yestidy. The goats'll be the death of me. That's why it was such a great help to teach you. You get well now, then you can get back to work."

I adjusted the wrapping on my head as it began to fall. "What is this smell?"

"Comfrey, borage, and yarrow, wrapped in honey balm, on your head. And hill wort. Other things. Guards against blindness with a fever."

I sank onto the pallet before the fire, weaker than I had known since the smallpox, and rustled betwixt the blankets. As I lay staring into the pulsing red coals, I thought, not one time had Birgitta threatened me with a stick. She was naught but tender kindness. What had changed? As hideous as it was to cut off my hair, I knew of that done for sickness, especially yellow fever. I felt puzzled at Birgitta's caring to have done it, for all I might have expected was that they'd throw me out in the snow to die. I watched her stir the copper pot and lapsed into dreamy sleep.

At length I awoke wrapped in a blanket in Birgitta's lap! Her head was leaned back at a sharp angle and she snored through an open mouth. I dared not move. I looked into her mouth and pondered the teeth, some of them still good, but a few looked black and there was a smell of old sourness coming from her. I felt embarrassed that I had peered at someone I barely knew and without her knowledge.

"Birgitta?" I whispered.

She mumbled. "What? What, Mary?"

This was the oddest predicament I had yet encountered, odder than being called "Mary" or milking goats. "I thought you hated me."

"Hated you, Mary? Why would you think that?"

I raised my face to hers again, and said, "You beat me all the time."

Her face bore confusion. "Bible says to spare not the rod of correction. You was given me to raise and train and care for. Beating is good for children. And gentler than my dada rolling me in a sack and kicking me across the floor. You're too big to sack."

"Sack?" I asked. I had never heard of anything so wretched. "I am *not* as foolish as a goat. I am clever. You could teach me *without* beating me." Care for? Train? I doubt that I hid my own confusion. "If I tried very hard to do what you wish, might you just explain it, rather than hit me with a stick?"

Birgitta wept. After some time she said, "I never had no child of mine. I always wanted a little girl named Mary. All 'as I ever knew is how to run goats. I'm old and these misses are not mine to guide and care for. I'm not allowed to correct them at all. Mary, if you'd behave without a stick, well, why didn't you say so? You was so mean and naughty. I wanted them to get me a nice girl, not a hard one."

Mean? How could I be anything but angry at her treatment? Overcome with emotion, I patted Birgitta's arm. "You were never a mother? Likewise, I was never a slave." I pulled up my feet to hide the stockings.

She closed her eyes and leaned her head back, speaking toward the gloomy ceiling. "Too late, now. Too, too late to be a mother. You see them girls. Addled, every one. We was brother and sisters, Master and Mistress and me, Haskens all. With no others in our town, they married. But I was older and I would have another, though he would not have me, so my sister was allowed a husband of our faith. A brother and sister should not marry lest they beget some defect as you see here. A brother and sister marrying is a shame, but for me to marry him also would be a sin." She stared at the shadows overhead.

I followed her eye's direction and grimaced at the shreds of spiderwebs clotted with dust and grease, hanging like fringe from the beams. Real silk fringe used to hang on my bedroom windows to keep out bugs and let in the breeze. "You are their auntie."

"Not the same. I am the old shoe they can't throw down the well and must feed. So I mind the goats. They said I wast ever lazy so no man would marry me. I shall train you to be not lazy, to work as the righteous ought. That way you will not be an old auntie to a passel of misbegotten brats. You will marry and keep house."

Was this training meant as good for my future? Birgitta fell asleep. Her face was pale, red dots of fever on each cheek, the skin had grown fiery. As she slept, I crept from her lap. My shoes lay by the fire and I pulled them on, thinking with curiosity at the change in my treatment. My hair had not magically regrown, but still, in my own heart things were different between Birgitta and me. I clenched my jaw, remembering that I was a gift, a toy for an old, childless spinster to play with, a game of false motherhood.

In the corner of the room, a bedstead where Birgitta usually slept was tossed and unkempt. I pulled the blankets back, curling my lips at the grimy bed, and I turned my gaze to the window. Like a plant under a rock, I felt I would die for want of the sun. A thin, gray light washed across the pillow. It was dirty in the center and worn through on the corners, stuffed with what looked like wads of goat hair. I pulled Birgitta's hand. "Come, lie down," I coaxed.

The old lady did as she was told, dragging her feet across the packed dirt floor as she said, "If you lie beside me it'd warm my bones—but my throat is raw as a burned leaf. I'd like a bit of warmed ale if it's about. That's a good girl, Mary," she said as I pulled the coverlet upon her, scarf and all. I found the pewter cup that had been polished for Reverend Johansen, poured a bit of cider in it, and laid the boiling rod in it until it quit sizzling. "Here, Birgitta," I said.

She drank it, lay back, and closed her eyes, in the heavy sleep of sickness. I built up the fire because she was cold. I smiled at the luxury of it as the flames claimed the new kindling. Master must have gone to town or he would be here by the fire, I thought. The rest of the family was upstairs, from the racket of them. I bundled up, wearing two of the girls' cloaks, and went to the woodshed three times, intending to lay up a store so I would not soon have to go again. I made room for the wood beside the hearth and under the eating table. As the house warmed, the voices upstairs calmed. Not a creature moved in the house. I felt proud of the warmth I had added without being told.

I decided I would do more work without a beating than I did with one. Patience had said, "Be clever," and clever I was going to be. The Haskens all together did not have one whit of cleverness. With no one watching me, I surveyed the house, silent except for scuffling from the goats. I took Birgitta's stick from her chair and opened the door to the goat room. With trembling hands, I milked four goats, which took care of all except for the one balky one. A kid, twice her size, nursed at the old doe and butted her, but to be milked she would not stand.

"Stupid," I called her. What was that goat's name? "Stupid!" I shouted. Stupid-the-goat kicked the bowl and sent it flying. When I fetched the bowl and began again, I whacked her leg as a warning. I saw with a new understanding what Birgitta had done to me. Was the old woman so stupid as to think a girl and a goat were one and the same? Still, waking up cradled in her lap had changed something within me, and I felt a strange mixture of longing and much-softened anger toward her.

After the milking I took a long drink of the warm milk. I wiped my face and burped. It felt so good to be full. I downed fully half the bowl. Never mind, I thought. I poured water into the milk to bring up the level. Just like Cora stealing Patey's shoes, I would make my every effort one to survive long enough to leave. The house had warmed as a spring day in Jamaica. I opened the front door, pulled in a kettle of snow, and put it on the hob to melt. I did not linger or stare into the distance longing for escape, for the cold was too harsh to even ponder it. As the day wore on I heard wolves, and pushed away any thought of escape. Summer would come. I would leave then, and be stronger. I got water and scrubbed my poor bare head, feeling chilled but good.

In a basket by Mistress's chair lay three turned-wood spools of thread. I helped myself to the white thread. I pulled off my petticoat and found the needle. I mended every torn place, stitching upon the old stitches so much so that there remained more stitching than cloth. I tore loose parts of my old silk gown and made patches to mend places where my treasures had worn holes, trying to make them look as if naught but a patch were there. I worked on my pocket; I wished I could take it to Ma and have her exclaim over it.

I held an image of Ma in my mind and looked down at the petticoat. There I saw, as if for the first time, the stitches she had done, so tiny and perfect next to my clumsier ones. The lines she had made were clever, indeed, as if decoration were their sole purpose, yet much was held inside, hidden. "Oh, la," I said, running my fingers over patterns of squares and circles, looped ovals with my clumsy patching blotting out the patterns. I sighed. Ma would be sad to see her work so battered. So dirty and ragged. How I had complained about this petticoat, even as the pirates broke through the walls! I searched among what remained of the silk. Finding a loose end of thread, I pulled it, and a piece as long as my arm came free. Part of it was still blue because it had been enclosed in a seam. I pushed the end of it through the needle with great care. Then, using a line I drew in my imagination, I followed the paths of Ma's stitches where I had darned the cloth so heavily. I tied a knot and laid my fingertip against my stitches where they began to mimic what Ma had put there. Her hands had created beauty in such a simple thing.

Days moved with tedium that I wore like a cloak. I dared not ask about Christmas, for the Haskens shunned the keeping of it. In my real home, the day was celebrated with a small feast and gifts of a shilling for the household servants, and a little special gift for us children. A shawl, some ribbons or lacework, a music box, a few chocolates. My favorite holiday, which Ma called "Hogmanay," Pa called "Shortest Night," and these people called "New Year," came and went before health at last returned to the Hasken household. I dared not hope for Hogmanay cakes or gifts from black-dressed, coal-carrying strangers.

As I milked the final goat that morning, I thought of last Hogmanay and Pa's gift to me. It was a clockwork music box with a painting of a lady dancing upon its lid. No finery such as that lay in this forgotten place. That music box was in some pirate's hold now, or sold across the sea. The Haskens' finest possessions consisted of a single silver spoon, a pewter mug, and two well-used wooden chargers in a chest of unused linens. My hidden treasures could buy and sell this entire house, I thought as I drank a third of the morning's milk, wiped my face, and carried it into the house covered with a rag.

Mistress was making bread and put it to rise under a dirty linen. She went up the stair. I watched her trudge away and wondered at how she tended her daughters as if they were helpless. While she was up there I added water to the milk to fill it up to the rim.

Birgitta stirred. "Mary, is the milking done?"

"Yes, Birgitta."

"Would you warm some? My breath comes so hard."

I made hot milk with tea and sugar. By the time it was ready the girls had come down. They had all suffered from the fever and appeared weakened, frail and thinner than before. Christine looked as if she had eaten nary a bite for three weeks. I poured Birgitta milk without offering to make more for the rest. No one spoke to me and I had learned at the cost of another stropping that I was never to address Mistress without being spoken to by her first. Answering. Never offering. A good slave.

On a gray heavy morning at the end of February, when the household was again well, Mistress ordered me to make posset. When I told her I had no idea how, she gasped and told me to learn how to create it. She warmed cider and put it in milk to settle in cups. We made bread, and bean stew, too. Company was coming.

When the sun made long shadows on the snow, Master arrived followed by five people wrapped in cloaks and blankets until they seemed like great beasts filling the room. He called out, "Mary! Come here!" A great unwrapping began with Mistress and Master helping them. Everyone called, "Mary! Come!" I scurried through them as heaps of cloaks and coats dropped onto my arms. I carried them to Birgitta's empty cot. I took the giant shoes and placed them in a stack by the door. They were a webbing of skin over wood frames, and had caught pounds of snow with their walking.

These people were Master and Mistress Newham, their daughter,

Thea, and their son, a boy as tall as his father, older than August. His name was Lukas. He had a gentle face and an easy smile and waving hair at his temples. When he looked at me, I felt suddenly clumsy, as if all my joints did not fit, a mismatched doll like Lonnie. I quite admired his temples, the cut of them, and his clean hair. I wore a kerchief and a house cap, but my hair, an inch long, felt as if it were announced before the world and he would see it and think I was hideous. I backed into the shadows. The last person with them was a woman but was not introduced. She sat by the door, a hood drawn. A servant, I thought.

"Mary?" Mistress called. "Fetch the cups." For several minutes I passed and poured and mopped up spills. For I did spill the cider next to Lukas's cup. He looked up at me just as I came to him and smiled at me. Mistress called, "Mary!" but that was no chide to me in the wake of Lukas's stare.

Lukas's gray eyes followed my movements and he had started to say, "Thank you," but his father stopped him before the words were out, saying, "No need to thank a servant for serving, son. They know their place better when you keep yours." Lukas then looked down his nose at me with almost a sneer when the cider dribbled down the cup, as if I were something less than he, as if I were not fit to pour his cider. I felt crushed in a way I would not have expected. I felt surprised, too, that I cared so much whether this impudent ruffian cared to have me pour his cup. Why, I had never spoken two words to the boy and he had naught to recommend him save a pair of gray, laughing eyes. What would I want with him or his favor? I turned my haughtiest stare to him, but whether he noted it I could not say.

I took the pitcher of cider to a side table and looked again upon the woman sitting by the door. At the moment I did, she raised her head and looked from under the hood. I stared into a pair of my own eyes! Patience! "La," I whispered. The Newhams had bought Patience. *The* Miss Talbot of Two Crowns Plantation sat by the door as a servant and not invited to table nor fed. Patey's hand went to her lips and she motioned me to keep silent. Could I rush to my sister and not suffer for it? I could see her hands, as raw from work and washing as were mine, although they had provided her clothing new and whole.

Once supper was served, I was given a bowl and I took it to Patience, motioned for her to follow me, and we shoved clear a place betwixt the cloaks. On Birgitta's bed we dipped our bread into the same sauce at last, leaning against each other in the only embrace we dared, shushed as mice. "Oh, Patey! I could climb into your lap."

"Best they know nothing of us being sisters. They might not let us be together."

"For a while I believed I had died and this was Purgatory. I have never been so cold. I am planning to run away when the wolves quit howling."

She licked her fingers. "Summer *will* come. The Newhams and the Haskens are moving to the wilderness with some others. The minister of their church is taking families to pioneer, and once the roads are clear enough for that, you and I can leave."

"Won't they want to take us?" I asked.

"We will leave despite their wants."

I smiled. My whole being felt warmed. "Do you have to milk goats?"

"No, Ressie. Do you keep geese? They bite my hands."

"No. They gave me to the old one, Birgitta, like a poppet. She named me Mary."

"The Newhams have talked of the Haskens' troublesome serving girl, Mary."

Mistress called, "Mary, the posset!" Lukas held his cup and I turned my head just enough to give the impression that I saw him not, and passed him with the pitcher. As I poured cider and served posset, I slipped three biscuits from the plate into the cuff of the pelisse.

Soon as I could, I sat beside Patience again. I put two biscuits in her hand. "They beat me at first," I said. "But less now."

"Mine do not," she said. "Although they might if they knew my shame. I suppose they will soon enough." She put an entire biscuit into her mouth, chewing it quickly.

I broke my biscuit and slipped half of it into my mouth. "I steal from them all the time. Stockings. Food. That is my shame. What shame have you?"

"We won't talk of that now. Ressie, I cannot bear to think that they beat you." She reached behind where no one could see and patted my back.

I ate the rest of the biscuit. "Are your people foolish? I think the very name Hasken must mean 'daft' in some other language."

"No. They are genteel, churchy, Pa would have said. I warn you, never speak of saints or holidays. Ma taught us a mixture of Catholic from her childhood and some from long ago, from the Old Way. Some African."

"Not a single crumb for Shortest Night. Anyway, everyone was ill with a fever. They cut off my hair."

"Oh, poor thing," she said, running her hands over my head. I closed my eyes, humming at the smoothness of her fingertips upon my brow. "It will grow. Keep your kerchief on and it does not show." She took my hands in hers and said, "I so missed Pa breaking open the holiday cakes."

"We shall go home, Patey."

"Mary!"

"Yes, madam!" When we were not fetching things Patey and I sat side by side for long stretches without a single word, breathing the same air. I whispered, "If you and I don't leave I will have to stay eight years."

Patey looked on me with Ma's eyes. "Unless a prince comes to pay your price."

I did not want a prince. Certainly not one as bowlegged and bug-eyed as Lukas. Perhaps there *were* other young men in the town, comely ones, smart and gentle as our pa. I remembered Patience dreaming for her prince back in England. Perhaps I was old enough to dream of a prince, too, but not Lukas. "What if I pay my own price?" I asked. "My price was five pounds."

She whispered, "What is the matter with your feet? You're limping."

"One shoe is too small. I change them from one foot to the other to let one foot rest." I held forth the foot wearing Lonnie's little crumpled leather bat of a shoe. Patience clucked her tongue and held up her feet. Her shoes were new and she had warm stockings of brown wool. I added, "I have stockings now. I stole them."

The evening was gone too soon. Patience helped them on with their wraps and giant shoes, and I held the door as they trudged out. Patey stepped close to my side, brushing against me with her new crisp clothes. It was as close to a hug as we dared. No sooner had I pulled the door in place than it opened again. Lukas stood with Patience's shoes in his hands. "Here," he said, thrusting them at me. "My father will give you these and provide others for our servant. My sister died last fall and she can have hers."

Oh, Patience! Her shoes! Though now she would go home in the most dreadful cold, other shoes awaited her there. Oh, how simple was this gift, and how valuable! I never imagined that one master might do such for another's servant.

Mistress began bundling the girls up the stairs. Birgitta stood by the fire, watching me as Lukas closed the door. "Let's see," she said. Birgitta snatched the shoes from my hands and made as if to throw them into the fire.

"My—their *girl* gave them to me, seeing I had only one fit shoe."

"This will just make some other way they can look down upon this family. Always with their noses in our business and in the air."

"Please," I said, "I could work so much faster if both feet had a good shoe."

Birgitta turned them this way and that. She handed them to me. "I suppose you'll be taller, too, and the clothes will fit better? Pah, little spider. Only let the mistress not see them. The daughters have naught so new or fine a pair between 'em. You'll need a longer skirt for to hide them." She said it almost as if accusing me of some crime.

"I might sew it all myself, if you would but guide me, Mother Birgitta."

Her face brightened at that, brows lifting, almost a smile across her mouth. "On the morrow. I'm tired. You've much to do." She lumbered to her cot and sat upon it. "I'll just sit a few minutes, then I'll bank up the fire," she said. But within moments she slumped over onto the blankets and a rattling snore came from her.

I carried her candle to the table so I could see to clean up the cups and plates. By then the entire household had begun to snore. I heard an owl cry and a wolf howl in the distance as I cradled Patience's shoes against my chest and crept up the stair to my little mat, so tired my ears had a strange sense of fullness and sound, like a hundred insects in my head. The wolf howled again, joined by a chorus of others. They sounded as if they were just under the window.

I thought about my sister and myself, all our travels, all our ways before then, and afterward being sold. I touched my skirt, feeling the petticoat stitching through the thin gown, the places Ma had sewn as if she knew I would live in such cold one day. My sister was not far away and not for long. Our owners were friends to each other and were going a-pioneering. Reverend would marry Rachael, a girl half his age. Lukas would travel with us wherever we were going. All of it made my heart warm and my face flush. I shook my head. He was probably drafty and dull-witted, too. I knew not what attracted me to him at first. My thoughts swirled like coddling posset and my heart ached for him.

When I emptied the morning pots, I put the broken, pinching shoe down the outhouse hole with the mess. After I finished cleaning the morning dishes, Birgitta offered me a bit of brown wool, quite plain, and guided me in the sewing of long side seams and gathering the waist at a band to make a skirt. I made my stitches as small and straight as I could manage. After a while she said, "You called me 'Mother Birgitta' the other day. I wouldn't mind were you to call me that."

I kept my eyes on my stitches. I had called her that with insincerity verging on disdain. I had also done it knowing the woman might be affected by it, and that it might soften my life until I could find a way to escape. Soft answers turn away wrath, Ma always said. "I shall, Mother Birgitta. I heard we are moving."

"We start a new settlement in the west. Rachael will wed Reverend Johansen in a few weeks. Mayhap Christine shall marry Lukas."

I nodded as if I were a wise woman consulted. "I think he *should* take Christine. She seems, most—inclined to marry."

"Most natural, you mean. The other is touched in some way."

I smiled. It was as if we shared a secret that bound us to each other, to agree to something as obvious as that Lonnie was not whole. When the skirt was done I believed by the look on her face that Birgitta felt proud of me wearing it.

When Mistress saw it, her face turned a dark scowl. I feared she would reach for the strop hanging by the chimney. "A waste, Birgitta, a sheer waste when that cloth could have made aught for the girls. And you! Mary, I do wonder but you've been growing faster than any of my daughters. Have you been stealing food?"

I feared lest the biscuits and the bowls of goat milk show in guilt on my face. I tried to make it as hard and blank as stone, like the pirate Aloysius nodding before Captain Hallcroft. I lowered my eyes. "I have a sturdy constitution and God's good grace to thank for my health, Mistress," I said with a curtsy. I kept my knees bent so that on arising I was not so tall. She said nothing but kept eyeing me so I added, "Perhaps, Mistress, the larger my stature the more work I can do."

"You've been stealing food."

"No, Mistress. I swear it." I was getting used to swearing promises that were as hollow as Lonnie's head.

She raised her hand as if to slap me and I cowered as she proclaimed, "No supper for you tonight." I looked at Birgitta, wishing for a sign she would feed me. Birgitta was my protector, but not in everything.

After that, I nurtured my hatred for them all while I stole more food. I took any morsels that I could tuck into a cuff or push up my sleeve, a bit of raw potato or a sliver of trimmed roast beef. I sucked on wheat grains as I had done on the pirate ship. When I milked goats, I took a hearty drink of the milk before I brought the bowl in the house. If I was going to hell any-way, I might as well go with a full stomach.

I hummed a tune and muttered words under my breath while I milked goats. It fit to sing, *"Damn your eyes, Mistress Hasken, damn your eyes."* Was I a villain, then? No, I decided. When I returned to Ma I would put off this hate and thievery as I would put off these filthy clothes and pitch them in the ocean. In the meantime, I practiced the salty words and curses I had learned, every one of them aimed at one of the Haskens.

Once the snow quit falling, a few days of warm rain turned everything to a blight of mud. The rain stopped and the air cooled, but for a few days there was blue sky of the oddest, pale shade of blue I had ever seen. With the thaw, a stream flowed nearby, and Birgitta sent me to fetch water from it rather than hauling snow. We were going to wash the winter's clothing, she said. I took two buckets and filled them half full as I had learned to do on the ship.

I made several trips, filling the cauldron as Birgitta stirred up the fire to heat the water. She added plants she had pulled and dried last summer, as if we were making dirty-clothes soup. Birgitta and I scrubbed dirty lin-ens against boards and rocks, hung things on bushes, while I carried pail after pail of water and kept the fire burning.

"If you intend to wash your raiments," she said to me under her breath, "do the underthings first. Then when they are dry you put them on and wash the outer. Pretty soon you'll be all dressed again, and since Master isn't at home, we'll start early and be finished. Tomorrow we begin Miss Rachael's wedding gown."

I rushed up the stairs, so excited about a bath and clean clothing Ma would have laughed. I worried about cleaning my things with all that lay hidden in them, but the only thing in danger of being found was my pocket. I took the tiny casket from my pocket and burrowed it deep under the bear-skin, wrapping it under three folds of the rug and piling everything so that it looked heaped. I smoothed the bearskin over it all and felt pleased at the result. I undressed and removed everything down to my skin, dressed my-self again in the brown skirt and pelisse.

I ran and fetched water and was just returning with it when I saw Mis-tress emerge from the house and walk toward the washing. "Mary," she called. "I want you to bring more wood. What's this?" She held the corner of my quilted petticoat.

"'Twas made by my ma, Mistress. Before I was taken from my home."

"These stitches are new. That looks like my thread."

It was, of course, but I lied and smiled. "My gown lies there, Mistress. I pulled threads from it to sew the petticoat. The blue there," I said as I pointed to it.

"This thread is mine."

"I swear it is not, Mistress." I bowed my head and curtsied again, and I made sure not to rise fully, keeping my feet well hidden beneath the brown skirt. "I *never* steal," I said, shaking my head.

A female voice from inside the house shrieked as if someone had been injured. "Look at this! Look at this!" I heard. Had she found my dirty stockings? My hands went weak and I let go of the buckets. One tipped over on my shoe, flooding it with water.

"Pah!" Birgitta shouted. "Look at that, now!" And she raised her hand to strike me but lowered it without doing so.

Rachael came from the house with something in her hands clutched against her meager breasts, her face brighter than ever I had seen her, squeal-ing with delight. She saw her mother and ran this way. "Mother, Mother! I couldn't find my rug, the Persian rug you said was my dower, until I dis-covered that Mary had been sleeping on it, and this was hidden under it. And look what's in it!" She held in her hands my mother's gold-cornered wooden casket with the pieces of eight worth two pounds inside. Rachael took the six shillings in her hand and danced around, chanting, "It's a dowry, a dowry!"

Mistress asked, "Where did you get this?" as she held out her hand.

Rachael placed the coins and the box into it. "Under my rug, Mother. Hidden by a thieving little servant girl."

I pretended bravery. "That box is mine," I said. "I will thank you to return it," and I held out my hand as if expecting they would.

Mistress held the coins, dropped them into the box, and closed it, shaking it, listening to the satisfying rattle of money. She wheeled around and loomed over me, saying, "Where did it come from?" Mistress shook the casket at me. "Speak up, Mary. You never have a want of words. Let's hear where you got this."

"My mother gave it me," I said, never taking my eyes off it. "When we were captured by Saracens. I have kept it in my pocket. It will help buy my price, when I can earn some other coin to go with it. I shall have it now, if you please."

Mistress said, "In your pocket? All this time? I don't believe you. Why did you not present it to us to keep for you if it was honest gain? No, you hid it like a thief."

"The box is worth some, too," Birgitta said. "This has gold."

I waved away the thought. "Gold? I think not. Pure brass. Who would give gold to a child? It was just an old casket Ma threw some coins in as I was taken from her. If there were gold in it, the Saracens would have had it. The English privateers did not want it when I offered it in trade for food. Why, they laughed in my face and threw it back at me. They had *trunks* full of gold doubloons. Why would they want an old box with brass corners? They would have *kept* it, if it were gold." I held my hand closer to the box, ready to snatch it from her fingers.

Mistress raised it up before I reached it. "You are a liar and a thief. You stole this. Perhaps from your last mistress. And you intend keeping it from me, who has provided you food and a home all these days? I'll take you to the magistrate to be hung if you so much as say another word about it." Mistress Hasken gripped Ma's casket in her fat, greasy fist and stormed into the house.

A stinging thud hit my shoulders as Birgitta brought her stick down upon my back. "You spider. You misbegotten pisspot! I ought to hang you myself."

"I did not steal it. It was my ma's."

"Liar! Liar! Liar!" she shouted with each swing of her arm. "I'll beat you so you never forget it."

I shrank to the ground under her blows. I counted them until I lost count. Later, when Birgitta had gone into the house, later, when I was alone, later, later, did I weep for Ma's casket and the two pounds of my price lost.

The next day, sore of body and soul as I was, Birgitta took me by the arm and stood me, sending me to work. I fixed my face like stone, barely moving my lips to speak. I muttered Birgitta's name without "mother" attached and said "yes, Mistress" when spoken to. I worked carelessly, spilling things, dragging clothing across the dirt floor, forgetting what I'd been sent for so that every errand took two trips.

Mistress insisted on inspecting my petticoat again, and I clutched the back of my chair as she raised my skirt and squeezed at it, terrified that her hands would find the treasures hidden and I would have no hope, completely adrift. But her hands were no more clever than her eyes, and she did not test the thickness. "This padding? What is it?"

"Woolen, madam."

"Woven? Carded? Think, Mary. Pah. You're as dull as a stump."

I shook my head, trying to remember anything at all of my mother's evenings spent on this petticoat. "It is two layers with a mat of woolen lint between them. The two are made into one by the rows of sewing."

"Not carded well, I think. Your mother wasn't good at it, was she? If indeed she did make this. You and Birgitta will make a petticoat like this for Rachael."

Mistress produced a hopsack full of goat hair that she wanted used to pad Rachael's petticoat, and we began matting it out, spreading the hair and pressing it in as evenly as possible. In the bottom of the sack, I found remnants of goat dung, dark and crumbling, fallen from the hairs at some earlier time. When Birgitta's attention waned, all of the dung found its way between the layers of linen, under the hair, so that it would add a certain air of elegance to Mistress-Rachael-the-Reverend's-wife.

Birgitta insisted I sleep with her to keep her warm. Fighting angry tears, I lay there as I was told. Soon as she snored, I crept from her bed and went to my own place up the stairs by the chimney under the bearskin. She said nothing of my absence in the morning. This I would use, I promised myself, my fists in tight balls, the knowledge that she was both forgetful and somehow longed for my affection.

CHAPTER 8

March 17, 1730

I expected Rachael to wed in a church at least or have a ballroom prepared for dancing. Instead, they went inside a house, to a man who put on his head a ratted old wig, and when he asked them if they intended to marry, Rachael and Reverend Johansen said, "Yes." They signed their names to a paper. It was the dullest wedding I could imagine. Not a note of music or a single sweet. I wondered how the parson came to be burdened with the Haskens' oldest daughter, but I saw no other single girl whose level of hopeless ugliness might make her willing to marry an old, poor parson. I felt sorrow for him, waking up next to a hag every morning.

Later, Reverend and the new Mistress Reverend sat before the fire talking of plans for their new home, the building of a meetinghouse, a garden, and when we would leave on the venture. I heard him say that he "would abstain from taking her to wife until it can be under our own roof." Both Master and Mistress nodded as if this made sense to them.

When word came that all was ready for the move, it took two days to get everything loaded into the wagon. As we walked away, the house looked as if robbers had ransacked it. Cupboards stood ajar, a rag lay there and a broken crock here. Fluttering like leaves before a hurricane, we set out on the muddy, rutted road that led away from the town. Family after family joined us on the road, with carts pulled by horse, ox, dog, or cow. One man hitched himself to a wagon and pulled it with his own legs. His wife and two children walked.

We walked for what seemed like hours with no sound but the complaints of the animals and the creak of the wheels. Birds overhead made strange calls. A rabbit darted from the brush and someone's dog chased it. Dark woods, so thick it made a roof over our heads, closed in upon us. In Jamaica, I was never without several strong slaves breaking out the forest for us to pass, my family never walking, always riding in a coach.

This was a land of cold, just as Ma used to tell in stories of Scotland and England. Was this also a place of brownies and trolls and the most terrible of all, fairies? Did duppies watch us? The forest seemed alive with strange sounds in dark misty dells just out of sight. I tried to remember the charm Patey and I had sung. I could not remember it. *"Gumboo, gumboo,"* I whispered, tapping one or the other of the goats with each word. I craned my neck at every turn to see Patey somewhere ahead.

Suddenly as a summer rain, a flutter of gasps and soft cries rose from our company. I looked toward the trees and the glade through which we had just passed seemed alive with movement. I thought it was rain, or wind, or a dozen wolves come for us. The bushes parted and the forms of men appeared, men with long black hair such as I had never seen, with faces painted red as a barn door. Some of them wore no shirts but breeches and vestments and leggings with wrappings on their feet. Bowmen all, they raised arrows toward us and we struggled keeping the animals straightened and still. The men were marvelous to look upon. The goats wandered as I stopped.

Reverend Johansen raised his hands and said, "Ho, brethren! Hello?" None of the men answered. He spoke again, first to us on the road, "Just some of God's children we call Indians. I will trust that we will pass safely. Pray, brethren."

"Indians," whispered Birgitta.

To the Indians, he spoke in his sermonizing voice. "We are pilgrims. We go to a new settlement west of here. I have already spoken with your chief men. We are no enemies of the Red Man. He assured us we may pass." The strangers spoke to one another in whispers. Reverend Johansen said a couple of the words he knew in Indian tongue. One of the Indians shouted at us. Running up and down the line of us, he waved his arm and menaced us with words.

"Let us move forward, friends," Reverend Johansen said. "Move on, making no alarm. Show them we are just travelers." The party started to move. The Indians stepped back, and with no more than the flutter of a leaf, they disappeared into the woods. The rest of that day we kept quiet and watchful.

"Birgitta? What is the name of the place where we go?"

"New Town."

A town? My heart lifted. "Where does it lie?"

"By Collins Pond."

"Shall I be able to send a letter from there?"

"Are you some queen of England to be sending letters about?"

I saw Patience walking far in front, but I could not leave the goats to go run ahead and find her. The strange sounds of the forest made me think I knew things that could not be known by mortals. We walked until the sun cast long shadows from the trees, dipping below them, and all was shadow and more shadow. We slept on the road itself that night. I sank where Mistress pointed, amidst the goats. Goats are naught but bones and bleating, and their hair was not warm nor their bodies soft. Of course, there was the smell, too, bitter as overripe vinegar, intrusive as bile.

The third morning, we came to a cleared place where several small houses, roughly fashioned of logs, clustered at the end of the road. I had never seen such houses, their only windows being places where the logs had been cut, and covered with shutters. I would be gone when the winter snow blew into those holes. The Haskens' goats went into a fenced yard. The settlement house was luxurious compared to what they had before, though it held no upper floor. Everyone was to sleep together on the floor.

No sooner had we gotten a few things put inside than I heard one of the girls scream as if she had been torn limb from limb. The air filled with the odor of a bear. I knew it from the skin under my bed, only this was earthier, potent, sharp as a foaming horse. I rushed out the door in curiosity to see Christine and Lonnie standing at the edge of the forest. Christine sank to the ground as if the heart had gone out of her and her knees could not hold her. Master ran toward them, carrying a pickaxe. Lonnie came running past me and flew into Mistress's arms while he ran to Christine, threw down his axe, and scooped her up in his arms. He carried her to the house and laid her before the fireplace. Mistress made a pallet on the floor and they laid Christine on it. She breathed with her mouth wide open. Mistress crooned and said, "Poor little thing. Poor thing. Birgitta? Is there water in the house?"

I got a bucket, saying, "Here it is, Mistress." I almost added "you old spider," but stopped myself.

Mistress dipped a rag in the bucket and wiped Christine's face over and over again. She sang to her and murmured things I could not hear. I stepped back. This was the first time I had seen her care for anyone. Still, I thought, with all those stories about wolves tearing people limb from limb, why would the girl not fear so to see a bear? People in the settlement came and many had opinions about whether the girls had in fact seen an animal or were simply overwrought from the traveling. Neither of them could give witness to what had happened, so it was decided that they'd only had a moment of hysteria. No one asked me if I smelled any bears about, so I said nothing. It would serve them all right, I thought, were the whole family to be eaten alive by a single bear and there in its great stomach they could bewail their circumstances as I had in the hold of a slave ship.

That evening Birgitta and I helped Mistress prepare supper. Lonnie went back to braiding her hair though Christine continued entranced. She wet herself. Everyone had to sleep upon the floor, but they made me sleep next to her and I squirmed there in the dark, trying in the crush of bodies to make room between us in case she wet again.

The banging and pounding of building another house began almost before the sun was up. After the day of seeing the bear, while Christine stayed quiet, Lonnie became talkative and rambled about, getting into things, poking sticks in a hornet's nest, putting her bonnet on a dog, dumping out the neighbors' milk jug. She was made my charge to lead and watch over just like the goats.

Before we had been there a month, life found its routine. We worked in the kitchen. Mistress kneaded bread. Lonnie braided Christine's hair. Christine knitted stockings. I did my chores happily wearing a new pair nearly every week. She stopped now and then and counted them over and over, trying, I suppose, to make sense of why she kept knitting but the stack never grew. There were still a dozen pairs in her basket. Yesterday I had gone through the pile of them, turning them all about, sticking one inside another at the toe and tying two in a knot, just to frustrate her. Then I felt guilty about such a mean trick on a girl who had lost her mind, so I offered to help her straighten them, carefully untying the ones I had tied. Christine smiled at me, and Mistress herself patted my head and said, "Good girl, Mary." Birgitta saw her doing it and rushed to me, copying the words and patting, so that she could claim my goodness, I believed.

One day as I came from fetching water, a great roaring, so close I felt the hairs on my head stand forward, made all of us jump as one. I smelled the bear the moment the roar stopped echoing through the house. Goats bleated, and the growling rose. I raced to the window overlooking the goat pen. The bear had already killed two! It was eating one goat and growled at another live one. I slammed the shutter closed with such a bang that cups flew off the shelf inside. The bear left its meal and came toward the window. I shall never forget the sound of its huge paws crashing and clawing at that shutter, wrenching it from its straps. The bear's foreleg and claws swept in through the hole, sending candlesticks and bread pans flying about the room. Its huge body lunged against the house and the wall itself swayed under the weight. Mistress and Birgitta screamed. Christine whimpered. Lonnie just sang merrily and kept on braiding, holding Christine in her chair by the hair.

Mistress said, "Mary! Fetch Master and the other men!"

"Out the *door*?" I asked.

"Go get them! Fetch Master Hasken as I told you! Get out that door or I'll—I'll." She left off speaking as the bear's arm made another grab, this time taking with it a pudding. One pewter cup dangling from a curved claw disappeared out the window.

"I will not go outside with that thing there!" I screamed. No matter that the bear was on the side of the house away from the door, the thing was as tall as the walls and I had seen it run before, faster than a horse in full gallop.

Mistress picked up a carving knife and came toward me. "You get the men, Mary. Do as you're told or I'll cut off your nose." The bear growled and Birgitta screamed. Mistress waved the knife at the door. "Back up, Birgitta, you're too close to the window. Mary, I won't tell you again. Run for help. Get out!"

"It will eat me! I shall not go!" I said. Watching that blade in her hand,

I held to the seat of a three-legged stool that was light enough for me to swing. I picked it up. "You go outside, Mistress. You are *grown*."

"You're young and fast. You can do it," Birgitta said. "Be brave. It's only a bear."

Christine slumped to the floor, jittering and shaking and drooling. The bear heaved its great weight against the wall again, and chinking fell from all around the room. Straw from the thatching sifted down upon our heads. Several pieces drifted into the fireplace and caught, leading fire out of the coals and spreading it onto the floor near Christine.

Mistress said, "Birgitta, open that door. Mary, run! Run, you little tart!" She waved the knife at me again and this time I held up the stool between us, the legs pointed at her. The bear reached into the window again. Birgitta beat at the beast's paw with the iron fire poker, which made it angrier and more intent on breaking the walls. The door stood open. The bear roared. Mistress came at me wielding the knife. With all my strength I threw that stool at her, turned on my heels and dashed out the door.

I had no idea as I ran whether I had hurt her or even killed her. I did not care. I ran for my life, skirting wide around the clearing but stopping to look over my shoulder as I approached the last log house between me and the crowd of men working on it. The Haskens' house was at one end of the clearing and the bear had not followed me. I ran straight to the side of Reverend Johansen and pulled his coat. I hopped up and down and my lips moved but my tongue had dried and grown hard and immovable as a pack of sand between my teeth.

He searched the faces of the men and knelt before me. "Speak up, child," he said.

I clenched my eyes and choked out, "Bear."

The men chased the bear into the woods again by clanging shovels and axes and beating barrels. Someone brought out a pistol and shot at it but no one knew whether or not the ball found its mark. Reverend Johansen told me in the presence of all listening to him that I had been brave to run for help. Our neighbors came to the house that evening, and as if they never tired of the story, they looked at every scratch the bear had left upon the house, the cookware, and the goats. They questioned me and many nodded their heads, saying I had courage to run for help with the monster at the gate.

When they said that, I looked straight into Mistress's face, wondering if she would say that she had threatened cutting off my nose to make me do it. I pondered whether that would make her look a fiend, and almost was tempted to offer the story. In the silence as she and I locked eyes, I thought that bearing witness against her cruelty might have revealed my threatening her with the stool and they would believe me to be a defiant and violent person. Was I? I could only say yes, but why risk another beating by admitting it? No one mentioned either the thrown milk stool or the waving knife. I decided that one did not exist without the other in that story, and keeping quiet was my best answer.

Reverend Johansen held up his hand. "Gentlefolk? As we build our meetinghouse we should also construct a garrison wall. Build it high enough to keep us from bears and thieves." I wiggled through their ranks, making myself as small as a mouse, to stand near Reverend Johansen. I liked his way of saying things so that people listened. I got an idea that grew as the men talked. I had been sold more than once like a barrel of oats, my ownership transferred from pirates to privateers to the Haskens. Why could I not be sold again to Rachael and Reverend Johansen? I could tell him about Mistress stealing my coins and he would listen. And if he would not, since Rachael had taken my coins for her dowry, I would steal them back.

That evening I waited until the family headed outside for the privy—and thank goodness for better weather and the use of it—before bedding down for the night. Birgitta bent over Christine, who was still mute and lay fixed with a huge cloth baby-damper. I went to lie in my usual place, between Birgitta and Christine. I whispered, "Mother Birgitta?" just to watch the old woman's face, to see whether she warmed to the title as she had before.

Her eyes opened. "What, Mary?"

"Do you think the new Mistress Johansen might need a serving girl?"

"Maybe. That be her own accord, now."

"I was just thinking, if she chose to buy me to wait upon her, Master and Mistress Hasken could have money to get Christine to a leech."

"We don't believe in leeching and spells, and Miss Christine has all the caring anybody could want. The Great Physician will cure her when He's ready."

I curled up my knees. I didn't know how to answer that one. "Mistress Johansen must be worried about her sister."

"Not likely. More worried about keeping the reverend close to her bed."

"Would Mistress sell me to her?"

"Sell you? Mary, you was give to *me*."

"Would *you* sell me to her?"

Birgitta looked stunned. "Whatever for?"

"She might be a lady, more fine, with her own maid."

Birgitta grunted and rolled away from me, facing the wall. "And I don't need help here? What with all these to see to and all that's left of me goats? Well. You can't—"

"I meant to please you. I thought you might want her to be a fine lady and all, since she is the eldest."

"You want to get out of work, since she is alone and you'd have no chores at all."

The family took their places at pallets on the floor. I leaned upon one elbow toward Birgitta, forcing myself not to shrink from her growing anger, as if I felt no concern about that but merely wished to please. I whispered as softly as a breath, "I do not want to be lazy. I would never want to leave you. I could only be happy there if you came, too."

Birgitta sat up then, staring at the fireplace stones as if there were some answer printed on them. After a bit, she lay down and muttered, "Well, there's no place to keep the goats at their house," and soon began to snore.

The new church house was going up, but all that existed now were rows of logs high as my waist. On Sundays the community gathered there with their slaves and made worship, with the wood chips of the coming church house perfuming the air. Rough logs made for seats and the sap from them soaked into people's clothes. They sang and prayed and Reverend Johansen talked and read from his Bible. During the hours of worship, some children ran and played, and those who needed one thing or another got up and came back at will. I was not allowed to run and play, nor to sit with Patience, for I had to mind Lonnie all the time.

Reverend Johansen opened his text and spoke in a somber voice that came from some unearthly plain. It echoed against the trees around us and raised my heart with angel's wings. "Psalm Sixty-two." He began to read.

After each verse he spoke at great length. I stared at his features as he told each phrase, as if he could divine the various natures of my sin. Lies and deceiving, these were my wickedness. By the time his speech was finished and he said "Amen," tears slithered down my face with abandon.

We picnicked on the planks of the new church floor. Christine leaned against a pillar sitting upon the ground. I covered her with a blanket and sat nearby where I could watch Lonnie prattling with a wooden spoon, and using an old, rounded knife, I nibbled at my portion of corn pudding.

A shadow darkened the air about me so that I looked up. Reverend Johansen stood over me the way Rafe MacAlister had once done. I tried to smile but did not speak. "Mary?" he began, "You seem touched by God's word. Was it the Spirit moved you?"

"I know not, sir. I feel it may have been something like it."

"Is that all you have in your bowl? Just corn pudding? Have you no meat?"

I bowed my head, afraid lest he be trying to have me say aught against the master. Even as I did I wondered if I would know a deceit or a true question, since my own heart was tangled in lies and conniving. "Mistress provides all I need, your lordship."

"I'm not a lord, Mary. You mustn't call me that. Call me 'Reverend' or 'Parson' or 'Brother Johansen.' Now. Would you have some meat if I gave it to you?"

"Yes, Parson. Gladly." He lifted half his portion of stewed meat into my porringer. I gasped. "Thank you, Reverend Johansen."

"There," he said. "That will help you grow up well and strong."

"Reverend, should I confess my sins to you? I have been exceedingly wicked."

"No, Mary. You confess only to God. Believe me, He has already forgiven you."

He seemed so kind, I almost admitted I had planned to steal the coins Rachael had stolen from me, but I decided that was a sin suitable for divine ears alone. Rachael had exchanged her life of crowded entombment for one little different from my own. Never did a day go by that she did not bustle about doing washing, digging a garden, sweeping and tending and carrying and cleaning. Her limp body firmed up and plumped up and her eyes even seemed not quite so crossed. Her temperament, however, was crosser than ever, as she was unused to the labor put upon her. I asked, "Could I not come and be your servant instead of the Haskens'?"

He smiled a kindly smile. He leaned forward and whispered as if it were a secret between us, "You are ever loved, little Mary. Not a sparrow falls from the heavens but that it is noted. How much more are you than a sparrow? I am a humble man and can afford no servants, nor will I ever own any slaves for I think it is a pitiful thing."

"Sir? Would you permit me paper and a quill to write to my ma?"

"I have none, child."

"How shall I ever get home to my mother?"

Reverend Johansen's face turned sad. "You will work off your indenture as others have done before. I did it myself. It is not forever. And you will pray that she is well and that you may find her when you have done your utmost in honest toil."

I set the plate down and sighed. "Was your mother alive when you finished?"

"Mary, I'm glad you asked me for the Psalms. It is a book of both great comfort and great chastening, and none should shirk the hearing of it." With that he left me.

It took the men four more weeks to finish the church house. While they did, Mistress and the girls worked at putting in a garden, and some days assigned me digging, or to keeping out birds and goats and pigs that came from one of the other houses. The air warmed. Rain fell, sometimes for days at a time, coming down in torrents much as it did in Jamaica. The trees budded and leafed out, and all the world was riotously green.

Only one goat gave milk by then, so Birgitta said it would be a lean summer until the does had their babies. The bear ruined other stores and tore through one home's doorway, which was closed by a blanket pulled and fastened on both sides, ransacking and ripping through all their cloth goods. Wolves howled at night, and owls, and the Haskens' house filled with bats. First one or two came in the morning to roost; before long there were thirty-one bats. I counted them every morning. Master was forced by his tender-voiced wife to collect scraps of any hewn wood from the church building and put a ceiling above our heads to keep the bats' spoilage from falling on the supper table.

I tried as much as I dared to work near Patey. To my joy she was growing stronger and plumper, too, and seemed recovered from our passage in the ship's hold, sometimes smiling. Once she laughed at Lukas, standing on his hands before her like a child showing off. As we carried buckets of water to the men chopping trees, she told me good tidings for the anniversary of my birth. I had turned eleven without knowing the day or date. "And when," I asked, "was my birthday?"

"I remember it," she said. "On a gusty, rainy day in March. Ma cried out five times. The sun broke through heavy clouds as if it pushed them aside and thrust itself upon the earth to shine upon your wee puffed and pinched face. You were ugly as a tortoise. Soon as it saw you it hid again."

"La, Patey!" I felt shock though she smiled. "Am I still so ugly?" I shuddered. Did I seem as hideous as these Hasken daughters? It was said no duppy ever peered in a mirror for fear of death by ugliness. Their faces reflected in a pond turned it to poison. Perhaps I was numbered among them.

She laughed. "Name a star in heaven without beauty. And yet, the sun itself had to hide when you were born. Not a bad way to start a life. But"— she mimicked Ma's voice—"'Twil be a burthen for ye, lassie." Then she began to sing one of Ma's favorite old songs, "O Waly, Waly." I joined her and we sang together, refilling our buckets and returning to the men. The whole place bustled with the work of living.

"Mary! Stop squalling that heathen jig!" Master Hasken pointed toward me with the axe in his hand.

I nearly dropped the bucket, my eyes large as apples. "Yes, Master," I said. "Beg your pardon, sir. It was just a song."

"We'll have no singing but for hymns and psalms as please the ear of God."

"Yes, Master," I said. I began humming the hymn of theirs I oft hummed to myself while milking, the one that fit the words "Damn your eyes, Mistress Hasken."

He listened for a minute then said, "That's better. Do you not know the words?"

"Only the tune, Master," I lied.

CHAPTER 9

April 29, 1730

After three days of strong wind and heavy rain, Reverend and Rachael Johansen's roof fell apart. The Haskens were first at their door to help, and they left Birgitta watching Lonnie so that I could be of better use. I took up a broom beside Christine who was well enough to sweep then, and helped Rachael sweep up fallen thatch.

I swept much the same as I had cleaned brass on the ship, moving with every stroke closer to the far corner of the house until at last I stood beside a trunk. Upon it was Ma's gold-cornered casket. When the sisters were outside I lifted the lid. I drew in a deep breath. My coins were no more than a finger's width from my reach. I no longer wore my pocket, for there was nothing to put within it. I picked up the coins, knowing I could slip out with them and hide them better this time, so they might never be found. This was no harder than stealing stockings, and these coins belonged to me. Would they know it was I took them? I put them back in the casket, intending to take it, too. A new thought stopped my hand. What if rather than stealing them I could get them to give it all back? What if I could prevail upon the reverend to do it?

I heard voices. I dropped the money, shut the lid, and pushed the box back into place so that it looked as if I had not touched it. If Reverend Johansen would give me my coins, all the better. If not, I would steal them another time. I pinched my lips together, and swept straw from the corner behind the trunk. The sisters returned to the house and I moved toward the doorway, pushing a foot-high pile of thatch and straw with my broom, passing them.

"Mary, mind you," Rachael said. "You're sweeping too fast and making dust."

"Yes, Mistress," I said. I felt her eyes on my back as I worked.

The next Sunday Reverend Johansen opened his battered book and said, "Psalm Forty-two. As the deer panteth for the water-brooks . . ." Thus began a talk about how like a lost deer our lives can be. I knew the words well, but it was grand the way he explained it. That day women brought food to the church house, for the roof was on and all was dry inside. When all sat, eating, I went to the well and brought up a fresh bucket of cold water, carrying it straight to Reverend Johansen.

"I shall cool your cup, Reverend," I said, "with a fresh pull of water."

He smiled and said, "Mary, you thought of my wish before I said it."

I poured water from the dipper into his cup and waited for him to speak.

"Very well, Mary. Was there something more?" He eyed my face.

"No, Reverend. I meant only to be of good service."

Three days later, Mistress Hasken sent me with a pail of milk for Rachael to use in her cooking. Rachael was in the garden and Reverend Johansen sat at their table, poring over his Bible. I waited at the open door for him to notice me. When a length of time passed and he did not, I tapped on the side of the pail, being sure to stare upward as if my attention had been caught by some sound or fluttering bird. Reverend Johansen looked in my direction, and upon seeing me his face softened. "Mary. It's you. Come in, child."

"I beg your pardon, sir. Mistress sends you this milk."

"Well, put it, ah"—he glanced over the room and its spare furnishings, without even a pail of their own—"set it on that chest. That will keep it off the ground at least."

I put the bucket next to my casket. "Here, sir?"

"That will do. Come sit by me, child. Let me rest my eyes from reading."

I did as he asked, sitting on the stool that I supposed was Rachael's place at table. I bowed my head, practicing both the humility I felt from his sermons and the forced broken spirit that becomes a slave in the presence of others.

"Raise your face, child. Ah. You look like, someone. Your face is dirty but your eyes are keen as a dagger's edge and I suppose your mind yet more sharp."

I had thought the same of his eyes. I faced him as I would my own pa. "I should like to ask you a question, sir." I felt my face assume an air of contrition yet I had come with a mission and I was not to be deterred. I was, however, going to be careful how I proceeded.

"There," he said. "Now you look even more like my child. I had a wife and family once. And a daughter about your size. Fever took them all. Put your lip back in and be pleasant. A petulant child is no honor to her parents. How do you come to know the Psalms, little one?"

"My mother taught me. We learned of everything in our study on the top floor of the plantation."

"Knowing it is wrong for slaves to be instructed to read and write?"

I straightened my back and blurted out, "I am not a slave, sir, and my name is not Mary. I am Resolute Catherine Eugenia Talbot, second daughter of Allan Talbot of Two Crowns Plantation, Meager Bay, Jamaica. I was not born to be a slave, sir. Not until my brother and sister and I were spirited away and brought to this cold shore to be sold like cattle, sir. My mother was an educated gentlewoman and my father the son of an earl. Their children were meant to be gentle and knowledgeable and fine." I bowed my head, wary of what that might bring me in the way of punishment.

Reverend Johansen straightened. "I see." He rubbed his chin with his hand and I could hear the rough beard in the silence of the room. He pulled off his indoor cap, revealing a nearly bald head with a slight tangle of long, thin gray hair. "I once was red-haired, redder than you, though now I am old and gray. My child was a little angel of rosy hue, as are you. Fair of face. Most fair. A father's vain wish fulfilled." He stood and went to the doorway, staring at the men raising yet another log in place at the garrison wall. His fingers tapped at the fat logs by his side and drew sap, which pulled him from his reverie so that he sucked on the sap at his fingertip and turned toward me.

I prepared to see anger on his face but instead could not read what was writ there. I said the words I had rehearsed. "When God's word speaks of deceit and thievery by falsehood, does it apply to all? Young or old? Masters or slaves?"

"Yes!" The word jumped from him without hesitation.

I remained silent and nodded. As I did so I marveled that I had learned such care in the company of pirates and brigands and Haskens. Nothing was more important than well-thought words.

He asked, "Have you plotted aught against another? Deceived someone?"

"No, sir."

He followed his path again to the doorway, avoiding the sap-dripping log. "Someone has deceived you, then?"

"An object has been stolen from me."

Rachael's voice came over the meadow, calling, "Do you need me, husband?"

"No, wife. Continue with your work, if you please. I am in prayer." He resumed his seat at the table. He closed the Bible and thrust it toward me. "Give me your hand." Did he mean to beat my hands with the book? I felt caught and resigned to take the beating I would receive. I held out my hands and closed my eyes. "Place your hand upon God's holy word, child." I laid my hand atop the book. The ragged leather of it, the faintest smell of ink and glue, the worn texture of the edges, awakened memories of the books at home, of Ma telling me how to divide numbers. "I ask you, with your hand upon God's word with fear of eternal fire in your heart, this question. Will you tell me the truth?"

"Yes, Reverend. When last I saw my mother she gave to me a pocket, and in it she hid a wooden casket with gold—gold-*colored*," I added, lest he count the value of it, too, "corners. Inside she placed two silver doubloons, stamped in the old Spanish way as pieces of eight, for me to keep against my freedom someday." I questioned blaming Rachael for this to her new husband. He might have affectionate feelings for her now they were married. So I said, "Mistress Hasken took my coins and my casket from the pocket and gave them to Mistress Johansen for a dowry, claiming that I had stolen them."

He peered into my eyes as if searching out some defiance or lie. At great length he asked, "Do you swear this before Almighty God?"

"I do, sir."

"You have been in this house before. Always in the company of others who watched you?"

"No. When your roof fell in, I was here often alone. Sweeping."

"And you saw the box and made this story to fit your wants? Or did you not think to steal the box again, to take it for yourself?"

"I did think it. Often. But 'twould not be righteous." My hand trembled upon the book.

"Can you produce that pocket?"

"I can."

"Bring it here," he said, motioning toward the door with his head.

I darted home. Burrowing into my nest of blanket and bearskin, I pulled up my wrinkled pocket. As I turned to make for the door again, Birgitta stepped in front of me.

"What's that you're doing, Mary?"

I smiled, knowing full well that a guilty flush covered my face. "Reverend Johansen has need of my pocket, Birgitta. He sent me to fetch it to him."

"What need has he of a child's pocket?"

"I don't know, madam," I said, and dashed around her. The girl-whipping stick swished through the air behind my head as I went. I walked in and placed the pocket in Reverend Johansen's hands with hopeful uncertainty. "This is it, sir," I said, as if it needed explaining.

He turned it this way and that, then poked his fingers in and turned it inside outside. "What happened to this? There was lining here. How does the inside of a pocket wear away?"

"It did not wear away, sir. I ate it. Some of us starved to death in the hold of a Saracen ship. I patched it with bits of my gown of blue silk. I—I also took some of Mistress's white thread to patch it there, which is one of the sins I have been repenting."

He moved his fingers upon it as if the feel of the fabric told him a story that his eyes could not. He turned it right again, took Ma's casket and slipped it inside. It settled in the place it had always been, corners fitting worn places on the pocket as the cloth aligned for it and nothing else.

"Come with me." Reverend Johansen slapped the cap upon his head, took hold of my hand with his, snatched up the casket and the pocket from the table, and marched the two of us to the common ground near the well. Where the common had been so trampled little grass yet grew. He held my hand up in the air. At that moment I felt the sap that connected our skins tug and loosen and stick fast again, and I enjoyed it. He cried out. "Hoi-ye, brothers and sisters!" Lonnie came with the first that heard his call. He turned to her and said, "Sister Livonah, fetch your mother to this place." To the rest he called, "Where is my wife? Bid that lady come." He led me to the step at the church house and we stood before the door.

Mistress hurried toward us, Birgitta rumbling and grumbling behind her. When Mistress saw me her face darkened. Reverend Johansen raised his voice as if he were preaching. "Fellow pilgrims, just as David, King of Israel, though he had dozens of wives, smote Uriah and took Uriah's wife to himself out of greed and desire, we must never take, out of greed and desire, from those who cannot defend themselves. This child, Mary of the Haskens, came on her journey to us, in possession of one thing. This." He held the pocket aloft, pulled Ma's casket from it. "Wife? Come here." He put the casket in her hands and at once I believed I would be hung. Waves of gray darkness washed before my eyes. He said, "Put that in the hands of your mother, Mistress Hasken, from whom you received it." If not for the reverend's strong hand holding mine I would have sat upon the steps, for my legs had not the strength to hold me.

Rachael whimpered and put her hand to her lips. She started to protest but she did not dare dispute her husband before the company. She carried the casket to her mother and held it out. Mistress stared at the box, glancing at me. Rachael said, "Take it, Mother. It is not mine."

When Mistress had the casket in her hands, she searched the faces of people gathered about but got no understanding from them. "Mistress Hasken?" Reverend Johansen began. "We accept and forgive the misplacing of a small article, even forgetting whence it came, but we know that our Lord commands, once the truth is found out, it must be returned to its owner. Did any in your family work, sell, or trade goods or money, ever, for the thing you now hold in your hand?"

"No, Reverend," she said.

"Yet, though it fit into the pocket owned by this person known to us as Mary, and its story matched what she has told with her hand on the Word of God, you thought it not fit to return it to the person who could have been the only source of such an object, and claimed such, but keep and thus further your daughter's material possessions?"

"Well, yes, Reverend."

I felt almost sorry for her, for she was confused by the parson's words, and had admitted her guilt without so much as a struggle of conscience. People made noise. Someone announced, "We need to build some stocks."

She blurted out, "I didn't know it was hers. She'd stole it and so 'twas my right as owner of her property. The husband and I paid good coin for her an' all of her as come with." By that time Master had come, and stood beside her.

Reverend Johansen said, "Brother and Sister Hasken, in indenturing this maid you paid for her strength and ability to work. You did not buy her possessions nor her virtue nor her soul." He was red around the collar and put his hands behind his back where both hands clenched in fists. "This is a human being, not a goat. Your duty to her is to feed, clothe, and educate her. Mistress Hasken, return that casket to its owner."

Mistress had no choice but to lay the casket in my hand. I closed my fingers upon it, feeling as if it held my ma's heart and soul, not just two coins. "Thank you," I said. Mistress bowed in submission, though not to me, but to some higher force found in the eyes of her fellow pilgrims. My eyes caught Birgitta's. She glowered with rage. I might well rue this action, though I had my two pounds and my box.

The air split apart as if rent by two great hands with the sound of a piercing scream. The cry was so violent it took my breath out of my body. The scream came again, and unusual smoke rose beyond the roof of the Haskens' house. The whole crowd ran toward it. Two men thought to carry buckets of water as the black smoke rose ever more ominously over the house.

With no one to watch her, Lonnie had fallen into the coals. Her gown had caught fire, and though she still breathed, there was not one place of whole skin upon her. Allsy, dead and pocked with pustules, was not so nightmarish as what lay smoking and moaning before us. She wailed, her air rasping and dragging in and out as she suffered upon the floor. They placed a wet blanket upon her to soothe the burns. Voices around me rose in prayer, simple, anguished supplication for an end to agony. Rachael threw herself down next to her little sister and wept, claiming it to be her fault, beating her chest with her fists, tearing at her hair until Reverend Johansen had to raise her and take her away.

In the midst of all the people gathered, talking and weeping, I was felled by the breaking of a stick across my back. Birgitta picked up another and laid her art across my shoulders with such fury I soon curled up on the ground as she cried out, "You were supposed to watch her! Because of you we had to come to the common. This is your doing, you wretched devil!"

I hardened my face to the burning behind my eyes and did not shed a tear. Someone stopped her, but not before she had brought me to a place where I wished to die. I groaned as hands lifted me to my feet. I held the pocket in my grasp. Lukas's father said, "There will be no more beatings today. You will sleep this night at our house. We will not weary our Lord with needless cruelty for which we will surely repent on the morrow."

Patience took my hand and, following the Newhams, led me to their home. She put me into her bed and, after everyone else slept, held me close and cradled me like a babe. I did not cry. I felt neither sad nor hurt. I did not know then that I could *not* cry.

"Ressie?" she whispered. "Take heart. Try to be brave."

"Patey, let me sleep. I will be good tomorrow."

"You are good, now."

I awoke snuggled next to Patey, so sore I could not move. She slept amongst barrels of provisions and boxes of implements. It was not luxurious but it had no goats. As I lay there, she slipped from the bed and tipped to the window where a little opening separated this room from the next, lifted the latch and pulled in the shutter. I saw Lukas lean his head through the opening and kiss Patience right on the lips! Not only did he kiss her but she kissed him in return. They kissed each other, murmuring, their faces touching or almost touching when they spoke, their lips all but nibbling at each other as a horse would search your hand for sweet carrots. I had seen Ma and Pa kissing in such a way, but any boy that I chose to love would have to settle for holding hands, and even then only if his were washed. Patey lay back beside me.

"Do you love Lukas?" I asked in the softest whisper I could manage.

"What are you doing awake?"

"I could not help it. Why were you doing that? Do you love him?"

"Kissing him keeps other things at bay. I promise and yet fend him off."

"Does he want to marry you? Does he have enough money to get us home?"

"His parents own me. I could no more become his wife than I could fly."

"Did he want to see up your skirt?"

"Where did you learn such a thing?"

"The women on the ship said that a fellow might give a girl something for a glimpse under a farthingale."

"I think you should go back to sleep."

"Are you going to kiss him again when I do?"

"Not tonight. I tossed a pebble at his sister so she will be watching; he dares not be caught. His parents would have him flogged. He burns with lust in his private chamber. Go to sleep."

It was not difficult to follow her order. I closed my eyes, imagining Lukas feeling remorse for kissing Patience. I smiled. It was good that he should suffer for love.

We buried Lonnie, the first of our dead, in a place beside the church house. After that, the reverend marked off a place and called it consecrated, where others would lie beside her in days to come. It did not take long for a second grave to follow. Four days after Lonnie fell into the fire, Goodwife Fischer was found having gone to her eternal rest one morning. Goody Fischer had been a frail, toothless woman who came with one of the families though she was no relative of theirs. No one cried for her.

The third death was a young man full of vigor and health. Foster Simon was his name. He was an apprentice carpenter and had gone with other men to deep woods outside our clearing to hunt a tree to make a table and chest. His father and brother accompanied the party and worked at felling it, but they started for home to bring others to help. Halfway there with his brother perched upon his shoulders, Foster remembered leaving his axe at the base of the tree. He put his brother down and sauntered back down the new-cut path.

When he did not return for the midday meal, the men called for him as they walked, and joked that he had probably fallen asleep. They found him, flesh bitten and torn, his neck broken. A bear had savaged the tree and huge scars on it coated with blood marked the place of Foster's death. I stood at the grave as they laid that young man to his rest. My arms and neck still bore yellowing bruises from the beating Birgitta had given me. As they started filling dirt upon him, his blood seeping through the winding cloth, I thought I would rather be in that cool ground beside him than working here.

Though Mistress kept me busy working, I searched out wildflowers and laid them daily upon the three graves. I did not know Goody Fischer, and Lonnie was so bothersome that I felt little but sorrow for the suffering she had endured and some gratitude that I did not have to sleep next to her. Foster had been little older than August, was both a young man and a boy, a stranger and yet part of this group to which I belonged. He had once helped me with a load of firewood and he knew "If I Wast a Blackbird." When Foster had smiled, two cunning dimples puckered his cheeks like an overstuffed pillow. I wished I had had a chance to kiss those dimples, I thought with a sigh. Oh, how handsome he had been.

One day, I lay down upon Foster's grave and stared at the sky. I patted the soil beneath me and felt of him lying there, snug and warm as if tucked in for the night. Clouds drifted overhead like a flock of animals, bunching and parting, bunching and parting. I knew then what Patience meant, for I knew I loved Foster Simon. My chest ached. I would never marry for my own true love was dead, just as in the blackbird song. My heart's wings would ever flutter over his heart, and the beauty of our tragic love would rise above any other love ever known. I sighed with the soaring emotion of it. Love so true and pure!

The next day I visited him and sat at the end of the mound over his feet. I swept clear a place with my hands and took great care to set stones upon the grave in the shape of a heart to show him my love. I heard Birgitta call and I stood to leave. "I will come back to see you soon," I said, brushing gravel and bits of dried weed from my skirt. "I wish you weren't dead. I will come and keep you company. Good day. And, I love you."

"Mary!"

"Coming, Birgitta! I love you, Foster."

Next Meeting Day, Reverend Johansen called to me, so I sat near him. "Mary, do you understand what death is? And do you understand what it means to let the dead rest in peace?"

Against my will my lower lip pushed itself out. "Yes, sir, I do most certainly."

"I'm speaking of Master Foster Simon. You have decorated his resting place and visited many times, yet you must know his soul is not there, and naught remains but his earthly form, turned already to dust. I ask you to let his spirit rest."

"Does my being there bother him, sir?"

"We don't know what the spirits know, but I think a fortnight of mourning is enough."

"I love him."

Reverend Johansen said nothing but smiled in a small way. "Child, if the dead do know, he will be warmed by that knowledge. You can carry that feeling in your heart and let him rest in the ground."

"I will not visit him any longer." Oh, my heart lurched with the agony of that terrible declaration. "I will still love him, though, with all my heart, forever."

"I think that is wisest," he said. "As for love, what you know now will grow and fashion itself anew each time you press your heart against the thought. I pray God that you will know the best that love has to offer when you are a woman grown."

I walked from the church and went inside the Haskens' empty house, for they were all still at the common meal. I took the iron poker from the fireplace and, using the tip of it, scratched the initials *F S* into the doorpost at a height that my hand would touch as I went in and out. The Haskens were tall. They would not glance down and see Foster's initials carved there for me.

CHAPTER 10

May 9, 1730

On the day the goats got out, only five feet of open space in our garrison wall remained to be filled with posts. I hated for it to be finished for it closed up the greenwood around about us. That day I was glad for it, though, for we had dozens of goats all running hither and thither through the houses and commons, tearing up gardens and messing on floors, making a stir on the morning's placid air. No one knew how, before the break of day, every fence in the compound had opened and every barnyard animal got loose. With the help of anyone who could wave an apron and chase them, seven of our goats returned to the fenced yard.

I discovered the tracks of one goat led through the garrison opening and into the woods. I ran to get Birgitta and show her that the goat was lost. I hoped that she'd say it was no use looking for it so I could get to other chores. One of my stockings had a hole in it and I meant to get a new pair from Christine's basket. To my dismay, Birgitta brought Mistress and they followed me to the opening in the wall. We walked several yards beyond it following the hoofprints. A few men kept at the chopping and fitting of the remaining log posts.

"Go fetch it, Mary. You don't have to go far. It's just there in that green place," Mistress said, pointing. "I have so much to do. Don't tell me you are too lazy to get a goat a dozen steps from the wall."

Birgitta twisted her face to one side. "I should have a man go with her, and I will go, too. If the bear is there, we'll scare it away as we did before."

"The bear *is* out there," I said, without address or bowing my head.

"Mary, do as you are told. I want you to help me with the sewing, Birgitta. She can go by herself," Mistress said. "It'll not take long." She turned to a workman. "You there? Bring your axe and help her get the last goat."

An old man looked up at her and heaved a great breath. "Which way did it go?" he asked. I pointed toward the greenest shrubs. He led the way.

I found droppings and they smelled fresh. "See here," I said, "toward the stream."

Mistress said, "Well, go and get it. We'll wait for you."

The man knelt and looked at the ground. "Stream's that way. I don't think you're going to find it. Fell in an' drowned, that's my thinking. I have work aplenty before me. There's no smell of bear in the air. Leave it be." He shouldered his axe and walked back to his chores with Mistress and Birgitta following him.

"Wait for me!" I cried, and ran toward them.

"Make her go or you will sleep in the shed this night, Birgitta!" Mistress called.

Birgitta's face showed how she hated being ordered by her sister. She turned to me, forced to comply though her voice was gentle. "Go fetch that goat, Mary."

"It has drowned. The man said it," I insisted.

Mistress whirled and leaned over me. "Do as you are told! *Your* care-lessness has lost this goat as it lost my daughter. As it lost my money—oh, I rue the day I bought you, you heathen wretch. Go and don't return with-out my goat." She turned to her sister. "See that she gets it," she said, then turned back to me. "If you don't find it I'll have them seal up the wall with you on the outside!"

Watching them walk away, I cursed them both under my breath with words I remembered the pirates using. It felt like power to say that the two old Hasken women should twist and dance in hell on the devil's prong, even though I was not altogether certain what it meant. I kicked at the goat droppings with my shoe. They were an hour or so old. "Nob?" I called. It was a foolish name for a goat. "Nob?" The closer I was to the edge of the stream, the more I trembled. I moved some brush, holding my breath, ex-pecting to see Nob standing there, munching away. Or, worse, what was left of Nob and the bear standing there, munching away. I looked behind me, wondering if the man with the axe was watching so he could run to my aid if the bear came and I wondered if I would hear the bear coming through the woods over the tumbling of the water.

I got to where a great tree had fallen, its roots lifted from the bank, making a muddy slide. The goat's hoofprints went there but it did not walk into the water; it kept going around the side. I heard the animal bleating softly. When I got behind the tree trunk, I could no longer hear the woods-men chopping logs or the sounds of the community, people moving about, animals lowing and clucking. The water murmured at my feet; down-stream, it rippled at a small waterfall. The tracks led on and I heard a goat bleat. On I went, listening and smelling the air for the bear. Still, I smelled nothing but the weedy smell that the bank of the stream always carried, and the whiff of a grown-up's sweat. I wondered, since I had now been in love with a man, albeit a young man and a dead one at that, whether I had grown up enough to smell like Patience. "Nob?" I called. "Nob?"

I went down the stream until it turned again to the left. In parted grasses where the reeds had grown tall, Nob stood chewing, tied to a stick. "God's balls!" I cursed. Why, who would play such a cruel trick? This could bring the bear just to eat the goat and, in turn, me! As if a cold blast of air took me, I wondered if Mistress were so cruel as to put the goat here and send me to it so I would be killed. I would show her a thing or two about bravery, I thought. With shaking hands I took his rope from the stick and turned to lead him home. I then let out a soft moan against the hand that wrapped around my mouth. The hands held me so tight I could barely breathe or move but I got the quick image of a dark man, wearing paint upon his arms and some strange pants, no shirting at all, with lines drawn across his face and chest. Beads rattled against his body as he held me tight to him. I smelled his skin as he nearly crushed the life out of me, and knew it was the grown-up sweating that I had smelled. I tried with all my might to scream and to fight away, but his strength was as two men and my voice stopped in my teeth.

My eyes searched the woods and stream and brushy green. From it, like plants thrusting up quick and brown, a hoard of dark brown men in feathers and paints and the strange pants arose. They made signals to each other with their hands, and began to move in the direction I had come, while my captor held me tight, my fingers snarled in the rope around Nob's neck. The goat had not been tied by Mistress but by them.

The hand that gripped my face loosened enough to let me breathe. The man shook me and said a word, squeezed my face and said it again as he turned to look me in the eye. Quiet was what he wanted. I nodded. He lessened his hold and I remained mute. He took his hand from my mouth and said the word again. I nodded again. He held my arms with both hands then, and I dropped the rope. Nob nestled in the grass to chew cud.

I smelled smoke. It rose in billows across the tops of the trees, bringing with it the smell of fresh green wood and old dry planks and the reek of scorched flesh. Oh, la, Patience! Oh my soul, my sister! I stayed still as stone. A bird called and another. Birds do not sing when there is danger about; even a child knows that. I realized I had not heard a bird in all the time since I left the garrison for the woods.

As the sun began to lower, the noise of many people tramping through the grass frightened away the birds again. Here they came, Indians. Behind them in a line walked people from our village, finally more Indians. They came leading cows and one of the oxen. They came with Mistress's goats. They carried two blunderbusses and bags of powder, bags of flour, salt, and dried corn. They laid them all in a circle and went over the stock of booty just as the pirates had on the ships. The settlement people who came to the green brush had blood and smoke and dirt smeared from head to toe. My heart pained me, wanting to cry out, Patey, Patey! My eyes searched each face, discarding each image until at last I saw her following Rachael, followed by another girl. An Indian man with a pole in his hand prodded her as they moved along. Mistress and Master, along with the Newhams, Reverend Johansen, and others I recognized, men and women and boys, were part of the second group. Birgitta was not there. I looked for her again, sadness and anger mingling in my heart. I grieved for a moment, but then I thought that the old wretch should have come with me to find the blasted goat. At least she would have been taken alive. Cursed be the merciless, I thought, changing the words from the Bible, for they shall receive no mercy.

The Indians bade us all sit by shouting orders and pushing people to the ground. Most of the people wept, even the men. Once all had sat upon the ground, the man who kept me led me to them and pushed me down amidst the younger girls. Other Indians arrived, carrying away all that they could from the houses. Iron kettles and bales of cloth, hats and coats and lengths of woven wool plaid I saw with surprise, for I had not seen such a cloth since leaving home. Ma had kept her lengths of plaid hidden between layers of linens. Just like my petticoat, Ma had always hidden things under other things, always kept those secrets that were dangerous, or precious, close at hand and yet hidden a breath away. I squeezed my legs together, taking pleasure as the hard corners of Ma's casket bruised my thighs.

There were about the same number of Indians as there were of us, yet they were all men and we were more women and children than men, and they were the ones with hatchets and blades and arrows. I wondered that Reverend Johansen did not speak to them for he knew their tongue, but he was far from me and I could not ask.

The sun slid from its heights toward the treetops, and the Indian men, quick as any woman in a kitchen, started a fire and butchered three of the goats. Mistress Hasken flew at them, her fists raised, crying, "My goats. My goats! You heathen scourge!"

I saw an Indian raise his hatchet as she came for him and turned my head away. I heard the thud and I heard Master Hasken groan in anguish. Heard her fall to the ground. Others began shouting at the other captives.

I knew without question that they meant for the people to be silent. I felt horror that Mistress Hasken was dead, yet it was because she had been stubborn and stupid that he had killed her. Why would anyone run against armed men who had already proved they had the will and more weapons than they needed to kill us all? Many began to wail and call out that we would all be killed.

One of the Indians stood before the lot of us and said, "Hello!" in a loud voice. "No more fight. No more die. Stay alive. No more fight. Understand?"

I nodded as if I had been instructed by a teacher. No lesson could have had more weight than Mistress Hasken's corpse.

Jabbing parts of the goats onto sticks and stretching them across rocks placed before the fire, the Indian men roasted the meat in a way I had not seen done before. I dared to wonder whether they would give us something to eat. I knew enough of hunger aboard the ships that it had impressed me with the stern belief that to live or die was nothing compared to doing either with a full belly.

They boiled dried seed corn in a pot with the goats' heads to make a porridge. When the sky began losing its last colors, two of the Indians took tin cups they'd stolen from the village and scooped them full of the porridge. One man chopped hunks of the open-fire-cooked meat into each cup. They lined up the littlest children first and fed them. I was one of the first.

Oh, what a glorious repast! Something in it was so filling and good with meat roasted instead of boiled, I could have eaten three cups of it. I handed my cup back to the bronze man who had given it, and smiled, saying, "Thank you, sir."

When I sat down, Rachael said to me, "How could you eat from them heathen curs with Mother just murdered before our eyes? You must have no soul at all."

I thought about turning away without answering her, or declaring I was glad Mistress was dead for she was an empty, clanging gong of a woman, but I said, "I was hungry and they fed me. It was a Christian thing to do and far better than I have been treated by some such as claim salvation."

"It's poisoned," she said. "I hope you die screaming." Then an Indian man came and said aught to her and she quieted, though she knew not what he spoke.

All the captives got the supper. Rachael put up her nose at it and would not eat. The man who offered her the cup passed it toward the next captive without even a raise of his brows, for he cared not whether she ate. The Indians did not eat of it but some of them prepared another dish, taking the goat liver, heart, and lungs to add to the corn porridge. They added some of the blood and cooked this a good while, and all of them ate it with such relish I wished I had a taste of it, too.

After all had been fed and there remained some of the stew in the pot, the Indians scooped up the last of it and held it forth, offering it with gestures to any who would have it. I gulped it with relish, even though the liver taste was strong. I had not felt so full and drowsy in as many weeks as I could remember.

The Indian who had spoken English before stood again. "No more fight. No run away. Warriors watch. Sleep now. Walk after sun come. No run away. Understand?" I settled in to sleep without much ado. Those among the group who felt terror at this captivity wept; some prayed aloud. As I closed my eyes my last thought was how I had exchanged places, indeed, with the women in the hold who knew how to be captive, who knew how to take anything offered without question. I felt grown-up. I even wondered if I looked as grown as I felt.

When the sun had barely greened the sky, they pushed us with their feet to awaken us, and distributed the cooking pots, sacks of corn, axe heads, and bolts of cloth among the captives. The men compelled everyone, even the smallest, to carry something. I was given a lidded iron kettle-oven with a handle, the kind Birgitta had called a spider, but then she called everything and everyone that when she was angry.

By noon all my fingers hurt. I switched the heavy iron pot from hand to hand, moving it from one knuckle to another, trying to favor the most sore places. I walked with a searing pain in my side, my legs trembling from exhaustion. Patience walked somewhere behind me. All stayed quiet. All walked in fear. We walked on without stop, walking until some of the weaker ones fell out, and the Indians put them upon their backs and carried them! I saw two girls and one grown man carried upon the backs of the warriors.

When they did that, the Indians also carried what the captives had carried, taking the boxes of sugar and bundles of tied onions. That evening followed almost the same as the one before it, with stew made from what we carried and two more goats. That night, even Rachael ate the porridge. The next day the Indians told the men captives, by demonstrating what they wanted, to carry some of the children. Master came to choose me, for I was the lightest burden, but I looked him in the eye and said, "I am not weary one whit, sir. Choose one of your own daughters." I picked up my kettle and started down the path, pushing to the front of the column behind the Indian man who had first caught me in the brushes. I put my feet in his tracks.

It had never before occurred to me that there were better or worse ways to die. Perhaps Mistress Hasken's death was merciful. At least, one quick fatal blow such as Mistress received would be preferable to the suffering agony Lonnie had endured. The first death I had known was Allsy's. We were ill at almost the same time with the same disease, though I recovered. I knew, I thought, what her suffering contained. I had heard men fighting and cursing and beating each other aboard ships. Hangings. Whippings with the cat. A quick blow to the head was a kindness, indeed.

These Indians were a puzzle too large for my learning to sort, too complicated for my mind. I wanted to ask Pa what was to be thought of them, since I could not fathom it myself. I thought of Pa, floating in the bay, face to the sun, smiling as if in sleep, the way he did on a Sunday afternoon, resting from the week's work in a hammock on the front promenade of the house. I thought of the crystal-blue waters of our bay, and the coral-lined coves, and the warm sun and balmy, fragrant breeze. Coffee flowers and roses, Ma's gardenia, almost too strong to enjoy except at a distance, plumeria and cocoa blossoms. "Oh, la," I said aloud. "When shall I get home again?"

An Indian came up behind me and said something that sounded to me like "Kzomi mannossa," although I could not speak the word again. He knelt and motioned to his back, and took the iron kettle from me. I nodded and climbed upon him. As he walked I leaned against his back and wept for the first time in weeks. My feet burned with the relief of not having to use them. My fingers throbbed without the narrow handle of the iron kettle cutting into them. My heart ached and ached and ached with the lack of some new injury to it, as if all the others were enough, stored there, just now felt, like a thorn that had worked its way through the sole of a shoe.

Oh, Ma, I thought, when I see you again, I shall never cease being good and kind and forever look upon your dear face, my most trusted and loved life's companion. How dear it would be to climb into your lap once more, held in that blessed peace.

We had traveled four days and slept in the forest three nights when on the fourth night, I awoke from a terrible dream of being in the Saracens' hold. Instead of the wee Irish girl being pulled from the cell, the men had come for me. Patience, in the dream, was not there to keep me from them. Instead of taking me abovedecks to be fed but thrown overboard, one man pulled my arms, one pulling my head, one on each foot, until I came apart in pieces like a wooden toy whose threads had sprung. I lay awake shivering, for I was lying next to the man who had carried me, and rather than curling up around each other as the prisoners were wont to do, the Indians slept like logs, straight, as if they felt no cold and needed no warmth. I wiggled closer to him, putting my side against his arm.

I stared upward at the sky. The moon was bright again, MacPherson's lantern, as it had been that night in Jamaica. I whispered toward it, "What have I done wrong to have ended in this place, O God?" Yet even as I said the words, I thought about Allsy and how I had been the one meant to die. How could I go back and trade my life for hers, even if I wished it? A person could not turn backward. Time went onward to tomorrow, and so if I were still alive as Patey said, and this was not Purgatory, it was still penance for having lived when others died. I sighed and raised my head above the man to look toward the place where the evening fire had been. The embers seemed alive, coursing red to black to red again, giving no light. I put my head back down. The man next to me snuffled a little.

What reason had I to live at all? I thought. "Oh, la," I said. "Ma, please come find me as soon as I can write you a letter." Tears slid from my eyes, one on each side of my face, and ran down into my hair. I rubbed at the right side, feeling the hair, now a couple of inches long. I must still look like a changeling without the bonnet.

I tried to fall asleep but fear came over me in a wave, and though I lay upon my back, my whole being felt weak. At first I believed I wanted to weep again, but when I breathed the more potent need was to scream. I smelled a bear. I leaned upon my elbow toward the Indian next to me and tapped him on the chest with two fingers. He sprang to wakefulness, hatchet in hand. I did not cry out. "Bear," I said. "I smell bear."

He frowned and grunted. They did much grunting, as a way of not bothering with words, I assumed, but sometimes a grunt and a frown spoke enough.

"A bear," I whispered. "You understand, a bear?" I sat up and made claws of my hands and opened my mouth.

The man stared at me, annoyed. *"Ashon,"* he said.

"Rarrr!" I said, in a soft voice, making my hands swipe the air as the claws of the bear had done. "Bear." As if the animal had heard my noise, a low growl come from the brush in answer. "Bear!" I shouted, and the same moment the man hollered, *"Owasso!"*

The Indians jumped to their feet, all holding their weapons. As everyone awoke, the bear shuffled into the clearing where we slept, and walked right upon Patience, going over her even though she raised her arms. The bear was so startled it stepped on other people, too, and backed up in surprise, rearing up on its hind legs. With but the moon for light, the captives tried to scatter. The Indians yelled and called to each other and three with their hatchets and one with a stone club fell upon the animal. The man with the club rendered a resounding thud upon the bear's skull. It reeled backward but roared and charged at him, wrapping him in its claws. Other men stabbed it while it fought the club-wielding man as if they were two men battling hand to hand.

Back and forth they went, around the campfire, and as the bear reared up, someone behind me, so close that the air next to my head trembled with the power of it, let go with an arrow that struck it in the breast. The animal swung its paw and sent one of the Indians backward into the coals. He cried hideously and rolled out of it, smoke coming from his leathern shirt in holes that went through to the skin beneath. Another man came behind the bear and climbed aboard its back, stabbing into its neck with a dagger. At last the bear weakened and slumped to the ground.

That caused the most terrifying effect of the night, for such a cry of howls and cheers rose from our captors that I thought Hell had come loose here in the forest. Before long, the fire had been rekindled, and while some of the Indians began to carve up the bear and skin it, others began a hatchet-waving dance around the fire. Now and then they swung their weapons as if fighting, and shouted, crying out to the sky. The fire circle grew to six feet wide, as wide as a man was tall. The kettles prepared, the bear's head went into one and four others each received a great foot. They filled the kettles again with fat from the bear's carcass, melting it just as we rendered fat from animals butchered in the settlement.

By sunrise, the special parts of bear's meat finished cooking and the rest of the carcass was dropped into a ravine. Only six of the Indians ate the meat and drank the broth it served. I could have gladly had some, but it was not offered. The original four men got some, as did the one who had knifed its throat and the one who had been struck into the fire. All the others saluted them and more singing followed the breakfast. During their celebration, I made my way to Patience's side. The Indians danced in circles, sometimes around the fire, sometimes just spinning in place.

"Dance with me!" I called over the din. "Let us dance, Patey!"

"No, Ressie."

"It is not a slave dance."

"No, I said." She held me to her then, hugging me in a way I did not expect and I fell against her. I watched from under her arm as the savages made merry, holding the bearskin in the air and diving with it as if they were great birds in the sky, calling, whooping, and growling at each other. The stink of bear now seemed like good stink.

One of the Indians saw us together and rushed at us. I fell away in terror as he grabbed Patey's hand and held it aloft, shouting. He dropped her hand and lay in the dirt. The man holding the bearskin turned and danced toward him and jumped over him. He swung it around Patience then jumped over his friend again.

All the Indians circled her, reached toward her, touching her arms and skirt and hair. She turned back and forth, frightened, holding her arms close to her bosom, tears upon each cheek. I heard her moan when one last man reached forth and touched her bonnet, pulling it from her head. Her long red hair fell from its binding and rolled down her back in curls. They stopped what they were doing and got quiet. When the Indians laid the bearskin upon the ground and bade Patey sit upon it, I felt proud for her and relieved, for I knew they meant her no harm. I suppose I might have been frightened for her, for later on that day I realized just how terrifying it would have been, had it been me they had chosen, but at the time I was most interested in the pantomime of the bear crossing Patience without harming her, and her rising up almost under it, causing the animal to rear and step away.

The man who spoke English came to her and said, "Gude woe-man. Shield of Owasso. Gude woe-man." He took a bracelet off his arm and handed it to her.

Patience took the bracelet and nodded, but I suppose she was too surprised to smile. She placed it upon her arm where it hung, for his arms were meaty and strong and hers as lithe and delicate as a deer's leg. He smiled then, pointed to her, grunted, and said, "Shield of Owasso," in English, and something else in their language. All the Indians got quiet, waiting for something to happen or perhaps for Patience to do something. When the quiet became long, indeed, she looked about her. The Indian man who had fallen into the coals sat alone, his face braced against the pain.

Patience stood and the Indians all made small noises, watching her. She went to the fireside and, with her skirt as a pot holder, lifted one of the kettles of rendering bear fat by the handle and took it to the bearskin. She went to the man with holes in his shirt and tapped on his shoulder. He looked up at her but did not move. The other Indians stepped back, as if they had no idea what she was doing, when I knew in an instant. Patey grabbed the man's shirt sleeve and tugged, saying, "Come here so I can help or you'll take a fever. Come on. Over here. Right there, sit," and she motioned to the bearskin. Indians gathered all around so I had to squeeze between two of them to see.

With tugging and motioning with her hands, Patience bade the man remove his shirt! Once he knew it, he did as she asked him, and though he resisted her pointing to the mat several times, at last she made him sit upon the skin. She dipped part of her apron into the bear grease, testing it so that it was not too hot, and began dressing the burns on his back. When the apron would not reach high enough, for it was naught but threads anyway and was sewn to her bodice in such a way that she could not remove it, she stopped. In a moment, she pulled her beautiful red hair over her shoulder and dipped the ends of it into the bear oil, using that to dress his wounds.

The sigh that went up from the Indians was as if they thought she was a saint performing some miracle. When Patience was satisfied that his back was as clean as she could get it, she rose and put the kettle back near the coals, now glowing from the earlier revelry. As she did, I moved toward her. She wrapped her arm about my shoulders. I held to her with both arms about her middle. She drew a breath and said toward the Indians, "If you will honor me, honor also my sister." She led me to the bearskin. One of them stopped me. No matter what Patience did with movements of her hands, he would not allow me to join her in sitting upon the bearskin. The Indian I had wakened with the news of the bear spoke up then, and told that part of the story. The Indians murmured.

Reverend Johansen stood in the circle of captives so I said to him, "Sir, I pray you, tell us what they say."

He shook his head. "The words I know are of some other tribe, I fear," he said, but in his voice I heard a tremble, as if the words were not Indian words at all.

One of the Indians spoke to the others and they began to pack up the night's merriment. They pushed Patience and me to the front of the line, and in a short while, before I was tired at all, my companion bade me climb upon his back again. I was happy to ride there, and fell asleep there, knowing Patey walked behind me.

If the Indians had a map, they consulted it not. I wondered if they traveled by the stars as mariners are wont to do, and it seemed they did study the sky at night when there were stars to see but most often there were not. Yet we moved through forest and marsh and glade as if they followed some supernatural guide, always with the sun rising on my right hand and setting on my left.

Each evening we ate stews and porridges. At last it came that they had eaten all the goats, a deer brought back by some warriors, and several rabbits and squirrels. I loved the squirrel best, but the Indians did not seem to like to kill enough for all of us. That day they brought the ox up and I knew it was for slaughter but I did not want to watch so huge an animal killed and gutted.

The Indians talked together for a while, pointing at the ox, gesturing, saying the word "owasso" a few times, but in the end they did nothing, and our fare that night was corn porridge. I was disappointed that there was no meat, but I suspected that "owasso" was the word for bear, and perhaps they thought killing the ox would draw more bears to us. I ate beside several of the Indians. I had not feasted so well in all these months since leaving Jamaica. We stuffed in the porridge, and when one man burped, I did likewise, and we smiled at each other.

Rachael and the reverend sat not far away. She frowned at me. "You do well to remember whose you are, Mary," she said.

I looked from her to the dark man next to me and thought of my coins. "I am mine own," I said. "I remember *that.* You belong to your husband and to these men. But *I* am *mine.*" She grunted. I faced the Indian man beside me. I nodded. He frowned, pushing his lower lip out. I copied his expression and no one told me to put my lip in. I knew for the first time that from then on, no matter what became of us, I belonged to no one.

They allowed us to huddle close together and I managed to find Patience one night. "Why, Patience. Your tummy is round. You have been eating extra food," I said.

"Hush, Resolute," she whispered. "Now is not the time to reveal my shame, for the Indians may do away with me, fearing I will slow this infernal marching."

"Shame? What shame have you in a nice plump figure?"

" 'Tis a child I carry within, sister. And keep you still about it."

I sat up straighter and leaned close to her. "A child? How do you know?"

"I just do."

"And how did it get there? Did God bring it to you? Did you pray for it?"

"Keep your voice down. No, I did not pray for it. I prayed against it but it came anyway. Now go to sleep. I have told you this so that if something should occur, you will know the source of my problems. Do not tell a soul for they shall kill me if they know since I have not a husband."

I lay beside her, my eyes wide open staring at the stars, curiosity flitting against my skull to keep me awake. What difference did it make if she had no husband? How did a girl come by a baby? Was there a clock that determined the time, just as winter comes before spring? I thought it would be ever so nice just to have the baby and not worry about a husband. We were too young for that. Would I have one? And would it be soon? I rubbed my stomach. A babe. But in this wilderness there would be all that crying and soiled linens to wash. What would Indians know about a baby? Why, they might handle it roughly and hurt it. I must keep the secret for Patience's sake and my own. Why, I might be carrying a baby, too, since we were sisters. Patience's babe would be born first, which was only right. We should think of a name for it. No reason to tell anyone until the time came. Perhaps we would be where we were going by the time that happened. I wrapped my arms about my sister and patted her secret, her roundness, smiling. Warm and happy, I fell asleep.

We pressed onward. My shoes split and stockings showed through the toes. My hands grew callused from the handle of the kettle. Every other day the Indian man carried me, as if I weighed not a breath upon his shoulders. Whether it was by raiding and stealing from some poor farmer they found in the wilderness, or by hunting deer or squirrel, we had something to eat every day. I began to feel almost kindly toward our captors. I hummed or sang every song I could remember, particularly the ones that I had been told not to sing. Some that knew my songs joined, but most were quiet, not used as I was to this captivity. I reminded myself of the women in the hold, who knew how to call for names and signal by drumming on the floor. I knew things I would never have learned in Ma's schoolroom.

One morning as I started in song, the Indian man I walked beside touched my cheek with his finger. "*Ah-shon,* be quiet," he said. The whole lot of them, every Indian, grew quiet. They pushed us into the brush. I was not far from Rachael and I heard her complain to the man who guarded her. He clapped his hand upon her mouth and threw her down, forcing his whole body upon her so that she could not move. Down our path came Indians, dressed differently from these, their faces painted in ferocious colors. Their hair was wildly set and I could imagine they had just left their homes for some errand, be it hunting or war, whereas our captors looked as weary and footsore as their prisoners. We waited a long time. Finally we began our walk again.

When we stopped to rest, Rachael fell against a tree and wept. Reverend Johansen tried to comfort her. She called out more. Even Patience went to her and tried to quiet her. I watched the Indians as they circled her. I feared lest they do away with her just for being noisesome. I was not so simple as to not understand that the Indians were hiding from the other group that passed. They did not want to fight them. I could only hope Reverend

Johansen could prevail upon her to quiet down. She turned on him, saying, "You did nothing to save me from being so ill-used by a heathen."

"I prayed mightily," he said, as if her having survived to complain were proof that it had had its intended effect. "We were all in mortal danger. Your staying quiet was to save all our lives. As it might be even at this moment."

"You are no fit husband who will not take up arms and defend his wife. If you had fought them we would not be here, forced to go mile after mile—"

"Wife, I cannot insist with more earnest appeal than I do at this moment that you stop speaking at all, or if you must, keep your voice down so that we are not set upon by other savages. If I had fought them we would not be here; we would both be dead."

She fumed, making a face so like her mother's I nearly laughed out loud. Rachael sneered and said, "I am so ashamed to call you husband. You worthless, feeble, wimbly old man. Coward." Rachael spat.

Reverend Johansen picked up a loose branch lying beside the path, raising it over his head. The Indians leaped forward to hack him down, until he brought it down upon Rachael's back as she turned from him. He laid her five whacks, the same as Birgitta used to lay upon me. "You will mind your vow of obedience and duty to me and to God, *and* you will bear in mind at this time that you live at the will of these strangers among us. You will behave as a minister's wife, sober, humble, and quiet. Your villainy could bring the murder of every soul here, and I will not idly have you throw away these lives."

The Indians looked from one to another. They lowered their hatchets and knives. One of them took the branch from the reverend and swung it again, giving Rachael another stroke of it, as if testing to see that the beating was real. She whimpered and hid her face. The Indian man nodded and handed Reverend Johansen the stick again. He pointed to Rachael, to the reverend, and to the stick. The one who had spoken the English words before raised his hands as he had done. "This land not our land. If Cayuga find on land, many die. You not fight, you not die. Three more suns. Not Cayuga land. Three suns. Understand?"

I was not sure I understood, but it seemed enough that Rachael's outburst had ended without bloodshed. What choice did we have whether it were three more days or a hundred and three?

For two more days, we traversed dense woods that slowed everyone, even the warriors. The food had grown scarce and many of them carried children and women upon their backs. At the top of the hill we had seen a city by a river. My own heart jumped with hope that here was freedom, at last. I would post a message to Ma. My legs wanted to run toward the beautiful city.

The third day after Rachael's beating, our walking seemed more treacherous than the many days before it. At least to the Indians, there seemed to be great reason for care and quiet, for we were headed for the city yet trying to stay hidden in the woods, moving in small clusters as if we were sheep. They carried no one, and even my friend who'd carried me or my iron kettle made me walk and carry it again so that my fingers ached. At long last we came to a great stone wall of a regal building, larger than any I had ever seen. I wondered if it might be a governor's palace. The Indians sent a messenger to the door, but it was not the man who spoke English. That, I found puzzling. These were not Indian buildings, I was sure, yet if he spoke no English he would be useless among these people of royal appointment. He went in. He returned. He spoke to the other Indians.

The door opened and the Indians herded us into the building. The door shut behind the last of us and the Indians filed up against one wall. I looked about but could barely see, for the brightness of the noonday sun had left me blind in the dark hallway. I rejoiced at finding something of civilization. Surely there would be hope for Patey and me at last. Beautiful colored windows lined the top of the wall and the sun shone through them, giving brilliant light and colors to the panes, yet not filtering down to where we stood. At the far end of the room someone opened yet another door and sunlight flooded into the place. The light revealed a massive room, lined with statuary and a few chairs and benches. At the far end stood an altar with a golden *crucifix* above it. Under the figure of Christ, a table full of unlit candles waited.

A gasp came from the captives about me, a sigh so deep and forlorn it pulled my heart. Many of the adults in our group dropped to their knees. Voices rose, then, men and women alike, declaring, "Papists! We are sold into the hands of the devil!"

Reverend Johansen stood, even as we watched a group of men in long black robes approaching from that opened door. "Children, listen to me.

No matter what they do, no matter what they tell you, remember always that lies and deceit are under the tongue of the pope of Rome. Sell not your soul for a piece of silver or a crumb of bread—"

One of the black-robed men said, "Sit, all of you. Welcome to *l'église de Montréal*. We will find places for you to rest. To sleep. To eat."

Master Newham asked, "And how shall we rest? We are captives and demand to be returned to our homes. To bury our dead. To take up our lives. We are not papists. We worship the true God."

Another of the robed men said, "We paid a price for you to save your souls from hellfire. The church in its mercy will clothe and care for you, sustain and retain you all the days of your life. We have paid your purchase price."

Then they went to the door whence we had entered and opened it, letting the Indians file out as if they were soldiers, as if they were in complete agreement with these men of robes. The robed men encircled the room, standing four abreast before each doorway. A man came in with rolled sheets of vellum under one arm and a quill perched over one ear, jar of ink in hand. He sat at one of the benches and pulled a table toward him. As he did so, another man held a candelabra high over his writing table. The two doors swung shut, plunging the room into darkness save for the candles, and the sound of heavy beams sliding into place echoed across the hall.

The first priest to have spoken said, "We will take down your names. You will follow Frère Christophe that way." He waved his hand.

A priest in the darkness called out, *"Ici."* No one moved. Then he said, "Come. Come forward." When my turn came to tell him my name, I hesitated. I was known by Mary. I detested that name, but it was connected to me among the people with whom I was familiar. He asked, *"Nom? Nom?"* and finally, "What is your name?"

"Mary Talbot," I said.

June the fifth, seventeen hundred and thirty, by the old reckoning, I was sold for the second time under the slave name of Mary Talbot to a black-frocked priest with ink-blackened fingers and a runny nose.

CHAPTER 11

June 6, 1730

The convent of Sainte-Ursule de Montréal seemed more of a great plantation than a religious order. Fields surrounded the walled interior where cosseted vegetable gardens presented an orderly and symmetrical invitation to the main buildings. The chapel, a rectory, a convent, and eight dormitories lay as if they were a head, a neck, a heart, and two rows of ribs. I was put in a room full of girls my size, assigned a bed, a set of chores—in the kitchen—and a companion. *La compagne.*

My *compagne* was Donatienne Flavie, a girl from the local town who had come there after her parents had died of typhoid three years before. She was thirteen and spoke French and English. It was her chore to teach me French, as much as possible, as quickly as possible. Our dormitory— housing the smallest girls—was closest to the nuns' convent, which was washed white but stained around top, bottom, and all the windowsills. Ours was a gray stone building that had once been plastered, even painted. Its level of disrepair seemed a fitting compartment for my spirits. The paint outside had peeled away, giving it the appearance of a spotted horse I had seen once. Patience lived with the older girls in another building. I only knew because I saw her coming or going, marching in a line of other older girls to and from the dining room. It was not permitted to speak to her, and though I stared hard at her, wishing my very eyes to poke her, trying to make her lift her face and see me, she never looked up.

"Do you have questions?" Donatienne asked as she helped me spread two blankets, one with a patch in the middle, across the small cot that was to be my bed.

"When shall I go home?"

She smiled and laid her hand on my arm. "Your *maman* and *papa* have died, little friend, or given you up because of their great poverty, or else you would not be here. This is an orphanage. You will have food to eat and a bed to lie in. You will be educated. Your soul will be saved from hell. It is not a bad place for poor girls *comme nous,* is it?"

"I am not poor. And I am not an orphan. My mother waits for me at our plantation in Jamaica. Meager Bay, Jamaica. I am only here to visit a friend."

"Who is she?"

"I will not tell you. Once I have found her, I will be leaving. In a gilded coach with eight matched black horses."

Donatienne's milky white face and chocolate-colored brows, lashes, and hair gave her an animated appearance. She appeared somewhat shocked at first, then puzzled, finally sympathetic, for all her emotions rushed to her face so that it told an entire story without a word. "I see. Little Marie. Poor one. You will come to understand. And you will weep. That is accepted. For we are all castaway here, and all love each other. If you feel sad, I will be your sister."

"I told you I will leave here in a coach and go home. Besides, I have a sister."

"You do not want me to be your sister?" Her eyes filled with tears.

I had not meant to hurt her. This girl was trying to be kind, but I had known so little of that recently that I felt puzzled at her and myself. What was it about saying I had a mother and a home and that I wished to return to them that made me seem some type of fool? "I have a brother and a sister and a mother. I need only send a letter and my mother will come for me right away. She may drive the coach herself if she chooses. You knew that not, did you? That women may drive?"

Donatienne brushed her tears away with both hands. "It will not make you feel better to pretend that," she said, "as I once did. It keeps your heart full of sadness."

I stilled my face as my mind worked on this. If she would not believe me I would keep my secrets to myself. Now that we were in a village, I would find a way to write a letter to Ma. I searched every corner of my mind seeking something to say to this girl. I said, "Then I will try not to, if you will not cry. There, now. Please let us talk of something else."

Donatienne smiled, her white face blotched with red flushes. "If you grow out of your clothes, you may have mine."

"I will not be here long enough to need them. But, thank you. Thank you."

"Say *merci*."

"*Merci*. I have another question. Are there any bears about?"

"*Non.* I have never seen a bear. Have you?"

"Oh, I am acquainted with bears." My lip trembled.

Every morning Donatienne and I followed a line of girls to the chapel. They said prayers I did not understand. They sang songs I did not know. They spoke in a mash of consonants and vowels that in my ears had not as much meaning to them as had the words of the Indians in the woods. "*Owasso, owasso,*" I chanted as I walked. After chapel, they served breakfast and there were two hours of education, during which Donatienne went over and over words and pronunciations, holding up one thing after another, pointing and gesturing. She was quite pleasant a person, and after such as I had been used to at the Hasken household, I fell quite into her routine and instructions. In the first weeks there, I was to do little but learn French and clear tables, unless now and then they had me bring in herbs from the garden.

I was glad to be in a house without goats, bats, or Haskens, and with a bed of my own that was off the floor. I was also glad to have so much less work to do, glad to have school even though it was in French, glad to bathe and wash my clothes, glad the only night pot I had to empty was my own. I was glad to know Donatienne, too.

They allowed me to patch my gown and petticoat. I did not want to lose my casket again, and so I laid lumps of tow around it, sewing over it until it looked as if the pocket were yet another patch on the old and outgrown garment. Donatienne showed me she also wore a quilted heavy petticoat similar to mine. I stared long at hers, not in great wonder over it but in thinking about Ma. What had she known? What land had she come from? I knew the name of it but not the place of it, not the being there. Scotland must have been cold, like Montréal, I decided.

I asked Donatienne for paper to write upon, but we were allowed only to scratch chalk onto slates. I could not send a letter on a slate. I looked for paper everywhere. Distracted one day by our lessons, perhaps because I tried to ask in French, Donatienne admitted to me the only place where she knew of paper was the rectory where the monks kept our records. I vowed I would find a way to get into that building.

At noon we had soup or stew, sometimes with meat, and bread rolls, which were often dry and had to be soaked in the soup to be eaten. Yet, having made many a meal of uncooked rice or hardtack soaked in my own spittle, dry bread and soup were still wonderful. Every evening ended with another piece of bread, often a fruited loaf of the type with which Patey had been rewarded on the Saracen ship, butter, a cup of tea, and another visit to the chapel for prayers. For many days I did not see Patience or anyone I knew. They were in the older girls' houses, I supposed.

Afternoons were filled with lessons and prayers. After a while, I could recite the prayers and sing the songs. I had no idea what the words meant, but I copied the sounds and joined in. I said my French prayers quite convincingly. I learned the names of some saints and surprised Donatienne with the few on which Ma had instructed us. Her favorite was Saint Agnes, who watched over children. I did not tell Donatienne that I thought Agnes had fallen asleep on her watch where Patey and I were concerned. I excelled in my lessons, determined that the nuns might question my spiritual devotion, but not my knowledge.

When we settled in our beds at night, I made up stories and told Donatienne about my life. I wanted her to know that I did not belong in this place, and that Patience and I deserved to be released. "Patience was a gentlewoman, you know," I said. "She was engaged to marry a prince, the heir to the throne of, of *Carbundium*. His father owns five castles, and she shall have her pick of any or all of them. With seven ladies-in-waiting at each castle. The prince angered an ogre who charged across the ocean on a ship with sails made of spiderwebs and witches' hair, and he stole her from the handsome prince. I saved her from him and I came along, too, to be with her, for I would rather be with Patience and keep her safe in this place, than back in the castle in Bariander."

"You said the place was called Carbundium."

"Bariander is a town *in* Carbundium." The story was getting unwieldy, and I gulped at my mistake. I should not have made up such long, difficult words.

"And that is in Jamaica?"

"No, that is the place where the prince lives. Patience and I live in Jamaica."

"What is his name? The prince."

"Theodore. Prince Theodore of Carbundium."

"Is he tall? Is he gallant? What color are his eyes? Say it in French."

"Not too tall. *Rose.*" I took a deep breath of relief. This, at least, was easier to remember.

"Red eyes?"

"*Bleu.* I meant blue."

Now and then, when the men worked in the fields I imagined Reverend Johansen out there, sweating under the sun with the others, his scrawny gray hair blowing in the breeze. Perhaps that one was he, or that over there. I missed Reverend Johansen. I suppose though he was not my pa, nor anything like Pa, he seemed more like a nice uncle, a real uncle, not like Rafe MacAlister. When I wrote to Ma I would tell her to come get him, too, and Donatienne if she wants to come along with Patey and me. We would be a little family. I would write to August, also, and he could come home. Perhaps Ma and Reverend Johansen would marry, and August marry Donatienne. Patience and I would be sisters all our lives and shun all men now that she had her lost love in England and I left mine in the graveyard at Collins Pond.

Some days all I could think about was that the building where the men lived was where I might find paper, quill, and ink. I took afternoon strolls up and down the length of the buildings, each day a few steps closer to the priests' dormitory. Sometimes one of them came out and I waved to him in a friendly manner, thinking that I must learn enough French to ask one of them to speak to me of the Psalms. That had made Reverend Johansen my friend, and it might work again. But their door was kept locked as if they were dangerous convicts. No one opened when I knocked.

In the kitchen during the execution of my chores, I sneaked half-eaten rolls and tidbits of mutton gristle or a leaf of parsley from the plates as I cleared them from the tables, folding the morsels into my sleeves. When I gathered herbs by the kitchen door, I put mint in my cheeks to suck on. When they made me work in the garden I ate the raw vegetables and sometimes even the leaves of them. One evening, Violette, a novice who was fifteen and devout, caught me finishing a carrot off a plate meant for a sick nun. They made me crawl on my knees up the center of the chapel for eating one carrot. In truth I had eaten nine carrots before anyone found out. But scolding and kneeling were nothing compared to what I had endured before. It meant only inconvenience.

The sisters bade me confess my theft and gluttony to a priest in a little closet, but I believed Reverend Johansen's words, that I had no need to tell any human being every sin I knew. In confession, I said, "Père Jean, I have stolen a carrot. I broke it into twelve pieces, one for *each* of the Apostles, and I *tithed* two of them, planting them again to grow two carrots out of the one, and I gave one bite to each of the *ten* most thin and starving girls in this place. They were hungry, Father Jean, so wretchedly hungry they had begun to eat their clothing." He said he had been told I ate it myself, but I cried then, real tears, and said, "On my honor, I did it only for the little ones."

"Marie," Father Jean said, "it was a cooked carrot. You cannot plant a cooked carrot. Do you add lying to your sins?"

I gasped. I had forgotten. "I did not know it would not grow, Father. I swear it."

Sister Marta, who supervised the kitchen work, decided I would be of more use in the weavers' barn.

The weaving barn, the *grange de tissage,* was a mass of confusion. Baskets overflowing with wads of yet-to-be-spun wool hung from walls at one end. Similar ones running off with flaxen tow clung to the other end as if they were bats in a ceiling. Cloth bolts filled bins and shelves in complete abandon. Coloring and dyes filled another room, and outside, great vats filled with horrific-smelling concoctions, far worse than anything I had known sleeping with goats, awaited processes I had yet to witness.

The sister in charge of the beginners there, which included two other children, a boy and a girl, and me, put us all to carding wool. Her name was Sister Joseph, which I found quite confusing. I did not ask her why she had a man's name. I decided to ask Donatienne when I got a chance. Sister Joseph asked me how old I was. Eleven, I knew. I wondered what would be the better answer for sympathy. "Nine," I said.

I still went to chapel first thing in the morning, took French lessons, and had meals. All afternoon I worked in the barn. I left every day covered in lint and fell asleep in my cot next to Donatienne. I needed her to translate what Sister Joseph said to me, but every time my *compagne* entered the wool room she began such sneezing and coughing it was as if she were breathing in poison. Her eyes swelled shut and her nose ran, and she grew faint of heart until they insisted she leave.

The two children were French but a third girl spoke English, and therefore had a *compagne,* an older nun named Sister Évangélique. Sister Évangélique was not patient, and she had no teeth at all, so all her words in either language were slurred and full of sounds that did not belong in them. I stayed close to Sister Joseph rather than asking for a translation. Both Sister Joseph and Sister Évangélique bowed their heads, their eyes wide, lips sealed, when Sister Agathe approached. I did not lower my head before her but stared straight at her when she crossed the room.

One time, right after morning chapel, Sister Agathe tapped me on the shoulder and said, "Your eyes are so hard. Your soul is far away, is it not? You must accept your life. So much sadness you have seen." She carried a large basket covered with a towel.

I smiled and said, "Not at all. I will carry that to the rectory for you."

"This is a bushel of laundry. Why do you want to go to the rectory? Every day you ask me to go there for something or other."

"I hoped—" I stopped in mid-sentence, trying to think up a believable ploy. "To find Reverend Johansen. I was sure he was with the Brothers." I smiled my most convincing smile. "He is my uncle."

"I will ask if you may visit him, since he is your uncle."

"Will you? Thank you, Sister," I said, and went skipping off to class. I stopped in mid-step so abruptly that my shoe left a mark on the cobble. It was not what she said that stopped me, but the sudden realization that I could not distinguish in which language I had heard it. Was I becoming French? "Oh, la, *non!*" I said.

After lessons, Sister Agathe took me to the rectory door, knocked, asked through the spy window for Reverend Johansen. She spoke in whispers to the voice on the other side so that I could not understand. Afterward, Sister Agathe said he worked in the vineyard with other men. I was not allowed near those men and they were not to come near the girls. "You are allowed to pray for him," she said. "Not to see him. We protect our girls from all contact with men." I did not have to pretend my disappointment at her words. One friend, no matter that he was old Reverend Johansen, made such a difference in my hopes for escape. As I walked away, I felt as if someone had hung a boulder about my neck.

The girls from the *grange* got potato soup with leeks at noon. If weather permitted we sat outside under a tree as if it were a picnic, always under the watchful eyes of *les bonnes soeurs*. Sister Évangélique knew English, and could tell Sister Joseph what we said. Christine came to my side one day, asking, "Have you turned Catholic?"

"I am only learning to comb wool, waiting until I can go home," I replied. "I have written to the king of England to notify my mother where I am. She will be here soon."

Christine's face registered her scorn. "Pah. King of England. I say you were always Catholic and destined for hell."

I shrugged and asked, "Have you seen Patience? *Princess* Patience?"

"She's in the sick ward with Rachael."

"What is wrong with them?"

"Only that my sister is married and therefore has legitimately gotten with child, and your sister is a slattern and will give birth to a bastard. She should be stoned."

When I spoke then it was more loudly, it was in French, and I turned my head toward the two nuns. "My sister Patience is kind and brave. Her baby is not a bastard. He is the future king of Carbundium." I left the small table and sat on the grass in the shade near Sister Joseph. I was not sure what the word "bastard" meant other than what I had heard aboard the English privateer ship. No child of Patey's would be called such. "Sister Joseph?" I began, my hand upon her knee. "I am convinced with all my soul the faith I have found here is the one and true faith. May I please be baptized?" I watched Christine's face curdle as if she had a goat's cud in her mouth. At the same time, both sisters patted my arms and head and smiled, crossed themselves, and kissed my hands.

Little fanfare accompanied my baptism. Patience was allowed to come as my next of kin, to witness it. I hardly knew her, for she was pale and swollen. Patience was getting near her confinement, she said. And so, while I was in the best graces with the nuns and the priest with whom I had contact, I asked permission to attend her birthing. They told me I could not. After that I relegated lesser sins such as daydreaming or sleeping during prayers to the priest's ears. I held no qualms at all about belaboring the ears of God Himself with supplications about returning home to Ma. I promised Him anything, even a life of poverty, if we could only get home.

In early July it was time to pull flax. Sister Agathe led the children to the edge of a field so large it seemed to go on into eternity. She showed us how to pull the plants, how to lay them thus and so. They did not come easily from the ground, and they were covered with tiny stickers. By the end of the first day I was sweaty and dirty, and my hands swollen and blistered, so that I had trouble getting ready for supper and prayers and bed.

Over the next days, I pulled flax until my fingers bled. I looked at the land laden with flax running waist to chest high as far as I could see. It went on and on, and as I bent to spread some that had fallen in a clump, blood marked the stalks I laid. I squeezed a fist and let it go. Fresh blood ran from cracks across the backs of my knuckles as I forced my fingers closed, and when I opened them it ran from open blisters in the palms. The hands did not seem to belong to me; their swelling made them foreign and unnatural. The sun was high overhead. Other captives, bent so their backs moved as bears, spread throughout the vast field, rose and bowed like birds picking for bugs. None of the *compagnes* worked in the field. No nuns stayed amongst the reeds and flax, yet a few watched us from a platform afar off.

I heard someone singing. It made me remember Patience saying she was no slave to be singing or dancing her grief away. With a great sigh I realized I was once again a slave and I began humming a tune, then singing the English words. After our noon meal, others sang, too, some together as a chorus, some just by themselves as I did. We worked until the sun crawled toward the horizon and one of the nuns came to the edge of the field and swung a bell. Everyone filed onto a path so as not to step upon the flax.

We washed our hands every evening at a large barrel of cold water. One day Sister Joseph tapped me on the shoulder so suddenly I thought she carried Birgitta's goat stick. I bowed my head and pulled my hands from the water, cringing away from the whipping I expected. "See here, Marie! Stand up straight and look at me," Sister said.

"Yes, madame. Oh, la, yes. *Oui, ma soeur.*" I switched from English to French.

"You are baptized. You will not sing the pagan songs here. You will sing only hymns to the Virgin. Is this clear to you?"

"*Oui.* But others sang *first.* I merely joined." I knew it was a lie. "Greensleeves," and "O Waly, Waly" were about longing and love, not worship. I had forgotten that some might know the English words.

"Will there be any more singing of unrighteous songs in the fields?"

"*Non, ma soeur.* I will not sing in the field." I hung my head, expecting a beating to follow the words. It did not. She had only her bony dog finger to tap my shoulder rather than a stick. I felt so exhausted. I pinched my lips and thought, Curses on you, Sister Joseph. I thought of the song I had used for Mistress Hasken. I puffed out a large breath. It fit, except that I had loved Sister Joseph. Until then. I stuck out my lip, thinking, No singing in the field. No singing the wrong song. I wished I were a pirate. I would sing the "Faraway Isles" song and "Blow the Man Down," even one they did not know I knew, that had all a woman's parts named right in the singing, "The Captain's Tart." I wanted to sing all the songs that insulted every ear on this land. Every place I was bound to, I knew all the wrong songs. My face reddened and I felt a flush of heat across my cheeks. Tears were welling and my lower lip quivered against my will. With great effort I tucked it under my upper teeth. I hated Montréal and I hated this convent and I hated Sister Joseph for making me work so hard.

Sister Joseph put one hand under my chin and lifted my face to hers. She said, "Now, let me put some salve on your poor little hands." She clucked her tongue.

One moment I was full of hate, the next, longing. I told myself I hated Sister Joseph, even as she rubbed salve on my hands. I hated her as she wrapped them in cotton lint and put a pair of black stockings on my hands as if they were gloves. I hated her as she led me to the dining room and sat beside me. After the blessing, I opened my eyes and saw that I had two pieces of bread on my plate and she had none. Oh, la. I wanted to climb into her lap and be comforted! I wept. If she had only stayed cruel I could have held only my anger and hatred, but instead I turned to Sister Joseph and asked, "Will you fix my hands again?" not because the bandages had fallen, but because I wanted her to caress and hold them again. She murmured to me as she straightened the stockings that I had worked so very hard, much more than the other girls, and that she was proud of me for such a great labor unto the Lord. When she had finished pulling the stockings in place, she hugged me and I loved her for it.

In chapel, I fell asleep during prayers. One of the girls awoke me when it was over and I stumbled as I followed the others to my dormitory where Donatienne waited to help me into my nightgown. She held in her hands the rough, gray thing as I approached the bedside. Exhaustion left me bitter and anger flooded my thoughts. "Leave me alone," I said. I swatted at the thing, sending it to the floor.

"What is the matter, Marie?" Donatienne picked it up, searching for the sleeves.

"My name is not Marie. I am tired. I have worked like a *slave* all the day long, and you ask me what is the matter? Leave it on the floor; I do not want your help."

"Very well. I will not help you." She laid the gown on my bed.

I hated that horrible bed. The small comfort that it was not a flea-ridden bearskin next to a chimney, nor a mat on the fetid floor of a Saracen bilge-hold did not make it *my* bed. My bed had coverlets of goose down and pink satin. My bed had carved and rubbed mahogany posts and a down tick and a cunning wee stair to get into it. *My* bed was on the top floor of a stone house on Meager Bay. "Do not look at me, either," I said, and burst into tears. Why could I not hide them now? Why was I no longer brave? Why did Sister Joseph not come and hold my hands in hers again? Such hard work as this day I hoped never to see again.

Donatienne mumbled, *"Très bien."*

I answered in French, "And stop saying 'very well.' It is not very well at all."

"Your French has improved. You have found your tongue."

My tears flowed in earnest then, and I blubbered, *"Je vous déteste.* I hate you." I turned away from her and pulled down my skirt, dropping the loose shirt atop it, both in a heap on the floor beside the bed. I pulled the gown on over my petticoat and shift. I kicked off my shoes but did not bother with the stockings for I could not use my fingers, wrapped as they were in other stockings.

Donatienne sobbed as she put on her own night clothes and climbed into her bed only inches from mine. "I am sorry if I have offended you."

Her words threw fresh oil onto the fire of my anger. "Pulling flax all day for two days, *that* has offended me." Uncontrollable tears annoyed me for a short time before I slept the sleep of exhaustion.

Some of the flax was left to ret or cure in the field; some was bound in bundles, wrapped in tow sacking, and sunk at the edge of the river in vast trays made of logs. Rocks weighted the bundles so that they stayed in the water. Mold and rot made a stench in the bundles worse than the garbage bins before they set them afire. That was the most valuable flax of all, for Sister Agathe said when it was woven it shone like gold.

Sister Agathe came to me one evening. "I have asked the Mother Superior if you may be allowed to visit your uncle. She made inquiries and found he is not your uncle."

I sighed. "I hoped if I said he was my uncle you might allow it. He was the minister of our community. He was kind to me."

"And so you have lied again? This time about something more serious than eating a carrot, no? You will spend tomorrow on your knees in prayer at the foot of the cross."

"Yes, Sister." I tried to contain my glee at facing a day without flax, but found on the morrow this punishment was not so easily ignored as before. The stones at the foot of the crucifix had been strewn with seeds, and I was not allowed to move them or to sit. I did not cry for myself. I laid curses to Sister Agathe on the deaf ears of the plaster man hanging above me.

Another Sunday came, a day warm and misty, the air reeking with moldering flax blown away by a light breeze, so that the whole place seemed lush and fragrant, verdant, full. The sun was high in the sky when prayers and Sunday's only meal of the day at mid-morning were finished. I walked to the vegetable garden hoping to find it unattended, but three nuns in gray bent there, praying over pease suffering wilt. The day warmed as I ambled the grounds. I came to a glade made by blueberry bushes grown overhead. An elderly nun sitting in an invalid chair slept there. Her blanket had slipped to her feet. I tucked it up over her shoulders. She awoke and smiled at me. *"Merci,"* she whispered, *"petite ange."* She fell asleep again as soon as the words left her mouth. More like *"petite sauvage,"* I thought. I wished I were an Indian with a tomahawk.

I picked a handful of berries and ate them. On the other side, a gate in the garden wall stood ajar. Beyond it stretched an open field of grain, silver heads waving under the gentle breeze like water in a bay. Bees hovered about a honeysuckle grown upon a discarded stile beckoning over a fence that no longer existed.

I wheeled around to face the convent buildings, aware that I was alone. I could see the upper floors with their open shutters, the spire of the cathedral. In the distance near the stables a man brushed a horse. Chickens pecked around both their feet. On this side of the blueberries, though, as far as I could see, I was alone at a path between fields. Once I stepped through the gate and stood on the far side of the wall, nothing lay before me but grain fields in all directions. Doves sighed and fluttered overhead, a pheasant cried out rising from his hiding place under the stile. I began to run.

As I ran from the convent proper, my face spread with joy. I opened my mouth to gulp in great breaths of free air. No one called me. On and on I dashed, my shadow before me as if a dark image of myself ran along as company, my arms swinging, my back warmed by the sun and the thought of freedom. *"Oui!"* I called out, with joy. I returned to English, crying, "Yes, oh yes, Ma. I am coming home!"

I ran until my side ached. The ground rolled lower at the end of the field, which stopped at a stand of maple trees. I might have dashed my brains against the colorless wall of stone on the far side of the maple trees, for I ran into it at full tilt, my hands breaking my fall. The wall was higher than the sides of the Saracen ship. I raced along it one way, then turned and went the other. I beat against it with my fists, growling like a wild animal. I jumped at it, trying to find a fingerhold. Here and there, a rock protruded, but putting my toes on it crumbled it from its place. I heard a dog bark on the other side of the fence. I called out, "Ho, there! Help me, gentlefolk!"

"Who calls?" a man's voice answered.

"Your servant, sir. Help me, please. They torture children, and starve us, and beat us without mercy. I was brought here by Indians. Save me from this, dear sir, and my mother will pay you handsomely. She is the duchess of all Scotland! Only throw me a line, and I will climb over. Take me away from this place and you will be rich!"

The voice laughed! "You will not find a one in this city who will go against the church!" His laughter and the dog's barking faded away.

I found a downed tree but it was too heavy to move. Another limb placed against the wall proved too thin to balance upon, and it cracked when I got half its length under me. Surely, there would be a gate in this wall. I began to run along it. The pain in my side grew until I slowed to a walk. I would return for Patience; I must make my escape while there was a chance. I went until I came out of the thicket of maple and entered low brush. The sun baked upon my head and I pulled off my cap and used it to wipe my brow.

I found myself but ten paces to a vineyard. I stopped at the first row of vines and ate an entire bunch of grapes, though they were tart and afterward I felt a terrific thirst. Across the vineyard I spotted a square place in the gray wall. It must be a gate! I started through the rows. My side gnawed at me. I tripped and fell, then rolled and sat in the shade of a vine. I would catch my breath. I meant to rest a while, but when I awoke the sun was low, the sky painted with pinks the color of the inside of a conch shell. I ate more grapes. I looked toward the gate but the shadows were so deep I could not see it. It took me until night fell to make my way across the vineyard in the direction I believed the gate to be. Crows fussed at me as if they meant to give away my escape.

Darkness fell without a glimmer of moon. I stopped at the last row. Something moved nearby and I sniffed for the scent of bear. An owl swooped from a tree and called, his wings catching the last of the light that lingered in the air and taking it with him, leaving me in darkness. I jumped at his call and felt a sharp stab. A nail protruded from the framework built to hold the grapevine over the ground in an awkward shape. It caught my left arm just above the wrist. Blood gushed from the ragged wound and I pressed my hand against it. I sank by the vine. The thing's branches were forced with cords into unnatural bends over the wood frame. Crucified, I thought. The wretched things had all been crucified.

I would wait until moonrise and continue, I decided, so I curled my arms about my knees to wait, pressing the bloody wrist against my skirt. The touch of a leaf upon my cheek brought me awake as if it had been a slap. I heard voices and peeked from my place toward the sound. The moon was so bright! "There! I see her!" I heard a voice from behind my head. It was not the moon but the sun! My heart sank. I lay upon the earth as if I were dead, wishing the ground would cover me there. Sister Joseph and Donatienne followed a priest, their skirts held high, revealing their little feet at my eye level, running so they seemed as puppets. I started toward the gate, trying to escape with them on my heels. Donatienne reached my side, her face red and wet. "Oh, Marie, you are safe!" I sank to the earth in a heap.

The priest raised me to stand. Behind them was Reverend Johansen. My face lit up with joy but he did not seem happy to see me. He turned on his heel, picked up a hoe, and left the three of them to walk me back to the convent. I felt overcome with emotion for myself and sorry for Donatienne, then. "I went for a walk. I got lost," I said.

Sister Joseph sat on the ground and pulled me toward her, hugging me, hugging Donatienne with me, squeezing us together the way Ma sometimes did with Patey and me. She murmured. She took me by the shoulders and gave me a shake. "You would not lie again, would you, Marie?"

"No. I will never lie again. I was not running away. I was lost. I am sorry," I said.

"I know you are sick for want of your home."

"I was lost. Must I be punished?" I asked Sister Joseph.

"Yes. Severely," she said with a frown. Then she smiled. "I think you must say a hundred prayers. Let us go and eat some breakfast."

Two days later, Sister Agathe called me from my work and said I was to go to the sick ward. Patience had been delivered of a baby boy. She added that it was important that I see my sister and kiss her good-bye, for the priest was with her.

I went to Patey's bedside. "La, Patience, you are so ill," I said.

She opened her eyes for a moment. "Ressie. Sit by me."

I pushed myself onto the narrow bed and she moaned. The others about us gasped as if I had hurt her. "I am sorry," I said.

"Do not leave me, Ressie. Please stay with me. Hold me. I am so cold."

I leaned toward her and laid my face against her neck. "Patience. Do not die. I need you so. The baby is well," I added, to cheer her. "And handsome."

"It is not my baby. It is Rafe MacAlister's baby. Tell the nuns to find him and charge him with the child's keep."

"How can he have aught to do with your baby?"

Sister Agathe put her hand on my shoulder. "Father is going to give her Extreme Unction. It will forgive her sins."

"Patience has no sins. I am the one who sins."

"You would not want her to go to hell. Step back before she dies."

I looked upon my sister with wariness and fear. Her face was indeed more pale than ever I had known, her eyes sunken and filmed worse than when she had had scurvy on the ship. "No, no," I whispered. "May I not stay with her?"

Sister Agathe and the priest frowned at me. I stepped away. He put oil on Patey's forehead and tried to get her to eat a bit of Eucharist. When he finished, I returned to her side and sat on the floor by the bed where I could hold her hand and wait. "Patey will not die," I chanted over and over again.

Suddenly I stood. I ran. First out the door, then to the chapel. I rang the bell to call a priest to the confessional. "Father? Father! Hear my confession." A candle came into the little cell with a man's form. "Tell God to let Patey live. I confess I have told lies. I lied about the carrot. I ate it myself. I lied to my *compagne* about my family. I lied about my ma driving a coach and my age and I told Violette how the dogs we owned would eat her alive once I get home. There are hundreds more, too. Forgive me, Father. Please do not let my sister die. Please!" The priest was one of the old ones. He could not understand my frantic mixture of English and French, and mumbled something I could barely make out. "You old spider!" I shouted, and ran from the chapel back to the sickroom.

Donatienne appeared carrying a bundle of blankets and two pillows. "I came to wait with you," she said.

"I am not afraid to wait alone," I said. Donatienne's face showed I had hurt her feelings once again. "What I meant to say, Donatienne, is that I did not want to trouble you. I very much wish you to stay."

She smiled and said, "I will make us a bed here." She put the pillows side by side. Laid the blankets next to each other. She lay upon them and reached for my hand.

I reached for Patey's hand and with the other I took Donatienne's while she talked about her father who was a tailor, and her mother, who bore seven children before Donatienne was eleven years old. All of them, father, mother, three sisters, and four brothers, perished in *La fièvre épidémique*. Their lives were gentle, she said. Not aristocratic, but pastoral. Earthy. Sleeping with the sun and moving with the seasons. When she finished I told her about playing on the beach and gathering shells. I told her about the taste of sugarcane. The food Lucy used to make us. I told her about

Allsy. When I said that she died, Donatienne wept. That stunned me so that I wept, too.

A nun came in carrying a candle and held a mirror to Patey's mouth and nose to see if her air moved. When they saw she yet breathed, they changed her dressings and I watched in shock at seeing so much blood. One time Patience groaned when they lifted her. I helped change the dressing, steeling myself against the horror I saw, trying to think that what my hands did would save my sister from death and that my hands must not carry their terror to my heart lest I die of it or faint and be useless to her.

The ceiling had been painted a vivid shade of blue such as no sky could ever be. It was hazed of candle smoke. My room at home had had a blue ceiling, too, but peaceful, cerulean, the color of the bay if a storm should approach at sundown and cast unusual lights into the water. The effect was supposed to be that one lying in bed had a sense of being under the sky, and therefore under the caring eye of their Maker. I saw spiderwebs an ell across, clotted with dust, smoked and greasy black. I patted Patience's arm and ran my hand down it to hers. Everything about her was sticky and moist. I held her hand to my face and kissed it. In the dim candlelight, I saw my hand blackened with her blood, and I rubbed it against my apron. I spat upon it, too, and rubbed more, imagining my face smeared with blood. "I will *not* accept your death, too, sister," I cried. "I *shall* not."

Once I asked a nun how the babe fared. She shook her head. I did not ask if it had died, for I feared Patience's words might have cursed the poor thing. I hummed to keep from letting in the thought that Patey had wished it evil and thereby caused its death just as she had brought a storm to the ship at sea. I rose and sat upon Patey's bed, leaning to press my cheek against hers and put my lips to her ear. "We have to go home, Patience. Get well. We shall escape, you and I. Do not give up, sister. I have seen the wall. I have found the vineyard and the gate. There is a way out of here, a way home." Patience's chest rose and fell in terrifying cadence, and my soul felt cold as the darkest day of winter. I drifted off and woke with a start. She yet lived. A greening sky showed in high windows where only black had been before.

After she had lived two weeks, they allowed her to go in an invalid's chair to the garden and I was sent back to the *grange*. To my surprise, other girls carded wool in my place. I knew not what I should do. I felt per-turbed at them for having my chair.

Sister Joseph met me with a smile and crooked her finger, motioning me into another area. "This, Marie," she said, "is a spinning wheel."

CHAPTER 12

August 18, 1730

He was named James and christened Talbot. Patience regained her health but she could not nurse her baby. The wet nurse brought from town spent most of every day and night with James's care. He rarely cried. He was rather charming, I thought, but I was soon bored with looking at him, though the nurse told me he would learn to smile and play some months away, and might be more dear then.

I sat with Patience in the sick ward each evening before prayers. Ra-chael seemed always present, listening to us, watching us. Sometimes we included her in our conversations. She was not stubborn and hardened as her mother, and, I thought, not quite as daft. My loathing of her softened. She was not even so ugly as I had claimed, perhaps only plain and doomed to grow thick and stodgy when she aged. Rachael said to Patience once, when she thought I was out of hearing, "How dear you are together."

I heard Patey say, "We are all we have left of family. She is my very life." It warmed my heart.

Rachael said, "My sisters never loved me."

I interrupted their talk with the robe I had been sent for. I said, "Here, Patey." When she drew her arms into it, I kissed her cheek and sat at her side. Rachael turned her face from us and stared into the room. Tears slid down her cheeks.

It was mid-August, the flax still lying in the fields, when Master Hasken and Reverend Johansen ran through the gate one night with the help of

MacPherson's lantern. None of us had heard any rumors of their plan, not even Rachael. The escape was on everyone's lips when we found moments to whisper to each other. For the next week, when I saw Rachael she was on her knees, pleading for her husband's safety, and in English, for her own escape. The constables from town searched ten days to no avail before they gave up. I learned that because I spent time every day in the sickroom with Patey, and eavesdropped on the sisters' whispering. They believed the men to be dead, for if not, surely Reverend Johansen would have returned by then for his expectant wife.

Once she had healed enough to work, Patience was sent to the weavers' barn, too. She sat in the very chair I had used, learning to card wool as I had done. I sat in the circle of spinning wheels, turning out yard after yard of woolen thread, alongside girls all doing the same thing, our feet making a rippling sound, treadling the wheels. I felt the nearness of my sister but so isolated from her at the same time. Now and then Sister Joseph came by to check on my work and told me different things, such as, "Hold the thread closer to your lap, and your arms will be less tired." Across the room, Patience carded wool in a circle of chairs, her back to me. She spoke not a word to anyone.

As the month of August drew to a close, Sister Joseph came to the dormitory and announced with anticipation in her manner, "The flax is to be gathered in." She clapped her hands, adding, "Tomorrow everyone will work outside. It will be so festive!" My heart sank. I had barely healed from the last outdoor work in the flax. A noise started outdoors, so that when we had our meal at noon, I went to see what it was. Men worked to set up tables of planks and rows of baskets in preparation for the morrow.

That evening I found Patience sitting in the garden beside the wet nurse who held James. The sun stayed up late now, and the air was pleasant. I kissed the babe and the nurse, too, before kissing Patey. She touched my face. I saw something hollow in her eyes that made me close mine and look away, fixing them upon the flowers about us. "How is my nephew today?" I asked her.

"Fine and bonny," she said. Her voice belied the emptiness in her eyes. "Come and take a turn about the garden with me, sister." Patience grasped my arm so that it was as if she led me about rather than having a stroll together. I said nothing, awaiting her words.

"Ressie? Have you the strength to suppress a secret?"

"More than you would suppose. I care not whether I add a thousand more."

"Look into the vegetable, there, as if we are discussing it."

I did, and even managed to pantomime and point at certain things for a moment. I asked, "What is your secret?"

She smiled. "I would almost think you acted full grown, so stern you are, little sister, except that a woman of cunning would not be so forthright in asking."

I replied, "In devices I am not lacking, sister. There is no bridge between us that must be carpeted for either a footman or a caravan."

Patience turned to me and yet turned her head away as she spoke. "Not only are you taller. My sister has grown inside. Here is my mind, then. Since I lay in childbed, the thought has come often to me that there is a way of escape from this place. We must speak quickly. There must be signs between us. A password. One word that will mean 'we must speak' and one that means 'it is time to act.'"

"What words?"

"Something the two of us know that will work into speech without halt, so that none know it for a sign. The signal to meet and talk shall be 'candlestick.' Collect anything you wish to take and keep your shoes ready. The other word is more secret and therefore more sinister. We will leave when you hear the word 'gumboo.' Meet that night by the graveyard's west gate."

"The graveyard? Why must we meet there?"

"It is not a place they would expect us to choose. You saw that there were new girls in the barn with us? While I was allowed to rest and tend to James, I watched the selfsame Indians who brought us here deliver these new conscripts. The man whose wounds I tended with bear grease recognized me. If people may come in, people may go out. Rachael Johansen will deliver in a couple of months; the Indians return then, too."

"Do you not think Reverend Johansen will return for her?"

"I know not. But she could not travel so soon. I plan only for you and me."

"We should take some food. I do not want to go on a ship in a cage. I want to go as ladies. Fed ladies."

"I would sell my gold rings for our passage home. I have asked to attend Rachael. I will be free to come and go in carrying out my duties for her. You do not need to do anything but wait for my word. I shall watch the moon after her babe is come. We will travel by bright moonlight. Do nothing unless you hear *gumboo*."

"And we could slip away?"

A voice behind us said, "Shall you slip away? Where to?"

I turned to see Christine Hasken there, and said, "To the privy, for we both have soured stomachs from the food we had to eat." I squeezed Patience's arm.

Christine said, "Leaving? Why, I thought you were a good little pope's child, Mary." She clucked her tongue. "What would Sister Joseph do if she knew? She delivered Thea Newham to one of the priests to be used as a doxy. Perhaps that would suit you?"

Patey shuddered against my side. "I don't believe that. None of us have been treated so."

I remembered Lukas's sister. "Thea Newham was a tart when she came here." I knew not if it were true; I meant to scald her. She bristled, but she did not try to slap me.

Christine said, "I care not whether you believe it. You are both stupid slaves."

I added, "Your sister Rachael's husband has run away and left her heavy with child. Fine minister of God, he is. You suppose he will come back for her?"

"He left with my father," she said. "The two of them will come back. They will take us away."

Sister Agathe approached.

"I am sure," said Patience, "that you mean yourself and your sister? You do not mean we three standing here?"

Christine closed her mouth and glared at Sister Agathe. I smiled at the nun, and said, "Good evening, Sister."

"Return to your rooms now, children," Sister said, and continued on her way.

Christine hissed, "There is nothing more savage than a Roman Catholic." She whirled around so that her skirt brushed ours, and left.

"How, Ressie, do you come to know what a tart or a doxy is?" Patience whispered.

"What is it?"

"Better you forget those words. The less you know of that the better." She pinched my cheek, but did not smile.

From my cot I whispered to Donatienne, "I heard the Indians came back with more children recently."

"Did they have feathers and make whooping sounds?"

"No."

"Then they were not Indians."

I did not want to argue with her. "I heard two men escaped from here."

She lay on her back. I could see the profile of her face in reflected light coming in a window. "Men sometimes find a way to leave."

"Would you leave, if you got the chance?"

"Where would I go? This place is my home."

"But if you had a home somewhere, would you not go?"

"We are not prisoners, Marie. This is an orphanage. We have no place to go to, and no one else who will feed an orphaned girl. Why, if they held the doors wide open I would not go through."

I wanted to say, "I was sold like an animal in a room by the outer wall. I still remember the old man, Brother Christophe, who wrote down my name and paid the Indians money," but all I said was, "Oh."

Donatienne was silent. I heard her sigh. She said, "Girls who leave here, the ones without castles and coaches, come to a bad end, you know?"

"What end? Do they starve? I would not want to starve."

"You know what I mean." Someone across the room snored. Two girls coughed.

"No, I do not."

"Lean close to me." She whispered, "They go to a bawdy house and take money to let men press desires upon them."

"What does that mean?"

"I am not sure."

"Oh. What is a doxy?"

She clasped her hand over her mouth with an audible gasp. "An English word. That is what they call those girls. Sometimes 'tart' or 'whore' or *'prostituée.'*"

"Christine Hasken told me that her friend Thea was given to the priests for a doxy." I lay on the cot when I said it. I was still uncertain of the meaning but I knew it was terrible. Something in the image reminded me of being on the ship, and that brought Patience's and Cora's nightly disappearances up the ladder to mind. Cake was their payment. I put my hand to my mouth and bit my thumb. Patey had said James was Rafe MacAlister's baby. "Does it make you have a baby? Having men's desires, I mean?"

"Yes!"

From across the room a girl's voice said, "Be quiet over there, you two."

I lowered my voice. "Christine is lying. Thea is not with child." Tears formed at the corners of my eyes, thinking Patience was a doxy. "Must they go to hell? Would God forgive a doxy?"

"If confession is made."

"That is good. Yes," I said, picturing Patience, "that is very good."

Raking and seeding, combing and scutching, beating flax with wooden bars, this was our festive outdoor work. The whole compound joined in. Baskets of tow and boon joined in long lines that formed a work route. The most experienced men did the hackling, bringing the flax across the board of nails to comb it into a long horse's tail they called "strick." The flax that had been spread in the field left a fiber that was a light silvery color. The other that had retted in the marsh by the river's edge was golden, and I saw what Sister Agathe meant about its value.

I counted every day, looking forward to the day when Patience and I would leave this place. As I imagined our journey home, my hands fumbled more; I dropped things. I mashed my finger in the scutching mangle when Patience walked past me carrying a large basket to the barn and whispered, "Father William has a new candlestick." I snapped up the next basket of tow from a man loading people's arms with baskets, and followed her. I had been there enough to see that there was order in the heaps and mounds of wool and flax, whether spun or woven or still in the hanks called "rovings." I could not suppress a smile when handing our baskets to the men stacking the work. "He has a candlestick?"

She brushed her sleeves and shook off her apron, her eyes downcast. "It will not be lit tonight. Tomorrow night seems likely." Her eyes moved to someone behind me and she said, "Nary you mind. Now, let us have those empty baskets to return to the field."

My feet moved as if they did not touch the ground. We were going at last! That night at supper, I asked Sister Joseph if I might have an extra piece of bread, but to my surprise, everyone had two pieces instead of one. I pretended to eat mine, turning the second into my sleeve for our journey. I hoped it would not be long before we would be dining someplace on lovely food. When I folded my clothes for sleep that night, I left my shoes close by.

Donatienne watched me. At length she said, "There is a rumor that two girls are planning to leave the convent. The nuns asked us who are your *compagnes* to question and to beg of them not to go to a life of great peril."

A chill swept over me as if winter had come into the room. "I know nothing of such a plan," I said. "I am so tired. Please let us sleep."

"Please don't go, Marie."

"The only place I am going is to bed," I said. I was glad the candles had been put out so she could not see my face.

"Sister Agathe said she will be watching for someone to try to leave."

"Did you tell her it was me?"

"No."

"Well, she had better watch someone else. Good night."

Though exhausted to my core, I lay awake for hours. At last, when sleep found me I dreamed of home, of running on the beach, but not with Allsy. I was running from nuns and priests and leering men like Rafe MacAlister who reached for me with clawlike hands. Their low voices called, "Doxy! Doxy!" as if it were my name.

In the morning, Donatienne said, "You cried out last night. You said, 'Leave me alone! Leave me alone!' in English."

"I had dreams. How do you say 'nightmares'? *Cauchemars.* Sometimes it happens." I was aware that today was the day of our leaving. I must not show anything on my face. "Did they catch those girls?"

"We will find out when everyone is seated for breakfast and they call the roll."

I pictured the roll call tomorrow. Patience and I would be gone. I smiled.

"Are you happy someone left? Don't you know how terrible their lives will be?"

"No, I am smiling because I think it is not true. I think that someone made up the rumor to make trouble for the nuns so one of them will have to watch all night long."

For the next three nights, I heard nothing from Patience, even when she had a chance to tell me it was time to leave. When I found her stacking roving and sorting it for color dyeing, I asked her, "Any candlesticks need polishing in here?"

"Yes," she said. "Take that one over there by the wall."

I was dismayed to find there was indeed a candlestick by the wall, much abused with soot from poorly made candles. One thing I had learned from living at the Haskens' house was that a candle could be made less of a mess by careful wicking. "Very well, then," I said. "You will tell me if there are any others?"

"Of course" she said. "Sometimes one moon is not as good as the next." She nodded at me, and turned to her work. I knitted my brows. It was meant to be a message. We would wait another month.

Now that the flax was in, I was put to spinning all the day. I spun not wool but flax, which filled a different distaff and a different wheel, and had to be done with a cup of water at my side. I learned to guide the tow onto the spindle, often so frustrated I groaned, wanting to pull the stuff and throw the water cup. When the nuns let me get up from the spinning wheel, I went outside and ran through the fields until the anger and frustration subsided. At times I ran with my eyes closed, wishing I would fall into a duppy's house and disappear from this place.

Another week passed and Rachael took to her childbed. She suffered a few hours and brought forth a son. It was only upon seeing the new baby, named Ezekiel, that I could tell the difference between Patience's baby and Rachael's. For all I had expected that Patience would produce a superior child, I saw that James was no bigger than Ezekiel, though he was some months older. Ezekiel ate and slept, fat and contented. James did not nurse without coaxing, and what went down him rarely stayed down. He was plagued with raw skin under his clouties, so that he was kept naked in a hamper placed in the sun. Patience was often not in the baby room when I went to visit her; she left James with the nurse.

The next full moon came and went. And the next. Between long days learning to spin, having my work torn apart and recarded to try again until I got the rhythm going with my feet and my hands, the farm harvest began. School receded to one hour, three hours of working in the fields, pulling turnips and carrots, bundling onions, a meal, three hours of picking apples, three hours of spinning before supper. Lugging pears and pumpkins, peeling apples, packing potatoes and parsnips in layers in the cellars, none of the work was easy. Yet, when I saw the girls and nuns in the kitchen, boiling applesauce, pear sauce, piling ever more wood in the stoves to keep the fires hot, though the day was stifling, I did not complain about my work.

On an afternoon during the last week of September, the sky changed. I could not say what it was, but I could feel it. There came a freshening of the air early in the day, and the wind came from the northeast. Why that should put me in bad humor, I knew not. I felt as if this new wind brought with it some unfortunate change.

I had in my grip a mounded basket of overripe pears, and the basket was losing its bottom so I was forced to wrap it up with my arms as you would carry a child. The pears gave off a perfume as rich as honeysuckle to the air about me. I made my way past the rectory, turned a corner, and stood face-to-face with Lukas Newham. "Oh," I said, "Lukas Newham. Fancy seeing you after all this time." I did not smile.

"Yes, Miss? Ah, the little serving girl. You have grown a foot taller, I'd wager."

I raised myself up on my toes, doing my best to look down at him. I felt conscious of my breasts brushing against the camisole. "You have also been cast into servitude, but I from a higher degree than ever your father's father had been."

He sneered. "You were always above your station." Then his demeanor changed. "How fares your sister?"

"Miss Talbot fares quite well, I am sure." At that moment a small pear, rosy and firm, slipped between the basket's cracked splines and rolled to his feet.

"Ah, an offering," he said, and picked up the pear, taking a great bite. "A peace offering, I wonder? The work becomes you, you know. Your cheeks have become full roses and your whole face carries a dust of freckling, just like a ripe fruit." He took another bite, juice running down his chin, his lips moist with it.

I liked the sound of that, yet I was not sure what my reply should be. Donatienne knew much about men and romantic overtures, and told me always to be cool toward them. "Your words are too impertinent. Now that you have taken a pear from my bundle, though, you may repay me a deed."

"What shall it be, little Rosy?"

I felt my face flush. "I beg you not to call me other than my name, Master Newham, as I shall yours. I saw you coming from the priests' door just now, and that means you have access to their quarters. I am told that in their quarters is the only place here to find paper and ink. Is that true?"

"It is. And you will not speak of where you have seen me."

"It is not a secret meeting, is it?"

It was Lukas's turn to blush, and he did, with great coloring. "You keep your tongue, if you know what's good for you."

"I do know all that is good for me, Master Lukas." I cocked my head and tried a guess. "You have met with a priest? Have you been baptized against your father's will? Have you consorted with papists?"

"You know nothing of which you speak."

"I know it is easier to live here when you take on their mantle as your own. I, too, have been baptized. Let us speak in English."

He did. "I have naught against my father. I believe there is more than what he sees in the Bible. There is much that is worthy here, and very old."

I thought for a moment, not knowing how to reply to him, yet not wanting to leave his presence. I asked the one thing that might be of mutual interest. "Have they surrendered your sister to the priests for a doxy?"

"No!" He threw the pear against the building, smashed pieces flying. "None of these fellows would! If they hold aught in their hearts, it is well reined and, and—"

"And yet you do not want it known that you have become a Catholic? Others of your community would condemn you."

"As would your sister."

I shifted the weight of the basket. "Why do you care?" My own heart leaped at the potency of that thought. It might be that he would wish for me to be near him, to long for my kiss upon his cheek. If I held my breath he might see in me some true beauty I might become. Perhaps if he did not, I could convince him of it. "Reverend Johansen and Master Hasken escaped with their souls intact, I suppose."

"I must go," he said, adjusting his hat.

"If you come here, taking instruction, others might hear of it."

"Not if you don't tell them," he said, but this time without a sneer, it was more a look of pleading.

"I carry a thousand secrets already. What is one more?" As I saw his face relax and his shoulders drop into their normal place, I added, "I have need of paper and ink. If you are engaged in study with priests, you might find paper and ink. And a post."

"They send out a post every month. Some to Rome, some to Paris, some to the colonies in New France."

"One more post is a small thing. I might keep your secret."

"I will get you the things to write a letter. When you have it, place it in that black-painted wooden box, there. Put the ink vial under this bayberry next to the wall."

"When?"

"You will have to trust me. I will get it to you."

I half closed my eyes, saying, "You will have to trust me, too."

He did not look happy as he strolled away. Myself, I had quite a grin. All I had to do was wait for the paper to appear. It was a change of the prevailing wind.

Lukas was true to his word. A small cloth-wrapped bundle appeared between the layers of my folded clothing—for now I had two sets kept in a neat stack under my cot that I could interchange or wear together when it turned cold—and I could tell by the sound without opening it that it held paper. I was pleased to find three small sheets, each about eight inches square, and a vial of ink for which I would have to find a stand before I could uncork it and use it. I would also have to find a large feather to make into a quill, but I had seen Pa do it often.

Donatienne watched me wrapping the papers back into the cloth.

I said, "It is a gift."

"We are not allowed such gifts." Donatienne turned to the window. "Marie? I feel you are lying to me."

"If I had stolen it, why would I let you see it now? It was a gift, I tell you."

"Then who gave it to you?"

"A man I know."

She clasped her hands on her mouth. "A man?" She walked around in a small circle, almost as in a dance step. "What man? What did he ask in return? If anyone has done anything to you, Marie, you must tell me at once."

"All he asked in return is that I tell no one of his plans."

"Plans for what? Escape?"

I could not defend myself without breaking the promise. "I cannot say."

"Did you know, Marie, that I am sixteen. Next year they will find someone for me to marry. If I am not in good favor, they may not look for a husband for me. They may think working my life away in a factory is good enough."

"I promised I would not tell. If you guessed, I could say what it was not, and not break my word."

"Was it a plan to escape?"

"No," I said firmly.

"Did he want to kiss you?"

"No. He wants to, to, change to Catholic."

"He made you promise not to tell that?"

"He was afraid I would tell his family. He wants to become a priest. He may go to divinity school in Paris. He told me."

"Are you making this up, again?" When I shook my head, Donatienne smiled and smoothed her dress.

"I should not have told you. I am ashamed I did not keep my promise to him. Do you think if a man wants to be a priest, he cannot love a girl?"

"Oh, they cannot marry, but I think some of them may have loved a girl. Maybe they could not win her heart, and so committed themselves to God instead. It's not unlike some women do, becoming *une bonne soeur.* Will you let me watch you write in English?"

"To Lady Talbot, Two Crowns Plantation, Island of Jamaica in Her Majesty's West Indies." I pressed the sheets under my waistband and in the dark of night when I was sure everyone was asleep, I climbed out the window by Donatienne's bed and headed straight for the rectory under a half-moon. I held my missal to the moon and whispered, "Get these to my

mother, please, sir. I know God is not the man in the moon, but I hope you watch your servant here with that great eye, and take pity upon her." I recited Salve Regina and Memorare under my breath. I stopped at the moonlit wall of the rectory. The black box awaited my letters. I kissed the paper before raising the lid and laying it inside. Other sheets of paper were in it, all folded and sealed. I stirred mine amongst them, making sure it was not on top. I tucked the vial of ink into the bayberry.

The moon was as high as it would get here, which was not overhead. The evening had a chill and I shivered. The path I had taken was shadowed by buildings and trees. I could go in the window opposite the one I left, and have more moonlight. I was not so much afraid of being seen, as I was afraid—now that my errand was done—of coming upon a bear. Granted, there were two high walls about the place. No bear had ever been inside them, but I felt overcome with guilt, certain of punishment well deserved, and a bear was a memory as stout as a Saracen pirate.

I passed the older girls' *dortoir*. White chrysanthemums ringed the well, glowing like a fairy folk's lantern. Two yew trees stood between me and my room. The shadows beneath them were blacker than the ink staining my fingers. I felt a prickling in my skin and the hair on my arms rose. Something moved in the blackness there. It might be duppies, I told myself. I took one more step and I was sure something was there. I sniffed. Just as I thought to cry out "Bear!" and run away, a human voice groaned. Another human voice laughed, a light, feminine laugh.

I traipsed around the first yew so the people there would be lighted with my back to the moon. A man sighed. People murmured. Scarcely had I reached my new vantage place than I saw two people, lying one upon the other, their skins bare from shoulder to ankle. They both wore shoes. They both had clothing wrapped at their necks, pushed up. In a tangle of legs and arms, they moved as snakes, churning like rippling water. If I moved or made a sound, my presence would be known. Was that why I did not move? Rapt with curiosity, tortured with both my lack of knowledge and the sure awareness that this was something I ought not to see, I froze in place. I fought a terrible need to make water. They made soft noises. I hiccupped.

Lukas jerked his face toward me. "Christ!" he said. The other person rose beneath him, a person with long, very red hair, so red that the moon's wan light painted it the color of blood. Patience.

"Resolute," she scolded, her tone both stern and quiet, "what do you mean by standing there watching? At least be decent enough to leave us our dignity."

"Dignité?" I said.

Lukas's voice said, "Convince her," and for a moment I heard scuffling and the drawing on of clothing. Patience appeared and Lukas's footfalls went away from us. She was panting as if she had run to my side. She smelled musky, as if he had sweated, skin to skin, and she wore his scent like a garment.

I said, "What was that you were doing?"

"Love. Only love."

"Ah. You stunk like that on the ships."

"This time is different. This time I chose it."

My insides felt heavy and hot; my hands and feet bitterly cold. "Chose it? And before you did not?" Memories came to me. The thought of what I had seen just now mingled with my confusion of thinking she had been dancing on deck. The words Donatienne had spoken, that desire was the missing ingredient in creating babies. Payment with cake. Cake and Cora's words about what the cake had cost.

Patey said, "Lukas is young. We are both young."

"Lukas wants to become a priest. He is going to Paris to become a pope."

She laughed so that even in the soft moonlight I heard the derision in her voice. "He told me nothing of that. It will not suit him for long."

"He made me promise to tell no one for the favor of giving me paper and ink with which to write a letter."

"A letter? To whom did you send a letter?"

"To Ma. So she could come get us."

Patience reached up her hand to slap my face but as she did I whirled out of her way. "Stop saying that, Resolute. When will you wake up and realize you cannot do that. Ma will not come. Ma is not alive."

"Do not say that. I hate you."

"It is the truth."

"It is not. She is alive."

"Do you not remember that night? Do you not remember the men who came through the wall?"

"You are so wicked. I wish you were never my sister. You do not want Ma to find us because you have turned into a doxy."

"It is near midnight, Ressie. Your bed is that way, mine is this. We should both go to them before I beat you for saying that."

"When I leave you will go and do that again with him." Words I barely knew flitted through my imagination. Whore. Slut. Doxy. Tart.

She laid her arm around my shoulders and gave me a squeeze. I twisted away from her and brushed her touch from my shoulder. She said, "Not tonight. You've rather interrupted the moment. And he'll be yours to command now, seeing you know a secret."

"Are you a doxy?"

She whirled me to face her, hands clenching my shoulders, and before I could move away again, she had slapped my face. "You best keep your judgment until you have had to tread the road upon which I have walked."

I felt tears going down my throat, but I did not cry before her. I said, "As you say. Is he the reason we did not leave? You wanted to be here with him to do that *wiggling*? Will we be leaving at the full moon *this* month?"

"I might leave with Lukas. I might not take you."

I shoved her with all my strength, wishing I could pummel her into the dirt. I turned and ran toward the wall of my dormitory. As I reached the closest window, I found the shutter latched from the inside. I went to the next, and Patience caught me and turned me around.

She said, "Please, Ressie, please forgive me. I spoke out of passion and not my love for you. Please, Ressie." The tears flowing from her eyes rained upon my face as she crushed me to her bosom. I cringed at the smell of her. But how could I not hold Patience? How could I reject her?

"Ho. You, there!" said a voice. It was Sister Agathe in nightgown, holding a lantern high. "You girls, there. What are you about?"

Her sight of us, I imagined later, we two clinging together and weeping, was all the explanation Patience or I had to provide for Sister Agathe.

We were sisters and met sometimes just to kiss each other and reassure each of our fidelity, I promised her. Sister Agathe wept sympathetic tears, patted both our shoulders, sent Patey home, and hugged me before leading me with the lantern to my bed.

Patience's handprint—in the morning a crimson stain on my face—was enough to convince Sister Joseph that I had a fever. She left me to bed the whole day. Alone in the dormitory, I wept. "Ma is not dead," I chanted. I tried to make sense of all the shocking things I had seen mixed with the wrenching fear that Patience would leave me here.

Donatienne brought me broth and bread at noon. "Are you worse?" she asked.

"I do not know," I said, for I did not. "I am sick unto my soul, friend."

"I will go to the chapel and pray you a Rosary."

"A whole Rosary? That is too much. Will you say a Salve Regina right here, so that I may fall asleep hearing it?" I said that, not because the prayers meant much to me; the meaning was in hearing a loving voice say them. I closed my eyes and pretended the voice I heard was Ma. Ma reading me to sleep. Ma singing her old Gaelic poems or her olden charms and prayers. I held Donatienne's hand and imagined Ma getting my letter, perhaps as soon as next month. Ma was not dead and I might be home by Christ-tide.

CHAPTER 13

November 30, 1730

November came in with All Saints' Day and went out with gales that lasted a fortnight. We could not have run away had there been a moon, for the winds brought sleet and hail, icing over parts of the fleuve Saint-Laurent as well as the animal troughs on the convent grounds. The wind brought a new plague amongst us, too, that needed no vermin to spread itself among all the children of the convent. *La rougeole,* the red sickness. We called it measles. I had had it before, but others had not. As I helped tend the many sick children, I realized that I had been away from my home for more than a year and I felt so much more than a single year older.

Baby Ezekiel died. Sickly little James did not. In fact, if he changed at all, once the fever left him, it was that he seemed a little more peaceful than before. Rachael grieved, though she was not ill, for she had had the red sickness as a child. In the weeks before Christmas, she held James and rocked him, even nursed him. Patience spent no time with him at all then. I decided Rachael was not a bad person. I felt pity for her. I began to take her little things as gifts, including my first bit of thread that was fit to weave. I considered it recompense for having stolen her mother's thread. Only now did I see the value of it and appreciate what labor it took to produce it.

After Christmas rather than Hogmanay we celebrated Mary, Mother of God Day. It was curious to me how that day happened upon the same day as the ancient holy day, but so it fell and I cared not to question it. We had no gifts at all, no games. Just more prayers than normal, more ritual. All our gifts were for the Virgin, who, of course, had no need of them whether she were indeed Queen of Heaven, or simply a woman dead. I felt peevish about being again denied my father's pleasantries and my mother's feast.

The days and nights of winter blended into one long, gray funnel of time. I spun linen thread, ever finer, until mine compared with any around. I was the youngest, the sisters declared, to make such thread.

At Michaelmas in 1731, when I turned twelve, I was taken to a new room and introduced to the great loom, a machine of clunking, banging, slamming parts, woven with miles of thread and moving things that seemed enchanted. I was also introduced to Sister Beatrice, the master weaver, and Brother Marcus, who had come to the convent as a captive but stayed when he found the life to his liking. By Good Friday, I had learned how to wind the warping board and had watched them warp a loom three times. Each time I put my hands to it, the thread grew tighter with every wrap, broke, or made sags. I lost count. I dropped pegs. I cursed aloud.

Sister Beatrice threw her hands in the air and left the room. Brother Marcus shook his head and said, "Take it off and start over. Warping the loom is the hardest part of weaving. Yet it is the first thing you must learn.

She has little patience left. See if you can learn so that when you are old, you will not have to leave the room in exasperation over a little girl. Peace is in the fabric and fabric must have peace. The loom will not work for you without it. Once you can do this, the rest is more simple. People say one day you will surpass Sister Beatrice, and she knows it. Now, try again."

Patience was sent back to the kitchen. I stayed at the loom. I seemed to be always growing out of my clothes, and I tied my hair with a kerchief like the older girls and women did, rather than plaiting two braids as the children did. There were days I forgot to look for a moon by which to make our escape. One day we found two girls had run from the convent under cover of night, in a bleak rain, helped out by two men cloaked in black. The nuns shut all dormitories for a whole night and day for prayer, they said, but imprisonment was truer. When the morning came and we went to chapel then to breakfast, we heard the names of the runaways.

I sat with Rachael at times, when my work hours were finished. She confessed to me that she had joined the runaways in meeting her husband and her father at the gate at two in the morning. She had brought with her one bundle. Baby James.

Her husband was incensed that she thought he would replace their son, she said. He told her to leave him at the gate and someone would find him in the morning. She would not, she said. For the sake of her own dead child, she would not abandon this one. Her husband fretted with great words at her, she said, yet given following them or staying behind with this child who so needed her, she believed she had no choice but to return to the convent. I patted her wrist, and to my surprise, she hugged me just for a moment. "You are a kind and loving person, Mistress Johansen," I said.

April passed, blown out by gales and rain. Then came summer and the flax.

Life at St. Ursula's was an unceasing parade of work, prayer, and poverty. My hands chapped and bled in the summers as well as winters. Sister Joseph was kind, as was Donatienne. I longed to go home, although for days at a time I forgot about Jamaica and thought only of warping and weaving and learning my Latin.

In 1732, I turned thirteen years old. That spring mold crawled up the walls inside the convent rooms. Donatienne coughed. A little at first, then a great deal, struggling for breath. I brought her broths and rum toddies from the kitchen. Every two or three weeks, a piece of paper and a small vial of ink appeared in the branches of the yew tree, like a Christmas trinket. I wrote another letter to Ma. I warped the loom. I had nightmares about shuttles flying at me and piercing me like arrows. I dreamed about being caught in the treadles and tangled in thread at the bottom where the weaver worked the hooks with feet tapping a rhythm like a jig. I dreamed the countermarche was a terrible dance that required me to keep my feet in perfect time with bobbins that bounced like rubber balls, falling out of their shuttles. The dance proceeded with words rather than music: beams, bars, beaters, heddles and threadles and racks. Tangled in thread, choking, I awoke, thrashing in my blankets, uncovered and cold.

In the morning, I found blood in my bed. I cried out, believing I would die.

After that, Donatienne and I were moved to the women's dormitory.

In the middle of May, Patience waited on the table where I sat, and said to me she had spent the morning polishing a candlestick, and that it should be shiny by vespers. I waited until our prayers were finished, and met her between the yews. Strange how that place had become a link between us, and I tried always to erase the image of her and Lukas there, though I never saw those trees, whether day or evening, that the image was not first in my thoughts.

"I had a message!" Her face glowed. "From someone who will help us escape."

"From Ma? Did she get my letters?"

"You will remember him when you see him. He will return in three months."

"Three months? I want to leave now." But in truth, Donatienne had just received word that a wedding was being arranged for her, and I did not wish to leave before Donatienne's wedding. "Is this man sent by Ma?"

"No. Stop being foolish, Resolute."

"Then how do you trust him?"

"I can trust him."

"No man can be trusted," I said, feeling myself far wiser than my sister with my new, matron's knowledge. I wondered whether it was wise to leave the leaving in her hands. Perhaps she could not choose our best future; perhaps I must choose my own.

Donatienne had met the man that she was to marry once before the wedding date. It had been arranged to take place in June before the flax harvest. His name was Julien Noël; his name was Christmas. Her gown was a simple borrowed frock once used by his sister, her veil a bit of light-weight wool.

I stood at her side, all the time thinking that she would return to the convent, yet at the same time knowing she would not. During her wedding, she coughed and coughed. At least, I thought, watching as Julien prayed the prayers and took the Communion, he did not seem either leering like Rafe MacAlister or mean like Lukas Newham. Julien Noël was but two-and-twenty, and she seventeen. During mass, I thought only of my loneliness. I had turned a woman, but my heart felt like that of a foot-stamping five-year-old.

When they arose from their knees, now man and wife, both appeared happy. I gave her a gift of my first yard of linen smooth enough it was allowed to remain and not be torn out for scrap. I had stretched it upon a framework of light wood. The yard of linen itself was made from a tiny bit of silver tow mixed with gold, for they would not let me have more of the finer thread from the fields until my work deserved the best stuff. Upon it, I had embroidered a man and a woman on either side of a house. An embroidered tree grew up one side and shaded the house, and in its branches tiny birds nested. That was a sign of good luck. Down the other side was a ribbon of honeysuckle with three yellow flowers, a sign of sweet happiness. Donatienne seemed pleased as she waved farewell.

That night as I lay next to Donatienne's empty cot, I wondered if Julien had already pressed his desires upon her. Brushing the thought from my mind, I recited the pattern for the tweed-style woolen the nuns produced to sell. *Blanc-gris-gris, marron-marron,* I chanted until my eyes closed.

When next I found paper and ink provided I would tell Ma to find me before they marry me to some townsman, too. I was thankful at least that Lukas had continued his ploy and brought me papers, still terrified I would let others of his community in on his religious change of heart.

The first flax harvest that summer was a large one. Four weeks we spent pulling and stacking, strewing and bundling for the marsh-retting. It was barely finished before the second harvest began. During this time all helped, even the cooks, so Patience was in the field at my side often. I asked her if the man who would rescue us had given her any new signs. No, she said. We must wait. He would come.

"Why wait?" I asked. "Were we not expecting to sell what we carry for passage home? We need no man to do those things."

"You know so little of the world. You will need a man to do much in your life. They hold the keys to all our doors."

"I belong to no one but myself."

Patience shrugged. "You do as well to complain about the color of the sky."

Perhaps the heavy work made everyone too tired to be watchful. No matter the reason, four of the company of slaves disappeared that week, three men and one woman. The next week, five more men went. One of the men was Lukas. When I saw Patey, we talked of their leaving, and I said, "It is time. We should press our luck and go, full moon or no. There is another week of flaxing I want to miss."

"They are posting watches at night now."

"They are watching the men."

"Word will be sent to our captors, the Indians. They will either find the missing people or bring more. I want to be here when they come. I have a plan."

"What plan?" I feared she had no plan other than to live in a state of expectation for the rest of our lives. Had she gone mad? "I shall go by myself," I declared.

"You will not live a week," she returned.

"I will go home."

Patience bent to pull the stalks in her hand from the ground, and said, "Where is home, Ressie? What have we but this place? I had hoped Lukas would take us with him. He promised to do it."

"Ah," I said. "*Lukas* promised." I felt disdain for Patience then, worse than any anger or puzzlement I had felt before. She had allowed him to use her for the price of escape. I knew what that made her in the eyes of God and the world. "Perhaps you sold yourself too cheaply, sister." She turned to me with venom in her eyes. It was the first time I knew my own heart as I knew my own hands. Her eyes met mine on the same level for I had grown to her height. I said, "If you slap me, ever again, I shall return you blow for blow. I will not be beaten by you or anyone for speaking the truth. You have no right to use me so ill." Patience straightened her back, dumped the armload of flax at my feet, and struck out through the tall plants, parting the flax, running from me. She took up a place between some other workers. I laid out the flax she dropped without shedding a tear, righteous indignation fueling my work as it did for the next several days.

Days turned into weeks and winter came again. My mind felt numbed to time and the rhythms of it I measured by seasons rather than days. I turned fourteen, and felt fully a woman, at last allowed to don the gray gown of our order. Before the summer flax harvest that year, we received word that Donatienne had died of consumption. I was not allowed to attend her funeral or burial.

On my fifteenth birthday, in the year 1734, Sister Joseph called me to her. I presumed that it might be something to do with my life there, my possibilities of a future placement in marriage. What she gave to me was a bundle of papers tied in woolen yarn.

"This day is usually reserved to assign you as a *compagne,* or to speak to you of coming prospects. Taking vows, marriage, or placement as a lady's maid. You have gone to great lengths to deceive your purposes here, Marie," she said. "These letters from you have been placed in our post box for the past three years. While I do not read English well, it does not take a scholar to discover the content of them."

"I only wrote to my mother."

"You procured costly paper available only to the Brothers. How did you come by these sheets?"

"I asked for them. From Lukas Newham."

"What did you give to him in return?"

"My word."

"That is all? He is gone, now. Will you tell me his secret?"

"Since he will not fulfill it, I will. He intended to become a priest. He said he knew of secrets that the pope alone should hear. He swore me to secrecy for the paper."

"We believe he dealt shamefully with young women in our care. Did he lay hands upon you? Did he beg you for favors, or take them?"

I could not stop the color on my face. "No, Sister. I am not to be had so easily."

"Why the wine upon your cheek, then? May I not assume that you are sullied or saddened by the efforts of that young man?"

"Not I, Sister." The image of Patey with him made my face burn. "I hated him."

Sister Joseph cocked her head and watched my heart play upon my face. She said, "Do you know of others whom he did sully? Tell me the truth."

I bowed. "Yes."

"Why did you not tell me?"

" 'Twould have broken my word to two people to do that. I was trapped for the want of a sheet of vellum."

"Several sheets, I see."

"Yes, Sister, though I did not steal them. He stole them."

"But you are wrong, Marie. There are other forms of theft, especially of the light you hold in your heart. It is dimmed by deception no matter how small. You have hidden one lie within another."

"Sister, what of my letters? To let my mother know I am alive?"

"No contact with the outside world is allowed for anyone. The paper will be soaked and the ink washed, though it will leave stains, as lies leave stains upon your soul, daughter. Leave here and go to confession now." As I passed the threshold, she said, "I thought you were above this sort of thing, Marie."

My work was doubled for thirty days, every moment of it spent fuming in anger, scheming to escape. I found every possible opportunity to pass Patience in the kitchen or at meals and inquire whether there had been a candlestick on a certain table or if one needed polish. I did it before listening ears. Sister Joseph thought I was feeling repentant, seeking out even more work to penalize my wicked heart.

When in 1735 I was sixteen, after the flax harvest I was almost glad to return to the peace of the great loom. The huge apparatus filled one end of the building, had rhythm and harmony in its beams. As I dusted the bench, I realized that the baskets and bolts that seemed tossed here and there made sense to me. If something tumbled against another stack, it was easy to see where it ought to have been. Everything had a place.

Winter came early that year and cold, wet winds blew as soon as September, bringing frost in the mornings. At breakfast on a stormy morning, I found in the bottom of my plate, under thin gravy, a piece of bread. Cut into the bread was a word that had grown so stale in my mind I nearly cried out at the sight of it. *"Gumboo."*

Patience cleared plates without a look in my direction. I might have thought it some accident in the baking, save when I handed her the platter, her eyes turned away but her fingers gripped mine under the plate and squeezed. "Thank you," I said.

"Not at all. What God provides, we will cherish."

My mind raced. I made mistakes in my weaving, causing three inches to have to be taken out. I dropped a shuttle and made a splintered notch on the end, broke a warp thread; almost fell from the bench when someone behind me let the door slam in a stout breeze. I told Sister Beatrice that I felt ill and she sent me to bed.

I patched my cloak, a rough black handed down, stitched layers of fabric together to hide what I meant to take inside my skirt and petticoat, and kept my feet upon a stool so that they would be rested for the march before them. While my weaving suffered from anticipation, my sewing did not and I finished everything, including bundling it, in short order. I folded it so that the pile beneath my cot appeared nothing out of the ordinary but it would be available in the dark of night.

As supper finished and chapel commenced, I thought of all the times Patience had told me before to meet her, even to make ready. There had always been something that got in the way. I expected that something would again break our progress, yet because she said it, I believed that the Abenaki warriors, many of whom were the same men who brought me here, were on their way with more captured slaves. What made today different from those other days, I could not ask.

After evening prayers, rain fell anew. I made a dash between our door and the older girls' dormitory. The nuns at the entrance were just putting wood in their stove, and told me Patience was working in the kitchen that night for our guests. Sister Évangélique said, "You know how travel is in this weather. They might not get here until tomorrow. She'll sleep in the kitchen."

"*Merci, ma soeur,*" I said, and made for the kitchen, fighting against the wind.

I found Patience standing upon a stool, reaching into a basket on a shelf high overhead. No one else was in the room. I whispered, lest others were just in the shadows. "Patience?"

"What!" she said, and toppled off the stool, thumping on the floor and overturning a basket of potatoes with her elbow as she fell. "Marie! You startled me so!"

"Did you not hear me come in?"

"I was deep in thought. Fetch that, would you? The potato under the chopping block." She stood and rubbed her elbow. "Glad enough the bone is not broken," she said.

I lowered my voice and asked, "Is this night *gumboo*?"

She whispered in English into my ear, her breath making a sound. "It is the night. There are always so many to feed, it will be noisy. In that basket up there I have hidden a monk's cloak much as the one you wear. No one knows I have it, however, and so it will be my disguise. I have a man's hat and a ruff. Are you wearing the petticoat Ma made?"

"Yes, though you would not know it for at least two layers of cloth cover it. I added a new waistband and hem, else it would not have fit."

"We shall leave when they get here. You'd best stay with me."

I said, "I have to fetch my parcel. And Sister Joseph will check my bed. Will you come for me?"

"You must be *here*. We have to run when the moment is propitious. Go get your things. I will hide you in the kitchen, in that alcove by the pantry."

"Do not leave without me, Patey." What I saw in her eyes made me cold deep inside. I felt as miserable and shaking as I had that night in the secret stairway behind Patience's bedroom wall. "I will have to slip out a window after Sister Joseph turns in. Promise me you will wait for me if they come while I am gone. Promise, Patience."

Patience narrowed her eyes and said, "If I go without you, know this. There was no choice. Now, run."

I splashed through runnels all the way to my dormitory. I knelt by my cot as was custom, crossed myself, prayed. As if she'd been waiting for me, Sister Joseph snuffed the candle on her table near the door the moment I arrived. I dressed in my night clothing, putting the gown over my petticoats and chemise so that later I could don the heavy skirt and short jacket. I changed my wet stockings for dry ones. I lay upon the cot, fighting the urge to sleep, curious at how I could close my eyes even in the midst of excitement. If Patey left without me, I would have only myself to depend upon. I would not wait, I vowed. After an escape they would watch for a while, but they would forget. They always did. Yet, perhaps I might do as well to stay and let the Sisters find me a husband. At least that would be a life. Two more years I shall be tied to the loom, two more years. What, I wondered, were the chances they would marry me to a man who would take me to Jamaica?

The midnight bell tolled. The room took on the quiet of resting souls and Sister Joseph snored peacefully. I dressed on my knees beside the cot, got on my shoes and tied my parcel of clothing. I looked toward Sister Joseph and bade her a silent farewell. I put up my hood, raised the wet blanket over my head, and pushed open the shutters at the farthest end of the building from her. It squeaked. I paused. The rain slowed. At last I stepped over the sill. Halfway to the kitchen, the sky opened and rain came as if it might never rain again.

I ran right into one of the yew trees; it was closer than I had imagined. I stopped to picture the place where the kitchen would be. I could just make out the shape of the other tree fifteen feet away. Not being able to see meant no one else could, either, safe in the cloak of rain. I neared the kitchen, raised the blanket, hoping for a familiar object. At once, a hand took my arm and fingers closed over my mouth, the blanket was held over my head and my whole person was quite lifted and moved. I fought mightily. I gave every effort to scream yet I was not able to make a sound.

In the midst of my struggling I heard a voice, a woman saying, "Resolute, be still. Keep quiet. Let her go, now. Not a sound, Ressie. It is I."

"Patience! Who had me? That was not you. Why was I captured that way? I had almost reached the kitchen."

"The others are eating. Plenty of people and food to keep everyone busy. We go."

I turned at her last words and ran into a man. Tall and hard as an oak tree, he was the source of the leathery iron hands that had taken my mouth and held me just moments before. An Indian man. I let out a gasp and drew a breath to scream.

Patience shook my arm. "Ressie! Quiet. I told you, we are leaving."

"Is he going to let us go? Is he here to capture us? Sell us again?"

"Run for the gate," she said, took my hand and pulled. With her other hand she clasped the Indian man's hand!

I stopped so suddenly I slipped from her grasp and the two of them nearly fell down in the mud. "Where is baby James?"

"He is better off here. Rachael will care for him. I cannot."

"He is your baby."

"You do not understand, I know, but he is better off here."

"What if Rachael runs away and leaves him? Is there a foundling home?"

"Then he will be kept here. Come now, Resolute, or stay behind. I will not wait for you and have us all found out. It will go badly for everyone if Massapoquot is found to be helping us."

This was not what I imagined. This was wrong. I had to turn back. I would let her go. If I went, I would never get home to Ma. I would marry some farmer I knew not, and bear children and grow old and die here in this frozen hell. "Baby James," I said again. "We will go get him."

"We cannot take a baby," the Indian said, in perfect French. I was amazed for I expected the same halting words they used in English. "We travel hard and fast. You must come now or stay behind with the child. No other choice."

"Ressie!" Patience shook my hand impatiently.

I could not see Patience for the downpour. "Are we going to Jamaica?" I asked.

"As close to it as we may," her voice answered out of the gray. She waited a few seconds, and when I could not answer, she took my shoulder and followed the length of my arm with her hands, grasping my fingers in hers. "Farewell, then, Ressie. I love you. I will always think of you. I have to go. God keep you, little sister."

As if unbidden, my hand squeezed hers. "Take me with you," I pleaded. With Patience on one side and a man I knew not on the other, they propelled me out the gate I had found long ago, into the hands of three other Indians. One led the way up the road, and turned into the woods where a narrow path cut this way and that. We marched through the dark night until the rain stopped just as the sky turned a lighter shade of gray. The air chilled so that our cloaks and coverings froze upon us, making tents of ice. I could not feel my fingers or my feet. We moved as shadows, on and on, until one of the men called a halt. I heard water. A river appeared out of the fog. Long bark canoes, two of them, waited at water's edge. The Indians put Patience into one canoe and me into the other. My heart sank. Would they take me into the woods and press me with their desires and kill me?

I sat in the floor of the canoe while one man before me put a rough deerskin with the hair still on it over me; a man behind me took up oars and rowed. As the hours passed I slept. The sun broke through the heavy clouds from time to time, playing warm spots upon my face. Home, I thought. We are going home. I thanked God. Thanked the Indians, too. I asked the Virgin to guide our canoe, whispering, "Ma, I'm coming." When the sun lowered, the Indians pulled their crafts to a bank and made a small camp. They lit a fire that seemed to give no warmth at all. Patience sat near the man who had caught me at the convent. I recognized him in the firelight. He was the one whose wounds she had tended with her hair. I whispered, "Patience, do you know these men?"

Patience smiled, her eyes alive and twinkling. "Every few months, Massapoquot and men of his tribe travel to Montréal to bring slaves to the convent of St. Ursula. We were part of one group. When they came, Sister Marta had all of us in the kitchen stay up for two days, waiting upon and feeding the men who had worked so hard to save our souls from Presbyterian hell." My mouth opened, appalled. She continued, "Every time I saw him, I felt something different. We began to talk. We knew each other. His name for me is Red Shield of Bear. When Massapoquot offered to come and take me I made him promise to get you, too. We have planned this for four years. That first rumor those two sisters would try to escape, that was you and I. But the weather was against us. Even the Indians do not go abroad when there is four feet of snow on the ground. I could not call you if there was no hope of making an escape."

"And they will take us to Jamaica?"

"No. But they will get us near Boston. There are ships there aplenty for you."

I huddled by the fire. "What about these other men? Do they speak French?"

"Yes, all of us," Massapoquot said.

I looked him in the face. "Why may I not ride with Patience? Why do I have to sit in the other boat?"

The man laughed. "Why would I have to do all the work? Why, you would make them feel as if they weren't useful."

There was so much to think about, yet I was so cold I thought I would die of it, and I could not think. Patience had left her own child behind. She would have left me, too. She had convinced four strange men to take us to Boston and no one had mentioned coins or gold. I wondered how much it would cost, or if she had traded her virtue yet again for this journey. I could not imagine how her mind and heart were connected to my own, for all the workings of hers seemed too foreign to grasp. What was to keep these men from doing anything they wanted with us and dropping our dead bodies in the river? I said a prayer for James and begged forgiveness for leaving him behind. We rode in canoes, then walked overland, with the Indians carrying the canoes on their shoulders until we came to another river.

Eleven days we went down the river, the men paddling, Patience and I frozen to the bone. Twice they made us lie down and heaped things upon us as if we were a pile of trade goods, and one of those times, Massapoquot had to talk long and fast to some other Indian men so that we could pass unmolested. The twelfth day they banked the canoes and hid them in tall brushy plants that overhung the river. Massapoquot said, "From here, travel slow. This is English land. You speak some English; you might say them we are not here to kill you, but Englishmen bad. They will kill, no matter you have their hair and skin. They not listen. You," he said to me, "choose you come with us. You choose. Not have to live with English. Think this."

"Yes, we will think on it," I said, trying not to appear as morose as I felt. I smiled at Patience, thinking that perhaps she had been right to trust him, or perhaps she had lied to them to get the Indians' help in escape. I wondered for the first time whether our absence had caused a stir at the convent. "My sister and I long to see our mother," I said. "I can smell the flowers of Jamaica, already."

We lived off dried corn bread and berries for five more days. We did much resting and eating, and though it was cold, they seemed in no hurry. We stopped at a road where the air was filled with the fragrance of wood smoke and bread baking. Massapoquot pointed. "There. English town. This place one road goes two ways."

Patience put her arms around me and hugged me. "Go to that house there, and tell them you prevail upon the selectman to provide you food and shelter until such as you desire to go on."

"Is my face dirty?" I asked.

"No. You look fine." She sighed. "Let me see you once again. Yes, you are fine. Almost a young woman. Another year, well and aye."

"Then I am ready. Let us go side by side, Patey. Thank you, gentlemen, for the journey. God will bless you for what you have done for us."

Patience said, "Go on, Ressie. I will watch you go, then, before we leave."

"You are not coming with me?"

"Ask for the selectman's house. Here, take this, too. I shall not need it."

"Patey?" Deep, wrenching, inconsolable sobs shook my whole frame. She removed her apron and fastened it about my waist as I moaned, "What shall I do without you, Patience Talbot? We are meant to go together."

She wept. The Indians wept, too, I remembered later. Patience said, "I am going with my husband, Massapoquot. We wanted to bring you to a safe place. There is a town not far from here. My old petticoat is sewn inside that apron. Everything Ma gave me is yours."

I stared at Massapoquot while pointing with one hand toward the house up the road. "Husband? What if these people are Quakers? What if they hate Catholics?"

"You are not a Catholic."

"I do not know what I am. I am lost."

"Someone moves in the field," one of the Indians said. "English. We go."

I bit my lip. She was leaving with Massapoquot. I felt as sure as if I had heard a holy voice, whatever Patience chose to do I must do the opposite for the good of my everlasting soul. As they stepped toward the woods, I stood fast. The men took Patey's arms and slipped into the cold shadows under dark red maple leaves.

The dappling of light and red as a screen before my sister, her red hair loose over one shoulder, painted an image as I could carry in my mind for a lifetime. She looked bewitched, fairylike, part of the forest itself, a face enchanted. *Au revoir!* I called. *"Au revoir."* I stood alone in a field of cornstalks and chaff, my heart broken, my eyes red. "Patience!" I cried. A crow flew overhead. Higher above, a *V* of geese squawked at each other. After many minutes, I pulled in my tears and pressed the backs of my hands against my eyes, cooling them, turned away from the woods, and moved toward the house.

CHAPTER 14

September 29, 1735

I knocked at the first door, an unpainted thatch of boards tied in place over a hole in a low stone cottage. The top half swung out at me. A gnarled hand held tight to a knot of rope, ready to pull it fast. A couple crowded themselves into the open half-doorway. They appeared more ancient than the sagging beams and rusted iron circle above the door. When I inquired were we not in a town, they looked to each other and drew back from me. "Are ye a witch?" the old man asked. "Come ye out from the woods like that, with no one to guide ye, and no horse, and naught but your bundle?"

"Did you kill our laddie?" his wife added. "He was thrown in a well by a witch."

"No, Goodman and Mistress. I was a captive, just escaped. I found my way here with the help of—of others. I am hungry."

The man twisted his sparsely bearded chin, then angled his head to ask, "A brownie are you, then? If we feed ye will tha' grant us a wish?"

"I am neither fairy nor brownie. I am but a girl in need of a roof and some soup."

"How did you know 'twas soup on the hearth?" asked the goodwife. "She's fey, I tell you."

"It is always soup," I said. "Oh, please, turn me not away. At least show me the direction of the town." Were I them, a young woman coming alone from the forest, not in rags but clothed and fair, carrying a bundle such as I had, may have seemed such an odd apparition I could not blame their superstition.

"Eleven miles. That way," the man said, pointing to a window on the back wall where the dull light of morning came through the only opening save the door.

"Is there a road, sir? I wish to get to Boston. I am told that it is a great seagoing harbor."

"Of course there is a road. This is not the wildi-ness, ye know."

"Will you gi' us a blessing ere you go?" the woman beseeched.

"I know not one," I said. I drew back.

"We've done ye no harm, little one. A blessing?" She came from the house then, with him on her heels, and bowed her head. I was at least a foot taller than either of them. The man looked upon me with fear but the woman was willing to share her dread with hopes of magic.

I imagined if I said nothing, they would think that I cursed them instead. I spoke a phrase of the mass: *"Gloria Patri, et Filio, et Spiritus Sancto; sicut erat in principio, et nunc, et semper, et in saecula saeculorum, amen."* I stopped myself making the sign of the cross, fearing that would give away the origin of the words.

The man waved his hand, one finger extended, toward the road. "Go on, now. Town's that way. Eleven miles. Ye will find the Great Road. We done ye no harm, remember that. No elf ever suffered at our hands, tha'."

The road wound through places almost too narrow for a horse-drawn rig, but it was not eleven miles to the town. Indeed, within half a mile I came upon a house and then another, their lands trimmed and perfect as the gardens at St. Ursula's. A woman waved to me from behind a split-wood fence. I returned the salute, then she called to me, "Are you travelin', then?"

"Yes, to Boston to find a ship," I said.

"Alone?"

"Aye, Mistress. Have I far to travel?"

"Boston? I think they say it may be three days by coach, two on horseback, and one on foot." She smiled. I supposed it was to be a riddle, but it was not clear. She continued. "Oh, don't look so sad. There's a town closer. Cambridge Farms, it was, in my father's day. Now 'tis called Laxton. The Boston road is not a road to travel alone, Miss."

Laxton? At her last word, the realization struck me that with Patience married in a way, I was now The Miss Talbot. "I am Miss Talbot, of Two Crowns Plantation."

"Nary heard o' that one."

"In Jamaica."

"How do you come here, then?"

"Captive." I looked at her house. There was no cross or crucifix over the door, but another horseshoe bent into an oval. "Sold to a Catholic convent in the north, and escaped now. I hope to return home."

A broad grin spread upon her face, lighting her eyes with warmth. "Are you hungry, Miss Talbot, as hungry as you are brave?"

"I am, good lady."

She cocked her head and laughed, as embarrassed as a child being praised. "Oh, come inside, dearie. I am no fine ladyship but I have on some bread and fine cheese. We'll make you a meal."

I sighed and smiled. "How kind of you, Mistress."

This time she giggled. "Come around to the door, then, with you." She met me from the inside, then, and welcomed me into a dear cottage so tidy and well appointed, though the furnishings rough, that it seemed a dollhouse. It smelled of what we—the French—called the "breath of heaven," fresh bread just from the oven. In the time it took the lady to bring bread and fresh butter to the table, memories of my time at St. Ursula rolled over me like a wave, and my hands trembled.

"Would you have cider?" she asked as she poured it into a gourd and handed it across the table.

"Well and aye," I said, and blushed, embarrassed at my words, for Ma's expression was so rarely on my tongue the whole of the years I had been away from English people. "The bread is delicious."

"There, you can call me 'Goody Carnegie.' Here's honey for you. Now," she said, "when you have broken your fast, tell us how you came to be here."

In as few sentences as I could manage, I did so, leaving out that Patience had left me and run away with the Indians. I told her I had come with strangers who had left me on the road to go to their homeland. Since it was another direction and I wished to get to the closest seaport, they had sent me on my way.

"And where was their home? Far from this town? For I would know everyone."

I nearly spoke the words in French, and caught myself at the last second. "They were not given to talking of it, and our flight was hurried. West, I think."

"Well, cheers that you got away! And would you not consider staying by here? There are those who might take you in. Laxton or Lexington, how e'er you call it, 'tis a nice town."

"Oh, I could not impose, Mistress. I only wish to find a ship on which to go home." I feared that by "taking me in" she meant as a servant or indenturing me against my will to pay for my upkeep. I pressed my hand under the table against my thigh where Ma's casket lay. "I have a small sum laid by. I would stay at an inn, if such were available. Of course, I should rather secure a coach to the seaport."

"Ach, a young lady alone at an inn? Heaven strike me dead this instant if I allowed such. No, no. If you must have a roof, you may share mine, but 'tis not a place for a proper young lady to reside. There are better, and there are those that would take you to the sea, child. Have you finished them vittles, then? Let us go a-calling."

Goodwife Carnegie took my arm in hers and led me up the road. About a mile on, we rounded a small hillock and came to a bustling town street. Dogs barked, children called out, and women called back to them from windows and doorways of at least a dozen houses storied high enough for three floors each. Farther in were a church building and a public hall, a well, and a trade-goods barn with three sides. Fruits in baskets filled the front stalls and people crowded at them. "Halloo," Goody called, and people in the square turned, staring at us, while children dashed by. "Halloo, see the young gentlewoman who has come to call upon me? Her name is Miss Talbot, and those of you who would meet her must be introduced by myself, first. She is *my* guest." She squeezed my arm and leaned toward my ear. "That'll straighten the curls in their wigs, dearie."

Within a few minutes, it seemed the whole town had gathered around, and a cadre of men circled at one side. One of them said, "Now, Goody Carnegie, this Miss will have to answer to the council, just as any would. And you, lady-child, where is your escort, your husband or father?"

"Indeed, I have none at present. Pray let me speak to you in private, good sir."

Another man said, "Be she driven abroad by some other town? Be she a witch?"

And another, "Why else go to Goody Carnegie's house first of all?"

"Take care," said another, "let us have her questioned by the committee."

Goody Carnegie said to them all, "If you will have a committee then I shall bring her. We will await you in the courthouse."

I felt more than knew not to question her labeling the small building to which she led me as a courthouse. There she bade me sit upon the steps until seven men approached us, one last of them fastening his jacket and trying to right an old wig that did not seem to fit him well. The others were wigless but bore in their demeanor and long beards the feeling of being a council of law. One man spoke, saying, "The Lexington Town Council is now in order. I am Selectman Roberts, and Misters Falwell, Erskine, Considine, and Jones are witnesses, as are Yeomen Franklin and Spotsworth."

Goody Carnegie grinned, showing yellowed and missing teeth. "They listen to me even though they don't like it. I've got land, y'see. Land talks."

A shortish man approached the courthouse and waved. "You there, come this way, if you please. We shall mount the steps there and you approach the bar this way." He pointed to a hitching rail in front of the building. "We will know your purpose here, and your comings and your goings, young Miss, Miss—"

"Talbot," I supplied. I told them all as well as I could, that my home in Jamaica had been ransacked by privateers, I had been captured, and, skipping the Haskens altogether, taken north into French colonies to an Ursuline convent. Several people gasped when they heard that last word. Then I said, "Another woman and I conspired with a team of rescuers to leave that place—"

"Wast it because you were taught an untrue religion? Because you were made to suffer papist rule?"

"Partly, sir, but most because I was not born a slave. I am a free person, the second daughter of Allan Talbot, Her Majesty's loyal—"

"The queen is dead," said another man. "These many years. Our second King George reigns in her stead now."

"How long a prisoner?" asked another.

"Five years altogether."

"And what is your plan for this place, seeing your first visit with any soul here is to a professed madwoman?"

"Madwoman?" I asked. "Goodwife Carnegie? She has shown me kindness but I knew her not until this morning. 'Twas her house first on the road. Another before it was empty and the one before that, a man and woman pointed the way to Boston. Before that, nothing but trash and dead animals."

A woman from the crowd behind me called, "Goody's not in her mind, lassie."

Goody Carnegie looked down from between two of the men's shoulders upon me. She smiled and nodded. "It's true what they say, my dearie. I have sometimes been troubled by a spirit of melancholy." She tittered, hiding a laugh.

"Melancholy is not madness," I said, then bowed my head when the men before me stiffened, but I continued, speaking my words clearly so I would not have to raise my voice. "I have known other people not so mad who treated me harshly. Goodwife Carnegie has been only kind. She has shown me here to beg your help."

"She speaketh with some foreignness of tongue," a man said.

"Imprisoned by Frenchmen five years!" said another. "Did you not hear her?"

"Do you speak French?"

"I do, sir." Donatienne's gentle face, her patient coaching came to mind. I said, "If I was to keep my wits I had to learn what was being said round about me. It was not torture, sir, but teaching as any of you would do."

"Will you say something?" another asked.

"What would you have me say, sir?"

The first said, "Give us an example, so that we may know it."

"L'Éternel est mon berger, je m'en veux pas. Il me fait coucher dans les verts pâturages."

"What say you, Gilliam, is that the French tongue?"

An old man nodded and smiled. "It is, indeed. The Twenty-third Psalm. Fine choice, Miss."

A chorus of murmurs surrounded me. I pointed my question to the closest fellow. "May I speak, sir?" When he nodded I continued. "Is this not the town of Laxton?"

"Some's call it that way, Miss. Properly pronounced Lexington."

I put on my bravest smile and said, "Gentlefolk of Lexington, I wish to return to my mother and my home. I have no escort, and I would not stay in a public inn. If I may prevail upon some kindness in this company to see me to the seaport, my only intent is to find passage home."

A man called from behind, saying, "Me and the missus be g'ang to Braintree on the morrow. Miss Talbot may ride with us to Boston."

"What be your age, lass?" a man asked.

"I prefer to keep that," I said. "It is a lady's prerogative, is it not?"

"You will stay with Selectman Roberts," one of the others said.

Mr. Roberts held up a hand. "We must think on this. Will you abide with us a night?"

Another chimed in, "That is the way it is done."

"Have you wife or family?" I asked. "I would not stay alone with a man, sir."

The men nodded and a few smiled. I had passed a test of my virtue. As selectman, it was Mr. Roberts's duty to take me in, I was told, but he was bound by convention, not law, and if I displeased them, he might change his mind. Mr. Roberts said, "My wife will see you are kept company, and indeed, my daughters and two small sons shall bear witness." He smiled at me and I could not help but return it.

"I shall be in your debt, sir," I ventured, though I wondered whether that was the best response as soon as the words came. "Then may we speak of a journey to the coast?"

"In good time, my dear. In good time. Autumn has near set in and ocean travel will be treacherous. It may be best for you to pass the time with us until spring."

I felt so free. The very air seemed to have light in it. Still, though I had no wish at all to wait longer, to convince these people to help me was my only hope. "I am sure you know more than I about ocean travel, sir, but I wish to go as soon as a ship is ready."

He seemed to pay little attention to that statement, and the whole lot of them accompanied me to the door of the Roberts home. It was a short walk. The house was large and made with an overhanging second floor, so that it looked like a cake sitting upside down. In the middle of the bottom floor, a carriageway led to a stable at the back. Mr. Roberts's family filled the house to overflowing, but unlike the Haskens' mean and cramped conditions, this place was lighted with windows by day and candles aplenty by evening, and there was not the smell of a goat anywhere near the place. The Robertses' daughters, aged from seven to seventeen, made much of dressing and ribbons and nosegays and lace. From eldest to youngest, they were Serenity, Betsy—whose given name was Elspeth, Tipsie—whose given name was Portia, and the smallest and most beautiful, America. The sons were Herbert and Henry. By supper that evening I had learned that the girls had been raised gentlefolk, though the two young boys, spoiled into naughtiness, teased their sisters, threw crying fits when denied their ways, and caused all manner of havoc at mealtimes. Still, they were not mean children, just untamed.

Alone in the washing room, I went to throw Patience's lopsided apron on the pile for the ragmonger. As I pulled it off and let it fall to the floor, it landed on the stones and made a clinking sound. I picked it up and pressed my fingers here and there and only then remembered that it had merely been a hiding place for her old petticoat, worn to shreds. I cut the apron open. Her treasures were still intact! Ma's silver casket had been fixed there by a patch of madder and black plaid. Ma's pearl necklace was there under a piece of crudest linen. The whole of it inside bore stains and grit and brought distasteful shadows and a feeling of fluttering darkness upon my senses. Finding this gift from Patey gave me hope for my future tinged with hurt at her leaving me. In an hour I had everything sewn into my gray skirt in pockets and duckets, just as Ma had made. It did not have to last long, as I meant to use the gold to buy my way home.

By week's end, we had discussed my traveling to Jamaica at least nine times, and seeing I was determined, nothing would do but that Mr. Roberts and his wife would accompany me to Boston to find a ship. I had to hide my disappointment when Mr. Roberts answered that he could not leave for at least five more days, yet the weather was increasingly bitter and I feared he had been correct about not sailing until spring.

On the day we were to leave, the girls burst into my room, chattering like a flock of chickens. Serenity, the eldest, looked upon my form for a moment, and then shook her head. "But you are so lithe! And that old gray wool! Too plain. You wouldn't want to be taken for a Quaker, would you? Oh, to have a waist as small as yours. Come with us, Miss Talbot." She pulled me by the hand and led me to her room, clucked and riffled through the gowns and petticoats hanging from the walls. "Try this. Take it with you, if it fits. It fit me two years past, but Betsy has already outgrown it, too, and by the time Tipsie can wear it, it will be out of fashion."

Under my weak protest, they pulled the pale blue satin and silk over my head, laced up the back, adjusted the shoulders just off the curve so that it made a cunning frame for a modest décolletage. Serenity pushed me before the glass. "Look at yourself now, Miss Talbot. Oh, my. None did this gown justice until today."

I saw myself in the mirror and stared longer than the nuns would have allowed, shivered with the sheer joy of wearing something lovely and light. It was the color Ma dressed me in for any nice dinner. I turned to Serenity. "You are kind. It is very fine."

"Let us do something to your hair. Come here, Betsy, and bring us a comb."

They fretted and fiddled, and finding my hair's nature as dismaying as I found it, they managed to get a chignon on the crown and pull out some curls at the temples and sides. The curls would not line up and fall "like good little soldiers" as Betsy said, but dangled by their own device, all askew and frothy. I smiled at Betsy and told her, "The more I trouble my hair, the more unruly it becomes. Please let us say it is finished, for it only will get worse." Once they were indeed finished, I admired my hair in the mirror and felt a swelling of what I may only look back on as vanity and selfish pride. At the doorway, I donned my black priest's robe over the gown, tucked my bundled clothing under one arm, and bade them all farewell.

I called to the boys, Herbert and Henry, "I shall not be pleased at all if you kissed me good-bye. I hate being kissed by boys." As I had expected, they both ran to kiss my cheeks and put their grimy hands about my neck for a caress. Herbert pressed a glossy, almost clear crystal stone into my palm, said it was a gift for my journey and not to lose it, as it contained magical powers. "Thank you kindly," I said.

As we rode in the barouche, Mistress Roberts said, "We shall miss you, Miss Talbot, for you have been a dear guest. If your travels ever take you this way again, do make our acquaintance anew."

"I shall, madam. You have been ever kind to me in my distress. I shall speak of your warmth and care to my mother and I am sure she will think you are splendid for it. Mr. Roberts, may I ask something of a business nature?" When he assented, I continued. "In preparation for some ill occurrence, my mother concealed some valuables which I have been provided in order to seek a way to return home. Is there a place in this Boston town to which we go, of a nature where I might sell or trade for coins for my passage?"

"You have them with you now?" he asked.

"I do, sir."

"Let no one know of it by any gesture or query until we are within a safe institution. We will go to the Seaman's Mercantile. Instead of going to the harbor at Mistick we shall ride up the Neck and into Boston proper."

"Thank you, sir."

"Not at all. It gives me a chance to see to my investments without worrying about boring *both* my lovely female companions, eh, my dear?" He winked boldly at his wife, who blushed and waved her fan at him. "Of course, you will have to let me handle the exchange for you. I will do my utmost to secure the right price."

"May I accompany you, sir? That way I could see how it is done, and be the more educated by your guidance." This played to his pride in a greater way than I had expected, and the man beamed as we rode the rest of the way.

I was not expecting Boston. First it seemed as if we had driven to the gates of hell itself, for the offal, dead beasts, garbage, and sewage at the edge of what Mr. Roberts had described as the "neck." Past these huddled ramshackle buildings, far worse than the log ones the Haskens had taken me to in the woods, but farther on, actual houses, small and humble, perched amidst well-kept gardens. Then we rounded a brushy, tree-covered knoll and turned to see the full of it. A city set on a hill, almost as if described in the Bible, with open windows and doors, and the sounds of life everywhere. The air was raw and damp and a mist softened the edges of the buildings. I saw spread before us a city of brick and mortar, cobbled streets bustling with carriages, smart whiskies pulled by a single stallion, and old farm wagons, the whole presence of human life being lived in a freedom and abandon I only dared remember from long ago.

When we arrived at the Mercantile, I huddled in a corner with Mistress Roberts and produced the pocket. Since Patience had abandoned both her legacy and me with such aplomb, it would be her things I sold first. I took the rings. Four were gold, I was certain, one containing a ruby the size of my smallest fingernail. Three more rings were silver or a whitened metal that might have been pale gold, for I knew of such and these showed no sign of tarnish for their years smothered in moldering linen. They were ornamented and, I thought, costly, too. I kept the pocket in my hands so that I could return the coins I got to it and stitch it shut after taking out what I needed for passage.

We were shown into a small room behind another small room, which had been gotten to through a narrow stairway. The place was stale and had no need of curtains on the windows for no light had come through that glass either way for what looked like a century, so thick was the grime. Mr. Roberts appeared to know the wizened fellow before us, but his appearance was so evil it drew me back to think Roberts had dealings with a man who might have been the most scurrilous pirate I had yet encountered. His name was Peterson Cole, and that name was on the board out front, yet I had expected a gentleman of some bearing to be at this trade, not the weasely bind-staff before us. Still, the two talked and shared a drink of brandy, pouring sherry for Mistress and me. I had not tasted the stuff before, and was not fond of it. I did manage to take polite sips, wishing I did not have to touch the cup with my lips, for I doubted it had been any cleaner when it was poured than had the windowpanes.

His shipments accounted, Mr. Roberts took some payment in stacks of gold coin. He eyed each piece as if expecting one to be a fraud, but each bore a nick on the edge, proof of the softness of pure gold. Then he introduced me without history, telling the man I wished to sell some jewelry I had inherited. I laid the rings before him. Mr. Cole squinted at the rings, then at me. He looked at them one at a time, and held the ruby up to the dim light from his window. "I'll give you seven shillings apiece, child. Take it. It's a bargain since two of these are obviously fake."

I straightened my shoulders and addressed Mr. Cole. "Sir, I am neither a fool nor a child. Any backstreet publican would do better than seven shillings. Good day." I stood.

Both men stood in response. "Now, don't be hasty," Cole said. "Maybe the light is poor. A Massachusetts gold crown apiece for the gold ones. That makes two pounds and six. What say now, Miss?"

I was tempted to say, "I say you are a fraud and a scorpion," but I kept my tongue.

Mr. Roberts's face held some distant chill and a brooding in his eyes, and he turned to me, saying, "I doubt any other transaction house would offer so little. If my charge here will allow, we shall seek another opinion in another exchanger's shop. I have to stop in Mistick this day, too, and the light is waning." An uneasy silence grew like a stench in the air while the two men eyed each other.

"A businessman must make a profit," Cole said. "Perhaps I'll look at them again."

The rings lay before me, all but vibrating with the lives lost in getting them to this place, glittering with the touch of my mother's hands as they lay there on the man's soiled writing-table leather. I said, "Five British gold guineas apiece for the gold rings, and four British gold sovereigns each for the two silver ones without the jewel. Ten British sovereigns or pounds—but they must be in the king's gold not the colonies'—for the jeweled one, for that is a ruby and the metal is gold. They are not fake."

Cole said, "I won't do business with a woman. Not even a woman but a child." He gave me a look that seemed to be bold rage and chilling avarice all at once.

Mr. Roberts's mouth dropped open. He said, "Well, she learns quickly, eh, good fellow?" His face grew just as steely and his eyes never left Cole's face.

At last Cole sneered, rolled his eyes, and capitulated. He turned to a cupboard at his back, opened a drawer, and pulled out three leathern bags.

He counted out the coins I had asked for three of the rings. As I did not move, he turned to me and said, "Take it or leave it. The other is a fake and I won't buy it for more than a shilling."

I picked up the coins with one hand and the ruby ring with the other. He let out a startled, "Hup!"

"I am quite happy with our bargain," I said. I placed the ring upon the first finger of my right hand and a warm shiver went from it through me and all the way to my feet. At that moment, I remembered Ma wearing the ring at a ball when I had been too young to see much but her hands and her face. And here I had almost lost it, trading something so precious for mere money. Never again, I told myself, should I look upon the things hidden in my petticoat as mere things.

That was to be my single triumph of the day, for at Mr. Roberts's insistence I waited with Mistress inside the coach while he inquired first with the harbormaster, then in a successively poorer line of taverns for captains or crew of any ships heading south to the Caribbean Sea. He returned to the coach and reported, then moved us forward another street or two. Not for six or eight weeks would anyone chance hurricane season sailing against the trade winds toward Jamaica. Not until spring. Not until May. Not without a load of trade goods and who knew when that would be ready? I felt near exhaustion as he returned the fifth time. I tucked my hand with the ring on it under my arm and held it close. The mist turned to rain.

"Now, take that sad countenance away, Miss Talbot. While you have passage fare, you must write your mother—we'll send it on the first packet south—and ask her to send you traveling money and a chaperone, and perhaps a guard. While you await her answer, you may stay with us this winter."

"Mr. Roberts, I owe you so much already. All this time I thought only miles and coin could keep me from my mother. Now the very weather conspires against me."

Mistress Roberts said, "Waiting is ever the hardest when one is young. But look, we will have visits and balls this winter to drive away the gloomy day. Young men with whom to dance. Would that not fill your days until a ship can be got? Write your mother immediately."

Mr. Roberts leaned out to the coachman and said, "I say, would you know of a scrivener about?"

"Aye, sir. Up by the Tri Mount."

"Take us there, man. There's an extra shilling in it for you."

The coachman whistled to his team and we jostled away from the wharves and the smell of old fish and seaweed. Through narrow streets up a hilly area, past modest two-story houses and into a street where neat shingles hung at the street level, the coach finally stopped in front of FOULKE AND HARRISON, ESQUIRES. We entered the building by a low front door which opened into a step-down. A man with black sleeve cuffs greeted us with a nod. Within three quarters of an hour, a formal letter was written to Ma and made ready to post on the next ship. Mr. Roberts paid for the attorney-at-law to dictate it and his scribe to write. The whole was an entreaty to Ma to send me plenty of passage money and a chaperone, or to come herself, how to find us on the road between Boston and Concord, and how the Robertses were happy to be in complete service to me as we awaited her reply. My heart all but stopped and I wanted to skip and dance about the room.

Mistress Roberts insisted that they purchase for me a wardrobe befitting a ward of theirs, a planter's heiress, and one who would grace their home for the next four months. "But I cannot pay for these things, madam," I said.

"Your mother will return it later. I am sure she will want you well treated."

We went to a haberdashery, a milliner, a dressmaker's, and a shoe shop, where a lady used paper and drew around my feet and Mr. Roberts himself ordered two pairs of shoes and one pair of white kid slippers to be delivered to his address every month for me.

CHAPTER 15

October 16, 1735

This was most like my true home of any place I had been in so long. My heart strained against my clothing, willing myself not to weep from home-sickness that had all but disappeared in the years at St. Ursula's. Before the Roberts family, I kept my face under scrupulous control, but alone, in my room or if they happened to be otherwise occupied—for the house had fourteen rooms and anyone might be in any of the three drawing rooms at any time—I oft gave way to my emotions. There was one thing I had learned about hard work and much of it. It kept the mind busy and the thoughts on the tasks at hand. Now that I had time to sew, or read, look out a window, or walk through their garden and pet the stable horses, I found my thoughts recaptured all I had lived through, oft with violent emotion attached.

I offered to mend or sew, but they would hear of me doing nothing more than artistic embroidery as befits a lady. Often as I plied my needle, I would catch a whiff of coffee or treacle cake and again I was a child, back in our parlor. I pictured Ma at my shoulder telling me to make the knots smaller, to thread the needle so, and to hold my work before the fire to see if ravels showed through the backing. Memories I had stored away seemed as real as yesterday, stitched in layers of suffering and loneliness. I thought of my own jewels, too, yet untouched, hoping I would know the right time to use them. I had Patience's money in my pocket and a ring on my finger.

I blamed Rafe MacAlister most for my suffering. I knew he had to have been at the bottom of it all. Next I blamed Patience, though she had wrought none of our misery; in the end she had deserted me to become the common-law wife of an Indian and live in the woods. If I ever saw her again I would spit in her face. I was also furious that the weather prohibited my travel, and prayed for spring as ardently as I had used to pray for escape. There were days it took much effort to hold the raging storms within my heart at bay, especially now that there was no Sister Joseph to scold me, no rock floor on which to kneel for penance.

Our days were indeed drear, though each one tried to lighten them in every way. Reading aloud, singing, or telling of some activity in town, we whiled away the time. To be a lady amidst gentlefolk was such lightness combined with such constraint, it made me almost wish for the freedom to flex all my limbs and do the dance of the loom, perched upon the bench.

Weeks passed and Ma had not written. One night as I slept, I saw Ma and Pa, floating faceup in Meager Bay, their hands clasped as if they had fallen in together; their faces smiled peacefully, and their clothing was that of their wedding portraits which had hung in our great room. I sat up, shuddering, weeping but not weeping; a groan escaped my lips, a sound of pain that came as if from the depth of my soul.

I lit a taper on the dressing table and looked in the mirror. I felt someone in the room behind me. I turned, calling, "Hello?" When I looked back to the mirror for a moment I saw my mother's face reflected before it became my face. The shadows of the room closed about me. I lit a second candle and walked the room with it, assuring myself that the shadows held naught other than darkness. When I returned to my dressing stool, the thought gripped me that if Ma did not write, or if she had not survived without me, I might indeed be orphaned. Who am I if I am not Allan Talbot's second daughter?

I spoke to my reflection. I pulled the candle closer to my face and studied the image in the pitted glass. "How shall I make myself into a woman? As I made an apron, as I made my own thread and turned it to a plaited cloth, hid my scree within, and then was abandoned by my only kin?" I had known both tenderness and a master's whip. I had seen God both served and flaunted and men scourged without mercy. I had seen mercy from these people, common colonists, not gentry, mayhap no different than my pa, working with his hands alongside his own slaves. I wondered for the first time whether he beat them, or caused others to beat them.

That afternoon I dressed in a morning frock; a light woolen shawl crossed my bosom, which now pushed roundly against the front of my chemise. I tucked my hair up into my day cap. The cap was made of delicate linen, starched and fringed with expensive lace from Belgium. I tied it slowly, watching the movement in the mirror. My eyes traveled from the face in the mirror to my own hands, and I held them around the candle flame, so that each finger was lined with deep shadow. I wondered how my hands would appear when I grew old, if I were to grow old, that was, and not die this winter of some plague or fever.

I drew in a breath, sat up, and said, "You shall be these things, Resolute Catherine Eugenia Talbot. You shall not bow your head to any. You shall live your life always with an eye to being of great age and having no regrets for things done or undone. You shall never give your conscience for a piece of silver or a place to lay your head." Tears blurred the image. "You shall bind no one as slave. You shall give of your hands generously but your heart sparingly. You shall never lie again. You will be a woman Ma would love for a sister and friend. You are your own." My chest swelled with emotion.

A call came from downstairs. "Miss Talbot? Would you have tea?"

Feeling the brush of Ma's hand against my hair, I raised my hand to touch hers. "Miss Talbot, late of Two Crowns Plantation, shall attend tea this afternoon with the family of the Selectman of Lexington, in the King's Colony of Massachusetts. She shall do her mother proud, and even more, she shall be proud of herself." I turned to the door. "Yes, thank you, I shall."

In early December of 1735, during a blizzard that dropped a foot of snow that never melted, word arrived that guests would come for supper and would be staying not far away. Herbert and Henry went about the house that day with shirttails flapping and shoes untied in open rebellion to the law laid down by Mistress Roberts. The house had been decked for Christmas, but at every corner new candles appeared with stubs ready for lighting. The young ladies were decked and perfumed, and insisted I do the same in another new gown of green watered silk.

A great noise came from below, a calling of names and a near riotous banging of doors combined with the sound of a carriage and six passing over the cobbled carriageway. Betsy clasped her hands to her face and said, "He's here!"

Serenity made a face. "Only that dreary old lord and his withering wife. Oh, and then, of course, young Master Spencer."

"Wallace!" Betsy said. "Wallace Spencer is practically betrothed to Serenity!"

"He is not," Serenity said. "But he does have a very well turned calf."

"Too bad about the other leg!" Betsy replied. Serenity tossed a pillow in Betsy's direction and both girls laughed.

I laughed, too, adding, "Betwixt the two of you I daresay he does not stand a chance." The others had already descended the stairs; we followed, I between the two oldest young ladies of the house.

Lord Spencer was away, but Lady Spencer acknowledged us with a slight nod. She was impressive. Tall. Aloof. I saw fire in her eyes. When Mr. Roberts introduced me to Wallace Spencer, the young man took my hand and bowed over it, discreetly touching his lips to my fingers. My heart leaped. I felt my color rise and could not take my eyes off his countenance when he faced me. His jaw seemed chiseled from marble; indeed, all his features had been sculpted most aristocratically, perfect, yet masculine in every sense. Hair curled at his temples as if it, too, had as wanton a nature as my own. The weave of his coat and trousers I recognized as being of high quality. The fabric was imported from France, I thought immediately, and tailored here. I wished to see it done, making gentlemen's clothing, for I knew about women's things, and curiosity cooled my cheeks.

"What? Have I bored you already, Miss Talbot?" Wallace Spencer asked. His voice washed over the room like warm water. "For I saw you flattered then disenchanted in the same moment. Oh, dear. I was hoping to charm all the young ladies in this house."

At dinner, Wallace Spencer sat next to his mother, opposite me. Thrice I caught him watching me. His eyes were warm. His lips smiled so easily in such a jaunty way, raised on the right side. That was proof to the world, said Mr. Roberts, that he was related to the Prescott and Davis families, old Boston, old grants, old Loyalists. I wrinkled my brow a little. I would let that information brew a while, and try to discover what those families meant to this one before I mused aloud.

Though none mistreated me and the days though short were merry, the house drew in upon itself with the confinement of winter. Wallace's presence was the pleasantest diversion, and I looked forward to his coming as much, perhaps more, than Serenity did. I kept my feelings hidden, for Serenity spoke much about her understanding that they were intended. Often he strolled with Serenity and me over the snow-packed road, short distances meant to stir the blood a bit before returning to the house for steaming beef broth in cups, or chocolate, or tea and cream. Since I told no one my age, Mistress Roberts decided I was as fully woman as Serenity and therefore must be of the same age. Serenity at seventeen welcomed my company, as it relieved her of having her mother present, and I was more likely a conspirator if he should happen to take her arm or hold her hand. In truth, he held both our hands, for the road was often slippery. When he left us, he kissed both our hands. I could not tell whether he gave Serenity the same tender caress with his fingers that he gave to me. I believed some secret passed between us that day, and my face warmed to a ruddy hue when we entered the steaming house.

Christmas season got under way on the fifteenth of December. We spent the day hanging the house with wreaths and garlands of holly and pine; the fragrance was heavy and sharp. Serenity turned eighteen the following day. Wallace had turned four-and-twenty that summer. He had studied mathematics and read law at Harvard, and yet was a gentleman and had no need of a profession. He did those things, he confessed, to placate a doting grandfather who nevertheless expected Wallace to be able to earn a living, whether he needed to do so or not.

Christmas came with puddings and pies stuffed with roly-poly and venison, roasted goose and pork. The smell of dried fruits bubbling in a crock of mutton or pheasant filled the house for days. Their kitchen made the gloom of the gray days so much more bearable, to have the smell of damp clothes and moldy windowsills replaced with the perfume of crackling fat and apple pies. Mr. Roberts had hired musicians who brought by cart a harpsichord, two violins, a viola da gamba, and the musicians to play them. By evening, guests began arriving and brought with them even more meats and succulents. Such merriment! Jigs, tunes, and reels they played for three hours, no matter that we were too exhausted to dance, and the music went on and on.

The music struck up a chantey I remembered. These colonials knew not the words and thought it was only a jig with a smart dancing rhythm. I laughed, remembering pirates bawling it at the top of their lungs, always followed by "The Captain's Tart." Wallace danced with every female in the place, merrily and with good steps. He informed us that he and his family would be lodging in Lexington until after the New Year. Everyone expected him to propose to Serenity on Christmas Day and announce their engagement, but he did not. Serenity lay awake at night and consulted her sisters and me, about what might be keeping him from making a proposal.

The Roberts family kept faithful to the First Church. Near as I could tell without asking many questions, it was a Protestant version familiar to me. I listened with half an ear to the words but concentrated a great deal on how they may have shaped these people so I would not be caught in childish mistakes, singing improper songs, or behaving in any way other than they. My reputation, I vowed, I would guard as sacred. Hogmanay had given way to Mary-Mother-of-God Day, and now Epiphany. By Epiphany Wallace had made no promise to Serenity nor asked her for one.

Winter, on its dull and lead-gray path, was now brightened greatly by the presence of Wallace. He joined me on a couch in the parlor one drizzling afternoon while his and the Roberts family were engaged in games of whist. His father, Lord Spencer, had come. The man was indeed a stony relic from some past time and distant place. When the latest trump was called and everyone stood for the making of a mulled punch, Wallace leaned toward me and said, "If you would, Miss Talbot, I ask you to be the bearer of a little secret for me."

"I should be pleased to do so," I said, expecting it to be something about the date he had chosen for his proposal.

While everyone was engaged in noisy conversation about the game at the other end of the room, he said into my ear, "I find that I have fallen in love."

"I should think that would surprise no one in this room, sir."

"With you."

I dropped the silver spoon from my saucer. The clatter it made upon the floor brought the room to silence. Both families turned to stare in our direction as I felt guilt and surprise color my cheeks. I stammered a moment, and then said, "Mr. Spencer has informed me that his winning the last hand has made him vainglorious. He wishes to be humbled by your having to, to listen to him sing." My smile fixed, I turned to him.

He cast his eyes on mine with such fervor I lost composure, but then, smiling, he stood and clapped his hands. "Well, then, Miss Talbot, what shall I sing?"

I retrieved the spoon and went to the table of meats and puddings. "I care not, sir. Ask one of the others to choose for you."

Betsy said, "Oh, do sing 'Greensleeves.' It is Serenity's favorite."

Though Serenity was in a near swoon, I doubt anyone could claim that Wallace's rendition was a favorite, but at least he knew the words better than he carried the tune. Through it all he managed to keep up a merry smile and did not gaze upon me again with those eyes. Then, lacking any embarrassment whatsoever, he said, "Ladies and gentlemen, one and all, I have decided to purchase an estate in Virginia. It is a plantation of some substance."

The Robertses crowded around him then, asking a hundred small questions, which Wallace answered cheerfully though often with the words "I know not." His parents were not surprised by the ploy, but had kept it for him to tell. I watched Lord Spencer. A more indifferent man I had never seen. I wondered why he was so often absent when Wallace and his mother visited us or we them. The word was that he had business in England. From the look on his face, I believed he was ponderously bored here.

Then Wallace said, "I will be leaving the first week of March to go south and see to the place. I expect to be gone two or three months at most."

Wallace had just proclaimed that he loved me and he was leaving. This was March so he would return in May or June. I had meant to be in Jamaica by then, but could I wait for him? Oh, whatever would I do that long without him? I made my way to a corner of the room, bumping into a footman carrying a tray of sweetmeats for the party. I could not retire without taking leave, but I needed a moment to calm myself.

The footman asked, "Miss Talbot? Are you unwell?" The crowd turned their eyes toward me.

"I am quite well," I said. I felt as if all eyes followed my every move. "Have I done something amiss?"

"No, no, my dear," said Lady Spencer. "Nothing of the sort." But her eyes went from Wallace to me and back to him.

I turned to Wallace and forced a lighthearted lilt to my voice. "What sort of plantation? What will be grown there?"

"What has always grown there, I suspect. Sugarcane and rice, but we are wasting Virginia soil not growing tobacco. Everyone else has.

That is the future in the colonies. I plan to put in extra fields of tobacco immediately."

Sugarcane. When he said those words the future bloomed before me, Wallace becoming a man like Pa, a warm and loving man, hardworking but gentle. My heart thudded yet I turned toward Serenity to see if his plan might affect her.

Serenity fought back tears. "A farmer? You are to become a farmer?"

"Not at all, Miss Roberts," he said. "I shall own a plantation. Others will do the work. Better you concern yourself with your fine embroidery and the ladies' arts."

Serenity's hand went to her embroidered collar, fingering my stitches there.

In March, snow became rain. Roads became mud. Serenity sang "Greensleeves" relentlessly, not realizing, I think, that the words of it depicted a jilted lover never to return. It filled me with guilt. I supposed that Wallace might write to me, or to her, and I would know his meaning by who received the first letter.

On a howling evening in late March, when the wind beat at the barren trees as if it would uproot them and gusts tormented the house so that the leaded windows bowed inward, I lit a candle in my room and said a prayer for my birthday. I knew not an exact date, only that between Michaelmas and Easter I was a year older. Seventeen thirty-six. I turned seventeen. Though they knew not my age, I knew that at sixteen a girl could enter betrothal. I was not betrothed to Wallace Spencer, I reminded myself.

I wrote a letter to Rachael Johansen. A few weeks later a letter came from her. She said as a sanctified person she was allowed correspondence. Then she told me news of everyone I had known. Her sister Christine had made her way in Montréal as a *prostituée* until she had been found raving and was locked in stocks. When she was released, she tried to stab a doctor conversing in the street with a priest, but managed only to damage his horse. Her father had tried to intervene and take her but she stabbed him, too. He was arrested for disturbing the peace but freed later, to disappear. She was hanged within a week. Reverend Johansen had died of a fever from an infected tooth, and Rachael had felt it was God's hand, and so had taken the vows of a sanctified woman, not a nun, never to leave the convent walls again. She planned to remain at St. Ursula to raise James and be mother to the infants left there by misused and desperate girls. I laid her letter on my bed table. I thought of girls like Patience, and their desperation.

My heart made a noise and sudden warmth shot through me. Would Wallace require of me that naked coiling as I had witnessed Patey and Lukas doing? Staring into the flame of my candle, I vowed that I would do what Wallace asked, even that, and give him children, as many as we would have. I let a vision drift before me of the one sugar plantation I knew, now removed to a place called Virginia, peopled with my children, my husband. And slaves.

I spoke aloud. "Allsy was a slave." I had never believed that Old Poe was anything other than a trusted friend, a second mother, a dear aunt. The fact that she had "cost" Pa by her death had no meaning to me other than the grief that death cost me. Allsy was as close as any sister. Shared apples and great pox, separated by smallpox, Allsy was African and had been my slave and I never knew. How would a plantation be run without slavery? Yet, if Wallace was to be my husband, he must be told about my feelings. We would own no slaves. We would have to employ workers who had a choice and were paid for their labor and never, never beaten. That settled, I rose from my knees and lifted the candle as I turned toward the bed.

A chilling scream pierced the air. I exhaled so that I blew the candle out, and dropped it. I was engulfed in darkness before the next scream followed it, continuing on with a long wailing, a moan that seemed to come out of the storm itself. I felt my way toward the door, hearing the rush of wind but feeling as if I were in the darkened stairwell with Patience, water crashing about us, making our way to the arms of the Saracen pirates. I reached through the doorway and touched the warm softness of another human. I gave out with my own scream of purest terror, just as that person did, also.

"Miss Talbot!" Portia's voice called. "I thought you would have a candle!"

I shuddered with relief and said, "Tipsie, thank heavens it is you. It went out. I was coming downstairs to fetch another." The voice in the storm screamed again, screeching agony and longing all at once. "What is that horrid noise?" I asked.

"It is Goody Carnegie. Gone mad again. Sometimes when the wind blows she runs about in the night. It's enough to scare a witch to heaven."

A light appeared before us, a double candle held by Betsy. "Tips, what a rude expression. With whom have you been associating who would speak in such a way?"

I asked, "That screaming is Goody Carnegie? But she's kind and dear."

Betsy said, "She calls through the woods, looking for someone who harmed her, they say. 'Tis also said she's running from witches from whom she's stolen secret poisons and potions. Or that she's a witch herself trying to catch a fairy."

Portia said, "I believe she's fey, and captured herself. Not a witch. That would be evil and she does not seem evil."

"As if you would recognize evil in anyone," Betsy chastised. "You are too kind to see the sin in others. You think everyone is as sweet and good as yourself, sister."

My hands shook with such trembling as if they were not part of me. While this conversation was softening my fear, I wanted light and much of it. "If you please, bring your candlestick in and light mine." The two girls followed me. I recovered the dropped taper, found two others, and lit them all. "Why does someone not help her? Is there no medicine for her? No person to keep her? Why, she will take fever in this cold."

"No one can help a madwoman," Betsy said. "Though if people truly believed she was a witch they would have drowned her long ago."

I thought of Christine Hasken. Hanged for stabbing a horse. Goody Carnegie, serving me bread and excellent cheese. I said, "What if we pray for her? Could we not do that at least?"

Both the girls looked at me with startled faces. Goody Carnegie howled again, much removed this time, so the wind carried the moaning under the eaves of the house and it no longer sounded like a human voice. Finally, Betsy placed her candlestick on my dressing table, hugged me, and said, "You are so dear, Miss Talbot. Kindness even to a madwoman. I hope you will always be our friend, even if you get home to your island."

The wind continued for several hours, and I slept little. I thought of poor Goody Carnegie. Christine Hasken knitting stockings. Lonnie, the wee dafty one. Birgitta and the goats. When I slept, I dreamed Ma cradled me in a hammock on the leeward porch of our house, and the smell of flowers lulled me to sleep. The smell grew stronger and more pungent. I awoke with a start. One of my candles had burned to the end, layering melted wax around itself, and Rachael's letter, moving in a draft coming through the windows, had gone over the candle and the last ember of flame had touched the corner of it. It had just begun to smolder, putting off that fragrance that replaced the flowers in my dream. I pressed the burned part and took off the ash, then smoothed the missal. It might have been moments from setting the room on fire, even burning down the house, perhaps killing me in my sleep along with all the others.

The feeling that I had looked upon my own death filled my heart with terror, filled my eyes with tears. I went to the window and pressed my hand against the leaded diamonds where now a pinhole of breeze came through all the day, air rushing in, not letting any out. How could so much air come into a place, and yet it felt as if I could not draw a breath? "Ma," I said aloud, "spring is beginning. I will come home this year. I will come to you."

Mr. Roberts agreed to take me once again to the solicitor's office, where, he said, he awaited word on urgent business. There might be a letter there for me, he said, as he had instructed any correspondence from my mother to be held there.

"But, sir, why did you instruct that? Am I not a free person to receive and profit from my own correspondence?"

Mr. Roberts frowned, but cheerily, although for a moment I saw that cold glimmer of steel, keen as the blade of a cutlass, cross his features. "Of course, Miss Talbot. Of course."

As we approached Boston, Mistress Roberts said to the air before her, as if in casual conversation with no one in particular, "I hear the Spencers are expecting young Master Wallace soon. I heard it from Anne Prescott herself."

"Indeed?" Mr. Roberts replied.

"Yes. And he will be calling within the week."

"Wonderful," he said.

She spoke again to the air. "It is of course known all about that he intends proposing to our Serenity. Her dowry is larger than anyone else's one could name. Now that he is landed, too, there should be no impediments to that path, which has been laid for five years at least."

"No, certainly. Of course," he added.

"And, have I your permission, sir, to call upon the dressmaker regarding some silk for a wedding gown for our most precious daughter?"

"Of course. We shall make that our mission and purpose. First, Cole's exchange for news of my trade investments, next the law office for some letters. Next, the harbormaster to see to Miss Talbot's passage home, of course. Then, and most important, of course, the best dresser in Boston. None but the best for our daughter. Is that woman you went to before of good use? Does she make the best patterns? I insist you find out who among the trades creates the finest gowns, my dear."

I knew something was afoot by all this foolish conversing over my head. They meant me to know that Wallace Spencer was taken. That they would stop at nothing for their daughter's happiness and that the dresser they had taken me to was second-rate. One better must be found to supply Serenity's gown. I stared out the window, and as I raised the curtain a bit more, the clouds overhead parted, sending a piercing ray of sunlight to my hand, reaching the depths of the ruby on my finger, giving me a warm rush with it. "I should think," I began, "that your daughters are the luckiest young ladies in this colony or any other, with such tender parents as yourselves." I turned to them and smiled, then returned to studying the landscape that traveled past us. Wallace had proclaimed his love for me. If he was true, if his heart was gold, their plans meant naught against his passion. My own love for him had blossomed these months of his absence—four now—into great longing that woke me at night with dreams of his visage before me.

The coach stopped before Peterson Cole's storefront. His SEAMAN'S MERCANTILE shingle hung askew. A hasp and padlock closed the front doors, and the windows had been barred from the inside.

"What's this?" Mr. Roberts exclaimed. He rattled at the door, shaking dust from its seams. "Open up, I say! Cole! Open these doors."

Mr. Roberts paced for several minutes before the doors, but no soul approached from inside or out to do his bidding. He pounded the door with his fist, causing Mistress Roberts and I to turn surprised expressions to each other. That was the way a common man might expect entrance, not a gentleman. The commotion he had created drew attention. Two men approached wearing high beaver hats, both dressed in somber but fine apparel. "May we assist you, sir?" one of them asked.

"Mr. Cole. My shipping investor. Where is he? Why is his office closed?"

"You have not heard?"

They drew him closer to the coach, unaware that but a curtain separated their voices from Mistress Roberts and me. She grasped my hand. I tried not to breathe so as to hear it all. "Cole had pushed risky investments—"

Mr. Roberts interrupted. "All investments are at risk."

"The ship *Carapace* went down in a hurricane, in sight of the *Oswego Carrier*. All hands lost, cargo sent to Davey Jones. The *Oswego* was lost coming into port. Fired upon by brigands in sight of the tower. Cole took his losses and absconded during the night last month. I've lost quite a sum, I don't mind telling you."

"Lost? All hands? And what, sir, do you know of the *Moravia*? She was armed as for war. Nothing or no one could take her."

The two men kept quiet for a moment. Then one ventured, "I'm sorry, sir, but I have never heard of that vessel."

Mr. Roberts's voice grew tight and rose. "But you are shipping men. I can tell by the cut of your coats. You know her. The *Moravia*. Think, man. It's most important."

"Unhand me, sir. I came to offer you friendly information."

"Yes, yes. Sorry. And Cole? You knew him?"

"Sorry to say we did. Both of us robbed by that gypsy fiend. If he is ever found he'll swing from a gallows if he's not tarred and feathered, first."

The other man added, "He's ruined four others in my acquaintance, sir."

Mr. Roberts entered the coach, ashen-faced and trembling. His mouth dribbled as he called to the driver to make haste to the solicitor's office. He rushed in, forgetting all propriety in seeing his wife and me through the doors. We made our own way indoors, to be seated in the anteroom for two hours while Mr. Roberts examined the lawyer and his assistants at length regarding his standings, his obligations, and his situation.

Mistress Roberts whispered to the air before her as she had done in the coach. "It seems no reason we shouldn't go ahead to the dresser's shop. Our appointment will be lost and I shall not be a welcome client then. He can take care of this business another day. He knew we had a most important errand today."

I said nothing. I sensed she knew little of his business dealings, nor could she read the disharmony upon his face. When at last Mr. Roberts emerged, he looked as if he had been beaten or had consumed ale all afternoon. He swayed upon his feet, grasping desks and railings for support. He said only, "Let's be going," without salutation or waiting for us to proceed ahead of him.

As I reached the door, the clerk, a young man in the office with a deformed shoulder, raised a finger, blackened with ink, toward me. "Are you the Miss Talbot residing with the Roberts family? I have letters for you." He leafed through a cubbyhole on his great desk. "Actually, one appears to be for you and one addressed through your concern to Mr. Roberts. Would you be so kind?"

"Of course," I said. The letters in my hands charged the air as if lightning had struck nearby. "Would you pardon my haste in reading them immediately, sir?"

He smiled at the use of "sir" and nodded, pointing with his good right arm to a small chair. I had barely sat when I tore loose the wax seal. The salutation concerned all the typical *"most gracious majesty's servant,"* and I brushed through that with my eyes, looking for word of my mother. Then I had to go back and read it again, for nothing in the heart of the letter was from her or about her at all. This was from the king's solicitor, now master of Two Crowns Plantation among six others in the West Indies, and concerned fighting off French and Dutch usurpers who would steal the land, and in the last phrase of the last sentence, *"due to the inconvenient loss of His Majesty George the II's previous conservator, the Right Honorable Allan Talbot."* Inconvenient? How the loss of my pa was inconvenient to the king troubled me not at all. Where was my mother? What of her escape? Had she found help among other plantation owners? Had he not looked or inquired of all the great houses in the parish? I slipped the seal of the other letter, and holding them side by side, at first they appeared identical, naught but the address was different. The one addressed to Mr. Roberts explained more than mine did, but it was significant, in that *"with all souls lost"* and *"the difficulty in defending the separate plantations from villainy, the plantation would escheat to the Crown. No compensation would be made to any claim on behalf of heirs."*

The coachman rapped at the doorjamb. "Miss Talbot? Mr. Roberts insists you make haste."

"Oh, indeed," I said, and followed him, having to bow under his upheld cloak. I climbed in, the close dampness adding to the crushed feeling in my heart. Mr. Roberts's face was so deep scarlet he seemed to be emanating steam from the damp curls of his wig. Mistress Roberts appeared concerned but confused. I bowed my head to be within my own thoughts, hiding my eyes behind the rim of my bonnet as the coach moved.

Mistress Roberts, after a great deal of throat clearing and fluttering behind a handkerchief, said, "May we continue to the dresser's, then?"

His answer was as much in sputter as it was in words. "What—of course—it cannot be—we are finished—this day—oh rue it. No."

Her face wore her disappointment as would a child's. In silence we rode for near an hour. I was not sure when I began to weep, but tears coursed my face freely, thinking of Jamaica. Of Ma. Of Pa and August. Patey. I raised my head to catch my breath and upon seeing me so encumbered with grief, Mr. Roberts himself burst into tears, sobbing and sighing. Perhaps he thought my grief was for his misfortune, though I knew it not fully, only that something had gone wrong with his shipping plans. Mistress Roberts wept also. When we arrived at their home, Mr. Roberts spoke to his wife as if she were a servant, saying, "Bring me port. Plenty of it. I must think." Then he closed himself in his study room, and while the rest of us supped, he called for another bottle of port.

Serenity and Portia chattered about Wallace, upset that their mother had not returned with samples of silks for a gown. I decided I must write another letter. I must inquire, perhaps through that solicitor, to the other great houses, and find to which my mother had retreated. I read the letters again at my dressing table. I should deliver the letter to Mr. Roberts, as that had been my intention before curiosity overtook me. "I opened it!" I said, startled at myself. The sealing wax was broken, half of it gone. Not enough remained to reseal it. There was no way to conceal that I had read it. The wax was still present on my letter, having been applied so that the bulk of it remained when I pulled the sheet open. I pried it loose with my fingernail, and holding it between two fingers over the candle flame, softened the back of it. Soon my fingers blistered, and I dropped the dab of wax. "Oh, la!" Now it was deformed and stuck to the table.

With a metal fingernail tool, I lifted it again and passed it over the flame, setting it on the ruddy place where the previous seal had been. It looked preposterous but it was sealed, drips marring the outer appearance so the whole thing seemed splattered by someone too unfamiliar with the task to be allowed in the king's service. Mr. Roberts, in his current state, might not notice. I would explain that in my excitement I had opened the wrong letter first. As I slipped the letter under the closed door of his study, I felt a great tug. I had betrayed my promise to myself not to be false. I tapped on the door.

"Enter." His appearance had changed markedly. He slouched in his chair, his wig on the desk at his elbow, port stains on his vest and coat, ink stains on his hands, and a great many paper rolls tumbling before him.

I retrieved the letter from the floor. "Mr. Roberts? I have received a letter from Jamaica. I opened it in my haste, before I realized it was addressed to you. I apologize, sir. It seems the current proprietor of Two Crowns Plantation did little other than confirm his presence there, rather than search the unscathed plantations for my mother's whereabouts—"

"Damn!"

I stiffened. "I am deeply sorry, sir. It was a lapse of my judgment."

"I don't want to hear about it. Close the door as you leave, Miss Talbot."

"Yes, sir," I said, as a servant would do.

"Wait! Hand me that! We are saved. That's it. We are saved! Now close the door, there. Be off. Good evening, Miss Talbot."

I placed the letter before him. My clumsy seal popped open. When I got through the door, Mistress Roberts was at my shoulder, dressed for bed and holding a candle. "What did he say?"

"Only to close the door."

"But what had he heard? What letter had you? Is this good or bad?"

I had no answer for her. All I knew was that it contained bad news for me. I said, "I know not, madam." She seemed so sad that I kissed her cheek as a daughter would, and bade her good night.

CHAPTER 16

May 2, 1736

The downstairs maid found Mr. Roberts first. It was noon when she braved entry into his study though he answered not at her knock upon his door. She was to be ever thankful, she told the constable and other men who came at Betsy's bidding, that as he swung from the beam, Providence had found it expedient that his distorted face turned toward the window rather than the door, or she might have lost her mind.

On the day Mr. Roberts was buried, spring gave way to light breezes and sunshine as golden and pleasing as a still-warm pie. There was discussion about his place of rest, but it was decided that his stature in the community deigned a consecrated plot near the church, for after all, they were not Catholics who purged those who for madness or sorrow ended their own lives. The entire town processed to the funeral.

Goody Carnegie, appearing as sound as any, greeted me with a wave and a smile of recognition.

"Good morning, Goodwife Carnegie," I said.

"Dearie! What a fine lass you are to remember me, Miss Talbot. How nice to see you, but such a sorrowful occasion. I am grieved at your loss."

"Thank you, Goody. How goes it with you?"

"Well enough. Well enough." She rolled her eyes a little. "Quiet, lately." An oriole chatter-sang overhead, perched on the edge of the church roof.

I smiled at her, seeing in myself a fondness for the poor dear, as I saw her tenderness, her brokenness. "Fair winds, then, and more quiet, for your future."

"Why, I thank you, dearie. Now, we should get back to mourning our fellow here."

As we stood alongside the grave and listened to prayers, robins chirruped heartily, larks and finches flittered with abandon, busy at nesting, and a black crow flew overhead, from north to south. I watched it go, rather than concentrating on the coffin below my feet. If I wast a blackbird, the song went, I would fly to the ship on which he sailed, find my love, and bow at his heel. If a blackbird could cross the sea, I prayed that one to Ma while they prayed Mr. Roberts to heaven.

Wallace returned and spring forced us to abandon our grief, for though we behaved with decorum, we could not deny the warmth or rousing thunderstorms or verdant fields and meadows alive with every form of life. Mistress Roberts sent for the dresser in Boston to come to their home and create a gown for Serenity. The cost would be paid on account, she said.

Serenity, Wallace, and I made it our business to go abroad in town twice a week or more, and to Boston for Serenity to have her gown fitted. That time we rode in the Spencers' new coach. While she was thus engaged, he and I sat in the coach and he moved from his seat facing mine to the empty one next to me. Though it was the warmest day yet, he pulled down the window coverings. "We are quite alone here," he said.

"Though much may be heard through those windows," I ventured. "Have you proposed to Miss Roberts, yet?"

"Do not toy with me, Miss Talbot. You know my intentions."

"I do. But does she? I trow that is her wedding gown she is fitting, and none other. She must be told. It is only right."

He said, "Alas for her. She may not marry for at least a year, with her father so soon dead." He smiled, took my hand and held it in his. When I made as if to take it away, he wrapped both his around mine so tenderly it made heat rise on my cheeks. "Ah. Perhaps you need some air."

"Perhaps," I said.

"Do you know my heart, Miss Talbot?"

"As it concerns Miss Roberts?"

"Silly goose. You know in days of old, a man and a woman would ply their troth by the fast holding of hands. It was a quite tender tradition."

"Along with a public blessing, it was. Here in this coach would not qualify, I believe. Tell me of your plantation in Virginia."

"Why don't I rather tell you of the other house I have purchased in Boston? It is that direction." He raised a hand across me to raise the window shade.

I followed his finger and turned my head. "Which one?" I turned back to him in case he had not heard me. As I turned, I found he had leaned in against me to better reach the window and was still in that place, so that his face was less than an inch from my own. I felt soft breath near my cheek, saw the lashes on his eyes, the delicacy of his chiseled lips, so near my own. I said, "I do wonder what is keeping Serenity."

"I bless whatever it is. The only serenity I shall ever know is in your presence."

My mouth was as dry as if I had breathed dust. "Sir, you must give me air."

In reply, he raised the hand with which he held mine, and kissed my fingertips, one at a time, while staring into my eyes. "I am bewitched by you, Miss Talbot. But surely you know that."

"Do not speak of this, Mr. Spencer, unless you will answer me in truth. Have you proposed marriage to Serenity? Have you let her believe you are intended for her?" I licked my lips, fighting the dryness of my throat.

"No to both questions. Naturally, their family and mine have been long acquainted, and as we are young people, it is customary to befriend—but let us talk of what I do have and wish. I have houses and land. I have horses and coaches to carry you about and servants ready to do your bidding. Will you marry me?"

I knew not whether it was because of the hesitation in my eyes, or in spite of it, but when his lips covered mine with such tender caress, such pure feeling, I let myself wilt, enfolded in his arms, and we stayed thus, our lips pressed tightly, for many minutes. When at last he pulled away, I sank, breathless, against his neck. The crisp-softness of his clothing, the enticing strength of his arms, the kiss I had just known, all seemed too much to think about. I could do no more than just stay right where I was for a hundred years. As I caught my breath, I said, "I will marry you, Wallace. As soon as I get to Jamaica and find my mother. When I return I will marry you. Providing you tell Serenity."

He pulled away, astonished. "That could take months."

"We are young. We have all the future. Come with me."

"Could you not send a letter and inquire?"

"I have tried. It served me not. Come with me. It will be a voyage to my past, and then I shall be yours for the future."

He seemed to be pondering this. "Dear Resolute. Dear one, do not place this yoke upon me, upon us and our future. This is too dangerous, too lengthy. I should not *allow* you to go, either. As an engaged person you will have certain responsibilities. I would have us marry this fall. You have often told me how the season suits you."

"We could marry in the plantation great house at Meager Bay. Ma would adore it." I clutched his hands and smiled my most beguiling smile at him.

"Kiss me again, and tell me you cannot wait all that time to be wed."

I kissed him again, and then pushed him away and said, "It is all I ask of you. Wait until I return, or *take* me to Jamaica. I have lived on no other wish for six years."

His breath came hard and fast, as if he had run to this place. His eyes seemed to have grown larger and darker, and he said, "When Miss Roberts is finished with her errand we will go to a shipping master and inquire. Now is the best time of year to travel. Marry in the West Indies? It seems the perfect solution. We would not have to tell Miss Roberts, not hurt her so greatly, just travel there with me as your escort, and marry there, and come back husband and wife as if it were a natural occurrence, the happy accident of travel. She will be much the less harmed and you will be out of their home and so will suffer no ill accusation. After their recent bereavement, it would seem cruel to break her heart, don't you agree? Of course you do. There, then. Dearest."

The door to the shop rattled the wee bell which overhung it. The heat in the coach, combined with the thought of traveling unmarried with him, left me near to fainting. "Raise the shade, please," I said.

"Of course." He reached across me again and planted a quick kiss on my forehead as he sat back in the seat across from me.

Serenity opened the coach door, all asmile. "Why, it is dreadful hot in here! Why did you have these closed on this side?"

Wallace said, "There were common people passing by and peering in as if we were a curiosity."

"Miss Talbot, I have brought you a gift." She placed a large round box in my lap. "I know it is soon after Father's death, but I saw it and thought of your fair coloring and knew it was the right thing to do. Please tell me you love it. If you don't I will get another, for I mean to give you something."

I opened the box, and feeling ever more guilt, I wept when I saw the delightful bonnet it contained. It was the newest fashion, small and costly, and in a shade called Prussian blue. "Oh, Serenity. It is exquisite!" As I sat, stunned, she put it on my head, tied the bow, and begged Wallace for his approval, which he gave with a nod, watching us all the time as a cat would watch two mice at play. When he informed her that our next stop would be one of the harbormasters, she did not seem at all disappointed. She was not happy about my going away, she declared, but made me promise to return and to write, which I did with some reservation and a twinge at my promise to myself about honesty. Serenity insisted she was happy to drive about with us, her best friends, all evening.

At the harbor office, though, Wallace bade us both sit in the coach where we opened the shades to get the ocean air; foul as it was with fishy smell and oils, at least it was cooler. When he returned, he said, "Miss Talbot, your passage is arranged. You leave on the *Aegean* in six weeks' time. She sails at high tide on June sixteenth or seventeenth. You must be here on the fifteenth."

I sighed so deeply I almost fainted. Home. Ma. Two Crowns. At last, at last. "How long will the voyage take?" I asked. "How shall it be paid for? What—"

"About two months. And think nothing of it. Anything you want onboard is already paid for. You will of course need a chaperone."

"And you arranged for me a cabin, not just a place in the hold?"

He laughed. "You have a cunning sense of humor, dear Miss Talbot."

Serenity took my arm and we hugged each other. I was happier than I knew I could be. So many wonderful things in a single day. I looked at Wallace and thought, Oh, my blessed betrothed, thanked him with my eyes and a small smile. We pulled away from the Neck talking of any and every thing and nothing of import.

Two days later, the Spencer family sent to me a gift of a traveling trunk for my voyage. When next Wallace called, I found myself surrounded by the Roberts family, with no chance of speaking to him privately. A game of whist, an afternoon tea, and a light breeze though it threatened of rain later, we girls were aglow with happy chatter. It was Herbert who caused everything to change. He came to Wallace, smirk on his face and hands on hips, and demanded an audience. "I will speak with you, Master Spencer," Herbert said, drawing himself up to his fullest.

Wallace said, "You address your elders as 'mister,' not 'master.' That is for boys. As yourself."

"I say, sir. I am now the man of this family. I just intend to know if you are going to marry Miss Talbot."

His sisters erupted in laughter. Serenity said, most condescendingly, "Herbert, that is not the type of question you ask an adult. You are far too impertinent." Uneasiness settled upon us all, then. Wallace excused himself early, before dinner, and his empty place already set at table seemed a burning firebrand in the room, a thing we could not explain or condone.

Before the pudding came out, I excused myself claiming a headache, but in truth it was my heart that troubled me. I promised them I would be recovered by morning if allowed to retire early. I had never before been given to fits of dramatic anguish, such as was common in this family. I had witnessed America Roberts throwing herself upon her coverlets and weeping, or the twins clubbing the floor with fists and feet and felt ashamed of them, yet I felt compelled to do just that. I supposed they were excused by their youth for such villainy, and composed myself to dress for bed and then sit at my dressing table and cry. A soft tapping at the door gave me to sigh, for I had no wish to discuss my sorrow, could not do so, for I knew not why I was disconsolate. "Please enter," I said.

Serenity opened the door. She had on her dressing gown of violet satin, the collar of which I had embroidered with lavish white and gold roses. "Why are you so disturbed? Was it because of what Herbert said? He is just a child, you know. You will find a love, someday. Wallace and I have been closest friends since we were children."

I felt my resolve for honesty melt like candle wax. "My mother is my only hope. At least you have yours here to be with you in any sadness or joy, to help you."

She made a sound, pursing her lips. "I never pictured Mother helping me. I hardly knew Father. He sat in his office and went to town. He treated us no better than he treated the servants. In truth I feel as if a great weight were lifted off my shoulders, not having to please him all the time when I never knew how."

I wept anew. "That is so—" I meant to say pitiful, but stopped the word. "Sad. My father was heroic and kind. He would sooner wink at me than scold me. It pains me now that I ever gave him distress."

"How sad for you."

I straightened in my seat. "If he had lived, I would never have suffered so."

She paced a bit, and then settled in the other chair, a cushioned wingback next to the fireplace. "What have you suffered? You seem so elegant. So knowledgeable. Two languages learned well, fine handiwork. Father told us nothing of whence you came, only that you were to be our ward. Only your want of returning to your homeland would suggest you were not as Bostonian as any of His Majesty's subjects."

"I have lived my life waiting to return home. I am going, thanks to Mr. Spencer."

A look of displeasure crossed her face, as if my saying his name were an affront to her. "He is most kind. You must have accompaniment, and protection. Perhaps Wallace and I should go. The West Indies? Could be adventurous. A memory to last all our lives."

"Serenity, I should tell you about Wallace and me."

"Tell me what?" She seemed to shrink into her clothing then, as if a blow had been dealt, a real blow, much closer to the bone than her father's death. "*He's* going with you? Is that it? But not I? Does he not intend to take me along? You have plotted behind my back, whilst I show you the tenderest affection?"

"I implore you, Serenity. I cannot deny our affections."

"Your affections? You have seduced Wallace? You cannot presume to speak for him as well for I have known him my whole life." She stamped one foot, rose and made for the door. My new bonnet hung on a hook near it. She clutched it and threw it toward the fireplace as she went out. One of the ribbons caught fire but I pulled it out before more damage was done.

Mistress Roberts came to me an hour later. "Your scheme will not happen. I have sent a letter to Lady Spencer with all the details. The only person who will convince me of it is young Wallace himself. I hope you know how ashamed I am of you. How sorry that we showed you all the kindness of family, to be repaid by this."

"Madam, he and I are quite in love."

"Love? What has that to do with it? Men have their dalliances. It means nothing compared to a proper marriage."

"But we will marry. In Jamaica."

"You shall not. He has promised Serenity. Even if you travel as a paramour with him and go around the world, you shall not marry him."

After that night, my presence in their house was tolerated but coldly. I made a promise to myself to suffer any bitterness until I could leave. For a few more days, I could stand anything.

Three days later, when Mistress Roberts's personal serving maid unbolted the door to a knock in the morning, I thought nothing of it until I happened to look up from my packing and see out the window. A file of eight uniformed men on horseback waited in two lines under the carriageway. It was too intimate a place for a cadre of uninvited soldiers. I joined the Roberts daughters on the stairway as Mistress came into the receiving parlor. We heard shouting, Mistress crying out. Betsy and Tipsie ran down the stairs and I followed close on their heels with Serenity, America, Herbert, and Henry.

The boys darted between us to plant themselves squarely in the midst of their mother and the men with whom she argued. Between Mistress Roberts's cries and the sobbing of the staff and daughters, what we learned was that Mr. Roberts had put up his house against the promised boon from a ship that did not exist. The Roberts family had been cheated out of everything by Peterson Cole, who before the ink was dry had sold the wager to another and disappeared. The new owner, Mr. Barrett, had called in the debt and was taking possession of the house and all its contents. We were to be put into the street that very day with what personal effects we could carry. Mistress begged for more time, but the man in charge told her she had already been given two months in which to make things right.

I ran to the carriage house. After I pleaded with the groom, he drove me to Lord Spencer's mansion on the finest avenue in Boston. I walked inside the cool entrance, breathing in the smells of wood and coffee, rum, tobacco, and old wool carpets. It smelled like home.

I followed the butler to where Wallace sat reading in a drawing room furnished in shades of umber, so dark that it needed candles lit at noon. "Oh, my dear," I said when I saw him. I ran to him and knelt at his knee. "There is terrible news at the Roberts home."

Wallace raised one hand. "Bring us tea, Oswald."

When Oswald left, I said, "They are to be turned out."

Then he faced me. "Turned out?"

"Soldiers came this morning with a magistrate and constable. Mr. Roberts had lost everything to the Seaman's Mercantile. The owner is calling in the debt, taking the house. Mistress Roberts has to leave immediately and will be guarded so that they take nothing of value." My heart was not brought down for them, for I had my own life ahead of me. I had Wallace ahead of me. I would be in the arms of my mother in two months or less.

"Are you asking me to take it on? You know, do you not, that I am dependent. I could not ask my father to assume such a debt."

"I am asking you to marry me now. Take me off their hands. We are promised. Let us marry and be wed, and they will have that much less with which to concern themselves. When I am come to Jamaica, my estate will be yours. Then if you agree with my wish to help them, we shall be able to do it."

Wallace grew still and silent. He lost all his merry ways and gentle looks. He said, "There's one thing to be said for changing horses in the middle of the lane."

Oswald appeared carrying a tray. I poured tea into the delicate porcelain cups. "What do you mean?" I asked.

"Nothing. Tell me how it happened, for I have been so busy preparing our new lives I gave it no thought at all. I knew the old man had a weak heart. It was spoken about town. He was known, you know, among *our* circles."

"His heart did not fail him. His financial partner did."

"I insist on knowing, dear one."

"I thought you knew and were just being polite. He hanged himself from a rafter in his study. Hard to believe the servants have not passed that around the town."

"Lord," he said, and downed the last of the tea in his cup.

I reached for his hand and he took it as I said, "Yes."

"They were notified today, this very day, you said, yet the magistrate insisted they had had prior knowledge? I must go there at once."

"I came in their carriage."

"Wait for me in the hall."

I felt hurt by his brusque tone, but thought of Mr. Roberts's manner of speaking. Perhaps it was the way with these New Englanders.

At the Roberts estate, soldiers stood by each door to the outside. Wallace marched past them as if they were curtains, going straight into Mr. Roberts's study. He sat at Mr. Roberts's desk and leafed through papers, tossing down one after the other, causing the stack to collapse. The letter from the solicitor of Two Crowns slid to the floor with several others. If I were to write to him directly, bypassing the use of the lawyers at Foulke and Harrison, I would need it. I put it in my pocket. By then the rest of the family had entered the room and he came up with one written in Mr. Roberts's hand, a sort of apology for the state of his affairs, and another from Mr. Barrett's solicitor dated two months prior. I said, "It is late, Wallace. There is nothing you can do."

Wallace turned a stern countenance to me as if he were a father, or worse, a master, and said, "Do not pretend to know what I am about. It makes you unseemly. A man's bride must not presume to know his business." Serenity gasped, threw her hands to her mouth, and ran out, sobbing. Her sisters and mother shrieked and followed her.

I felt chastened as if Birgitta had thumped me with her stick. My heart wrenched in its place, tears welled, and I felt shocked. "Of course not," I said.

He managed a smile but I could see through my own tender feelings that it strained him to do so. "First lesson. When it comes to business, you mind your tatting."

Why they let Wallace go through their father's and husband's papers, scattering them as any mouse searching for crumbs might do, I surmised was the result of years of convincing that anything a man said or did was not to be questioned. I wondered then if I would ever have the patience to bear such indignity as they, and with such peaceful countenance. Was it true what Patey had said about needing a man for business? I hoped his sharp tone was due to his concern for the family.

Finally, he held up a sheet of paper and said, "So it is the Honorable Alexander Barrett who has claimed this house."

Mistress Roberts returned in time to hear his last words. Her face streaked with tears, she held a kerchief to her mouth. Her hair hung in frenzied coils, her fichu askew.

"I don't know how he could do this," I said.

"Legally," Wallace said. "That's how. That rascal gypsy Cole no doubt convinced both men the risk and the ship were real, took the cash, and left. Now Barrett has no other option but to foreclose to recover his losses." He stood and straightened his coat, moving toward the door.

"But," Mistress Roberts asked, "could he not see we've lost everything if he takes this house? Where will we live? How shall we eat?"

I said, "Could you speak to Mr. Barrett for Mistress Roberts? Or introduce her to him so she could ask for the house?"

Wallace's eyes searched mine. His expression told me I had overstepped yet again. He glared at me while addressing her. "I will see what I can do, Madam."

Mistress Roberts hugged her daughters joyfully, one after the other, praising Wallace even as he made his way out the front door. He borrowed a horse and rode back to town, leaving me there with no further words. She thanked me for bringing him there, though she caught herself in midsentence. "Though I am still peeved at you for taking him from my Serenity. If it weren't for you, we should have no fear at all of losing this house."

I said, "I assure you with all my heart, if I could have stopped our falling in love, if I could have known, if I could have saved Serenity—"

Serenity had returned, and now stood behind me. "Oh stop," Serenity said. "If you believe what you say, then walk back into that woods whence you came and never return. Leave him to me where he belongs."

"Would you have me out on the street?" I asked, cursing the plaintive note in my voice. I had wished to remain aristocratically above begging.

"Yes!" cried Serenity. "We are all on the street because of you, you witch."

"No!" cried Betsy, America, and Herbert.

Finally, red-faced, Mistress Roberts added, "*We* are not as those who would throw someone out into the street. Now we are to become beggars among our friends."

I squared my shoulders and walked up the stairs to finish packing the trunk the Spencers had supplied me. It was full of clothing that the Robertses had purchased. In it were also my petticoat and Patience's apron. I took those from my folded garments and bundled them into my two smaller parcels.

One of the footmen carried my trunk down. I carried two hatboxes and my parcels. I bade farewell to a maid. She said, "How elegant, your ladyship. It's like you was in a story falling in love with a prince. He's ever so elegant. You shall be very happy."

If happiness was measured in money, I shall, I thought. I wished Donatienne were here to talk with. Will I be happy with Wallace? I wondered. His kiss, just the memory of it, sent trills rippling over me, as if I had leaped into a cold stream and a warm bed at the same time. Was not desire also the promise of a blissful marriage? "Yes, I shall, I expect," I said, pushing from my mind the image of a yew tree and Patience beneath it.

Mistress Roberts saw me by the trunk and shouted across the drive, "And not a tender word to our guest about love or devotion, no! Just a quick order. Oh, a fine life she'll lead, charged around like any alewife and full of child while he goes riding about the countryside."

I said nothing but closed my ears to her taunts, satisfied that it was justified, and partly the voice of a childish old woman who did not understand Wallace, or my love.

In the midst of wails that reminded me of my capture by the pirates, the Roberts women and two boys were pushed outside with what clothing and sundries they could carry in their arms. The servants were also put out to try their best at finding a new position. The soldiers made sure we were not pilfering the silver or gold ware. A rider came, a messenger. The master of the guard took the note first, and then gave it to Mistress Roberts. She wept anew. "Children? My children, we have no hope. We are out. We will go to my cousin Alora's house in Cambridge. *She* is fond of me, I think."

The coach Wallace sent for me arrived in the midst of turmoil. I asked the coachman to drive the Robertses to their cousin's home in Cambridge. They packed themselves in it so we were crushed like candles in a box. On the way I tried to assure them that they would not perish. They would have to find a new way to live, that was all. I said what Patey had told me, adding words of my own advice, "Be clever. Watch always, see what is around you and care for each other. That is your best hope." All I accomplished was sending them into gales of tears. I left them at the door of a modest house, three stories tall, with neat and well-kept vegetable gardens on the south and west sides, and some very surprised relatives. I knew enough of the raising of food to see that these gardens were a substantial boon for any family, and that they would fare better than many others might in their situation.

It was late afternoon when I arrived at the shipping office near the harbor. My dear Wallace swept me into his arms with a freedom from propriety that astonished me. It felt daring, bold, as if our passion were unleashed. We ate beef pies with beer, our last meal on land for quite a while. The ship would sail on the morning's tide at seven. After we chatted about possible food aboard the ship, I asked, "Where shall we sleep this night?"

"Here on the bench, I suppose, with the others." Then he laughed and said, "We'll away to my house, have a proper supper at eight, a nice bed, and Barnes will awaken us in time to come back. On a bench? I believe you would have done it, you silly goose."

I said, "Oh, you were teasing? It would be no worse than some nights I have spent, and better than others."

The grin on his face turned to stone, just for a moment. Then he looked down at his lap and back to my face, his smile as warm as ever. "Tell me about those places. Since having disappointed the Roberts family with the prize of a rich husband for one of theirs, I have heard a great many libelous and bilious rumors regarding your past."

"I know nothing of their rumors but I will gladly tell you the truth. I was captive almost six years. Hardly a life of crime and thievery."

"Captive? As in a story? By whom? Tell me."

"No, not as in a story. My family was torn from our home by Saracen pirates. Then the ship was taken by English privateers. My brother made to be part of them, my father killed, my mother abandoned. My sister, Patience, and I were sold as slaves in a colony of Reformed Puritans, and then captured again."

"Slaves!" His eyes formed narrow slits, just as a cat, half asleep, watching, waiting. "But you are educated."

"I was beaten and starved so that I thought I might die. I was captured by Indians and taken to the Canadas where French nuns made me work in fields until I was sunburned and sore, then work at a loom day in and day out for a crust of bread and a bit of thin soup. I was educated there. All that is behind me now."

"But, you seem—you have every appearance of aristocracy. The right hair, the perfect form and size. And you were a slave?" He said it with such revulsion I felt shame.

I wanted to explain, to tell him what I had endured to come to the place where I was, and how enduring it had shaped me. "I was. It was terrible. This is a good time to tell you, also, that I would have it that we keep no slaves, ever. I will not own anyone but myself."

"As a slave, did you have to perform everything you were told to do?"

"Of course."

"Did your master require you?"

"Every sort of work. Milking goats. Washing and carrying for their lazy daughters. He made me charge his pipe."

"I know something of what a slave is to do. He made you do what to his pipe?"

"So he could smoke it."

"And did you?"

"Yes, quite often. I met one fine man there. Reverend Johansen. He was ever good to me. He spoke to me so kindly. I was glad of his friendship but of course when we were carried away to the Canadas, he could help me no longer. He died recently."

"I see. What other men were there?"

"Even though the house was so tiny, people stayed overnight often. We had to sleep one upon the other. Lukas Newham claimed to love my sister but he was false. Some others were gentlefolk. Even my master, though I hated him and he beat me, was so kind to his children. You should have seen him when Lonnie fell into the fire. Birgitta beat me, too. They went to the wilderness to form their own town. That is where the Indians took us. They made us walk for over a month."

"Indians took you? Barbaric! What did *they* do to you?"

"Often they carried us. They were not so terrible as you might think."

"I dare *not* think of it, dear one." He took a long, last drink, finishing off his tankard of beer. "This is very sad news, indeed. Very sad."

I laid my smallest bundle on the table before me. Upon it, tied so that I could reach it quickly, were the two letters, one to me and one to Mr. Roberts. "But I am alive, Wallace. And I love you. That is all that matters, now."

"What is that you have, Miss Talbot, my dear? Did you write me a love letter?"

"No, though I should have liked to had I thought of it. These contain two addresses of the solicitors in Jamaica to whom I shall apply for my estate."

"Apply? Why must you apply for it? Let me see them. I am already so distressed hearing your tale that I can hardly bear more. Why did you not bring them to me so that I could take care of this for you? You know you have no head for business. May I?"

"Of course," I said, and pulled them both from the bundle. "I merely wanted to have the office names so that when we get there I might find them."

As he read, his face lost its warmth and he pursed his lips. He made a fist with one hand and read the letter again.

"It is rather complicated," I began.

He raised his hand to quiet me. "Wait here," he said.

"Where are you going?"

"Business. I must check into this. Wait here for my return." He dropped two shillings on the table as payment for our repast.

"Yes, of course," I said, watching the coins twirl in ever shrinking circles, closing, closing, until they collapsed, one upon the other.

"Wait for me, here," he repeated. He stood and adjusted his hat.

"All right. I will wait for you, Wallace." Then he was gone.

An hour wore past, then another. Finally the publican himself told me to either order food and drink or wait by the door. I had one look at the two women standing by the door, speaking to each man who arrived or left, and told the man I would have another beef pastry, and that Wallace would pay for it when he returned any moment. I asked him to see if Wallace's coach still waited outside, for I might wait at his home.

"No coach," he called from the doorway, and went back to his stew pot and kegs.

I listened as a watchman called out the hours. At midnight, the inn was empty and the publican came again, this time not so politely, saying, "Time you was making your way on the street."

"I cannot," I said. "I promised Mr. Spencer I would wait right here. He will return any moment. I believe I hear his horse now."

"You has been put out. Are you blind as well as thick? And I be putting you out again. G'out there and find a brick to stand on. You be 'ant g'ang to fetch that half a crown what left earlier."

I pulled myself up. "You shall not address me in so vulgar a manner. I am betrothed to Wallace Spencer of the Boston and Virginia Spencers."

"I'll address yer ladyship anyhow I be want to do. Out with you, wench."

He raised his hand to strike me, and I took up my parcel and bundle. Wallace had put our trunks in the harbormaster's office, but my petticoat and apron with hidden treasures I kept by my side always. Whether the man might have struck me, I would not know, but I was cast out the door into shadows and smells that turned the world back into my deepest and most hideous nightmares.

People clutching each other passed by me, the smell of drink hard on them. Where there were two men they were singing. Where there was a man and a woman, they performed coarse teasing and fondling of each other before my eyes.

At long last the watchman returned, and I called to him.

"Get off with ye!" he shouted. "I got no truck with hoors."

"Please, sir, I beg. Find a magistrate for me. A wagoner. Or take me with you to someplace safe. I need to board the *Aegean* by five in the morning, there to wait for my betrothed husband."

"Fah! Betrothed cuckled worm!" he said and held his lantern over my face.

I tried to still my fears and plead to him with my eyes. "I was to await him here where we ate supper, but he has been detained. Please help me, sir."

"Ye ain't a doxy. No, I can see ye ain't. And right here? Awaiting his lordship? With no carriage or trap? What kind o' folk are ye? Be ye fair?"

"Fair? I suppose some have called me thus."

"And if I take ye to the ship ye'll do mischief to her sails and her crew, and toss 'em over for changelings and selkies."

I smiled. I knew whereof he spoke. "I meant other than what you speak, sir. I have fair hair and skin, but I hold no enchantments, only hopes. I want to get home to the island of Jamaica. My beloved promised me that I should be allowed to see her before we marry and he has arranged us both passage on the *Aegean*. She sails at dawn."

"That she does. All right. Blast me but I believe ye. Follow me."

I supposed later that I had been a fool. That this stranger could have led me anywhere he chose to be ravished and murdered in a thousand different ways. I trusted him for no reason I could name then or later and, gratefully, I ended up at the harbormaster's office where a sleepy clerk gave me his seat. I reached into my pocket for a penny for the watchman's effort, but he refused it.

"I still be not certain ye're real. I will take nothing from ye, miss, which might bring me a pot o' trouble until I can get rid of it."

"Your kindness has saved me," I said, and leaning toward him, I kissed his whiskery cheek.

He huffed and puffed like a teakettle, then went out the door, turning first to the right, then left, and went whistling on his way.

A hand jostled me awake, my head banging the wall behind me as I opened my eyes. "Miss? Are you boarding?"

"Yes," I said, rubbing my eyes. "Yes. Is Mr. Spencer here? We are to board the *Aegean*."

"You'll have to wait here for him, then," the man said. "Just better stay awake."

Five came and the sun rose at half past. Six came and I could see a great ship in its mooring, gangways crawling with men loading her as fast as any could. My heart beat the time, minutes, minutes, seconds more. The loading seemed to slow. Panic filled my soul. I took my parcels in my arms and hurried down the dock. A stern, loud-voiced man stood at the nearest gangplank, writing things on a paper held on a small wooden board. "Passenger?" he barked at me.

"Yes, sir. My name is Miss Talbot of Two Crowns Plantation, Jamaica. I am traveling escorted by Mr. Wallace Spencer."

He looked over his papers. "Spencer? That name is removed. Talbot? No passenger by that name."

"What do you mean, removed? Please, sir, look again."

"We have five passengers. No Talbot. Spencer was registered as 'gentleman and wife' here but fare is rescinded. Have ye the fare?"

"How much is it?"

"Fifteen pounds ten will get you there without starving."

I gasped. I had less than a third of it in coin. I thought of the pearls.

The brooch. Home. "I could get it if you will wait for me. I will find a jeweler."

"We sail with the tide, come hell or high water."

"Would you buy pearls? Trade them for the fare?"

"Mayhap. I'd have to see 'em. Who's going with you?"

"No one."

"No unescorted women. If you wasn't a whore afore you got here, you'd be one by time you made the bay in Kingston. This is no place for you. Go on home now." He proceeded to go down his list and call orders to people who could not have heard him, ignoring me as if I were just another plank of wood before him.

I dashed toward the office. There I spied my trunk outside the door. A paper tag fluttered from one of the locks. I took it up to see my name there, with *Aegean* under it, a black waxy *X* marked through the entire thing. My pleas to the harbormaster to take my pearls brought me nothing. I turned from him in tears.

An hour later calls of "Away! Away!" came through the doors and windows, and the whole human population of the docks rushed to see the *Aegean* depart. Her sheets fluttered with the sound of a flock of thousands of birds. They caught the slightest breeze and filled, making a wake in the harbor. "No!" I called. "Oh, Wallace, where are you? Our ship is leaving without us!" None could hear my cries over the din of voices. My life was shattered. Where was my beloved? He must have been set upon by vagabonds or highwaymen, or perhaps his horse stumbled in the dark, leaving him dying in a field. I felt almost aswoon with panic. Where was he? I watched the *Aegean* until she vanished in the mist. Land across the harbor made all ships turn to meet the open sea and for a moment I saw sails reappear. When they faded from view, so did all my hopes. I sat upon the trunk and fought away tears.

After a time, I straightened my shoulders and told the man in the office I would return for the trunk. I meant to go to Wallace's home and make sure he had not perished. I stopped a coachman. "How much to get me to Boston?"

"Where is your husband?"

I rolled my eyes. "I haven't one, yet."

He whipped his team and moved away with a clatter.

I hugged my parcels and walked, getting away from the docks being my only thought. I walked past buildings which hours before seemed sweet with promise. Now they were filthy dungeons full of vile people. Not at all sure I was going the right direction, I made my way through the streets of Boston until I turned down a narrow lane and saw the familiar sign of Foulke and Harrison. As my hand touched the door, I knew that without Wallace, I would still find a way to get home. I opened the door sheepishly, to find the crippled young man there at his desk, writing something in a beautiful hand, copied from a terribly scratched note.

He looked up and smiled, saying, "Good morning, Miss Talbot."

"Hello, sir. I am sorry; I know not your name."

"Daniel Charlesworth, Miss Talbot. At your service."

"Mr. Charlesworth, is Lawyer Foulke in?"

"No, I'm sorry. At court, probably all day."

"Oh, that is unfortunate. For me."

"Is there something I might help with? I am reading law, and I understand confidentiality. Of course, I am but a clerk, and if you'd wish to—"

"Oh, would you?" I pulled the letter addressed to Mr. Roberts, unfolded it, smoothed it. Wallace had left it crumpled on the floor when he left. "You see, I wanted to get home. Home to my father's plantation, that is. Something has just occurred." There, I paused, fighting tears. "Please tell me what this means, this word here." I pointed to "escheat" and watched him move his lips as he read and reread the paragraph.

"'Escheat' means it moves to a former claimant. Essentially, the king has withdrawn ownership of the plantation from your family and has taken it back in his possession, to do with as he wishes. Your father, being deceased, has no further claim."

"What about my mother? She is alive. What about me?"

"It does not recognize heirs. If your mother was not in possession of it when the solicitor arrived, she has no claim, either."

"I have a brother."

"Where is he?" Mr. Charlesworth's face brightened.

I could not tell him August Talbot was gone to be a vagabond privateer and might be long dead, too. "He went to sea," I said. "I know not."

Mr. Charlesworth's expression mimicked the sinking of my heart. I saw then that he was quite young, little older than I. "Oh," he said. "If he could be found, there is a chance, with a suit against the king's exchequer, not with a great possibility to win, mind you, but perhaps possession could be returned. I think Mr. Foulke would advise you to go on with your life and give that property up to the hands of Providence."

"Going home to Two Crowns Plantation is all I have lived for, for six years. My mother is there."

"The plantation is not, however, in her possession."

"How much would a suit cost against the exchequer?"

"Several hundred pounds."

My shoulders slumped and I turned away. I saw in my mind's eye Wallace reading that letter again, my imagination renewing the memory as if it had occurred in broad daylight rather than a smoky seaside tavern. I had told him of my past and he had shuddered. I had shown him the letter about my future and he had left me. Had his love been for me or for an estate in the West Indies? I turned to Daniel Charlesworth's open, kind face and knew. Wallace had desired my dower more than my lips. I tried to still them from trembling. "You are so kind to have helped me, Mr. Charlesworth."

He smiled, and an endearing kindness glowed in his eyes. "Not at all. Please come back if you decide to pursue the suit."

"I shall. Thank you."

After another hour of walking, I was back at the reeking wharves, piers, and noise of the seaside. Was it my fate to be as wanton and depraved as Patey? As Christine? Wandering the wharves begging a coin? In that hour, I had laid out the events surrounding these letters again and again, and saw clearly that Mr. Roberts had expected I would have money, an estate, parents to whom he could apply for remuneration of my expenses at least, perhaps even a way out of his debt if my father were a peer of the realm. When I had approached him with the epistle, his hopes were dashed with that word "escheat," as were mine. He took off his dressing gown sash and stepped off his desk into eternity.

I walked into one harbormaster's billet after another, leaving note after note on paper torn from the letter and nailed to the wall, stating, *"August Talbot. I am in Lexington. Resolute."*

CHAPTER 17

June 16, 1736

I inquired of every person with a chaise or wagon I could stop, whether they might be on their way to Lexington. A man driving a small cart with a woman on the seat beside him offered to carry me across the Neck to Mistick, sitting upon sacks of oysters. Three shillings.

"Two," I said. "It is all I have left." It was an easy lie. If they knew I had more it would cost more.

"If all you have is two shillings, why do you want to go to Mistick? Why don't you just throw yourself into the sea?" the woman asked, and laughed.

The man said, "Oh, leave her alone, woman. We don't want to go to Mistick, either. I have to take those oysters in the cart to sell. I hate the things, meself. You can ride for two shillings, then. We are going to Lexington, only my woman there meant to hold you up for another shilling, you being dressed so fine."

"I would it were possible. I could give you another penny, if you would like."

"We would like, your highness," the woman said, and cackled. She had no teeth at all. "Pass it over."

I climbed upon the sacks of shellfish and handed her a penny. A distant thunderstorm lit up the sky in random sheets of lightning accompanied by the sound of heaven itself tearing open. We reached the Lexington-to-Concord lane as it began to sprinkle. "It will be good for the oysters but not for the horse," the man said. By the time we made the town limits, the rain was fast upon us. In its wailing winds, I heard Goody Carnegie howling. The man and the woman crossed themselves several times and began saying Our Father aloud. I thought, Catholics in this Protestant place. They would not show their real selves without a great deal of fear. When I tried to tell them not to be afraid of poor Goody, they looked on me as if I were mad, too.

"Why are you not afeard?" the man demanded. "Are you a witch?"

"I told you never to pick up a stranger!" the woman said, and beat him three good whacks about the head.

I was wet to the skin, exhausted, abandoned, and terrified. I held by my promise to myself to be honest and in control of my mouth but I had no reason to curb my bravery. I said, "What is there to be afraid of? It is a storm. More I should be afraid to be in the hands of strangers. You make the signs of papists and I know what dangers lurk there." At that moment a woman's moan split the air and was followed by a clap of thunder that made their horse bolt and fart and nearly jarred me from my seat.

"Do you not hear the cries of the madwoman?" the man asked, shaking his horsewhip at me.

"I hear," I said. "I am not afraid."

The woman hissed at me and held a twig broken and bent into the shape of a cross before her, waving it about. At last they pulled up before a public inn. Light flowed from the windows carrying merry, drunken singing that seemed to chase away the worst of the storm. She slurred at me, "Get off. We've carried you longer than your shillings and a penny allowed."

"For the travel I thank you," I said, "but for the insults I do not. Will you be purchasing a meal here in this inn?"

"Will we not be shed of you if we do?" she asked.

"I only want shelter from the rain, same as you. I will stay far from you both, and I will tell *no* one *you are Catholic.*" Fear passed between them with a shared movement of their eyes to each other and to me.

I followed them inside though I could not imagine spending a night in such a place. Even Goody Carnegie had warned against it. It was vulgar and foul and I pushed to one side away from the oystermongers. The innkeeper would allow me a seat on a bench, and shoved a man, drunk and smelling of a latrine, onto the floor. "I shall be happy for that, sir," I said.

"What of your parents, there?"

I looked where he pointed to the oyster man and woman. He had assumed we were a family. I was tired of being angry and sharp-tongued, tired and sore of heart in every fiber of my being and did not wish to correct him. I sighed and said, "Those two? They are angry with me. I left to marry a man and they brought me all the way from Boston in the storm before I did. I have learned my lesson. Please be kind to them though they shun me."

He nodded. "Aye. I've a daughter almost your age. I am glad they caught you before you made a crashing mess of your life. You must not be a bad sort to admit it." He took them each a cup of ale and a small bun, with his compliments, he said. They looked upon the offering warily, then their eyes turned to me. I nodded, then leaned my head against the wall and in the revelry of the inn's drunken din, I slept.

I awoke and left the inn at dawn. Before I had walked half a mile, the toe gave out on one of my shoes and mud crept in between my toes. I reached the familiar—Lexington's center cobbled street—then came to the avenues branching it where there were finer houses. Beyond that, a few more houses, two cross streets, and I turned down the lane where the Roberts had lived. Rather than soldiers at the gate, there were liveried footmen. Mr. Barrett had moved in. No such grandeur had been the Roberts legacy, even when they thought they were well off. I wondered if Serenity had taken that costly wedding gown with her as she fled.

I gathered my courage and approached the door, ignoring the footmen as was proper. Not having a stick I rapped at the knocker. A butler came at once. "Miss Talbot of Two Crowns Plantation to see Mr. Barrett," I said.

The butler peered down his nose to right and left for sign that I was accompanied, as a lady should be, yet he continued, unperturbed. "This way, Miss Talbot."

Once he had closed the door, he said, "Is Mr. Barrett expecting you?"

"No, I fear not," I said. "I lived in this house, you see, as a ward of the Roberts family. Of course, I had no idea they were in such peril. I came to inquire if he would assume my wardship. I have clothing. I have means. I have only the need of a roof until I get home, for which I shall be waiting only until sailing weather. May I speak with him?"

"I shall see if he is at home."

The man left. Of course, he meant "at home" to me. If Barrett had no intent of seeing me, he would not be home. And he was not. I looked into the butler's eyes for a sign of understanding. They were cold as a January morning as he closed the door to me.

On the road, every man or woman I encountered was too occupied to bid me the day. I remembered when I had first come, how although Goody Carnegie might have been considered a madwoman to be feared, she was able by request to cause a meeting of a council, and to find me a place to stay. If she were not tired from her night of howling, she might at least tell me where to go next. If Wallace loved me, surely he would be searching for me. How was I to save myself now? Would he not think kindly of me as I thought of this poor woman? I only need awaken in him a bit of pity for my circumstances.

It took me another hour to find her house. The storm had torn a large tree loose from the roots, smashing it across the Concord road that ran to the northeast. At last, I found her, sitting before her fire weeping as if her heart had been broken, her door ajar, leaves, dirt, whole branches, even a dead bird blown in by the winds. The gale had tattered her table and filled every cup with sand and grime. I knew not whether she were really mad. I knew not how to speak to a person who was so. I put my bundles on the floor, sat upon one, and waited.

The old woman rocked on her stool, moaning, crooning, *"Fawn-de-la, nah greit. Muirneach my babe, bye-baby-bye. Cush-nah, babe."*

"I am so sorry, dear Goody," I said in a low whisper.

She looked startled. "She was so bonny, my babe. So winsome and merry."

"How lovely she was," I said, nodding as if I knew. "Just a small child?"

"Yes. Small as a puppy. Tiny like her great-grandmother. A wee bairny."

I stiffened. I had not heard that word in so long. "Are you better now?"

"I am, dearie. Usually after such a storm I have to weep until I can weep no more. You have broken that part of the curse."

"I have done almost nothing, Goody Carnegie, except believe you. Is it your child, the one whom you mourn?"

"My only child. My wee one. My very heart I would give for her."

"And you did."

She looked upon me, startled, and a glimmer of a smile appeared at her lips. "Aye. I did that. Heart and mind, of mine, both went into the grave with her. Would you have some tea? It *is* a mess in here." She arose and started dumping sand and leaves from the teacups. "I haven't put the kettle on this morn."

"I will help you, if you like." I meant to be reserved, to keep everything hidden and held, both my shame at being treated so by Wallace, and my guilt in taking his love, if the fault were partly mine, from Serenity. By the time we had breakfasted on tea and bread—I did not tell her my cup had sand in it—I had explained what happened in more detail than I intended. In all of it, Goody Carnegie remained quiet and thoughtful. I wondered if perhaps she could not comprehend my words. Finally, I said, "I need an honest way to earn thirty pounds or more. I want to go home to Jamaica."

"She is not there."

"Madam?"

Goody shook her head. "Nothing. I get things mixed sometimes, now and long ago. I see it as if it is happening right before my eyes again and again. Sometimes when I awaken I am in a different place than when I lay down."

I nodded as if this made perfect sense though I did not understand at all. I supposed she had not heard me. I said, "At your word, men in this town gathered and listened to me. You must have some influence. I have no right to ask your help but I fear I have made enemies and there is no one else I know. Some might help out of Christian charity; some would not for the same reason. There are people here very devout and others up the road who thought I was a fairy."

"They only listen because they are afraid. That's the Boyne family. The old man and woman. Their son went down a well and they believe it was fairies did it. Or I."

"I am afraid my reputation is a rat's nest already. I know no one who would trust me save yourself. I have some skills, though. I sew, embroider. I can spin and weave, too. If you know someone who would take me in as a servant, paid, so that I could save fifteen pounds—"

"You can? Here I thought you were a lady."

"I am."

"I meant not that way." She scratched her head ferociously. Her hair was matted and snarled, looking like a giant gray animal perched atop her head. "Well, you *could* live here with me but you wouldn't want to and I would not want it, either. I get too sad, and I fret, and talk to myself and to people who are not here, but I think of them then I talk to 'em. I could not pay you but I could give you the other house to live in. Come here." With that, she was off, marching up the road, her hair flying in the damp morning.

I grabbed my parcels and dashed to catch up with her as she prattled on and on. "At least you'd have a roof. I don't live there, o' course. Haven't since the time of my sorrows, and won't ever again. It is haunted, you see, and sometimes the spirits in there chase me, when it is raining heavy. They won't bother you; it's me they come for. If I could move away to another country I would, to be free of them."

"But how would I earn money?"

"I'll show it to you."

The day went sultry before we had gone a quarter mile. I pictured that perhaps she was taking me to one of the ramshackle hovels I had passed before I got to the Boynes' house. Goody Carnegie turned up a lane which climbed a small hill and circled it. I was hard put to keep up with her, for her nightly jaunts must have put strength in her legs, or else it was true what I had heard that sometimes the mad are unearthly strong.

"Much farther?" I asked, when she came to an abrupt halt.

"Here it is," she exclaimed. I saw nothing but a pile of old leaves on a heap of ivy. At one length, an embankment of stone came from the earth, and next to that some stones had been laid so that I saw there was once a wall. She smiled, her grin higgledy-piggledy with missing teeth. "Help me push away some of this frittery." As we worked, uncovering I knew not what, she gained strength, and happiness began to color her countenance. "Oh, it was where I dreamed of being, always. A bonny house."

Sure enough, after some tugging and disturbing a large wood rat, a stone wall came out of the leaves, here a corner, there a window grown about with ivy, and at last a wooden door, shorter than my chin.

"Of course," Goody said, "there is a hole or two in the roof. You'll need a thatcher."

I strained to look through the doorway to see anything of a house before me, feeling that she was so unhinged she may have seen this as a palace, indeed. The small square of stone was built into the side of the hill, using the granite outcropping as part of the wall on one side. It was stuffed with rubble, old furnishings, rags, nests, and the smell of various kinds of vermin. I backed out, and as I touched the door it fell from its one remaining hinge, stirring up a cloud of leaves and dust within.

I held the doorjamb and my heart gave a great thump. Over the center of the doorway above my hand, an icon was affixed to the frame. It was a horseshoe, hammered narrow, small enough to fit a young colt. Cast in iron and forged atop it, a spider. Its legs held the sides of the horseshoe, its head pointed down at the open doorway. "It is the sign of a weaver," I whispered to no one in particular, perhaps to the spider itself. Had I gone mad, too, just from being near Goody Carnegie? Had I caught her bafflement as I had once caught smallpox?

"It is, indeed," she said, and began humming. "I am glad that remains. Belonged to my great-gran, back in the Highlands afore they come. She brought it here. Fairies won't cross iron, you know. There should be something at each window, though that is the only door. Yes, this house shall be yours, dearie. Oh, it is grand, is it not?"

"Mine? Oh, Goody, I am not sure how to thank you. Although I suppose I should be going on now."

"It is a good house. It once held much love and happiness. And where would you go? Back into the woods? You'd perish there. Into the town? Same result."

As a slave, I had been housed, and in a manner, fed. As an Ursuline conscript, others chose what I ate, when I slept, and provided everything while I worked as a laborer. Here, in this place, I was free, but that meant I was to both decide and provide all my own means. "I see it *is* a good house," I said, feeling condescension in my tone. "But the roof?"

Goody went on, as if she'd continued while I had been caught up in reverie. "There is a well. Comes in the side, there, by a stone way." She led me into the building. It was deeper than it appeared from the front. Inside and outside, the walls were overgrown with weeds and ivy, the floor strewn with a few bits of left-behind furniture, a tub with a hole in the bottom, and an old bedstead. She went on talking. "Open this gate, see?" She pulled on a rusted hinge, which to my surprise opened. Water from a running stream had been somehow caught uphill and forced through a round spout of stone behind the gate. It emptied into a deep granite bowl that drained back through the wall to a trough outside, much clogged with debris and leaves. "Water's good. A roof can be fix-ed." She drew out the last word into two syllables, the way Ma did when she was tired.

I could not say if that were the reason my aspect of her seemed to change but at that moment it did. I felt I had been pulled toward her dreamy world of possibilities and must return to the real here and now. I said, "I have no way to eat or to make a living here. I must find a position where someone will pay me for work."

"You have a little coin. I've seen it. You will buy flour and make bread. By and by you will walk to town and buy meat and pulse, and cook in the fireplace. Anything can be done if you have a will for it." The woman eyed the rock walls as if they made a beautiful castle.

I said as gently as I could, "Yes, it can. But even then, that takes money." I stifled a shudder. It would take time. And a roof. And knowledge of housekeeping, of which I had none. Oh, why had I been confined to the weaver's barn rather than the kitchen? If I had done as I was told, and not stolen so much food, I might have learned so much.

"Buy yourself a spinning wheel, two goats, and some chickens, and work hard every day. Sell what you get in thread and eggs and cheese. It is an old truth that 'thee must spend a crown to make a pound,' and it will seem at first as if you are going backward in your plan. If I had any money—"

"Oh, no, I would not presume upon you in asking for it. Even if I sold all I had, it is not just the money I need. I need a companion willing to travel, too."

She put her head down but turned her eyes up toward me with a childish look of apology. "I won't go over the sea."

"I understand. It is dangerous and difficult. I would not ask you to take such risk."

"You're a kind one, you are. Now, why don't you live here, dearie? We shall be neighbors. This house is over a hundred years old and she's had more than one roof before. I shall give you this house as long as you desire to live in her. If you leave and I'm still alive, you give it back to me. If I am dead, it is yours forever. I have no children, no niece or nephew. Use the money you have to get what you need to make your living and bake your bread. In the fall we'll press cider, and make beer, and put aside roots."

Fall? I should not be there that long, I vowed. Fall was the time of stormy seas. It was already mid-June. I would only stay as long as it took to get home. At that moment, four large pigeons fluttered through the beams over our heads and landed on the dirt floor of the place. I said, "I think perhaps I should inquire about a position in town."

At that moment she seized my arm and held it fast. "I was trying not to tell you this, Miss Talbot. You will find no position in this town or any nearby. Talk from the Roberts family is that you caused them rack and ruin, killed the old man, stole the swain from the daughter, poisoned the dog, and spat in the eyes of the old woman as you left."

"I never!"

"You best see what you can do about living until you can make your money. You have no choice except the old one that has been the choice of ruined women for all time."

"*Prostituée?* Oh, la. I would rather perish."

"Folks will be rude to you. But you show them you are none of that other."

"Why do *you* believe in me?"

She chuckled and winked at me. "I know who you are. I saw who you was at that funeral, saying 'morning' to me with no care for eyes upon you. I have no one left in this world. No one speaks to me as I expect they will do to you, but I have this house and all that land there, back to those trees. Forty-two acres in this tract and another five full of bog berries, by the place I am now. This used to be a fine farm; my grandfather's and his father's, worked out of the woods with his own hands. That house I live in is on it still, but I had to live where there weren't so many ghosts."

"This is so kind of you. I cannot pay you for it. I have done nothing to deserve it."

"You have done enough. I have reasons for doing this. We'll write the deed so I may stay in my house until I die. It is a good and kind thing you do for me, to take it. Please take it. I beg you. I will only stay until I die."

I could do naught but follow her, for without another word she pressed me on the path toward town. We walked to the town center and to the magistrate's office. There Goody Carnegie signed away her family farm to me with the contingency she had before named, that I stay until she died or turn it back to her. The man was perturbed at her. Whether he disliked her in general or me in particular, or the plan of hers that caused him some trouble, I could not say. It took three hours, by the time he got done looking this up and consulting some of the same men who had studied my answers when I first arrived. All had to see the papers and read what was writ there before I was granted the privilege to do the same. When I had the papers and deed in my hand, I looked them over. Goody Carnegie was

saying something about my putting these in a safe place when my eyes
caught the words "four hundred and twenty" before the word "acres."

I whispered, "Goody, this is a mistake. Look at this paper."

"Hush now, my dearie. Cush-na, by baby. Be only quiet before the magistrates."

I raised my brows, and turned to the men. "Is this correct, sirs?"

"It is," one answered me.

His answer did not bring me comfort. I felt I was being ensnared in
some trap. Yet, by that time I knew how to get to Boston, so I stilled my
hands from shaking, holding the papers. "Good day, sirs," I said. Then I
stopped at the door and added, to smooth my way in the future, "And God
keep you all and yours. Thank you for attending us today." I should have
said more hearty thanks to this daft old woman, I told myself as we walked
the road in silence. As a gift it was as perplexing as it was generous, for I
knew not how I should live in a roofless stone shed full of rats and pigeons
and the stray catamount or bear. Nor did I believe that anything so enormous came without obligation. There was also her vow that the place was
haunted and her own stormy jaunting through the woods to contend with.
I was not sure I had the heart for it. It was, however, a place to be until I
knew of a better place to be. "Goody?" I asked as we ambled back down the
path toward her house. "Why was he so hesitant to make the changes to
your deed that you asked? Are the men of this town so full of hatred for me?"

"Ach, no. It's not me they mean to harm, neither. It is my land that
raises their ire. They want it, you see. If I should die without an heir, it will
belong to the town. They could either apportion it amongst themselves or
set something upon it, such as a school or a community farm. It is good land.
High and flat, already cleared for the most part. A stream that flows year
round. You have woods, too. This is enough for today. I am so tired. So very
tired." She opened the door to her house. "Eat with me, lass."

"Shall I help you with bread?" While I sliced bread she had made, she
cut chunks of cheese, which she had also made, and I admired the knowledge she contained.

Goody poured cider, sniffed it, and said, "Gone hard. 'Tis twice as
good."

I hesitated a moment before the food, thankful for the simple grace of it, thankful to know this most peculiar woman. "May I ask you a question, friend?"

"Aye," she said, smacking her lips after a long draught of cider. "Anything, friend. Long as you do not ask to sleep here."

"I do not question your wonderful gift to me of a house and land. You said it was forty acres, yet the deed given to me lists four hundred and twenty. The other five you said is in truth fifty. I would have begged you for but a place to lay my head. Why mislead the amount yet make so generous a gift?"

She smiled and turned her eyes to the cheese before her, pushing it on her plate with one finger until it made a complete circuit of the cracked old dish. "To watch your eyes. I saw no greed. No grasping. I saw you were but stunned and perhaps unbelieving. If evil led your thoughts, I could have changed my mind with no more word than that I was yet mad when I said it."

Goodwife Carnegie intended that I sleep in my new "house" yet I could not. The house was home to many creatures with which I had no intention of sharing my bed. I slept that night under the great tree by the door of the stone house, placing boughs for shelter and a hiding place. I vowed I would sleep as the Indians had made me do, glad the night was warm, glad I smelled no bears. Only in the morning light did I marvel to myself that I had slept deeply, unafraid, unbothered by dream or squirrel.

My breakfast was an apple Goody had sent with me when I left her home. My one complaint was that it was too small. I started in with the old broom handle, pulling back vines and rubbish, dragging everything out of doors where I could sort through it to see if there was aught that might be of use. In the corner by the old bedstead, I found a rotted pair of boots. I got to the front corner and took away a nasty vine full of thorns that had grown over a rotted woven blanket, which seemed to have been stitched with padding in it, just as Ma had made the petticoat. When I moved it, a rat darted at my ankles, clawed at my skirt a moment, and I shrieked in terror that the thing would climb my clothing. It tangled one foot in my stocking as it struggled to get away, and I swung the broomstick at it. The rat ran from me and out the door into the light as I hit my anklebone with the stick. Grimacing, I used the stick to raise the blanket.

A spinning wheel.

I pushed away dust and leaves, dragged the thing to the center of the room, and pressed the pedal. It gave an awful groan and the leather strap fell away. I pulled it into the light. The thing was old, painted black, decorated with delicate lines of red with tiny green leaves. All was sound except for the spindle, which some animal had gnawed, yet it still went into its place, still could hold wool. A spindle could be gotten. No doubt Goody must have forgotten and would want it. I sighed, for far more than the land she'd tempted me with, this was something I knew I could use to my advantage. Later, she helped me replace the leather strip that moved the wheel, and clapped her hands when I pushed the pedal. This was not my home, I repeated with each step.

The next day Goody and I started at sunup and walked all the way to Boston. We arrived when the sun was well overhead and the day had become warm and misty as a baker's kitchen, with a threat of impending rain. We found a jeweler. I spent many minutes eyeing his stock, memorizing his prices and wondering what he might give for what I had brought. I sold three more gold rings for ten pounds and seven. One of the brooches from Patey's apron was one I remembered Ma wearing. A sapphire, as crystal blue as a Jamaican lagoon, surrounded with gold and small clear stones that might be diamonds. I would not part with it. The other brooch meant nothing at all to me, so that I sold for another sovereign. Altogether, I had enough to get a passage home for two people, if I could find another ship sailing there, another captain willing to take passengers, and a person willing to travel with me as an escort.

I persuaded Goody to go with me to the harbormaster's offices where I had left notes for August. In one of them, the paper was missing. I asked a man there if someone had taken it, and he shrugged as if I were no more than a squawking gull.

Goody said to me, "You put them notes there? You writ them in your hand?"

"Yes."

"Then we need more notes. We need to get a woodsman and a thatcher."

"I need to think," I said. She had granted me a miserable hovel in which to live, but I did not want to spend my few coins to live there. I had no kettle, no cup, not a knife or a trencher. No bed but pine boughs. I rubbed my head, not because it pained me but just to close my eyes from the sight of her for a moment. I also needed to believe that perhaps my brother had taken the note.

Goody Carnegie said, "Oh, let us have some cider and a bite. We'll find a nice place and share some victuals, you and I, and talk of all that you must do. I brought bread and cheese." We bought a flagon of ale, rather than cider, and it was fair stuff for I liked it better than some I had tasted before.

She gulped down the ale and smacked her lips. "Ah, look at them all. Staring at me as if I was the devil himself."

I looked about the room. "I am sure we are not noticed here," I said.

"They're lookin'. I feel it. Lookin' under their eyes, down their noses, up their sleeves. Ha."

A shudder of desperation came over me. If she were to appear to be drunk in public the innkeeper would toss us on the street like tinkers. I had to turn her speech to something other. "Please tell me what it was you meant to say earlier. You said you would tell me 'what to do.'"

"I'll whisper so's they can't hear us, dearie. Now. You got a place to live and you'll come to me and learn some to cook if you don't know. What can you make?"

I thought. "Posset. Hasty pudding. Boiled chicken. Mixed eggs. Roasted goat."

"Ah? I love goat. Now. With what could you earn your bread?"

"Spinning, of course. Sewing. Embroidery. But any woman does that. Weaving."

"Weaving and spinning they do, also. But not fine. Can you do it fine?"

"Yes." I did not want to do that, nor to spend my precious coins for a wheel or loom. I wanted never to touch another wheel or loom.

As the ale affected her, her light accent deepened into a brogue. "There's a look on your face, dearie. What would you do, lass, if you spent all you had to get there and dinna find what you were searching for? Even if you did not return here, how would you live? Do you think the only thing you must do is arrive, and someone will take care of ye?"

"My mother."

"Aw. I tell you, that is not enough. You ken yourself she is not at the plantation. She may well be somewhere, earning a living or kept at another fine house, but you cannot assume it will be so for you. You must ha'e more than your passage. You must ha'e a boon. A way to preserve to yourself a life o' yours. A means to go on if all comes to fail. That's where a woman falls. That Mistress Roberts, what could she 'a done if she had a boon put by? Buy up her *own* house and not be turned out, that's what. Give yourself the time to put by more and enough to go on, so that you are not put out. Where would I be if not for that? A woman is a fool that lives from penny to farthing and n'er looks to the possibility of loss."

"Wallace told me when it came to business to mind my tatting."

"Ah. A flapjack for his tatting!"

People did turn then, staring at the source of their disturbance. I whispered, to pull her closer by having to lean in to listen to me. "Is it then lady-like for a woman to earn money? I trow my pa swore to me I should never earn a ha'penny."

"Wherefrom are you? Did you never struggle to survive? Did you unhinge your wits, and let the wind blow you where it lists? No. You made up your mind to go on. I'm telling you. A woman's business is business. Think about what you'll do if all your plan to go home comes to naught. I have given you this place because my own bairny cannot have it. The Crown may tax it out from under you. If you don't think of these things you will be on the street a vagabond, a whore, a fortune-teller, or drowned for a witch if you make your means by aught else. Even if she marries, a woman must know of thrift and house. Now, tell me, what would you do to keep yourself?"

"Could a woman make a living as a weaver?"

"There are those. Find a way to add more color than what is available on the ships from France. You will have to risk the coin you have to find out."

My mind raced like a shuttle flying through the warp, seeing designs on the future. "I will save back enough for my passage and a little more, if all else fails. I will write and hope for word from my brother. I will spend what I must to keep myself."

A smile spread upon her face as if a sun rose in her eyes. She dropped the fog of ale and madness. "That's my girl. Let us work, now."

We set about making out notices—just two—one we would place on the town board here in Boston, one to be nailed on a post set near the cross-roads in Lexington. We walked to the craftsmen's road, a bustling place, noisy with the sounds of men's work: anvils clanging, a wooden board falling and someone cursing it, the rumble of a sawmill. Goody lifted her nose and smelled the air. "Would you know a dyer's if you smelled it?"

We asked at the woodsman's shop if any knew of a thatcher. The thatcher was working so we left word with his wife, so large with child she looked round as a fish barrel. She knew a woolery where we might find wheels. I bought all the wool hanks they had—filling two bushels, plus two bushels of well-hackled linen. I purchased a flax wheel, and we took the small parts in a crate, the rest we had to carry. Goody and I lugged the bushel baskets, the crate, and the wheel. After we had walked three miles, a young man came upon us from behind. He offered to carry the load for us, and at last added, "I'm plenty strong. Your grandmother is old," said he. "She is weary from carrying this load."

"No," I said. "For you could as well take my goods and run into the woods, and we could not chase you without losing the rest of it."

"Go on with you," Goody Carnegie said. "You heard the lass. We need no help." When he had gone, she asked, "Why did you turn him away? I am sore tired, carrying these."

"He asked for nothing in return. If he had said, 'Give me three farthings to help you get your load to town,' I would have believed he simply wanted the farthings. No. I believe he wanted to steal from us."

"You will get along, I see. There's the girl."

With luck, two boys came alongside us, carrying between them a loose basket with two squawking geese inside. "Pleasant day, misses," one boy said. He had a missing tooth in front, and half the other greatest tooth was eaten away with decay. "I'll take half your load for a shilling. My brother can carry our ma's geese." We let him carry the wheel and two bushels, so we had the crate and a bushel to trade between us. The boy left the wheel at Goody's door, too, not shirking the last steps. I gave him the shilling and Goody gave him an apple.

In a week I had turned the wool and flax to thread, and carried them back to town in one of the baskets. I sold them to the woolery and bought as much as my three baskets could carry plus another basket. I did this for two more weeks, and by the second week of July I had a purse of nearly five pounds. After two more weeks, I asked at the woolery for a loom maker. I was sent back two streets near another wood shop.

The loom maker, who insisted he not be called "sir," or any salutation other than Barnabus, was a wizened creature who wore a long robe like the priests I had known. His shop was a muddle of pieces, jumbled and confused bits of wire, tools on the floor and on tables, burned-out tapers having waxed everything to the tabletops. Little light came through the blackened windows and balls of some kind of animal hair drifted about the floor. "My wife of thirty years has died. These three days has she lain in her grave. I can do nothing. Nothing. Please go away."

Goody said, "Had she been sick a long spell, Barnabus?"

"A year to the day she died. One year. I have done nothing, all these many months. I'm no weaver. Now if you will leave an old man to his grief? Go down the street to Vicksley's. He's no good but he needs the work. He's got fourteen or fifteen children. Maybe eighteen. Who counts?"

Goody Carnegie looked the more sad and said, "And you have none? Oh, you poor man. Poor man."

I walked toward the back of the shop while they spoke. There in a small room, a loom such as I had never seen took the whole of it. A passage had been cut through the wall so the weaver could climb through it upon the bench. Another passage existed on the far side where the finished cloth could be taken and new warping placed. It had to have been built in that space. Dim windows filtered light upon a bolt of fine linen, so delicate, so intricate a pattern that it must be for some fine use. I memorized it, the warp in black and gray, the weft in four subtle colors. Raw silver and black, threes on threes, raw golden in twos and tens with a single strand of bloodred crimson splitting the pattern.

Inspiration came as if a moment of prescience had descended upon me. "Barnabus," I whispered. "Perhaps you can do nothing because this cloth remains unfinished. Perhaps you cannot weave this, for you are the loom maker, not the weaver. I am young but I have been a master weaver for four years. If I finish this cloth you may sell it for a great deal of money. It will allow you to carry on, having your wife's work completed and off the loom." I smiled and peered into his eyes. I couldn't say why I liked this old man. He was balmy with grief, that was true, but I had been so, myself. "No one else you shall meet would be able to finish this linen cloth. Your wife had the skill to make the finest cloth in the New World. I am her second. When it is done I believe you will work again."

"That was ordered some sixteen or eighteen months ago. Who counts? And she could not work on it at the end. I cannot pay you to do this."

"You said that you cannot use the loom yourself. If I finish this cloth, would you give to me this loom? It will have earned you a living, it will continue to earn me the same, and it will no longer be filling up this room with its sad reminders of what you have lost. What say you?"

He mumbled something, and then asked, "How long will you take?"

"I will start tomorrow. I ask no money. Only the loom itself."

Goody's face beamed with happiness. She clapped her hands softly. "That's my wee Abigail," she said.

Barnabus appeared worried, but he said, "I will do this as you ask. We shall see if you arrive on the morrow. We shall see what skill you have. If you ruin this and I have to pull it out, I will not do business with you again. But if you can complete this, I agree that I will take this loom apart and carry it to wherever you direct, and rebuild it there for you. You must have a room large enough for it. Do you?"

"I have one room," I said. "It is enough. I shall be here, early."

As we left his shop, Goody linked her arm in mine and patted my hand, saying, "Oh, Abigail, I knew you would find a way. I knew you could get along."

"Goody Carnegie?" I started to correct my name but I sighed, then said, "Thank you for believing in me. Now I must decide whether to return to Lexington or stay in Boston for the night, so I may begin work in the morning." Thunder beat against the heavy clouds that had formed while we were in Barnabus's shop. Above them, lightning made the clouds glow as if they were pillows cast into a fire, not yet caught in flame but touching the embers. "Goody, what do you think?"

"You should stay here. I have to go. Leave me. Leave. Abigail, I have to run away, don't you see? I have to run and not hurt you again." She tossed my arm from her and backed down the street, her face contorted in agonies only she could know.

"Please stay with me and let us find a place to sleep."

"Don't come near me. Don't touch me!" She screamed and loped down the road, disappearing between two houses.

I could not catch her. Wind tossed my bonnet, and I had to clutch my bushel basket to keep my goods inside it. My feet carried me to the Spencers' home. Why, I could not say, for I dreaded meeting Wallace again, yet I so needed help, any shame he might heap upon me would be worth a place to lay my head. By the time I knocked at the door, rain began to fall and lightning flickered. It felled a tree somewhere on the far side of the town common with the sound of a mighty cannonade, yet no one went to douse the flame, for the rain finished the business.

Lady Spencer was busy in the library, and the butler bade me wait in a small parlor. It was poorly furnished, not at all like the one in which I had met Wallace. When at last she entered the room, she looked on me with icy recognition. "How kind of you to call," Lady Spencer said, "and in such atrocious weather. Some compelling reason, perhaps?"

"There is, madam."

"I see. Won't you have a seat? We do not drink tea in this house. Do you drink coffee?"

"Thank you, madam. But I would not sit for I may dampen your upholstery."

She waved her hand, both dismissing my concern and signaling for the coffee. "This is not the *fine* parlor where I receive guests. Please be seated. While we are waiting, perhaps you tell me of the urgent nature of this call before Oswald returns."

"I was most pleased to find you at home, Lady Spencer," I began, for she could well have told Oswald to inform me she was not. "I know you have no reason to oblige any request of mine. I require a small room for a few weeks. I have promised an old man that I will finish the weaving his wife began. It means a great deal to him. I need a place to stay in Boston to do this."

"How, hmm, altruistic of you. You say *that* is the urgent business?"

"If I finish the work, he will give me the loom. With that I may make a living."

"Ah. So now rather than a lady you show yourself to be a tradeswoman?"

"No, madam. I was born a lady. Ladies must eat. If no one supports them, or provides what they need, even a lady might learn a skill."

"Why do you not tell me the name of this craftsman?"

"Gladly. He goes by Barnabus."

The butler brought the coffee. As he poured, from a corner of the hall where he had left the door ajar, I could hear footsteps passing. When he left us, Lady Spencer said, "Barnabus? I know him. His wife died and left my linen unfinished. I intended twenty-two yards for a summer frock. *You* can finish it?"

"I was taught to weave in the convent in New France. That was but one of the reasons Wallace thought me unfit to marry. I intend to work until the cloth is finished for the payment of the machine itself."

"And you want a room in my house?" She stood and paced in a small circle, then sat again, took up her cup and sipped. At length she said, "That is the extent of your request? A room? You ask no money, no—no other entanglements?"

"If I may, a meal each day would be nice. If Barnabus had a wife with him I might stay there, but it would not be proper. Though, if it is not convenient—"

"Wallace will be in Virginia for the summer months. I see no reason you may not stay in this house. He's bought his own, at any rate, and does not sleep here. We have several unused rooms with beds and furnishings. At the top of the stairs, there, turn to the right and take any of them that suit you. I suggest the last one, for it is on the easternmost wall, and if you are to work in a trade, the sun will awaken you at tradesmen's hours."

I smiled. "Thank you, Lady Spencer. This is most kind of you."

"Not at all. Lord Spencer is in London for the foreseeable future. Supper is at seven. I do not enjoy the habit of tea at four and supper at eight. Bad for my gout."

A smile brightened my face, and it felt as if it came from the inside out. This was a woman, though not to be called a friend, who at least was genuine and honest with me. If ever there was a person I could respect it was a fair, honest one. "I am so thankful. Now that I know the cloth was meant for you, I shall labor even more carefully on it."

She nodded. Her face seemed to tighten around the mouth, then she gave a small laugh and a wry smile lit her eyes. "You see, I was quite certain you had come here to tell me something far different. I supposed you carried Wallace's child and for a handsome sum would go to another town and not destroy our family name. When you said you were compelled to come here, I thought I knew. Hmm. A room. Just a room." She cocked her head and looked askance at me, then nodded, saying deliberately, "We will do that."

Lady Spencer sent for my trunk to be delivered from the dock to her house. I worked in Barnabus's shop six days of the week, commencing at seven in the morning and ending at six every evening. At noon he brought me bits of stale bread and boiled carrots, saying that this was his wife's one requirement of him as she wove and she insisted it kept her eyesight keen. Sundays, I accompanied Lady Spencer to Boston's First Church for hours of sermons, songs, and prayers. Some of it enlightened me, some sobered me, and some bored me. At supper every night for the first ten days Lady Spencer asked the progress of the cloth. After that, she spoke to me of whom she had seen about town, who had called, and what news she had from either her husband or Wallace in Virginia, and that their sugarcane was growing well. After those days, she talked more of herself, and as she did, she plied me with questions of my life, not in the colonies or the Canadas, but the plantation at home.

She took a drink from her third glass of wine that evening, and asked, "And why, if you know, were your parents there?"

"Madam?"

"Displeased Georgie-porgie? Or was it fat Anne?"

"The king, madam?" I tried not to register the shock I felt at her villainous familiarity with the monarchy. "I know not."

"My father, my brothers—one of them was hanged, you know, in Newgate. And I might have been as well, for I would have carried a pike with them." She downed her glass and rang the bell at her side. A man brought her brandy, and she bade him give me some, too, and then filled her own glass more full. "After Widdrington was taken, and Radclyffe, my natural uncle, you see, for they were not too particular in those days, and Charles went to France, the lot of us were transported here. I know about being transported. I know about losing your home, young woman."

"Yes, madam. Which Radclyffe was your uncle? James? My father claimed himself a son of the cousin of Edward, the second earl."

Lady Spencer laughed. She smiled upon me with genuineness that made her stern features almost beguiling. She asked, "Is Talbot your true name?"

"Yes, madam."

"We are cousins, then, Miss Talbot. My name of birth is Mercer. My mother was a Cameron. I married Lord Spencer on the night before the Battle of Preston."

"Cousins?" As she named off those names, I pressed the fingers of my right hand against my lap as if to press the names to memory. I had a feeling they would be important to me and that if she were not so full of wine she would not speak this way. I said, "If you and I are cousins, then I am a cousin to Wallace, too. It is good we did not marry, then."

"Marry? Hah. It is good you did not marry but not for that reason. Wallace is not the man his father was, nor his brother Edward. James Edward Stuart Spencer we named him. Of course, you understand the name if you are a Radclyffe. Blast, how the good ones seem to die young. Wallace is clever and ambitious. But Edward . . ." She tapped her brandy glass and a man filled it again as she said, "Edward, now he was a *son*. Edward died five years ago, when Wallace was but a lad. You would have done *well* to marry Edward. In fact, I would have insisted upon it. You are not so close cousins that it could not be. Indeed, many a royal bed is shared by closer. And you, my dear, have a sauciness that would have complemented Edward's depth and humor."

"Madam, I—"

"Now, let us speak no more of this. Wallace, I fear, shall go instead for that ninny Serenity Roberts. He claims he loves her, but the truth is that her mother married again, to a man of great means. Oh, never mind. What does it matter?" She finished the brandy yet again. The butler refilled it again, too. "I see that you are indeed the kind of young woman who should make any mother proud; you must take care for the good do die too soon, dear." She looked so sad, peering into the brandy glass. A moment passed in silence. A single tear ran down her face.

"Madam, I fear you are disturbed by something."

"Disturbed? Why should I be disturbed? Wallace has ordered the purchase of two dozen more slaves than he already had. That makes eighty on one plantation alone. His father allowed it and so I cannot forbid it. Got them from Africa. And how was he to pay for it? He told me that place would be making a profit within six months, but it has not. He has torn out the sugar his father planted and put in tobacco, but it will be two years before he pays for a single pipeful, I tell you."

"Because of poor sales of tobacco, madam?"

"Because of slaves. I hate the very thought."

I nodded, though I had no wish to discuss something that touched my most painful memories with a woman deep in her cups. "Lady Spencer? Should I help you upstairs to your room?"

"I think you should."

I left her at a dressing table and went to my little room, closing the door and feeling an immense peacefulness come to me at the sound of the latch. Lady Spencer had laid out to me things of her heart as Donatienne and I had done. This was a trust which did not come often, regardless that it came upon the wings of the grape. I would hold it sacred.

In all the time I worked for Barnabus and slept at Lady Spencer's home, I did not see Goody Carnegie.

CHAPTER 18

August 18, 1736

On a Wednesday four weeks after I began it, the cloth was finished. Barnabus declared my work superior to any but his wife's. On Thursday, it was delivered to the dressmaker for the use of Lady Spencer, and a good deal of money was paid to Barnabus. That very day he began disassembling the loom, even replaced a raddle with worn pins, the brake, and two heddles. I tried to memorize every part as he moved this to loosen that. He whistled happily as he worked, but then at supper on Thursday he said it was bad luck to break anything down on a Friday. He would work on Saturday and by Monday, he would be ready to deliver it, so I drew a map so he could find the house. He filled my basket with thread, then, so many spools I feared it would tear loose from the handles. "Never mind," he said. "I will bring the rest with the loom. Grace be on you, Miss Talbot. And thanks."

"And on you, Barnabus. I thank you, likewise."

"I see orders undone and work unfilled. I have much to do." He bowed over my hand and said, "You are always welcome."

Lady Spencer allowed her coach to bear me and my trunk to the stone house on a small hill in the center of the Carnegie farm, which was now in my name. She also supplied me with a mix of odds from the kitchen, a roasting pan, a good iron cooking spider with a legged lid, four spoons of differing size, two knives, a pronged fork for meat, and a table and chair.

As I rode in the fine coach down the road toward my own house, I felt fine and well fed, contented with my own good work, happy to be on my own, and assured of my future success. With the price that linen had brought, I knew that if I made more on my loom, in just a few months I could have money to sail around the world if I chose. If I had to winter in the colony once again, I would spend it weaving and spinning, and would have a just sum of money to show for it when the first ships sailed in the spring.

For now, the late summer of 1736 had come in heady abundance. Dragonflies, attached head to tail, came in the window of the coach and swayed to and fro. As I passed Goody Carnegie's home, I waved to her from the coach. "Hello!"

For a moment she seemed stunned, and then she called out, "Abigail!" and clapped her hands together. "I shall come for tea, dearie!" she cried. "This very day."

While I had been gone, Goody Carnegie had had the thatching fixed. She walked me around the inside square, pointing to every new bit and tie. "It will be so snug for winter," she said.

"It will," I agreed. Her joy at having me there was contagious, and I took some pride in setting out the things Lady Spencer had sent with me. We supped on bread and cheese, ale and honey. When she left I found a niche under the rafters where a small stack of coin could balance upon the sturdiest beam, and not be seen from below. Only someone who knew of their existence would reach into that small place; someone with no fear of spiders.

I spent my days spinning. I sang every song I knew, keeping the wheel running. I swept my little floor twice a day. I cooked on the big hearth, hung my clean vessels on the walls where pegs had been inserted between stones, then went back to spinning. By the time Barnabus arrived with a wobbling, squeaking cart pulled by a large dog, the stone cottage was worthy of being called a house, although I had to stand the door in place, and block the entrance with barrel staves and brush each night.

When Barnabus finished assembling the loom it took up a full half of the house. I reached out to touch it and he and Goody both let out loud noises. "Wait, wait. I have spent these days fixing and waxing it. Don't ruin it after all that work. It must be blessed before you touch it," he said.

"Yes," Goody said. "The weaver must not touch it until we say *Beannachd Beairte*."

"I know no prayer called that. Is it a charm?" I asked.

Goody began to speak and Barnabus joined her with the second word. They took my hands in theirs, and with the ring we made, held them above the loom's bench and treadles, saying, *"Fuidheagan no corr do shnath; cha do chum 's cha chum mo lamh."*

The two of them turned and stared at me. "I don't think she knows the words," Barnabus said.

"Three must say it the first time," Goody said. "I should get Mrs. Boyne." And she dashed out.

"While we await her," Barnabus said, "I would ask some water for my dog."

I fetched the animal water, and gave it a bun from my pocket. My breads were not yet as good as those Goody Carnegie made, but the dog ate it happily.

Once Mrs. Boyne arrived, the three of them went over and over chants to bless the loom again, to bless the cloth I made from it, and to bless the wearer of anything I should sew, until I could repeat them from memory. It was more difficult than learning French, for the words had combined sounds that came not easily from my lips. At least they had a rhythm, I thought. In my mind, I pictured sitting atop the weaving bench, hands and feet busy to the pulse of the chants. That made it all part of the fabric of my mind.

Two days later I had not touched the loom, afraid to begin. I had forgotten the blessing. The odd words would not stick in my mind in the way of the smoothness of French or the static of Latin. I had to fetch Goody, and strolled down the hillocks into the misty vale where a stream at the bottom was fed by the same waters that ran by my wall. Up the side ran a path to her house. And there for the first time, I spied a wee stone upright, in the woods. A headstone. Upon it was carved quite a detailed skull set amidst angel's wings, round about which grew vines of ivy. Overhead a holly bush shaded it from the oak and beech, and at the other side, five maple trees stood in attendance; this was a secret glen but ten feet round, made just to encircle its habitant. Beyond the maples, a scattering of five other stones, some of whose names had long ago worn away, raked the ground like great knuckles reaching through the soil, barely showing their curved tops above piles of fallen and rotted leaves. The name upon the center stone before me was *"Abigail Thankful Grace Carnegie. Born March, 1719, died January, 1721."* She had been born near the same time as I.

When I reached Goody's house, she was in her garden. Perhaps, I thought, I might take her to the stone and remind her of the dead child. Perhaps she needed to remember I was not her daughter.

"Goody, please come with me," I said again.

"It is not good for a girl to go alone through these woods and down into that mist. Fairies inhabit these woods. They will not let you go about for long without following you, perhaps attaching to you. Ask me not again, girl."

"But I have found a wee grave. I think it is your Abigail."

"That means nothing. This day, and a thousand others, have I held her upon my knee. She walks and wakes and abides with me as much as not. It is only when the wind blows that she goes with them and I must flee."

"Do you mean, you know she is dead?"

"She's nothing of the sort. Only buried. That means nothing. Fairies don't stay buried. Nothing of the sort. I have cheese to press. Come with me or leave me be, but do not pass through that hollow again. Come around the path."

"Will she come to you when I am there?"

"Abigail, now, do not vex your mother. I have cheese to press."

By the first of September, when the air was heady with mists that parted by noon to reveal the earth, I had gotten the stone cottage quite to my purposes. It remained a rude structure, dark inside for I had no candles. Keeping out the rats and birds, squirrels, and a raccoon I had evicted from their long-time abode continued to be a constant source of aggravation. Yet I had a hearth and water, cooking implements, two spinning wheels and a loom. I warped the loom by the dim light from the window. Did my spinning in the doorway and began weaving with memory more than sight.

On Sundays, I walked the length and breadth of the land, avoiding the misty hollow between Goody's house and this one. I did not consider this my land, rather thought of it as lent to me. However, I was free to make use of the apples, grapes, strawberries, and pears. Goody helped me gather plants for dyes and then I was able to create some browns, one a reddish hue and one a yellow-brown. I collected the berries I knew as *bleuets* though Goody feared they were poison. I experimented with them in making a dye, and found that I could boil a quantity with bitter apple and while it did little but gray the wool, it put a deep blue shade into my linen. I spun four or five hours a day until I had enough to warp my loom with twenty-yard strands of the dark blue linen thread. Then I set about weaving six plain strands to one blue. It made a pleasing shade, a unique look, and I knew that twenty yards of it would bring me a goodly sum.

On a hot September morning that threatened rain with large, dark clouds, a man and girl came by herding nine goats. They had some water and an apple apiece, too, and stayed a bit to rest before they went on down the road. While they stayed I heard much from him about the road from Concord to Lexington, and what went on from the Indians about, the danger of an alliance with the French and Iroquois tribes. I gave him five shillings for an older ewe and a younger one, along with a buck.

It was the custom in this country for any laborer seeking wages to walk up and down the lanes looking for work. Goody cautioned me against tinkers and tradesmen alike, for a young woman alone was prey to any who might throw her down, she said. Always say there was a man about. Anyone who lived nearby would soon learn otherwise, but a stranger from some other town might be less likely to hurt me if they thought so. I was not afraid. The goats made a racket when any person approached, and Goody insisted I have geese, too, for that very reason. Soon, during the warm hours my yard was full of the sounds of a country home.

On the last day of September, in the birdsong-laced coolness of an early morn, I pushed the shutters open at the window to find a grizzled face staring in at me. I screamed and banged the rickety shutter back into place, latching the dogs. "Go away!" I shouted.

"I come for to do your work," the man said. His accent was thick, the *r*'s rolling like a syllable of their own.

"I have no work for you. Now go. You will wake my husband and he's a cruel giant of a man. He will break your bones if you wake him." Only then did I hear the geese awaken and the goats begin their plaintive call that warmed me as if a child called "Ma-ma."

With shaking hands, I put water in my kettle and stirred the coals. I needed more wood from outside, but I got a flame going and found a burned limb in the ashes to lay over it. I listened at the door and the shuttered window. I had not heard the man walk away, but neither had I heard him come, and the animals had slept through him arriving. I shuddered. His face had been savage—more frightening to me than an Indian in paint and rattles—for he was a wild-haired, dirty, one-eyed tinker with the look of a pirate if not the smell. I put my bread and a pear upon the trencher, and blessed it. The water began to boil. I had no tea or coffee, but some herbs, mint and comfrey and rosemary, and so I poured the boiling water over them. I listened again. Sipped. Took a bite of the bread and one of the pear.

The knock on my door caused the barrel staves that held it to fall from their places. I took the teakettle in hand, my skirt over the handle, intending to throw boiling water at the man, and picked up an iron rod from the fire. "Who is that?" I called.

"I have business with the man of the house, woman. Tell him the carpenter he sent for awaits."

"He sent for no carpenter."

"I'll talk with the husband, Winnie."

I gasped. Unless a shortening of Winifred, on our island that was a name called to unknown peddlers' children and stray dogs. "Go away. We have no need for a carpenter."

"You'll go awaken him, I think. And you do have need, I can see."

I beat the iron against the stones to sound threatening. "Go away, sir."

He knocked again and the door fell in at my feet with a great dusty whomp. He said, "It seems you *are* in muckle need of a carpenter," as he stepped in. His huge body emphasized the small room, half taken with the loom, my table and chair between me and him, my back to the fireplace.

I drew myself up and held out the iron. "You have not been invited. Now go on with you." I backed against the fireplace, the terror of my last moments filling me with desperate strength. "I will not be taken easily."

He looked about and made out that I was alone. "There was notice in Boston that Miss Talbot on Carnegie Farm had need of a woodsman. I am he. I have come with my son. Because you claimed your man asleep, I've waited here on your doorstep for over an hour. Since there *is* no man about, I'd speak to *you*."

There were two of them? My throat went dry so that I could not speak. Gray clouds swam before my eyes. "Get out," I said.

When I awoke I was outside, lying on the granite stone that made my threshold, while some other man fanned my face with a piece of a ragged woolen cape.

They muttered some strange syllables to each other, and then the younger of them came from my house with a cup of water. I was afraid he would dash it upon my face but instead he dipped his dirty fingers into it and drew a cross upon my forehead and another on my bodice. Pushing them away, I scrambled to my feet. "I say, sir. Stop that. Let go." I had dropped the kettle and saw with a twinge that it had a dent on one side now. I picked it up, still hot, and took the iron poker and swung it at him. Patience's words of long ago came from my mouth, "Back away from me, man, or I shall tear out your hair and cut you up for the sharks!" Then I added on my own, looking at the poker in my hand, menacing it toward the younger man. "And put out your eyes!"

At that, both men appeared so startled they dropped their hands, looked at each other, and the old man began to laugh first, carrying the younger one along in his mirth. He laughed more and more heartily, tears rolling down his cheeks, leaving clean streaks. "Well and aye, that's a fine way for a gentlewoman to talk! It's a Lowland rebel we have come to serve, Cullah, my boy!"

The young one's laughter making it hard to speak, he blurted, "You've led us to the wrong house, Pa. Lady Spencer told us it was peerage we was to work for. Is this Granuaile or Ann Bonny we have found? Some Campbell witch?"

I laughed not. "Get off my doorstep," I said, "or you will see how a lady may defend herself if need be."

The ugly man set down a crate he had fixed with rope and sash upon his back as he bent to retrieve his Monmouth cap, much worn and greasy. That was proof he had been pressed aboard a ship at one time, I believed. The crate seemed heavy, near the size of a coffin, for it spanned from above his head to his knees. The younger fellow carried another nearly its size, with a broadaxe lashed to the side of it. Over one shoulder he had a leathern pouch. I stammered and said, "How would I know you meant to work when you break down a door?"

The older man said, " 'Twas not a door but a failure that was knocked upon, and it wouldn't take more'n a birdie to do't again." The younger one then handed me my house cap, the white linen kerchief I wore. I had not known it fell, and embarrassed, I dropped the poker, set down the kettle, put the linen on, my cheeks hot and tears rushing.

The younger man said, "Were you going to put out our eyes with *that*?"

Pressing my teary face against the corner of my elbow, I went to the door. Although I pushed it into place each night, I had never had to lift it from the ground. It was heavy. "I shall thank you two to put up my door."

The old man reached down with one hand and lifted the door as if it had been a leaf. "Your ladyship, we are but yours to command." Then he burst into laughter again.

At that the younger one took off his hat and swept it below a grand bow. "We are ready for our tea, now, mistress, and then we will begin our work for you."

At that mocking gesture my fear flamed into rage. "Insolent fop," I said, "you are too late. The thatcher has come and finished, and I am too poor to pay for expansion of the third-floor tower as yet. Before I spend money on the *second* story, I would make a trip to Jamaica and claim my mother and my estate from the Crown. *And* before I do that, I would make my coin by weaving the finest linen ever made in this bitter cold, godforsaken colony. Until *that* is sold, I am too poor to buy coffee, but if I had a single leaf of tea I would not part with it on your account."

He bristled and his eyes flashed with anger. "Pa, we have worn thin our welcome."

"Ah, no harm meant, lassie. Here is the letter from the Lady Spencer for our vouchsafe." He procured a tattered and squashed bit of script from his vest and handed it to me. "Ah. Well. Can you read?"

I opened the seal. "I can, quite well, thank you. In French, in Latin, and in English."

"There's a vexation, son," he said. "A woman who has been to her books will never have any sense."

It was indeed from Lady Spencer. These louts were her prized carpenters, she said, the older one for any sort of structure, the younger for fine custom casework and joinery. Their names were Jacob and Cullah MacLammond. They had set out in the middle of the night to arrive here by dawn, and on her instruction bound by her for fifty pounds' worth of repair or building on "my home" in Lexington.

I put the paper before my face to hide my expression from them and closed my eyes, trying to fathom the intent of Lady Spencer in combination with the annoyance of these two men. If she had indeed sent them to me, would she have instructed them to treat me as some savage wench? Frighten me? Or was their clumsy jest only that, a greeting *en plaisantant;* and perhaps they believed I had been awaiting their coming?

The young one said, "Come, Pa. We're paid whether this Miss Talbot prefers our working for her or not. We mean you no harm, Miss Talbot. Personal charms be—"

"I know not whether you speak of your own charms, sir, or mine. However, you cannot blame me for fright on seeing a man's hoary face in my window before the light of day. Your own mother might scream at such a sight. Now, which of you is Jacob MacLammond?"

The older man said, "That would be myself, Miss Talbot."

"And what do you intend to do here?"

"Well, as far as a third-story tower, I doubt fifty pounds would cover that."

I looked from him to the younger MacLammond, who was still glowering in anger, and decided to address Jacob. "What was the purpose, then, of that *mascarade* of speaking to a husband?" I shuddered that the French word had escaped my lips, though I knew no fitting one in English.

Jacob squinted with his one eye. The face before me I saw now was not so much born ugly as it was scarred beyond the point of human features, as if a bear or some other devastating catastrophe had raked him. When he spoke, it was evident deeper scars had fixed themselves to bone beneath skin and wrinkled his visage unnaturally; his mouth widened too far on the left side. "Just a precaution if it should prove I had the wrong house. Wouldn't want to have some fellow come out for me with a pistol."

While the thought crossed my heart that I should spend some of my money to own a pistol, I offered them breakfast such as I had, of pears, bread, and small beer. Jacob MacLammond surprised me, taking a bar of tea from his pack, and though he apologized for the saltiness of it, I made a hearty brew of what he shared.

The young one, Cullah, kept quiet as we ate. I had many chances then, by sidelong glance, to weigh his appearance against his father's. Had not age and some accident misformed the father, they might have been brothers separated by but a few years. I tried to keep my eyes averted as his father ate with gusto, but faced his son as the younger MacLammond had been trained in table manners. At least I surmised so, until he turned to me upon finishing the small portion I had provided, and asked, "How do you come to live alone, young Mistress? Are you widowed? Why are you not indentured or a ward to some benefactor who will watch over you? What is your means, here?"

"Boy!" his father shouted. "Lady Spencer sent us!"

He said, "I want no part of work with a scald or a gypsy. Nor a seductress."

"I will answer," I said. "I understand. I am alone because I was abandoned by those who helped me escape from the Canadas. I was a prisoner of the pope."

"Who helped you escape from the papists?"

I paused and looked the man in his one eye for a moment, because he did not say the word with the affect of nearly spitting it as if it fouled the tongue, as most Protestants did. "I will tell you truly, sir, if you will bind me a promise that you tell no one."

Cullah asked, "Is it some shame?"

"No. Well, it is. Will you both promise?"

"By my good eye, I will, then," Jacob said.

"My sister and I escaped the convent with the help of two Indians. She married one of them and left me at the field behind the Boynes's house."

Cullah smiled and said, "Oh. Well and aye, then. I feared you were going to say she married some English cod." Both men laughed. "Do you have wood stock with which to fix this?"

"No, sir. Goody Carnegie—"

"Ah! That one's gone afey," said Jacob. "She's known far and wide."

"You know her, then?" I asked. "Well, when she is in her mind, she is not daft at all. She has offered me this house as long as I intend to stay. She is not fey."

Cullah closed his lids slowly, as if sleep had come upon him as I spoke; when he opened them, he said, "So you answer one question with a reply to another."

"I meant no falseness by it," I said. "I was beginning to answer but taking a long way around it. My only means is her generosity and the weaving I plan to do."

Jacob said, "We've rightly got better manners than has been shown, Miss Talbot. We have been already well paid. We'll work the fair amount of it for you as whatever suits your fancy, and improves this house. The boy here is not much good at felling so it goes to me to bring down the trees for your work, but he turns a fine table leg."

"Really, sir, I need no work."

Jacob raised himself from the table and, using one finger, flicked crumbs of wood from the very beam on which I had stacked my coins. From his bag he pulled an iron hammer. With a mighty swing he sank the head of it into the beam. "Rotten to the core," he said. "Been thatched, aye? But the wight that thatched it did nothing to replace the rotted beams. Let me look a bit. Aye. Aye. Well, there won't be a tower for fifty pound, but we'll do what we can for you. Replace the rot. Make 'er sound."

Jacob seemed to be measuring with his hands, his lips moving soundlessly. After great length, he said, "It will take a month. That's without fixtures or furnishings, you understand, but we'll fit what we can for cupboard and larder."

Perhaps this was something I could do in return for Goody having allowed me this house. If Lady Spencer had paid these men to work on it, I could return it to Goody better than I found it. "All right, then. Can this be done without disturbing the loom?"

Jacob studied it. "We build a roof under the beams, at the top posts there. When we take down the thatching, there will be a mess like a hay-stack turned up, but I can save your work. Then we will put it right, and take down the false roof. It can be done."

"When will you begin?"

Cullah rose and moved behind his father. He wrenched out the hammer embedded in the beam. Shreds of wood that came with it fell as dust. While I knew little of wood and its crafting, I knew a beam was not supposed to powder. "We just began," he said.

Outside, they opened their boxes of tools, axes, and blades of all types. While they made a survey of the land for suitable trees, I collected my coins. I saw them looking at the enormous beech that overshadowed part of the yard, but I asked them to leave it. I went for Goody's home, to tell her of this news. She returned with me, abeam with joy. She claimed that my coming had brought her more luck and then some. She pointed them toward the woods that stood on her land, and said they could use what they needed there.

In just a few hours, they had a shed built within the stone walls that roofed over my loom from anything above, and they began tearing down the thatched roof. The shed was hot as an oven inside, but I worked in it, thankful for it. Then after a time, I found the rhythm of the loom echoed with the rhythm of axes striking the trees. I lost myself in my work, and was startled when Jacob and Cullah came to the place, weary, sweating, and smelling badly, and asked me for some supper. Then both of them laughed and Cullah pulled forth a rabbit he had killed and cleaned.

"I have never cooked a rabbit," I said.

Over the next weeks, Jacob and Cullah turned my tranquil life into havoc. Every day my work at the loom started with one blessing and I put the shuttles to rest with another. Every day the music of weaving was but a trill above the booming of hammer and peg. The granite walls of this house served now as a foundation, and another, larger house grew atop it like a mushroom. Stairs and another door opened to the world from atop the rise upon which the granite abutment had made a wall below.

Between building, Jacob and Cullah hunted. We ate more often with Goody Carnegie than not. I was glad of her presence. More than once I had come outside to do some little chore and found the both of them work-ing without shirt or hat, clad only in breeches and heavy boots.

Cullah lost no chance to shed his coat as he worked, and after he had asked me to bring him water more than one time, he crafted a bucket to keep at his side. As wood dust and flecks covered him, he often took the dipper and washed himself. I had never seen so much of a man, his body, his skin, other than swimming with my brother and sister. Even then, August was a boy with spindle legs and a narrow build, a pointed chest like a bird. Cullah was of some age I could not guess and did not dare ask. What I knew was that his body rippled in the sun, dripping water. Dark hair made a diamond on his belly and coated his arms, catching the sawdust and wood chips so that he looked as if he wore a feathered armor. His long hair he bound carelessly with a leathern thong. Though he shaved his face almost every day, a dark beard as menacing as his father's threatened his countenance by evening. He was altogether vulgar in appearance. A brute to be used as one would an ox. Across his back and one arm a band of white scar no wider than a good thread lay, testament to some old wound.

Jacob caught me observing it one time as I stood behind Cullah as he poured water over his sweating back while I held another cask of water. Jacob said, nodding at his son, "Fell from a tree, he did. As a lad. Means nothing." Hundreds of scars, like those on his face, webbed Jacob's back. He'd been mercilessly used.

Yet, as I crawled into my bed, just a blanket on the floor by the loom, I fingered the tiny scar I had on my left hand, remnants of the nail holding grapevines crucified under a full moon. I thought of no way a fall from a tree would produce a fine line that stretched across a man as if he'd been caught in a warp thread. Jacob's scars were a different thing altogether. I wondered if he had suffered as did the man beaten to death under August's eyes. I thought of Foster, killed by a bear, and others I had seen with scars. I remembered Patience lovingly bathing the wounds of the Indian man.

That night and many that followed it, I fell asleep thinking of Cullah. What meaning his odd name might have, whence he had come before Lady Spencer knew him, what his age might be, and whether he were really the son of Jacob, who was nearly as brawny as Cullah. The third evening of thinking thus, I had a mysterious dream of home. Rather than Allsy running, holding my hand, the hand I took was rough and large, attached to an arm with a scar upon it that matched mine, yet the faceless person to whom it belonged was lost in some sort of mist.

The next morn, I hummed softly as I prepared our food and began my day's work. To my surprise, Jacob heard me, and with Cullah both knew all the verses to "O Waly, Waly." The two burst forth in song as if the need of it had been held, steaming, under a lid, waiting for release. For some reason, it made me feel so homesick to hear a man's voice the way Pa's would have done, carrying on with his work, a tune on his lips. Then Cullah sang another, all in some tongue I knew not, a melancholy melody that made the heart ache and tears rise. It fair took away the hours and my hands upon the bobbins worked as if by magic, disembodied, as I felt the tunes course through me.

The sky threatened rain early in the afternoon. Goodwife Carnegie walked my path. Only when she called to me did I wonder at having it seem "my" path. Strife drew her face into a frown. "It comes. The rain," she said.

"I know. Please, Goody, stay in my home and run not through the forest. I fear much for your life when you do that."

"I cannot. I cannot."

Jacob frowned and worked his chin with a grizzled hand. I offered him the water bucket, but before taking it he said, "There's much to fear in the woods, lass, but sometimes there is more to fear in the mind."

Goody looked upon him, trembling helplessly. "It is neither memories nor ghosts, the phantasms haunting me. They are real. They come for me when the wind blows."

"*I* would keep them away, if you stay with me," I said. "Whoever follows you through the storm will feel my wrath."

From the corner of my eye I saw Cullah smile. "Aye. I've known it, lady. A firm redoubt it is."

Goody said, "I came to see your progress, whether you can stay during the rain, but I see you have no shelter yet except over the loom. Come you all to my house. Follow quickly before it arrives." Then she hurried in the direction she had come.

Cullah peered at the sky and sniffed deeply, then said, "It looks to be a killing storm, Pa."

Jacob wiped his face. "We'll see your loom is covered, and get the animals in."

I went with him to chase the goats into the wee shed he had built for them. I had insisted I would not have goats in my house so they had their own cunning little shed and yard. Jacob chased down the billy and then went to collect their tools. He kept them oiled with bear grease when not used, and I saw him fetch the pouch of grease.

When I shut the goats' door and he'd latched the bar across it, Cullah said to me, "I believe what you said. She's not truly mad."

"I know only that she is called mad by the townspeople yet they will listen to her with some respect. Other than when it storms, she seems to me given only to the madness caused by loneliness. I have stayed in this house simply because it made her happy. I need to earn my fare to Jamaica, but more and more the thought of deserting Goody Carnegie saddens me."

He pulled on his kirtle and worked at lacing up the front. As he did, he cocked his head. "When do you go?"

"I know not. I must have a companion with whom to sail."

"No honest captain would take you alone."

"I have left word for my brother. It would be fitting if I could go with him. He went to sea. Years—ago."

He must have seen the sorrow on my face as I said that. He smiled, saying, "He'll try to find you, if you have left word. I'd never leave a sister such as you. He will come."

I felt heat rush from my bosom to my forehead in the glimmer of time it took for his smile to form. I smiled in return. "That is kind of you, sir. Yet, the sea is a dangerous place. I lost my pa to it."

"You have no fear of staying with the old woman, then?"

"No, but you and your father must come, too. If you sleep in the woods you will be all night in the storm."

"Would not be the first time," Jacob said. "Or, we have the goat shed."

"Please. I cannot bear the smell you would wear. Goody bade us come," I said.

"You have no fear of staying with us, then?"

My hand flew to my mouth to hide my shock. "Oh. It cannot be. Goody goes abroad during storms and we would be alone. I know not what to do."

"Bundling board?" Cullah suggested, his eyes merry.

My face must have glowed like an ember, for his flushed dark, too. Cullah followed me to where Jacob waited uneasily at my doorway. He had stowed his tools inside and barred it. "I've made sure the loom will stay dry, Miss Talbot. She's made off with your cooking spider and half the haunch you'd put in. If we're to eat this night, we'd better follow the crone."

Without thinking, I laid my hand upon his wrist, hard and muscled as a horse's leg, saying, "Goody is naught but kind to me, as are you. Please do not disparage her."

Jacob gave a wan smile, and patted my hand with his other one. "Maybe, as you say, the townspeople respect her because they fear her. Ah, well. Let us go to her."

As we made our way, the rain held off though the clouds lowered and darkened. Goody fretted in her first room, tossing about blankets. I saw she'd been trying to arrange one to hang in the midst, as if to create a separate place for privacy. "Aha! You're here. Woodsman, have you got a nail?" Jacob searched his pouch and came up with one. Goody said, "Don't gape at me, man. Put this blanket here so's our miss may have a place to sleep. You men will be there by the door and she will have this side."

We ate our supper as the storm brewed, sharing her good bread, so light it seemed meant for some royal personage. At first we all stayed quiet, the men intent on cleaning up every last drop in the pot. Then Goody laid out cheese and apples. Thunder rolled across the sky like a cannonball across a deck. Her hands trembled. At length she said, "That is all I can do for you. Sleep if you can. I must go. The wind. The wind comes. And the voices. The fairies will not let me stay."

Jacob stood holding his arms forth, barring the door with his body. "Stay with us, lady. We will help you fight them. Banshees or fairies, the devil himself, whatever it is that comes for you. Then mayhap you will be freed from them."

Her cry was terrible, rending my soul with memories of being on ship. "No! Did you bring them here to torment me?" she aimed at me. "Are these the ones, these men, be they changelings come in disguise?"

I stood, too. "La, no. Goody, these are the woodsmen come to fix my little house, the one you gave to me. We accepted your offer of safe harbor while the storm rages. Please stay with us."

The old woman shrank inside her clothes, until she had none of the form or vitality we had just seen. I worried she was indeed the changeling she claimed she feared. At once a crack of thunder overhead affected her as if it bore grapeshot; the contortions of pain on her face grew so dire I feared her death.

Cullah stepped toward his father. "Let her go if she must, Pa. She is compelled."

" 'Tis only thunder, Goody," coaxed Jacob. " 'Tis the Lord throwing stones at bad angels. The wind is but His wrath, clearing ghosts from the trees."

"They'll come for me," she whimpered. "If I am near a fire or hearth, they'll come. Out of every nook and shadow."

"Light candles," I said. "Have you more candles? We shall stay with you all night. Light lamps, light candles, and we will block the hearth with charms and prayers."

"There are not enough candles in all of Christendom. I have no fear of the road, only this hearth. Open the door to me in my own house, you brigand!" A gust blew against the house, shaking the shutters in their dogs. Lightning filled the room for a moment with blue, illuminating even the motes in the air; the cannon roar of thunder deafened me and something like an inhaled breath snuffed every flame, all but the fire in the grate. Goody picked up the long-handled fork she called a tormentor from the crane and held it at Jacob as if to run him through. Jacob moved not at all. Cullah slid his feet noiselessly toward me so that he was but a foot away, and leaned on the table with one arm as casually as if it meant nothing, but I read the intent in that strong arm stretched before me. He meant to keep her and her weapon from me. I said, "Dear Goody, please tell us what you fear. We may help you."

She howled as if she were a wolf over a killed deer. The sound faded to a moan that wove itself into the wind as it howled through the eaves of the house. "Let me go! You cannot stop them. They know what I have done. They made a changeling of my babe, new as it was; in the midst of a storm they took her. I knew it was they. I only held her to the fire a little to chase them away, to make the fairies leave her and return her to me. She cried out in an unholy voice, so used was she by them. I don't know, I don't know!" Her voice trailed off and she covered her head with her arms. Then she drew in a strong breath with a shriek. "I don't know why it happened. I dressed her in white. I offered them gold and rosemary. Gave the babe hairwort and periwinkle. Oh, but I could find no dog's head! I called the chants and charms until I was hoarse but she would not stop her changes. Only a little more fire, a little more, I thought. They caused the dress to catch fire. Abigail! Abigail. The fairies took her breath away in the fire. Now they're coming for me. In the winds and rain, they chase me, trying to get the one that leaped from the fire to my heart—"

With that, she knocked Jacob a strong whack on the knee with the tormentor and threw it wild across the room. As he bent to rub his knee, she thrust herself past him. The door swung on its hinges, banging into place. I rushed to it and opened it, Jacob and Cullah behind me. Leaves blew in as if borne on fairy wings, like the souls of hundreds of duppies intent upon populating the house. Lightning flashed about the yard and sky as one, as if the storm had sat upon the ground before us.

"I'll go for her," Jacob said.

"No," I countered. "Leave her be. She had better run." I felt ill, as if I could cast up my food, stating, "She put her child in fire." Nothing I had ever known could compare. No Jamaican, African, or Guinean chant required such. Neither Protestant nor Catholic. I stared at the door, my brow furrowed, my chin taut with unspent tears. We watched the rain begin now, gentle for but a moment, then a torrent from on high engulfed the world before us. None of us could speak. At last the rain came aslant, and we shut the door. "Lock it not," I said and turned to them. "She may return before daybreak if the storm stops." I mopped my face upon my sleeve.

We made beds, honoring the blanket Goody had hung, though I slept in my clothes, awake long after the men's snores rattled dust out of the thatching. I placed a knife from the worktable under my pallet. Whether I feared Cullah or his father, or Goody Carnegie more, I could not have said. I wished I had stayed in my own tiny place, tucked under the false roof over my loom.

My loom. My cloth. My home. Was this my home, this terrible place?

CHAPTER 19

October 3, 1736

Goody did not return the next morning. We left as soon as it was light to see if aught needed care at my place. Since it was still raining that evening, I fed her geese and chickens, and she did not come home then, either.

Jacob and Cullah slept at Goody's house that night. I slept alone in mine. All those days and weeks before they had arrived, I had little noticed the lack of other human beings there. Then with the rain, I felt closed in, confined as if in the cattle hold on the ship. Jacob and Cullah so far away. There was nothing they could do in the rain, for certain, yet I missed them.

Rather than my usual singing, I wept as I worked. It was as if all the sadness, all the lost people of my life, came to my mind's eye in somber dirge. I felt so alone. Still, my hands worked as if they belonged to the loom and I merely oversaw them. The rain did not stop for three days. The men returned every afternoon in the downpour, to report that Goody was still gone, to see that my temporary shelter was still holding, and as Jacob said, "To be sure that I was not carried off by salvages or beasts."

The morning of the third day, a knock at my door stopped my hands. I had my hand on the latch to open it before I realized that it might not be Jacob or Cullah, for they had long passed the need to knock, and usually just opened it with a call to make sure I was not in a stage of undress. I was most surprised to find eight black-frocked men under spread cloaks. "Miss Talbot? We would have a word with thee."

Eight more people had no room for foothold in this stone house, filled as it was with the loom and the false ceiling. Four came in, one squeezed himself out of the rain at the door, and three peered over his shoulders. They were the men from the town who had met me when I first came, missing, of course, Selectman Roberts, but adding one in his position, the newly made selectman, Mr. Jones. They had heard, and would tell me not from whom, that I was living alone in the woods with two men not my relatives, in the employ of the devil spinning gold out of flax. I could happily report their missing men were at the Carnegie house, and put on my cloak to take them there to show them.

At Goody's house I was relieved to see her, ragged as a beggar but sitting between Jacob and Cullah, drinking tea from a cup by her fire. The men spoke to each other, satisfied that no illicit behavior had taken place here. I had to wonder what had caused this sudden interest in the condition of my integrity yet I was far too busy to tarry over it. As the men were finished with their inquisition, they bid us good day.

At the end of the path from Goody's door to the road, one I remembered as Mr. Considine turned and said, "You understand, the committee cannot allow unrighteous action within the reaches of the town? 'Tis bad enough that Goodwife Carnegie has given you her property, but that she holds with old ways. Witchcraft and transport with the devil follow those who do. It was only, Miss, that some sea captain had been asking after your whereabouts. Wallace Spencer declared to us that you were of the highest virtue, and that it did not mean what we took it for. We had to be sure."

"A sea captain? Who? When?" August had found me! My spirits soared but the man simply shrugged. "I have witnessed no devilment except her own sorrow affecting Goody Carnegie, but I assure you, sir, I hold no ill will toward you for your concern on my behalf."

"Good day, then."

"Do you know anything more of the sea captain?" I called toward his back.

"See that you attend church more regularly, Mistress," was all he said.

In Goody's house, as we baked and ate, we chatted about the silliness of that visit. She called me Abigail twice. As we spoke, two men, not the ones before me, kept coming into my thoughts to interrupt my speech. Wallace had defended my honor? Yet, he had left me because he thought I had none. And then, the sea captain. Who could it be but August? August, come for me at last. My heart swelled. Laughter came easily. Birds sang and my spirits rose on their melodies until I felt as if I enveloped all before me.

I looked upon Cullah, speaking with his father and Goody. What a bonny young man he was. His eyes sparkled when he laughed, as eagerly as they flashed like flint when he was angered. His hair was as unmanageable as mine and his father laughingly said something about his last having cut it with a broadaxe. I could barely hope my spindly brother had grown to such a good height and broad shoulder. When August came, I would make him a fine linen shirt just to fit him.

When at last the rain stopped and the world outside was a pit of tarlike mud, there was no work to be done with the wood wet and swollen, Jacob declared. He told me they would make a trip to Boston town for hinges and iron-worked handles for the doors. I asked if we could go together.

I took my cloth from the loom, forty yards of fine gold-white linen. I had thirty-three yards of good wool and fifty yards of fine wool. I wrapped my linen carefully in layers of wool, and folded the woolens within sacks of tow. We left in the early morning mist, a fog so thick and cool that the air swam before us as we moved through lowlands by the marsh on the road to Boston.

To ready for the trip I had folded my skirt up and held it with small ties of yarn, hidden in pleats and folds, covering my petticoats with an outer skirt made of roughest sacking that, when in town, could be folded up and tied. The sky was clear, but as we trudged through a world of mud as I could never have imagined, the road so cut with the travelers and wagons and slow going for all, the travel was too much labor to talk or sing as before. I pined for the seacoast and home. Nearing the coast I could sense the difference in the air; albeit grimed with the presence of so many people, it still held the smells of the shore.

Stopping at a pathway between houses, I folded up the mud-splattered sackcloth, let out the yarn, and dropped my better skirt over the sacking. I was proud of this linen, finely woven by my own hand and stitched in good style. Plain in design, but not without ornament. I had taken care, though I had done it with so little color available to me, the frills and embroidery in natural colors but intricate patterns made a statement I thought elegant simplicity. No Quaker garb, this.

At Barnabus's shop I sold my woolen for silk thread. I sold my linen for an alabaster vial of indigo, dyes of black and crimson, plus twice as much fine linen tow. I put my coin, nearly ten pounds in value, in my stockings. When I required Jacob to go to the wharves to see if any had left word from my brother August, he was not pleased to do it, but we did walk there. Now little was left of my notes, the ink faded almost away. One was missing. Could I dare hope someone had found it and knew the writing, knew August Talbot and showed him? Might we meet him on the road?

Jacob shadowed me as if my safekeeping were his sole charge. I asked him if we could call at Lady Spencer's home. I meant to renew myself to Lady Spencer, to ask her to speak to her acquaintances about August, and failing that, whether she knew of someone traveling to the Indies to whom I could apply as companion.

Jacob insisted upon the tradesmen's entrance at the back. I left him and Cullah at the path and went straight for the front. Oswald opened, wearing his usual stony expression, his nose almost too high as he looked over my clothing. I said, "Please tell Lady Spencer that Miss Talbot of Two Crowns Plantation is calling."

He bowed without a word, leaving me in the foyer. I supposed Jacob and Cullah went to the back of the house. I checked for mud on my hem. Oswald took me to the better parlor this time. On seeing her my spirits lifted until I discovered Lady Spencer was not alone. Wallace stood near the fireplace not far from Serenity Roberts. Mistress Roberts, America, and Portia sat together on a sofa. I bowed to each in turn. Oh, my heart. I came near to making some whimper at seeing handsome Wallace so elegantly turned out, so finely dressed in satins. His chiseled mouth smiled at me with warmth and surprise, and I was filled with the memory of his lips upon mine. I felt my face coloring and turned away from him.

"What a lovely surprise, Miss Talbot," Lady Spencer said, her tone cool.

"Thank you for receiving me, Lady Spencer, but I cannot stay. I called only to ask after your health and that of your company. I leave you my best wishes." I forced myself to smile at Mistress Roberts. America grinned merrily at me. "Good afternoon, madam. Young ladies. I hope your family is well."

Lady Spencer said, "Wallace and Miss Roberts have just announced their engagement to us. We are all most joyful over it."

A pain pierced me. I fought to control my lips' quivering. "A most joyful occasion," I said. "Congratulations to you, Wallace. Many happy returns."

Serenity smiled at me with the look in her eye of a cat having stolen a juicy morsel from the mouth of another cat. She held her hands in her lap, curled, like paws, I thought. "Thank you, Miss Talbot. We shall be supremely happy. We will marry in a month and journey to Wallace's plantation."

"Only a month?" I asked, fixing my face in a smile that hid my surprise. "I am sure you will have much to do in that time, creating a trousseau. How fortunate that you have your mother and sisters to help you."

"I hear you are a seamstress now. And a spinster. A weaver, that is the word."

America said, "And you live in the woods with the crazy granny and two louts."

"America!" Mistress Roberts's hand dashed out to pat America's arm in rebuff. "We have not heard anything of the sort."

I turned to Lady Spencer. "The committee came to my dwelling, Lady Spencer. I am sure they were satisfied that such is not the case."

Serenity said, "We wish to buy fine linens. I want the whitest white. What do you have to sell? I shall need a seamstress for the simples. Of course, a *qualified* dressmaker will be doing the fine garments."

Lies slid from my mouth as rain fell from the clouds. I formed a face of curious puzzlement. "To sell? Why, Serenity, I have no wares to sell. I sew for myself as many women do, from the governor's wife to the poorest milkmaid. If you wish to buy you must seek a merchant." I raised my hand in a slight gesture I thought showed off the ruby ring on my first finger.

"I would hire you to make the simples."

"I am not for hire."

"Mother, make her sew for me," Serenity said. "Wallace? Surely you must insist that this girl create my goods. I told you she had done my 'broidery before."

Wallace turned to her with that visage of boredom combined with irritation, the face I had pictured so many times after that night he left me at the inn. "Did you not say, ahem, you were *not staying*, Miss Talbot?"

Lady Spencer gasped at his rudeness and I saw a red flush rise above her high collar. "I have some very good claret we have all just enjoyed. Sit here, by me."

Wallace forced his beautiful, haughty lips to smile when I joined his mother on a settee. Oswald brought me a goblet of claret. Wallace and Serenity moved to another part of the room. Mistress Roberts and her other daughters sat stoically, as if not sure what their next moves should be.

In a moment, Lady Spencer tapped my skirt with her fan and nodded so slightly I might have misunderstood, were it not for the movement of her eyes. She said, for all the room to hear, "I can see you have had the good fortune to have Johanna the dressmaker create this for you. The fit is exactly the way she creates my gowns. Johanna does not take everyone. Clever to use such light linen in this heat; even though it has rained, the room is stifling today. Perhaps you embellished that frill yourself? Well, why not? A lady may be able to do the finest embroidery and not call it huswifery. Excellent. You have a brilliant hand."

"I made it myself, Lady Spencer," I admitted.

She mouthed the words "I know," then whispered, "Johanna has been busy with a newborn. Nothing like the talk of ladies' garments to bore my son to tears. I presumed it would leave us some privacy."

Wallace and Serenity moved from the empty fireplace to a window. The others were conversing and not watching us. I lowered my face and my voice. "I have heard of a sea captain making inquiries of me. I hope it is my brother. Even so, I have enough money now, to return to Jamaica. If you know of any who travel to the Indies and might take a companion, I should be thankful for reference."

She whispered, "I know nothing of any sea captain. But you'd leave your house? I suppose the work done was not pleasing to you?" She appeared distressed.

Tears brimmed and fell. I dabbed them away and sipped the claret. "I thank you sincerely for the work done, but I have the feeling it is still Goody Carnegie's house. She wishes me to stay. She is lonely. I—I do want to go home, Lady Spencer. My one wish is to see my mother. To touch her hand one more time. To lean my head upon her bosom to beg her forgiveness for it having taken so very long for her youngest child to return."

Lady Spencer's eyes filled also. She stared at the fireplace where Wallace had been, proud and spoiled. "When my youngest child leaves this house, I feel certain he will never return to it."

"Is it ever thus with children? A mother cannot know if they love her until they are grown?" I thought of Patience, gone to a life that seemed to me a horror. What would Ma think of her actions when she heard?

"It is. Let that be a lesson to you. Once they begin to walk, they are no longer your babes but little men and women placed upon the earth to seek their own means."

"Mother?" Wallace called from across the room. "Shall we have more wine, or will we be having another for supper? I will send word to the cook."

I stood. "Let me not intrude on your happy celebration further. I bid you all a good day."

"Call anytime," Lady Spencer said. "And do have one of your servants send word when I may be received by you. I shall inquire for you about the other matter."

I knew that she was aware I had no servants. I supposed she said that to make me seem elevated before Wallace and Serenity. "Lady Spencer, Mistress Roberts. Serenity. America. Portia." I waited until I was nearly at the door, Oswald's hand upon the pull, to say, "What was it you were to plant, Wallace? Oh, yes, some vegetable?"

He appeared stung. "Tobacco."

"Tobacco. Very well. Best wishes for your marriage. May it be *ever* so long," I said, with a face as near to Oswald's demeanor as I could manage.

Jacob and Cullah waited on the street; Cullah sat upon a stand meant to allow gentlemen to alight their horses more easily. One of his large boots lay before him, and on that foot he pulled a new stocking and a finer boot made of soft leather. "Ah, they almost fit," he said. "With a little lint in the toe, it will be fine."

"Good trade, son. Ah, you're found out. Miss Talbot, good day. And did they give you good table?"

I shook my head. "Naught but a single glass of wine."

Cullah said, "You should have come with us to the kitchen. We had such a repast that we may never need to eat again."

"Ah, you're always hungry, boy. Put away them things and give the missy something to eat. That's the good of going in the kitchen door. A few kind words to a cook and we've got plenty in the kit for the road."

"I have a pie here. I think it is beef," Cullah said.

"I cannot eat on the street."

"Too proud?" Cullah asked.

"Proud enough not to be branded a lout for bad manners in public.

You yourself ate at table, not on the street like a vagabond," I said. We found a bench under a tree. Once I had half the pie and gave the rest to Cullah, I moved my money to my pocket, put my dyes and bundles in Jacob's pack, and we started for the house in Lexington. That house. That place where I slept and cooked and wove cloth. Where I waited for my brother. Waited for calm seas. Waited for these cocky woodsmen to finish their noisy labor and leave me in peace. August was coming, that was the one happiness among all the thorns left in my soul by Wallace Spencer. My heart was full and my feet felt heavy with the weight of it.

The road was not much used, and we found long miles without another soul, so Cullah sang. He tried to teach me some of the words to his sad song. After one particularly bad try, he took my hand in his, faced me, and said, "Watch what I am saying."

"Could you not write it down?"

"I never learned. Just pay attention; if you can learn French you can do this." He said the words slowly. I repeated them, then more quickly, then with the melody. Suddenly I realized I had heard some of the syllables before, in the chants and charms Goody Carnegie used for every occasion. We sang it again and again, until I had it. He did not let go of my hand. It was only at my door that I realized we had strolled hand in hand and arm in arm like lovers most of the way. Cullah's father had followed two steps behind, neither speaking nor slowing. I took my hand away, blushing.

Jacob gave me my bundles. None of us spoke. At last I asked, "Ah, shall we have some supper?"

As Cullah was nodding his head yes, Jacob said, "We'll be sleeping at the goodwife's house from now on. We will let no man pass the road without knowing what he is about. No more committees will darken your door."

"But my brother is coming. You would not stop *him*?"

"It might be your brother. Might be some other wight."

"No one else would search for me. It is August."

Cullah said, "What is his look? How would we know him?"

I cast my eyes about. "He was fifteen when last I saw him. His hair was not quite as dark as yours. He was not tall. Very big feet. He had a mole on one cheek right above his dimple, so he looked something like a painted doll when he smiled, and a scar over one eye where he once got a fishhook in his brow. I suppose he might be taller, now."

"Perhaps," Jacob said. "With big feet, a boy often grows into them."

"Would you allow me to measure you, so I could make him a shirt?"

Cullah's face warmed as if he stood before a fire. "One man is not like another," he said. A low, rumbling sound came from him, a laugh.

Jacob grunted and said, "Measure me, lass. I'm the best measure of any man."

Cullah's eyes flashed with anger. "I didn't say I would not do it."

"You did." Jacob's manner bristled, too, as if he were ready for a battle.

I said, "I will measure you both, then, to make a shirt for August." Before I had finished speaking Cullah stripped off his coat and drew a deep breath, expanding his ribs, setting his shoulders well back. Jacob growled and took off his own coat, standing beside his son with a frown on his face and his eyes on the ceiling. I used a thread, knotting it for shoulders and arms, length and girth. While Jacob's face registered a snarl, Cullah's seemed merry indeed.

We began work again after a couple of days of dry weather. I set my loom to make the finest linen I had yet warped, thinking of a shirt for August. Before that, though, I had miles of thread to spin. Jacob and Cullah slept at Goody's but worked the day through at my house, and within the week Jacob began the thatching of the upper floor. Cullah was still hard at work on something inside, but I had no time to dandle about and watch them, for I had those many yards of weaving to do for August. The noise of their work bothered me not at all now. Three days passed as if but an hour.

The clatter of the men's tools had quieted for an hour the afternoon Goody came calling up my lane. I had had to take time from my spinning to tend my goats, and had a nice pan of milk to carry to the house. "Abigail? Abigail?" she called.

It vexed me to answer to that name, frightened me, in a small way, that she might find too much to be similar and I would suffer Abigail's fate. I called to her, "Goody! I am in the goat yard."

"Never you mind, dearie," she said, grabbing my shoulder roughly. "In the house. Hurry. Bar the door, bar the door. Abigail, they are coming."

I searched the sky for clouds but found none. "No one's coming, Goody. Unless it is Jacob and Cul—"

Goody Carnegie pushed the milk pan to the ground, wrenching it from my fingers. "Abigail, listen to me. Where are the woodsmen?"

"In the house." I felt before I heard the concussion that stopped her speech. I thought perhaps I had imagined it. That she had taken a fit. Had had a shock. Frozen in place, she had become a pillar of salt, a Lot's wife to mark the way to my door. "Goody?"

Her mouth moved. A whimper escaped her lips. Goody fell to the ground, a fountain of blood sheeting across her back. I screamed. Ran toward my door. On the lower level, the stone walls had been filled in—the ample window was now but an air hole. The door had a bar but it was heavy and hard to place. I heard a man's voice in the woods. Another answered it back. The timbre was wrong, for Jacob's or Cullah's voices. In the darkened inside, I looked up the staircase. Any who might circle the house could come in. I looked upon my loom, my spinning wheels and baskets. If Indians intended to steal me away again, I would not be found.

I crept into the fireplace, still warm as it was, and pulled baskets of thread behind me. There were too many embers. It would light the baskets and burn me alive. I sought to crawl beneath the loom, but had not got under when a hand, strong as iron bands, took my ankles and pulled me forth. It was no Indian, though, but a white man. I cried out with all my strength, and the wretched fellow laughed, hoisted me up, crushing the breath from me, and started up the stair. My strength was no match for him, but I could kick against the wall and knock him off balance and I did, four steps up. We tumbled down the stairs, him cursing and furious. At that moment another man came down, but this one saw the barred door and opened it, shoving me through to the outside.

There, a third man joined the two. Rafe MacAlister. He had grown grizzled and fat. He missed more teeth and had a cotton eye. The three of them dressed in seamen's motley, though Rafe wore a new-looking cocked hat with a cockade of red satin.

I screamed and had to fight my feeling of faint. "You! What do you mean by this? Your ruffians have—"

He cuffed my face with the back of his hand. "Quiet. Yes, that's you. That's who I been looking for. I'll have you this time, I will. And growed right up, hain't you? No one to stop me but the old one and she's not really feeling up to it." He laughed, that same old sound I remembered so many times in our parlor.

"What do you want with me?" I asked.

"You are mine. For a debt long unmet. You think your father was some kind of walking saint, don't you? Well, the wretch Jacobite owed me, cheated me out of my position, my land, crawled over the necks of my family to get where he was. Him and the lot of 'em. Caused my sisters to be transported, my mother and brother hanged, my wife run through by the queen's guard. My children slaughtered and fed to the pigs."

"My father would never do such as that."

"Not now. He's keeping Davey Jones company at whist, I hear." He took my wrist in an agonizing grip.

"Unhand me, you pirate."

Rafe laughed, low and menacing, the stench from his mouth more vile than before, and he leaned toward me. "Not until we've had the sweets we come for." He ran his free hand under my skirt and between my legs. I kicked at him as he did but he was too strong. He hissed, close to my face, his breath that of something long dead, "I swore to myself I would have your father's head on a pike and your mother's eyes on my shoe buckles. I swore I would kill him and destroy his children and his children's children. You are the last. You'll get what's coming to all of 'em."

I cried out with the roughness, pain, fear. His brigands stood on either side of me, holding my arms, and commenced to tearing my workday gown to shreds in their hurry to get at me. I begged Rafe to stop. I screamed, prayed, cursed him. The villain tore open his trousers and was upon me and I nearly naked, squirming beneath him, when at once he gave a loud grunt and fell from me.

Standing behind him was Cullah, clad in only his leathern trousers and work boots; he'd kicked Rafe in the head. Immediately Cullah was set upon by the other two villains. I picked myself up, gathering what shreds I could find of my petticoat. Rafe shook himself and joined in the fight, when from the beech tree a roar more bearlike than human made both him and me turn toward it. I looked up to see Jacob, swinging a sword as tall as himself with the speed only a man used to such a weapon could employ. It met one of the brigands right across the neck. The pirate's hat flew up and

across the yard as his head rolled from his body, down his back, and came
to a stop at my feet, his eyes blinking three times in surprise, before they
shut for all eternity.

Rafe pulled a pistol from his coat and fired, but missed. Cullah sprang
at him, knocking him sidelong with the stock of an axe. As he did, the third
man circled behind and the head of Cullah's axe found home in the man's
shoulder as Jacob lunged for Rafe. Jacob's greatsword pierced Rafe's upper leg. Rafe cried out, taking yet another pistol from his vest. This time
Jacob sent the pistol and the hand that held it deep into the woods with a
swing of his blade. Cullah chopped his man in the throat, not severing the
head but putting an end to his fight, and the two woodsmen circled Rafe
MacAlister on either side.

"You've no call to come here, villain," Jacob said. "You'd be the sea
captain looking for our lass, here? Your need for revenge will be your un-
doing."

"What's the scuffle? I suppose you're bedding the wench?" Rafe asked.

He cradled his bloody, spurting arm in the other, wrapped in his coat,
and still spoke as if he would bargain for me. As if I were a slave. A chunk
of bread.

I said, "Is it not enough that Saracens took my father's land? That pirates sold his children as slaves? Is it not enough that my family has lost all
that you have lost?"

"I will eat your liver while you die like I did your mother's." All the
while, he circled warily between Jacob and Cullah.

Cullah looked at me for a moment, then turned to Rafe. "You'll go to the
gallows, that's all you will do."

I said, "My mother might see fit to repay you, if what you say is true.
The land has been forfeit to the Crown. You could seek recompense from
the king."

"God's balls, you are a fool besides being a dirty little whore. More
fool than your father, curse his eyes. Maybe as tasty as your mother was,
though. I rutted her before she died and after, too. She's deader'n a tinker's
damn. Put down that claymore, Scotsman. Christ. I have need of a drink."
Rafe shrugged and actually smiled, as if making friends with Jacob and
Cullah were that easy.

I shook in every fiber of my being. It took all my strength to continue standing.

Jacob lowered the sword. As he did, Rafe said, "So tell me. Is she tight as a new sloop? Have you both been well satisfied?" As the words passed his lips, he used his last strength to find a dagger under his belt and thrust it at Jacob in a mighty lunge. When he raised himself Cullah reacted with what I could only imagine might be the speed and instinct of a lion, for he whipped that broadaxe across the backs of Rafe's knees, crippling him, sending him into the dirt.

Jacob looked down at his side where Rafe's blade had slashed him. Rafe groveled on the ground, howling in pain and anger. Jacob and Cullah exchanged weapons, tossing them to each other. Cullah raised the sword high, the basket hilt covering both hands. Jacob stood upon the man's legs. Cullah put one foot on his chest and leaned on him, the claymore across one arm as if he held a religious article. He said, "Have ye a god, ye bastard?"

"Go to hell," Rafe snarled.

"No," Cullah said, quietly as if he were in conversation in a parlor. Then he plunged the tip of the sword through Rafe MacAlister's throat and said to him, "Go to *your* god, then. If he lives in hell, so much the better. You'll feel right to home."

I ran into the stone house and fell against the fireplace hearth, holding a remnant of my skirt to my face. I wept. Later, wrapped in a blanket, I wept more, resting in Cullah's arms, on a settle in the top floor of my house, next to the new fireplace where cider bubbled. I felt as if the shaking would never stop, as if I might die from it.

After the sun went down, I accepted the hot cider. By the light of four candles, I replaced a clumsy bandage on Jacob's side. Cullah went out, saying he would create a coffin for Goody, and it took but a few moments. "She was light as brush," he said. "Bones and worries, all that was left of the woman."

I heated water and then turned my head as the men cleaned the sweat and blood from themselves. I wanted a bath, too, but it was not possible with them inside, and it would have to wait. I supposed later that they had done something with the bodies of the three villains. I did not ask.

Cullah made beds for the three of us on this new floor of the house, hanging a blanket for my sake, as Goody Carnegie had done. We spoke not at all, but pointing and nodding, we made for bed. Before I went behind the blanket, though, I saw Jacob and Cullah had both brought their boxes of tools and both boxes had been opened and laid out. They had false frames in them. Under the woodsman's tools, a fold of plaid lay unwrapped, displaying an array of blades of differing sizes—swords and daggers, dirks and pistols. A brace of leather had held the claymore in place, though with the clatter of hammers, bits and drills, no one could have heard it rattle. In Cullah's box lay more plaids and a large silver buckle, with a set of pipes and two glistening swords.

I lay on my pallet staring into the darkness. I did not weep, then. Poor Goody had gone to her Abigail at last, and perhaps was at rest. No more would she cry through the woods. I had to get away from this terror-filled place of cold and gray and wickedness. Rafe MacAlister was lying; I knew my mother was still alive. The men talked in whispers in their strange language. Then Cullah called, "Miss Talbot, are you asleep?"

"No."

"We were almost too late to save you. I am truly sorry. I hope, that is, I pray, that, that you were not much harmed."

I said nothing but squirmed on my pallet, thinking of that vile part of Rafe MacAlister so close to me. If not in body, could a spirit be raped? For if so, then I was much harmed.

He went on, "You see, we had had no need of the weapons for so long. The false bottoms of the chests were secured and hard to open. I am terribly sorry. We would have come sooner."

Jacob added, "We did come soon's we saw them from the rooftop, but getting our weapons took too long. I apologize, too, lass."

"I am still whole, if that is your worry. I am only broken of heart and soul. Only that."

"*Men* may die of that," Jacob whispered.

The fire crackled in the grate.

"Men are weak," I said, not hiding the anger in my voice.

"Well and aye," answered Cullah. "My tears for you were about the other, and yet these words you say are the more sad." His large hand breached the opening where the blanket hung, twisting by its own sagging warp, away from the wall. I saw it, outlined from the light of the fire; I remembered my own hands cupping a flame long ago. He turned his hand and reached as if to beckon me, and against my own impulse, but feeling so bereft of hope, I reached for it. Instead of a hearty, strong grip, he held my hand with the tenderness I would use to lift a fledgling bird back to its nest. I held on as his fingers closed over mine.

I fell asleep with the words ringing in my head, "Ma is not dead."

CHAPTER 20

October 20, 1736

I wrapped clean linen around Jacob's middle, stretching my arms so far that it was as if I hugged the man. "You must have been a soldier," I said, stifling a shudder when touching his back webbed with white scars far worse than his face.

"It is better you know little of that time. Let it be that my son and I have built a house for you. We work for Lady Spencer. We are woodworkers."

"You are Jacobites."

"Aye."

"Freemasons, too?"

Jacob looked surprised. "Aye."

"And what *are* your real names? Were you transported here or did you flee after the rebellion? You thought I had not heard of it? My father talked of little else. My mother also. How did you come by the scars on your face?"

"You are a right pressing little lass."

"It is my nature. I know this much. A MacLammond is the son of Lommond, from the shores of Loch Lommond. Highlanders. Argyle and Donald, they were my mother's people."

Cullah said, "Ceallach Lamont. It means war. None of those are my real name. It is Eadan. I'll thank you not to use it."

Jacob moved my hands from his chest and pulled his shirt over the bandage. "It was a crazed flight through the nights to the sea. Captured and sentenced by the magistrate right there on the shore, we were both to hang again, but we were put aboard a filthy transport to the colonies."

"In the hold?"

"Aye."

I nodded. "I was in a hold. More than one. It was wretched. Patience nearly died."

"They sought to make a puff of my boy. When he fought back, the bosun's mate slashed him with a sword. I killed the man. They took the cat to me. Tore out my eye. Bled me near to the bone." He grinned. "The mate had beaten another boy to death, causing the crew to tramp upon his wee corpse and grind his grease into the deck. When I was thrashed, the crew mutinied. Took the ship and sailed to Virginia. Took the captain to the authorities but they only fined him and commenced to put us all in jail. Hung a few. My boy slipped out of their hands. When they went to send me to the gallows, he argued with the magistrates. When that didn't work, he found a pick and dug me out of the cell. We are wanted. Unwanted, too, I expect. The names of Brendan and Eadan Lamont will get a man hung. Jacob and Cullah MacLammond are just two woodsmen making their trade serve to fill their stomachs."

Cullah looked up from working the edge of his axe with a stone.

"And what is a puff?" I asked.

"What?"

"You said they would make a puff of Cullah. What is that?"

"To use a boy as a woman. Filthy sodomites. Oh, lass, I've blighted your ears. No way to speak to a lady. I beg your pardon."

I was puzzled, and it must have shown. "Let us speak no more of it, then. How shall we explain to the ministers the death of Goody Carnegie?"

Jacob walked to the window and opened the shutter. "We'll lay her in that hollow below her own yard, by her child. Found dead. Buried. We'll ask them to come pray for her but I doubt any will. Town'll be relieved. I am, too. It is no good to have much exchange with one taken to fairies and there's naught to be gained by too much truth."

"And where are those men? Did you bury them? What if someone finds them?"

Eadan-Cullah said, "Someone will find them, to be sure. I put them in a field, the three propped as if they died there. Built a fire between their feet and put it out. Set out their packs for a nice supper. Put a dagger in the first man's hands and an old axe in that sea captain's. Wasn't one I use, just something I found in a river. It will look as if a terrible fight took place between the men, the one still owning his head being the winner, though he bled to death with MacAlister's gold chain in his hand. Found that in a river, too. Someone will find them and sort it all out and be quite happy to report that is exactly what happened, though he will not remember seeing a gold chain. He'll be paid well for his honest testimony."

I rubbed my hands together in clean water. "You mean someone who finds the dead men will steal it? And you set it there as a trap to keep him quiet? Who would steal from the dead?"

Jacob only smiled.

"You have a low opinion of mankind, sir."

"Well earned. There's more to our tale. I stole the Scottish Stone. Even the knave who has it now, on these shores, would not admit to that. The wight claims to be a Templar and he's hidden it in a glade on a long island to the south. Now we have opened our confidence to you. Can we expect your word that our secret will be safe in your hands?"

"My pa was a Jacobite and a Mason. My ma was a Radclyffe and a Jacobite. I worry for the disposition of my soul, the way my talent for telling only part of the truth has flourished under practice. You have nothing to fear, sir. I have carried secrets my life through." I knew as good as daylight that they, too, held my life and repute in their hands, for they could easily denounce me through the countryside as a wench who had bedded the two, and I would be from then on as outcast as any leper.

I prepared us a meal, my mind busily stirring the previous conversation. Cullah and Jacob sat by the fire in silence until I called them. Though they had built the chimney up from the bottom level, at one end, a second wall made a safe place, with its own exit to the rafters overhead, from whence a person in need could make their way to the outside, and a cunning little stairway that looked for all the world like one of the beams. I stood at the top of it and looked down. Every step had its wee niche. I could escape to the outside, just as Pa and Ma had made in the wall of Patience's room.

Cullah had created furnishings I never expected, two items referred to in this area as settles, which, when placed before the fire had the effect of collecting the warmth and keeping it by the persons sitting there. They needed cushions, which I would have to make later. There was a table, two small stools which might have several uses, and a cupboard built into the wall by the chimney. He raised a cloth to show me another. A chest, carved all about the four legs and front, with my name cut into the top, decorated with two geese or hens, some bird I dared not guess for fear of hurting Cullah's feelings.

"It is lovely," I said.

"Miss Talbot, you are the blithest maid I have ever known." His voice was lower, silken, and gentle. "I would that you kept it for a marriage chest."

"Well, then. It would make a fine one. I have no marriage in mind, but I suppose someday that will come. I will take it with me to Jamaica."

A parade of emotions traveled his face then, and at last he turned away, speaking to the fireplace. "We cannot keep living here. Our work is finished, though I'm glad we waited this day."

"Lady Spencer was generous. It is a nice house," I said with my eyes on Jacob.

He looked forlorn. "If you leave it, now we have built it, what will become of it then, lass? We cannot own it. I have it that Goody Carnegie left the whole of it to you."

"I cannot keep this house and land. It is not mine. I have a home in Jamaica."

Jacob took my hands, and as tenderly as he could look through his one eye, he nodded and said, "You yourself said the plantation went to the Crown. No English king is going to give it back to you, a girl, who can neither prove its ownership nor work it if you did. Providence has placed you here, in this land. I am not asking you to have my son, that's a matter for your heart. But I am asking you, as would a father, an uncle, a friend, to think on staying here. You have means to work and live. Risking everything to go to some far isle on the hope of finding someone who is probably long dead is foolish."

Having his son? Was that what Cullah meant by a marriage chest? Had

I not seen it in his eyes or heard it in his words? "My mother is not dead."
Yet as I said those words, the image of Rafe MacAlister squirming on top of
me, the image of him doing the same thing to Ma became blurred until I
thought they were one and the same. I felt the demon's weight again, saw
Ma's face close-up, covered with tears and blood, her own blood. I pulled
my hands from Jacob's and rushed to the hidden stairwell, feeling the stony
wall of the chimney, its warm rocks, except for the drip of water, the same
temperature as long ago those had been as Patience and I descended them.
I looked down into the rocky room below where the loom awaited me.

I saw her. Ma. Sprawled on the floor, the dagger to her own bosom, the
vile and rough hands upon hers, raking it back and forth, crosshatching
her bodice with blood. And the ripping of her skirt, the crying out for Pa. I
saw her in my lower room, dragged toward the hole in the wall, then drawn
back, limp and unmoving. I saw Patience's bodice, crushed against my
face, her hands forcing my eyes away from rape and murder, suffocating me
until I fainted. Patience crushing me again in the hold of the Saracen ship,
ready to kill me to keep me from a fate such as our mother suffered. And that
wee redheaded girl who insulted me on the boat. And the other woman.
And all who perished.

I awoke with a man's arm across my body, holding my shoulders down.
I screamed and scratched at his face. "Miss Talbot, Miss Talbot," called
Jacob. The man, yes, I knew him, the one-eyed woodsman and murderer.
His son, slasher of tendons and poser of corpses. Had they raped me or
were they about to? Had I fallen into their perfidy by my own ignorance?
Had they plotted treachery with Rafe MacAlister?

Jacob clutched my hands to keep them from his face. I burst into tears.
"Ma! Oh, my ma!" I know not how long I wept. I know that I awoke again
and it was dark, the snores of men round about me, filling the air. I awoke
again, painfully thirsty, my tongue stiff and hardened, split in the center
and dry, but when I stood I could not tell where I was. The hold of some
ship? I felt the walls, all unfamiliar, as if someone had spirited me away.
There was no water. No fresh water unless they let you up from the hold.
The floor rocked. Dolphins cried and gulls answered. I found my way to
the side as the vessel pitched and turned. At the side was a stairway, and
down it, my mother cut and bloodied, holding an empty cup. My thirst

o'erwhelmed me but I could not drink. She called my name but so afraid was I to go to her that I could not move. Then Patience tried to smother me, and I awoke.

"Miss Talbot?" A gentle hand brushed hair from my face. "You fell here, and we let you sleep, but maybe you would rather get to your bed? Look, I have made you a real bed, not just a pallet on the floor. Let me help you."

I opened my eyes. Who was this man? Yes. This was the son. The one sliced across the back for refusing to be abused and abased. "Cullah?" I asked. "Is there water?"

"Ah, you know me at last. Good. I will fetch you water."

"Where is my—" I started to ask for Ma, but I knew. Oh, I knew. So I asked instead, "My cloak? I am cold."

"Would you sit by the fire?"

"Yes." While we sat there, Cullah and I, I told him my other secrets. Of Patience. How she had run away with the Indian man. How she had broken my heart and spirit so many times before, but that I believed I had not understood her, with the understanding I now had of life. I told him of August, whom I never expected to see again. Told him of living on hardtack and rum. Of picking flax until my hands became great mitts of pain. Of thinking all this time Ma lived and waited for me. Of being punished for eating a single carrot.

"Many's the lad," Cullah said, "hanged at London town for stealing a rabbit."

"My mother is dead," I said, tears brimming anew.

"Mine is, too."

At that, I gave myself completely to weeping and sorrow. He told me of how it happened with her. How they'd fled, him barely a lad, and her swollen, carrying another baby. Soldiers had caught them and she began to miscarry. They put her in prison where she bled to death. He said, "Never would I have believed a person, any person, could hold or lose so much blood. I have bled people since then. Seen animals slaughtered. But Pa said, because she was with child it was life's blood, that it comes from heaven itself, and so the bleeding was two people slaughtered because the wee one bled to death, too."

For a long time, then, we held each other, not as lovers but as friends, as brother and sister might, our tears wetting both our shoulders.

At last I said, "The way Jacob told it, I thought you were one of the fighters. I watched you against those three. You are a warrior."

"He has taught me since. A man has to fight. There is little else for one not born to title and land."

"I was born to title and land, and I have now naught but a loom."

"So, you will fight with your loom."

I thought that was foolish, but I said nothing. Instead, I asked, "Why do you carry pipes?"

"You saw? How did you know what it was?"

"There was a painting in Pa's study. A man in kilts playing pipes."

"It makes a sound to wake the dead and call forth the living. Puts the fear of hell into the heart of any Englishman."

"You are an Englishman."

"I am a Scot. I will never be an Englishman."

"My pa was English. My ma, Scots. I thought they were the same. The only people who seemed different than us were the Africans. Now, I am Jamaican but you and I both live on colonial soil."

"Soil the English took from some other poor farmers."

"Cullah, if you're never to be English, why do you wish to live here? Why don't you go home to Scotland?"

"It is as Pa said. We don't live to go somewhere else or to do some future thing. We fight if we have to, but we try to make a living. This is the life I have."

"For seven years, I have only been able to go on by thinking that this was not my life. That I had something to go to, to escape to."

"That is hard. As if you're living but not alive."

"What will I do, if I do not long to go to Jamaica? Who am I if not Allan Talbot's second daughter? Where shall I be without Two Crowns Plantation?"

"Why not be Miss Talbot the weaver, of Lexington and Concord? Maker of fine woolens and linen, keeper of some acres of forage and pasture, hills and forest, and a wee graveyard? Why not?"

"I am not made to be a tradeswoman. A crafter. I was born a lady."

"And so you will not be a tradeswoman. You will be the planter's daughter who has a skill and uses it wisely. You will find another reason to live."

"I am being punished by God."

"Hah. That is why almost everyone who meets you thinks you to be the highest and noblest? Goody Carnegie gives you her family land. Lady Spencer treats you as an honored child. Even the old buzzards in their plain garb come to find you in sin and as God would have it that is the night we slept with Goody and you were safely in your own wee house. Your house. You have a surfeit of good and call it punishment. Are you quite sure you are not really an unhappy fairy?"

"No, I am not."

"I have to admit, at first I thought you were."

"Bless me. Why?"

He grinned. "Never had I seen a lass as cunning as you. So fair, it was as if you sprang from the light flickering through a maple leaf in autumn. So clear of complexion, I thought you'd skin made of milk and water. Your hair is, is—" He stopped, suddenly embarrassed. "Beg pardon. I didn't mean to speak so personally."

"You are forgiven. Please. Let us have some food."

But as I turned to straighten my gown, my eyes took hold of his. In a moment I remembered Wallace using the ruse of reaching across me to take a kiss. When Cullah leaned his head toward me, pausing, hesitant lest I push away or call out, I needed no ruse. His lips enveloped mine and I pressed against him, held securely by his strong arms, feeling the soft stubble of his chin. He raised one hand to cradle my face and I leaned against it, and though the kiss lasted far too long to be proper, when at last he pulled away, I closed my eyes and pressed my head against that hand.

He laid his cheek tenderly against mine and whispered in my ear, "Miss Resolute Talbot, thou art the blithest maid e'er walked the dews of Skye."

"That sounds almost like a song," I said.

"It is. That is the English for that song I tried to teach you."

"I will not be happy when you are finished working on this house."

"But, we are finished. We would have gone before now were it not for your fit."

"Fit?"

"Well, what do you call it? Your spell. Your grief. I went through the same though I was but a boy when my ma died. For two days you had frightening dreams, for you called out. But you seem better now. We have work to do."

"But where will you live?"

"In Concord. We have a shop there. Where did you think?"

CHAPTER 21

October 30, 1736

They were gone. Jacob and Cullah, the woodsmen. Brendan and Eadan, the rebels, the warriors, the hunted murderers. Gone to Concord. I wandered for two days, missing Cullah. I hung on a peg the shirt I'd made to his measure but for my brother. On an early afternoon when the day had been warm, I took flowers to Goody's grave on All Hallows. I laid a sprig of yarrow upon the grave of little Abigail. Then I walked to Lexington to attend church on All Saints' Day.

Overhearing gossip, I learned that, as Cullah had suspected, Mr. Considine had recently found three vagabonds dead in one of his fields and named the place Sad Field. He claimed they must have been drunk and fought each other due to their poverty, for they had nothing of value betwixt them but their weapons, old and worn as they were. Immediately afterward, he purchased another tract of land that met one boundary of the Carnegie Farm, having, he said, payoff of a long-forgotten but very good investment.

I collected pears and apples and dried them, storing them in rough bags hung from the rafters. On Saturdays, Cullah came to my door and brought with him some little box or shelf he had made. Wooden trenchers and spoons. The odd iron hook he said was "left behind" from some work they had done during that week. Last week he brought me two gallons of vinegar. One time he brought his father's great tool kit, and from it drew a pile of staves from which he created for me a barrel-vat for dyeing cloth. When I told him the dye would soak into the wood and all my cloth would become the same color, he only smiled and said he would make another for every color I wished to create. I prepared supper for him on those Saturdays. We ate in the cool of the afternoon, and then he swept the crate upon his back and walked back to Concord.

On Sundays, I walked to town and went to Meeting, not for spiritual renewal but for companionship. Fall turned the night air sharp, though the days stayed pleasant.

I set about my work with renewed energy on Mondays, and by two weeks' end had thirty yards of fine linen. I mixed dyes and tested the results on scraps. When I had just the right shade of rose—darker than the blush on a dogwood flower—I added blue to make lavender. I wrote the formula and mixed my brew. I held my breath as I plunged the length of fabric into the new barrel. Only then did I see how smoothly Cullah had planed and shaved the wood inside, so that it had no burrs to catch the thread.

When an hour had passed, I rinsed the cloth and laid it upon a rope Cullah had strung from the wall to a tree. When it had dried I laid it upon my table and took the one thing yet unused and clean, a fifth new trencher Cullah had left me, and put it upon the cloth, then drew around it, making circles. On each circle I drew a leaf on the left with a posy by it, and then with a spoon for a straight line, I made dots where I would put flowers and leaves. When I sat to embroider I decided that this would be a very fine cloth, and perhaps I would take it to Johanna the dressmaker myself, not sell it to Barnabus. I mixed threads to create subtlety of color that pleased my own eye, all the while thinking that if it pleased only me I should be out the cost and labor of creating expensive fabric. If others found it to their liking, I would charge more than I had ever asked before, for I intended to embroider every yard—all thirty—so that any lady could have the largest farthingale on this continent and still make use of it.

When my back ached so that I felt I needed to move or be forever frozen in place, I cleaned out Goody's house, aired the blankets, and washed everything else. I stored candles, candleholders, and a little mirror, her leech book of herbs and poultices, most of which was writ in some tongue I could not read, in a rough chest. I made sure to be finished there before the sun began its descent, for I had no love of the shadows that haunted the place. If my house was really the place where she had burned her babe to death, it had no feel of it. It was Goody's own hearth that caused me to shudder upon opening the door. I was only too glad to close it and place the largest log I could move against it, wedging it into the mud to hold it closed.

That evening I sat before my hearth stirring apples and molasses with some Indian flour into a hasty pudding. A drop bubbled and popped upon my hand but landed where calluses had toughened the skin and I licked the sweet pudding without pain. Though it was November, there had been no snow, no storms. As I thought that, tears welled and spilled down my face. Loneliness echoed in the empty house.

Then and there I made up my mind that in the morning I would pack my things and go to Boston, find the first ship heading south and get aboard. With calm weather, there had to be someone headed south. I remembered Jamaica. I saw my mother killed and all these years I believed the lie I had told myself. I sat at my flax wheel and pushed the treadle. The familiar whishing that had kept me afloat all these weeks now seemed accursed. Goody Carnegie's words rang in my memories, too, of what I would do if I got to Jamaica and found nothing the same. How adrift I might be there, worse than here where I at least knew how to make do.

"Why does not Cullah return?" I said aloud. I felt more alone than at any time yet. I wanted him to come and build something. To hammer away all day. To tell me his strange stories in the evenings by the light of this fire. To kiss me. Did I love him? A woodsman? How could I love a simple woodsman? I had loved before. Always it was simply the first or closest or only single fellow in my acquaintance. I ate my supper alone and closed my door and windows for the night. Was love but a feature of vicinity? Perhaps if I stayed onboard a pirate ship I would love a pirate. If I lived in a castle, a prince.

Suddenly Wallace's face loomed in my imagination. How sorry I might have been, though crushed by his rejection, to have married him and learned only later of his unspoken scorn for me. How thankful I was not to be yoked with such a mate as he. Yet, just thinking of Wallace made warmth come to my face, my lips. Thinking of Cullah only brought me a storm of emotion, like a gale with no direction, this way then that, turning, changing, loving and longing—and fear.

As I lay abed, I decided I would *not* find a ship on the morrow. Instead, I would make inquiries. I would find out more about the two MacLammond men, before I lost my heart to one of them. Perhaps I was not in danger of losing it at all, but simply wanted to stretch my legs and go abroad in the town, something besides being shut inside spinning and weaving the day through. That was not uncommon, was it? La. Was I lying to myself again? If I was so practiced at deception that I was the person most deceived by my own lies, how could my heart ever be trusted?

It was a fair walk to Concord but I got there in less than two hours. At the first store of trade to which I came, I asked whether MacLammond the woodsman came there. The answer was no, but not just no. The storekeeper had naught but evil to say about the MacLammond men. I asked at another but that man had no knowledge of them at all. Then I found a church by a well. The bucket was empty so I lowered it and drew from the dipper a cool drink. Then I went inside, meaning to rest. The vestibule held a bench for just such a purpose and, opposite it, a board papered with notices. I sat on the bench. My eyes had barely gotten used to the darkened interior, when I saw the letters *AT* on a small paper. I held my breath while I stood and raised the more current notice. A soft moan escaped my lips.

August Talbot here this day, 9th July, 1736. Made inquiries to the Whereabouts of his Sisters, the misses Talbot of Meager Bay, Jamaican West Indies.

I went to a door in the far end of the building and rapped at it. An old parson opened, saw me, and quickly donned his wide-brimmed hat. I called out, excitedly, "Father? I mean to say, sir? Tell me, quickly, what know you of this note?"

"Pardon, Miss?"

"Do you remember the man who left this?" I handed him the note.

"No. People come, of course, all hours. The door is always open. Being at the crossroads, naturally, some of those are years old. I wanted them to move the board outside but people said then the rain washes all the messages away."

"Well, it would."

"Yes, I suppose. Who was it you were looking for?"

"The man who wrote this note."

"What's he look like?"

"I, I know not. He was but a boy when he went to sea. Did you see him? Did you see who left this?"

"Sailors sometimes come here looking for people. They all look alike, sailors. Put on it how to find you and pin it back up."

He offered me a quill, so I wrote, *"Take the bridge to Lexington and go through the town. Ask for the Carnegie house. I shall wait for you. RCET."* Then I asked him, "Reverend sir, may I ask whether you know of a man named Jacob MacLammond, or his son Ea—that is, Cullah?"

The man squinted as if weighing his words. "Have you a message for them, too?"

"No. I am inquiring of their character. They were recommended to me by Lady Spencer of Boston." I searched for a quick lie. "My auntie with whom I lived has died. I have heard they do woodworking and turnings and I have need of such. Of course I must be careful who I let into my house."

"Did the person you heard this from tell you what to say? I'd pay attention to them, if I were you."

"To say, sir?" It was my turn to squint. Was he asking me for some secret word? Some key that would tell him I could be trusted? "I know only that they came once from Scotland and choose now to live here. I need them to, well, build a chest. A chest with shelves." I steeled my face but felt as if the falsehood shone brightly.

The parson folded his arms, used his thumb and drew a small cross on his sleeve.

I smiled and said, "Reverend sir, men fight their wars and carry their causes. I am not looking to pass along any messages or codes, I am simply looking for a man to build a linen press. You do understand?"

"I do indeed. Jacob and Cullah MacLammond can be found at the end of the lane there. Where you see the two stores and a sign with the raven, turn to the right and go down three more doors. It's noisy. A woodsmith's shop is hard to miss."

"Thank you, sir." I started out the door and turned. "Can you tell me why the proprietor at the place on this road, that way"—I pointed—"thought so little of them that he all but cursed them to my face?"

The parson made a face that was more a grimace than a smile. He whispered, "Every just cause begins in the midst of those who thwart liberty and justice." Then he nodded, not as one agreeing with his own statement, but purposefully as if to convey more than his words. "The man you spoke to is a loyal British citizen. Yet, I knew him in Scotland by another name, as did your woodsmen. He's determined to rid himself of his old acquaintances and prove his new loyalty. Sometimes associations can result in a misfortunate stretching of the neck."

"Indeed." I was not sure precisely what he meant, but I would question no further. "Good day, sir, and I thank you."

"I say. This sailor you wish to know about, he is someone you trust? If he returns, give me some question to ask, the answer which only he will know."

If the man wanted secret words for everyone, so be it. I would know August when I saw him, I felt sure. "Ask him the name of his wee sister's friend. If he answers Allsy, it is he. Good day, then," I said, and I made my way toward the MacLammond woodshop.

I knew I needed a linen press. I still had no idea what I would do on again seeing Cullah. He was not my kind. He was strong and hearty yet not honest, for both the MacLammonds' lives were cloaked in lies. As was mine, I supposed. He rescued me, that was true, but gruesomely. Oh, la. What had I to do with a man like that?

At the shop, wood shavings spilled into the street freely. A sign scratched on a plank with charcoal warned all passers that to enter the shop when hearing any machinery was dangerous. A system of moving pulleys and ropes hung from high overhead, a fire burned in a stone cairn near the door, and a shrieking, grinding sound came from somewhere behind the two double chests and a dusty settle on display at the front. I stepped behind those and held a linen handkerchief to my face to relieve the sawdust. In the back I saw Jacob concentrating on something before him as he worked his foot on a pedal that resembled the one on my spinning wheels. He let off his foot and it turned back toward him, then he stepped on it with great fervor, causing it to spin again, holding the knife to it. I waited. The din would drown any shout, so I waited and watched as he worked on the spinning log with a blade that seemed to be only sharpened on the tip.

I saw no sign of anyone else in the shop, but I meant to speak to Jacob at least. When at last he refrained from stepping on the treadle again, the wood on the spit began to slow and he dipped a rag into a pail at his side and held it to the piece, once again keeping the motion alive with his foot, this time using both the forward and backward spinning. At last he slowed the piece with his hand and said aloud, "There it is. Very fine. You thought you could confound me, but I have you." He unfastened the wood, full of spools and knobs, and held it against another, his eye roving the pair for disparate spools. He flicked his finger at something, turned it around, and set them down.

"Jacob?" I ventured.

He jumped and dropped one of the posts. It landed in a pile of shavings. "Who calls me?"

"It is I, Miss Talbot."

He squinted and then smiled. "Miss Talbot! Come in. What pleasure to see you." He came brushing wood shavings from his clothes. "What would you have of me?"

Suddenly struck dumb of lip and empty of mind, I stammered, then said, "I came to Concord to buy some salt. I used the last in dyeing and I need more salt and a linen press. What is that machine? It is curiously like a spinning wheel."

"No doubt the first turner of wood thought of that when he created this. Or perhaps some poor muddy potter was the model. The post fits in here, and with these chisels I carve it while it turns. Ingenious, isn't it?"

"Indeed. You see, in walking to Concord I thought I might, out of curiosity, see just such a tool. I have heard of them before. What is it called again?"

Jacob nodded and shook sawdust and shavings off himself. "Lathe. Shall I tell Cullah you called?"

"No, please do not. I shall be on my way. I mean to purchase salt. Good day." I turned to leave, pulling my skirts tight to go through the furniture stacked in the front.

"What about your linen press?"

"Have you one for sale?"

"Made to order only. Tell me what size you need. Will you want it of hickory? I have some spalted maple with figures in it. Will you see it?"

"I do not know what size. What size are they, usually?"

"He's taking dancing lessons, Miss Talbot. You will find him in Cross Street on the upper floor of Larson's fine musical instruments."

I turned. "Jacob, please do not brand me a wanton by informing him that I stopped here. I shall be in different mercantiles, and if our paths should cross, well, that will be as it may."

"Have no fear, lass. I know you only came to witness the lathe first-hand. 'Tis no crime to expand one's education by observing the working class and their methods."

He had said it with something between a smile and a sneer, and I could not be sure of his meaning, so I said, "Then perhaps I should provide you lessons on my wheels and loom in the future, sir. Good day."

"Good day, Miss Talbot. A linen press is best if it is not too tall to reach into. Cullah will remember your size."

"I see. Good day." I hurried across the street.

Jacob called, "Two pounds for maple. One pound and five if you want cherrywood."

I had to cross another street and encountered a group of Quakers who would neither pardon themselves nor acknowledge my existence. As they went their way, a young man, probably no more than eighteen or so, stared from under his broad hat toward me. I kept my eyes turned away until the last moment and then looked directly at him, which caused him to flush deep as wine. I smiled inwardly. He was a pretty boy but I had no use for children, I told myself. The mere fact that I could cause a boy to blush with a look was only proof that I was no child myself any longer. The boy tripped and bumped someone. I could hear a woman scold, "Friend, watch thy step. My hem is torn."

When I had my package of salt, a small wooden round of molasses, dried cod and oysters, and a paper-wrapped parcel of embroidery silks, I started for home. I walked slowly. I passed the music shop where Cullah was learning what—to dance? The shuttered windows hid only a dark room, now. I said aloud, "I only came for a linen press." My heart recoiled in a twist of pain.

The cloudy, gray afternoon was drawing in. It would be light for but a few more hours, I dared not wait much longer to start home. I strolled slowly down the street. At the last church on the end, the reverend was saying some prayers and a few people had gathered inside. I said a quick prayer myself, in hopes for August returning, hoisted my package onto the other arm, and walked toward home, looking over my shoulder for Cullah.

Since his father had seen me would he not have told him? I asked him not to say I called, but he could naturally have mentioned that I came about that chest, and to see the lathe at work. A person would, in polite conversation, say those things to a fellow. I quickened my steps until I nearly ran.

When I reached my door, I threw my bonnet on my bed and went to feed my goats and geese. Usually I took care where the food scattered, but this time, I simply upended the scraps I had for them in a heap and went in the house. I barred my doors and windows, and lit a single candle. Far in the distance, a wolf howled. The candle guttered and died, and cold fear chilled me through. I stirred the fire and lit another candle. Snow began to fill the corners of the windows.

CHAPTER 22

November 16, 1736

An autumn festival, the note said. A country dance. November 24, the last Saturday before harvest ended. Cullah came to my house a few days after I went to Concord, bringing the invitation. In truth it was but a leaflet scattered throughout the town, but for me it held portent. He carried his woodsman's box with the axe attached to the outside. He brought a gift of beef, hung so that the outside was dried. It would be excellent roasted, though he said he would not stay while I cooked it; he only meant it to sustain me. He said Lady Spencer herself would be attending, so I would be in poor form not to come. He would come with a conveyance, he said, to take me to the dance. As he talked, I pondered whether I had time to finish the embroidery on my bolt of lavender linen and sell it. I had taken the new silk

I brought home from Concord—a skein with a thread of real gold—and made one more rosebud on each of the one hundred forty-seven circles that crossed the thirty yards. There were three left to do.

"Why do you come with such a heavy burden? I have no work for you," I asked, though my heart fluttered with joy.

"There is word that the woods are not safe. Indians have taken two from the road, one was found slaughtered, the other not found. That is why I came as soon as I heard. Promise me you will not venture on the roads alone."

"Indians or no, I must get some goods to Lexington where I have promised thread to a shopkeeper." I was already imagining opening my trunk, dancing in fine slippers left from my days of being a desired guest of the Roberts family. He watched me with the delicacy of a cat drooling over a wounded mouse, so I said instead, "Look at this." I unfolded the linen upon which I had labored these weeks. I felt the same as I had the day I ran to Ma with my picture of Allsy and me running across the beach, showing my work for his approval.

He reached for it, then drew back his hand. "It looks soft. Very fine."

"Thank you. It is all right, you may touch it."

"No. My hands are rough. I would hurt it. You should not sell this. You should wear it yourself. The color suits you."

"Do you think so? I should love it. But, I could sell this for several pounds more than my own gowns cost."

"You think too much of money. There is more to life. I, I would buy this cloth and give it to you if you would promise to make yourself a bonny gown and wear it."

"Oh, I could not accept that."

"Why? Is my money not sound?"

"There are laws. Sumptuary standards. This cloth is for nobility."

"I have it on good authority that your family includes a couple of earls and a duke. Peers of the realm."

"Who are all rotting headless in a midden outside of Newgate."

"Sell me this cloth, then."

"I cannot, Cullah."

"I will pay good money for it. Three pounds and seven."

I wanted to lead him away from this subject and my plans. "I have a gown to wear. Perhaps you are insulting me that my own garment is not good enough to suit you. Besides, how do I know you know how to dance?"

"I have all the latest steps. Five pounds. I shall give you five pounds."

"Oh, la!" I was shocked. That was what I expected to ask for the cloth, not what I expected to get for it. "You are persistent, sir."

Cullah smiled a genuine grin that showed his well-set teeth and sparkling eyes.

Then I smirked and said, "You do not have five pounds."

"I am known for my persistence, but honesty, too, Miss Talbot. Now, do we have a bargain? Will you wear it? I have bought the cloth and given it to you as a gift."

"There is not time to make a gown in two weeks. I have other work to do. I must, as you know, make my own living. Perhaps I should not go to any dance. My hands are rough. I have no ladies' gloves. I have no one to dress my hair but must depend upon myself. My bonnet is old. I have too many freckles."

"I have something for you besides the haunch of beef, then. But, I will give it only if you promise to wear this cloth on November twenty-fourth. You will be taken by coach, and no drop of rain will dare fall upon you. I was told this might be something a lady would use." He pulled from his box a parcel wrapped in leather. In his hand the leather wrapping sprang wide and within its folds nestled a great length of ribbon of deepest forest green. It was one of the colors of my embroidery on the lavender linen. There was enough to trim my bonnet and a gown, so that it cunningly set off the colors of the embroidery. I felt myself near swooning with longing to wear something so elegant.

"You, Mr. MacLammond, are attempting to buy my condescension to your plan."

"Is it working?" The boyish charm in his eyes belied other things I knew of him.

I smiled. When I smiled, he did, too. I reached for the ribbon and said, "I will say this, then. I will accept your gifts of ribbon and beef. I will trim my bonnet with one and my table with the other. As to making myself a gown of this cloth, I know not whether I am able to do such sewing in but two weeks. I would need hoops for a proper farthingale and cords for the back and the stomacher. Lace for the sleeves. But, I will consider it. If I am able to get it done in time, I shall. I will have to have muslin for a pattern. I will need to go to Lexington, then, to purchase the goods to do it and you said it is not safe to travel. Will you take me there?"

"When?"

"Tomorrow."

"If I return to Concord today, it will be late before I can arrive again the morrow."

"You could sleep at Goody's house."

"Not alone." When I said nothing, he said, "Now she's dead, the fairies scurry in the joints of the place. I could barely stand it with my pa there. That place does not rest easy. I could sleep here."

"I would be ruined if you slept here."

"I would make you my bride this day, Miss Talbot."

Warmth mixed with fear filled my heart. I pictured the blushing, stumbling Quaker boy, far nearer my age than Cullah. He was a man, not a boy, and anything he desired I could not hold from him long. I drew myself up as if no fear ever crossed my mind. "I have not been asked to wed, nor have I given such a word to you. There is no priest about, nor a witness. Have you come here to destroy me, then?"

He exhaled, making a noise through his lips. "I would sleep with your loom in the lower room. You bar the door above. You have my word as a gentle suitor that I will not harm a hair on your head. Though given any piece of bark I could manage to make you a bundling board in a trice. It would be a, a loving way to sleep." He took my hand and kissed my fingers, too tenderly, so that heat passed over and through me as if the sun had burst through a heavy sky on a cloudy winter's day.

I said, "New Englanders are prodigiously fond of that contraption. It is a wonder every maid has no less than seven children before she is wed."

"Some may," he said, and laughed.

After some talk, I felt safe, even confident of his promises, until I said, "Good night, then," at the top of the stair, preparing to close the door.

"There is only so much temptation a man can withstand. Better place the bar."

I slammed it in place so he would know it was there. The brigand. The lout. Commoner. Villain. But as I climbed into my bed I felt his presence in the room below me as if the fire in my grate were stoked up for a bitter day outside. To turn my thoughts from him, I imagined making myself a gown from my finest-made cloth. During the night a thrumming from my own insides awoke me, heated desire clawing at my ribs like a caged animal. It took me a moment to connect the feeling to the presence of him below, but the image of Patience writhing with Lukas under the yew trees filled me with disgust and made me shake my head and turn over, determined to sleep.

We departed early for Lexington town. I found the things I needed and spent time studying the gowns of ladies I saw, although most of those on the streets were but servants fetching and carrying. I bought a pair of delicate gloves at a reduced price because they had been torn by a careless customer wearing a ring. I could fix the rip easily enough.

The sun lowered as we left for home, and we walked the road nearly alone.

My mind was full of measuring and where to put tucks and flounces when Cullah said, "There's a wicked wind."

"What?"

"Do you not hear it? As if Goody Carnegie is crying on the wind."

"Perhaps we need a charm against evil, then. Or a prayer, if you be so inclined."

"I never was one to memorize prayers. It always seemed to me at the times I was in greatest need of God's helping hand, I couldn't remember the words. My prayers wouldn't come except in a scream. Otherwise, I try not to bother the man, like some who has got to ninny over their porridge every moment."

I leaned toward him and chanted in a low whisper, *"Gum-boo cru-ah-he na clock. Gum-boo du-he-he na'n gaul."*

To my great surprise, he answered with, *"Gum-boo loo-ah-he na lock, Gum-boo tru-he na'n loo-ee.* I thought you knew no Scots."

"I did not know it was Scottish. Ma said it was Gaelic and as a child I thought that was African. *Go-intay, go-intay, sailtay, sailtay, see-ock, see-ock, oo-ayr."*

Whether because of the charm against evil on the road, or because we seemed so strange no one would touch us, we made the house safely and in good order. "Now go on with you," I said. "I have a great deal of work to do if I am to wear a new gown in two weeks."

"You are quite sure I could not light a fire for you tonight?" The smile on his face was so dark it seemed more foreboding than well-wishing.

"Good day, Cullah MacLammond. I shall await your coach on the twenty-fourth. If I cannot finish this gown I will wear something else."

"I bought that cloth."

"Let me see the color of your gold." I held forth my hand. "A proper lady's gown is no small feat, yards and yards of cloth, tucking and lacing and twiddly stitches."

"I will have to pay it in partials."

"I suspected as much. Then I may have to wear it in partials. I merely promised I would try. Pity you did not buy a professional seamstress, for I am slow at it." When he was a few feet from my door I called, "Watch for Indians on your way home. See if any of them have aught in coin you could borrow against your debt."

When the embroidery was finished I held it to the light and admired it. Oh, la! This was cloth for a noblewoman or the vest of a lord. Perhaps it was fitting, then, that I kept it, as a marker, a passage, to my own life.

I made the construction of a new gown my highest goal; it was finished the night I went to the dance with Cullah. His father drove the coach, accompanied by that old parson I had spoken with, so that everything was quite proper. The parson did not recognize me, so I left off questioning him whether he'd seen August.

Cullah did not mention the gown, though he did remark on the ribbon on my bonnet. He seemed at first distant, and sat out more than one dance to confer with the old parson. I said to him that he wore those new boots well and that I hoped he had indeed learned to dance in them. And in truth there was no step at which he was not adept, though he turned about with many girls more than me on that floor. I felt eyes upon us when we danced, and then it seemed they were on him even when I sat. I had to go to the balcony more than once to catch some fresh air, for the place was stifling. He drove me home, begged again to spend the night, and left me, whistling one of the reels loud enough to keep the Indians and fairies at bay. It was the most diverting evening I had ever experienced, with enjoyable food and gracious music.

Then, I did not see or hear from Cullah for a week. I worked at first cheerily, but as time wore on without a word from him, I grew pensive, and felt I had been tricked into this work and the waste of that rich cloth I could have sold for a goodly sum. My trepidation turned to anger, and I put the gown away in my trunk.

One gray morning, I caught the smell of snow coming on the breeze, as subtle as a rose. Something in the breeze carried the faint taste of mint and comfrey tea. And that day, there came a conveyance such as I had only seen in town. A flat wagon, driven by Cullah himself, came rattling up to my house. "Pa told me you have need of this!" he called from the seat. He took down pieces of wood, shaped and honed, carved with designs in parts and painted, too. As he got each piece on the ground and put it into place, turning screws and tapping here and there, a chest began to take shape.

I thought he had brought the old chest in the front of his shop, but this was a new linen press and not the same size at all. "I did not order this," I said. "Though it is nice."

Cullah faced me and said, "Jacob said you saw the ones out front. They're just examples. I thought, after I was here last, that you need something to put your work into, so it doesn't come to stacking it on the floor. I measured the place by the loom. If I'm any good at my craft, this ought to fit in it."

I watched him tug the chest through the door and wiggle it into place in its corner by the loom, so snug as if it had always been meant for that spot. I could not help clapping my hands happily. Such warmth spread through me, I wanted to hug and kiss him. I closed my eyes, thinking, do not lie to me, oh, my heart. Bear no false witness of my feelings, for I fear that I love this man.

He stared into my eyes, a mixture of emotions playing upon his face, and then said, "You went with me to the dance with no ill effects. But I have told you my wish that you marry me. I tell you now that I will wait for you to have me. Until the day you tell me to stop waiting, that you love another, I will wait."

"You do not ask whether I love you."

"If you grow to love me that would be excellent. For now, that you tolerate me would be enough. I know I love you with my very core. Everything I have and all that I am I would give to you. I will hold that love sacred until you tell me it is all lost. Until you say you love another. That day I will bury it. If I must wait until the waves stop coming from the sea, so be it."

"You give very little quarter."

"Love and war. No quarter given, none asked."

"Cullah. Eadan. Is there any other thing in your past than that which your father told me?"

"Such as a wife and seven children?"

I laughed. "I was thinking since Jacob took the Stone of Scotland perhaps you'd stolen the crown jewels. *Is* there a wife?"

"No. Although I have, well, learned a few manly arts from a tart or two."

"And would you be inclined to return to them, say, when I am sick on childbed?"

"What kind of rogue do you take me for, woman?"

"I want a man who is steadfast and chaste. Past tarts excused. Future tarts will be cause for great strife and a clout on the head. Before drawing and quartering."

"Miss Talbot, you are a stern taskmaster."

"I shall need a stick, then."

"I will fetch you one."

"I shall marry you, then."

He gasped with a look on his face that made me see him as he might have been when but a child. "You will?"

"Despite my lack of arts and understanding, sir, I find that I love the very sight of you. The way your hair will not part straight. The way you laugh. I cannot but move my hand across my loom that it is not touching your cheek."

Cullah sank to one knee, looking for all the world like a man in a painting before his lady. "When? Today?"

I laughed. "We must post banns. Let us choose a day together. Christmas is coming. That would be a better time."

He smiled and his eyes filled with tears, saying, "I've kissed you before. Will you not kiss me now, my troth-ed wife? I do fear I shall die for want of it."

I thrilled at his words. "If this be life or death, perhaps a single chaste kiss to keep you alive." Our kiss was not chaste, nor was it singular. I fell into his arms as rapt as ever I could imagine love to be. While I concentrated on the soft warmth of his lips, my mind raced ahead to what marriage might bring. Passion filled me that seemed only assuaged by forcing my entire body against his, and I did it, his arms encouraging me, until I had to pull away, weak and shuddering.

His wide shoulders seemed like the very frame for which I had traveled all the steps of my life up to this moment, to lean upon, to depend upon. This man was no boy and no narrow-shouldered gentleman of the realm. Everything about him was strength and work, his hands callused as my pa's had been, his eyes merry with the joy of hard work and the satisfaction of producing beautiful goods. The very smell of him was pleasing.

He whispered against my head, "We could make a public announcement at Lady Spencer's winter ball."

"What ball?" I asked.

"Mid-December. You are invited."

"And are you?"

"I will be there. It would be right for your family to announce it. Since you have none, I will ask Lady Spencer to do your honors."

"Cullah, that would be wonderful."

I wore the lavender dress to the ball, and this time decked it with Patey's string of pearls, putting the sapphire brooch at my décolletage, the ruby ring upon my finger. I topped it with the hat trimmed in the velvet ribbon, to which I had added embroidered edges. Cullah and Jacob both seemed to take a glance at me and turn their heads as if in shame or embarrassment. I asked, "Is something amiss?"

Jacob stopped the horses before the mansion. Cullah pursed his lips, asking, "Will you be ashamed to be seen with me?" He looked down at his secondhand boots, polished with beeswax so heavily that he smelled of honey.

I pulled up my skirt and stuck out my feet in their old leather shoes, cleaned, but not so much as a wisp of wax on them. "Are you shamed to be seen with me with these shoes? The slippers I had counted on split apart. I hoped you brought some of that wax to use on the way."

He shook his head. Looked into the woods then down at his rough hands. Felt his chin, as if the beard betrayed him, too. "No one will see your feet. No one will take their eyes off your form and face. Dancing lessons are not enough. I see it now. I am but a carpenter, Miss Talbot. I shall wait for you outside with Pa."

I closed my eyes for a moment, feeling such a part of his heart already linked to mine, that pain seemed to come from him to me. "Our Lord was a carpenter. If you will not go, then I shall not go in. I shall wait with you. There could be no reason to go in without you, for I would dance with no other, and I will be seen by no other."

Cullah lifted my hand and pressed his lips to my fingers in their fragile gloves. A bit of rough skin on his thumb caught in the lace glove and pulled a loop of fiber. He gave a sigh. "My hands are too rough to touch you at all."

I said, "The gloves, my love, are to hide my own calluses. Say you will go in with me or we may as well stay here."

Jacob whistled at the horses and said, "You will go in, son, or I'll box your ears."

"Well and aye," Cullah said, "well and aye," though he did not appear satisfied.

The Spencer home, fitted out for a ball, was grand beyond any that the most fanciful story could have drawn. All the ladies were decked in perfection, and I counted myself among them. The only thing missing for me were more stylish slippers, but still, I had a serviceable pair of shoes in which to dance, and my feet would feel none the worse on the morrow. The men tried to equal the ladies in their prim wigs and gilt shoe buckles. A few, I saw, wore no wigs, and so Cullah did not seem out of the ordinary.

The Roberts family was attending. Serenity and Wallace had returned from Virginia for a visit. Serenity's midsection was well swollen with child, which at first seemed not amiss until I counted months, and remembered their marrying without much of the usual delay or planning. Depending upon when the babe came, I realized, it might have been made soon after his leaving me at the docks. Perhaps even before. Perhaps that would explain the level of distress the family had shown me? Others whom I met from Virginia that evening, men and women alike, had come quite bedazzled in lace. Wallace, of course, was dressed to his fullest flattery. As Serenity sat, swollen and pale, he danced, his carriage perfect as it had been before but now slowed and meticulous with the Virginia planter's mien, so that he caught attention from men and women alike.

I tried to avoid their presence in order to have a pleasant time. Alas, that was not to be. During a lull in the dancing, Lady Spencer sent Portia Roberts to ask me to come to her side. When I did, Serenity and Wallace stood by her, along with another woman I did not know, a dark-haired woman with high cheekbones. She wore an exquisite gown of the same fine cut and craft as Lady Spencer's yet without the ermine trim befitting a lady's status. When she introduced me to the seamstress Johanna Parmenter, Mistress Parmenter bowed slightly lower than I had, and smiled most courteously.

As we began to talk, Cullah excused himself and said he had to speak with Lady Spencer. I knew of this, of course, for he wanted to ask her blessing on our betrothal. It seemed needless to me, but since she favored both of us—and that was her own choice when she could have easily banned me for the spurning by her son—I would be thankful indeed for her blessing.

Mistress Parmenter led me, taking my arm in hers, away from the Spencers to an alcove. "I asked to meet you for a purely selfish reason, Miss Talbot."

I smiled, trying to place my emotions in reserve the way Lady Spencer did. "How may I please you, Mistress Parmenter?"

"I must know where you got the fabric you wear. France? It looks French. It must be. But you have paid a fortune for it and yet wear it so modestly. Perfectly elegant taste. Most women would add so much ruffle they hide the beauty of the fabric for which they have paid so dearly."

"I would rather not say whence it came."

"I must know. I swear I will keep your secret. Was it contraband? Oh," she said, turning around me, as if inspecting a model. "Your lines are sleek and yet in style, and the ribbon, so subtle. But I apologize; it is not comely to observe so closely. It is only that I am allowed by Lady Spencer to come here to observe the fashions, so as to keep her in perfect currency of habit."

"Oh. You are a *dressmaker*?"

"I am."

"Then I will tell you the fabric for this gown came from my own hands and loom. I am a weaver."

She frowned with a critical eye, leaning close to my bodice without any shame. "And who embroidered?"

"I did it myself."

"Alone?"

"I have worked on this for many weeks. I am not by birth a craftswoman. I am permitted to wear this, even by sumptuary propriety."

"I should say you are. But, la, you have been taught by a master."

"I suppose. Some of what I was taught I have refined out of stubborn intention to create the finest cloth."

"Do you have more? I will pay you twelve shillings a yard for this."

"I have only some left, perhaps five yards. I would sell it for fifteen shillings. Each yard."

"Done. When will you have more?"

"Do you want it exactly as this? I could create indigos and cream, or crimson, besides this purple."

"The purple is divine, but I will take anything you create. Twenty yards of any color will do. Did you make your hoops and panniers, too? I thought as much." Suddenly she leaned her head away from me, observing me again but with a strike of scorn on her face. "You are, then, a competitor."

"I wist not, madam. I have no wish to fit ladies' gowns and keep up with style. I would sell you my cloth, only spare me from having to sew tucks and whalebone for some lord's spoiled daughter with bad taste and too much coin."

Mistress Parmenter laughed and tapped her cheek lightly with her fan. "If you will promise to sell only to me, I will give eighteen shillings a yard. You may vary the design as you choose, as long as the amount of embroidery is about the same as this. Excellent work. I will not press you for speed, but if you will allow me to say that I purchased the cloth you wear from a specialist in France, so that I may show it and speak of it, I will have orders waiting within a week for everything you bring. We will both be well suited."

"I prefer not to lie."

She smiled and gave a low laugh through closed lips. "Then you will not. I will handle that for us both. If any asks you, simply say what you wish and shake your head at the boldness of a woman in business for herself. Let them think what they may."

"I am sure I will have twenty in a month or less."

"Excellent." She threaded her arm through mine again and led me back to the dance floor where the dancers were in form for the final turn of a rondo. "Lady Spencer will direct you to my shop. There is no storefront or sign on a street. I work from my home, with fitting room and all. It allows a certain mystery which ladies who can afford my services find attractive. So, we shall work in mystery, too, in trust, with nothing written. I will trust you and you will trust me, and if at any time you do not feel so, you need only say and our contract will be dissolved."

"Agreed," I said. My heart swelled. I could never have hoped for such a contract, such a link. Such a price!

A candle near her guttered, flared, and went out. She moved her eyes slowly from it back to me and said, "Of course, I will say so, too. Are you able to keep a secret?"

"Like the night keeps the dark," I said. I smiled at her and gave her my fullest attention, even though as I turned I saw Cullah approaching. His face lit with excitement as he raised a hand to wave at me, but I felt it was vital at that moment not to lose her eyes' hold on my own. "Can you get me a better price on the silk embroidery hanks than I have been paying at the general mercantile? A merchant's discount, perhaps?"

Johanna waved to someone across the room, while saying, "Of course."

"With a penny's profit or so for yourself."

She turned to me again. "Of course," she repeated, and this time laughed openly. "You are young to have such a mind. We shall enjoy doing business together, my dear Resolute."

"I agree, Johanna. Now I must see what my beloved has to say to me, for he is trying hard to get my attention."

Mistress Parmenter moved with the grace of a swan through the room and seated herself next to an elderly blind woman. I smiled at Cullah, for he was as animated as a child with a candy. "Is Lady Spencer to announce us to the crowd?"

"No, it's not that. She said better to post banns in the usual way, for to announce us would not suit her son and his wife. She wishes us the most happiness, however. All that. But Resolute, no, Miss Talbot, oh, Miss Talbot, I must tell you. I have found him. I have him."

"You found whom? Is Jacob here?"

"No. Please, ask me no more questions. I am struck dumb. He is here." Cullah turned to someone behind him, a man tall enough that his hair showed above Cullah's head, yet his face was unseen. His form was more slender than Cullah's broad shoulders. The man was dressed in lavishly expensive and comely attire, yet with not the Williamsburg delicacy of Wallace. His clothes were a daring style from some faraway place: heavy blue brocade and cream color set off with a dashing maroon sash, under which he carried a short-sword. His face was bronzed, his eyes creased from too much sun, and he had a narrow, white scar from his hairline to just under his left eye. His visage carried an air of worldliness that set his features with age that seemed far beyond the youth in his dancing blue eyes.

The man turned his head one way, then another, eyeing me with gaiety and pleasure. Though it was not displeasing, it was uncommonly difficult to bear without turning away. He smiled broadly. At that second, he began to speak, and I saw he had a dimple on one cheek. "Resolute?" he asked.

My soul burst with the word as tears flew from my eyes and I cried out, "August!"

My brother swept me in his arms with no more care for decorum than the pirate he might be. No matter. No matter. I cared not the least. Here at last, my own brother, August Talbot, whole and hale and swinging me and my hoop skirts as if I were a bell tolling the return of a sailor long lost at sea. I cried out with joy. I held him with ferocity. When he put me down, all eyes were upon us.

I turned meekly to Lady Spencer, aware that I might lose her friendship by this odd display of bad manners, but the look on her face was one of triumph and a secret plan fulfilled. She held a glass of champagne in the air and said softly, "Here, here."

The cry was picked up by people all around the room. Applause and laughter filled the hall, and the story of our separation spread about the room with plenty of ornamentation by the time we heard it. I held August's arm tightly in both hands. He was lean and lithe and whole and alive. Gold chain glistened across his chest; he wore gold shoe buckles. I held his shoulder and shook my head. "I can hardly believe it is you."

"And I, you," he said. "Oh, it has been seven years too long."

"But you live, as I do."

"And what of Patience?" he asked softly.

"I know not where she is or if she lives. She left me on the path to Lexington."

"And you waited for me all this time? Your note was brought to me."

"I will have to tell you the whole tale, August. It is not a simple one. But what of you? How have you fared?"

"Excellently, once I overcame a certain obstacle. Uncle Rafe was—"

"A fiend. And are you still going to sea? Have you a house here?"

"I have two ships, my girl. No house."

"You must stay with me, then."

"I have quarters in town."

"But I have a house."

"A house? All your own? Well and aye, my girl. I should have known you would find a way to thrive. And a husband?"

I turned to Cullah. I said, "We are not yet wed." Then to August I said, "Two ships. Two? Oh, la! You shall take us home to Jamaica! Take us with you! I have money to pay passage if you wish. August, take us home!"

August's face went cold and all the merry light drained from his eyes. "Ressie. There is no home for me but the sea. Why would you and your betrothed want to go to Jamaica? It is not a place for an honest woodsman and a gentle young lady."

Tears flooded my eyes and poured down my cheeks. "Do you know about Mother?"

"I have seen her grave. I had its location from Lucy, one of the slaves, when I freed her with some others back on the island. I put a stone there with her name carved. I stood at Ma's grave and said a prayer for her."

I felt Cullah's hand on my arm. I trembled. His hand was so warm. My chest ached as if I were run through with a cutlass. I closed my eyes and said, "I want to go home." When I opened them, Cullah's face was all I could see.

He said, "Would you leave me, then?"

I hesitated. "No. Come with us. We three shall go. We shall be happy there."

I heard August's voice. "I have made our graces to Lady Spencer and family. I told her you were too overcome to continue to dance."

For the next four days, in my little parlor, I heard all about how August had grown up aboard privateers' ships until he had earned enough in wages and booty to buy his own rigs. He had fought Rafe MacAlister across the Atlantic and the Caribbean seas, had marooned the blackguard on a low-lying cay off the southern colonies, but from there Rafe had made his way north to find me.

I told him that Cullah and Jacob had killed the man, and August nodded, holding his mug of beer high. "My best to your man, then, and his father. No fouler devil ever stepped aboard a deck than MacAlister. Yet I never knew what his reason was to chase me all over the bloody, pardon, sweet sister, all over the forgotten sea."

I told him what Rafe had said to me of our mother's death, too. I did not tell him what I had suffered. August grew quiet. In those moments of silence, we exchanged looks that imparted to me some of the haunting sadness in his eyes, and I understood without hearing every dire nuance.

The house had seemed roomy enough with only myself, and had not lessened by Cullah's presence, but August seemed to fill the room with vibrations and light. When we had our fill of sad things he told me of adventure and gold, treasures and battles, and that he had made the Cape of Good Hope once but swore never to sail it again. August said he might purchase a house in Boston to be near me, though I told him he had a house in Lexington anytime he wished.

"When do you marry?" he asked.

"Soon," I said.

"I plan to sail before the snow flies again to get out of this heathen cold. I would be favored to leave you with a chest or two, to keep for me, if I may. I like your man. A straight and square fellow. And not a seaman; so much the better. And do you love him, or are you at least well suited to each other?"

"I do love him. But not as I thought love would be. Not so that I cannot think or carry on. I love him practically. I appreciate him, and I like his character. I am not charmed out of my mind by his presence."

August laughed. "That sounds so like you. Always a head on your shoulders. Why stoop to dashing charm and passion when you can have a solid, hardworking husband?"

"Why, indeed," I answered. The memory of Wallace's kisses flitted before me like a moth that had been disturbed and settled again in a new place. I said, "I saw Patience swayed into doing things unconscionable because of passion or love or whatever it was. I am perfectly happy to find love that comes with steady and honest good thought. Have you a wife?"

His eyes shaded then, growing darker as if a veil had pulled across them. "No."

Within a week, Cullah nailed our marriage banns to the door of the church. We spent days, he and Jacob, August and I, discussing where we should live, how we would make our ways together as one. It was decided that since I was literally the "lady of property," he would live in this house with me, and add to it. August asked him to build a wing, too, saying he would finance it, so that he had a place "in the country," to visit. Jacob declared he meant to live in Goody Carnegie's house. Cullah blanched at that thought, but Jacob said he knew ways to keep fairies out, and that he feared nothing with or without skin. Cullah's knee touched mine under our table when he said that. I knew Cullah to be mindful, indeed, of things which skin could not contain. Haunts, ghosts, fairy folk. The man was strong as any warrior, but worried about the wind.

When I asked what was to become of their shop in Concord, they both heartily agreed that it was time to move it to Lexington. The town had grown. Any who knew of them would come there, and those who did not would learn.

With more good fortune smiling upon me, the choice—on Cullah's insistence—that I had worn my own creation in the lavender embroidered gown, had filled Johanna Parmenter's slate with orders. She sent word within three days that customers waited anxiously for as much as I could turn out, and I could easily have a fortune by spring.

On the twenty-ninth of January, 1737, at noon I donned my lavender gown, my jewels, and a pair of white kid slippers that August carried in his trunk, to pledge my life and my fortune, my body and future, to Eadan Cullah MacLammond. I was yet seventeen, he twenty-five, though he looked younger than my brother who was twenty-three. Even as the minister said the words, I wondered what a marriage was to a man with so many names, and was I really now Wife Lamont or Wife MacLammond? Wife of Cullah or Eadan?

We celebrated with a small dinner with August and Jacob, and to my surprise, Johanna Parmenter came. They three left after the sun began to set. I could not be sure but there seemed to be a little too much fraternity among the three of them, and I suddenly wondered why I had met no husband of hers, since I knew she had had a babe. I wondered if it would be my brother she would bed before dawn.

Once again I was alone in the house with Cullah. All my previous desire turned to fear. Faced with the reality of him, the close physical presence, this surrender—filled me so with dread that my knees shook.

"I must clean the trenchers," I said.

Cullah removed his scarf and opened his collar. "I will help you."

"No. It is woman's work, and I am not ill. If I were, I would let you."

He put one hand upon my shoulder. "Will you come to me?" he asked.

I kept my eyes low and whispered, "If you will kiss me."

"I will kiss you."

I raised my face to his. Three candles—for I was sparing no luxury on my wedding day—gave a golden light to the room. He smelled of rosewater and beeswax, and I smiled, thinking of his boots, so shiny that he did not want to wear them outdoors, and had put on his work boots to walk out and put my goats into their shed. Cullah pulled the trenchers from my hands and set them before me on the table. He turned me to him. Then with more delicacy than I had used to don them, he raised the string of pearls from my neck and held them to his cheek. "They are still warm," he said. "They smell of you." He kissed the string of pearls as if they made a rosary, and then laid them on the table as he inspected my bodice. "I look at all these ties and ribbons and I am lost. I would help you but where do I begin?"

I smiled. "Kiss me again, and I will tell you," I said, then I fell into his arms as he complied.

"You are trembling," he said at last. "So am I."

"I have not," I started, but found my mouth dry and my tongue stilled.

He smiled. "I know you have no experience. You promised that for a kiss, you would tell me which cord to pull."

I pulled first at the cords that bound my stomacher to the waist. Then I loosed the sleeves. He pushed them back and down. "This next," I said, "is a ridiculous contraption of fashion, making it seem I am half caught in a birdcage. It is only two ties; one in front, here, and one you will have to find in back by my waist." In a moment, I felt the hoops and panniers fall to the floor and my skirt sink in on itself like sails in doldrums. I opened the skirt and stepped out of it, standing before Cullah in my shift alone.

The season had turned, the week before. A chill crossed me with the natural moistness of the shift after wearing a heavy dress gown. My nipples made two hard buttons that held the shift from my body. With the candles behind me, he must see through the light linen shift! My trembling increased. "I am so cold, now," I whispered. "I should wait in bed for you to undress."

He flung his shirt over his head and pulled me to his bare chest, holding me closely. My hands traveled the curves of his muscles as a blind woman would explore a statue, finding every swale and swell to my great liking. Then he sat upon the bed and pulled off his boots, letting them hit the floor with a solid bang. Cullah smiled and patted the bed beside him. "Come to bed, wife, but pray, for a moment, endure the cold and let me have a look at you."

He reached upward and pulled the shift over my head with no more care than he had his own shirt. It caught in my hairpins and sent them flying about the room like so many scattered grasshoppers. My hair fell upon my shoulders, and I pulled at it as his eyes traveled the length and breadth of me. "Oh, my love," he crooned, "you are so much more beautiful than all my dreams, all my ponderings and imaginings." Suddenly he straightened his back and his face showed mistrust. "Are you not a fairy? You must tell me if I ask, for fairies cannot lie."

"Oh, husband. I assure you I can lie and that alone proves I am of this world. It is my abiding sin and I struggle with it daily. I promised to be true to you, and with all my heart, I vow honesty and loyalty. I am no fairy." I drew in a breath so loudly it was as a sigh on the wind, for at that last word with one arm he drew me to him. His lips suckled one nipple as his fingers dimpled and caressed the other. The sound of his breath stopping and starting as he pressed and rolled his face into my breast gave me fear, but the feeling of pulling and suckling drove me mad with heat and a softening in my knees so that I nearly fell upon him. "Eadan," I said, surprised at the depth of my own voice. His hand against my back slid to my buttocks and explored the curves of them as I had his chest only moments before. "Eadan, my husband, take me to the bed, for I am chilled."

His powerful arms swept me up and over him, putting me gently upon the bed on the side against the wall. He doffed his trousers and curled under the blankets next to me. "Shall I build you a fire, Resolute, my wee wife?"

"I shall require a fire this night, and many others, I trow." He kissed my lips, and as he did I found his hand and put it against my breast again. "What is this fire, Eadan? What is it?" I could not contain my own longing. I cried out. I kissed him.

Eadan's other hand slid down my belly and rested between my legs. Rather than the violence and affront I had felt when touched thus by Rafe MacAlister, when Eadan moved his fingers through all my hidden places, as if he knew them but at the same time as if he had waited his whole life to find them, I felt only joy. He said, "All fire, especially this fire, is God's gift to mortals. We want it even before we know it." He stroked. My back drew into an arch, even against my bidding. He did it again.

"You must stop," I croaked.

"Why?"

"I shall perish."

He laughed softly, his voice so low as to be barely audible. "Take me with you." Then he rolled atop me, kissed me, and thrust himself inside me.

CHAPTER 23

September 1737

In the second week of September our first child tumbled into this world, nearly missing the sheets prepared for him. A boy. Eadan brought me beer-and-barley soup while I nursed. Jacob wanted us to name the babe after him. I had wanted him named after his father, but both men wore me down. Brendan Fergus Argyll Lamont, the third generation of Lamont clan on this shore, would be known to the world as Brendan MacLammond II. The four of us made a family. Well and aye.

Mrs. Boyne, our closest neighbor, had given up on the thought that I was enchanted, and had instructed me in the finer points of motherhood such as binding the babe's belly, healing my sore breasts with sheep fat and just-sheared wool, and drinking plenty of dark beer. Mr. Boyne kindly sheared one of his sheep himself, just for me to have the new wool.

With the birth of my child, I felt a terrible guilt and longing for James, Patience's child. I sewed him a little coat from the new wool. I made a second cap of warm wool. I packaged them and sent them to the Couvent Sainte-Ursule in Montréal. Every year, I promised myself, I would send a cap, a blanket, something I could make with my own hands, so that the boy would always know the touch of love from someone of his own blood. At Christmastide every year I would also send Rachael Johansen a letter and a scarf I had made.

MACLAMMOND was printed on the shingle before my love's shop in Lexington. Nothing more was needed. Jacob often spent some days at home, rather than the shop. Cullah complained sometimes about his father shirking his labor, but one evening when the light was just so from the window, I saw that Jacob's eye had clouds in it. That night in bed, I told Cullah and asked him to stop harrying his pa for the work, that I could use him at the house. Warping the loom was painstaking and detailed, and Jacob could mind goats and repair fence while I worked.

When he was not working in town, Cullah enlarged our home until it did indeed carry a third-floor tower. He told me that hearing the baby cry gave wings to his hammer, a feeling of urgency that the family would grow and need room. If someone ordered a fine maple or walnut chest, the scraps went into a bin. From them he built boxes and shelves, spoons and bowls. From his own stock, he created beds with posts to hold curtains, until our house resembled no less than the Roberts home had been. I was so proud of my house, of my husband and child, of my life. I attended meeting on Sunday when it pleased me. My husband worked hard and was known for honesty and generosity. I made the most beautiful linen in Massachusetts Colony, though Johanna continued to insist she purchased it from France. I had been trained by French weavers, so what was the difference?

Brendan was a quiet baby, sleeping much of the day, so that in short time I felt healed and went back to my work, this time only spinning and weaving in two-hour bits. Still, it was possible to finish a couple of yards a day at the loom, and I had lately been concentrating on woolens, for, with the approaching cold, Johanna had told me there was more call now. She had asked me to try the variation called linsey-woolsey, but though I had provided her with twenty-five yards of it, it sold slowly, only four or five yards at a time. I also made rougher brown wool for men's and boys' coats. That sold better.

I had had seventeen yards of black wool for capes on my loom when Brendan was born. Every morning I blessed the loom and touched the iron spider over the doorway, every evening I put it away with the second chant.

My Cullah never left for his shop without touching the doorpost and blessing all who passed thereunder and he never came to bed without thanking God for another day of good hard work, a project finished or a new one begun, and a wife and home to keep him through the night.

From the Boynes we learned also of their tradition; though they were Irish they could boast of three generations having been born on the land whereon they lived. Their beliefs in old ways were woven with the ways of Indians, the English, and some distant north folk. Mrs. Boyne could speak of them with great detail yet could never tell me whence they lived nor how long past her knowledge had come.

Jacob believed she unwittingly carried Norse tales as some of the Irish do, indeed some Scots also, for the heat of Viking blood was strong, he said, and he believed he saw it powerfully in my strawberry-and-flax-colored hair.

When he spoke of such things, he would raise his cup to Cullah and say, "Son, blessed will be your sons that carry her blood, and may your daughters all take after you, for that will be the strength of this family. A merry day, a merry day, I tell you, when you brought this lass to wife."

If Jacob's only thought was to endear himself to me, he made good work of it.

Every month I called upon Lady Spencer and showed her samples of my work so that she was always the first one to apply to Johanna for a gown of some cloth that appealed to her. And then one day, to my great surprise, Lady Spencer called upon me.

It was a bitter and windy day in March, the roads still frozen solid enough that horses' hooves sounded as if they traversed a pavement. I was in the midst of kneading bread when the coach appeared, and when I heard it I rushed to put a fresh apron over my waist and a clean lace cap over my hair.

Lady Spencer admired Brendan, commented on the style of my home, particularly the curtained windows and woven damask-covered bedsteads, but other than that stayed but a moment. As she stood at the door, adjusting her gloves, she turned and said, "The town council has been meeting lately. I find that it is best to listen but do nothing."

"Their meetings concern me? My husband?"

"Tell your husband I believe he is a loyal subject of the king."

"Yes, Madam, I shall."

After she left, simply waiting for Cullah to come home was beyond my strength. I had to do something. I put the bread to rise and changed and wrapped my babe, then walked to town. I found Cullah standing at the lathe, and I was careful not to make any sudden noise or movement that would distract him from the spinning form and the razor-sharp blade in his hands. I watched him. His shirt had come apart at the shoulder again. His apron wore into it, and as I observed I thought of how I might restitch the place so that it could withstand the wear. His work took him from one tool to another all day long. A frost of wood chips had caught on the back of his hair. When at last he let the machine spin to a stop, I stepped forward. "Husband?" I called. "I must speak to you."

He welcomed the two of us with a broad smile. When I told him of Lady Spencer's strange visit, his face showed his concern, yet he said, "I am lost for a reason to it. Loyal subject of the king? Which king did she mean?"

I drew in a breath. "I know not."

"Did you say anything to her?"

"Nothing more than bidding her good day."

"If anyone comes to the house today, you must turn them away. Either arrange it so that you seem not to be there, or bar the door and tell all that they must come back later when your husband is home."

"Cullah, what is happening?"

"Maybe nothing. I'll come home by way of Pa's house and we will talk."

Cullah did not come home that night. Though Brendan slept, I could not. There was no moon, either, and though I hated to waste it, I kept a candle going the night through and dozed in my chair by the fire. Finally, in the early dawn, just as he and Jacob had once arrived at this place, the two of them came a-clattering in. Brendan was hard at work on his breakfast, so I said nothing when the two men laid their belts at their chairs and drew them to the fireplace. Much as I wanted to cry out at them to explain how they could have kept me in worry the night through, I meant, first, to wait for them to speak and, second, to keep Brendan quiet, for he was finished nursing and nearly asleep.

I laid the babe in his cradle and pulled the kettle from the hob. Then I poured hot water on the last of the tea leaves we owned. Market day I would have to get more.

Cullah at last said, "I have spent the night with Apollos Rivoire. He is a Freemason in Boston. Do you know what that means?"

"No."

Jacob blew on the tea I poured for him. He said, "It means we are trying once again to fight the Hanoverians for the right to be our own people, have our own laws, and rule our own land."

"War?" I said, too loudly. "Do you mean we shall have war with the British army?"

"Not here," Cullah said. "Scotland. The Highlanders are rising. Forming up the clans to drive the British from their land. The French are our allies, and have always been. I, I gave them money to send over, Resolute. I had to do this."

"And to do this you spent all night in Boston? Without thought of your wife and babe? How much money? Are we to be put out of our home for some pipe dream of your father's? What of you, Jacob MacLammond? What part do you play in this? For Cullah would have no memories on which to draw. The dreams of free Scotland you have spoken about at our fire are your dreams, not his."

Jacob snarled. "It is not a dream. It is God's will."

"How much money?" I demanded.

"Forty pounds," Cullah said.

"Fort—" I sat hard in my chair, the feet out from under me. A year's income gone on some barmy dream of an old man and his memories. "Forty pounds," I said. "You did not think to speak to me before you ventured everything, no? Who is Rivoire?"

"The silversmith."

I gripped the edges of my seat. "Oh. Fine company, then. Maker of wealthy people's trinkets. He can afford to support something in a country across an ocean which we will never cross, on a land we will never see. He can throw money at windstorms for all I care."

"I'll hear no more about this, woman," he said. "It is done."

"Why did it take you the night through to do this? Where have you been?"

"We had to run from the soldiers and constables. We took swords he had made, pistols and muskets, clothing too, to a ship sailing for Mull. It left on the risen tide at midnight. The rest of the time we've spent coming home to you and now and then hiding, of course."

I put a hand above my eyes and pressed against the pain throbbing there. "Smuggling muskets? Hiding? Now and then? Of course. A ship bound for Mull. With forty pounds of hard-earned gold belonging to us upon it. Well. So the silversmith makes swords in his secret workshop. And you two have been smuggling arms to a foreign kingdom. Cullah, the Scots want to overthrow King George? That is treason! You could both hang! And, oh, Eadan, whatever shall we do without your money?"

Jacob cleared his throat. "They are not after killing the king. George Second has nothing to fear. We want our own king of Scotland, James Stuart, returned to the throne. We want no English soil; we want our own land back. And this family shall do as we have *already* done without that money, for 'twas hid by me *before* we come here, lass."

I stared hard at him, unable to keep my lower lip from protruding as if I were five years old. "I do not believe you. Cullah just said he gave our money."

Jacob said, "Well and aye. I had put it away for Brendan's school. But this—"

I poured out tears that surprised even me. Brendan stirred at the noise as I wept with full heartbreak. My son's schooling had been sacrificed for Scotland's king? No doubt some knock-kneed dimwit of illegitimate inbreeding got on a pox-eaten slattern by that devil Cromwell or one of his minions. I wished the ship to sink. I wished James Stuart, whoever he was, to hang. I wished Cullah MacLammond to fall down the well.

Cullah said, "The Rivoires are Huguenots," in a reassuring tone.

That meant nothing to me. I cried all the harder, making quite a racket.

"We are invited to supper tomorrow. Some of the townspeople will be there. They are much eager to meet you, Ressie. You must."

I was so angry I could hardly speak. At last I said, "What is a Huguenot?"

"A Frenchman."

"I have a child to nurse."

"It is a dinner for certain people. So that we are all in one accord. It is done."

"Even if I spend the entire evening in the kitchen with our baby in my lap and my breasts ogled by every butler and servant?"

Cullah bristled. "I'll kill 'em. Anyway, Brendan will not misbehave. He's a bonny good laddie."

"He is neither good nor bad, he is six months old. There is throat distemper and influenza in Boston, and consumption and measles. Why did you do this to me?"

He leaned back in his chair. "That's a fine thing. What, are you too highborn for the likes of them? You are invited to dine with the best of society, decent people who would take you right in, and you think it is a sentence."

"It could well be. And I said it not because they are not worthy. I am nursing!"

"I am going to work." He stood up, and moving angrily, took his belt and slapped his hat on his head. It landed wrong and he straightened it.

"That is a good thing, Cullah MacLammond," I snapped.

"Well and aye," he said, and slammed the door.

Jacob sat at the table and after a while he raised his one eye carefully to peer in my direction. I pointed to the door and said, "You had better go find some work, too, for this boy is going to school and if you just wagered Harvard—yes, I know about Harvard—if you just wagered Harvard on some daft, worm-eaten, bowlegged king-in-a-kilt, you had better get it back by the time the boy is old enough to need it."

"Woman, you've got a tongue on you like a fishwife."

"Well and aye. You knew that before you moved in. Go to work. Out with you."

He slammed the door, too, but called through the wooden barrier, "I have had no breakfast but the sharp end of your tongue!"

"Forty pounds," I shouted in reply, which woke up Brendan, who cried, and I sighed, changed his clouties, and rocked him again. I did not spin or weave the whole day through. I wandered the house, the yard, the small barn. I thought and thought about what had gone on. To what kind of man was I married? Was there a charm for a man who had lost his senses?

The morrow came and I found with some dismay that I did not fit well into my lavender gown. I left the panniers on a hook and loosened the stomacher, and still no help. I wore a simpler gown, still well made, but not lavish, and I put a parcel of extra clouties for Brendan in our small wagon. Jacob stayed at the house. I barely spoke to Cullah all the way to Boston. To say I faced this evening with strangers and a nursing babe at my breast with dread would be too soft.

What I discovered, however, was that Monsieur Rivoire was glad to have someone to whom to speak French, though his wife was English and they had long ago Anglicized their name to Revere. Their tiny lad was but two and was named Paul. Though they were stern Protestants, their loyalties lay not in their religion but in Masonic code. So this was what drew my Cullah and his father together with these odd fellows, I marveled. While their little Paul did his best to play peek-at-me with Brendan, who dutifully laughed at his new playmate, I talked with Deborah, Paul's mother, and other women there.

So we were part of a new society. Making our way home at nearly midnight, my babe close in and warm under many blankets and a great rug, I
watched our breaths mingle before us. The night was crisp and the cold
hurt my cheeks.

After a long silence, Cullah said, "When they ask of us, we give. And if
we ever have need, we have to but ask of them and they will give."

I said, "Deborah Revere came from a very wealthy family. Easy for her
to give."

"He married well."

"No one can say you married me for money."

"I married you to have someone to cuff me about."

"This society, these people, they have secrets."

"Aye."

"And you acted as if I were an outsider. As if you have secrets from me.
I am on your side, Cullah MacLammond. Did you not know that?"

"You would not have agreed to what Pa and I did."

"Of course not. You do not ask why, you just want blind obedience?"

"Certainly. That makes life easier." He smiled then, and turned to me
and winked.

I said, "You should have married a horse, then."

"Hear that, Sam?" he called to the horse. "Sam says no, that he cannot
make a hasty pudding to save his life. No. Had to marry you. Bewitched by
a wee fairy."

I made my voice stern as I could. "If ever something is amiss, if you
need me to meet you in secret, or you need me to understand something,
you must give me a word."

"What word?"

"My sister used '*gumboo*.'"

"That's likely enough."

"She cut it into a piece of bread. That was when I knew we were leaving
the convent. Before that, if we were to meet to talk, she said 'candlestick.'"

"If I use the word 'cross' and it seems out of place, that will be a signal
and you will meet me in our parlor, or our kitchen; that is better."

"All right."

"And if I use the word 'sword' you will immediately go to our bedroom."

"Yes. And what then?"

Cullah looked at me and grinned, wrinkling his nose mischievously. "Prepare."

I gasped. "I have married a heathen."

"Aye. One who can wield a sword well." Cullah nudged my side with his elbow.

I felt my frown start to break. He was laughing but I felt angry still. I did not want to let go of the anger and its hold on my heart. "Oh, leave me alone, Cullah."

"I cannot do that. You've married a heathen and I'll not *let* him leave you alone. I'd ask you to forgive me if I knew all I need forgiving for." The horse snorted loudly.

I said, "There is a *list*."

After a while he nodded and said, "Ah. Good thing I can't read," and nudged my side again.

Our days before Brendan's arrival had rolled in and out, my heart full of this new life as wife. I learned much more about cooking for men, particularly making everything in greater quantities than I expected. I tended geese and goats and added chickens to my flocks. I found I liked hens and their dear sounds. To say we never disagreed would be a lie; of course we argued. But each day I found new things to admire about Cullah, things that in knowing made a great difference to me in how I felt about him, and had I not known, I would have been so much less in favor of my choice of him.

In between working at his trade, he worked on our house, ever building, planning, talking about this and that. I learned from him as if a school of woodcraft opened on our supper board each evening. I knew the differences between a raised panel and a cove molding, an ogee and a wooden Dutchman, and I knew to never, never set a plane upon anything not made of wood. He had a head for money and business and could estimate down to a farthing the cost of a paneled room, a barn, or a cradle, multiply a goodly sum for profit, reduce a percentage to slight his competition to win the project, and still make us a fine living.

For my own weaving I thought only in terms of cost against materials. A penny for a farthing, and waste was my mortal enemy. A needle that went dull I sharpened until it was too small to hold. When Cullah said I was not making enough profit for the hours I spent in embroidery, he told me how to account for each figure upon the yard, and how to price the fabric. Johanna was furious when first I raised my price, and threatened to buy from someone else, making me fear for our future. I wept bitter tears, thinking my husband had been too demanding, not understanding the nature of women's business and that it was different from men's businesses. The following day she sent a boy to my house with a message begging forgiveness, assuring me that my price would be met. Cullah seemed to me a simple craftsman, but perhaps I had judged too soon. Perhaps he knew people far better than I.

That night, I tucked our babe in his cradle and stoked up the fire while Cullah put the horse in the barn. He came up the stairs with icy hands, and when he formed himself next to me like two zigzags woven into the bed itself, our places so known that the ticking seemed to shape to us, his knees felt like blocks of ice against the backs of my legs. I sighed, listening to the rhythms of these two asleep, the babe's soft snore promising to become more resonant with age.

I had left a candle to burn to the wick and to be cleaned out for a fresh taper in the morning, so there was still light near the bed and the reassuring smell of bayberry wax closeted my little family. I laid my hand upon my husband's arm, knowing, as if my hand lay upon some wild animal, the fibers of him, the bone and tendon, the sun-roughened skin and thick hair on his forearm.

I had been lost. Adrift. Captive. Abandoned. Without cunning or force, Cullah MacLammond had claimed me and captured me. Contrary to his words, I was the one fairy-fettered by him. I was part of this place now. Irrevocably, unchanging, I had become part of a land of cold and snow and thatched houses just as those of which Ma and Pa had once told me of old England. This New England had claimed me. I had only to wait to see what we should be to each other.

CHAPTER 24

May 7, 1738

"The king is mad," my brother said under his breath. "First he hires me to do a thing and then tries to hang me for doing it. Resolute, don't embroider the bloody thing, just sew it up. And hurry."

My hands trembled and my throat clenched. Much as plying my needles and thread were to my life, I had never sewn human flesh, swollen and running red upon my kitchen table. "They will not find you. Cullah built many a hiding place in this house."

"Where is he?"

"Coming."

"Did he see?"

"He saw."

"Will he give me over to them?"

"My husband is a good man, August Talbot. He would never betray you. Be still. There, now the baby is crying. I cannot get the knot to stay."

"Leave a tail on it and tie a square knot. Nothing fancy. I'm not a pillow slip."

"Your skin is tanned and tough as a hide and the blood is so slick."

"I hear horses." He stood so quickly the three-legged stool tipped over and he pulled the needle from my fingers. It swung from his arm like a tassel.

I said, "Follow me," and across the kitchen to the stairs to our basement we went, where, halfway down, I pushed aside a square panel in the wall. "Step up here. Watch your arm."

"If it comes open I'll hire another seamstress."

I pushed the panel in place and got back to the kitchen, took the haunch of goat from its hook in the fireplace and flopped it onto the puddle of blood on my table. I had just set the stool aright as the door flew open. Three men dressed as yeomen charged into the room, short-swords drawn and ready. One of them said, "We're looking for a ruffian, Mistress. A pirate who goes by the name Talbot."

I gestured with a large knife. "I am not he," I said. I began cutting into the haunch, mingling the goat blood with my brother's. "You let in flies. Close the door."

The answer took them so aback, I believe, that they stammered and looked to each other for a moment before he went on. "Goodwife, did you hear a horse go past?"

"Not a sound but my babe crying. Search the house if you want." Indeed the plaintive wailing stirred my heart, but I had to continue my ruse of urgent meat cutting.

At that moment a bang and several small thumps came from the back of the house. The men hurried across the room toward the side door just as Cullah came through it and greeted them with a shout. "What's this? Who are you men? Robbed in my own house?" He pushed past them carrying a shovel coated with mud. I knew he had been in the low section, burying the sack of gold for which August had nearly died. "Will you look at this, wife? Talmadge borrows my only iron shovel and returns it like this! I swear he'll have the use of it no more."

I saw his gaze pause at the pool of blood and the goat shank on the table, and I said, "Will we have enough firewood to get this cooked by suppertime? And look you there, take care what you are dropping on my floor, husband. Brendan is creeping now. As to what these men want with us, it seems they are looking for a lost horse." Actually our son was walking, too, but I was playing a part, and I knew even if he came down the stairs he would do it backward on all fours.

After a few threats and questions, Cullah convinced them that he had been doing nothing more sinister than fetching his shovel, ill-used by a neighbor. The men left after warning us again to beware of rovers and picaroons traveling the countryside.

August stayed in his nook while the baby played, ate his porridge, was washed and dressed and put to bed. When at last the house was quiet, Cullah made a birdcall. August came forth. I set a plate of meat stew and beans before him, poured him a flagon of ale, and took a fresh loaf of bread from the coals.

That evening, by the light of a single candle, Cullah, August, Jacob, and I talked of how we would see August to some safe harbor out of the reach of colonial constabulary until he could hear from the minister in England and get his commission again. I felt proud of them both, and a little afraid of the meeting, as if I were pouring grease into a fire. They were both dangerous men.

"Of course you can stay," Cullah said. "But it would be best to wear a farmer's clothes and work our fields, if it's to be for a while. People in Boston know you."

August smiled. In the light, his grin made an old scar on his face shine like a ribbon of satin. "A farmer? Yes, a farmer."

"You will still have to explain to the town council who this man is living with us," I said. "No stranger may stay here without supplying a witness to his character."

"You'll do that for me, won't you, sister?"

I smiled. My brother's character was not something I wished to know too well. I loved him. I would hide him. Help him. To vouch for him with a clear conscience was another matter, but that, too, I would do.

"It's still hard frost," Jacob said.

Cullah said, "The ground will break soon. It's the only other occupation that will explain the swarthiness of your face. Ressie, how many days until a full moon?"

It was not lost on me that I sat surrounded by villains of a sort, and full of child and nursing another by one of them. Only a handful of people living knew of Cullah's identity as Eadan Lamont. I was not drawn to him for that. No, I loved Cullah for everything else he was, tender, courageous, a savior in times of terror, a willing bearer of the scars upon my heart. We fit each other like butter in a mold, pressed together; where one lacked the other excelled. My life was filled with learning to be a woodsman's wife, owner of a farm, watching the moon for times to plant, to break ground, to harvest. I kept goats and geese, chickens and sheep. I raised flax and fruit trees. Most of all, I spent any moment I could at my wheels or my loom, spinning and weaving. The work had left its peculiar scars and calluses upon my hands. "Another five days," I said.

That evening at our fireside, after Cullah left us to put the horse in the barn, August said, "I still find myself surprised at your house and home, Ressie. Cullah is a good man. I wish I knew what became of Patience."

"I told you what became of her."

"I meant I wished I knew whether she was happy. If she is not mistreated, I should be happy for her also."

"As the wife of an Indian? I think mistreatment is her only lot. She chose it."

He was silent long enough to make me less sure that he agreed with me and only wished not to argue. "There are women who refuse to marry at all."

"I considered that."

"Yet you chose to become a wife."

"I did. Cullah—I loved him at once—he was honest and bright and steady."

August smiled. "He reminds me of Pa."

Tears flooded my eyes. The babe within me wriggled as if awakened by a great noise. "I had planned to marry a planter with a cane field."

"This is better," he said. After a long silence he said, "I had planned to marry a duchess with a merry eye."

"What became of her?"

"Other men caught her eye, too. For all her wealth and charms aplenty, I would not be a pitied cuckold."

"I will introduce you to a noble, honest woman."

"You would sentence one of your friends to marriage to a seaman? No. I prefer to find home here with you, leave the sea when I should and the land when I must. I will be the bonniest uncle any children could ever have, and their benefactor when I am dead."

I gave him blankets to make a bed by our fire. While he was busy, I said, absentmindedly, "One thing I know, our son will learn to read and write, so he can do more than make an X for himself. I will teach him myself, as Ma taught us."

Cullah had returned and heard it. "Will you have him outreason his father?"

I paused before answering, as I had seen Cullah do at times, when he wanted to be sure to be heard without raising someone's ire. "His father is intelligent and knows how to calculate things beyond my schooling. That our son could go to school I can only dream. How can one man's X differ from another's, without a witness? But a signature, that is your own hand. I can teach you that, and him, more, as well."

"I'll not have you teach me it."

I bridled inside at his words. His pride was hurt by such a simple thing. This was a mere trifle in the fabric of our lives, and I would not have him angry over it if I could. "Then I shall not if you do not wish it. You took dancing lessons to escort me to a country dance. A lesson in signing your name is about contracts and business. Far less important than dancing."

"Leave it be, Resolute."

"Well and aye, then." I would not argue with him over our table, nor did I want to exchange more about it in front of my brother. I put the babe back in his bed, poured the men more cider, and me some ale. Afterward the men laughed and joked while I lit candles then cleaned the trenchers.

We named our second son Benjamin. Every time I knew another birthing was before me, I wondered if this time I should breathe my last. It serves no woman to look upon her life with much expectation. Women as well as men may be felled by accident or by disease, but no woman asks a man to risk his life and the lives of his children just to bear them. Men believe that their strength is in their sinews, mastery of trade or horsemanship, and skill with a sword or pistol. Some would say their brawn is displayed in witty reasoning and conversation, while women know, be she queen or fishwife, that her greatest strength is in her heart. She lays down her life to bring forth a child, and then rises up and does it again. My brother congratulated me on the effort which elicited the screams he had heard, along with my surviving what he, with complete aplomb, called torture worthy of any rack.

By the light of the first spring moon, August worked side by side with Cullah and Jacob, planting corn and other vegetables, flax, barley, and oats. At the end of the northern field, the men worked with shovels around some object buried in the ground. Something round and heavy, that clanged when struck by the spade. It was a bell. Buried deep, it was not large, probably from a ship. The clapper was rusted away. In the mound left at the mouth of the bell lay a rotted leather pouch. Cullah laid it in my hands. I coaxed the bag to open, but it was so hard stuck it would not give to gentle prodding. I pulled it to find inside a little piece of leather, on it, two Xs, below them, a smear of brown.

"Is that blood?" I asked, with the babe suckling under a shawl.

Jacob looked at it this way and that. "I think it is. Two people signed their *X* and made a blood oath, and laid this bell atop it. It meant something to them but you'd have to find someone who knew the Carnegie family to explain it, if there are any left."

August made a face and said, "There's a body buried somewhere about, I'd wager. Someone swore in blood to keep a secret, and that usually means a murder."

"Ah, bury it back," said Cullah.

"No," I said. "Bury the oath, if it pleases you. I want the bell. Put it by the back door and I shall clean it."

"What do you want with a rusted bell?"

"I can call you in for supper by use of a mallet and this bell."

"Ah, woman. It will sound like you're calling a church meeting. Besides, I am no farmer to be in a field all year. I go back to my craft soon as we get this planted."

I winked at him and turned, going back to the house, sure that he would bring it for me. That evening he brought the bell, cleaned of all soil, and other things that he had found buried in the field. Five cannonballs, an iron hook with part of a key still on it, a metal ring about five inches in diameter, and a two-and-a-half-foot-long cannon without a frame or end. It was a piece that I knew came from a ship.

I laughed and asked, "Cullah? Where is the booty? No chest of gold?"

August froze in place. "Are you saying it is gone?"

Cullah said, "Your box is safely tucked under that beech tree at the bend in the stream. Your sister has a sense of humor."

A few evenings later, when Cullah came in for supper, we had not sat long before we heard a stirring from our animals. Just like people, they like to settle in after dark. Geese make a good alarm, for no one enters a yard without their sounding off. The goats added their bleating to the noise, and soon the whole barnyard was awake and calling. Someone knocked on the front door. Jacob stood, pulling a small dagger from his boot, then sat again, with it hidden by his arm. August and Cullah stepped into the shadows of the pantry and pulled swords from the lintel, waiting. Jacob nodded. I opened the door.

A man in a tricorn hat with a long black cloak nodded at me as he removed the hat. His face was as dark as an African but his features were sharp and chiseled rather than rounded. His long, straight hair was pulled back into a tail and tied with a fresh ribbon. "Evening, madam. The Guinea sent me here."

I knew that was a code connected to my brother's business. I did not like that he worked in secrecy and darkness, but I had grown used to it. "Come in, sir. Will you have supper?" I asked.

The messenger looked at Jacob and asked, "Is there a man about? Another man, I mean?"

August stepped into the candlelight. He did not try to hide the sword in his hand. "There is another, sir. You look fresh from the sea. How goes the wind, sir?" he asked.

"Fair and steady. East by northeast; freshening."

August put forth his left hand, the right still ready with a sword. "Who sent you?"

"The Guinea, sir," he said, clasping August's left hand in his own left hand.

"And his name?"

The man grinned, showing a full set of very white teeth. "They that know him call him 'Guinea.' He said you would know him by another name. I am to hear it from you before we finish here."

"Would it be Tig the Fiddler?"

"Aye, it could. Captain Talbot would know the more of it."

"Signed his papers as Carlo Delfini."

"Aye." The man handed him a folded paper. As August flipped it open and read it, the messenger pulled forth another paper. "You'll be wanting this, Captain Talbot."

August read with concentration. His commission as a privateer had been reinstated. The dark man handed him a pouch, too. August upended it and poured a stack of gold coin into his palm. He selected two of the largest coins and gave them to the messenger, saying, "Wait for me outside."

"At your service, sir." The man placed the coins into the lining of his hat, put it on his head, and without so much as a nod to the rest of us, closed the door behind himself.

August disappeared almost as quickly, and reappeared from the hidden alcove in the stairway wearing his own clothing, short breeches and stockings, a flared coat I had cleaned and patched, and a new linen blouse replacing the rough woolen farmer's garb. He looked every bit the sea captain.

He laid his broad cockaded hat on a stool and put the rest of the coins back into the pouch. That, he presented to Cullah. "For your help and house, friend."

"I'll not be paid for doing a good for my family. Or for anyone."

" 'Tis not payment. You've done as you could for me. I do as I can for you. Please." August shook the sack toward him. It struck me then, the difference in the two. August was tall and lean, dashing and dark, sleek and swift as an adder. Cullah was wide shouldered, broad chested, formidable in a fight, like a bull enraged. When they had dressed alike, my heart had told me they were alike. I knew that judgment was flawed.

Cullah took the gold and then August was gone into the night. I watched him ride away with the same mix of longing and anger I felt every time he left me. I felt cross. It seemed to me that what I wanted most in the world was having everyone always to abide with me. "Cullah, you must be careful with that."

"I will. Here. Put it where you hide the other money. And count it first."

I opened the bag. Without pouring it out I saw at least a dozen gold crowns and more than that of doubloons. "It is at least twenty pounds. You told me you needed a new blade for your saw."

"Two men in town owe me for cabinetwork. I will wait until they pay. This will go toward our sons' schooling if we leave it be."

As we readied for bed, Cullah lay in the darkness, his face searching the ceiling. I crawled in next to him, but his arms did not reach for me. "Good night, my love," I whispered, and rolled to face the wall. I was exhausted. I would have had him if he had reached for me, but if he would not, I would sleep hard.

"Resolute?"

"Yes?"

"Write it, then. The letters that make my name. I watched him read that paper. It is important. I have no time for schooling. Never have. But you write it on something I can carry to the shop. I will learn it."

In a few days, Cullah came home, puffed himself up, and said, "I signed an order for seasoned hickory today."

As the meaning of that dawned in my heart, I swelled with pride for him. "Fine. Very fine, husband."

Cullah added a room for my brother's use alone, should he ever have need again of a safe harbor this far inland. By the time Benjamin was six months of age, our house had eight rooms including a kitchen under the same roof, not counting the lower stony level where the loom sat.

In the summer of 1739, I lay thrashing and sweating in our bed on a mercilessly hot night. Some, I have heard, plead for death, preferring its quiet knell to even one more hour of childbed. By dawn, when the world had a gentler coolness and a light breeze came in the windows, the babe was born. A woman child, at last, I thought, with great swelling of my heart.

Cullah was beside himself with her wee presence. He stared at the little mite as if he had never imagined himself the father of anything but an army of brawn and bone. Jacob marveled at the fineness of her fingers, long and straight, as they explored his face and clutched his hair. He wanted to name her Mary Barbara, after his mother, but that made me cry. So, in a spell of quiet when all the children slept and the three men in my life sat upon the foot of my childbed, I told them stories of my captivity, and how Birgitta had called me "Mary" by her own whim. I could not allow my first daughter to bear the name Mary.

For almost a week we bantered about names, though we had worked on that through my expectation, too. At last I said, "Eugenia Gwyneth is my choice."

Cullah put his hand against his chin. At length he said, "It is a good name. A fine one." He picked her up, as tiny in his hands as a loaf of bread. "Gwyneth? Eugenia? Gwenny, my love? Wee darling, Eugenia Gwyneth. Besides, she likes it. She smiled. And don't tell me any prattle that it was just her tummy bubbling that made her do it. Yes, she's our wee Gwenny. It suits her ladyship fine."

"Eadan, you are smitten beyond all reason." I adored him for the way he adored Gwyneth. Yet, fear clutched at the back of my neck as if it were a hand, or a strike from old Birgitta's goat stick. Best never love a child too much. Best never think they are yours to keep. This one was not a week on this earth, and might be snatched away from us any moment. I knew so many women, now, who suffered the loss of so many, sometimes three or four children carried away in a single night by some scourge or other. As Cullah placed Gwyneth in my arms I snuggled her to me and kissed her perfect little bald head. Kissed her pinched-shut eyes. No, I will not love you, I promised myself. The women in my life whom I have loved, even those I have not, have all left me for death's dark shadows. I whispered, "Gwyneth, leave me not." The babe smiled again. "And be not so pretty a thing that your father's heart breaks never to mend when you do."

I studied her little form with apprehension that I had not felt at the births of my two sons, for though in the years of their births the chief source of our income had been the making of small coffins, we had been left un-scathed. This year of Gwenny's arrival was a year of no plagues, no fevers or distempers other than mild cases of quinsy or colds. That alone filled me with dread. This delicate woman-child had no reason to die, had been born with a shield, I thought. At least for now.

At least for now.

By May of 1746, when I was twenty-seven, we had five children. Brendan, Benjamin, Gwyneth, Barbara, and Grandan Stuart, a wee boy with his father's dark hair already thick upon his head at birth. Our lives were peaceable though I was always tired. When I looked back at those days later, I wonder I ever made it through a day. My house was never clean. No furniture went without scratches. The winters were long indeed, with the children confined indoors. Yet, never did I feel as haggard and as filthy as I had living in the Haskens' house. My children's clouties were cleaned daily, and Cullah built a walk-through to get to the barn where we boiled and soaped daily.

We heard of Indian attacks, but they were always some distant place. New France had spread to the west, but none of that affected my family. We feared little, and life was pastoral, gentle, broken only by a squabble among the children.

My husband and I had rare cause to disagree, but then, we had rare time to speak to one another. Other than my consternation at Jacob adding some tale or other of ghosts or fairies to frighten the children into being good, I felt happy. I wove when I had time, simple cloth for children's clothing, though I made myself notes of things I had seen or imagined and wished to try. A silken weft on threes. A line of indigo, heavy-twisted, on tens. I spun if the children were quiet or asleep, though sometimes I fell asleep at my wheel. I even learned to knit in my sleep, I believed, often sur-prised at what I had done though my mind felt no more lively than a turnip.

One summer's day Cullah came in the door and said, "Wife, bring the children here to me." I thought at the time it was an odd thing because every day, unless one of them was asleep, they came running to him when he returned from working. Grandan was nursing at the time, and I had long ago left off covering myself unless there were strangers in the house. The baby slupped at my breast and for a moment Cullah lost his grim expression and smiled, though it was but a moment. "From now on, your grandfather Jacob is coming to live in this house. He is getting old, and I want him to be here."

"What is wrong?" I asked.

He turned away as if there were some answer in the stones of the fireplace. "I'm worried. He's old. Some preacher walking the streets today spoke of doom. The Highlanders are gone. Not just defeated, butchered to the last. Culloden field. The British have killed us. My God. There is not a clan left, Ressie. Not a man left alive. Not a babe."

"Was this the cause for which you sent forty pounds? La, husband. Do not weep. Our lives are good, Cullah. There is corn growing in the garden, our little ones are—"

"Stop! Say nothing more. You will pull ghosts from the trees by saying aloud we have some they want to prey upon here. I have to tell Pa. All our kin are dead. Do not wait up for me."

"What about your supper?" I asked, thinking that was what he meant.

"I'll have it with him," he said, and charged out the door.

Never mind that I had been in this house during many a stormy night. This night, terror struck me as I had not felt in a long time. Moments became hours. I lit candles, three upstairs and three down, to quell my fear. My heart beat so that everything I or the children said was muffled by the pounding of it. The storm began in earnest just as darkness drew in upon us. Though this house was not drafty, the wind came from a different direction, it seemed. An explosion of thunder came with a gust that snuffed every candle. It sent me back in time to being that small girl in the hold of a ship under cannons blasting away. Lightning flashed, for some seconds charging up the room with blue light, then blackening everything beyond what we expected. Benjamin began to cry, and because he did, Barbara and Gwyneth also cried. Brendan made a brave effort to keep his face still, but as I got a taper lit, I saw him turn away from me and wipe at his face with his cuffs. I cleaned the little ones for bed and sent the two older boys upstairs.

If Cullah were here, he would make them jolly, I thought. Cullah and Jacob would tease them and tell them God was beating bad angels with his fists, or blowing ghosts out of the trees. At last, seeing no other way to calm them, I called all the children in with me. Every time they heard thunder I bade them shake their feet to mimic God kicking bad angels out of heaven, and soon their tears became laughter. Grandan slept and soon Barbara did, too. The storm slaked, and the children calmed. The two oldest boys slept. Gwenny stared. "Close your eyes," I said.

"Where's Pa?" she asked.

"He's coming with Grandpa."

"When is he coming?" she pleaded.

I caught myself. It was as if she, too, knew something was amiss, felt that this strange night could be the end or the beginning of something dark. I smiled and said, "I am sure that with the storm, Grandpa said to him"—I mimicked Jacob's accent, rolling all the *r*'s to great effect—" 'Cullah me boy, we shan't go out on a colly-waddler of a night as this one. Just you sit by me fire while I tell ye about a real storm. Let's see, that was in forty-three. Or was it twenty-three? Well, never mind. That storm was so bad, the wind blew so hard, it blew a stone castle all the way from Jamaica to Lexington. And you know what was in it?' " I paused, for Gwenny had heard the story before.

"A princess?"

"Yes. And do you know who she grew up to be?"

She said, "A knight's lady, who maked her own clothes and those of her bairnies, jus' like in the Bible, she work-ed day and night to do it."

"You know all my stories," I said, kissing my fingertip and touching her nose with it.

"Tell me again about the little girls running across the roof to see the ocean."

"The widow's walk was high up, on the tip-top of the castle. It had a staircase that went through a dark attic and came out on top where the sun was hot and seagulls turned cartwheels all day long."

"Just like Brendan does?"

"Exactly. Though they were birds and had no such long legs. They put out their wings like this."

Gwenny stretched out her arms and waved them about. "I want to fly," she said.

I could not keep the smile in place. A quick image came to mind of all the little tombstones I knew, their carved baby faces couched by feathered wings above engraved names. "It is not in God's goodwill for people to fly, Gwenny. That is for birds. People have something much more important to do."

"What? Sewing and numbers and weaving?"

"Perhaps." I heard the door open below.

Gwenny sat up and said, "Papa!"

I heard no familiar voices. In fact, no voices at all. "No doubt the door simply blew open. Keep quiet and let the other children sleep, now. You should be asleep, yourself. You stay here and I will go and help him and Grandpa off with their wet things. You keep my spot warm, all right?"

"I shall, Ma."

"Good girl. Bless you, my Gwenny. I will be right back." Then I left with a single candle, leaving one alight in the room over the heads of our dear little ones. I crept down the stairs holding my breath and trying to make no sound at all. At the foot of it I peered into the parlor. Two large figures crouched before my fire. I spoke no word. My hands trembled at my lips.

One of them straightened up. "Colly-waddler," he said. "Pure colly-waddler."

"Jacob?" I whispered, now mindful of the children.

The other man turned. Cullah. "Oh," I cried, and ran to him, setting the candle upon the table before I flew into his arms. "I was so frightened."

He smiled down at me, pulling off his cap and cloak. "Now, Resolute, I told you where I was gone. You didn't expect me to trudge uphill in mud from one little house to my own in the black of night in the middle of a storm, did you?"

"But so long? You could have gone to Boston and back in that time. You terrified the children with talk of ghosts before you left."

The look on his face changed and he studied my eyes. "You are afraid," he said. "Poor wife. I terrified you, too."

Jacob knuckled Cullah in the arm and said, "You'd a done better by her to stay with her during the storm and get me in the morning. There was no reason to rush."

"A fellow in town was speaking on the corner near the shop where I could hear him the day long. Gave me to fright of the old ways, the fairy ways and the small people, brownies in the shadows, you know. He preached so well I thought the devil was at me."

I rubbed my forehead, trying to hide my astonishment. "Have you eaten?"

"We did," Jacob said.

"Well, come up to bed then. We shall have to carry all the children to their beds for they are all in ours."

After that time, on Cullah's insistence, Jacob lived with us. I watched my husband change somewhat. He seemed suspicious of everyone and everything outside the circle of our hearth, and began a series of changes to the house. Where there was an ample room, a new wall was built a foot or so away from the old, with shelves and notches in the paneling to lift and move things, so that every square of panel hid a secret box as if his new fears could only be assuaged by building places to hide. Some of them could have hidden one of the children, some were too small to house a thing larger than my hand. On the outside, too, he built an addition that would look to the world as if it were always part of the saltbox house, yet it enclosed a stairwell to the barn. The two of them worked through the rest of the summer on all the little secret places of this house, until it was as honeycombed as the home in which I grew up, in Jamaica.

I asked him to put a siding of rock around the original house where I worked. In it we could store all things of value which might be lost in a fire, such as the deed to this land and our marriage papers. I stored the old tattered petticoats, the pearls, the brooch, and the ruby ring, along with Ma's other jewels in their caskets on a shelf behind the loom. All I had to do if I wished to wear them was take a piece of wood from the wall which appeared to be a brace. Behind that, a flattened piece of lead flashing could be moved, and it revealed a slot where I could push a narrow stone aside to the little crypt. Before I closed it that first night, with a satisfied smile, I also placed within it thirty-one pounds in gold coin as savings against any need in the winter to come. Cullah and I spent hours devising hiding places for things large and small.

Fall turned early so that by the third week of August we were chilled at night and needing blankets put back upon the beds. I awoke one night in September with a familiar flutter in my belly. I stood and looked out our window upon the full-moon-lit fields below. A child. A sixth child. Oh, la, I thought, and sighed, leaning my head against the panes of glass. And the little one not out of clouties, yet.

From the dark, Cullah's voice asked, "Resolute? Where are you?"

"Here."

In a moment he was behind me, his great hands warm on my shoulders. "Can you not sleep?" he asked.

"I felt a babe."

"Is he not in his cradle?"

"No. Another babe. A new one. I felt the flutter."

The thrill he used to show was gone, as this was now so familiar, but he smiled as he rested his cheek against mine, wrapping his arms about me from behind as we looked out the window. "I will have to build the tower your ladyship once asked for."

"Well and aye," I said, with a tired smile. "This one will come too soon and there will be two in clouties at once."

"No matter."

"Not to you. I wash them."

He patted my arm and led me back to the bed. "It's time to take in a girl, then. A maid. Apprenticed out, you know, same as with boys. There are likely girls in town. I will ask about for you."

After he had asked throughout Boston, Cambridge, and Lexington, fate decreed that it was America Roberts came to live at my house. She was the last of the Roberts girls, all her older sisters already married. Her mother was caring still for the two boys until they could be apprenticed, yet her new husband refused money to send them to any worthy professional man, so they would have to be attached to a tradesman.

I lay awake one night, restless at having America in the room we had made for her in the attic. I wondered if she felt as I had when sold to the Haskens. At last, I could lie there no more. I got up, put a wrapper about me, and took a candle up the stairs. At the attic door, barely tall enough for me to go through without lowering my head, I paused and tapped. There was no answer. The girl was asleep. I chided myself on foolish worries. Being with child had often kept me awake with goblins of the mind. I turned on the stoop, just as the door swung inward.

"Yes, Mistress?" she asked.

"I came to see if you are warm enough," I said. "Sorry if I awakened you. I could not sleep thinking you might be cold up here."

"As long as I undress quickly, I am warm enough once I have the coverlets on."

I held the candle up to see her face. "Do you have need of another?"

"No, Mistress."

"You will tell me, please, if you do? And tell me if any of my children are cross with you, or tease you? I will not have them being unkind or rude. You are not a slave. You shall withstand no ill-treatment in my house. Report it to me at once."

"Thank you, Mistress."

"And, America?"

"Yes?"

"I will get another bed warmer that you may use each night."

"Thank you, Mistress. You are far more kind than, than I had expected."

"Good night, then."

I was not a lenient mistress as mistresses go. I bade America clean floors and launder from morn till night, taught her to bake before the hearth and to season meats and puddings, that last with an eye to her fitness as a wife someday. We purchased an extra brass bed warmer, which she could fill with coals any evening she chose to carry it upstairs, and every evening the bed warmers stood waiting their charging by the great hearth like so many muskets waiting for their soldiers to do battle against the cold and damp. In most chores she was compliant, even happy. America could have gone to any home as a maid-of-all-work. I did not ask why it suited her to work in my employ. If ever I thought of my life at the home of her parents, it was with a mixture of thankfulness and sad regret, anger and pity.

CHAPTER 25

October 4, 1746

After the first chill of fall, an Indian summer came upon us, and the balmy days with cool nights, gentle breezes, lifted Cullah's dark spirits, for he had not been the same since the news of Culloden, worried every night about lurking evil. I tried my best to entertain the family with stories of Jamaica, and was surprised, now that I had an audience, how much I remembered. The colors of the place came back to me as I spoke, and I imagined embroidering with those shades, when I ever had time again to work at my own craft, and just the thought of it filled me with joy.

The next morning being Sabbath, we were up early preparing for the Meeting. Jacob and Cullah went to the field to hitch our wagon to the one plow horse we now owned. America was busy trying to get Barbara's and Gwyneth's plaited hair to stay under their caps, for she had not done them well and she kept having to start again.

I put Grandan into new clouties and went to replace my house apron with a clean one. Cullah came through the door. His countenance was ruddy, his eyes flashing. He lowered his brows when he saw my face and pointed to the door at the stairs to the lower room of stone. "It is about a cross."

I said, "America, take the children out to the wagon."

"It is a *gumboo* cross," Cullah said. "They should stay inside the house."

"Stay in and bar the door," I told her. When I caught the look on her face, I said, "Ask me no questions. Do as I say."

"But Mr. Jacob?" America asked.

"Do as you are told," Cullah commanded her with a voice so low it gave me even greater fear. Then he turned and went ahead of me down the stairs. As I reached the floor, he made sure none of the children or America could hear him before he said, "Soldiers are approaching from Concord. It looks to be at least a dozen. They are armed."

"Perhaps they are but passing us on their way to Boston."

"Pa has hidden in the woods. Are you able to proceed to Meeting without me?"

"Of course. But if you wish not to go, we shall all stay here."

"It would be better for the children not to be here to witness, well, anything."

"Eadan." I looked at the fear mixed with determination in his face and said, "I will do as you say, then." I started up the steps but turned halfway up.

He stood upon my bench and pushed back the panel in the ceiling, then drew out his broadsword and axe. I raced down the few stairs and threw myself against him. "Promise me, husband, promise this, that you will not value your honor and your pride above the life of your children's father."

"Resolute, a man without pride and honor is not a man, and not fit to be a father."

I held his face between my hands and kissed his lips, trembling as I did. I whispered, "Wear my kiss upon your lips then for a trophy if you would be a knight. Weave your strength with my love and with God's wisdom for a shield if you would be a living one." I sped up the stairs, determined not to look back. And I did not.

"America, we shall proceed to Meeting. I will drive the wagon," I said to her, with as much confidence in my voice as I could pretend, for I had never driven a wagon, not one time since we married. The children clamored but I said, as I shook the reins, "Your papa has much to do this day and wishes us all to partake of the blessings of Meeting Day. We will see him later. Then we will have a celebration."

"What of, Mother?" asked Brendan Fergus. "I say, what shall we be celebrating?"

"I suppose we shall celebrate a warm ride for all it is winter a-coming in. We will have a fine supper, and I will make sweetmeats aplenty for you all. Now, speak to no strangers on this road, unless I give you leave." The horse stepped out, lumbering, gentle. He turned his great head and looked back at me with a quizzical face, if a horse can have such, and continued on his way. I added a lilt to my voice. "Everyone? Faces front, hearts on the lessons of the Sabbath."

As we reached the joint of the road where the Carnegie farm path met the Lexington–Concord road, a group of soldiers in bright crimson, bearing muskets and swords, caused such a noise that our horse turned his head to see them. I had no good hold on his head and when he turned the reins fell from my hands. He thought the slack rein meant he was doing as he ought, and he turned into the soldiers' ranks.

The Redcoats shouted, waving their arms about and calling me to halt the horse. One of them grabbed the horse's collar and nose-rigging and pulled him to stop, saying, "Mistress, you was asked to stop this horse and wagon!"

"I have lost the reins," I replied.

He blew upward, tossing his amber curls. "Well, then. 'Ere you are. Now, where are you off to, Mistress?"

His lowborn Cockney accent was so like those I'd heard aboard the privateers' ship that I got a clutch in my throat hearing him. I said, "Church meeting. Lexington."

"Go there often, do you?"

"Every Sunday as we can manage."

He nodded in the direction I knew was the road to Lexington. "It's that way, Mistress."

"Yes, I know. I lost the rein when he looked to see the spectacle of your coats and the turn was made for me."

"Well, back him up and on your way, then. We have business at the house down the road. Do you know the house I mean? The one far and awa' too castley for its own good? Now 'as orders to billet this company of men, since they 'as so much room."

I froze still as a stone. He waited. He said again, "Back 'im up and be on your way, Mistress," but this time there was a note of threat in his voice.

"I know not how to back him up, sir. I am not privileged to have much experience in driving and my husband has gone to work."

"On the Sabbath. That's strange. Might be arrested for such, where I come from."

"Truly?" I tried to replace the terror I felt with a look upon my face of surprise and humor. "You must all be devout, then, and I am pleased to make your acquaintance. If you could but help me get this wagon turned, I should say a prayer for you when we get to the church."

"You ain't some papist?"

"No, sir."

He handed his musket to another and shoved at our horse's wide chest, kicked at his hooves, and got him to back the wagon enough to pull his collar and get him righted. The soldier handed me the reins but I was caught with dire worry, and after we passed a small curve in the road, I got the horse to stop. I turned to America. "They were going to my house, of course," I whispered. "If all they want is billeting and Cullah meets them sword in hand, he will be killed for nothing."

"They were staring at me in a way made me feel most naked, Mistress."

"Your master will protect you and I shall, as well. No one under my roof shall be harmed, but I must warn Cullah before they get there. If he tries to fight them, they outnumber him so greatly it will go badly. Help me turn this horse about."

"Me, Mistress?"

"Yes. Hold these reins and I will push the brute about as that soldier did."

She gasped but did as I asked. I climbed down and strained against the great beast with all my might. At length he turned and I returned to the seat, flicking him soundly.

The Redcoat soldiers heard the horse as we approached, and moved to the sides of the road for I then had no control over Sam; he would do as he wished with us at his top speed. We sailed between them, past them, crying children and all, before they could react in any way that would slow Sam. He was slow and huge and powerful, and once he got started, he just did not stop. I hoped Cullah was able to hear the racket, for we made good time, and though the soldiers ran behind us for a little while we outpaced them. At the house, I pulled with every fiber of my being and Sam adjusted his pace not at all. "Stop!" I cried with all my strength. I screamed.

Cullah came running from the house, his axe in his hand. Seeing the horse out of control, he left the axe in a bush and ran for us, took the animal by the collar, and got it stopped. I leaped from the wagon and ran to his side. "Put away your weapons. The soldiers are on their way but they are not after you. They want billeting, Cullah. They are not here to fight you. There are twelve of them. Please do not fight; they will kill you. Cullah, do you hear me?"

"I hear. I will have no soldiers in my home." He shook my hands off. "You should have gone on as I told you to do."

"Then you would have come out swinging a sword and been killed. I had to warn you. Gentle words are all you need."

He lifted the squalling children from their seats and America and I bustled them into the house, down the stairs into the rock basement, and then settled them on blankets as if we had planned something special all along. I raced to the kitchen and fetched treats for them, a jug of milk, a handful of candles in my pocket, and carried them down again. I placed all at the disposal of America, kissed each of my children though the littlest ones still wept and clung to me and it tore my heart to pull their wee fingers from my clothes and hair. I joined Cullah at the front door just as he tucked his claymore behind the cupboard and opened the door.

The soldier who had helped me turn the horse in the road stood there with a haughty sneer. "That's a fine 'ow-de-ye-do," he said. "Fine, indeed. Are you the owner of this house, then? Your name, sir?" Before Cullah could answer the soldier went on, "I'm Corporal Landon, charge 'o this company, sir, and these orders say you are to board six of us for six months. That's the rule. Your house 'as been judged big enough for that."

Cullah gritted his teeth.

I said, "Let me see that, Corporal." I read the document and turned to Cullah. "Four months, Mr. MacLammond. Four months, Corporal." He had a crooked nose and was missing one of the larger teeth right under his nose, so that he whistled when he spoke. Just another freebooter on land rather than sea.

"Four, then, Mistress," he said, cocking his eye at America.

She slid behind the door and peered from its edge.

Cullah said, "That means you'd be here until after January? And, the man who wrote these orders for you, did he not reckon we have nine people already in this house, and another coming? Did he not think to ask whether every corner were already full?"

"I am a corporal, sir. I do as I am told. I do not ask the captain whether he 'as inquired of the 'ome owner of 'is available floor."

I handed the man his paper. "I have no extra bedding or blankets and I will not do your washing."

His eyes grew cold as he looked down at me, for he was a short man, but still taller than I. "It says billeting, Mistress. It means accommodating. Your orders are to accommodate six men 'ere in the 'ouse with food and warmth such as can be 'ad. We 'ave no beds on our backs as you can plainly see. An' you let one o' 'Is Majesty's soldiers die of frost lying on your floor, it's 'im that'll pay with 'is neck stretched, I reckon." He jerked his head at Cullah.

Cullah's face did not change a whit, as if the threat meant nothing to him. "You will do your own washing and not burden my wife with your dirty drawers. You will keep clean in your person, and above reproach in every action. You will harm no person in my home and you will be polite, chaste, humble, and quiet. I will stand for no profanity under my roof nor in front of my family wherever they may be."

The corporal put the folded order in his pocket. "You people are right 'andy with the orders. Men? Make off with the rest of you, to the next 'ouse."

That would be Jacob's house, I thought. Goody Carnegie's collapsing house, empty and unkempt. I said nothing. If they meant to stay there, they would have to fend for themselves, indeed. My mind was already humming, trying to think where we should put them all. Six men in my house! Six men would fill up the house with no one else there, and there was America to think of, her young and untouched state, how to keep her safe from any ill-meant attentions. The stair to the attic could not be guarded from our room. She would have to sleep in the top room of our little tower. It was but a closet, meant to use to see across the landscape and down the road a small way, not large enough even for a girl as slight as America to stretch her legs. It was reachable by passage through our bedroom. I would put the children into two rooms rather than three.

The soldiers might be alone in the house if we went to meeting. My heart gave a great thump. We had always kept Christmas in the small ways Jacob had told me, with small gifts and a pudding, and the burning of a tree, though it was outlawed in all of Puritan Massachusetts. There would be no Christmas, no gifts for the Christ Child, no Hogmanay. But my children would be so disappointed if we held it not at all.

To say that billeting soldiers made bedlam of our lives would not do it justice. For three weeks of cooking, cleaning—and I kept my word, showing them the washtub and scrubbing methods—just having them in every corner had turned our snug family into snarling cats. The children fought, hit each other for toys, and bit each other when I was not looking. Cullah snapped at me for no reason, and I nattered at him over carving a new spindle for the flax wheel, knowing I had no time to spin and had not touched it in months. At last I heard myself as some harried shrew of a wife, and burst into tears, begging his forgiveness.

Brendan was enthralled with the soldiers, their uniforms, their weapons. He tried on their coats, marching about the room holding a real sword tucked in his elbow. The rest of the children grew pensive, especially Gwyneth, who started sucking on the ends of her hair, even pulling it from her cap to get to the ends, no matter how often I tied it up. And then one day America ran into the house, leaving the front door ajar, bumping Barbara over in her haste, which sent the babe to screaming. I picked up Barbara and followed America. I reached the last flight of steps above our bedroom just as the girl slammed the miniature door to her tower chamber. Barbara still wailed, but by the time we reached that chamber she was becoming amused by being jostled upon my hip up the stairs. I talked to her as I went, "There, there. Hush now. It was an accident, poppet. Shush, shush."

I opened the door and ducked to creep inside the tiny room. I found America huddled in a ball as far from the door as she could be. "What happened?" I asked. I set Barbara down, who began crawling, exploring the place. I petted America's back as she sobbed. She raised her face. It was not bruised but her lips were swollen beyond anything that even a bee sting could do. The front of her bodice was torn and part of her shift had been pulled out of the ripped place, the shift, too, ripped and frayed.

"He said I should let him have a feel of my bosom. He said feeling girls was not wrong. I told him to unhand me but then another grabbed my arms and held me fast. They pulled at my titties. They kissed me and put their tongues into my mouth, though I spat at them and bit them. One of them got his mouth on me and bit my lips so hard I thought he would bite them off. Then he grabbed my, my—I cannot say it."

"How did you get away?"

"They heard Master Jacob coming. They threw me into the goat shed and blocked the door with a post and left me there. Master Jacob opened it and I ran."

I turned at hearing Barbara cry out, "Gom!" which was her name for Jacob. He stood behind us on the stairway, having followed the commotion. Babby made her way toward him and I nodded, hoping to convey to him that I thought everything was soon to be in order. I said to America, "Did they do other things to you? Did any of them open his pants?"

"No. They cursed me and said all they wanted was a friendly feel."

I put my arms around her. "There was nothing friendly about that. This will not happen again. For now, change your clothes and I will make you some coffee. Bring me that bodice and I shall repair it and embroider it, so that this damage is replaced with something beautiful."

I hurried through the house making sure all my children and Jacob were indoors, closing every shutter, and at last barring the door. One of the soldiers tried entry and then beat against the door. "Let us in!" he called.

"Go to the devil and shake yourself!" I cried back at him.

Jacob roared with laughter. "You heard the mistress of this house! Do it!" The man outside beat against the door thrice more and then all was silent.

As the sun lowered, another time someone tried the door. Cullah's voice called out, "What's this? Who has barred my own door from me?"

I stepped out, and told him of America's sorrow. "They can sleep in the goat shed tonight. Tomorrow you must find their superior officer in Concord and have them sent somewhere else."

"I'll talk to them," he said, and turned about without even setting down his pouch. He came in for supper an hour later, though the soldiers did not. In fact, I saw them not at all until the next morning when they applied for some breakfast, all of them shivering, filthy, and bearing blackened eyes and blood-stopped noses. The saucy corporal walked bent as if he had been kicked in the middle by a horse.

America told us which of them had held her and which had torn her clothing. But in truth, Cullah said, when he confronted the men all of them came to each other's aid, and he'd had no choice but to give them all a good drubbing.

"All at one time?" Brendan asked him.

"Aye, boy."

"Six trained soldiers?" his son asked again.

Cullah appeared insulted. "What are six lobster-backs to a braw and hearty Scot? Slavering ninnies. Long as they did not have time to load a musket, I had naught to fear." I laughed but with bitterness. I felt proud of him yet worried that he would bring more retribution upon himself. The Crown would endure no thwarting of an order of billeting.

One day as I went up to clean ashes from the hearths, I caught the corporal creeping up the stair, opening the door to my bedroom with a wary hand. "What say, there?" I called. I gripped the ash bucket with both hands, ready to throw it.

He gave a short laugh. "Pardon, Mistress. The boys have need of a stone to sharpen the cutter he gave us to make firewood with."

"The stone is in the barn, along with the other tools."

"Yes, Mistress," he said, smiling, and sauntered back down the steps to return to his chores.

America became as a drifting shadow, terrified to come from the tower room without her hair under her cap and fully clothed, when before she had joined us at breakfast in a shawl and wrapper. She told me that now she lived in constant fear. I showed her how to open the wall in her tower room, to find an entire flight of stairs that would get her straight into the barn on the ground floor. The barn already looked as if it were joined to the house, but the little hallway that allowed us to care for our animals without braving the cold was narrower on the inside than it seemed from outside. I showed her the key to opening the cupboard in the kitchen, which had a room behind it from which a person could, by means of eyeholes, see the kitchen and parlor along with outside by the front door. I showed her how she could stop on the stairway to the loom, turn to her left, push aside the board, and through that opening find herself above the loom on a solid floor in the room where August had hidden. A small window that appeared as normal as any from outside lit the room. Below the window sat the locked chest where Cullah kept the pipes.

In this dark place lit by a dirty window and my single candle, I felt as if time again had rolled in upon itself, as if I stood in the hold of the *Falls Greenway*, the deck shifting and rolling, the low ceiling overhead dangling with cobwebs and filth from above. I heard Patience's voice when I asked, "Were you trying to knock my brains out?" Patey had said, "If that was what it took to save you." And I had cried and pushed her away, thinking her nothing but cruel, believing she hated me. I looked now at America, trembling, her small bosom heaving from imagined torment, for she was old enough to know what a man meant to do with a maid, whereas I had not known. Tears filled my eyes and my whole frame shook. Patience had not hated me. She had loved me. I wrapped my arms about America and held her as if I were Patience, as if she were me, patting her back, soothing with murmurs like doves' sounds. I said, "We shall be strong of heart. Those men may be stout and more in number than we, but they are foolish and ruled by lust. We shall have the day because we shall be ruled by virtue and wits."

"Mistress?" America asked with a whimper in her voice.

"Yes?"

"You are so kind to me, Mistress. I shall not forget you as long as I live. I shall always love you."

Well and aye, I thought. If a lass had someone to care for her, she stood a chance in this life. I said, "Do not tell the children. They are still too young to keep this place a secret and might want to play here. If there is need of them coming here for safety, that will be soon enough for them to find it out."

"Is there a secret place in the barn, too?"

I smiled. "You have seen the flat place on the east side? It is cold and wet, and would suit for the direst of need, but you will not need it. That place is to store old farm equipment." There was, of course, another place above it, dry and secure. I could not have said why we built it so. It kept us both happy to know it was there, as invisible as a fairy's breath, and large enough for our family to sleep within.

One late November evening, when a bitter wind howled outside and cries of old haunts murmured through the rafters, only five of the soldiers came to supper. "Where is Ross?" I asked, for by then I knew them.

"He claimed a fever this morning. Lazy lout."

"Well, I am not traipsing all the way to the attic," I said. "One of you take up his supper." We finished eating. The soldier named Collin took a cup of ale and a trencher with a piece of venison and herbs in sauce up the stairs. In a few minutes he came down, his hands still full. "Well?" I asked. "Did he want it not?"

"He won't be wanting any more now, Mistress. Ross is dead."

They buried him down the hill by Goody's grave. We discovered that of the men staying in Jacob's empty house, two had died already, and the other four were ailing. Within two days, Brendan and Jacob had a fever and a hard, dry cough. Cullah came down with it the same day as America, Gwyneth, and Barbara. I recognized this from what other women had described. We had contracted throat distemper.

That evening, after an afternoon of plaintive wailing, my precious Barbara died in my arms and dear, tiny Grandan got fever. While I tended him, my head ached, my ears hummed, and dizziness caused me to lose footing as I tried to nurse him while moving from the parlor to the kitchen. Benjamin and I began coughing the next morning, and a couple of the soldiers did their best to bring us warm ale and boiled potatoes they made. Fever raged through me along with chills, sweating, but a nursing babe cannot be denied, so I took him to my bed with me, and I held my darling Grandan as he took his last ragged breath. We had our other children now on pallets in our bedroom, and that night, Cullah, coughing as if he would turn himself inside out, dragged himself from his bed to adjust Benjamin's coverlet and found our second boy had left us, too. I was too ill to weep. When I woke and sobbed, I fainted.

I took to my bed as Cullah and the last whole man of the soldiers lit a fire in the graveyard yet again to soften the earth for another grave. I do not remember them burying the children. I knew not whether any of them lived. I thrashed, for I remember my hand hitting the wall and something making a loud noise. Soaked in my sweat, I could not eat and did not want the water on a spoon someone tried to force between my lips.

I was told that one of the soldiers went to Concord for a doctor, but the man would not accompany the soldier to our house, for the town was full of it then, and there was little to be done. Children lived or died at the will of God. Adults took it and had half a chance, but most children below the age of twenty perished.

The ache I felt in my back and arms was treachery, but the ache in my throat and belly alarmed me even in my sleep, but I did sleep, unable to do anything else. I felt the warmth, though, slickness flooding around me.

The hands, gentle but strong and somewhat fumbling, moved me back and forth, a sort of soft tumble, as they cleaned around me.

When at last I could raise my head and take my own broth from a spoon, I no longer carried a child. Jacob, we still had, as well as America and our two, Brendan and Gwyneth. Cullah would speak nothing of it all. I took his hand and we wept bitter, wearing tears, until at last he left me there and I wept until I slept again, in that dark, dreamless void of illness that is more a treading the line between living and dying than true sleep.

It was the eighteenth of December when at last I rose to don clothes. I had lost all my motherly plumpness, and though I had mourned the loss of a narrow waist that allowed me to show off my lavender dress so long ago, I now mourned the sallow, shrunken hag I felt I appeared. Cullah, too, seemed drawn and wretched, America dragged herself from one chair to another, Gwyneth whined every moment she was awake, and dear Brendan alone seemed ready to return to life. I took no joy in anything. My babes had been buried before I saw them dressed and cleaned for their last repose, I remembered in a mysterious, cloudy way. I spent days weeping or on the verge of it.

Of the soldiers, four remained alive on December twenty-sixth. That day I told Collin Trask and Corporal Landon to go in the woods and cut a tree and bring it to the hearth for Christmas. I was not going to deny my remaining children a bit of plum pudding, a shining shilling, and a warm fire. In a place where celebrating Christmas was a crime, I made us criminals, witnessed by these men who had the power to arrest us, these harbingers of death who had already done worse.

Corporal Landon nodded, said nothing, and did as I bade him. Collin scratched his head and said, "I've never had Christmas before. Will there be pudding, Mistress?"

"I will do what I can, son," I said, feeling so ancient that this boy but fifteen years younger than I seemed as a child to me. I made a small pudding with hard rum sauce, and Cullah lit it the way my pa used to do. I watched the blue flames lick the edges, remembering how the rules dictated it should be the size of the smallest child's head, and though the others moaned with delight I wept at the table. Cullah's face washed with red; he could not stop his tears. The children and the soldiers thanked me for the pudding, but I ate none of it, apologized for having a headache, and went upstairs to bed.

1747

In January the soldiers moved on. We had done our duty as subjects of His Royal Majesty, George Second. They had brought with them ravenous appetites for food, randy attitudes toward our ward, and death itself to my babies. No matter that they had softened their manner and tried their best in the end, my heart was hardened to agonizing iron. I watched them go and had to stop myself from spitting on their heels. They brought this corruption, this devil's wrath upon my family, and I hoped they all died screaming.

Cullah spent the rest of that winter repairing and sharpening his tools. He also worked the blades of his battle-axe and claymore, dagger and dirk, and a short-sword he brought from town. I worried, for he neglected his shop, and orders stood waiting for furniture, paneling and trim, and, as always, coffins. I brought the woolen wheel upstairs to sit by the great fireplace after supper while the children read me their lessons. Before our season of illness, Cullah had listened to them, amazed, I think, that they could read, and enthralled by the stories they read aloud. Now, for hours before we went up to bed, he stared hard into the fire itself, paying no attention to the children or me. On a night in late February when a blizzard howled at our chimney, I asked him, "Why must you sharpen those again? You should be after the miller's chest of drawers."

"Three times in February I heard an owl after the sun rose. I saw a black cat on my way to town, walking back and forth as if to dodge something in the road, then it turned back and made tracks in the shape of an arrow."

All those portended death. Death had been at work in our house aplenty. "Why did you not tell me before this?"

"I didn't want you to fear. I believe war is coming."

"I fear your reticence more." At length I said, "I know no fear. Three of my babies have died in my arms, and me powerless to ease their suffering.

Part of me lies buried in each of their graves. I am dead already, husband. Tell me not of war. Death is not my enemy. Living is."

Cullah's head rotated without expression, his eyes wide and staring like the owl his movement mimicked. His eyes brimmed with tears and he said, "Do I mean less to you, then? And Brendan? Gwenny? Are we not worth your taking one more breath?"

"Of course the living are in my heart." I looked down at my hands and took my foot off the treadle, letting the wheel slow to a stop, its comforting clicks slowing, slowing, running out of time as the ticking of a great clock winding to a stop. "I did not mean that, Eadan. But you talk of war as if we must prepare for it. I will not think of war nor plan for it. War, you say? What should I do if you were killed? I would keep Gwenny and Brendan in until they are apprenticed, and then I should wish to die."

Cullah's face contorted with pain. "My pa is old but he is with me, yet. Upstairs, sleeping, sounding like a band saw shearing planks off a tree full of burls. His wife, my mother, is dead. His other sons, too. Now he has buried grandchildren. Even though I am a man, and I do not need him to keep me, I want him alive. Whether I live or die, your children will want you alive as long as you can stay alive. I want you alive."

Tears dribbled down my face and fell to my bodice as I said, "I am no use to you or anyone."

"That is a fairy talking, trying to fool me," he said. Then he rose and knelt at my side. Taking my hand in his, he kissed my palm and then my fingers, folding them until my hand was as a small apple cradled in his hands. "You are so sad, so full of grief. I know better, my fair one. Believe me in this. You have no need to be of use. You have the need only to be."

I fell into his embrace, burying my head against his neck.

"Hush now. The bairnies will hear you and then how would they feel?" He pulled himself back and smiled at me, the saddest, most burdened smile I have ever seen. "See then? That is Resolute. That is the wife I knew."

I heard a sound behind us and turned to see America Roberts on the steps, watching us with rapt attention. Her eyes glistened with unspent tears. "Beg pardon, Mistress. Gwyneth is crying. She says she wants her babbies. I gave her her merry poppet but that did not soothe her and I don't know what she means."

In that moment, Gwyneth herself peeped from behind America's bed gown, holding on to the girl's legs. We held out our hands to both of them, and Gwenny ran to her pa, saying, "Pa? I want our babbies. Get them out of the ground now." America nestled close to me and I put my arm about her.

I asked, "Is Brendan awake, too?" as Gwenny then climbed into my lap and put her thumb in her mouth, gripped a strand of America's hair, and snuggled betwixt us.

"I know not, Mistress," America said.

I turned to Cullah and said, "Perhaps he is too grown to let us know he mourns."

Cullah nodded. "Boys spend too much time crying. Their hearts are too big and there is so much they cannot understand. Then when a man begins to mature he believes he must not weep or he will lose his manhood. Sooner or later, he discovers that sorrow does not destroy it, but when it is all new to him, this growing, this strengthening, it feels too breakable to risk. His fear is so great a burden that he must carry it inside until sometime when he is sure that he will not become a boy again for it."

Though Cullah prepared for war, though he haunted the woods with his pipes, and harried trees with his broadsword and battle-axe, war did not come. Not then.

Three soldiers came in July with another order of billeting. Cullah took his claymore from its closet and sent them flying for their lives through the fields. Jacob said, "They will come back with more and arrest us. If they do, I will go with them and hang. You will hide, Cullah."

Cullah clapped his father on the shoulder and said, "No. If they return, we shall tell them I could not read their orders, and thought they meant war upon us. Then we will say we gladly will allow them billeting here, and they will cause us no problems at all, I think, now the fear of Eadan Lamont is in them."

I shuddered and turned away from them as if men's plots and power felt too brutal to behold. At least, the soldiers did not return.

Cullah returned to his shop. His sadness, rather than warping his work, made him put his heart into every piece. No longer was his furniture merely good, simple, and useful. He spent more time designing it, making drawings, sanding and polishing, as if everything were done for one of our lost children. The finished work was endowed with some ethereal quality of form and air, as if tables' legs floated their platform, rather than held it. Chests rose to heights so tall that it took a step stool to reach into the topmost drawers; he carved shells into rich mahogany and black cherry cabinet drawers and put brass pulls in the centers, topped them with lathed finials fine as a wisp, and worked rosettes that looked like petals. The legs upon which each piece stood seemed too delicate to hold it. His prices went up and up, for his work was sought among the gentry of Boston, and to own a MacLammond highboy or table became a boast. No one asked why the mark he made on the back of each chest was a small thistle with *EL* in the center.

Cullah told me he had an order from the house of Spencer in Virginia, after having shipped a marvelous pair of matching chests to the house of Fairfax, the largest plantation in that province. "Imagine," he said. "The old rotter, spending money for my work. I believe I should deliver it myself." He said it, though, without a smile. Without joy. It was as if the sadness of his heart showed in his craft so that an inanimate object like a clover-shaped lampstand vibrated with his emotions.

With no more clouties to change and wash, I had time again to weave. My weeks of spinning wool had left me with plenty of supply, so I dyed the yarn black and made fifty yards of it by August. I embroidered it with black, so that it seemed richer than it was, a pattern that could not have been woven in.

This day, this muggy, misty August day, soon as Cullah had gone, I fastened my shoes to set out to the field, and heard a great din from the yard. There might be a bear in the goat yard, or a fox in the henhouse, so I grabbed a broom. Anything I could not chase with a broom, I would not chase at all, preferring to lose a goat than my own hide. I peered out the glass in the parlor, and saw the form of a man moving between the trees.

I ran the stairs two at a time, roused the children in their bedrooms and pulled them into the hallway with me. Someone intent on doing us harm would go up the main stairs. I called, "Brendan? Gwyneth? America? Follow me."

Down we went, into the room behind the kitchen cupboard. I looked out the glass again. Here came the man. An Indian slipping from tree to outbuilding, now crouched by the wooden fence at the goat shed. I got behind the cupboard and pulled it shut.

Before much time had passed, I heard the familiar squeak of the door hinges. The Indian was in the house. No one followed him. From where I stood, I could see him moving with the stealth of a cat, listening, sniffing the air. He looked into the pot of beans on the hearth. He moved the cask of dried fish from where I had left it, and even peered at the cupboard, so that I drew away lest he see the reflection of my eye through the hole. He did not go up the stairs. He stopped at my spinning wheel and rotated the wheel with one hand, jumping back as it made its ticking sound. From the basket on the floor he took a roll of woolen thread, the finest I had made, and pushed that into his waistband. Then he walked out the door, leaving it ajar, the children huddled together. I ran to the window to see him dart into shadows by the barn and from there into the woods.

Later, when I got the children from the cupboard, I tried to cheer them by making sport of any robber who came but to steal yarn.

Brendan said, "He's going to make a braw nightcap for his bairnies."

Gwenny added, "Do Indians know how to knit and tat, Ma?"

We laughed. But I asked Cullah to buy us a pistol, and to teach me how to fire it.

That September old Barnabus died. He was found stretched out on his floor by someone peeping in the window, as if he had simply chosen a strange place for a nap on a warm afternoon, hands clasped upon his chest, a faint smile opening his lips. Cullah and I gave ten shillings for him to be buried beside the wife whom he so loved. We tried to get the man's huge dog to come with us, but when we got to the edge of town the beast took off into the woods and we could not find him though we searched an hour.

That night following our burying Barnabus, we lay together for the first time since our poor infants had died. I felt little pleasure from it as I had before. He stopped and rolled over, staring at the ceiling. "Wife?" he said.

"Yes, husband?"

"My heart is not in it. I cannot."

"Mine is so blackened, too, that I want to lie near you, nothing more."

After so long a time I thought he had fallen asleep, he said, "Resolute? I want to read more than my name. I want you to teach me to read."

I leaned upon one elbow and looked in his direction, though the room was too dark to see him at all. Leading with my lips pursed, I planted a kiss, surprised to place it on his eyebrow. "If you wish it, I will do it. I will become a teacher," I said, and patted his beard, which had grown quite stout. "Although if you are to be my pupil, you must be sheared. I find too much wool does make the mind linty."

After a moment of silence he drew in a breath and laughed a single loud hurrah, following it with a ripping gale of laughter. "Perhaps I'll tie bonny ribbons about the mat so that it tickles my lady's fancy."

I laughed, too. Then I said, "I insist on shaven pupils, Mr. MacLammond."

He reached out into the darkness and patted my arm. "Then if it cannot be skinned, I shall at least cut it nicely. Will that suit you, Lady Lamont?"

I followed his tease. "Aye, Sir Knight of the Realm, it will."

"You will have to let me do the learning of it in bits here and there. Slip me a paper with something upon it. I do not want my children to know their pa cannot read."

I suspected they already knew. "Discretion shall be our word."

"I thought our word was 'sword.'"

"Oh. Oh, yes, it was."

"I love those old days, my Resolute, those days before we knew such pain and grief. We have lost them forever before we realized how happy we were."

"Aye."

"Would they could come again, I should never again be angry for a farthing shorted on my bill. I should never again curse the cold or rain or the heat of summer. If I could have them back, I would suffer no sadness upon any of our hearts."

"Oh, Eadan. I do love you with all my heart. I love you more than I knew I could love anyone." I lay back down upon my pillow. "I fear I shall spoil our children now."

"Aye. It matters not. Life is short and must be lived. We must not let them become lazy or cruel, but beyond that, give them what they want."

After a long handful of moments, I said, "Eadan? Give me a child."

"What?"

"Give me a child, husband. I beg you. Give me a child." I placed my hand upon his chest, right above his heart.

He felt in the darkness for my face and kissed me slowly, tenderly. "Is that your wish, wife?"

"Most earnestly."

"I am but yours to command, then."

CHAPTER 26

Michaelmas 1750

At last, in 1750 before I had turned thirty, Brendan was thirteen and Gwyneth was ten, I gave birth to another boy child. We named him Benjamin after our other Benjamin. That year, too, Brendan went to apprentice with his father and with that, Cullah confided to me, he apprenticed not only as a woodsmith but as a Highland warrior. Cullah slowed his business to spend two hours every day away from the shop with Brendan, teaching him Gaelic songs and charms, and how to fight with everything from a battle-axe to his bare hands. The boy grew quiet, taller, and along with a wisp of dark hair on his chin, a seriousness came to his face as the boyish joy left it.

Father and son became inseparable. I felt the loss of my boy. It was as if he saw that he was to become a man, and that women, particularly mothers, had no place in that. Perhaps that was true. I remember the battle I faced for so many reasons in just weaning him. This was another weaning. While I yearned for the lad's head upon my breast as of old, I thanked God that he had a father. Without Cullah what would Brendan have done?

That year, Jacob's eye had gone white. He had lost stature and strength, too, and slumped over, feeling his way about the house and grounds with hands outstretched. It was as if the manhood and strength that took hold in the younger Brendan drained itself from the older Brendan to achieve it.

Cullah came to me one morning before leaving for the shop. He held a leather piece, folded about a roll of plaid. "It's gone to moths and rot," he said as he opened it up. He spread the cloth wide. "Can you make this?"

"Of course I can," I said. "Mostly blue, with a strand of white and then red, four blacks, five greens. How many yards do you want?"

"Maybe a bit longer, another yard would help. And more than one. Make the same for Pa and my boys. When it is done tell me and we will hide it. And you must tell no one as you work on it. It must be done in secret, even from the family. Resolute, I don't want the children to remark to some playmate that their ma is making plaids in the basement. And there is that girl, too. We don't know but what her loyalty might change with the attention of some young swain. What I'm asking is against the law."

"Then why are you asking it? You have carried this old plaid around for years. Why, now, do you need a new one?"

"War is coming."

As I readied for bed that evening, I wondered if my husband were going mad. I asked God in my prayers whether the curse on this house, or Goody Carnegie's spirit, or some other shade of evil had attached itself to him. I thought as I warped the loom, perhaps he believed that by being ready for war, he could forestall such an event.

Cullah renewed his practice of the pipes. To my greatest surprise one day he came home from town with a drum so large Gwenny could fit within it if we had let her go in. He had made drumsticks upon his own lathe, and began with a simple pattern to teach Brendan how to hold and play the drum.

In the evenings when Gwenny was sent to bed, Cullah learned not just to read and write in English, I taught him some Latin and French as well. The French were, after all, Scotland's allies. This fact, we cautioned Brendan, was not to be spoken of before others. He looked at me with the most serious face, that tiny fuzz of darkening hair upon his lip, and said, "Mother, I swear to you, I carry a thousand secrets already. One more is nothing for you to have a care about."

I sat up straighter, feeling as if I had just heard my own words from my son's mouth. "Well and aye, then, Brendan."

By 1752, for reasons I could not comprehend, the prices of all my wool and linen doubled and then doubled again. It took a shilling to buy what a farthing bought a few months before. Our money dwindled, not in the amounts, for I guarded and counted the coins once a week, then placed them back in their little hole. The dwindling seemed to come from some incredible force, something that made everything cost more and, consequently, the money worth less.

By the end of that year, too, another shock came to Lexington town, for the man who had been the minister at First Church for over fifty years suddenly died. The Reverend Mr. Hancock had always appeared to be older than Methuselah. What did surprise Cullah and me both was that the church came to us for a share of his funeral. We gave them two pounds and seven. Deacon Brown received it with a frown. "Will that be all?" he asked. "You know the value of our money is dropping daily by the regulation of currency. It will take two hundred and twelve, we calculate."

Cullah said, "I will give you three pounds then, but I would rather see that his widow had food and clothes this winter, than to clothe a dead man, no matter who he is."

"Mr. Hancock's widow has asked for five hundred bricks for the burial place."

"Deacon, I am a working man. You know we honor the man as you do. Besides, a widow that presumes to need five hundred bricks for a single grave must be sending his horse and buggy with him." Cullah smiled.

"Will you not preserve your standing in the church, then?"

My mouth fell open, but I could not speak. Cullah said, "I hear the talk about being 'tight as a Scotchman,' as they say. I think my standing is justly served by this donation. Now, sir, will you have supper with us?"

In the Year of Our Lord 1753, when we heard the king had changed the calendar in a confusing eleven-day jump, I was thirty-three at Michaelmas. Shortly after my birthday, I bore the girl who was to be my last child. We waited to bestow her with a name, so much had we feared putting another child in the grave. All that time we agreed to only call her my ma's word

Gree-a-tuch, as if she were not real. When she had lived until the first of May, we named her Dorothy Ann. Dolly, for short. I kissed her warily, fearful of the pain of loving her, though love her I did; fearful lest she hurt me by dying.

America Roberts lived with us still, a young woman of twenty. Her suitors had to pass muster with Cullah, who enjoyed meeting them at the door, sweating and shirtless and smiling with the claymore in his hand. I would send him to dress for supper and the hapless young man would be forced to partake of our company as well as America's. The only one she seemed to care for was a young ministerial student from Cambridge named Arthur Taylor. But he succumbed to smallpox the following year. It swept through the colonies, taking half of the families we knew with it. For reasons we knew not, its specter spared the loss of any in this family; though my Brendan was ill it was not severe. All the others had no illness at all.

America sobbed night and day for five days. Then she put up her hair and went back to work. She had learned to weave good woolens, and with dyeing and spinning, was every bit as perfect a hand as my own. I told her that twenty-one was not old and she must not resign herself to a spinster's life unless she desired it, but she swore she did, and I said no more after that about it.

In 1754 when Dorothy Ann was two, Benjamin five, Gwyneth a comely fifteen, Brendan seventeen, and his father forty-four, two uniformed soldiers came with another order, this time wanting more than bed and board. The town of Lexington had been required to supply a certain number of soldiers to be pressed into war, they said, in service of the king against the Iroquois and all Indians. Cullah told them he needed at least a week to close his shop and set things right with his family. The soldiers agreed to it and said they were marching as far south as Braintree rounding up all able men over the age of sixteen, and would take my men along with them on the return trip in ten days' time.

When Cullah ordered Jacob to stay with me, he frowned and threw his slipper into the fire on hearing it. Jacob was now blind. He could no more fight as a soldier than he could fly off the roof. I saw my men as prisoners. I hated everything about this, not the least their peril, not the most, their similarity to my capture.

Brendan blustered about the house, more pleased to be a soldier than he could name. That evening he proclaimed at supper that he was never so glad as to throw off the woodsman's apron and sawdust to don a red tail-coat with white and blue trim. He polished his buttons, took his hat on and off until I told him he would wear it out before the morning. "Mother, all my life I have waited for this. I was born for it. I shall make you proud and I shall rise through the ranks. They will salute General MacLammond of His Majesty's own First Regiment of Foot." He snapped a salute as if to that image of himself someday in the future.

"Meanwhile, son," I said, "take off that coat and let me fit it to you."

"No, Mother. I shall grow into it, I am sure. Don't cut it down."

I looked toward Cullah. He pursed his lips. "Well and aye. Add some padding and stuff him up some. Perhaps he'll look so frightful they'll all surrender on the spot."

"Who are we fighting, Pa?" Brendan asked with an eager grin.

"I know not. The king orders his subjects where he may." Cullah busied himself putting a keen edge on his fighting axe. I thought of his use of that grim tool so long ago. He was still strong and straight as an oak tree, if a little wider around the middle. An ominous enemy to be sure, but a ball cared neither for strength nor training. A ball pierced with no regard for the strength of the man who fired it or the age of whom it struck.

"At least," I said, taking Brendan's coattail, "come here and let me trim this odd piece. Whoever sewed this left a snip here. It would not do for a general to have threads hanging off his coat."

In the years since we started our farm, Goodman Considine had died. His daughter married a man by the name of Virtue Dodsil whose greatest happiness in life was farming. After supper a knock on our door opened to neighbor Dodsil, who was somewhat younger than Cullah but older than I. He was, we believed, a superior man to his late father-in-law, and honest. "Dodsil, come in, come in," called Cullah.

We served him ale and asked if he would have chicken stew, but he took the ale alone. Then, he would not speak unless America, the children, and I left the room, and while that was not customary in our house, I bowed to proprieties and took them—minus Brendan, I saw with surprise—to the upper floor.

America and I sat at embroidery. Gwyneth sat with Benjamin and

Dorothy Ann and told them the stories that I had told her so long ago. After two hours, we put the little ones to bed and I bade good night to the young ladies and went to my room. When Cullah came to bed I was near asleep. The sound of the door latch was all it took to make me sit up. "What news? Is Virtue conscripted also?"

He sat on the end of the bed and pulled off his boots and shirt. I touched his back. He sighed. "Ah, Resolute. Yes, he is. But this is not what I expected." He doffed his trousers, raised the blanket, and rolled into the bed. Lying on his back, he took my hand and said, "I cannot fight the French."

"The French?"

"Over in the Ohio Country, they put in charge some green fellow with no more sense than a goose who got himself pinned between French missionaries and bloodthirsty Indians. They drove him and his lobster-backs across the river back to the colonies and made a shame of the lad and the few soldiers that lived. His name was George Washington. Hell of a bad way for a man's name to be remembered, is it not? Now Parliament has sent a pack of new generals and fifteen hundred more soldiers across the sea. They want to take Québec, Montréal, all the way north into the far Canadas. They intend to drive all the Frogs from these shores along with driving all the Indians from the land between British provinces on the coast and the French territory far to the west. It is rich with furs and gold, they say, farmable land, plenty of rivers to run trade goods to the ocean as far to the south as the southern oceans. Lands I never heard of before: in the north is Nova Scotee, colder than a Viking could stand; in the south, a port called New Orlean, where Dodsil said all the people are descended from golden Indians as tall as giants. The army will destroy them all, Dodsil says."

I asked, "A land so vast. Can there not be something done just to portion it out? Can it not be shared? Why should there be war?"

"He says the French are bribing the Indians not to trade with the English. That they are taking up all the port cities and closing trade and soon there will be no more goods sold to English. A cup of molasses has doubled in price."

"I will do without it," I said, though I rued the words even as I spake them. Living without treacle would be harder than living without salt. "How long will it take to take the land from the Indians and French?"

"Blast everything, Resolute. I cannot fight the French."

"The English and the French have always been enemies."

"As have the English and the Scots. How can I raise arms against men who fought and died beside my people? I cannot forget Culloden."

I stayed silent for a long time. At last I said, "Could you not refuse to go?"

"And be hung for it."

I sighed, flopping my hands upon the coverlets. "Our son thinks he will become a hero. I would rather he became a Quaker."

"I will not wear a red coat. I will take my plaids and my pipes. I will fight with the Scottish regiments against the Indian tribes. I still do not know if I can slay a Frenchman."

"Are there Scottish regiments?"

"Aye."

"And will you take Brendan with you, then?"

"I will take him if he will go."

"Just tell him and he will go. You are his father."

"No more. A boy that goes to war is no more a boy. He must decide."

I thought of August, and how he changed in just a few short weeks from a happy boy to a tormented boy, then grew to be a man with a deadly gleam in his eye.

Next morning, when Cullah told Brendan what he'd told me and laid before him the plaids I had woven, Brendan's face wore his dismay. When Cullah wrapped the plaid around him, though, his expression changed. He said, "Will you keep this coat for me, Mother? If the Scottish regiment doesn't get much fighting I will come back for it."

May 21, 1755

In the company of thirty of the king's men, my husband and my oldest son left this house. I watched them go, the one steadfast and powerful, the other slender and jaunty in his new kilt, a musket over his shoulder as if it were a fishing pole. I knew that the army would have paid our way if I had chosen to go with him. I could have abandoned my children to America's care and gone as a camp wife, but the thought of that was too pitiful to entertain for more than a moment. I had a two-year-old babe; I had Gwyneth and Benjamin, still too small to apprentice for at least five years. Would my man find another woman to wash for him? To do other things for him? To lie down for him? My heart sank. My prayers were not for his life, then, but for his heart. His life, I believed, was safe in hand. I went out to the road. I feared not that Brendan would forever remember his mother, for what child forgets her? I trembled. I would not stop trembling, I vowed, until they both rested before my fire again.

I held in my hand the snow-white cockade Cullah had taken from his good hat. He gave it me as he left. A spot of white was a signal, a sign of a Jacobite. I set it upon the mantel board over the hearth and leaned it against the clock August had sent to us for Hogmanay this year. I had never had a clock before, though I remembered one similar in my parents' home. Now and then I stood watching the gears move, the links on the weighted chains rising and falling as it worked its way around the hours. I loved the ticking of it, like a heart. Alive. The white cockade seemed to watch me in return.

Wee Dorothy Ann called me back to her side with a plaintive wail that a child has for a short time. When I looked into her eyes I saw Patience staring back. As I pulled my bodice open, I felt guilty for I was glad that Jacob was now blind and I was free to nurse her before my own fire as if he were not there. Soon enough she must be weaned, I knew. I counted on America's help at both the loom and for the care and schooling of the children, but nothing filled up the emptiness I felt. Nothing I did kept me from staring down the road. Terrifying dreams plagued me, until I resorted to asking Jacob about signs and portents from the old ways. On his advice I kept onions over the baby's bed. I kept two knives crossed on the kitchen table while I worked and put horseshoes over every door. I crushed the shells of every egg I cracked, small enough that no witch could write our names upon the fragments. Still my dreams tortured me with images of Cullah and Brendan fallen in battle, their bloody faces looming toward me from behind trees. Sometimes in the dreams, I heard babies crying so that I got up to see what was amiss with Dorothy, only to find her deep in slumber.

I did not visit the graves of my babes in any weather other than bonny and sunny and bright. I did not visit them when even was setting or dawn just broken. I went there just in the bright of a clear midday, when all of nature seemed lit with God's grace. As summer wore on, we were often surprised with quick rain showers, as if a single cloud came upon a place and began to weep, then, finished with its mourning, moved on. It was on such a day I had gone to the graves, leaving America watching over the sleeping Dorothy, who was at last weaned, and the other children who were at their books.

At the headstones of my dear ones, I said a prayer for each and I paused at Goody's grave. I knew not what to think of the old woman who carried so much lunacy, and kindness, and guilt within her. I felt a darkness come over me, and paused, wondering if it were the presence of evil. It was simply a cloud hiding the sun, changing the angles of the light in a way I had not before seen in brightest noon. Prickling ran up the sides of my neck to my hair. I finished my prayer with my eyes open.

At the edge of the small clearing, where trees and brush met with a rise in the ground on one side and a granite outcropping on another, forming a *V*, I saw another stone. A headstone. Overgrown with ivy, it seemed to face the hillock, rather than the flat. I went toward it to see if aught were writ on the opposite side. The sky darkened yet more. A mist of rain sprinkled down upon me, speckling my gown.

I bent over the stone. Nothing was there. It was old indeed. A forgotten grave. I straightened. The rain had quit, and I turned to leave when I brushed against a man. A tricorn hat he wore upon his head. His ankle-length cape of black wool brushed against my skirt, my hand, my arm. I saw the cloth flutter. I opened my mouth to beg his pardon before I felt the shock of meeting someone in so isolated a place. But, there was no one there. It had been a specter. I looked toward the footpath I had traversed to get there. The rain had dampened the ground, but I saw no treads upon the speckled soil other than my own. I remembered no face, nothing corporal at all, save the fact that he was walking quite resolvedly toward me and his cloak touching my own.

I hurried down the path. I prayed aloud, at first in English but then French, and then Latin, walking faster yet, for those were the prayers drummed into my head, I knew them by rhythm, by chant, even more than I knew Ma's or Jacob's old Gaelic charms. *"Sancte Michael Archangele, defende nos in proelio; contra nequitiam et insidias diaboli—"* I broke into a run, gasping the rest, saying, *"Satanam aliosque spiritus malignos,"* as I got to my house. The wee ones had gathered in the parlor, with Gwenny and America, and I stilled my face against the wooden door before I turned around and greeted them with a smile.

After that time, I could not visit the graves of my children. I remembered Cullah's saying that oft, when he needed most to pray, all that would come out was a scream. When the memories of that brush against the black cloak came to me, the only prayer that came with it was a terrified scream that played against the ribs surrounding my heart. I decided to say the Rosary and to beseech Michael the Archangel every day for my husband and my son. I would also beseech the old charms against fairies and say the Protestant prayers, as well. Let someone tell me a woman may not think of her son and husband in battle with any prayer she can, and they will have a williwaw on their hands.

CHAPTER 27

October 2, 1755

Not long after that, I carried my flax wheel up the stairs to the parlor to work; America worked at embroidery, Gwyneth sat at the woolen wheel. Jacob snored before the fire in a settle. I saw my daughter as if for the first time since the babes had died. She was a child no longer, fully as old as I had been when I came to Lexington town, as old as America had been when she came here to apprentice. Her figure was slender as a willow branch but filling. "Gwenny?"

"Yes, Ma?"

"Have I ever told you the charm against evil from the old ways?"

"I do not say it for it is thought to be witchery to know those ways."

"The old ways are merely old, not witchery. I learned it from my mother and she was no witch. Goodwife Boyne knows a hundred more."

"She is quite odd."

America chuckled. "She is at that."

I said, "Gwenny, you are old enough to go out to a house."

She brought her wheel to a stop and looked up. "Would you send me away?"

"It is thought best for young people, to see how others may keep a house. To learn and make up their minds for their own way. You do not have to if you do not wish it."

"I do not wish it. With Pa gone, and Brendan, too, you and America would have too much to do. It is hardly kept together now. What would you do, bring in a boy as apprentice gardener? Grandpa cannot teach him. A boy would be worthless."

I smiled and straightened my back then dampened my fingers yet again as the thread sought each drop of water and stretched itself as if it were a living thing onto the spindle. "The women in this house have a way of speaking their minds that may not be thought well of by society."

"I care not a whit about society."

"Perhaps you have not met the right society. I wondered if you thought of going out."

"What could I learn there that you have not taught me here? Was I not also attending you at the birth of Dorothy Ann? What more is there to learn?"

I took a deep breath. "There are secrets of this family, of this place."

"I told my friend Elijah that I knew a story about a castle in Jamaica and he said it was foolishness."

"Then you need more intelligent friends, Gwyneth." I talked to her about trust. About hiding things, about knowing things that others may not know or might even ridicule her about. She seemed to take it all in with little expression.

Gwyneth said, "Ma? Why are you saying these things? It is true what Pa said? Will the Indians come here and try to kill us? I know about the cupboard in the kitchen."

I let my wheel stop. After a while I said, "There are many reasons why you may want to hide. Some traveler demanding entrance. Soldiers demanding billeting."

America said, "If your mother had not hidden me, I would be dead by now."

"Why?" Gwenny asked.

"Because the soldiers here wanted to abuse me. I would have killed myself."

"Those fellows? Why, I thought they were so merry. They made me a swing on the big tree out front. One of them carved me a wee dog from a block of wood. He was one that died, though."

"You were a child," I said. "Thank heavens that they were not completely depraved and harmed you not."

In the morning, I showed Gwenny the other stairs and the hiding places that I had showed America years before. This time, the room above the loom held nothing but spiderwebs and Cullah's empty chest. When I saw it, I sighed. In the years since first showing it to America, Cullah had lined the room with fragrant cedar, and now it held shelves on which to store bolts of wool. I smiled. Better to be prepared.

Gwenny put her arm through mine and said, "Ma? Do not weep. Pa will return, I know it. Brendan will, too. We will be together again."

Just before All Hallows, I received a letter from Rachael Johansen. James Talbot, Patience's son, had reached an age and chose to leave the convent. I had long entertained a wish that he would seek me out, find the woman who had so often sent her heart to him, and her letter said she asked him to do just that.

While Cullah was gone, my visits with Lady Spencer took place as regularly as I could manage. Then the first week of November, I received a messenger with a note from her. It said she was ailing and begged me to call upon her. I wanted nothing more than to be with my old friend one more time if her days were numbered and few upon this earth.

Her old butler, Oswald, had been replaced with a new man, Rupert. Rupert had a clipped manner of speech, though he led me to Lady Spencer's presence with more grace than Oswald had used. I found her seated before a window, a large rug covering her feet propped upon a cassock. "My dear!" she called. "How pleasant to see you. How is the new darling? I am sorry. I have forgotten. It is a boy?"

"A girl, Lady Spencer. Dorothy Ann." She was two years old, but I said nothing.

"A fine English name, Dorothy. My favorite aunt was named that; my sisters and I called her 'Dolly.' I shall look forward to making her acquaintance. I want you to visit me again, Friday week, Resolute. I shall be having a dinner attended by important people to whom I want to introduce you, if you have not yet met them. My son and his wife will also be here. That means, of course, you will have to suffer the presence of fools, but we will negotiate those waters easily enough. It will be enough that you come. Now, that is Friday, and the following Saturday, then, the last Saturday before Advent, I shall have entertainments yet again but it will be held at Wallace, Lord Spencer's home. Yes, you did not know my husband has died? Well, ours was a marriage of convenience. Convenient for him and profitable for me. Wallace is now Lord Spencer and I am throwing the ball in his honor. I wish you to be in attendance, and I hope you are able to accommodate me on this.

"We may as well speak now of the reason I asked you to call. I have invested in a shipping venture. It is risky, but what have I to lose? Only this house, which my son does not want anyway. I have put it up as collateral against a shipment of silks and spices from the East in India, fruits from the West Indies. They are running against the East India Company. Do you know what that means?"

"Only that everything in the colony depends upon East India Company."

"The British are trying to throw the French out of every place they have a foothold, including this continent. The Indies. Bengal. They are bathing the provinces in India with blood. Lord Clive is gone back to London from his post in Bombay and so the place has gone to complete riot and the company is too busy shooting Frenchmen to hire privateers to ship their goods or to defend those who would. There are a few willing to risk their own necks and they demand bounty for it. That means the ones that are left are murderously foul and it is a dangerous ploy. I found a captain willing to make a run for it, and I am paying him double for a cargo, providing he brings it back dry. His name is Talbot. You know him?" She smiled at her tease.

"Well I do, madam." I said it as much for the sake of listening servants as anything, for she knew my brother visited me whenever he was in port.

Her voice softened. "I have decided to do something meaningful with my last years and my last wealth. A woman may do few things that stand up over time if her children do not do her proud. I will tell you of my will and how I have it arranged. If our dear captain brings home this ship, this house and grounds become his." She raised her hand at my expression. "Now, not a word. That is my choice. My son, of course, knows nothing of it yet, and if some calamity occurs to the ship, he never will, for the house will then go to him. We shall believe nothing bad will come of the voyage, and plan for the best. When the ship comes in, the cargo is yours though not without strings attached. While your man is in the north woods hunting Frogs, there is much work to be done here in Boston. Part of that work is for you to thrive, for only if you are received in the highest society will you be able to do the rest. There will be silks on that ship for you to sell but also to wear.

"Johanna the dressmaker is retiring from her trade, and others have surpassed her in style at any rate. Have her apprentice, Constance Cousan, a Frenchwoman, create for you something with a pleasing and modern décolletage. You will hold a store of silk that can be sold for a great deal of money as well as used for your own betterment. If you sell it, do it before they raise the tariffs yet again. Better yet, do it secretly and pay no tax. Every day the Crown thinks up one new tax and another, and it will only get worse. They are fighting wars on every side, Russia, Saxony, even the Swedes and Austria again, and flint and black powder costs dearly. They will come to this colony, and all the others, to fill the coffers for this. I want to ask you to keep it out of the royal treasury any way you can. I believe in the liberties granted to all English citizens. Besides his being mad as a hatter, there is something quite rotten in the courts of good King George. Quite rotten indeed."

"I will do my best, Lady Spencer." I wondered why she did not trust Wallace, her only living son and heir, or some lawyer or friend. Was I being told that I was such a friend?

"I want you to call me by my given name. We have known each other long enough, do you not think? My name is Amelia."

"That is lovely. Thank you for this courtesy, Amelia. And for your great faith in me. But this is so unusual. May I ask why?"

"Why would I offer you my given name? No, you mean why give away my house and goods. Well, my dear, I hope you never know. Let us simply say that my son and his lovely wife are back in town. We have had a discussion which left me little choice."

The thought of the treachery Wallace could carry out made me feel dark inside, as if his name brought a shadow to the room. "Do you know when to expect the ship?"

"It was due in port five weeks ago. Now, be not frightened. This Captain Talbot is quite the seaman, I have heard. His men like him. He presses no one to join his crew. They line up for the privilege. He will arrive." She smiled and nodded. Rupert poured more coffee.

I could say nothing. I knew not whether her words encouraged me as much as they stunned me, for this seemed out of place with her protected demeanor. "I am sure he shall. He must."

"Let us have the coffee, shall we? At least it is one thing that does not set fire to my gout."

Four days later, a public coach pulled up to my door. The sky seemed to rest upon the chimney itself, and a leaden mist swirled on the ground. August stepped from the coach, thin and weary, with a slight cough, but otherwise well. He had bathed and shaved, sported new clothes and a warm smile as he hugged me and kissed the children. I had not seen him in two years, and while I knew his life was fraught with dangers as can only be seen upon the high sea, I had felt no concern until Lady Spencer had intrigued me with her recent confidence. The idea that he had been a privateer on the side of British law had always made me feel safe. Knowing he was now skirting that law, and could hang if caught, made him more of a rake and a pirate in my eyes. He bowed upon seeing America, and I watched his face, wondering what I saw there.

The following day a flat wagon appeared at my door, loaded with so much from August's cargo that we had to move and restack everything in every room of the house. My home looked like a mercantile. We settled in that evening over stew and beans and bread with the children gathered round. He had much to tell, as did I, and he was displeased that Cullah and Brendan had been taken to war.

Friday, as I prepared to meet the coach to travel to Amelia Spencer's supper, August suggested that he stay at home with America and the children, for he still felt as if he had caught a cold on coming into the north Atlantic. He laughed at himself, saying, "I have been shot at, punched, kicked, and stabbed, but what lays me down like a withered crone but a New England ague!" Dorothy had a sniffle, too. I hated to leave her, but my heart told me I must, sure as it told me we would probably all catch the cold and have a week or two of sore throats and running noses. I was thankful it was nothing more. Just a cold. All else I felt was uneasiness akin to Cullah's constant fear of war, a mysterious note in Amelia Spencer's words that left me no choice but to go.

Just after sundown, the racket of a team of six came up the road. "Be you Mistress MacLammond?" the coachman called while doffing his hat. He was a well-dressed fellow, though sunburned as my brother.

"Yes, I am," I said.

"Lady Spencer sends her regards. I'm to take you to the house, Mistress." He got down and helped me into the coach.

I had dressed carefully. I wore fine black linen with a thread of pale blue worked in as a tiny, discreet stripe and with a middle shade of blue ribbon edging the ruffled sleeves and the seams of the bodice. It was, I thought, an elegant but modest effect. I wore no jewelry other than my ruby ring but I had pinned the white cockade from Cullah's best hat to my neck as a brooch. It was a sign to Lady Spencer, I suppose, but more importantly it was a connection to him, and I had been feeling in need of my husband's strong arms as I rode to town to see what had become of Wallace and Serenity.

As I entered the drawing room, Serenity turned toward me once, twice, and then arched her eyebrows dramatically. "Ah, it is you! I thought perhaps a Quaker schoolmistress had come to call upon our family."

I calmed my face as I knew how to do so well. Serenity's intent had been to insinuate that my clothing was plain, drab, even ugly. I knew otherwise. It was the sort of insult for one child to make to another and I would not stoop to considering it worthy of reply. I said nothing, but made my way between her and Wallace to sit in a chair beside Amelia.

Time had been kind, even effervescent, to Wallace. He had grown more dashing, more vital. Without a wig, his dark hair now sported a pair of dove's wings, that elegant note of maturation that put a streak of white at each temple. His figure was trim as ever, and the two of them were resplendent as peacocks in pink brocade silks and lace. Their children paraded in to offer greetings, then the youngest were sent to play at games in another room. The greatest change was in Serenity. She had grown fat as a brood sow, barely able to move in her corsets and laces. She propped herself in a couch and took up most of it, called for a footrest, and grunted, hiding a belch.

Serenity said, "Well, how good to see you, Miss Talbot. Oh, what was your married name again?"

"MacLammond," I said with a small smile.

"Mackle-mond." And so it went, Serenity interviewing me as if she meant to hire me for some position, and I answering her queries with care and a smile. At last she offered me an invitation to a ball they meant to have at their home in Boston on the Friday preceding Christmas. "Unless," she said, tittering behind her fan, "that does not give you enough time to find the loan of a suitable gown. In which case your regrets will be accepted."

"On the contrary," Wallace said. "No excuse will be adequate to deny us your presence. It is so boring here nowadays. None of the old people are around. All drummed into service, apparently, against the French."

I turned to him with a wary feeling. "As is my husband. I am glad to see your service is already finished."

"What? No, no. They came around Charles City, of course. It seemed a good time for a six-hundred-mile trip to visit my ailing mother, did it not, my dear?"

Serenity nodded approvingly. "But that is why Wallace thinks none of the fun people are here anymore. They've all gone to war. Isn't that tragic?"

"It is indeed," I said. "Would you permit me to bring my ward? She is of age to be out, though not given the privilege." I wondered what Serenity would say upon seeing her sister or whether they kept correspondence and she knew of the girl's place in my home.

"It wouldn't be a place for servants, except as attendants," Serenity said.

"She is not a servant. She is a young lady without means for a coming-out ball."

Serenity looked at Lady Spencer with a roll of her eyes. "Very well. Bring whomever you wish," she said.

"Thank you. I shall bring my daughter, too, then. It will be her first event and she will turn sixteen just before it."

Serenity's whole being sank with her sigh, though she smiled. "How lovely."

Dinner guests began to arrive. Lady Spencer had arranged a violin duo to play at the far end in the large parlor while everyone gathered. The two men had worried looks on their faces as they worked their bows up and down the strings. I longed to sit and watch them, for I had never heard such music or seen such playing. Too soon we were ushered to the dining hall.

Boston town could boast itself of lavish wealth. My gown was out of style, and too plain. Serenity's flourishes and lace had been carried out in some form on every woman there. I was a wee blackbird among fluttering silks and whispering brocades. My only comfort was that I might be unobtrusive for it. Lady Spencer took my arm at the door. "Help me, would you please?" she asked, leaning upon me. She introduced me all around.

As a well-dressed young man passed the doorway, she caught his eye and said to him, "May I present Mistress MacLammond, Mr. Hancock? I trust you will value her friendship as I do, may it be sometime in the future."

Mr. Hancock wasted not a second in flying to my side to take my hand and bow graciously above it. He held it while smiling into my eyes with a warmth that reminded me so of Cullah. How I missed the touch of a man's hand, even a young man's. He said, "Good evening, Mistress MacLammond. From this night forward, on Lady Spencer's word, I shall be at your service." He was alarmingly attractive, I thought.

"How kind of you, sir. Are you related to the late Reverend Hancock of Lexington town?"

"My late father, good lady. I have been living with my uncle since he died. I am your servant, Mistress MacLammond."

When the supper was finished and the ladies had retired to another parlor, Lady Spencer addressed the men, already getting out their tobacco. "Gentlemen, I bid you good evening. You will please excuse me for my health does not permit me to remain up longer, but make yourselves quite at home. Rupert will see to anything you desire." We made an appearance at the room where the ladies prepared to wait out their husbands' pipes, then Amelia asked me to help her up the stairway. Her maid showed me to a room. This time I was not to sleep at the eastern end where the sun could awaken a tradeswoman, but was taken to a suite next to Lady Spencer's own.

No detail had been spared, for I was provided a night shift of clean new linen, and a featherbed with downy coverlets. I sank into the bed and closed my eyes, fighting sleep that threatened me the moment my head touched the pillow. August was alone in the house with America Roberts. Jacob was there, true. And the children. And August had a cold. But what was that to a man? I sat up, against the roll of the featherbed, overcome with fear that no bundling board could dampen the ardor that might be running rampant in my home while I was away. I lay against the pillows. It was late and I was exhausted from the wine and heavy food. America Roberts was a woman grown. August was uncannily handsome in a devilish way. Nothing I could do from this side of the down-filled counterpane, eleven miles away, could change anything. I raised my hands for a moment, then lowered them, resigned to let them control their own lives. My eyes closed and for the next few hours, I slept the deep, safe sleep of a small and innocent child snuggled in satin bedding on the top floor of a house overlooking Meager Bay.

While Gwyneth was thrilled beyond all telling with her invitation to Lady Spencer's Christmas soirée, I had to beg America to don the gown made for her and accompany me. At last, it was August's promise that he would escort us and she would be no wallflower that convinced her to go. We hired a nurse and a cook to make supper and care for the little ones, and warned both ladies to take none of Jacob's jests to heart. Sitting in the coach, we were a collage of color that gave light to my spirit. August dressed in stunning scarlet velvet. America was in forest green with emerald and gold trim, Gwyneth in pale pink with white lace peeking from every seam, and myself in deep rose silk with subtle coffee-colored lace. The pearls, the sapphire brooch, the ruby ring added the right touches. I let the girls wear Ma's rings, too, and pinned a circlet of ribbons in Gwenny's hair held by Patey's smaller pearl brooch.

I felt queenly in the dress, and I wished so that Cullah were here beside me, though I feared he would have declined this invitation, afraid of the company of wealthy people. I felt none of that; in fact, I felt more at home than ever, as if these were my people and this was how I had been meant to live. A twinge of guilt caught me in mid-thought, yet I felt no resentment of my home and my living; it was merely that I knew this life, too, and felt I could move within it had I the opportunity to do so. I folded my hands in their new silken gloves, thankful that no callus could show through.

While we rode, Gwenny amused her uncle by practicing saying, "Thank you, sir, yes I should like to dance," using different inflections. Then she turned to me and said, "Ma, what if they dance something I do not know?"

"I suppose you might watch it and see if you can do it for the next time."

America said, "If the man is a good dancer, he will lead you through the steps. Do not worry. But Gwenny, you should call your mother 'Mother' rather than 'Ma' at least for the evening."

Gwenny asked, "Are you going to dance all the dances, Miss Roberts?"

"I am older and you are far too beautiful for any man there to look upon me."

August smiled at America but said nothing.

"Not at all," I said. "Gwyneth is young as a rosebud, to be sure, but America, you have lost none of your attributes and that gown is exquisite on you."

"Mother? I wish I could have a lower décolletage like hers." Gwyneth plucked at the lace lining over plump little breasts tucked into a neckline as pink and frothing as the treasures it tried to hide. Constance had had a way with Gwyneth's gown that followed my wishes and yet still did not detract from the young lady my Gwenny had become. "It makes me look flattened out as a boy, the way this fits."

"When you are older." I looked at my daughter, so charming in her gown, and too winsome with her pouting lower lip pushed out the way her mother's had been wont to do. "Any man there who mistakes you for a boy would do well to cast himself into the sea for not only are his eyes useless but his reason is gone."

August sighed as if he were a little bored with all her prattle, but to soothe her he said, "I brought only one dagger and a dirk. In the presence of your charms, dear girl, I feel unarmed against the threat of certain attack on your behalf. Perhaps I can find loan of a cutlass or use the andirons for a cudgel."

"Uncle!" Gwyneth said, but she smiled behind her lace fan and asked me no more foolish questions.

Snow fell about us as we traveled. The house where the coach stopped was lit as if every chandler in the colony had made his year's profit in providing candles for the one night. A handsome man in livery met us with a folding shade to keep the snow from our faces. I paused to glance at him as he passed my hand to another servant. His gentle accent when he asked to help us down gave me pause.

"Sir? I have lived here awhile but I call Jamaica in the West Indies my home. Do you know the place?"

"Beg your pardon, Mistress, I know nothing of what you speak."

"Your accent reminds me of the people where I lived."

"Forgive me, good lady."

"Not at all. Sorry to have been mistaken."

"Yes, madam. No mistake at all, I am sure. Good evening, Mistress," he said, and bowed as if I were royalty.

I stopped on the steps of the house to watch him tuck the step into the coach before it drove away, as stiff and perfect as any. Lady Spencer had coachmen that she paid. This was Wallace and Serenity's home, the one he had purchased when he'd asked me to marry him. That man was a slave.

America saw the look on my face and asked, "Is something amiss?"

"No, nothing. His voice reminded me of someone. Let us go in and introduce you both to society, my darlings. I wish your father were here to see you, Gwenny, although he would not approve of that neckline, far be it that you would want it lower."

August extended his arm to me and the girls walked arm in arm until the footmen at the stairs took each of their hands. We made our way into the gaily done hall. The introductions were formal. The steps leading into the ballroom were dramatic, and placed just for the effect of making each guest seem as important as the last. When I handed the man the card with our names on it and he read it aloud, I watched Serenity's face. Her mouth opened at her sister's name and a small, unladylike squeal came from it. She swept America into her embrace, then kissed the air at America's side curls on both sides of her face.

I found myself asked to dance by many of the men I had met at Lady Spencer's dinner the previous month. After a couple of hours, Wallace himself asked me to dance. He was smooth in the steps and light-footed, so that I found myself following my own advice to my daughter, and was able to keep up. I had always felt I sensed rhythms well, but while this was more challenging because it was new, it was quite pleasant. When our last bow was taken, he took my hand and said, "My dear Resolute, dancing has brought a most becoming flush to your face." He kissed my fingers, bowing over my hand. Then he leaned forward and whispered in my ear, "Is it not interesting how private one can be in a room full of people? I have longed to see you again. These years have made you more ravishing than ever."

I knew not how to respond, so I smiled and curtsied. His words left me unnerved. Had I given him some indication that I welcomed such a remark about my person? Was it so obvious that I missed my husband, that any rake who meant to take his chance felt he could woo me with delicate words? I felt more distressed than flattered by him, and sought to disappear from his view then, weaving through people until I found Amelia Spencer.

I sat by Lady Spencer and tried to forget about Wallace. Everywhere, the slaves in livery performed as clockwork soldiers, wound up, in their white wigs and gloves, their handsome tailcoats unmoving though they hurried from one end of the ballroom to the other. A young woman with wide eyes and long lashes carried a silver tray to and fro, collecting empty glasses and saucers with fragments of food. The music played. Instead of being a lady and having every whim catered to, or aching at a loom, I imagined myself trussed and powdered, made to carry sherry glasses as if they were the crown jewels. Was there a goat-beating stick somewhere in a barn? A cat-o'-nine-tails hungry for any hint of impropriety? I knew how hard it was to obey as an obstinate little girl. What made a grown and brawny man take on as if he waited upon a king for every guest? What scourging awaited the slightest wrong move? Were these men so happy to be escorting ladies to a coach, rather than sweating in a cane field as my pa had kept them, that they performed like courtiers? What did that say about my father? I loved him still, but it had been an enormous plantation. What inducement made them work?

"Are you tired, my dear?" Amelia asked.

"I was deep in thought. Old memories. Such a grand affair, this. It reminds me of when I was a child, and that of course reminds me of my parents, now gone."

"I wish my Edward were here to enjoy life with me, too. It helps me to think that he is here, just lost in the crowd somewhere, brought by my memories and love. Perhaps you could think of them that way, and not let so much sadness rest upon the day."

I smiled. "You are right, Amelia. And you are remarkable. I shall do as you suggest." If I could keep my mind on the time and place before me, I thought. But, though I made effort to appear engaged with the dancers, applauded the music, and smiled, I lived for a while that evening in a house on Meager Bay. My mother was somewhere in the crowd, a beaming hostess. Pa would be dancing with Patey across the room.

Late into the evening, I saw the serving girl again. She looked as before, her face a mask of stone. Upon her tray, a single crystal goblet stood in the center, and she was abruptly forced to wait in front of me as dancers twirled past. Once they moved on, she stepped forward, right into two young men jostling each other, coming from one of the side rooms. The tray tipped. The goblet hit the floor with a crash just as the orchestra stopped. Eyes turned this way. Horror filled the girl's face. I stood and stepped over the goblet, forced myself to bump into her then move to one side. "Oh, la!" I cried out. "I have dropped my sherry. Please do fetch me another, would you? Here"—I pushed at the broken glass with my toe—"someone will have to sweep this up, too."

Another slave appeared with a small dustpan and a brush. The girl looked into my eyes for just a split second, then lowered her long lashes and said, "I will send it immediately, Mistress." I heard Jamaica in her words.

Gwenny approached, her arm upon August's, her face flushed and moist with perspiration. "Mother? I should like to go outdoors and cool off. Uncle says I must not."

I said, "That would harm your health, Gwyneth. It is bitter cold outside."

She curtsied, laughed, and changed her tack. "Uncle August is quite a gallant. He knows all the dances. I will have no problem now with any of them."

"Is that so?" I asked, turning to him.

August said, "It is only to save her from the rubble at this party. Not a one of them suitable as a potential husband for her."

"Oh, Uncle! I quite enjoyed speaking with Mr. Hallowell and Mr. Hancock. Did you see him, Mother? Mr. Hancock? The dandy young man in the cream coat?"

"I believe I have seen him," I said. I saw in her face the longing I had felt when first I loved a young man already in his grave.

"Oh, Ma, there are only three more dances. I could dance until the sun comes up!" Almost as if on her words, the young man with unruly hair approached us. I recognized the young John Hancock. Without the wig he had worn before, he seemed younger still. His cream-colored clothes were expensive, despite his somewhat comical hair arrangement. As he bowed and asked her for a dance, I decided that the hair gave him a look of startlement, and I felt a sense of pleasure and amusement as they went to the floor. Then I accepted my brother's hand and danced a minuet during which I was astonished at his gracefulness. When it was done, I hugged him and kissed his cheek, so happy was I to have him home again.

The party had grown in excitement, and every inch of floor held a foot tread in the next reel. I watched every square. And suddenly I could not find Gwenny. I located August, smoking a pipe at a window where he had opened the pane a couple of inches to draw in fresh air. "August? Where is Gwyneth? After that minuet I have not seen her."

His face lost its charming appeal and assumed the character of a hardened man used to having his orders followed. "You." He accosted the man next to him. "Have you seen the young lady coming out tonight, in the pink and lace frock?"

"Yes, sir," he answered. "Fair as— Pardon, sir. I saw her, but not since the minuet."

August's face became frightening. "Find her. Search the house."

The young man ran to do as he was told. I laid my arm upon August's, finding it held none of the comfort as before, but was gone to stone. "I am sure she is dancing," I said, trying to smile at another man who was now backing away at the tone of August's order. "At least be discreet, sirs."

August strode about the room, through the reel itself, upsetting three of the squares, and walked right through the hall made by dancing pairs, his eyes this way and that. I began scouring all the side rooms that led from the ballroom to alcoves and windows. At the far end, I opened the door to a room so dark that were it not for a reflection on her pink silk from the hall behind me, I would never have seen her. August reached my side as I threw the other of the double doors wide. There stood Gwenny in the arms of Wallace Spencer, his lips upon hers, his embrace swathing her. He looked up without a care on his face.

"Mother!" she whispered, her eyes wide and terrified. "I'm sorry."

August pushed past me and said, "Unhand her, Spencer."

"This is my house," Wallace replied, though he did let her go and began adjusting his coat collar and vest, brushing at his sleeves as if she had left something there by her touch. "And the lass wanted her first kiss. She'd chosen someone quite unworthy to give it to her. Now, let us have no more about this and return to the ball."

I rushed to Gwenny and clutched her shoulders, searching her face. I heard August talking to Wallace behind me as I asked her, "Did you ask him for a kiss?"

"No, Mother, but when he kissed me I couldn't let go."

"Where is the young man?"

She began to cry. "Out the window. Lord Spencer hit John in the face and tumbled him off."

I went to the window. The young man lay sprawled below. "Is he dead?" I asked.

Gwenny cried louder. "I don't know. He might be." I turned. August's and Wallace's voices had grown louder and the music stopped behind the door.

"Are you challenging me, sir, in my own house?"

"You must apologize to my niece."

Wallace snapped his fingers and from behind a set of drapes appeared two armed guards. He smiled. "It is a party, sir, and the crowd is quite gay. Kisses and little freedoms are part of the happy occasion. But to insist I apologize for kissing the child of a slave?" He hissed out that last word as if there were nothing lower on earth. "You, sir, astound me. Step aside or throw down your glove."

At that, the slick of metal against metal heralded the two guards drawing small swords. August seemed not to watch them at all, but I felt he sized them up. He said, "Sir, I am sure you are aware that dueling is against the law. Perhaps we should meet alone at another place to finish our—discussion."

Wallace looked at me with cruelty in his eyes. "Over a petty wench? I doubt you know who her father is, but if you should find him, tell him for me she is a choice little peach waiting to be plucked."

I gave a cry of shock.

August said, "He is trying my bluff." He turned to the two men with swords at the ready. "Captain August Talbot, at your service." One of them developed a rain of sweat from his brow, his sword hand trembling. August said, "Ladies? I suggest you find Miss Roberts. Our host seems to have lost affection for our presence."

He pushed us behind him as he backed out of the room. I shielded Gwyneth with my body and she turned her face toward the wall as we edged toward the large hall. August told the doorman to get a torch and help him find the poor man lying in the snow. America joined us and we followed him, tramping through snow and damp in our thin slippers. At last we came upon him. "Is he alive?" I whispered. "He is a most gentle man, the son of a minister."

August jostled John and patted his face. He was but a boy, I thought, perhaps just a year or two older than Gwyneth. "There you are, good fellow. How is that head, now? Quite a blow you received."

"Sir, I beg pardon," John began, his speech a little slurred.

"Not at all, not at all," August cajoled. "Hit your head, did you?"

"I fear I have had too much wine," he said. "Oh, look, my new coat. Is the ball over?" He caught sight of Gwyneth and squinted as if trying to remember something. She turned away. "Miss MacLammond? At your service, I think. My head feels as if hit by a cannonball. I have been so hard at the books I have not danced or had wine in three years. I am quite embarrassed to have made such a fool of myself."

August said, shouldering up the boy, "I warrant you had a great deal of help. Someone scuttled your jib and sent you off the boards there. Let us get you to a bench. As the morrow is Christmas, you may rest."

"Christmas? Alas, no. I must be in Meeting at the earliest. Oh, I shall rue this evening, I fear. Oh, please forgive me." He spoke to Gwenny.

As we rode home, I asked August, "What do you know of that man?" The mere fact that John Hancock was no doubt on bad terms with Wallace

Spencer made him all the more appealing than had his cream-colored coat and breeches.

"Spencer, that hack-slaver? As black a bilge rat as Rafe MacAlister."

"I meant Hancock. Other than that his hair was astir, he seems gentle and striking fair. I might be pleased to have him suitor to Gwyneth."

August chuckled. "You choose well, for he's heir of the richest family on this shore, I would wager. Half my cargo is whale oil and rum to England from the Hancock company. Would a minister's son want me for an uncle?"

"He might make her a good husband."

"He might, indeed. There. She is asleep now. As is our America. The shame will be when anyone finds out what happened."

"You are not really going to duel with Wallace, are you?"

August smiled, letting the expression harden on his face. "I might look forward to it. But sister, it is against the law. And I would never do aught against the king and Crown." He pointed with one finger toward the ceiling and the coachmen.

I mouthed, "Can they hear us?"

"Assume it so," he whispered. "At any rate, though a first kiss ought to be a delightful mess between two untried and willing souls, it was but a kiss, and there will be others. You have pretty children, Ressie. Very pretty."

"Are you fond of America Roberts?"

"Well, of course."

I raised my brows.

He said, "Not that way. She is too beautiful."

I wondered if some disagreement had occurred that night I left them alone with only blind Jacob and the children. "You danced with her several times," I prodded.

"Were you counting?"

"Yes. And what man scorns a beautiful woman?"

He shifted his legs and said, "The cold this time of night is cruel, isn't it? It is well past midnight. Don't tell me you shall turn right around and make your children go to church meeting? I don't intend to go."

"Fine example you are, uncle."

CHAPTER 28

January 18, 1756

August meant to stay with us until Cullah and Brendan returned. Everything changed the second week of January, when a sudden thaw left the roads passable but not yet muddy. If he had been present, rather than down in Boston at the harbor on business all day, he might have balanced things, or taken them into hand himself. Jacob was not in the house; he was feeding the goats and fowl, doing the milking. The children were upstairs with America and Gwyneth at their books. A gig that I recognized as one of the Spencers' pulled up to my house. Serenity alighted and left the entire rig with four men and six horses stamping against the cold, waiting in the road.

I invited her in, of course. It was what must be done. "Will you have coffee?" I asked after she had been seated.

"Tea, if you have it. All England is mad for tea now. We were there last spring. Oh, have you ever seen Hyde Park in spring? Just lovely. You cannot imagine it if you have not been there. You must go sometime."

"I have no tea but there is coffee," I said, "and biscuit." I heard children playing overhead and smiled. "My youngest two. Benjamin hates being confined to the house in this weather. They are playing at knights and castles as they learn their history. I believe we are up to the reign of King John."

"I do not care for coffee."

"Well, then. Beer?"

"No, thank you. I am on my way to Concord to see a dear friend of mine. And my mother is ailing, did you know? I am going to interview another doctor for her."

"Yes, I knew. Lady Spencer—"

"Not Lady Spencer. I mean my mother, Mistress Roberts-Brown. Quite lost her mind, poor soul. Rambles on, saying the same things over and over." Serenity seemed to be squirming in her seat. Something had brought the woman here, that I knew.

"How sad." To be kind, I said, "Often when people are old, they forget what they have just said. It is not madness, just aging."

"Well, that may be so for your mother, but my mother is daft as a drunkard most of the time. I hope I never live so long as to become idiotic. I was quite taken with your gown. Who made it? Oh, dear. That's not why I called. Oh, well. You know, don't you?"

"Know, Serenity?"

"Well, that we're apologetic. Wallace and I are monstrously sorry for the incident that happened in our home and trust you will say nothing at all about it. We are both very sorry you became upset. There. That's it."

"Is that why you called?" I asked, bridling a cauldron of anger that she was stirring. Perhaps she was only here to forestall another meeting between Wallace and my brother. "Why, Serenity, you cannot be sorry that I was upset."

"Why not?"

"You cannot apologize for my feelings. You may apologize for your actions. You may even try to apologize for your husband's taking advantage of my daughter and disgracing her, and throwing an honorable young man out a window with a fist to his jaw. But"—I slowed my words, emphasizing each one—"you may not apologize for my feelings. My feelings are my response to your husband fondling my daughter. He all but called out my brother to a duel. No, Mistress Spencer, you must apologize for your husband's actions."

"Well. Well. I told him he was mistaken sending me here. You are not our level of society. You were a slave. Everyone knows what slaves are like."

"Why, Serenity, I lived with you. I was your companion and friend. Indenture was in my childhood. Perhaps I lack understanding, not being so refined as yourself. What are you implying?"

"Your children are from all different masters."

"How many children on your plantation look like Wallace?"

Serenity stood with a hop, nearly tumbling over the chair in which she had been sitting. "How dare you."

"Fifteen, by now I should say, at least."

She stomped toward the door. There, she stopped and looked from her gown to a bolt of fine blue wool I had laid there on a small table, waiting to be wrapped and taken to town. She gasped. They were the same fabric.

She whirled at me. "You may think you belong in our society, Miss Talbot, but you do not. You are nothing but a tradeswoman, a crafter. You and your family will never darken the door of my home again."

I thought of Lady Spencer's grand home, now already pledged to my brother, and realized that Serenity had no knowledge of that. "I would not let Gwyneth's shadow fall upon so much as your coffin. I am a crafter. Had not the Crown taken my plantation from me, I might have grown up to be much more like you, Serenity. So for that, I am thankful I learned to weave."

She sniffed, patting her own cheeks as one might soothe a pensive child. "One must make allowances for the lower class of society. God sent you to be a slave so you could learn to weave and make your living outside of good society as a crafter."

"God sent me to be a slave?"

"Otherwise you'd have become a slut."

At my side on the table rested a bowl of apples, most of them soft and awaiting cooking down for apple butter. It was done before I knew it. It was done as if someone else ran into the room and put the apple into my hand and pulled my arm. I threw it at her with every ounce of strength I had. I roared at her, "God sent you this apple, then, to teach you manners!" The fruit hit Serenity at the base of her lower lip and splattered upward across her face, causing a tiny cut in the lip at the same time. A drop of dark red appeared on her lip.

Serenity shrieked for her men, and proceeded to feign a faint on my doorstep, her face filthy, and her wig falling off sideways. The man holding her right arm while her backside slid into mud at the doorway asked, "May we bring her inside, madam?"

"No. I will help you get her into the coach. I think she will be most comfortable in her own home. She was rambling on about madness in the family. Repeating herself. I believe the woman is having a spell. Quite incoherent, perhaps mad. It runs in the family, you know. Get her home and I insist you send for a physician. She needs a vigorous vomit and a good bleeding. See to it that a doctor does it as soon as she gets home." We got her into the coach where she tumbled down against the seat as a child might sleep.

The coach left, though I did not enter the house until it was well out of sight. "Jacob?" I called. "Jacob, I must talk to you." I told him what I had done, adding, "Oh, Jacob, they will come for me. If we were in England, they would transport me here. The Wallace Spencers have wealth and position. I am doomed." My children came down then, and I was forced to confess another time. "Children, your mother lost her temper in the most terrible way. I was insulted and did not forbear to take it quietly. I should have asked the woman to leave. Or merely told her I was not pleased with what she said."

My little Dorothy said, "Ma? What did you do?"

I drew a deep breath. "I hit Mistress Spencer with an apple. A mushy one. Right in the face."

"Yippee!" Benjamin whooped. "Did it make a big mess and bust out all her teeth? I want to see that!"

"Oh, son. I am so sorry I did it. Gentle people ought not to behave so."

"What did she say to you, Ma?" Gwenny asked.

"She said she had come to apologize for what occurred at the ball—Wallace Spencer was too proud and sent her—and then she apologized for my upset, not for your affronting."

Jacob said, "It isn't like you to be offended over mere words. I have known you to be almost stoic when faced with a braggart or a lunatic."

"But she was neither. And her husband took evil advantage of my precious Gwenny. Besides, that was not all she said. She said God had made me a slave and that was where I belonged." I burst into tears. "Oh, my dears, they will come for me. I could hang for this. My poor babes. You will be motherless and scorned. I have ruined us."

"But Ma, it was just an apple," said Benjamin. "I threw an apple at Thomas Bedford's sister Nanette and it had a worm in it. All I got was that Thomas's father flicked my behind with a switch a few times."

I bit my lip from the inside.

Jacob said, "Well and aye. If your mother gets a switch a few times, we won't think the worse of her, will we, children? After all, she was defending our family honor and your sister's name." Of course, all the children agreed with that, but my heart broke so that I wanted only to go to bed, and left America and Gwyneth to serve them supper.

America brought me tea and a bit of pudding. "I am sorry," she said. "I cannot help but think she deserved even more, but I wish I had been the one to deliver it. Then you would have nothing to fear."

That evening, when August rode home on a fine stallion, leading another horse he had bought, I was forced to tell the story yet again. August's understanding was far different than mine, as was his response. "No one will arrest you," he said, "if I have to load muskets and fight them off."

"August, we cannot do that."

"Then we will take your family and disappear. Or you will hide in one of your many priest holes. You built them for just such a purpose, did you not?"

"I would not break the law."

"It was what the wench deserved. If she were not wealthy, no one would give another thought about it."

"But she is wealthy. She will do something."

"I will duel that fat fop over it. That will settle it. It must be done before the magistrate is called in."

"I will not have you risk your life on that account."

"You risked yours."

I sighed. "I am undone. I am undone. I need Cullah. He always answered cunning with silence, and it was the right thing. I have never been able to master my own tongue."

August laughed in a knowing way. "Only this time it was your hand, I think. Like a good cider, my little sister, you are very sweet and a wee bit spoiled, hiding a hogshead of black powder and cinnamon in your stays."

"August! The children will hear."

He laughed again, a bit louder, and said, "I wish that they had heard you bewend the hassock-headed bitch. You have a talent for it; it would have improved their education."

I clapped hands over my mouth, but felt a laugh similar to his welling up from the terror within. I giggled through my tears. A pirate bold is my bonny brother, I thought.

"There," August said. "It was only a matter of time before you let go of your fear and took this for what it really was. At best, a matter of honor. At least, two housewives squabbling."

"August, how low."

"You could claim it so, and given fifteen minutes before any judge, she would show herself to be the lower of the two."

The following day August left early again, claiming he had an errand in town that could not wait. He returned at evening with no explanation other than "business."

The next two weeks dragged past in long dreary days, some so gray we all felt compelled to sleep most of the time away for the sun barely changed the color of the sky at all from night to day. Only the lowing of the cows brought us from sleep. America tried her best to soothe me at every turn.

Two soldiers came on a Friday morning. They delivered to me a paper with the words "Writ of Summons" upon it in large hand-scribed letters. I was not being arrested, I was being sued for damages to the person of Serenity Spencer. Grievous injury, it said. Violent attack. Bloody mutilation. I closed my eyes. In my childhood I had seen bloody mutilation. "What manner of lies is this?" I said aloud to any and all. "This is nothing but falsehood. Nothing but confabulation. What shall I do?"

The soldier shrugged. "Appear in the court when it says to appear, Goody. Else we come and haul you in a cart, tied and bound to a tree. Good day to you."

Tears rose in my eyes and I closed the door. For several minutes I could not speak a word. I stared at the floor, horrified at what I had done. The sound of my own breath going in and out filled the room. I closed my eyes and turned my face upward, so wrought with anguish at my own being, my many faults, that no prayer came to me at all.

And then I heard, "Haff. Haffa. Ahah! Mama, hap!" I opened my eyes to see my Dorothy, her face an open display of shock and disbelief. On a low stool, a candlestick had lost its taper. Dolly's wee skirts and petticoats smoldered and exploded into tongues of orange flame. Her face at that moment registered only surprise.

I fell upon Dorothy, tearing the flaming cloth with my hands. I crushed her to me, pressing the fiery ash against my body, setting alight my apron, my house cap, and my skirt. Dorothy wailed now, terrified at the fire as well as what I was doing. I flung burning fabric away and crushed her at last against the floor with my own body, forming my arms against her tiny ones to smother every last bit of flame.

I felt more than saw my other children, my men, America, all standing, helpless, watching, chasing and stamping cinders of burning cloth. I stammered out, "Get—water." I rolled off Dorothy and she let out a wail that came from her soul's core. I stood her up and pulled again at layer after layer of burned petticoat and stockings, until, even as she wailed, half the poor mite was naked before us all, pink and scorched. Only then did I breathe. She had lost most of her hair back of her ears on the whole expanse of her head. The skin there was blistered and red. Her face, thankfully, untouched and whole. Her legs had blistered in rising whitish lumps, though her back seemed unscathed, for the fire had stopped at the sash of her pinafore. "Oh, baby," I said. "My baby. Whatever possessed you to step over a burning candle?"

Dorothy cried. It would not have mattered if she could have explained her action. Children did things because they knew no fear, they had no judgment, and they cannot look forward in time, not even one minute. I bathed her backside with cool water cupped in my hands and she cried all the harder. Gulping air, at last she let me bind her sore legs with clean linen bandages. I held her in my arms and rocked our bodies together, singing "O Waly, Waly," until by the second verse, she slept.

I shook my head and said, "I could not move fast enough."

August said to me, "Ressie, you were like a wild animal. You saved her life."

America said, "Now she is sleeping. Will you let me clean your wounds?"

My hands hurt mercilessly. I had blisters, too, though the tops of several of them had already opened and torn away; they tormented me most thinking that my babe felt such burning pain. As America dabbed at my hands and face with wet cloths, I felt every sting as if it were Dorothy's. I asked, "Have I my hair?"

"Yes, in the back. Poor thing, the front is gone. Also your eyebrows and lashes. They will grow."

"I have to go to town on Monday to appear before the magistrate." I sighed. "I will look a madwoman even if I wear a new cap, pulled low. If I must, I will powder my face. All I care is that Dorothy is well."

That night Dorothy glowed with fever as did I. In the morning, I bathed her with woolen pads soaked in cool water before the fire in my room. She cried as if I tortured her, revived enough to eat, cried more in distress, then slept again. August was away from the house early in the morning, but did not tell me where he was going. America and I tried to salvage what could be had of my clothing, for not a scrap would I waste. All of it would make something, even if it were a pot holder. I sat at length and studied the stool where the candle had been. I wanted not so much to place blame for the accident, but to prevent its occurring again. All I could figure out was that someone had moved the candlestick from its usual place on the mantel to get at the box on which it sat, and had not put it back.

I looked inside the box. Tobacco. Perhaps August had reached into it, and not thinking about the whimsical nature of children, had busied himself with a pipe, even lighting it with the candle, and set it by his feet on the stool. Dorothy had been used to playing upon the steps and jumping from the second one to the hearthstone. With the stool there, she may have thought it nothing new, or perhaps thought she could jump high enough to get over it. Had he been so careless as to endanger my child?

Just the day before, when she was playing at dancing, I had said to her, "Oh, my, how high you jump! Look at my Dolly fly up, as a wee jumping jack." Perhaps she thought she really could fly. There was no end to the guilt I owned this day. If my precious Dolly should die from this, I thought, I shall throw myself into the sea.

Monday, America Roberts and August came with me to town, after she had helped me dress and hide my missing hair with a lacy cap. She put my bonnet on but I could not stand for it to be tied against the raw red skin under my chin and neck so I tied it loosely as some wore for style, and hoped it not too brazen. I was dressed as if in mourning except for the white cockade at my throat.

On the way there, August tried to convince me things would turn out for the best, but when I walked into the town hall I thought I should faint. I kept my eyes on the floor until I heard them read a statement that included my name. Then I looked about. I saw Serenity and Wallace Spencer, clothed in new luxury, matching brown silks with gold embroidery. Lady Spencer accompanied them, too, seated on the front row of benches before the table of judges. I turned away. I must look a drab old crow. I touched my bonnet. I had not powdered my face except to hide the red of my forehead, for I knew that I might be moved to tears in this procedure, and that would leave streaks that could not be explained. I must seem a horror, I thought.

I sat between August and America, who patted my arm and tenderly held my hands as if she must have sensed they felt burned and painful, though I wore gloves. Another man rose and read another statement. My head spun. I held August's arm so that at one point he patted my hand but loosened my grip. He smiled when I complied. I tried to return it, but I doubt that I succeeded. Before me sat men in long wigs and black robes, making judgment against me and my household for all time, I feared. Such gloom took me as I had never before known. I saw my poor hurting babe, first, then thought of all my children, even the ones long in their graves. I wept, thinking of Cullah. August shook my arm. "Listen," he whispered. "You must listen."

Serenity moved to a chair in the center of the opening between the magistrates' table and the bar that separated them from the rest of the people. She acted as if it were difficult to stay conscious, and patted herself, fanned herself, though it was so cold our breaths bathed the room with a foggy softness.

When the magistrate prompted her again, Serenity said, "I had gone to call upon Goody Mackle-man, there, as a kindness and courtesy, although it was beneath me to do it. The minute I came through the door she hurled such curses and threats at me as to nearly cause a lady of my gentle up-bringing to succumb. She might have even tried to cast a spell upon me, I do not know, for I have no knowledge of that sort of devilment, being a God-fearing wife and mother. She then began to cast apples at me, crashing my mouth and face. She bruised me and caused blood to cascade down my gown. This tooth, here"—she pointed—"is chipped now. If you don't hang that woman you must at least run her from the town. Tarred and feathered. Yes. Send her from the town and confiscate her property." She nodded at Wallace after saying that, smiled, then resumed a somber face.

One of the magistrates seemed to be staring, not at her but at August. I whispered to him, "Will I get to tell them the true incident?"

"Just wait," he replied.

The first man spoke again. Now I saw he was the lawyer representing Serenity. He reiterated everything she said. I winced as the magistrates nodded as if it were the truest case they had ever heard. The second man rose again and made different remarks sounding more as if I had been wronged and acted on impulse. "Who is he?" I asked August.

"Your lawyer."

"Did you hire him?"

He turned to me, cutting his eyes at an angle. "No," he mouthed.

"Who, then?"

"Sh-sh."

One of the magistrates crooked a finger at me. "Goodwife MacLammond, is it? Yes, Goodwife. Please come and sit in the witness chair."

August led me to the seat, still warm from Serenity's broad beam. "Yes, your lordship?" I said.

"We are not lords. You will address this assembly as 'Your Honors' or 'Honorable Sirs.' Now, please answer to this assembly. First, what church do you attend?"

"First Church, Your Honors."

"And do you tithe?"

"When there is coin coming in, Your Honors, but sometimes my husband and I have been paid in sacks of grain or lambs. It is not always perfectly divisible; I cannot divide a single lamb, but make effort to account fairly, with some to the poor fund."

"Have you ever attended a Quaker assembly? What about papist? This charge says you cast spells of a pagan nature and know all kinds of chants and are familiar with diverse concoctions of the Roman Catholic Church. That you had been known, when you abided with the Roberts family, to pray to candles. How do you answer?"

I touched Cullah's white cockade at my throat for strength. I hoped I could answer tenderly enough that they would hear my words. "Honorable Sirs, some of you were present when first I came to Lexington. You know that I escaped with my life and nothing else from a French convent in the Canadas where I had been taken as a child by Indian captors. A child learns what she is taught, but I never prayed to candles, Your Honors. I prayed to the Lord God. I was taught to speak French and Latin. I learned prayers in Latin, sir. Latin is not a language of the Roman Church; it is taught in Harvard along with Greek. When my escape was made, I was introduced to First Church by Lady Spencer, here in this room. I have never willingly attended any other."

"Did you throw apples at Mistress Spencer?"

"One apple, Your Honors."

One of the magistrates sank his head into his hand and clutched at his mouth with his fingers as if deep in thought, or perhaps, I thought, trying to hide laughter as I had done as a child. He was next to ask, "And did you curse at her and cast spells or at any time threaten her with cunning words or charms?"

I thought of my loom blessing, such an ordinary part of each day. I decided to lie. "No, Your Honors. I know no cunning words or charms. Goody Spencer threatened me, sir, and gave insults though her pretense was to apologize for her husband's having taken liberties with my daughter when we were guests in their home."

"What insults? Pray let us have an accurate statement. The gentlemen of this court are not so immured to the evils of this world that they need fear what passes between goodwives in a squabble."

I thought over their words. They were likely to be more offended by the Roman Church than they were by what I considered the greatest offense, accusing me of being fit only for slavery, so I chose my words. "If you please, Your Honors, after acknowledging her husband's fondling of my child, Goodwife Spencer said it was good that I had been taken to a Romanish convent, beaten and deprived and forced to learn that catechism, being taught to weave so I could become a crafter and a slave rather than assume the titled position I was heir to. She said had I not been forced to weave in a French Catholic convent I would have been a slut." Gasps and fluttering filled the room behind me. "She said God had sent me to the convent because I was not fit for gentle society though she knew and accepted me, the daughter of a plantation master, as her landed superior a few years ago. It was her mother who threw me from their house when I lost my fortune to the Crown. Goody Spencer insulted me most grievously, Honorable Sirs. I picked up the apple. I threw it and said, 'If God sent me to the papist Catholics to be taught weaving because I was not equal to you in grace, then God sends you this apple for you are not equal to me in manners.' Those precise words."

One of the magistrates who until that point had seemed asleep, roused himself and leaned forward, saying, "What about the despoiling of Mistress Spencer's gown?"

"She made as if to faint as she left my house, and sat in the mud. The four coachmen had some struggle lifting her into the coach. It was mud, and not blood, upon her gown. Have her produce the gown and it shall be proven."

Serenity's lawyer exclaimed outrage at my lies and deceit. My lawyer said nothing. The magistrate in the center of the table looked from me to others around the room. Then he said, "We will confer. There will be silence in this room."

All the men at the table began writing on papers before them. They passed them up and down the row. Each read the others' opinions. They wrote yet again, and the same thing occurred. Finally the chief magistrate said, "Goodwife MacLammond? Approach this table and stand before us. Turn and face this room, the members of whom represent your community, whose laws of peace, sobriety, and sanctity this body is charged and incorporated to protect. Goodwife MacLammond, by your own admission you are found guilty of bodily harm and insult to the person of Mistress Wallace Spencer." Tears dripped down my face. The salt burned against my reddened cheeks as I stared at the floor before me. He went on, "However, this body finds that the words used against you to demean you and slander your character, though they were not heard by others, were of a nature to bring a person to their own defense."

Serenity gasped and Wallace stood. "Your Honors," he said, his voice forced into a guileless melody, "you cannot mean you disbelieve my wife's account?"

Serenity's lawyer stood and touched Wallace's arm to quiet him. The lawyer said, "If the accused is guilty, it is necessary for you to pass a sentence."

The magistrate glared at the lawyer from under great brushy brows. "If the plaintiff will remain silent, we shall do that."

The lawyer representing me stood, too. He held a paper in his hand. "Your Honors, I believe there is more to this examination than has reached the ears of the magistrates here convened."

"One moment, Mr. Charlesworth." I looked up, startled. It was Daniel Charlesworth, the clerk with the withered arm at Foulke's, a man I had known in Boston so many years ago. Now in full wig and robes, his face softer and heavier with age, it was he. I raised my head and stopped weeping. The magistrate said, "Goodwife MacLammond, for taking action against a woman of high standing with a piece of rotted fruit you are sentenced to one hour bound head and hands in the public pillory which stands hard by this building. This sentence will commence upon leaving this room. There you will consider your temper and your tongue and contemplate Proverbs, chapter fifteen, verse one, 'A soft answer turneth away wrath, but grievous words stir up anger.' And, in consideration of that very proverb, though your action was of violence that cannot be overlooked, this body of magistrates believes that your anger was kindled in such a manner that to any righteous woman must have been outrageous. Therefore, your sentence on record is one hour but the time to be served is reduced to ten minutes. The claim is so adjudged. Now, what is it, Mr. Charlesworth?"

"It should be known, Honorable Sirs, that the claimant's spouse, Lord Wallace Spencer, has filed a deed of severalty on the property owned by Master and Mistress Cullah MacLammond. It would be to the Spencers' great advantage to cause her such embarrassment that the family would leave, deserting the home and lands forfeit to an attachment such as this." I turned to Wallace, my eyes wide. Would he stop at nothing?

"Let me see that," the magistrate said. Mr. Charlesworth handed him the paper. "I see. Well, sir. This is ridiculous. Everyone knows Miss Talbot was willed that farm by Goodwife Carnegie, and then by marriage, she and Mr. MacLammond have owned the Carnegie farm nearly twenty years." He tore the paper asunder and said, "Let us have no more of that. Mr. Spencer? I suggest you take your delicate wife and yourself back to Virginia, where you may be quite better received than in Lexington. Despite the respect and admiration we feel for your good and generous mother, this society prefers our own. This court is dismissed. Bondsman, take Mistress MacLammond to the stocks."

I went willingly. America Roberts followed, turned her face, and would not speak to her sister. August and Daniel Charlesworth followed her. The bondsman took my arm and led me to the platform behind the building where stood the reeking pillory. I looked upon that instrument of shame as if it were to be my rack of torture. People did die in such things. Crowds might laugh or taunt, but I had known them to become churned up to throw stones, or eggs, rotted fruit, decaying dead animals, dung, even pumpkins if the pilloried person were hated enough. One time an idiot had been sentenced to serve twenty-four hours after being found in some carnal act—I know not what of a certainty, but it involved an animal—and as he stood in the stocks he was stoned to death.

I climbed the steps. A crowd assembled, growing moment by moment. I wondered if the smell coming from the place was emanating from the platform or the crowd. Did they carry rotted fruit and dead cats or did I smell the remnants of some past judgment, still oozing under the planks even in the cold? America moved ahead of me and put her shawl over the rough wood on the neck trough. I removed my bonnet but left my cap in place to cover my missing hair, and handed her the bonnet.

The bondsman took the shawl and gave it back to her, saying, "Not allowed." He thrust my hands through the holes and shoved my head toward the groove meant for the neck. After he closed the wide yoke, pushed the tenon through its hole and bolted it, he pulled off my gloves!

I moaned aloud against my resolve to stay silent no matter what occurred. My blistered hands had bled and oozed as I wrung them in the hearing. The cloth stuck to them, forming a crust that he had torn open. They bled anew now, and it appeared to the people below that he had somehow injured me. Someone threw an egg at the man and it splattered the back of his coat with foul-smelling contents. That started a clamor, and my knees weakened, expecting that to be but the first of many such insults aimed at me.

I could see nothing but the gray boards on the platform. I heard boots upon the boards, felt the vibration of someone moving around. Was the bondsman preparing something else? Did he carry a whip? Would he remove my cap, too, revealing more shame? To be a woman without hair was to be an object of ridicule forever. No matter that the back of it was done in a roll of braids, the front was gone, blistered under the cap, making me look like an elderly man with a natural tonsure of receding hair. I panted, bracing myself. All of a sudden, the crowd quieted. Someone draped a coat or a cloak across my back. The garment had just been worn and removed by some person; it felt warm as an embrace. I waited. Silence grew until I heard my own heart beating.

Then I heard someone say, "Time is completed."

There had been not one stone, not a potato, not a voice of derision. The bolt was opened, the tenon pulled, and the yoke raised. I lifted my head, my neck gone stiff and painful. Oh, la! I stared straight at the back of Lady Spencer herself, supported by a walking stick in one hand and Daniel Charlesworth by her other arm! She had stood on the platform in front of me so that no one dared throw a thing.

I turned around. August had kept guard of my backside. Rather than his more sober tricorn hat, he had donned his captain's hat with its gold braid and plume, and thrown his bright red coat across my shoulders. He faced the crowd a moment more, then turned to me and smiled. Across his brocade waistcoat, two wide leather belts bristled with three pistols and a dagger. At his side hung a tasseled cutlass, partly unsheathed. His hand rested upon the hilt of it, and he cocked it, but he held the other hand out to me and I took it, marveling in the size and strength of it.

"All is well," he said, loudly enough for the people to hear. "The people of Lexington, I find, are most congenial and quick to forgive small offenses."

People in the crowd said, "Aye, aye," and a few clapped. Then August held out his other arm to Lady Spencer, who took it, to the gasps of people below. Daniel Charlesworth took America Roberts's arm, and the five of us left the place in Lady Spencer's gig. I sat in silence, feeling stunned relief. August played the gallant with Lady Spencer with perfect deference and decorum, despite that he looked capable of rendering asunder any who stood in his way.

At Lady Spencer's house, she called for wine to be served in the parlor, and though I sat with them, I felt separated and shattered still, as if I moved behind a gauze, as though everything were too polished and too loud, affronting my senses.

Daniel told us how he came to be a lawyer in full, now, and that Lady Spencer had sent for him to come from Boston, with little knowledge other than what August had given her on Saturday. By today, Monday, Daniel had come to my rescue. He had queried some friends and found out about the suit to take my land, as that was what had postponed Serenity's charges as late as they were, else it would have happened in a trice.

"Why would Wallace do that?" I asked.

Daniel smiled with one corner of his mouth raised wryly. "He wants that land, as do many others who believe the old stories about it. The

Carnegie place used to belong to someone named Goodman Smythe. A common enough name that it means nothing. The rumor was that the name was falsely used, that he had been a pirate and knew Edward Teach and was of the same caliber, and that Smythe had buried treasure on the place. All accounts, though, were that he worked diligently and as hard as any farmer to try to make good of it. He never lived higher than his farm allowed, which was quite modest."

I laughed. "We found a brass ship's bell and a couple of cannonballs, a metal ring of some sort like an ankle iron. If he was a marauding seaman, he left little behind."

Lady Spencer said, "I always believed that rumor was false. The man was a humble yeoman and worked himself into an early grave. His son went to a trade in New York but a little while later was killed by a falling tree; his daughter married Matthew Carnegie."

"She was Goody Carnegie?"

"Yes," she said, "poor thing. No one knows why she went so mad. He left her after about a year, alone with the house and land. Left for the frontier and never returned. It was a wonder she lived so long, but blessed peace that she is at last in the ground."

I nodded. I knew the reason for Goody's madness. It would serve no one to tell it, and I was too exhausted to want the small thrill of owning some dreadful gossip. Was Matthew Carnegie the specter never at rest over the graves of his child and wife? A chill drove me to shudder, but I brushed it away.

Amelia said, "You, my dear, do live beyond a farmer's wife. I fear it is my fault."

When America, August, and I arrived at last at home, the children gathered, all questioning at once about what had happened in town. Jacob had let them play and dabble as they might, and the only one who appeared presentable was Gwyneth. Rather than ask for explanation, she put her arms around me and hugged me, and in that simple act, made all of it worthwhile.

When the clamor of our arrival had passed and the children were in bed, August and I sat together at the fire. His face grew cold as it did sometimes. "It is not finished," he said. "The Spencer plantation in Virginia ships a great deal of tobacco and rum to England. I sense a downturn in their profits coming. Ill winds they be a-blowing."

"August, you must not," I said, stunned. "Vengeance is not the answer. You will be fanning the flames of a feud between us and Wallace Spencer. Gwyneth is not so harmed. Cullah is gone and Jacob cannot see. I fear what Wallace may bring upon my family when you are away."

"Don't preach at me, Ressie. I see the venom in your eyes even now. You'd have him over the coals in a trice. Saturday I ordered my ships made ready. I have the names of the vessels that take his cargo. We sail next week as soon as we're provisioned. I shall levy a tax upon the Spencers that they will not quickly pay."

I searched my heart. I should be happy to think of him acting out retribution upon them but I felt broken of spirit, weary of hate and intensity, and not willing to perpetuate the whole affair. "I wish you would not."

"What about Gwyneth's honor?"

"Of course I value her honor, but, August, I do not want you to be arrested. I need you. Cullah and Brendan will return, then go."

He sneered. "I answer to no one. I have word the *Blue Dawn* left port in Hampton, Virginia, bound for England ten days ago, loaded to the waterline with Spencer's barrels. Winds are up. With good sail and all watches on deck, I can overtake her before she reaches sight of land. They will expect no trouble and will not be watching. We shall see her on the bottom before so much as a pipeful reaches the coast." He stared hard into the fire, the look on his face one of fury barely contained.

"Do you not feel enough has been done?"

"Never."

"I paid my due. Leave this be."

"He will pay his."

CHAPTER 29

February 25, 1756

August had been gone three weeks or so—it was a bitter, late February morning when the Reverend Mr. Clarke, the pastor of First Church, called. I could not say that I felt changed afterward but I wished the blot I had brought upon myself would go away. Reverend Clarke assured me it would. "It will be talked about until some other thing comes along. Have no fear. Hold up your head, Goodwife. You have paid your debt to the town and now to your God. No one condemns you."

I bridled my anger and served him tea, though I felt a childish want to scold him in return. I knew I had been wrong. I felt mortified.

When he left with a small napkin wrapped around half an apple pudding, I went to the barn and began collecting eggs in a basket. The sounds of the chickens and geese murmuring at my feet lulled and soothed me and the dozen or so eggs in my basket made me think of pies I might make. I began to sing. The barn door creaked. I looked up. It moved back and forth in the wind. "Reverend?" I called. "Have you more to say?" The door creaked again, swinging to and fro. "There you are, you silly girl," I said, to a speckled hen. "Two today? Did I miss your nest yesterday?" I reached in and pushed her off the eggs she sat upon. The hairs on my arm stood up. I shook off the chill. The door creaked again but I ignored it. I clutched the eggs in my left hand and turned to put them in the basket draped over my right arm. I dropped the two eggs. They made a gentle-sounding crush as they hit the hard-packed mud floor.

Standing in the sunlight of the open barn door was a man. An Indian. He wore leggings and breechclout. His face tattooed, his arms glistening with grease and full muscles bound by a band on one arm, he stood stock-still as if he had come for the eggs and had been caught off guard by my presence. I was aware that someone had made the sound of a whimper of fear and that the sound may have come from me.

"Talbot?" he asked.

"What?" I stammered. "What do you want?" I raised my brows and held the basket of eggs toward him. "Are you hungry?" I asked, gesturing with the basket.

"I find woman-child Talbot."

"What do you know about a girl named Talbot? Who are you?"

"My mother woman-child Talbot. She sends one find other Talbot. Her name now Weenak-echon. Willow Bend Down. Mother old name Shield of Owasso."

I drew in a breath. "Shield of Owasso? Red Shield of Bear? Patience Talbot? You—you are her son?" I stepped toward him.

"Where woman-child Talbot?"

"I am she. Resolute Catherine Talbot. I have a husband now. My name is MacLammond."

He broke his stony look with a sly smile. "Mack. Lamb-ben. Talbot now Mack Lamb-ben. What means Mack Lamb-ben?"

I thought a moment and saw Cullah's face before my eyes, my Eadan with claymore ready, his image bristling with the ancient danger of a Highland fighter under an echo of skirling pipes. "It means Warrior."

He seemed to be thinking. "Woman named Warrior?" He looked about the barn. "Sister of Shield of Owasso called Warrior." He turned back to me. "Woman named Warrior, sister Willow Bend Down old. Our people war. Old ones and babes killed by English. Old mother wishes come to sister Mack Lamb-ben. Cannot run, much bend down."

"Patience is alive? Shield of Bear, I mean. English are killing your babies? Your old ones?" It was too much all at once. "She comes to me?"

He nodded. "Willow Bend Down come this place. You keep? Keep safe?"

I could see him better then. My eyes had adjusted to the glare behind him. "Are you the man who came here before? You came to the house and took yarn?" He understood not. "You go there"—I pointed at him, at the house, made a fist—"took wool."

He smiled. Why, his eyes shined merrily, his teeth clean and straight, and the face of him not at all threatening! He said, "Skimp wool. Not good to sew, too much breaks. Willow Bend Down tell sister who make skimp wool."

The smiling dolt had just insulted me. I sharpened the tone of my voice. "It is not meant for sewing, it is wool for weaving. It must be fine to make—oh, what am I saying? Forget the yarn. Where is Patience? Where is Willow Bend Down?"

"Come," he said, and motioned to me with his hand. He still smiled.

I moved toward the door. He pushed it wider. There stood a woman in deerskins, bent over, crouched under a heavy bearskin cape and holding to a walking stick. Her long, braided hair was motley with red, gray-white, and yellowing strands. She wore grease on her sun-darkened arms, a band around her head. She had a tattoo of a solid black line across her face as if another band encircled her cheekbones and crossed the bridge of her nose. When she saw me, she straightened a little and raised her face.

The man spoke to her. I recognized when he said "Mack Lam-ben," but nothing more. The woman nodded. She spoke to him and raised her arm, her hand uplifted. He gave the same gesture, even more slowly, as if he were trying to press a memory into his heart. Then the young man looked warily about the place and trotted into the woods where he disappeared, leaving me staring at this creature before me. She stared back, her eyes of pale green searching my face. I pulled my cap back. My hair had not faded as hers had, having rarely seen the sun upon it. I stepped closer. "Patey?"

"Ressie?" Then she muttered something I could not understand.

"*C'est moi.* Is it you? *Est-ce vraiment toi?*" I asked. She spoke again, words that seemed more clear but were neither English nor French. "Can you speak no English at all?" I asked, leaning down so our faces were at the same height. I knelt in the dirt. She did the same. When we were both on our knees, we leaned toward each other, staring. At last, I said, "Patience? Patey?"

She nodded. At first hesitantly, then assuredly. I smelled on her the wilderness, smoke from a thousand fires, blood from butchering animals, sweat and sunshine from all our years apart. We fell into each other's arms, both breaking into loud weeping. As she cried, I smelled something else. A sour, death smell, a disease. No wonder she could not keep up. Patey had come to me, had been brought to me by a son half Indian, half Talbot, not willing to let her be left behind to face the ravages of war.

I made room for my sister at one end of the parlor. With Jacob's help, we created a bed where, I remembered—before there were children, before there were additional floors to this house—there had once been a bed. Our first. Patience stayed in it, much of the day. She seemed so weary. Then in the afternoons, when it warmed, she rose and sat in my chair by the fire.

Little by little, Patey regained her speech, and she seemed to long to tell me all the years of her life gone by. In short tales by our evening fireside, she told me of her husband Massapoquot, of their nine children, and of the one young man who brought her to me. She would not tell me his name, but said, "Call him John."

When she had eaten good broth and bread for a few days and seemed more well, I at last asked her, "From what are you ill?"

"I have a stone in my stomach, that is all I know." She had found her English words, though she spoke slowly.

"I will take you to physicians in Boston."

"No. Look at me. I am more Indian than English. One look at the mark upon my face and they will either turn me away or put me in jail or a lunatic hospital. If you will have me leave you, I will walk away and die as my people have died for all of time."

Her people? How could she believe that Indians were her people? Talbots were her people. Earls and nobles were her people. I felt so distressed I was sure it came out in my voice. "What causes stones in the stomach?"

"The sachem did not know. He said I may have eaten a stone left in some beans and it grew in the place where a child should grow. Or, I may have eaten the seed of a wolf, because sometimes it feels as if I am being chewed from inside. I fear I am dying."

"Oh, Patience. Do you feel better at all, after the bath and the soup?"

She smiled and winced. "It would make you happy if I said yes."

I bowed my head and held her hands in mine and pressed them. How alike we were, yet no longer the same skin. We both had calluses in different places, but her hands looked tanned as if by a leather worker. The skin even on the backs of the hands was thickened. I leaned toward her, and as if I had asked her to do the same, she inclined herself toward me. We touched our faces to each other. I held Patience and wept sweet, bitter tears. So much time gone by. So many things we never shared. Yet it was her choice, I reminded myself, and that, too, brought tears to my eyes. Now that she was returned, she would soon die.

My children were both awed and terrified of her. America conquered her timidity soonest, as would be expected. Sometimes, Patey rocked the littlest ones, and that included, to his great joy, Benjamin. Unlike his uncle August expecting him to behave in a manly way, Patey petted him and let him return to baby ways as much as Dolly. After about a fortnight of that, he grew tired of babying and told her he had quite grown up.

"That is good, little Ben," she said. "If you would like to be held, that will be good as well. You may choose."

"Why do you do that?" I asked. "We thought it wise to prepare him to be a man by not letting him act a child."

"But he is a child. An adult has life hard enough. Let them have their comforts when they are still soft and weak. There is no good come of beating a child but filling him with hatred and, and, I cannot remember the word. Resent."

"Resentment? We do not beat our children, Patey."

"Most English do. It is said they eat them in times of famine."

"I have never heard of such atrocity. The only people who ever beat me were the Haskens. I don't think they were English."

"It is said."

"Patience, there are hideous things told about Indians, too."

"They are not true."

"Your son said they meant to leave behind the old and the babies to be slaughtered by the soldiers."

"The ones who stay tend the young. That is the way of the people. It saves those who can run, who can fight, who can have children to replenish the people."

"They would have left you to die."

"Just to mind the children. It is the way."

A great stabbing pain shot through me. "Were you ever sorry you left me?"

She looked at me, her eyes filling with tears. "You? Always I regretted leaving you. I missed you. But, I had a good life. I was loved. Really loved. Not just by a man, but by all the people. I would never have been loved by the English here. It was my greatest sacrifice, leaving you."

"It has taken me a long time to feel I belong here. Often I still do not feel it. How could you belong to, to, such a life?"

"I was loved," she said again.

Gwyneth spent six weeks swooning and crying, and every time anyone asked her what was amiss, she said, "John Hancock has never called upon me. That horrible Lord Spencer has ruined my life. Now I am not good enough. Not rich enough. Not pretty enough." I knew she was distressed by what had occurred at the ball, but I told her it was, after all, something in the past. I assured her that the affront by Lord Spencer could never have diminished her in John Hancock's eyes. He was young, perhaps too young to fall in love the way she dreamed it, and she herself young enough to fall in love again. I did not say aloud that I believed if Mr. Hancock would only tell her she was not in his heart and mind and never would be, as harsh as that was, at least her heart might break and then mend. But no, because he neither wrote nor called upon Gwenny, she was convinced that he would if he could, if his studies had not hampered him, or if he could find our house, or if he had not found someone prettier.

Patience smiled at her, even laughed sometimes, and chided her with, "There are too many pretty boys around for you to only look at one. You see this mark upon my face? This was given to me when I married. It is like the ring your mother wears. It signifies to everyone for all time that once a woman marries she is never the same. You must choose carefully, for you, too, will be marked for all time when you marry."

"Did it hurt, Auntie?"

"No. I did it for love. There was pain, yes, but it was not the kind that hurts deep. I chose it. Your mother thinks it makes me ugly." Patience wrinkled her lips at me.

"I never said that!" I protested. "It but makes you look like you belong more to some other life than here. It makes me feel foreign from you." Finally, I said to Gwenny, "Daughter, if John Hancock had an eye for Gwyneth MacLammond, nothing on earth would keep him from our door." She cried bitter tears and told me I knew nothing of the human heart.

Patience seemed to rally some strength, but then by the end of April did not leave her bed for four days. Against her wishes, I sent for a doctor from

Boston. The man, Dr. Witherspoon, came with two other physicians, a Dr. Banbridge and Dr. Crawford. The second two were students, and they spent two hours examining and questioning her. At last, Dr. Witherspoon led his fellows to the door of the parlor and we all went outside. He said to me, "She has more than one disease, I'm afraid. Cankerous stones and parasites have infested her intestines, her gut. The infestation is so severe that to remove them would kill her. She's weakened and malnourished, not for lack of your care but because the disease organisms digest her food and leave her starving. Does she cough?"

"No," I said. "I don't believe I have heard her cough. She is quiet."

Dr. Crawford said, "No doubt due to abuse by the Indians who kept her."

"She has not spoken of any abuse, sir. She claims to me that she was as well kept as any white woman." I wanted neither to defend Massapoquot nor condemn him. I only asked, "What can be done for her?"

"Keep her clean and warm. Cleanliness is not only good for the soul, it prolongs the body. Beef broth. Warm compresses for pain. If she will drink a glass of vinegar every day, it may drive the parasites out. Very little else, actually," Witherspoon said, shaking his head. "How did she come to be this way?"

I detected in him more compassion than the others so I addressed him, though I intended the others to listen. "Thank you for seeing my sister. We have traveled a great many miles, she and I, from whence we began our lives. She was born in England, you know, on an estate. We were both taken to Canada. They, the Indians, let me escape, though I know not why. Patience chose to go with them."

"Tragic," he said.

"Doctor? Will my children have been exposed to some pestilence?"

"I do not believe so. Boil her bedding and shift, just to be sure. When she dies, burn everything."

I paid them each two pounds and bade them farewell. Patience sat up after they had gone. She stared ahead, her eyes fixed on some thought, perhaps. "Ressie?"

"Yes."

"Do not let them touch me again, those duppies."

"Duppies? Patience, those men were doctors."

"Duppies."

"I will not let them touch you again." I went to her and touched her head. She raised her arm and surrounded my hips with a caress. I sat upon her bed. She reached for me and put her face on my neck, weeping bitter tears, hard sobs stifled by her weakness and pain. I could do little else but hold her and weep, too. In those moments, time itself dissolved into liquid that was all at once both the present and long past. We held each other, our eyes closed against the light, caught on that terrifying staircase from which the only escape was plunging into darkness. I forgave her every ill-thought act of her youth, even as I grew amazed that I remembered them, and all the anger I had felt at her for the decades behind us melted into the honeyed light of time.

CHAPTER 30

June 6, 1756

Hard against my heart as May began to wane was one simple fact. The year of my husband's and son's impressment had passed. Brendan and Cullah should have been home but they were not. I would not think of them lying dead, I told myself. I patted Patience's head, fed her some chicken soup, then went to help Dolly learn her letters. Benjamin came to me and asked if he could see Auntie Patey.

"Of course, son. There she lies. She's quite ill today."

"I wish she had not got so ill, Ma."

"I do, too, son."

"I love her."

"I do, too. She is kind, my sister." I saw him take the chair where I had been, watching over his aged aunt. She slept, her ravaged insides placated at least for a while with the soup. I wondered at this son of mine. Our older boy wanted to be a soldier from the time he was a lad, and would have brooked no patience for a sick old woman marked by a life so different from ours. Patience had been so lovely as a girl; she was haggard now. This boy, my Ben, had a different heart. "Perhaps," I said, "you will be a doctor, or you will help people in some other way."

Benjamin looked up at me. "Maybe. I thought I would build things with Pa. Is she going to die?"

"We all shall. Our hours are not measured for us to know."

From then on, my life seemed full of the business of itself, though every stone of it was mortared with thoughts of Cullah and Brendan returning. I taught my children such schooling as I knew in English, which was little indeed. As I tried to explain things to them, at times I found it difficult to find other than French words. I cared for my sister, who seemed to regain some health in the following weeks. I called upon Amelia Spencer, finding in her the mother I had missed so often. I embroidered a linen for her table and presented it to her and I sewed slippers for her swollen and sore feet, padding them well with carded wool with the oil left in, to soothe her gout. It seemed I had a mother and a sister again. And, much as I longed to be held and coddled and doted upon, they needed me to do for them. Thus did I find myself mother and sister to them.

Jacob had been able to find his way around the barn and do the milking by guiding his hand along the walls. I sent Gwyneth to milk now, and sometimes heard Jacob scolding her for it, which she bore with much grace. It was Gwenny who thought to take Jacob's hand and lead him to the cows and goats. She who held their heads while he milked. She whom he came to lean upon. In my heart, every bird cry, every wolf howl, every bleat of lamb and sputter of hen called for Cullah. I who according to my daughter knew nothing of the human heart, felt it break many times each day.

Then came a day at the end of June when I heard another birdcall, familiar only to a family who had known the birds of Jamaica. I asked Jacob to go to the back door and hold up a bucket, the signal that all was well and August could come to the house. "Patey?" I called. "Wake up, Patience. Our brother is home."

"Brother? Do you mean your husband?"

"August Talbot. Our brother. Let me help you to a chair."

August came in looking sore of heart and soul. He took my hand and kissed it before he sat, placing his hat upon his knee. "Have you anything on the fire, Ressie? I am famished. Is your man about?"

"I will get you a plate. Cullah is not home, but there is one here you must see."

He stood, his eyes flashing for a moment as if I had betrayed him. "Someone here?" Then his face softened. "Sorry. I am too easily startled. You have had another child?"

I laughed. It had been far too long since Cullah and Brendan left home. "No. Do you remember a promise you made long ago? You said you would 'go around and return' for us? For Patey and me."

"It was not possible. You know that. A boy's promise truly meant. Patience—"

"Is here." I stepped aside. Patience raised her head.

August flew to her and knelt before her tiny, bent frame, leaning toward him as she tried to rise from her chair, though she sank back in it. For a moment, he cocked his head this way and that. She remained silent as he observed her. At last, convinced of whom he saw, he held out his hands. Patience laid her hands in his. Hers had grown softer in the months at my house, and paleness had replaced her swarthy and freckled arms. He dwarfed her in size. Scarred and browned, tall and rugged, a man capable of ruthless revenge, this hard man burst into tears, pressing her fingers to his eyes. "Oh, my sister. My sister," he sobbed. "Forgive me, Patey. Please forgive me. Oh God, how I have paid for leaving you. Can you not scorn me? I deserted you. Can you let me care for you now? Patey, forgive me."

Patience's eyes filled with tears, too, and with one hand she motioned for me to join them. I sat upon the floor beside my brother. The three of us together after so many years. So many miles. So many tears. After a great deal of weeping, which started all the children and even dear old Jacob sobbing, too, Patey said, "August, you did what you had to do. I am the only one who must be forgiven. I left, too. I deserted Resolute, still barely a child, not a mile from this very spot, when I should have cared for her. Look around you at what she has done." Patience lifted her head and looked about her.

They both turned their eyes to me as if I held some magic in my being. "I am not holy, nor always good," I said. "I have sinned. I have buried babies. The wonder is that we have each other at last."

"She is a gentle mother," Patey said. "Strong and merciful."

"Ressie has acted a mother to me for years," August said. "Ah. A-hah." He sputtered and wiped his face, as if he were surprised at his own weeping. "There's a good man for you. Blubbering in your lap. I should be happy, not like this."

Patey gave him a small and gentle smile, so like Ma's had been, and said, "Your tears are a precious gift to me." That started another round of sobs, until we laughed at each other, kissing each other's lips and cheeks, mingling tears and joy.

At supper we shared all our stories of how Patience came to live here, and how August had fared on the high seas. He swore that he had now crushed Wallace Spencer, though I doubted it. I feared more that in taking Spencer's goods, August had wounded an enormous bear, and made the man angrier than ever. He was adamant that it was less a worry. However, he intended to stay in his rooms at my house for several months, he said, and conduct some business from here. Then he proceeded to go back to the woods after dark with Jacob holding a lantern for him, so he could return with a heavy chest. That he put in his room in an armoire.

The following day, dressed in brocades, sporting gold buckles, August accompanied me to visit Lady Spencer. Patience refused to go, for she was so ill, but I feared she might not be received with that great black mark across her face. In her formal parlor, Amelia reclined on a couch and did not rise to greet us. "Come, my children," she called. "I have been waiting to see you. The two of you together. It is a great treat."

August bowed before her, then stayed upon one knee. "Your ladyship, I fear you will not say it when you hear what I have done."

"No more about it. I know." She waved her hand. "I have the papers ready. This house is yours, as long as I may live in it until I die."

Just as Goody Carnegie had bequeathed to me her home, this woman was giving her house to my brother. "I do not deserve it," he said.

"Deserve? I promised it in return for badgering some English trade. You, Resolute, must remain charming and wear silks. You must be received in society. Never forget, either of you, that there is always something greater than yourselves at work in the world. Look for it. Seek the whole truth, rather than letting the wind blow you as it will. Both of you are uniquely traveled, schooled in life in ways no scholar knows. Now, enough philosophy. Bring me some water, there, please, dear. With the lemon. Yes. This heat. I can no longer drink coffee but would you have some?"

"If you please, Amelia," I said, "we should be glad to have the cool water also."

Lady Amelia Spencer passed into eternity the first of July, 1756. The entire town of Lexington and half of Boston attended her funeral though no one had the effrontery to request that the townspeople pay for it. The conspicuous presence of August Talbot, and likewise conspicuous absence of Wallace and Serenity, made for much gossip, which enflamed even more when it was made known that August, a man of questionable character and loyalties, had been made heir to her property. A man approached the two of us after the burial and said, "What, sir? Are you so bold as to attend? I have a price on your head."

August turned to him with a wry smile and said, "And you, sir, name the price and I shall pay it. Then you will leave my family alone."

After Lady Spencer died, I began to have dreams from which I would awaken shaking and terrified. The dreams were so real, full of smells and textures, tastes and sensations, that during the dreaming, I thought the events were real, and was only soothed when I wakened, covered in sweat, often sitting up having knocked my arms against the wall. In one nightmare, I descended into dark woods where a cave opened before me and I slid down, down its muddy maw against knives, pitchforks, hay hooks, and daggers lining the walls. I never saw the bottom of it; I tumbled and slid, helpless, trying to avoid the cutting implements on the sides. There I saw Cullah, his face smeared with blood, running, frightened, dying perhaps, crashing through the woods as fast as a man could go, his claymore in his hands. Brendan was not with him. August and the rest of my family would come running, greatly disturbed by my cries.

At last America offered to sleep with me, and that next night when I awoke crying, she took my hand. "You were calling for Master Cullah," she said.

It was then that I realized the nightmares which seemed to have begun when Lady Spencer died all felt as if I were to be trapped, lost, captured, and only Cullah could save me. Every night from then on, I prayed for them the last thing before sleep. If ever I forgot, the cave and the blades were my home for the night.

It was a sad day for me when August moved into Lady Spencer's grand mansion in Boston. He promised he would not leave the city without telling me, but I would not see him every day any longer. He came and went through all my life, I suppose. Sometimes there were years between times I saw him, sometimes just weeks. Yet, now, with him so close but not in the rooms built for him under my roof, I felt as if he were lost to me.

By September, Patey seemed to shrink into the bedclothes as her breath became more and more labored. Many afternoons I spent reading to her, brushing her hair, sponging her clean, not knowing whether she even knew of my presence. With Amelia gone, there was little reason to go to Boston, and I began to neglect attending Lexington church. Indeed, it seemed I did little but cook and clean and tend Patience, but how could I do other?

In September, also, America Roberts agreed to marry Daniel Charlesworth. I was taken by surprise, for all this time I had imagined a well-concealed romance had carried on between her and August. He said nothing to me about it, until at last in exasperation, I had asked him outright, "Why did you not propose marriage to her while you could? I know she loved you."

"One of the reasons I wanted to move to Boston, Ressie, is that I have a woman."

"When will I meet your wife?"

"Not my wife. She is my woman. She goes with me. She asks little and takes little in return. Miss Roberts is a fine lady, Ressie. And yes, I see it in your eyes. I loved her once. Love her still. Too much to marry her."

"But why let this happen?"

"She deserves the life of a lady. That, I could not give her. I will go to the sea."

"You were born a gentleman."

"Do not ask me to unlearn what I have learned of life. It is who I am."

His words had stunned me. I went to do the milking and all I could think about was that what he had learned of life was who he was? Was that who I was? I asked America later if she were not affrighted that their children would all have a shrunken arm like Daniel's, for I remembered Lonnie Hasken's lopsided body and I was sure it was that way from the womb. I was ready to press her with insistence that she make known any feelings she had for August, and to reveal what he had told me about his feelings for her. "No," she said. "Daniel's shoulder was caused by being stepped on by a horse when he was but three years old. He was not meant to survive, but eventually he learned how to do almost anything the other boys did. He graduated Harvard when but sixteen. I fear only that he is older than I and that I shall have him not long enough."

"Are there—no—others whom you love?"

She sighed. "There was. Once. I think you know. Your brother does not love me. Please be happy for me. Daniel and I will make a good home. He is kind and intelligent. Goodness and caring, that is more important than, than passion."

I could not speak for several minutes. At last, I talked to her about her linens and laces and about making a special mantua for her wedding. And then I went to my room alone, where those words "I shall have him not long enough," and "more important than passion" made me weep as I had not done since Cullah left.

The Reverend Mr. Clarke performed the ceremony on the first of October 1756, followed by a small supper at our house with sweet cake in my parlor. He spoke to them of fidelity and honor, and prayed with their three pairs of hands clasped after Daniel placed a gold band upon her finger. August stayed nearly invisible in a corner of the room; his eyes like slits, he watched with the mien of a hungry wolf. I was relieved when Reverend Clark left us and the couple readied to leave, stacking two trunks in a coach. None of America's family had attended. It saddened me so to see America and Daniel leave for Boston. America had been part daughter, part sister to me. "Visit!" I called. "And tell me when your child is coming and I shall attend your lying-in!" I knew not if they heard me over the horses' hooves, for they smiled only upon each other.

Patience had stirred not at all the entire afternoon, though all the merriment took place around her. I feared she had died during the wedding, but when I touched her head, she raised her hand and gripped mine. "Are they gone, then?" she asked. "Noisy peahens woke me up. Is it evening?"

"Yes, they're gone. It is warm out."

"Help me up. I would see the stars."

August and I raised her as gently as we could, though it still pained her. I said, "The sun is not yet fully down. The stars may not show for an hour or more."

We made progress to the door so slowly it awakened in me the memories of teaching my children to walk their first steps. Here we were holding Patey for perhaps her final ones. She sat upon the bench by the doorway. I asked, "Would you have a cloak?"

"Yes. August, tell me of the stars."

I returned with the cloak over one arm and a cup of hot tea with sugar in it to the cadence of August pointing to stars and telling how they guided him across the seas. Patience tilted her face to the sky and listened as if the words came from it, as I draped the cloak upon her thin frame.

She whispered again, "Bring me a cloak, Ressie. I am cold." Her voice seemed unearthly, spectral, so very quiet and yet the words as penetrating as if she had shouted them in my ear. I fetched another, my warmest woolen cloak, and August and I dressed it about her shoulders. "Tell me which ones you would follow to the West Indies, little brother. What star leads to Jamaica?"

August began to explain, his eyes toward the sky. I put my hand upon his arm. "Brother," I said. "She listens no longer. She is on her way there now." Patience had slumped against the wall, and was near to falling off the bench. She was gone.

In a week, August sent word by way of the dark, chiseled-faced man, who had once brought him a message here, that he would be sailing on the next high tide under a full moon. That would be in only three days.

By October fifteenth, I began to weep and I could not stop. I had lost Lady Spencer and Patey to death's dark cavern, America to marriage, and August to the sea, and still my men did not return. Jacob tried to reason with me but I would have none of it. I believed Cullah and Brendan had been lost in battle, or died of disease, or wounded, bleeding upon some rock. Why had I not left all and gone to them? Why had I not followed my men into war? Other wives did. I was bereft of my greatest love. I took no joy in anything, and though the sky was dark and gray, the mist heavy, I sat by a window and stared out into the mist for hour upon hour, hoping to make them appear. They did not.

This October seemed eternal. Daily snows and rains, first cold then thaw, icy storms and howling winds followed by false summers, ended with snows a foot deep. I had Jacob and Gwenny, Benjamin and Dolly, but my fears of losing Cullah and Brendan stretched beyond all reason. Gwyneth moped. She gave up on romantic notions about Mr. Hancock and she busied herself sewing and spinning, milking and leading Jacob about, giving him patient help when he could not fill his pipe or if he spilled food from the wide knife he used instead of a fork or spoon.

On All Hallows' morn, we attended Meeting. Coming home the road was half thawed and muddy, treacherous for old Sam pulling. We did not get home until mid-afternoon. That day, I should have gone to the graves of my dear ones, dressed them with care for the following day, All Saints'. Patience's stone was only just set there in place and had never been dressed for the holiday. I packed my basket with broom and hand rake, gloves and a jug of water, and several rags to clean the stones. But by the time we had changed our clothes, the sunlight was fading; there was little time. The children dawdled. Jacob seemed preoccupied with trying to get the door hinge to stop squeaking and of course the sun lowered every minute we hesitated. "Will you all hurry? I do not want to be so late there is not enough light! Children! I will give you a scolding you will not soon forget if you do not get your shoes on your feet and come to the door this instant! It will only take an hour or so. You can give that much to your loved ones."

Jacob addressed me. "I will go with you but I tell you it is better to wait. Hear the wind? You have Miss Gwyneth and two small ones who need protecting. I am no use. Wait, I say."

"Tomorrow is All Saints' Day. It cannot wait. The day is the day and it comes whether we prepare or not."

"I know it is."

"I shall go by myself, then. I am not afraid."

Jacob breathed slowly. "Feel the air? It is thick already with souls rising. The sun is lowering, too. It is dusk already. I can tell that much without an eye for the air changes its lilt. The souls walk the earth, Resolute, from now until midnight, drifting through the mist and fog here around the house. Why would you attend them at the grave? Better to bar the door and say some prayers. Open it to no one, no signal, even if they make themselves to sound like one of the children."

"Will you not go with me, Jacob? I am determined."

"Woman, I tell you, no." The call of an owl, already hunting, flying low, came from the big tree by the house. " 'Tis a spirit e'en now. You will be caught by them, taken to the dark world. How will I, a blind old man, ever get you back for my boy? It is almost never done, saving someone when they go down with the fairies. They'll make you ride a flaming buck for all eternity. The Old Ones are about, I tell you. Stay. I am too old and blind to catch a horse or a hart with my bare hands and pull you from it. Stay, Resolute."

"Meeting ran much too late. How will they know I prayed for them if there are no fresh signs of care on their graves?"

"They will know. We shall go in the morning. After it is light," he cautioned. "Tonight, one whiff of darkness, one whirl of mist, any small fingers of ivy may twine about you and you will be theirs."

I nodded and sighed, then turned to see to the children. Dorothy and Benjamin listened, eyes wide. Benjamin's eyes held terror and suddenly filled with tears. I looked into Dorothy's eyes for fear, but what I saw was my reflection in the stubborn confidence of one who accepted her grandpa's fairies and brownies with the pursed lips of a skeptic. I smiled at Benjamin, two years older than his sister yet petrified with fear. I thought, it was true that men were weak. They are noisy, and big and strong. Perhaps all his noise about keeping the fairies at bay was Jacob's own terror.

I clapped my hands, smiled, knelt before the children, and said, "We shall all stay inside and cook apples in the fire for our supper. A picnic on the hearth, how will that be? I have cinnamon and you may add all the sugar you wish. Now, no tears. No one is going to be caught by the mist and carried to the fairies. Hush, now, Ben. Jacob, you shall have them weeping all night long. It is just a story, wee ones. Well and aye. You may both sleep in my bed this night as we wait for the saints to arise at midnight." I could not say that that plan was for their comfort any more than for my own.

The night fully closed in and darkness came. We ate apples, and Gwyneth told the wee ones stories. She mixed tales of fairies and ghosts with stories from the Bible, making all sound gentle and sweet for the children. She made the real terror of a changeling into a gentle story of a childless couple who adopted a fairy who kept them rich with stores of milk and butter—so different from real fairy pranks of stealing children and substituting some old demon fairy for a babe, or like Goody Carnegie, fairies capturing people and cutting their minds loose from their bodies. Queen Esther saving her people from doom. Duppies whose worst crime was stealing candy and hiding it in the trees. When I saw Dorothy sound asleep, I said, "It is time for all these lovely stories to go to sleep, too, along with the children hearing them. Off to bed."

The wind wailed under the eaves. A puff of smoke exhaled into the room from the fireplace as a gust pushed at the chimney. Leaves swirled and brushed against the door and windows. "Mother!" a man's voice cried from outside the door.

Gwenny gasped. I looked at her, clenching my teeth to keep from shaking.

Jacob stiffened where he sat, and said, "Answer not. It is a spirit."

Cullah's voice cried out, "Ma?" It was Cullah. He called again, with a sound as if he were just on the other side of the wooden door, his voice pleading. "Ma, are you about? Won't you open the door?" It was Cullah! But Cullah's mother was long dead. His mother had never been here. I bit my lower lip.

Benjamin had been ready to fall asleep, but he cried, "Pa?"

"Benjamin, for the love of everything, please make no noise," I said. "We must not answer. It is All Hallows. The voice you hear is not your father, though it sounds like him. He would not be calling for his mother, son."

A hand rapped at the wooden door. The bar rattled in its slot. Then fingers tapped on the glass window. Gwenny screamed soundlessly, her fist against her mouth. Dorothy slept on the settle in a heap of quilted blankets. Jacob's face was wild with fear. He felt at the hearth and picked up an iron. "Open not that door, Resolute," he whispered. "Don't let it in."

The rapping came again. Insistent. Loud. The voice called, "Mistress MacLammond? Open the door! Please. It is late and I am cold. Only let me in, Mother. Ma?" The bar shook so hard I rushed to it to stop it from falling loose and letting the thing enter the house. Cullah's voice called, "Is this not the MacLammond house? I have hunted far and wide this night. I saw the candle from below in the dell. Mother?" Then the voice took on a cry of impatience, as from a child, mixed with sorrow and rejection.

"Mother? Open the door. Oh, Ma, leave us not out here to die. Only let me in, I beg you. If this is not MacLammonds' house, please leave us not here to freeze this dark night."

It was Cullah; I would know his voice on my dying day. He must have been slain and was even now walking the earth on this Hallows' Even. I could not pray. I could barely breathe, but I choked out the words, "Go away. In the name of God go away, you."

"Ma!" There was a rushing clump and a bang, as if the thing threw itself against the door. "Ma, let me in! I beg you. We have come such a long way."

Jacob said, "They will tell you anything to get you to open the door. Let it not in, Resolute. It said it came up from the dell and that there is more than one. That is the graveyard. On your knees, children, and pray them away."

Gwenny did as he said. Benjamin burst into loud sobbing as Jacob started saying Our Father. He panted a few times. "Our Father," and after but a few words he slipped into Gaelic. *"Arr uh nee-ehr, air nee-uv."*

"Ma," called Cullah. "Please let me in. It's been so long, Ma." The voice began to weep! "Ma-ma?" I reached for the latch on the bar at the door. Its cries broke my heart.

"Stop!" screamed Jacob. "It's a trick, Resolute. In the name of God, don't open it. We will not open! Do you hear, spirit? Your tricks do not work here. Go and menace some other for by the name of God we shall not let you in."

"I am not a spirit, sir!"

"At midnight," I whispered to Jacob. "At midnight the hallows return and saints rise to heaven. Then if Cullah is still there—"

Jacob hissed at me, "It is not Cullah, woman."

Then I thought to ask it questions. "Who are you?"

"Brendan MacLammond."

I sank to my knees then. Was my son killed, too? "Whence came you?"

"From a river and a fort, north in the Canadas. My father follows me. My friend accompanies me. We will perish if you let us not in, for we are starved. Mother, please believe me."

"It is All Hallows," I called. "I cannot open the door."

The voice was silent for a long time. "Mother? I didn't know what day it was. Oh, how may I prove it is I? *Gumboo!* By the sword of Eadan Lamont and the cross of Holy God, I tell you the cross of *gumboo* binds me to you and him."

I looked at Jacob. He raised his face to me as if he felt my stare and he whispered, "Ghosts would not call on the name of God. Nor fairies. It sounds like Cullah." I threw the latch and lifted the bar. Behind me Jacob took a firebrand from the hearth and held it high, ready to fight off the minions of Satan if need be.

Into my house walked a man wearing a filthy plaid. He had a young man's beard but his face was so dirty it matched his hair and I knew him not. He was tall and thin but broad of shoulder, as if not yet filled in. He wore English boots and a tattered leather shirt under the long plaid across his shoulder. He held the door ajar. "Ma!" he said with a great smile. "It is I, Brendan. Oh, but you had me so afrighted, thinking you would not open to me. Hold a moment. I have brought a man with me. He's been wounded but holding up. Rolan? Can you make it here?"

"Brendan?" I feared touching him, but if he were my son, I should want to hold him as any mother would. Was this my son or a fairy? Did I dare believe it?

At that moment a gaunt fellow appeared dressed in ragged summer linens that had once been tan. His beard, too, was one of youth, but longer and fairer. He shivered as if the bones of him could rattle together. I would not have thought it possible, but he was thinner than the first. Nothing but bones and filth. He had an oozing wound on his neck wrapped around with what looked to be a man's old stocking, for the toe of the sock stood out at an angle like a flag and still bore imprints of dirty toes. He tried to bow but could not move his head. He said, *"Plaisir de vous rencontrer, mademoiselle."*

"Not 'mademoiselle.' She is my mother. Ma, this is my friend Rolan. We've come from the fighting. We've done with it. I tried to turn him in but they told me to kill him, and I nearly did. But he did not die. My time was up, you see, and he was my prisoner but we got separated and we were both afraid of the Indians. We had to get away from the Indians for the army left us abandoned in the woods. We had such a long way to go and got to be friends on the way home. Since I am not a soldier anymore, I'm my own master again and I chose to call him friend. Well and aye."

The blond man said also, "Well and aye, madame."

"You are French? *Français? Vous êtes français*?" I asked. "Brendan?" I asked the first man. "But your voice, it was Cullah MacLammond calling me. Or, I thought, calling his mother. You frightened me to my death. It is you, Brendan my son?" I raised my arms to embrace him.

"Ma, better not touch me until I have a chance to scrape a few layers of dirt. I've been itching. Oh, so great to see you all." He turned to Jacob. "Grandpa Jacob? You believe I am myself, don't you? Have I changed that much? Gwyneth, you? Ben, don't cry. Be a good wee man, there. It's I, your brother. Where's little Dorothy-dolly? None of you know me?"

I said, "My son went away a boy. You have a man's voice and a man's body. I did not expect that a year and a quarter of fighting and foraging would put height on you. To appear on All Hallows, we could not be sure it was not some spirit. Or that your father had not died and his ghost came to torment us. If you are not Cullah, where is he? And close the door. We do not have wood to heat all of Lexington from our hearth."

The man laughed. "My mother would always be practical." He smiled and closed his eyes, tears emerging from them, coursing through dirt and making clean stripes on his face. "I am home." He dropped to his knees. "Thank God I am home."

Jacob went to him then, put his hand on the man's shoulder and said, "My bonny wee Brendan?"

Brendan stood, a good foot taller than his grandfather, and smiled. "It is," he said. "Have you aught to eat?"

I shuddered. It was told in these parts to never, never feed a fairy. You will never get it out of your house if you do. I closed my eyes. "What time is it?" I asked no one and everyone.

"Well past midnight," Gwyneth said. "Surely the hallows have gone back to the grave now. Ma? Grampa Jacob has nailed iron rings over every door. No fairy will go under iron. He couldn't have come in, had he not skin as ours."

"Would you at least feed my friend?" he asked.

I said, "We had apples with cinnamon for supper. Push up the fire and I will get some long forks for you."

They started in roasting the apples. I could not bring myself to believe this was my son; though he seemed like him he did not look like him or talk like him. But no duppy or fairy would sit so close to a fire. No ghost would want to eat. I watched them a while, then asked again, "Where is Cullah?"

Brendan squinted and said, "He's coming. It is taking much longer for him to travel with the people going with him. He told me to get Rolan to some shelter and food and go on ahead. I didn't want to leave him, but there were reasons. Oh, that is good. Have you bread, too? And cheese?"

"Would you like some ale warmed?" Gwenny asked.

"I will take it any way it comes, warm, cold, or frozen solid," he answered.

While I cut slabs of bread and cheese, she poured tankards for him and for Rolan. Rolan took a cup from her with a sheepish nod and said, *"Merci."*

I asked, "Do you want to clean up? We might retire upstairs and leave you with clothes and water mixed with vinegar. I have sponges and soap. Your wound," I said to Rolan, "needs dressing."

"Madame?"

"Votre blessure a besoin de bandages."

"Oui."

I turned to Brendan. "Will you be all right to stay down here tonight? It is late. We will make your bed tomorrow. For now, wash yourselves and sleep in these blankets by the fire."

"Ma?" Gwyneth began.

"Up to bed, children. Benjamin? Wake Dorothy and take her by the hand. You both sleep with me tonight. Jacob?"

Brendan said, "Good night, Ma."

"Good night, Ma," Rolan mimicked.

When we got to the top of the stairs, I pulled Gwyneth into my room. Jacob came up behind, and bolted the door, while unlatching the secret passage to the tower room and from it to the stair down to the barn. We would not leave, but it would be there if needed. Then we arranged for him to make a pallet in one corner, while the children all took my bed, and I slept curled up on a chest with a blanket.

Morning came late, and the clouds had not parted, indeed the cold wind that blew in brought winter with it, and two inches of snow. If we had left those men in the parlor below to face the winter night, they would have died. I would have acted less charitable had not there been a familiar ring to his voice. So, when I descended the stairs to find someone I now recognized as my son, clean shaven and wrapped in a blanket, with clean hair, my heart felt as if it swelled in my chest. I smiled. "Brendan," I said. "Oh, please forgive me for not recognizing you. I had no idea you would change so much."

"Well and aye, Ma. Why did you keep insisting it was Pa calling for his mother?"

"Do you not know? Your voice has gone so low I thought it was your father. You sound exactly like him. I am so pleased to have you home, son. So thankful."

"I am happy to be home. I was sore afraid you would have more soldiers billeted here, and poor Rolan would have to be turned over to them. He is supposed to be my prisoner but he's an all right chap after you get to understand him. Farm boy from the south of France, pressed to be a soldier just as we were, and shipped here to fight us."

I bent over the bed where Rolan slept. His face and hair were clean but not shaved, and the dirty bandage was still about his throat. I touched his head. He had fever. "Why did you not change this bandage?" I asked. By then, the rest of my family started meandering downstairs.

"He said he would tend it. He let me wash first, and soon as I got shaved, I fell asleep. I slept like the dead until just before you came down."

"Rolan?" I called. The man did not move. "Brendan, get me that vinegar and some rum. I will change this. You had better pray for him if he is your friend, for to get a blood fever in the neck, he will never last."

I thought I had witnessed all the worst that man or animal could bear in the way of sores and disease, but I was not prepared for what came away in the filthy stocking at Rolan's neck. I was glad he did not seem to feel me tending him and glad I had not yet eaten. Once I got fresh linen wrapped about him, I hoped he felt better, for I knew I felt better, but whether or not he felt relieved as I, I could not tell. I tried to wake him and held up his head to put a spoonful of rum between his lips. He swallowed it, opened his eyes for a moment and mumbled something, then fell back to sleep or swoon.

I took my scissor and trimmed the beard on his neck and then trimmed all about his chin, as well. I combed his hair and braided a queue in the back, tying it with a length of woolen yarn. "Why are you doing that?"

Gwenny asked. "What difference does it make how the man looks if he's sick unto death?"

"I am not doing it for his grooming, Gwyneth. It is to keep the hair from tangling about the bandage or just getting in his face. Keeping the bandaging and wound clean are most important now, and it will need to be changed again in a few hours."

"I'll do it," she declared with a conviction that brooked no response.

Brendan told me about his prisoner. Rolan Perrine was the second son of a farmer. He had no interest in soldiering, while Brendan thought of nothing else. Rolan was a terrible shot, and more terrified of killing a man than facing a noose for desertion. He had admitted to Brendan that when he had him in his line of aim, he had pulled the barrel high so as to fire at his officer's command yet not kill anyone. Brendan laughed deep in his chest. "Fine soldier, this fellow. If he killed anyone it was an accident. The most effective weapon he used on our men was being too thin to see behind a tree. Me, I, well, have you any of those flat cakes you used to make?"

"Yes. See if Rolan will have another spoonful of rum while I make the batter and start the iron heating."

Rolan did not die that day or the next and he was still alive when Sunday came and able to sit up and eat broths and pancakes. I begged Brendan to stay with his friend. "I never miss Meeting now," I said. "Do not look surprised. I have sent many a prayer heavenward on your behalf. And your father is not home yet. Your uncle sails under more danger of his own making. There is more to living in a town than I knew when you were young. Things have happened. It is important to go and to give to the poor and to keep in good graces with all who know us."

"But you always said to trust your own heart."

"That is true, son. I do not do this for trickery but to make myself known. If people have your acquaintance and friendship, they are not so quick to believe falsity. Last month across town, Goody Meacham was tried for witchcraft because she argued with a neighbor whose dog killed her goose. The neighbor's child then died and his cow had a calf born with two heads. No one knew her. No one came to her defense. She might have been hung had not the judges disagreed on whether she looked the part of a witch. I never want to be in a place where no one would come forward to say to a judge that they have known me to be righteous. A life well lived, in some respects, needs witnesses."

Brendan cocked his head. He watched me pour batter on the hot iron, turned back to my gaze, then he said with a laziness to his voice that belied the workings of his brain, and that I recognized in the son I knew, "That will be something to think about. I believe you are right. Evil loves darkness and good the light. Is that cake ready to turn?"

I smiled and flipped the flat cake over. The other children gathered around and ate, and after breakfast Jacob said he would stay with the boys while we went to Meeting.

Eleven days after Brendan came home, I was out in the barn when I heard a voice in the woods, singing the "True Lover's Farewell." I stood in the barnyard and looked in every direction, for the voice echoed all about. I had forgotten what a nice voice he had to listen to, every note on the right pitch. "Cullah?" I spun on my heels as I called with all my strength. "Eadan!" Searching the meadows and fields, I saw him at the edge of the woods. He had a huge sack over one shoulder and his sword lashed over the other one. What was more, he was clean and his beard neat, his hair in a tail at the back under a tricorn hat, wearing not his tartan but new clothes made of skins. He stepped out toward me and I to him. Then he put down the sack and sword and ran full out. "Eadan!" I cried again. At last his arms closed about me and swung me about, both of us wanting to melt into the body of the other. "Husband. Oh, my husband, you are home."

Close up now, I got a look at his eager expression, his weary eyes. He said, "My Resolute, thou art the blithest maid e'er walked the dews of Skye." Then he kissed me so hard my lip felt crushed. He swung me into his arms and hefted me two or three times, then said, "Beauty walks in your being. Light as a fairy. Are you sure you are not a fairy? I am enchanted by this maid, who weighs less than a pennyweight of feathers."

I laughed again. "I have so much to tell you. Take me to the house."

"Oh, wife, I have some to tell you also. Is the boy here?"

"Well and aye."

"And his friend? Did he live?"

"Yes. And well. He is with Gwenny in the barn, milking."

"The two of them alone?"

"Well, Cullah, he's so ill."

"Not that ill. Let me greet my bairnies, then send one of the other children, no, send them all to keep them company. We have aught to speak of, alone."

I smiled. "How came you to these clothes? And to return cleaned, and"—I sniffed—"you smell as you did on our wedding day."

"Ah, so many questions. Would you have me covered in filth and gore? I stopped and enjoyed the kindness of others so I would not frighten you. Come along, Resolute."

We held hands and found our children. I told them all, Jacob and Brendan included, the silliest things and promised them treats and puddings and sweetmeats aplenty, if only they would go and watch Gwenny and Rolan milk the cows. When the last had gone toward the barn, Cullah and I raced up the stairs and bolted our door.

A couple of days later, when we settled our fluttering hearts and had time to speak of other things, I asked him, "Husband? How did you fare? I feared so often that you would be called less than a soldier for refusing to fight the French."

"I found that I could fight anyone who pointed a musket at me. A man's will to survive is greater than his cause, I reckon. Armies count on that, lest no one would fire and we should all sit and have a game of whist and call it finished. One man fires and the lot of them feel threatened. I told Brendan to watch for that. Never to be the first to fire, unless there is no choice, and never under any circumstance be the second, for the first could have been accidental until you know. Many a battle was worked to our advantage by officers who knew that. One shoots from a crafty position. All the men hiding in the brush and trees then are threatened and fire, giving away their position. Now, that is enough battle strategy for my wee brain. Tell me, gentle wife, of what has happened in my home?"

It was not easy to confess to the one I loved yet another way my angry tongue had worked to my disfavor. He listened to the story of the stocks, and the safekeeping by my brother and her ladyship. In the end he laughed. I could but ask his forgiveness, and plead that I lost my senses for lack of his presence. I told him of Patience and August, of my sister's death and my brother's vengeance against the man who would have despoiled our daughter. All the little things we had left unsaid, we said. The way the summer turned. The way the air smelled this November, so like other Novembers that it carried with it the promise of roasted meats and sweet pies as well as blizzards and long, long nights.

"I can think of ways to fill a long night," Cullah whispered to me.

"I can think of one," I said. "I hope your nights were not so long while you were gone."

"Every one of them, an eternity without you," he said. "And you are worried that I have played the rogue? Fear not. I simply added each night to those I will spend with you from now on. I will never again leave your side, my Resolute, not if dragged away by a team of horses."

CHAPTER 31

January 20, 1757

It was against the law for us to feed and house Rolan Perrine. He was, after all, either an escaped French prisoner or a deserter, so whichever side got hands on him would execute him forthwith. He did not wish to return to the French army, or return to France a pauper, or to go north to the Canadas or escape to the wilderness. I wondered if he thought he would not survive the trip, or if the terror of soldiering was too much for him, for he was a pleasant young man, and well versed in the raising of all types of plant and animal. He loved the land and wanted nothing more than his old farmer's life. The only chance for him, now that his neck began to heal, was to become as "English" as he could. I once was to become French, I told him. He remarked how the world had turned.

We gave him many suggestions for overcoming his accent and speech. We dressed him like every other man about and burned what was left of his clothing. The more we spoke with him, the more he looked about the place, he said he would love to stay at a farm like ours. So we hired Rolan

Perrine, a farmer's son from France, to farm our fields. He would live in Jacob's old house, as long as he felt no fear of spirits, and he would plow and plant, reap and bundle, in return for the house and food. And we would help him to become English, starting with his name. He became Roland Prine.

From that time forward, Roland Prine spoke of nothing but soils and fertilizer, rain, moon cycles, asking when was the last frost, when was the first? What did the neighbors grow? What crops had failed, what pests were about? He went to meetings with us at First Church but spoke not at all, and put himself in the path of other men who knew farming, so that by the time in April when it seemed the frost was over and the moon was right to plant, he had already broken the fields. He put in barley, wheat, corn, and two acres for naught but vegetable for the table. Every remaining inch of land went to acres of flax. I felt a mixture of pride and despair, and finally, great resignation at the prospect of its harvest.

I said to Roland, "We will have enough for three families."

He said, "Then, if my mistress will agree, we shall help those who have less."

"Well and aye, then, Roland," I said.

"Well and aye, Mistress."

That summer our land produced more than seemed possible. Had Roland not been there, we would have suffered, for that summer prices doubled and then doubled again on all house goods we did not grow ourselves. A bushel of wheat quadrupled in price. We ate luxuriously of Roland's tillage so that we were quite plump, stored for the winter, but also gave much away that harvest.

Cullah said to me one morning, "This is not right. He works the land with old Sam to help, and we eat of it. For the trade of a place to sleep? That is meager ration."

"Should we pay him, too? We could sell the vegetables, and give him a share."

"Aye. Let us do that. Gwyneth would be good at that. Now that she has come into full bloom, I doubt any could get an ear of corn sold faster."

By the spring of 1758, before the month of April had gone halfway, the roads and hills gone to mud, Roland asked Cullah for Gwyneth's hand.

They married April twenty-first, after he had gotten the land broken up for another year's planting. We gave them a quarter of it for themselves, and Cullah, Brendan, and Jacob would build them a bonny house. As they clasped hands and prepared to walk to the little old cottage now made into a bower, we gave them each our blessings.

Dorothy said, "Learn to make good pudding, sister, and come home sometimes."

Ben said, "I shall make a hobby horse for your babe when I apprentice with Pa."

Brendan gave them both his hand, then kissed his sister. "Aw," was all he said.

I told them I loved them. Cullah said again, "I shall build you a house."

Jacob stood up, hobbled to the door, and said, "Now, Gwen. I knew you when you were born. Now you're wed. So don't be an old sclarty-paps, and come see your grand-par when he gets old."

We all laughed, so relieved of the sweet sadness of her going.

"I will, Grandpa," she said. She had tears in her eyes. She mouthed to me, "I am so happy, Ma. Farewell." Then she turned away.

I studied my hands. My fingers still pained me from embroidering her new shift and gown. And Jacob was so old. Bent. He walked with a stick now, all the time, but he promised to help all he could. My Gwyneth, the child that I had feared so for her life, was now carrying my life into the future. I felt a rush of sentiment I could not place, and with it, a strong wish to return to Jamaica, to tell my mother, "Oh, Ma, I have a beautiful daughter. Today is her wedding day. Oh, Ma, life has made me a mother and you a grandmother, and perhaps soon I shall also be a grandmother. Oh, Ma, hold me close. Let me rest my head upon your bosom for a moment and be a child again, and hear your voice singing to me." Tears ran.

Cullah put his arm around me, saying, "She will be fine. Don't worry. She will make a good wife. You have taught her well."

"Yes," I said. "She will." I laid my head against his chest. "Cullah? How is it possible for me to feel so young and so old at the same time?"

He scratched his head and turned to look at my eyes. "Are you ill?"

I laughed, though more tears flowed. "No. I am only a woman, and we are complicated devices."

"Well and aye, my love. Well and aye."

· · ·

That summer when the wheat was green, the flax a sea of blue, and the barley still not more than a hand high, Brendan joined the British army for good. The war with the French had simmered down and yet new recruits were always needed. Because he had proved himself with valor during his previous stint, he was made a lieutenant and sent to Canada to relieve the forces at Montréal. I sighed. Montréal. I knew so little of the place, and yet it was so familiar. All so long ago and far away as if it were a story I once heard. I wept with his going for three days. And then I put on my apron and returned to my life and my loom.

The house felt quiet and empty. I taught Dorothy reading lessons and arithmetic and embroidery. Benjamin learned his lessons in Latin well. I hoped he might proceed to college. He might have the makings of the highest calling, a minister of God. I asked Reverend Clarke to speak to him, though yet a boy, for it was not too soon to plan. Jacob, of course, had never regained the forty pounds he had once promised, but no matter.

Town meetings went on now sometimes more than one a month. One night after being quite late returning from town, Cullah turned to me as we lay in bed and said, "Ressie? What do you believe?"

"On what subject?"

"I mean, what do you believe in? Do you believe there is a thing that is ordained and true and noble enough to die for?"

"I know you believe it. Men do; that is why they fight wars. Jacob fought for his beliefs and you ended up here."

"I am asking you, wife. What do you believe in so that you would risk everything? Would you pick up a musket and kill a man?"

"Why do you ask me these things?"

"Would you?"

"For my children, yes."

"There is talk. Among our friends in town. Talk of acting against the Crown. Refusing to be subject to another tax. Another war. No one in Parliament has ever been to this coast, did you know that? Everything costs more and more. Today I could not buy hinges because they weren't to be had. If I must make them or buy them secretly, it will cost dearly, and I cannot sell my furniture for a price people will pay."

"What do you mean to do?"

"Nothing, yet. The talk is just there, that we could band together to force prices down. Don't buy British goods. Make our own or do without. Or depend on people like your brother to bring them from France or Russia or the Indies."

"What goods are British?"

"That's just it. Almost nothing and they buy and sell to us for three or four times what it's worth. Cauldrons. Snuff and snuffboxes and shoes. They have passed a new law that no tradesman is allowed to make ironwork. Piggins and bars must be sent to England and we must buy it back after being worked. Any man caught working iron shall be arrested and tried for treason. Anyone buying iron from other than England faces the same. Not a horseshoe! We will have to take that iron we found in the fields years ago and melt it in secret or face arrest for having it."

"You will wake the children."

"Not a candlestick, I tell you. Not a single hinge. We have to be able to make our own. Don't try to sell your cloth; even the silks from Lady Spencer will be taxed for half their value and I cannot pay it. We will be arrested if we don't pay. Trade with the neighbors and don't go to town. I heard from young Paul that their taking our iron will be the subject of the next town meeting. It will amount to having to smuggle home a crane for the fire or a shoe for a horse. There will not even be coin, but we will have printed money on paper that could catch fire like a twig. I am joining the rebellion. The whole of Lexington must be in one accord on this, for we must act together or hang separately."

"The Quakers do such. They do not trade with outsiders. I do not know about iron, but they make shoes. But, Eadan, what is this talk of dying?"

"Sometimes I lie awake at night and think I am dying. Or I will be dying. And that war is coming. Everything feels so unsettled. Everything."

I lay there, silent. To me, until he said this, everything in life had felt so settled and happy. Cullah was home. Brendan off on the career he chose. Gwenny married. Ben declining Latin nouns faster than I could think them up. Dorothy doing her first sampler. The land at last farmed and producing well. Life was good. "I am sorry for you, husband, to be so troubled. Perhaps you are worried so because of the hinges, and there will be some in town tomorrow. You have to wait."

"Or I will design a lid for a box with a hinge built into the wood, and I will not buy a single British hinge."

I knew I had to proceed with care in the words I chose. I heard the longing in my own heart all these years, so afraid people would leave me, that I feared even a momentary distance. Perhaps having lived in war brought the same. "Do you think, because you have seen war, that you cannot rest? That you think all the world must have war now? That perhaps you cannot lay down your sword?"

"I do not like being so fenced by their rules of trade. I am no longer allowed to sell to my neighbors for barter, did you know that? It will get worse, too. I am sure."

"The speckled hen hatched her clutch today. Twenty chicks."

"Why are you talking of chickens when I am telling you the business is troubled?"

"Because your home is not troubled. We will overcome this, husband. We are so wealthy. You have provided all this and more, August has filled my shelves with goods to last our lives through, and your business will continue, too. Please sleep peacefully, husband. Please. Your war is over. You are home. I am here." Even as I said that, I felt amazed at referring to myself as a stronghold for a weary soldier. I wanted him to protect me, not to need my hands for his safety.

Cullah blew upward against his hair. "I am worried."

After a long time, when I could not think of any good answer, I said, "I love you." I curled up next to him, and soon enough he was sleeping. I did not. I heard again and again his words "what would you die for?"

After Christmas 1758, ice hung from every tree limb, even from the poor cows' noses as their breath froze within them. With snow a foot deep, one day I went to our larder and took stock of what we had left. Roland came to the door as I made a list, and asked me to come to their house for they still lived in Goody Carnegie's place. Gwyneth was ill, he said, and wanted me to come.

When I arrived there, Gwyneth told me she had too soon dropped a babe. I wept with her, for it would have been my grandchild, yet it was so early, perhaps less than two months of life. Roland took a pickaxe to the graveyard, and though the ground was frozen solid, with setting a small fire for a couple of hours, he got a hole dug no bigger than a rabbit would use, but it was enough. It was buried in an unmarked grave. I would not let her watch while he did it, for Roland and I agreed it would be better were she not to even see the mark of his moving the ground. I did not know what other women did with such things, but it was done. He told me I might return to the house and make Gwenny some tea while he set the brush about and tossed some snow over the place so it would vanish into the rest.

Snow began anew, so it would not be difficult, I thought.

After a few minutes, Roland came to the house. He took off his hat and coat and sat by the fire, his face an image of despair. He said, "It is snowing more. Would you like us to walk you home, Mother?"

I smiled. Neither of us was comfortable with that title yet, I believed. "That is not necessary. Gwenny needs to rest a couple of days."

"It would be better if she rests at your house."

"Certainly you may come. What is the matter, Roland? *Ne mentez pas. Je vois que vous êtes inquiet.* Something is amiss," I said.

"*J'ai vu un homme dans un cape et un chapeau noir.*"

"Roland," Gwyneth said, "do not speak secretly to my mother."

I stared into his eyes without looking at her. I believed he was trying to decide whether to tell her. If I knew my Gwenny, she would want information just as I would, and then could make up her own mind how to respond. But she was in a weakened condition and emotional with grief. I said, "He said there was a shadow by the graveyard. It frightened him but it was nothing."

Roland repeated, "It was nothing."

"Do you mean the man in the cape?" she asked. "The spirit of a man is there, looking for something or someone. When Barbara, First-Ben, and Grandan died, Brendan and I sometimes went down there. If you walk next to the rocks, a man passes by."

I heard Roland sigh with relief. "You are not afraid?"

"No. His cloak brushes my side, and he does nothing but keep walking."

I shared their nervous laughter.

The year's first town meeting was held late in January of 1759. Benjamin had a sore throat so I stayed home. When Cullah returned I waited until the children slept and we were alone in bed before I asked, "What news of the meeting?"

"The king is mad," he said.

"I meant something I had not heard before."

"British ships have stopped five traders outside of Boston and commandeered both their goods and their crews. Captains who would not surrender were clapped in chains and their ships sunk. One was killed as he fought back."

"Do you think August was among them?" I willed myself to dismiss the thought of him killed, though if there was one who would fight back, it would be my brother.

"I know no names of ships or men."

"If we went to Boston, might we learn the names?"

"If I know your brother, though they have him in chains, it will not be for long. All the confiscated goods are sold at insane prices, and people are paying them. I cannot imagine a woman so desperate for perfume as one in Virginia I have heard about this day. Six pounds and ten for a bottle no bigger than a finger."

I laughed with derision. "Ha. When perhaps a bath might serve the purpose better," I added, and rolled over onto my side. "It was probably our beloved Mistress Spencer."

He formed himself to me, his head raised above mine on his hand so that he could whisper, and said, "There is other news. I brought home a pamphlet for you to read in the morning when there is light. I have to return it tomorrow so the next family may read it. There will be a new tax now, on every tree I cut. Not enough that I break my own back or hire a man for sixpence to cut it, but I must pay a tax as if the king owned the tree itself though it is on unclaimed or private land where I have paid for a right to cut lumber."

"That is ridiculous."

"There is more. The British army is landed. They say there is too much snubbing of our noses at the Crown. They have put an extra five hundred men in Boston."

I felt myself begin to tremble, but I tried to sound as if I cared not at all. "Boston? Is it so dangerous a place?" I thought of August. How long would he be able to skirt Wallace Spencer's reach?

"In Boston, newspapers and pamphlets come out every week with articles about the army trampling the common rights of every British citizen. Someone sent a letter of complaint to the House of Lords. Their reply was to send more troops, with promise of a thousand more by the end of the year. No doubt they will live with us again."

"This is ludicrous."

He shrugged and said again, "The king is mad."

By the first of March, Gwyneth and Roland's new cottage was nearly finished. All that lacked were furnishings, but Cullah worked on what they needed from his shop. In April we received a parcel from August. It took two men to lift it from the cart and set it inside my door. "Will ye have me cleave 'er open, Missus?" the driver asked.

Just knowing August was enough to make me wary of that. "No, thank you. My husband will take care of it when he comes home. Would you have food and cider?"

He smiled. "Thankee, kindly, Missus. 'Ow 'bout you, boy? Want to eat? 'E don't talk much, now. Our Davey boy 'ere is good and honest, though 'e needs someone to 'old a steady 'and on 'is rudder. A bit loosened in the noggin, 'e is." The man accepted a plate and took the bread, formed it into a roll around the meat, and passed to Davey. He made a similar roll for himself and they both drank heartily after wolfing down the food. As he finished, I took two pennies from my pocket and offered them to him. "No, thankee, kind lady. I been well paid afore-hand. 'Is lordship what asked me to deliver these goods 'as instructed me to not accept your money but with delicate thanks, as 'e 'as give me a week's wages to do this 'ere."

"He is a generous fellow, that," I said.

"'E is, indeed, Missus." The fellow and his helper went on their way.

Cullah returned home to find the crate sitting in the parlor doorway. I could not move it. "Have you ordered something?" he asked.

"My brother sends his regards, and apparently his worldly goods. It took two men to get it there. I do not know what it is, Cullah, but I trow you must open it right there and we shall unload it a piece at a time."

"Do you think he smuggled himself to us?" Cullah took a wedging tool and worked at the nails until he got the top off the box. The first layer was a sealed paper flat upon a woven blanket. He handed me the letter. "Better read that," he said.

Gentle R, I trust you have means to hold this until the blackbird calls. Keep it as clean as can be managed. There is something in the smaller casket for your house. I will come for it. Forever your humble and affectionate servant, —A.

Cullah raised the blanket. We looked in, then at each other without a word. Below the blanket was an artillery piece. A cannon, so new it shone. A small iron version of those I had seen on the ships, but new, unused, and cushioned in wood chips, wrapped with rope for lifting. He tugged on it. "I will have to get Roland."

It took both of them with Jacob helping to get it from the crate and into the parlor by the fireplace where it sat like a monster with a single great eye, staring at us.

I asked, "Should it not be in the barn?"

Cullah said, "He said to keep it clean, which means the house. You wouldn't want it to rust, after all. How about the basement?"

"You cannot expect me to trip over that thing daily."

Jacob said, "Put it into the false wall."

"I would have to get it up the stairs," Cullah said. "What is your brother thinking? British soldiers could arrive tomorrow with no warning. It is a cannon and it is iron!"

"Perhaps we should have left it in the crate?" Roland asked.

Cullah grimaced. "We would have had to step around it until he comes for it. That could be weeks."

"Or years," Jacob added. "Is there still room beside the hearth for the inglenook you meant to build?"

"Aye, there is."

"Roll it over next to the wall and build over the top of it."

Cullah's eyes widened and he smiled, even winked at me. "Ah, that's my pa. Fine idea, there." Cullah did not go to work in town the next morning. Instead he set about making a new settle built into the wall beside the fireplace. It had to be high enough to put the cannon under it and close the lid to make a seat.

"I know you know your work," I said. "But the wood in this room has been here for years. The wood you are using is new. Look at the framing against the floor." There the green wood looked almost cream colored against the aged hickory floor.

He cocked his head this way and that. "You're a clever lass, my Ressie. I will pull off the old trim and use it against the floor. A little black paint on the rest of it will do to cover up the newness, and we'll scuff it up a bit, too."

Just as he said that, Benjamin came into the room and asked, "Pa? Why do we have a cannon? Who sent it to us? Are we going to shoot it?"

Cullah looked at me, stunned. "Well, he's not a lad anymore, then. Get your sister and we will have a talk."

"Oh, Cullah," I whispered when the boy went for his sister. "What if they tell other children?"

"We must convince them both not to do that. I think there is no other way but honesty, at least as much as they can bear. And then, we shall appeal to them with our trust. Perhaps a bit of fear. If they are made of good fiber, they will have courage. If they are not, we can do nothing but hope the other children think they are lying."

He sat them down and explained as well as any could that their uncle's business was sometimes dangerous. That the high seas were full of pirates who meant to murder and steal, and that to be safe, all ships carried cannons. Uncle August had bought a cannon for his ship, and he was on his way to get it, but until he came, we could not speak of it.

"Why can we not speak of it?" asked Dorothy. "It is stirring to have it. I want it to *pah-boom*!" She clapped her hands.

I interjected, "Dolly, it is indeed stirring to have it. If you tell anyone we have it, though, the pirates might come to get it and steal you away, make you a slave and beat you, just as in the stories I told you." I saw horror on my children's faces, but I felt no guilt for causing it, for this was all our lives in the balance. Now knowing about the cannon, they had also to know how dangerous it would be for word to get out of this room about it.

"Even my friend Isbeth?" Dolly asked.

"Yes, even Isbeth. No one else must know. It is our secret. A desperate, stirring secret." Even as I said that, I began to feel a mortal fear that she would not be convinced to refrain from the childish joy of telling a secret.

Benjamin said, "I shall never tell. You may count on me."

Dolly nodded, adding, "Me, too."

I forced myself to smile as if I had perfect confidence. "Excellent," I said. "Now, both of you put on your hats and go collect eggs. I think I shall make some custard tonight. Do not come back until you have every egg in that henhouse." As they headed for the door I called out, "Do not forget to take some to your sister!"

That evening, Benjamin said, "Ma? Pa? I have a plan."

We looked at each other then faced our wee son.

He went on. "I know it is hard for little'uns to keep a secret and our Dolly is prone to tell things."

Dolly made a face at him. "I never told about you getting on the barn roof."

My mouth opened and Cullah said, "On the roof? Boy, you might have fallen. You'd be killed if you fell from it. Did you not think of that?"

Benjamin sighed hard and rolled his eyes. "I did, sir. And I did not fall off. There is a place to stand that is flat. I could see a thousand miles up there. About the secret. I have told Dolly that we have a pact about the thing and never to speak the word"—he whispered—"'cannon.' If ever she wants to say the—ahem, thing—in our inglenook, she is sworn to give me a high sign by touching her bonnet twice. I will return it if all is clear. If it is not clear, I give her a low sign, touching my elbow, and she will know that we both know a secret and are to keep still without speaking of it."

Cullah said, "That is an excellent plan. Teach us the signs so we will know, too." So, my children came up with a better way than we had, to foil the pirates with which I had frightened them, and to foil themselves against letting out our secret. "Now," Cullah said, "show me how you got onto the barn roof. I feel, just as such a clever boy as you, I too might like to see a thousand miles."

It took a week, but Dorothy tired of the game and quit giving us all high signs every few minutes.

Later that week a committee of officials appeared early at our door before Cullah had finished breakfast. By the time they left, we stood silent, becalmed of even the basest of courtesy. We had been handed a printed and smeared "Notice of Taxation" that levied a tax upon every acre we owned and gave us but thirty days to come up with five pounds to place in the hands of the provincial treasury. Cullah glared, and said, "I would like to know how they think a laboring man can give six weeks' earnings every year and still feed a family. Have we that much in reserve?"

"Yes," I said. "Though only in what August sent."

He stuck his chin forward. "If you will, my dear wife, count it out in the smallest coin we have. Ha'pennies and tuppence. Copper. Better yet, printed notes. Let them have the worthless Massachusetts paper if we have aught of that. Here's one in my pocket. Use it to start."

Every week that went by it became harder to afford things we used to spill. Flour and salt, sugar and tea. We tried to sell our vegetables but people did not buy. Beer was so high we bought cider, and Cullah built a cider press so we could make our own, but we could not make enough in one harvest to last a year, and it would get hard so soon that at times the children went to bed drunk. The work of flaxing had been so difficult that we ended up with little to spin, and we did not plant it that year.

I had never made my own candles, but the price of them now made them so dear I sought to buy wicks instead. The wicks and molds cost what a six months' supply of candles might, but I could get many times that, I thought, if I could but grow clever at making them. I soon discovered that I detested making candles. The smell of tallow was revolting and I spilled it so often my floors were slick. I moved the process to outside the barn. Though in appearance it could be said that I had indeed created a candle, the results were smoky, melting tapers that burned to the stub in an hour. I soon lamented buying the molds and wicks for I could have spent the money on real candles.

Gwenny and I worked together then, when she could. We went with the children hunting bayberries, and the poor ones worked their best, coming home scratched and sweating. When they complained I told them of my years picking flax, and warned them not to cry for a scratchy bayberry bush was nothing to a flax field. Getting the oil from the berries meant an extra day of boiling, but it made better candles, sweet smelling and twice as strong.

Everywhere I looked, I found ways to scrimp. Making do became almost a religion to me. I felt proud of the things we undertook, the things we all learned together. Proud, but meager.

The tax collector came while Cullah was gone to work. I counted out printed banknotes adding up to two pounds eight, then stacks of pennies and ha'pennies. He asked me for a drink. I pulled water from the well and gave it him. "Have you no ale?" he asked.

"Ale? All we have is in your hand, sir," I answered. "We have had no ale in this house for a fortnight. We drink water. Consider it God's ale. Quite calms the spirit with no chance for drunkenness."

"Tea?"

I had tea, but I was too angry for courtesy. "Who can afford tea, sir?"

As he walked away with two months of Cullah's earnings I winced under the weight of this new sort of poverty in a way I never had when I was starving. I remembered the slave woman saying, "We know what that cost. You eat it." I sat on a stump in the garden where my family's labors barely wrested aught for our table. I had to sit a while and remember. Even asking my own memory what it was that connected it to this. At last I realized that poverty was a kind of captivity. Then I picked up my hoe and went to work. I dared not complain to Cullah because I was so angry it would bring out my worst nature. I cut a new line in the earth for yet more beets and parsnips. Carrots, potatoes, beets, beans, and parsnips. Perhaps squash this year. Squash did not keep well, but it livened the blood. Yes, I shall plant squash. "I shall ask Roland," I said aloud to the soil, "to procure some squash seed."

In the distance, a bell sounded. This was not Sunday. It could only mean some alarm. Over the tops of trees to the west, a haze of smoke drifted skyward. I ran toward it, not setting down the hoe. People came from all around, gathering as neighbors do, to the house of Virtue Dodsil. It was engulfed in flame. A spark from the chimney had caught the thatch. All of them were out, except for the house cat. There was little that could be done other than watch the place burn to the ground. Virtue himself stood before it, his whole body atremble like I have never seen before. He shook with such violence he had to shift his feet to keep standing.

I said to him, "Will you come to my house? At least for a few days?"

"No. We will live in our barn. At least we have that."

I returned to my home and loaded my arms with blankets we could spare. Some new that I had made, some old to be placed upon the ground.

I had woven goods aplenty, but little else to give. His wife took them with somber thanks. Then she looked at them more closely and said, "These are new. You didn't mean to give us new blankets, did you?"

"Yes," I said. "Emma, you need them."

"Mistress MacLammond, Resolute, you are wondrous kind."

That night, I lay awake thinking about our roof. "Cullah? I want you to build the chimney taller."

"It is tall enough, Ressie. Dodsil's roof caught fire because his chimney was full of holes, not because it was too short. Our chimney is good."

"It is very old. It was here two generations ago."

"It is two feet thick on all sides. Sleep, wife."

CHAPTER 32

May 18, 1759

Sunday at Meeting, Reverend Clarke spoke with fiery words about the freedom of mankind. We of Lexington town were convinced there was no distance at all between our rights as British citizens and our godliness. One night at a town meeting, he had us shaking in our boots when he said, "Goodman Parker has been held, used most dreadfully and badly beaten, and charged with treason for carrying our minutes of the last meeting to the town council in Boston."

All around the room, talk grew more heated. Cullah proclaimed that he was loyal but would not be crushed by the iron boots of the British Crown. I wondered at that because Cullah would never profess loyalty to the English Crown. Jacob listened, but said nothing. Scriveners wrote with mad excitement, taking down all that occurred. At last, Reverend Clarke asked for someone willing to carry our notes to Boston. "We will have two copies prepared, so that one may perchance get through. Two messengers. Who will go?"

Cullah stood and shouted, "I will go. There's one man for you."

Jacob's face brightened. "I say, I shall be glad to go."

Another man across the room shouted, "Take me. I'll make it through."

I pictured them slinking through the woods and brush, Redcoats on their tails like dogs after a fox. I stood. Amidst the shouting men, it was a while before anyone noticed, even Cullah seated next to me. I stood upon the bench where I had sat. The din about me shrank to almost nothing.

Reverend Clarke asked, "Goodwife MacLammond. Have you aught to say?"

"Yes," I said. "Take me. I go to Boston every week. Put the papers in my handcart, and I shall walk there as I do every other time, with my child upon my apron strings. The soldiers will be looking for men carrying parcels, or horses with packets. I will stroll right up to the door and bid them all good day along the way."

Nary a foot moved nor a sniffle was heard. The rumble of men's voices began as faraway thunder mixed with laughter and rose to a terrible pitch. "A woman? A woman! A message taken by a woman. It's terrible. It's ungodly. It's wonderful. It's brilliant. It's heresy."

I stepped off the bench with Cullah's help. His eyes flashed with more anger than I had ever seen. I had thought I was presenting a brave and unique solution. I had no idea he would be so alarmed. He folded his arms and looked straight ahead, the muscles in his jaws making his beard move. Jacob said nothing.

At last, Reverend Clarke held up his hands. "We will vote on this suggestion." Vote they did. It was given to Cullah to carry one packet, to another man to carry the second. As we rode home, he simmered, not speaking.

We climbed the stairs and I felt the stunning blow of his silence as if he had slapped my face. I undressed for bed, unsure what to say or do. When he removed the packet from his coat, he slipped it underneath the top drawer of the tall chest by the door, where it would rest below the drawer and above the dust cover. I watched, rapt, but he blew out the candle before he turned toward the bed. We lay side by side. Still he spoke nothing, and touched me not at all. At last, I could bear it no longer and I said, "Cullah, I do not know why you are so—"

"I have never been so angry with you in all these years, wife. Never once have I had to still my hand from throttling the stubbornness out of you."

"It seemed a good plan."

"Speak no more of it. Bad enough that you raise your voice in Meeting."

I wept openly, sobbing, my elbow above my eyes like a child.

"You made me a fool before the whole town," he said. "Or do they think I am the coward who put you up to it? At the least, I am now a man whose wife must outthink him in public at the cost of her hearth and home. Is that what you think of me, Resolute? Am I but a fatheaded gob to be outdone? You made me a henpecked gamock before the church by your scorn for my offer."

"Scorn? I meant no scorn." I had felt enthusiasm. I had thought it called on my courage. I turned away from him and faced the wall. Between my sobs I gasped out, "I have never thought of you with scorn. What I said makes sense to me, still."

"You could be captured and taken and beaten, in the name of God. Flogged naked in a pillory with none to protect you this time. Or worse. You could be a-abused!"

"I have been beaten before, Eadan. I have been beaten until it tore the clothes from me and I could not stand."

He went silent again, and I felt his anger rekindling, for his whole body trembled. When at last he spoke, it was in a whisper. "Abused, too?"

I turned to him, my own anger showing now. "You were with me on our wedding night, husband. You answer that question, was I virgin or not? When I said beaten I meant beaten until not one inch of my body was without bruises."

After a long silence, he asked, "How old were you?"

"Ten or so. Eleven. No one cared when my birthday was, so I lost track sometimes."

"A babe. No older than our Dolly."

"A slave."

He sighed. "The thought of you in the hands of British soldiers makes me weak, as if I could die from the image alone."

"If I made you feel foolish, my dearest husband, I am sorry. I thought only of a plan to get the message through, not meaning to step on your pride. You were not angry that other men offered the same."

His great hand lay upon my shoulder. "Men die for their causes. I was feeling proud and brave, then, to offer to carry the message. And yes, my pride was big enough you could not move without stepping on it." He laughed softly. He kissed the top of my shoulder and put his hand over the place he had kissed. "Would you have me believe you were feeling proud and brave, as well?"

I rolled over to face him. "And why not? You asked me not long ago what I believe in, what was there in life that I would keep so close as to die for. The more I heard tonight, the more I knew what it was. I have been a slave, Cullah MacLammond. A caged captive. I believe in liberty."

"They call it treason."

"You have joined the rebellion. You came here to this shore as a rebel Scot. Do you think freedom is a cry that exists only in men's hearts? Do you think women know nothing of slavery and bondage? It is worse, for we are subject to the whim of any master, be he a lord or a husband. A woman must abide as she can. You are a kind and loving husband, but it is not always so. Even a pious man may be a tyrant of a husband and a ripping bad father. Do you think I could sit there these many weeks, and listen to those words, hear you speak of your worries and of war, and not be moved?"

"I thought women cared for nothing but children and home. And sometimes—"

"What?"

"Sometimes finery. I did not say it because I know you are not vain."

"Simply because a woman cannot swing a sword that is taller than a man does not mean she cannot feel those same stirrings that you feel in a battle. She must fight with cleverness instead of muscle."

"Unless she's Saint Joan."

I stopped my tears and said, "Saint Joan the lunatic." I sighed. The moon was bright and I could see his face outlined in faint blue light coming through the window. "I am no lunatic, though I know I can be brash. I, too, shudder in terror at the thought of you carrying messages through the forest at night. Do not roll your eyes at me, Cullah MacLammond. I do. It is not your courage I doubt, but courage will not stop a ball. We must be united. We must trust each other, just like our bairnies giving each other signs and signals that all is well. Never think I would do aught to shame you. If I can help you, you have but to call upon me. That is what I meant tonight."

"Then never put yourself in danger from soldiers. Never do it, Resolute.

I would be undone. Our children would be orphans, cast out, for I would meet the headsman for what I should do if you were taken from me."

He pulled me to him and held me as if I were a treasure so delicate it might disappear on his touch. He said, "And how, in this dark room, did you know I rolled my eyes? Are you sure you are not fey?"

"I have lived with you these many years, husband. I did not need to see your face to know it." I hated it when we argued. But I loved it when the harsh words gave way to reason and the anger was replaced with embrace. He chuckled, a deep, warm sound, and sang a wisp of a song to me, kissing my head. And we slept.

Cullah carried one message to Boston and then two. Sometimes word came and he walked there and back through the night, sometimes he simply put what looked like a blank sheet of paper in his work pack and left it at a public house near his shop in Lexington.

That August, Gwenny and Roland had a baby girl. She lived but three weeks, and then died. We knew not why. She was buried next to our babies down in the sleepy and misty hollow below the empty house.

My brother August arrived in September to spend a week with us, and then spend the winter in his new mansion. He was well dressed but carrying a small trunk holding, he said, no legacy of his occupation, which had turned to piracy against the British. He would dress like a simple man at our home. He had lost two ships to the British navy, now confiscating cargoes right and left of any who carried goods to the colonies in America. August asked to see the gift he had sent before. Cullah lifted the seat where the cannon lay. He leaned in and inspected the piece then moaned as he straightened. "Couple of broken ribs, that. Hard for me to bend, still."

Cullah said, "Soldiers arrived with a tax order two days after this new seat was finished. More came for billeting a day after that. I put your crate in here and nailed the lid shut as they were coming up the road. Never thought about it again."

August took a pouch from his coat. "I cannot keep it in town for my house is searched regularly." He opened the pouch. "Here. Doubloons. Spanish, mostly, but no matter."

I opened my mouth, but Cullah spoke first. "August, how did you come by this?"

My brother made a movement that looked as if he settled his head painfully upon his shoulders. "It came from a Tory hold after being stolen from an honest privateer. One minute they contract men to patrol the seas and the next they hang your whole crew for doing exactly what they'd been assigned to do. You may find it causes raised eyebrows to spend doubloons, but they're worth more than a sovereign apiece. Melt them down. You'll find the silversmith in Boston town willing and discreet. You know whom I mean. The time will come when it will take a bar of gold to buy a loaf of bread, mark my words. Take no paper money in exchange from now on. Only gold and silver coin. No bill will be worth the paper it is printed on in a year or two."

"The cannon," I whispered. "Is worth—"

August smiled with a cold hardness. "Its weight in gold. Aye. Cast iron. I will have sixty of them in a month."

"What do you plan to do with them?" Jacob asked.

"I am outfitting a ship, that's all."

"Under their long noses?" I asked.

"And under their long guns," August added. "Resolute, I have no intention of putting your family in jeopardy or even the slightest suspicion. It was wrong of me to assume we agreed upon a subject of which we have never spoken. It makes you a conspirator of sorts. I'm sure there is a lawyer somewhere with a name for it. Cullah, Jacob, you men have helped me immensely."

Cullah said, "I thought you to be a contracted privateer."

"Until the Limeys began to waylay their own contracted captains like myself, and using the word 'tax' rifled our trade goods so that we were left with only half of them to show. The East India Company controlled every grain of spice, every inch of silk, and had doubled and tripled the prices. Once I got back into port, I owed the port taxes on the whole of it and they'd gone up fivefold. What they left me with, after three voyages, was debt that would sink a fleet. All I have left is that house of Lady Spencer's and the trifles I have stored here."

"August, you are not planning to take on the British navy?" I began. If he had lost his ships, he must be in terrible straits. That would be as if Cullah lost his shop and tools, his house and family. How lonely my brother seemed. How sad, too. "Wait. If you have lost all, how are you buying a ship and forging guns?"

Cullah raised his hand to me. "Leave this, wife. We will ask nothing and know nothing if asked. I know this kind of anger. Sir, go with our blessings, but if you change your mind and wish to leave the sea for a quieter life, you are welcome here."

My brother smiled at my husband, and I felt sadly left out of their unspoken communication. "If I don't come back," August said, "open the other trunks I left upstairs. You never have, have you, Ressie? I thought not." He looked deep into my face in a way that felt almost as if he saw something I would not recognize in my own soul. "Ever I should meet a woman like you, sister, I would come home from the sea and never let her go. Trust is the one thing in a woman I have never found, so much that I have thought it was not in women to trust or be trusted. If ever I do not return within three years, everything in the trunks is yours, and the Boston house, too. I will have a will made in Philadelphia and recorded there so it will be kept out of the hands of Tories. I'm going there to buy iron and plenty of it. I should be back in six weeks."

I said, "Wait. We have a cannon, too. We found a small piece in a field. And the cannonballs, take them and melt them down for your purpose. They are all rusting in our barn. We meant to have them melted but that is no easy thing with something as obvious as a cannon."

At the end of seven days, two wagons approached our house, stopped, and one man left his wagon, climbed into the other, and drove away without a word to anyone. In the back of the wagon left behind were a set of similar clothing, a slouching, misshapen hat, and boots that were more wrapping than leather. August asked Cullah to help him roll the cannon in the blanket and get it into the wagon. He also took the old rusted small gun we had found long ago, the cannonballs, and the iron ring. In the morning, looking like any poor wight off to market before daybreak, the cannon nestled hidden in a load of hay surrounded by enormous barrels of salt cod, August left us, bound for the ironworks in Pennsylvania. We spoke words of farewell with our eyes locked. A fearful silence fell over us then, and no cheery waves accompanied his going.

I took Cullah's hand as we watched August's squeaking wagon roll away. "I do not understand him, husband. His anger seems more than revenge upon Lord Spencer."

"This is not about Gwyneth. It's about your brother. If I had had everything taken from me, I might feel the same. It feels even now as if the

Crown could take everything a man has, all he has worked for, take it all so a fat sow in a silk coat is not inconvenienced by the national debt. Someone somewhere is getting rich by all this confiscation."

"Do the English not pay taxes?"

"Never enough for a king intent on ruling the world."

"Goody Dodsil told me she heard there will be yet a new tax of five pounds per household across the whole of Massachusetts. She has no way of making five pounds."

"Five pounds to someone who has twenty thousand a year is pittance. Five pounds, if you haven't got it, is a fortune. Aye. We will pay her tax and ours."

"Aye. Find a way to sell the silks before they all go to worms." To change the subject I said, "I do miss my brother. If he would come home from the sea, he might meet a nice woman. He loved America Roberts."

"He is a hardened man, wife. What woman wants to share a man with the sea? He wants what I have with you. He will never find it if the only women he meets are in seaports pursuing a huzzy's trade."

"Do you trust me as he said? I never considered myself trustworthy. I spend my days trying to make up for all the lies I have told."

"You have done that and more." He raised my hand to his lips and kissed it, then looked at it as if it were new to him. "These wee fingers were never meant to have such calluses. They belong to a lady born. She should have all that is gentle and beautiful about her."

"I do. I have you."

"I am getting old, Ressie. I will turn fifty after next year. I have not provided for you as I intended. Without America Roberts here, you have no one to help you at the house. And now there is all this messaging to Boston. I am tired. I am going to tell them I will no longer carry messages."

"Are you ill? Is there something you have not told me?"

"No, I am not ill, though I just watched August grow old before my eyes. When your brother arrived and smiled at you, he seemed no more than a youth. When he said farewell, he looked older than Pa. I saw myself grow old with him. Perhaps we should take in another ward to help you."

"I would like that."

"I will ask at the town meeting next if any have a daughter ready to go out."

Cullah missed the next town meeting, though. Jacob slipped in the barn and broke his leg in the biggest bone above the knee. It did not come through the skin, but I could see the lump in his leg. He groaned like a child, with tears in his poor blind eye. We sent Benjamin scurrying to town for a doctor. By the time the doctor arrived, Jacob had begun to sleep fitfully in a way I feared was not rest but near death.

The doctor said it might kill him to set the leg, but that it was also the only thing that might save his life, for the leg was blue and would go to infection if he did not bleed to death first. It was given to Cullah to hold Jacob's chest and arms braced against himself, to me to hold Jacob's good leg. The doctor began to pull. No matter what he did, Jacob's wrenching and miserable screams broke our hearts yet the bones would not set together. At last, after one long, dreadful pull during which Jacob kicked as wildly as any horse with the leg I was holding, groaning and grimacing so hard that even with a wrapped stick in his mouth, chips of his teeth fell from his lips, the leg was set. Cullah had sent Benjamin and Dorothy to get wood for a splint from a shed by the house where he had some planks left, and they got back just as the terrible operation was performed. Both children burst into tears. The doctor put the splint on either side of his leg and wrapped cloths around the leg to hold it in place. "Do not loosen that binding. If you do it will come unset, and if it should come unset," he said, "he will die. Better pray for him, even so." He bled Jacob seven times before the old man calmed and slept.

After the doctor left, the leg swelled and swelled, above the wooden battens, around the wrappings. After three days of breathing hard and moaning like a woman in childbed, Jacob called out, "Mary?" one time and then slept the sleep of the ages.

Cullah dug his father's grave on a bright, sparkling day, a day that seemed as if all the world should be at peace and happy. He sweated and his legs shook, but he would not stop until it was right. The children did not run and play and it seemed no matter what I told Dorothy, she would not believe that the doctor had come to help. She believed, because old Sam the horse had been put down the year before, that the doctor had come to kill her grandpa because he was old and his leg was broken. I was taken with a sadness that surprised me.

Once our funeral was finished, Dorothy ran across the fields, desolate with harvest already gathered, to Gwyneth's house, and stayed there for a week. I missed her. I knew she was grieving but until she decided she wanted to come home, it was good for her to be with Gwenny.

A week later, I walked to Gwyneth's house. She and Dorothy and I shared tea and we wept for Jacob. We talked. We smiled a little. Then I left my daughters and returned to my home. My empty home. I stirred the pot and waited for Cullah, and thought what a great emptiness was left by Jacob's passing. At last, I sat at the front door, on the chair where Patience had died. I held my hands folded at my heart, and ached for all who had passed from my world.

People from our congregation did not leave us bereft. Every three days or so for the next four months, someone came with a cake or a sack of meal, a clutch of eggs or a noggin of rum. It was good to know now that we had made a place in the hearts of our community. I counted the worth of that place more valuable than the sack of doubloons August had left with us.

When I walked to Boston every other week, I took a doubloon to Revere's shop and had Paul exchange it for minted Massachusetts coins by weight. The doubloons he could melt down for the gold and filigree a mantel clock or make bars for trade. When I entered the shop, he either found a way to pat the top of his head as if it were a nervous habit, or to touch his left elbow. Every time someone made either of the signs, the "high signs" to me, I thought of how clever my boy Benjamin was and it was easy to smile as if nothing in the world troubled me, though it was not safe to speak openly at the moment.

Christmas in 1759 found us gathered at our fireside with Gwenny, round with child, Roland, and Brendan home from battle at Ticonderoga. Smallpox, he said, had fought on the side of England, but cost the British army dearly in terms of men lost. He had a month's rest leave coming and was glad to take it. I repaired his uniforms and sewed him many pairs of new linens and stockings until he laughed and said the generals were not outfitted so fine. When he left, I tried to keep myself from weeping, but it was not to be. He was a jaunty soldier, a man born to it.

In late March of 1760, the new year turned and Gwyneth's babe was born. They named her Elizabeth Victoria, as English a name as could be. In private when we left them, Cullah winced. "Could they not find a good Scots name for her?" he asked.

"She has your features," I said. "So pretty a wee thing."

"Not as pretty as her mother," he fumed. "Gwenny was beautiful from the first moment."

"Grandfather, you have become a curmudgeon."

"Grandfather?"

"Had you not realized it? Your daughter's daughter makes you a grandfather."

Cullah smiled with one side of his mouth. Then with both. "Grandfather," he said. "Grandfather."

Our house, a quarter mile off the road from Lexington to Concord, could be seen on a clear day from the road, and was sometimes sought by travelers, so it was not a great surprise one day at noon, while Cullah was in town building a warehouse for a man named Parker, that a strange fellow approached me while I pulled weeds in the garden. He watched me, saying nothing, for so long that I felt uneasy. He was rather short of stature and wore a flat parson's hat but nothing else in his attire marked him as a cleric. At last I asked, "Are you looking for someone, sir?"

"Is this the woodsman's house?" he asked with a very French accent that made my throat tighten.

Had someone come looking for Roland? I said, "It is. Cullah MacLammond."

"C'est moi, James Talbot de Montréal."

I stepped closer to him. My hands began to shake. I questioned him in French. "Tell me how old you are."

Before he answered me, he pulled from his loose shirt the very first knitted cap I had sent him as a baby. It looked completely unworn. "I was a little too big for it when it came, *Tante. Tante* Rachael saved it for me to bring to you."

I could not decide whether to embrace this strange man, but I did say, "Stay with us a while, James, please. Are you traveling farther?"

"I hoped to go to New Orleans. I can read and write, or I can work in your fields. I wouldn't be a burden to you."

"You will be no burden. Stay a few days at least."

In the hours before Cullah came home, while I baked bread and roasted our supper, James and I spoke of the people I had known at the convent, how for years he had steadily made his way here, learning English as he went, working at farms for food, forever heading south, to me. He slept on our floor for two nights. Then Cullah told him about Goody Carnegie's old house, and James asked us if he could work for us and stay in it. So rather than a girl to help in the house, at least now we had another man to help on the farm. No one said anything about how long he would stay, nor whether we should pay him, for he refused that immediately. Only that he would stay until he did not.

And then the king was dead.

A new monarch was enthroned in 1760, the year I turned forty-one years old.

George Second was replaced by George Third and still the word from England was, "The king is mad." New King George's first act toward the colonies was to levy upon us a sugar tax, making treacle as dear as thread. It forced up the cost of making rum in New England, and traders from the West Indies carrying sugarcane and treacle to us had to build new storehouses for their gold. The cost circled the ocean straight to England so the king's proclamation cost even the British people dearly for their rum and sugar. Traders carrying rum to England returned to the colonies with their ships awash, their ballast bags of gold. The Crown would allow no sales of wool or woolen products, meaning the cloth I wove; all thread and cloth had to go to England for assemblage, just as iron had to be sent there to make implements. All of it came back to us, of course, but at twelve or more times the cost of keeping it here and doing it ourselves. I felt stunned. Now it wasn't just the silk. I could not sell my own weaving without becoming a criminal. Cullah had built a false floor in our small wagon as if that were naturally what we would do. I wrestled with my heart. My yearning to continue as I had always done measured against the promise to myself to be honest and above reproach.

And then one day Emma Dodsil, Virtue Dodsil's wife, tapped at my door. She carried a bushel basket of eggs. "Mistress MacLammond?" she called. She was trailed by three of her children, who ran off to see my newborn goats.

I let her in. "Oh, you poor dear. How have you done since the fire?"

"I have come to try to repay your kindness, Resolute."

"That is not needed, you know, Emma." In truth, I wondered what I would do with all those eggs. And how on earth could the ones on the bottom of a bushel still be whole with the weight of all the others on top of them?

I poured us ale and we sat quietly for several moments as she looked about the room, guiltily.

At last Emma said, "These are boiled."

"All right. I will make a pie of them."

"These are not the gift."

I lowered my head. "I do not understand, Emma."

"I have done work. It's nothing much." She lifted the rag of hopsacking holding the eggs, and underneath them were folded clothes. "I made these things from our remnants." She lifted forth an apron, a child's pelisse, and a kirtle. "I sew, you see, and now it seems I am able to provide more than we need. I, I have heard that you sometimes go to Boston to trade. If you could sell these, I would give you half the money. That is my gift, for—"

"Stop. You know that is against the law, now."

"Yes, Resolute."

"Who told you that I do such a thing? Do you suspect me of not being loyal to the Crown?"

"Oh, no, Mistress."

I noted how her friendly familiarity had gotten formal when I confronted her motives. I rose and stood with one arm against the mantel of our fireplace. With my other hand, I touched the rim of my house cap twice and watched her from the corner of one eye as I pretended to stir the bean pot. She made no like movement. I said, "I hope your family has stayed warm with the blankets I gave you."

"Yes, indeed, Resolute."

"It is only against the law to trade in such. I am still allowed to make them for my family and my friends. It was a gift to you from our best, Emma. Nothing less than any neighbor would do."

"Of course, dear friend. I meant nothing by it. It's just, we have need of so many things. Prices are so high. I hope you don't think I would do anything against the law."

I turned to face her and smiled. "Absolutely not. It was but a misunderstanding. I am sure you need the money." I wondered if she might even be paid for witnessing against any neighbor thwarting the law. Lest my words seem like the accusation it was, I added, "We are all finding prices higher. Doing with less." We finished our ale and she packed up her goods, with her cloth of boiled eggs atop the basket so it looked as if that were her only burden. As I watched her call her children and walk away, the smile left my face. I would have to be far more discreet in everything I did and said from this day forward.

Before long the ladies to whom I sold cloth made it clear whether they would flaunt British law or not. I came very near to being caught trading in woolens one day. I rolled a length of wool in a sack, and once in Boston, placed it in the coal bin of Constance, the dressmaker. I made other stops and returned, to find inside a pouch holding a pound and ten shillings. Then the next week when I repeated the charade, I opened the coal bin and found the pouch, but in it were two colonial paper notes, virtually worthless unless I were to trade in Loyalist shops. I took the money and boldly walked inside. I wanted gold, not paper, and I would have it. There were four people in there, three women and a man I knew not. I handed Constance the notes. "For my bill," I said, then whispered, "Would you please change these for gold?"

Her eyes narrowed. "Whatever do you mean? I carried no credit for you, Mistress MacLammond." She raised her brows to the man. He stepped closer to me.

I felt the hairs on my arms rise and a tingling took my fingertips. Angered, fearful, I said, "No, no. Fancy that. I have gone to the wrong shop. It is money I owe the butcher. What a silly mistake I have made. I'm sure the only things you butcher in this shop are ladies' gowns." I made my way to the door, re-solved never to trade with Constance again. I felt doubly sad for it, though, knowing that the split between Loyalists and the rest of us would only deepen.

CHAPTER 33

January 2, 1765

Five years can pass like the blink of a cat's eye. I had not opened the chests my brother left with me. Though I spoke not of him, he would return, I knew, for when he was not with us, I heard about him instead. He had gained repute as a smuggler, and it was sometimes said with a low voice and a wink, "This be got by trade or by Talbot?" as a way of acknowledging the fact. He was hailed for it. Though I feared for him, I took pride in his reputation, too. Every day I held his image in my mind's eye and thought of him standing on the foredeck of his great ship, the wind filling the sheets as she moved across swells. I pictured him happy, standing there. Each woman I met, I considered as a bride for him, but none was fitting. None could replace his first love, the sea.

During those years August made furtive sorties on land. Sometimes he boldly occupied his house in Boston. Often he unloaded his "trade" on the harbors. Once in a great while, he came in the dark of night with a wagonload of things to put in the double floor of our barn, or the upper room over my loom, or in the eaves where Cullah had built shelves then closed them off from view. While Lexington had once seemed rather isolated, and its only thoroughfare simply a path between Concord and Boston, now with a great influx of poor people we were hailed night and day by straggling travelers, so that I told Cullah we might as well open an inn, but he did not laugh at my jest.

Gwyneth had three more children, so that her life was constant in duties at home. I knew well the exhausting toll that took on a woman, so when Dorothy, by her own choice, lived with them I tried to believe that she felt no less love for her father and me. But she was twelve and still had not recovered from Jacob's terrible death. She told me she would never marry, that she wanted to care for her sister's children, and felt happy there.

Benjamin was apprenticed, not with his father but in Boston with Paul and the Revere family in the silversmith business. It worried us both that without Benjamin or Brendan, we had no hope to carry on his work when Cullah grew old. It came to me that someday our land would lie fallow, but I pushed the thought away. We had Roland, a good farmer, and now James, too. James had chosen to live in and repair Goody Carnegie's old house. He kept secret his Roman Catholic ways and worked with Roland, tending sheep and cows, hoeing weeds.

In the midst of what seemed to be spreading poverty, the call and need for cloth grew. I turned to my loom and my spinning as I had not done since before the children. At the same time I developed a web of women whom I trusted and we traded and bartered for goods so much that I might see my own cloth worn by a magistrate's wife who had traded a sow to the undertaker for some porcelain and the porcelain pitcher was on my table

full of milk, the cups holding settling posset. I spun every moment I was
not occupied with something else. I wove yards of motley and yards of fine,
yards of linens as dainty as a shimmer, and woolens of every sort. I wove
black and tan and gray, and I wove plaids of tartans when Cullah could
remember the setts or patterns of color. If he could not, I made up my own
pattern of color from what I found pleasant. I wove linen with silk chasing.
I loved that best. It was almost embroidery, doing chasing work.

"I want a girl to come in," I told Cullah one night, while I cut chunks of
lamb for a stew. "I need help with the work. When I am spinning, the
weeds overgrow the garden, and while I cut out weeds, the sheep have gotten into the corn. Then the cows, the cows seem to need me there. They
give better milk for me than for Roland." That was not true. I knew that
what I wanted was not so much an apprentice as someone with whom to
talk. Cullah worked in town. "Remember?" I said. "You were to ask about,
but Jacob fell. His death changed everything."

"It did," he said. "I am lonely. I expected my boys to follow my trade.
But since they have not, without Pa here, I am also too much alone."

I put down my knife. "We could force Dorothy to come home."

"She'd be unhappy. Might grow melancholic." Cullah looked at me
with an old familiar longing. "I'd have been happy if you'd had more children. I did my best."

I smiled. "You did, indeed. Perhaps we must be thankful for the quiet
and a full night's sleep."

"Every season has its beauty."

"You are become a philosopher, husband. Will you ask in town, then?"

April 2, 1765

Often, Cullah stayed in town and did not walk home until late at night. If
ever I questioned him, he smiled and said, "It's business, Mistress MacLammond, keeps me from your bosom," or, "Not to worry, Goody MacLammond, your husband is neither a reprobate nor a drunkard. He is merely
the most hated thing, a patriot," and tell me nothing. I wanted to cudgel
him into speaking it, but there was no use. I knew the man I had married
by his stubbornness as well as by his face.

In spring he spent two nights away from home. When he got back in the darkest hours before Easter morning, April 7, 1765, he came with the oddest burden I could have imagined. Two sack-back and two comb-back Windsor chairs. They were large and comfortable. He had placed them back to back and putting his hand through the rungs lifted two in each hand and carried them all the way from Boston down a narrow path that led across a swamp, a bog, two neighbors' farms, and through the woods. I asked him, "You brought them from Boston?"

"Aye."

"And why, on Easter morning, did you feel you must do that?"

"I made these chairs. Each one took a week's worth of labor in itself. A good chair is the hardest thing there is, and these were my best work. I couldn't let them burn."

"Why were they going to burn?"

He cast his eyes about the room as if, I thought, trying to come up with a believable lie to tell me. "They were in the governor's mansion, and there was a fire."

"Who set it?"

"The Committee of Safety. It's as well you know. We lit a candle for the cause of freedom, that's all. I am taking these to the attic, and I ask you to come with me and help me lay something atop them. But ask me no other questions, wife, for I have been abroad for two days and I must eat and get to work now or seem conspicuous."

"It is Easter Sunday. If you go to work, not only will you seem conspicuous to the soldiers, you will be called to question by the deacons. Nevertheless, husband, if you sold them to the governor, and you've taken them back, you stole those chairs."

"You've a bitter tongue, Ressie."

"Aye, well, I live with a thistle." More and more I thought of Scotland's symbol as indicative of her people. Rugged. Uncrushable. Beautiful. Armed with wicked thorns.

"I made them."

"He paid you for them. That means you stole them."

"Well and aye. There were too many high spirits last night. I didn't think clearly. At the last I couldn't watch my work go to the flames. Risked losing the hair off my back for them."

"You have to give them back."

"Will you allow me at least to say that I saved them from the fire? Must I confess all and be hung?"

"You heard the call to fire and saved them. That will serve."

"Aye." He kissed my cheek. "You are my rudder in an evil sea, Ressie."

After the Easter sermon, Reverend Clarke received a note from one of the deacons. We sang a hymn. Then he announced that Imperial Governor Thomas Hutchinson's mansion in Boston had been burned down and messages had been left stating it had been done by the Sons of Liberty. No one made a sound. I imagined that some cheered within themselves, some were saddened, even angered. Some wept, but that, I knew, was no indication which way their feelings leaned. I stayed myself from any expression and looked at my prayer book. I noted that the singing of the next hymn was so rousing as to shake the glass in the windows.

Cullah drove our new third-hand wagon to Boston the next day, whistling, as he carried the four well-made chairs to the governor's new temporary quarters. The buggy had a seat for two with a shade behind them, and a place to stack things in back. He tied the chairs with as much gentle care as if they had been children. No questions were asked, he said, for he had found the menservants at home, and he left the chairs amongst their congratulations for the salvage.

He left for his shop carrying his toolbox on his back on a Monday two weeks later, a beautiful April morning, the kind of morning when the whole earth seemed to be celebrating its life and warmth. All the pear and apple trees had blossomed, frost was but a memory, and birds pecked at our windowsills. I had kissed him and he slapped my hip playfully before he left. I collected eggs. I put out bread dough to raise. I swept the floor. In that much time, less than two hours, he returned to the house, his face pale and wan, his right hand wrapped in cloths none too clean, and to my horror, he had lost half the littlest finger on his right hand to a whirling blade. I cleaned his wound and wrapped it in linen bandages.

"Ah, I'm a terrible fool," he said. His voice barely hid his pain.

"My poor husband. It must hurt so dreadfully."

"I cannot hold a sword now."

"But you can. You will."

"It will feel different."

I looked hard into his face. "Why do you need to hold a sword? Why did you not say a saw or an axe? Or a plane or chisel? Why did you say a sword?"

"Cooper and Prescott came by the shop just before I did this." He held his bandaged hand up. "There is yet another new tax. It was passed six months ago without a single man from the colonies to question it in Parliament, without any of us knowing it beforehand. Every piece of paper must bear a stamp and every stamp must be paid for. A penny for a receipt. A pound for a license and three to sell a piece of land. Ten shillings for a pamphlet and five pounds for a newspaper! It will drive the newspapers out of business, and it is meant to do so, for they speak of nothing but angry outcries against the king. They say there will be open rebellion this time, far beyond this colony. War."

A chill ran through me. "But, how did that make you cut your hand?"

"While they were talking across the street from my shop at Elliot's Wheel and Carriage, Tories went in, front and rear, and confiscated all the wheel rims he had. Claimed they were illegally gotten iron not from England but made in Philadelphia. It caught my eye. I was trying to look as if I did not notice, for they aimed muskets in every direction, even at a young woman crossing the street with her bairny at her side. I looked away for just an instant. With a band saw, an instant is far too long."

"I should say. Were they English wheels?"

"No."

"Will Goodman Elliot get his wheels returned?"

"He's out his inventory and can't make his orders without wheels. Now they're so high, he said, when he finally delivers the coach he has made no profit at all. Ressie, a man cannot stay in business making no profit!"

"Will you have some rum and willow water for the pain?"

"Well and aye. It did not hurt at all, did you know that? It felt like nothing, until now. Now it feels as if the devil himself has chewed it off." I poured rum. Mixed him a toddy of willow water. He took a long draught of the drink and coughed. "Ah. Would you give me cider instead? I am not fond of this stuff. I feel it already, making my brains spin. I heard your brother is in Boston." He coughed again. "The army has ransacked his house but not found him, yet Hancock just got a load of spices from Talbot's ships."

Ships? August had recovered his losses, then. "Will he come here?"

"I don't know. I do know this. There is talk of rebellion in every quarter. Your brother is planning something that might get him an appointment with the hangman."

That, I knew, I could not change. August would do what he willed.

The Reverend Mr. Clarke came to visit and spent a long afternoon with Cullah on the bench outside by the parlor door. I knew nothing of what they spoke. The gentle rumble of men at talk felt soothing to me, same as it had when Pa had had ships' captains in our parlor. It troubled me a great deal, though, when they lowered their voices and I could hear nothing but an odd word. I told myself the Reverend Mr. Clarke would never do anything against the law, whereas I did not believe that of my husband. Yet, the two, with heads together and voices lowered, made them seem more alike than not. I tried to go about my chores and ignore them. Was that always the way with men? Were the soothing rises and fallings of their voices indicative of plots of subterfuge and rebellion?

After Reverend Clarke left, Cullah took to his chair before the fireplace, and stayed there for five days. In pain, perhaps, or sulking, or both, perhaps. I could not guess at his malaise, and he would barely speak at all until I feared we might have to send for a doctor, that he had some sickness of heart or mind that time and clean bandages could not salve. I carried his meals to him, for he would not so much as come to the table to eat. He refused Gwenny's invitations to their home. He stared into the fireplace whether a fire burned there or not.

In the warming of May, after working in the field alongside Roland one long day, James seemed exhausted. One thing I had discovered about him already was that the man could stand little in the way of nervous excitement. He was a fair farmer, but not energetic, as if he'd never known a man's strength. He worried that the cause of distress in our household was his presence, but at last Cullah told him what had happened. He asked him, "Will you swear to keep our secrets, keep our home as if it were your own?"

I repeated it all in French. James agreed. "Of course, sir," he said. Simply because this man was related to me, being a nephew, did not make his allegiances ours or ours his. He smiled, laughed a little, trying to make light of it. In his smiling face, I saw Rafe MacAlister's grimace. A coldness came into me at that moment. I feared I would never look at James without seeing his father, again. I resolved to guard well my actions.

That evening as I sat to spin and he sat spellbound by the flames, I imagined Cullah standing at the great saw with its blade encircling a gear in the roof, the only control of it a brake pedal. It ran by a waterwheel, or if the stream was low, by apprentice power on a spoke. This time of year there would have been rushing water, making the blade run faster than normal. British soldiers had been searching the shop across the street, ransacking the place, and my husband had been distracted. Distracted by guilt for his part in burning the governor's mansion? Had he stood there pretending to work, all the while terrified of them repeating the same orders at his place?

That summer, soldiers walked every street of Boston, every avenue of Lexington. County lanes were as often trod by Redcoats as by farmers. I created bolts and bolts of cloth. Cullah had made me a wheelbarrow with a false bottom that fit the rolls of cloth. I carried some of them to Lexington town, sold them in private homes as if I were a fishmonger, or took them to Boston under layers of ragged but clean muslin surrounding tarred canvas, and topped with old vegetables. Sometimes the vegetables, so oft used that way, grew limp and withered. Once on my way to Lexington, when stopped by a gaggle of six young soldiers who inspected my load, I told them in a rather silly voice, "Your Honors, I be just a poor goodwife. This is the best I got. It wo' not bring me a farthing but maybe sixpence for someone's pigs to eat."

"What's under the top, there? I see some cloth." His accent was Irish.

I smiled and cocked my head as if I were simple and I mimicked Mistress Boyne's manner of speech. "Why, it is cloth, you clever one! 'Twas once a cloth from the altar at a papist shrine. And there is something under it! I got a cat that was kill't by a fairy down in the dell by the grave of a witch. There's a power to that one. I have seen her meself, a-prowling the land on a winter's eve. The cat is to keep fairies awa' from me whilst I walk. 'Tis the only way. Would you like to touch it? Marvelous charm, it is. If ye take one of the worms and put it in your collar, you cannot be shot by elves on your journey. Tha' knows what a pity elf-shot is."

The men wrinkled their noses and backed away from me. "Be off with you, woman," one said. He turned to his mate and whispered, "What a creature!"

I nodded and smiled, and walked on, amazed myself at the drabble that had poured from my lips without so much as a pause to concoct it. Sister Joseph would have been appalled.

He called after me, "And for Christ's sake, go to church. Damned colonials."

When I met him at his shop, Cullah took my barrow and said, "I was thinking that you work too hard, always at the cloth. You will cause yourself to go blind."

"I will be careful, husband. I will rest my eyes."

"There. Working, working. Resolute, my wee wife, you are as determined as a badger, and for what? Our children are grown."

"I suppose I cannot stop. I feel I must work at something." And like a chant or an old string of Latin prayer, the sentence finished itself in my mind as, "or I shall not get home to Jamaica, to my mother," and that surprised even me. It was true, now that I was alone so much, the children gone, those old words echoed more and more.

Meanwhile, Cullah had continued talking and I had not heard anything until he said, "You need a diversion. Let's stay the night in Boston. I'll drive the wagon. I have chests to deliver. We'll bed at your brother's house."

I stopped walking and said, "I have no way to dress my hair in the morning. What shall we eat?"

"What is the fuss with hair? Women fiddle for an hour and then cover it with a cap so you would not know if she were bald as a pumpkin. If your brother cannot give us meat, we shall eat at an inn or a stall in the street. He has had provender at our table often enough, August could grant us a stale crust and a noggin of something. I must get there today, Resolute."

I said nothing still. What could he know about my pride? My hair?

When we got to Boston we went to Revere's, and Benjamin showed us a hammered brass charger he had created. I was so glad then that Cullah had come with me. Our son was growing so quickly. Seventeen already, and tall as his father, but with my lighter hair and skin. We all went to have a meat pie and ale at a nice tavern nearby, but Cullah grew more sullen as the meal continued, until he ceased speaking at all.

When we returned, Deborah Revere herself met us, smiling, and she kissed my cheeks. "Come next Thursday to our supper. Dining at eight o'clock. There will be music by seven, so come early. We are having some new music done." She looked from my face to Cullah's. "It will be a good place for all our sons."

He glanced at me. "Then they shall all be there, madam. We have a daughter of a good age, too."

"Of course. Then I shall expect, what, four of you?"

"Yes," I said. "Thank you so."

She cast her eyes around the place. "There shall be excellent company, Mr. MacLammond. Twenty-one of us, sir. Good day, then."

"Good day," Cullah said, as my mouth was open to utter the words.

When we left her presence, I tugged at Cullah's sleeve. "Tell me, husband, what wounds your spirit so? Is it your finger causing such distress?"

He did not turn to me, or smile. "It is that I see my children, Gwenny's bairns, and I do not wish them to grow up in a land such as this. I did not mean to be harsh to you. I am worried about the future." He chucked the reins. "It's intolerable."

He tied our workhorse and farm wagon at a ring several doors away from August's home. The street was lined with hansom carriages, and music poured from the open door at Wallace and Serenity Spencer's house. Candles had been lit in several downstairs windows and more of their guests had just arrived. I pushed aside the knowledge of it coming from their house, and stepping to its beat let the music lift my spirits. I said, "Was it not excellent that we happened to go to Benjamin's workplace in time to see Mistress Revere?"

Cullah said, "It was no accident. I was promised to go there, today."

"Promised? For what purpose?"

He looked about the street, his eyes wandering to some flowers overhanging a ledge outside a window three stories up, but he muttered, "Mistress Revere has given me a message and we must attend that supper even if we are standing at death's portal. The sons to whom she refers are not our children. Nevertheless, our son Benjamin must be there, likewise Dorothy. We must see that she is dressed as befits a child of royalty. And you, too. Have you got a new gown? Silk? Something with the finest trim?"

"It is but ten days away. I have some embroidery work, a stomacher, and some silk fillets made that I meant to sell. I can make the colors work for a mantua and wear my old petticoat with a bit of ribbon. There remain three bolts of silk from that stock Lady Spencer left to me. Dolly and I shall create her a gown from those."

"See those flowers there? Why do you not plant some of those?" he asked, as three men in fine clothing walked past us. Then he lowered his voice again. "I suppose I shall need a coat such as that?"

"That I can do for you. So much for lessening my work, though."

"It is important."

"What is twenty-one? She said there would be excellent company, twenty-one."

"Did she now?"

"Eadan," I whispered, as we walked along, "that was a message, too."

We stopped at a stall to look at straw baskets a woman had for sale. "Have we need of a basket, wife?" he asked me. He raised his voice. "How much is this one?"

I said, "It seems we have much to carry and I shall not know how to take it all." I was sure by my tone that he knew I meant I could not take his subterfuge.

The woman at the stand put down her basketwork as if having customers annoyed her. She took the basket from Cullah's hands, turned it about, and said, "Two shillings and sixpence."

He answered, "That's a fair price, I suppose. Have you any others at that rate?"

"Choose the one you want and I shall give you a price, sir."

"Would you sell them all for twenty-one pounds?"

She carried on as if he had just haggled her out of the sixpence. "It'll be three shillings, then. And that's one got buttons on it. It'll do nicely for your lady, there." She smiled at me.

Buttons? What basket was made with buttons? I frowned in return and tried to force myself to retain composure if I could not smile, for here, suddenly, I knew it was some kind of code they spoke to each other.

"Three shillings, then," Cullah replied. "That seems fair." He reached into his pocket and put the coins in her rough hands. I cringed as his fingers touched her palm, so blackened with her work that her fingertips and chopped nails seemed to have chewed their way through filth to emerge rusty-pink from black gloves.

We walked on. "Three shillings for a two-shilling basket?" I asked. "Twenty-one pounds for the lot?"

Cullah took the basket from my hands and then said, "Hold this, dear wife," and handed it back. Then he removed his kerchief from his neck and folded it, placing it in the basket. As he did so he leaned close to me. "The extra coin is payment for her services. The woman is a widow and sells only a few baskets a week. Eating is a good inducement to keeping loyal. Excellent company means that there will be British officers at the Reveres' soiree. Twenty-one is the wharf where a ship laden with buttons will dock some night this week. Buttons are kegs of black powder. The basket seller will pass the word to a man in the committee named MacGregor, a Presbyterian from Enniskillen. Now you know all. Are you satisfied?" Cullah took the basket from my hands as if we had performed some ritual. "There," he proclaimed a bit too loudly. "This will work wonderfully. Fine purchase, wife."

Satisfied? I was struck dumb.

"Now, since we are on the subject," he went on, his voice barely audible. "It is high time you and I had an understanding, wife. Though my pa and I came from supporting King James and the Jacobite cause, we, you and I, and our kin, are Protestants. You must know your own father was, never mind the rest back in Lincolnshire."

"I know not what my father believed. I know not what I believe."

"I need your promise that your belief includes something broader. In the Lexington Committee of Safety, there are Christian men, churchmen who are Romanish but hiding it, some who are Quakers and hiding it, two Lutherans, hiding also; some are, good God, Baptists, and some are drunkards. There is even one who claims himself to be a disciple of Charles Wesley, and was transported here for that. It matters not how they call upon their God. It matters that we trust each other."

"Trust and watch," I added.

He smiled at me but the look in his eyes was of guile, not of humor. "Do you know something I should know?"

"I know this, husband. When it was convenient, I was Catholic. You are paying that woman to keep quiet? That tells you nothing about her loyalty. Whoever comes with a larger purse will have it next. When it bought me another biscuit, I learned my Catholic prayers and said them cheerfully. If I had been held by Gypsies or Indians I would have done no less. If a child without real malice can do such a thing, a man or woman with a motive can do more."

He squinted as if that were difficult to hear, then picked up the handles of the basket and we started down the road. He said no more. We walked slower. I began to hum to myself, the tune of "If I Wast a Blackbird."

"Do not sing that song," Cullah said, "unless you are in danger."

"That is a sign, too? You men have some things to learn. The women I know have more subtle signs."

"Well and aye."

I was more than a little surprised to see Rupert, Lady Spencer's butler, answer the door at what was now August's house. He was liveried in quite a different style, and in colors that shot a pain through my heart. I recognized my father's colors of the coat and our coat of arms in an embroidered crest upon his waistcoat. He did not recognize me at first, but when he did, he suppressed a smile. "The master of the house has asked me to tell all callers he is not at home, sir and madam. If you will please follow me, I will inquire for you."

We followed him into what had been the grand parlor. Where Lady Spencer had done the place in muted colors, August had had colorful paintings, upholstered couches, and velvet drapes brought in. A huge rug made of two animal skins sewn head to head filled the center and the bold black and white stripes of the creature seemed to point in all directions to the four corners of the room. Animal tusks crossed over portraits of Spencer ancestors. A breastplate from a suit of armor with a pole-sized piercing in one side hung at the mantel flanked by Chinese vases and heavy silver candelabras. Garish war shields and crossed spears had been mounted over the doorway. Everything seemed exotic and luxurious, as one might expect of the home of a man who traveled to the farthest reaches of the world. At one end of the room, rolls of papers drifted back and forth upon a massive desk-table, moved by some unfelt draft.

I waited by the front window. Cullah was in a far corner, inspecting a cabinet. "This chest is fine," he said, pointing to the piece before him. "That one over there, worthless. It should not even be in this room. Look at those tenons visible. Anyone should know to shave up the grain and lap it over. But this, this is a work of mastery. The finials are so small they might topple from it."

"And they do, regularly," came a voice. It was August. "The blasted maid seems to do her dusting with a scullery mop. I've had to scold her three times for breaking things. My dear sister and brother-in-law. I am glad to see you both. I do apologize for not being able to entertain you this evening." The coat he wore, though it was embroidered silk, was a dressing gown, not meant to be seen in public.

"Oh, August," I exclaimed. "Are you wounded? What has taken you?"

"Some tropical blight, I reckon. It will pass."

"May we impose upon your hospitality to spend the night?" Cullah asked.

August closed his eyes and opened them with such weariness I felt we should walk home instead, though it was late. He said, "Of course. I am always at your disposal. I will have a room laid for you, and a table. Forgive me if I do not join you. I was having broth before the fire in the opposite room."

I looked into his eyes, and at that second, I believed he was lying. "What illness has brought this?" I asked again. "You have been shot?"

"No, fair sister, I have not been shot."

"Stabbed, then." I shuddered. I looked up at the armor over the fireplace, the obvious hole that meant death to its wearer.

Cullah said, "Ressie, leave him be."

"Men! Secrecy when it is not warranted. Such dim-witted arrogance they cannot speak what is most obvious. August, are you dying?"

"Perhaps," he said. Then he winked. "We are all dying, you know. At the moment, I am suffering the effects of the best medical treatment money can buy. The fools tell me I have the French disease."

"French? Why, what—" But I knew what he meant. French disease, Dutch plague, Prussian blight, the Spanish pox. The rotting scourge of men who consorted with low women, and of women consorting with the syphilitic vermin inhabiting the wharves. I remembered anew what Wallace had done, the villainy of leaving me alone at midnight on the waterfront. "August, no," was all I could say. I sat abruptly upon a couch.

"Fear not. You cannot catch it from me by being here. In a few days, I am assured, I shall be presentable again. Thanks to this physician, I shall forever smell like brimstone from the netherworld, never taste anything again nor make water without agony, but I shall probably live a few more months at least. With any luck I shall be hung before I go mad." August rubbed at his clean-shaven chin and said, "Oh, my dear. I have upset you. I apologize, sweet Resolute. Please do not trouble yourselves. Now, please excuse me. Rupert will attend your stay. Good night." He left the room and entered the smaller parlor across the hall.

Cullah turned to me and I to him. I made toward the small parlor room across the hall, but Cullah caught my arm. "Leave him."

"But Cullah, I wish to speak to that doctor. I heard voices. There is more than one other man in there."

Cullah shook his head. "Let us admire the trophies in this room."

After about an hour, Rupert returned to the parlor and escorted us to the same dining table where I had once enjoyed Lady Spencer's hospitality. A cook brought us vegetables with tiny slivers of meat, and fresh, hot bread. It was somewhat spare, considering the elaborate gilt surroundings, but no doubt had had to be cobbled up out of whatever was left from noon. Rupert himself poured us Madeira, a wine of a sort I had never tasted, sweet and savory at once, dry upon the tongue enough to make a person wish for more.

Cullah watched me and finally told him, "Enough," when he had poured my third glass. "Bring coffee, if you please."

We retired after coffee to the bedroom which had been Lady Spencer's room. Comforted, if not sauced by too much wine, I pulled off my gown, and we slid in our shifts and shirts into a downy bed tick. I did not remember my head touching the pillows when I awoke with a start deep in the night.

I lay in the bed trying to return to sleep, but I could not. I arose carefully, not to awaken Cullah. I felt as wide awake as if it had been midday. I knew I would not go back to sleep, but I knew not whether the worry over my brother's illness, or his odd behavior, Cullah's secret message to the filthy basket woman, any of these, were the culprits robbing me of a night's rest.

I took up the extra blanket folded across the foot of the bed and wrapped it about my shoulders, then went to the window and looked out. The moon above the house behind this one was just rising, the tip almost invisible at first, being no more than a quarter full. I watched it rise, curling like a shaving of wood over the ridge of the house the way a chip came from Cullah's plane, until the whole of it showed, adding feeble light to the garden below.

I opened the window, careful not to waken Cullah, but wondering if the night were pleasant enough to leave it open. When I got the sash raised and found the air brisk but not bitter, I smiled, enjoying the coolness against my cheek. I leaned out. A candle blazed in the window below my room, and as soon as I saw it, it went out. August must have kept up half the night, ill, I thought. I heard a series of soft clicks, and I leaned farther out.

A form, a man, left through one of the tall windows on the bottom floor. He held a shaded lantern in his hand, tiny sparks of candlelight showing through its pierced sides. He wore a low-crowned, wide-brimmed hat, so it was impossible to see his features, yet, I felt, more than knew, that it was my brother. He made his way on a cobbled path toward the back of the yard where the stables were, but stopped abruptly. He turned and looked about himself, scanning the bushes and hedges for movement. I pulled myself inside the window frame, thankful that the moon held little light that might betray my presence. The man studied the house, his hat brim at last rising so that he could see as high as the window where I stood. He watched the window a long time. In the faintest moonlight, I believed I saw a sword tucked into his belt, not in a scabbard, but right under the sash.

My heart beat faster and harder. Had he seen me? Why would I fear that so? If that was my brother, and this his house, why would he slip from a window in the middle of the night? Why not go right out the front door? Could it be that August was asleep in his bed and someone had robbed him and was now escaping? The night watchman called out just then, "Twelve o' the clock and all's weh-hel!" The man below turned away and darted into shadows, and from there, I could see him no more. I stood at the window until my feet felt as if they had taken root into the wooden floor. I could not decide what to do. At last, I imagined that if August were asleep in his bed, I would know that it had been a stranger, and I would awaken him and Cullah. If I found August not in his bed, I would assume that he himself had crept out of his own house under cover of darkness.

I felt my way across the room and stepped into the hallway where a single taper burned on a stand. We were above the bottom floor and on a gallery from which several doors opened. I knew the last one, where I had lived when I worked for the old loom maker Barnabus, would be too small.

Besides, if my brother were wont to keep late hours, he would not choose that sunny room.

Since August had provided us with the grandest room, I chose the next door. I tried the latch. It opened. I pushed. The hinges squeaked. I summoned my last bit of courage and held the candle high. An empty bed stood at the far end of the room. It was not even made up for use, but had blankets and pillows folded in a stack at the foot of it. I tried the next door. A bed was laid out in that room, but had not been slept within. Yet, as I looked about, I knew this was not a room well used, for no clothing hung on hooks, no belt or boots stood by the cold fireplace.

I peeked into the gallery before stepping out of the room. I tried the next door and found the latch had been locked from the inside. I felt at odds with myself now, foolish, and decided against going to the next two rooms. I turned and nearly bumped right into a man. I covered my mouth with one hand and stifled a scream. "Cullah!"

"Wife, what are you doing creeping through this house at this hour? The watchman just called one of the morning."

"I could not sleep. Come back to our room. I must tell you something curious." With the door closed, we sat upon our bed. "I opened the window for fresh air, and—"

"It's none too fresh in this town."

"Aye. But I was watching the moon rise, when I saw a man leave this house by one of the windows in the study below our room. He did it in quiet, in the dark, and he looked up at me."

"Did he see you?"

"I think not."

"Well and aye."

"But Cullah, what if the house has been robbed?"

"Why were you abroad in your shift down the corridor?"

"I thought I should find August, or not, to make out what happened. If I found his room, and he was there in bed, I would alarm him to the intruder. If he were not there, I might suppose the figure leaving the house to be him."

"You cannot leave this alone, my Resolute?"

I frowned and my shoulders dropped from their tense, raised shape.

The blanket dropped off one shoulder. "This is something you knew about?"

"Yes."

"You trust me not at all, Cullah, my husband?"

"I trust you, but the fewer people who know things, the better. If you know it not, you cannot be questioned. You cannot give word against any."

"You will find no man alive more able to hold a secret than I. You understand me so little, husband? Do you not see that in keeping all this from me, I imagine only terror? If I knew the things that work in that head of yours, I would rest easier. I think that you have no thought for my soul, my inner light."

"Careful. You will sound too like a Quaker for some."

"August is not sick, is he? Why would he want me to think that?"

"He believes you would then feel it was God's mercy if he were killed on his mission. And, he assumes you might ask for prayers for his health, which you might, and that would give credence to his ruse. Besides, he would not have you mourning him as a life half lived, nor cursing his devotion to making this a free country from England."

"Treason."

"Yes. Secession from the empire. And the lot of us are in it. Hancock and your brother have been outrunning and outgunning the East India Company. August has another ship fitted with forty guns of his own, a sloop he named *Westwind,* just to do battle against the English navy in the East. He has gone this night to have her unloaded."

"In wharf twenty-one?"

"No. It is always backward. In wharf twelve. And do not ask me to tell you which one is given that number for I do not know. They change the numbers regularly." Cullah breathed and nearly put out the candle flame; his sharp exhalation caused a ribbon of melted wax to run over and onto my hand. "Ah, I'm sorry, Ressie. Let me take the candle for you." I rubbed the hot wax, trying to spread it fast enough that it would not have time to burn, while he placed the candlestick upon the table by the bed. "Now you know. It is a small thing, my part in this, for I would have stood by your brother and swung a sword, and I may yet, but all they have asked is that I carry the word. Now you, my wife, are not only an apple thrower, you are a traitor, too. None of this will come cheaply. Our own son a Tory soldier. I did all I could to keep it from you—"

"But you could not, for I would not have it. I can stand against anything, husband, except the distance you keep between us by not telling me things. You made me no different than an acquaintance."

"I made you safe." He raised the coverlets. We settled into the bed.

"You made me sad."

"If I am caught, they may now come for you as well."

I laid my head upon his shoulder, nestled in the cove of his arm. "You will not be caught. And, I work hard to be honest, Eadan, but it takes constant guarding of my tongue. I am a considerable liar. If I am caught, I will deny knowing. I will not deny you, but I will deny my knowledge."

"I will not deny it. I will stand."

"Cullah."

"Ask me no more, wife. I am grievously tired. As you should be, after the firkin of Madeira you had tonight. Come here to me and rest."

"I am glad my brother is not going to die."

Cullah's answer was to stroke my hair.

"I will tell him in the morning," I said, "how happy I am."

He kissed my head. "You will ruin it, then. Do you not see, Resolute? You must affirm what you have been given to see as truth. That is the lie you must tell. You must act as if a player on a stage. He wants the world at large to believe he is no longer able to command a ship or to fight."

With that, he drifted into quiet slumber. My hand upon his muscular chest moved up and down with his breathing. I thought upon every word just spoken between us. In the morning, we left without seeing August at all, but before we departed, I placed a note to him upon the desk at the end of the parlor.

> *Dearest August. May you find your health renewed soon. Perhaps the physicians may have some new cure. At any rate, please visit when you are well enough to travel.—Ever your faithful and true sister, R.*

CHAPTER 34

June 22, 1765

I went to work on a gown for the Reveres' evening with a heavy heart, hoping every moment to hear from August, fearing to learn the worst. A few mornings later, Cullah opened the door to a knock. I was standing behind him, expecting to find August in some new disguise, though I wondered that he had not given his usual birdcall first. A Redcoat soldier stood there, smiling. "Brendan!" we shouted simultaneously. My heart leaped for joy. Oh, so many nights I had lain awake wondering if he yet lived.

Brendan pulled off his hat and hugged us both. He was so tall and regal in his uniform. Gold braid glistened everywhere. He snapped to a salute. "Pa. Ma? I have brought you an even greater surprise. Wait here."

He returned to the coach and opened the door, helping a young woman from its interior. She in turn looked back and helped a small child down, dusted him off, spoke in his ear, and held his hand as they approached, her arm upon Brendan's arm. The woman was well dressed. Her bonnet was exquisite. Upon her face, a deep vertical scar over the left eye was covered by an eye patch of white linen upon a cord. The patch had been embroidered with cream-colored silk so that it was more a testament to how she meant to be seen than a testament that she could not see. I liked that about her right away, and I thought of Jacob, remembering what a fright he had appeared when first I met him, his grizzled eye socket unhidden for all the world to gape.

"Mother and Father," Brendan began. Only then did I catch how clipped and precise his manner of speech had become. "I would like to introduce to you my wife, Rosalyn, and our son. He has turned three years. Quite a little man already. He's named after the story you used to tell, Ma, about the boy who rescued all the captives from the ship lost at sea. Meet Bertram Willow MacLammond."

"Madam? Sir?" the woman said, and curtsied most gracefully.

"Oh, la!" I cried. I fell upon the girl with hugs and kissed her cheeks. I cared not at all for scars. Cullah took her hand and bowed over it, and gave her a wisp of a kiss on the cheek. "Oh, oh," I said again with my arm about her shoulders. "Rosalyn. Rosalyn. Why did you not write us, son, of such fine news?"

"But I did, Mother. I wrote you when I married and again when Rosalyn was ill. Then when Bertie was born. I sent another letter to tell you we were coming to visit. Now that I'm stationed in Boston proper, with all the buildup, you know, I was so excited to come I could not wait."

"Bertie?" I said, and knelt before the laddie. "Bertie? What a fine name you own. Just like a name I used to know." I felt such a tug, both joy and pain in my heart. The real Bertram Willow had died on that Saracen ship, in so forlorn a place. Died with my father. In telling my children fanciful stories, I had created of his name a boy full of great feats of seamanship, a heroic Ulysses. It was always one of Brendan's favorite stories. "Well, Master Bertie," said I, "I think after a long ride many boys might like pudding with milk on a fine afternoon such as this. What do you say?" I held out my hand to the child.

He took my hand with all the conviction as if he had known me from his birth, and said, "Yes, Mistress. Thank you kindly."

"Why," said Cullah with a laugh, "he's a bonny wee gentleman already." He smirked and added, "The letters did not get through if you didn't pay the cursed stamp fees."

"Come in, come in. We shall have sweets!" I called over my shoulder. "I have made pudding this day for your pa, who is mending after an accident. Follow Master Bertie and me!" I was overjoyed to spread linens on beds for them, using my best and newest.

After supper we talked until Bertie curled up on a blanket atop the inglenook by the fireplace; we talked and laughed and whiled the time until the clock struck one in the morning, and heard how Brendan had met Rosalyn after the war. She told us she had been injured as a child by the lance of an Indian. The next day, Cullah took Brendan and little Bertie with him to his shop. I was happy for that. It would give me time to talk to Rosalyn, but more important to me, I hoped it would raise Cullah's heart and remind him of the work he had left to do.

Rosalyn helped Dorothy and me to create her a gown after a new fashion they were wearing down the coast rather than a mantua. My own gown was a sack dress, gathered in back in box pleats with a couched and embroidered stomacher all made from rose-colored silk moiré, and I relished its elegance as Rosalyn helped me try it on. We had dinner in our house, my old table swaying with the load of food and surrounded by Gwenny's brood, Brendan's as well, and Ben and James. My new daughter was ever pleasing so that I liked her a great deal. I was sad to see them leave, but much encouraged that they would be but a couple of hours' walk from our house.

The evening at the Reveres' home was as so many others had been, with one great change. The room was full of British officers and their ladies, all trying to assume airs of condescension toward us poor colonists. I soon became bored by the small talk and fluttering of the younger women, and sat myself beside Deborah for a while. When a friend called her away, a woman came and sat in Deborah's chair, fanning herself from the flush of a dance in too tight laces. "Good evening," she said with a merry smile.

"Good evening," I returned. She had a decided accent, though not a British one. I suspected she was from one of the more southern colonies, but from the cut of her gown, I wondered if she had just landed on one of the ships from London.

She smiled gaily and said, "Oh, let us not stand on ceremony. I am so tired of some of the women here with whom I have acquaintance. Margaret Gage. Married to the stodgy owl there by the hearth, gesturing with the glass of port. They will have to throw the rug out for the ragpickers after his windy speech to that poor man. Look at him spilling wine with every gesture!" The gentleman to whom she referred was in military uniform, decked with gold braids, paunchy, white-haired naturally rather than wearing a powdered wig.

The lady herself wore neither wig nor cap but a turban wrapped with gold braid and hung with tassels in the new Arabian style. Her hair had not been curled or coiffed but hung from the turban in random disarray like a courtesan or a savage. Smiling, I nodded, curious at such presumption. I looked into her eyes and saw something that opened, as if a trunk lid rose within them, revealing a sparkle of candlelight as if through a shaded lantern flickering there. I said, "Yes, I know of him. General Gage. My husband served under him at Ticonderoga. Good evening. I am Resolute MacLammond. Married to the braw Scotsman by that table, the one with dark hair bending with a kiss now, serving a plate to that girl."

"She's stunning! Are you not jealous of your Scotsman's attentions to so delicate a flower?"

I laughed. "She's our daughter."

"Ah. Good. Excellent." The lady laughed again.

I saw at once her charms were in her disarming manner, though her figure nothing special. She spoke with a delicate lisp, though not a brutal one; it gave her words a soft slurring sound. Her rose-colored gown was near the same shade as my own. "I cannot say I had any idea this evening would be so lavish," I offered. "I will be happy to introduce you to anyone you wish of the colonists."

"I came from quite respectable Presbyterians in New Jersey, though there is the rogue or two, just to keep things interesting. This town is lively. So close to the shore you can smell the ocean some days. Tell me, do you know any truly rapacious ogres?"

"Madam?"

"Surely you know some of Boston's most illustrious gentlemen? I'm looking for one who is a villain at heart for a particular sport of mine, and not the one you think. I find that really devilish men seem to find either simpletons or hags to wed, one who is too stupid to see what he is or one who, if she is clever, is more evil than he. If you know someone here, I should like to meet his wife. I enjoy a good joust."

A chuckle crossed my lips then. "I enjoy them most in secret. I have to live among these people, and I have made enemies enough in my time here. It does not prevent me from imagining, as you say, a good joust. Or a lovely afternoon hanging."

"Ha! I knew I liked you at once. Would you call upon me? Please say yes. I want to know your dressmaker and your husband's tailor, for his coat is exquisite—if I could get Thomas out of that scarlet and into something more delicate, I am sure he would grow to love it. I am so anticipating making acquaintances here in the colony. We have been here but a month and it is dreadfully boring sitting with the macaroni stew."

"Pardon? Macaroni stew?"

She patted my arm with her hand, small and manicured. "The gaggle of girls married to all these officers. 'Macaroni this,' and 'macaroni that' as if they had the vocabulary of a flea. I adore your gown. I see we have similar tastes. What do you think of this turban affair?"

"It is most pleasing, Mistress Gage."

"Now be honest. And call me 'Margaret.'"

"Well, it is unusual. Flattering but, well, Margaret, you catch me off my guard."

"Good, I meant to, for I am secretly quite rude." She smiled again, winning, open. "I'll wager you have more spirit in you than you like to admit. Quite a labor, keeping the horses in check, is it not?"

"The turban is breathtaking, and your hair, so bold."

She leaned toward me as if we were young girls sharing gossip. "You are prevaricating, dear. Would you say it is 'wenchy'?"

"Oh, not at all. Well. If I may say, it is rather savage."

She laughed. "Good. My husband adores it, though in public he criticizes me roundly for it. All the while, see there, he looked again. All the while he complains, he is stoking up the fires for later."

I blushed deeply.

"Oh, how attractive your color becomes when you are alarmed so. Please do call upon me. I could not bear it if you refuse."

"I shall."

"Send your man around to my house in the morning. May we say, Tuesday afternoon tea?"

At first, I reckoned she meant Cullah, then my face dropped as I realized she meant a servant should search out her house and then direct my coachman to it. Had I a coachman. Or a servant. "I will be there."

"Bring your daughter if you'd like. She's charming."

Margaret Gage and I became friends within a couple of weeks. I called at her house, which was not as grand as I expected it to be, and she called upon me, as well. My home could be described as little more than a humble country house. More than a cottage, but nothing like those in Boston. She was gracious in every way, and accepted the cakes and ale or pasties and coffee I offered with aplomb. I guarded my words with her still, and I suspected she knew as much. She, on the other hand, guarded nothing from me. And one day she chided me that I did not have help in my kitchen, but did all myself. "Help in the country is harder to find. My daughters have helped."

"You need a girl in."

I promised her I would think about that, and later, when I was helping

Gwyneth shell some pease, I mentioned it to her. Within a week, with no explanation other than "it seems the right thing to do," Dorothy moved home. She put her things in Gwyneth's old room at the front of the house. I was so happy I sang the day through, though neither she nor Gwenny would admit to their having talked about it. I did not like the idea that my daughters would speak around my knowledge, but at last I accepted it as their having grown so close during the last years.

After the sun set the next Sunday, a wind came up. We were preparing for bed when I heard a strange bird calling outside. It called again. A few minutes later there was a knock at the back of the house. Cullah went outside and around the house. In a few minutes, I heard cartwheels crushing gravel in the road, and the clomping step of a heavy horse. It went past the house and toward the barn. The sound drifted into the wind. I heard nothing for an hour, and then the parlor door swung open. Cullah held it wide. In stepped August and the man who had delivered the message to him before, their arms loaded with heavy crates.

Dolly came down the stairs. "Ma? What is wrong? Pa? Oh, uncle!"

"Get on your wrapper," I called to her. "August Talbot, what have you? Come here by the fire. Will you have something to warm yourself? Brother, will you not introduce your friend? Come. You are welcomed also." How joyful to see him alive!

August and Cullah exchanged looks, but finally the man said, "Call me 'Nathaniel,' Mistress."

"Ressie? I have put quite a stock into your barn in that upper room. Have you a place in the house to hide a few crates? It's going to Parker's warehouse tomorrow night, but for now it would be better these were watched by other than geese and cows."

"Of course." I led him to the panel halfway down the stairs. Nathaniel crawled into the room and lit a lantern, then Cullah and August passed boxes to him.

August looked at me from the corner of his eye. "Powder cartridges and shot."

I nodded. We gave them the remnants of our supper and filled their cups with cider. I had baked bread that day and there was plenty to fill in what the meat could not. We made up a bed for August in Benjamin's old room, and one for Nathaniel on the pull-out stand there in the parlor. I had long ago burned the ticking upon which my Patey had slept, but we replaced it with a few blankets and he promised he would be comfortable.

While I watched them eat and presided over the laying out of blankets and bedding, I could not but feel atremble at what the two men wore. They had long black capes and each wore a beaten but black tricorn hat, just as the one in which our graveyard ghost appeared. Their shirts were black as well as their waistcoats, stockings, and trousers. Both also had wide black kerchiefs around their necks. August carried a leather pouch, rough sewn and oft patched, all stained black, too.

"And, my dear sister," said August after draining his cup. "I have brought you a gift." He pulled from his pouch a smaller cloth sack and handed it to me. "Taken from the captain's quarters of His Great Buffoonery Wallace Spencer's *Long Ridge* out of Jamaica with a hundred barrels of sugar, and I fear, not a ha'penny of tax paid for any." He and Nathaniel laughed conspiratorially.

I slipped the drawstrings and looked inside, then let out a long breath. "August. Cashews! Quick, Dolly, get me a skillet. But"—I stopped, my nose into the sack—"these are stolen?"

"I didn't take them. Some outlaw pirate did. I came by them honestly. A gift from your brother in thanks for all you have done."

"August. If we eat these we shall be guilty."

He cocked his head at me. "I didn't say I stole them. And don't eye me like that, I did not give him a taste of my blade. I traded a sash for them."

I roasted and salted two handfuls of the cashews, sizzling them in their own oil until the house filled with the buttery fragrance. Then I poured them into a trencher and we all sampled. I said, "I have not tasted these in thirty years. Oh, dear August." Then I closed my eyes and my mouth for I could say no more. The taste and smell carried me home, long ago, far away. Warm breezes laden with flowers, sea-green lagoons, hot spices, and the murmur of voices from the kitchen as our women shelled and roasted cashews. Tears ran down my face. Cullah spoke to the men while I drifted on a sea of memories.

Before dawn, I made a large breakfast of meats and tomatoes, beans with onions, and Indian flour cakes dipped in treacle thinned with rum. I served also coffee and hot milk with nutmeg across it and lump sugar in the bottom of each cup. My brother and Nathaniel left while it was still dark in order to arrive at home before anyone saw their strange clothing. Cullah waited until they were gone down the road to pick up his leather apron and sack. He said, "Three men will come to take the shipment into Pennsylvania. They will give you the signal of a white feather in their hatbands. Feed them if you will. I trust them, but keep Dorothy in the house."

"Who is it? Someone we know?" Dorothy asked.

"One of them is one of the Revere boys. The other is your brother Benjamin. The third is a rake and a scoundrel of passing fair. Son of one of the Prescott family. It's better you don't see them, and cannot say when last you did."

Dorothy pursed her lips. "I like Samuel Prescott."

"Aye. I thought you might. Good day, wee one. Help your mother."

"Do you not trust me, Pa?"

He smiled with one side of his mouth. "With my life, yes. But with your pretty face before three strong lads on their way to a foreign land, one of them who might lay eyes on a greater prize than what's in the barn? I'd have to hunt them down and kill one of them and then where would be your uncle's plan?"

"I'm not a child, Pa."

"That's the trouble."

I put my arm around Dolly as he left and I whispered, "Your presence at the Reveres' dinner persuaded half the young bachelors of Boston to become Sons of Liberty."

"As they should," she said. "I would have no man who did not believe in my father's cause."

"I thought you were determined never to marry?"

"I was a child then."

After Margaret's insistent urging, I told her she might be amused to meet Serenity Spencer, who was now living again in Boston while Wallace conducted business. Why, I could not fathom, but though I told Margaret only about my past with Serenity and hinted that I had as a child been enamored of Wallace, her eyes sparkled like diamonds at the prospect, and so she made a date to call upon Serenity provided I would accompany her.

"Was he handsome?" she asked with a sly smirk.

"Very. He is still, I think."

"The devil, they say, goes about in finery."

"And if you believe Beelzebub is as cunning as he is attractive, then I think we have found him."

"Delicious!" Margaret crowed, and clasped her hands to her bosom.

I drove my wagon to August's house and he came with me to the Gages' home. He looked the aristocrat in every way except for his darkened skin and the scar on his face, but it made him present as bold, rakish, and dashing to my lady friend. The air was alive with the fire of their attraction to each other. It grew to the point that I felt odd, as if I should excuse myself and let the lovers at it, until I reminded myself that Margaret was married. For her own sake, I stayed in the room to keep them from each other and we sipped Madeira as sweat flushed my face. Thankfully, August found reason to attend to some business or other on foot, and left us alone.

When the door closed behind him, Margaret turned to me with guilty eyes.

I said, "My brother thinks you quite the beauty."

"Oh? I hadn't noticed." Her voice trembled.

"I think, dear friend, you are lying. The air in this room stifles me."

"Resolute, you shock me." Margaret blushed and went to a window where she appeared to be watching August walk down the road. "Any woman would be flattered by the attention of so vigorous, so dangerous a man."

I stared into the bottom of my glass of wine, looking at my fingers through the glass below a filter of red where they appeared as if they were washed in blood. I wondered if anyone could see that I was closer to August in spirit than to any good church woman. Perhaps I was as dangerous as Margaret. I wished I were at home.

Margaret said, "Let us go immediately and call on the harridan of whom you spoke so highly. Imagine, consorting with Lucifer himself, and still whole? She must be unbelievable. If we arrive at two rather than three, we may find out all sorts of delicious things. I know it is just a few houses down, across the street, but I prefer to arrive in style." As the coachman drove us around the block, I fanned myself and turned my thoughts to preparing to see Serenity. If Margaret longed to search out trouble, she would surely find it there.

Their butler admitted us and showed us to a well-laid sitting room. He scuttled off to find his mistress with a concern on his face that brought a flush to Margaret's cheeks. She wandered about the room, pausing before large, life-sized portraits of Wallace and Serenity. "He's quite smart. What say you, Ressie? Are these good likenesses?"

"Good? I would recognize both of them but the artist has been kind," I said.

"Ah. I do so like a kind painter rather than an honest one. Are they recent?"

"I do not see that it is long past. Perhaps a handful of years."

The butler arrived with a tea service. "The housekeeper wishes you to refresh yourselves. Madam is delayed a moment more."

"Thank you," Margaret said. "We shall pour; you needn't wait."

"Yes, madam," he said, and left.

We drank the tea. We waited. We took a spin around the room, looking at the vases and portraits, the sculpted figurines, the furniture. A clock in a case taller than Cullah sat at one end of the room. It chimed three. Margaret studied it. "Do you think it is correct?" she mused. "Even if we had arrived on time, she has kept us waiting. I say, this one is more than a little trouble. Let's see the house. Perhaps she is asleep in her ale somewhere."

I was shocked to see Margaret open one door after another, surprising the cooks in the kitchen, a maid dusting books in a library. I could do naught but follow her, for I had rather be found with her than alone in the sitting room. At the end of the great hall, Margaret opened yet another door, her tiny, gloved fingers still upon the latch when we saw through that breach Serenity, a riding crop in her hand, standing above a young African woman in neat maid's livery, cringing on the floor. Wallace stood beside Serenity, her arm caught in his hand, the riding crop still poised to come down upon the woman beneath them. Margaret stepped into the room, pulling my skirt so that I followed her, and we watched the scene before us as if it were acted on a stage.

Serenity said, "No more. I will not have it. I will not have her! Do you hear me? No more!"

"What is it to you?" he said, with a low growl in his voice that chilled me. "Mind your business, woman, and leave her to me."

"After I catch you in the act? My God! In the very act in my private salon! Leave her to you? I would sooner burn her at the stake!"

In all of this, the African showed nothing on her face. Margaret elbowed me and arched her brows.

Serenity struggled against Wallace's hand, and finding she could not free her arm, kicked the woman with her foot. "I have guests coming in a few minutes and I will have to entertain all the while knowing what you are about. You make my skin creep! Get her out of my house. Out of my house, now!"

Wallace said, "I paid for her. I'll keep her."

"Either get the slut out of this house or get yourself out! Sell her for nothing, the worthless sack!"

"I'll buy her," I said.

The two of them turned, red-faced, as Margaret gave a squeal of glee and clasped her hands upon her mouth. I said, "I will take her. How much is her price?"

"I paid twenty pounds," Wallace said.

Serenity said, "Sixpence!"

I reached through the slot in my gown to the pocket and pulled out a sixpence. "Here," I said, holding it forth.

Serenity looked from me to Margaret and back to me. "What are you doing here?"

"Mistress Gage asked me to accompany her, to make your introductions."

"But you are not expected until three." She shook her arm from Wallace's hand.

"It is quarter of four," Margaret said. "We waited to be received by you, but apparently you and your husband had household matters to discuss."

"Here is my sixpence," I said. "I insist you give me my girl."

Wallace stormed, "No, by God, the wench is not for sale."

Serenity grasped the coin from my fingers. "Sold! Take that tripe from my floor and never let me see her again." She kicked the woman again and the poor thing curled more into a ball. "Baggage! Slut!" She turned toward Wallace, her lower jaw extended. "Thank you very much. Now I have been made a fool before a new acquaintance, Mistress Gage. What is it about Boston that makes you into such a lusting baboon? I repent the day I married you, you cur!"

Wallace made a smile that was more a sneer and turned to us. "I believe I have enjoyed quite enough female company this afternoon. Mistress MacLammond, please take your purchase and excuse me. Mistress Gage? A pleasure, I am sure. Good day."

Serenity screamed at him. "Where are you going?"

"Out the door. You will hear from my lawyer in the future."

Serenity dropped the riding crop and pulled herself to a chair, falling into it. "I hope a carriage runs over him." After a while, she looked at us. "Get out," she hissed.

I went to the woman still curled on the floor and touched her shoulder. "Come with me," I said, motioning. "Come on, dear. Serenity? Give me a bill of sale."

"Why don't I throw rotted fruit at you instead?"

I picked up the riding crop and pointed at the desk with it. Her eyes widened and I saw fear in them. "There is paper and a quill before you on that table. Write it. Purchased, this date, for sixpence, one African woman named, what is your name, Miss?"

"Tassie," Serenity said, curling her lips. "Her name is Tassie." She scribbled, dipping the quill, dropping blots everywhere and blackening her fingers. "Take this. Take that blackamoor and never let me see her again."

Margaret and I took Tassie's arms as if we were three friends, and we led her from the room. At the front door, Margaret asked her, "Do you have anything to get? Combs or stockings? Anything that is yours?"

"No. No, Mistress."

Margaret looked at me behind Tassie's head, and motioned with her eyes to the carriage out front. When we had gotten in it, Tassie held her head down without looking around. Margaret said, "Well, Resolute, dear. I meant to meet this Mistress Spencer for some jolly entertainment and I believe this afternoon you have given me enough to fill a shocking novel. At any time if you know some other woman who is even half as frolicsome as Mistress Spencer, do include me in your visitation." She smiled so it brought dimples to her cheeks.

"I was astounded at what just occurred," I said.

Margaret giggled. "I loved it!" We drove to her house, then she asked her driver to take me home.

As the coach turned, I feared the girl had fallen asleep. I touched her hand. She jumped. I remembered the goat-whacking stick, that shape and size of a riding crop, and how I would often be so tired after a beating. She sat there in sullen quiet, expecting every touch to be more of the same. "Tassie?"

"Yes, Mistress?"

"Is that your name, the name you were born with?"

"You call me anyt'ing you wants, Mistress."

"I want to call you the name you choose." I felt stunned. I had bought a slave. I owned her. My ears made a noise as if waves from the ocean washed through them. I continued, "And, I want to set you free. I do not know how to do it yet. It must be done legally but I know a lawyer who will help us. Do you feel able to speak to him now?" I reached out and with my finger touched a red, welted line across her cheek. "If you would rather rest a few days, I will understand."

I felt more than saw a mosaic of suspicion and joy playing upon her face. "No, Mistress. Now be plenty a good time."

"I thought so." I pulled the bell chain beside the coach's window. The driver pulled the horses to a halt, and I sent him down a corner toward Daniel Charlesworth's office. "Where will you go?" I asked.

"Don' know, Mistress. Home?"

"Jamaica?"

"How did you know?"

"Wallace Spencer got all his slaves from Jamaica. Aren't you the girl who dropped the wineglass?"

"If you please, I never dropped a glass, Mistress."

"Oh. I thought I remembered you. You were but a child then. I pretended I had dropped the goblet."

"I did not break a glass, Mistress."

"Very well. Do you have any means to get home to Jamaica? Do you have the passage money? Do you have aught to do once you arrive? You must think on those things. You have been a slave. Once you are free, there will be no roof over your head, no matter how miserable. You will have to make your own way. The ways for a woman are few. I could arrange to pay passage for you, but I cannot protect you on the ship or ever again once you arrived there."

"I need to t'ink on that, Mistress. You mean to let me free?"

"I do."

"Why would you do that, Mistress?"

"I wish it."

We stopped at the office where Daniel had worked, though he rarely came in, calling himself retired. A clerk handed me a form of freedom, a transport, an identification document, and said that if I would fill it all out, he would record it then and there. I turned to the girl. "What would you have me put down as your name?"

"Tassie is a slave name. You give me a name, Mistress. I be happy with that."

"When I was a girl, my best friend's name was Allsy."

"That be good, Mistress."

I started to write Allsy on the line given for the name of "person" and stopped. "Allsy is a slave name, too. Are you sure you want that?"

"Give me a white woman's name, Mistress. Give me something so white that it feels like snow on glass."

My eyes opened wider in surprise. "If I change Allsy to Alice? Does that sound good to you?"

"Alice. Alice. It's the sound of snow." She smiled, then turned her face from me.

I thought a moment. "It is indeed."

She nodded, whispering, "Alice."

I wrote "Alice" on the line. "Do you know how old you are?"

"Maybe thirty. Twenty-nine maybe. I was twelve when Master took me. I—I do not know how to count."

I wrote on the paper. I handed it to the clerk, and he wrote again upon another form, passed it to me, and said, "That will be five shillings for filing, and one pound more for the stamp tax, madam."

I reached into my pocket. I had nothing left in it but one of the gold Spanish doubloons I had carried to take to the Reveres' next time I passed by. "You will have to take this," I said.

He disappeared for several minutes. Alice held her Free Status paper as if it were a butterfly that might vanish in her hands. After a while, the man returned and counted out a few pennies into my hand, which I returned to my pocket.

Outside the door, I turned to her. "Alice? I am not cruel enough to say to you that I have done all I can for you and drive away, leaving you on these cobbles, your fate to the winds. You do not have to do anything today. You do not even have to choose what you will do in the future, today. You are free to go, free to come. I need a girl at my house. I will not own a slave, and I do not own you now. You are not bound to come home with me. If you wish to, you may. I am sorry but you may not come as a guest. You would have to work and help me, but I will pay you four pence a day, and I will not ask you to do anything that I do not do also. I have plenty of work. I have a husband, a daughter still at home, and a business weaving and spinning. You could come now, and then decide to leave, and that will be all right. You may want to leave this very moment, and that is all right, too. So I ask you, will you come home with me for a time? Come and see if you wish to stay?"

"Mistress, I want to go home to Jamaica."

How those words twisted my very fibers. "I know. Do you have family there?"

"Maybe. Maybe they's alive. I wish it, Mistress."

"How long since you have seen them?"

"Seventeen years, I t'ink. If I come with you, I can go home tomorrow?"

"Yes. That paper there assures everyone you meet that you are a free woman of color. You keep that sacred as a duppy charm."

She smiled. She was quite comely. I shuddered, thinking of why Wallace had kept her in the house. Thinking of that day he believed that because I had been kept a slave I had been used so. Alice said, "I come with you, then, tonight. Tomorrow I go home to Jamaica."

"Tomorrow."

Alice did not leave the next day. She spent a tentative week, terrified of Cullah, terrified of Roland, even afraid of Benjamin when he visited, and Brendan, too. She scurried about, cleaning, baking breads, sweeping, and washing clothes. She asked me about how she could get passage home to Jamaica. I told her what I knew, and how to find out more later on, should she decide to leave, about what the fare was, and where the boats landed. She was so frightened that it made Cullah troublesome.

He asked me one morning after she left the kitchen with a basket to collect eggs, "What does she think I am? A goat?"

"She thinks you are like Wallace Spencer."

"I don't want to have a woman that foolish in the house."

"She is not foolish. She has been a slave a long time. I told her she is free. If you want her to leave, we are free, too, to send her away."

He gave a great sigh. "Every other time I come home you have brought in some poor soul. Are we to be an inn for the desperate from now on?"

I thought a long moment. At length I said, "Yes." He smiled.

After two weeks, I came in from hanging linen outside to dry, to find the kitchen empty and the front door wide open.

"Alice?" I called. No answer. I called up the stairs. "Alice?"

She was not in any of the bedrooms, nor in the attic. The comb I had given her, the extra skirt and apron, the cloak, all had been removed from Dolly's old bedroom where Alice slept. The bed had been made up neatly. I went down, and down again, to the loom. By the time I reached the front door again, I was winded. I sat upon the bench outside the door. She was gone.

I went back to my chores feeling lonely. I sat at the kitchen table shelling dried beans into a bowl. The door behind me creaked open. A dark-skinned hand came around the door, pushing it slowly. Alice stepped in. "Mistress?"

"Yes, Alice?"

"I walked near all the way to Boston town."

"Did you?"

"All that way, I thought more than I could t'ink before when you asked me to stay or go, to make up my mind. All my life I go where I am told. I didn't know I could do it. If I am by myself for a while, I can t'ink up and down a t'ing from both sides and I can make up a decision in my mind. If I am free, here is what I made up my mind to do. I come to ask you to hire me to keep house for pay. If you like my work, as you have seen it up to now, I make up my mind I have need of pay as a free woman. If you hire me I ask one pound a month."

"That is less than I pay you now."

"Only a little. That is what free housemaids in town gets. One pound a month. I don't aim to be fancy, I want what they gets. I want to be a housemaid in my own shoes."

I knew what she meant. I had not heard that expression since I was small. "I happen to be in need of a housemaid. I believe I will hire you,

Alice. You will work as the family does, five in the morning until eight at night. You may have every other Saturday afternoon off to do whatever you please as long as it is in good moral character. And if you decide you wish to leave, and you have done a good job, I will recommend you to other households providing you give me half a month's notice. Agreed?"

"Agreed, Mistress."

"Put your things away. You will find a room at the top of the stairs where the, the previous housemaid stayed. It is all ready for you."

She smiled. "T'ank you, Mistress."

Fall of 1767 settled in with its gales and flutters of snow followed by warmer days. The garden lay exposed, pumpkins strewn amid dried vines, yellowed beans clinging to poles and cornstalks, dead at the foot but still recklessly in bloom on the tips. Harvest meant constant work. One day as Alice and I picked through cooked pumpkin chunks to crush for pies, testing them with a fork to see if they were done, a wagoner came up our road stirring dust that floated in the misty air. It made a cloud that traveled to where Dolly sat reading aloud the newest pamphlets from Boston, by the doorway under the climbing vines. There were two men. I said, "Go inside. If anything happens, bar the door quick as you can and run upstairs. Alice, ring the bell in the kitchen window with the mallet by it, five rings, to call Gwyneth and Roland and tell them it is dire. Then get yourself upstairs, too. There is another bar on our bedroom door up the stairs. Use it, if you must, and wait in the hidden stairwell."

The driver came to me just as she got within the house. He tipped his battered hat, which once had been cocked all around but was lapping behind and gave him a comical look. In case that was meant to be one of August's "high signs" I put my left hand against my chin and touched my elbow with my right fist, changing it as if I had started to cross my arms and changed my mind. "David Cross, to see Jacob Lamont."

I hesitated. Was that a signal? And was Cross his name or was that also a sign? "I am sorry, Mr. Cross. I do not know a Jacob Lamont." And I did not, for Jacob's Lamont name was Brendan like our son's. "Perhaps you have gotten the wrong instructions." His hands did not move. I touched my cap, wondering if he would respond with the sign that August and all our family and friends used and never told to strangers.

He did not touch his hat again, but said, "No, no, Mistress. I have been this way before. Ain't there a man living here name of Eadan Lamont, then?"

I meant to let my face freeze in its expression. I know not whether it was successful. No one was supposed to know of Cullah's real name. No doubt our children heard me call him "Eadan" now and then, but never those two names together. "You ask too many questions, sir, for a stranger at my gate. Good day." I made as if to go into the house. When I turned, from the corner of my eye I saw that something or someone moved under a tarpaulin in the wagon bed.

"Tell him I got somewhat for him. It has been a long time in coming. Tell him I will wait for him."

"You have the wrong house, sir," I called, then rushed within and barred the door.

To my surprise, I heard the wagon rumbling away. I ran to the stairs and went up, to the room where our children had slept. The window faced the road. I opened it and hung a white napkin from it as the men in the wagon disappeared down the road.

Later, when Cullah, Brendan, and Bertie came home and I was preparing the table for our supper, I told Cullah about the visitors. Rosalyn sat in silence. Cullah grew quiet, but I recognized it as the quiet he assumed when he felt most threatened. "I know no David Cross," he said.

After our son and his family had retired and we lay in bed, Cullah said, "He asked for Jacob Lamont, then Eadan Lamont?" He rubbed his wounded hand with the opposite one. "Did you offer him food or drink? Did he beg any?"

"No. Cullah? How far back goes your name MacLammond? The man knew you and Jacob, I could see. He had no white ribbon or feather. He made no repeat of our signs, in fact, he did not even doff his hat from politeness. What is there in your name, husband, that you have never told me?"

"Nothing, wife. You know the truth. I was a lad when we left Scotland under the name Lamont. Perhaps he is but a friend too stiff in his speech to convince you to let him in the door. It would not be the first person you have turned away for rudeness."

"You do not believe that any more than I."

He was quiet. Then he said, "If aught happens to me, I have given a friend a letter to your brother, in hopes that he will be able to preserve you. I have made a testament and willed you the farm but you cannot work it enough to pay the taxes. If you must, prevail upon Brendan or Gwenny to live with them. Benjamin should be able to make some living in about five years. Of course, Dolly may marry and be able to take you in. Though I think she will never marry."

"Who is this friend who has your letter?"

"Young John Hancock."

"I wish he would marry our Dolly. Gwyneth was quite turned by him once."

"Too late. Married in England and just returned here."

"Do you think he is loyal to the Crown?"

"I think he is loyal to his purse. But he deals with your brother often enough. August Talbot is now captain of Hancock's sloop, the *Liberty*. It is running Dutch goods and British tea enough for the whole province."

Moonlight gave a pale blue gleam to his profile. "Running stolen goods?"

He laughed. "You wouldn't think that of your own brother? No, no. Not stolen. Smuggled in without taxes. Most of the town of Boston covets his presence at their tables. He is become a heroic figure."

"And what of this Mr. Cross?"

"I don't know him." He rolled over and cradled me in his arms. "Wife, I ask you not to worry about him. I will see to the fellow. He has either got the wrong man, or he thinks he may take some advantage of us. I am satisfied with that explanation for I am not a man to be taken advantage of."

"I ask you for your honest answer and you tell me not to worry."

I heard him swallow. "I have been honest with you, Resolute. I was but a boy when I was sentenced to hang alongside Pa. We escaped. We survived getting here. Changed our names. No one could know me by that old name. No one could charge me with rebellion against the king for that king is long dead. This king, this king troubles me a great deal, but I have done my grumbling in secret except for attending town meetings. Let us speak no more of it tonight."

"And learning to shoot a musket from John Parker, well and aye. It troubles me that 'cross' was our secret word, and that he gave it as his name."

"You will have it out, will you not?"

I said, "I will."

"I will not work at the shop till I find an answer for you. Will that please you?"

"Yes."

"Will you sleep then?"

"I may. We must change our secret word. If he has it, and is using it and it is not his name, I could be fooled by it. Let us use 'birch tree' instead."

"Well and aye. 'Birch' it is. Sure you would not rather have 'walnut'? 'Elm'?"

I placed my hand upon his shoulder and left it there. "Do not laugh at me, Eadan. It gives me such pleasure to speak your true name. It fills me with fear to hear it from a stranger."

"Wife, I tell you, you needn't fear. I am here. And you were right, I have lost a bit of finger but I can still wield a sword." He chuckled. "Either sort."

"What? Oh. Oh, that."

"It's been a while, but I remember how it's done. I feel young tonight. We call ourselves the Sons of Liberty, and thinking of myself as a son makes me feel like a colt."

"A colt. Well and aye. You are a fine one, Eadan. We are old. We should not."

"Once, you said that we should not for we were too young."

"Too unmarried, you mean."

"I offered you a bundling board. I seem to remember you preferred it not."

"Because, husband, did you not guess my meaning? Were you so foolish as to think I might trust a bit of board to keep us apart?" I felt brazen. "Did you not know I burned with lust for you? Perhaps we are not so old, even now," I said.

I awoke in the morning with the slight ache of body that the act of love often left me. The sun had spread from the tops of the trees across the fields in striping that ran counter to the plowed rows, so like a woven pattern. Chickens in the yard made gentle noises. I looked out and saw Alice in a warm cloak heading toward the barn with the milking pail. Wrens and finches chirruped and flapped at the berries on a bush next to the kitchen window. From across the field at Gwenny's house, cows lowed, expecting milking. My hair was long enough to brush against my knees, and I held it back as I knelt to bring the kettle to the table. As I filled the kettle from the water bucket, Cullah arose and came behind me, his familiar smell, familiar touch, so natural that I did not stop my action but moved as if we were one. He wrapped me with his arms, his two hands crossing and each taking one of my breasts, giving a light squeeze through my shift. I murmured, "Think not that I am so easily had again, sir knight."

"My princess," he said. Cullah kissed the back of my head. "I am but a poor—"

His words were stopped short by a shout from outside.

"Eadan Lamont! Come forth! In the name of His Majesty, King George the Third, you are under arrest." The voice drowned in a thunder of horses and the rattle of their riders' sabers against boots.

Steady tramping of foot soldiers filled in the rest of my terror. "Cullah! Hide. Go for the barn through the back stairs."

"Get my sword," he said, fastening the button on his pants. "And my pistol."

"No. I shall send them away. Pretend you are not here, Eadan. Hide and live."

"I'll not hide in my own house. I'll not hide behind my wife and my wee daughter." He threw wide the kitchen door, taking a meat cleaver from its hook.

I stood in the doorway. "Cullah!" I shouted. Then I screamed it.

Cullah stood in the yard. Seven soldiers in uniform pointed muskets fixed with bayonets at his midsection. Three officers on horseback stayed upon their mounts behind the foot soldiers. Behind them, a wagon, the driver that man known to us as David Cross. I could see the wagon was now loaded with things, but I could not make out the nature of the things. It looked as if they had taken down a household of furniture. I bit at my rolled fist and held to the door frame.

Cullah said, "What do you men want here?"

One of the men on horseback said, "You are under arrest, Eadan Lamont. Put down that axe and surrender."

"Arrest for what?"

"Put down the axe."

Cullah slipped into the guise of nonchalance I had so often seen him use. He shrugged. "This is no axe," he said. "It is but a kitchen tool. If it were an axe, you men might be in danger of me throwing it. Put down your muskets, men. There is not any reason to try to seem so threatening." Then he spoke to the man on the wagon seat. "You there! David Hardesty! I know you. Ah, you were my friend a month ago. Yesterday you came to threaten my wife, an innocent British citizen. What have you in the wagon?"

The British officer snarled, "Quiet, you!" He pulled a paper from his coat pocket and began to read. ". . . sundry acts of rebellion against His Majesty . . . as a treasonous act have with others ransacked, fired, and destroyed the home of the Provincial Governor of Massachusetts . . . and are known to this plaintiff to be an escaped, condemned prisoner of the Crown come under cover to this colony . . ."

My knees lost strength. From beyond, I saw Roland and Gwyneth coming this way, hurrying, their children behind them, except for the smallest, still sleeping in his crib. Still unaware of the world that had dawned this beautiful day.

Cullah shouted over the man, "You have riffled my shop! I recognize that chest, those gears of my tools. You've torn my saw and wheel asunder, you fool! It cannot be rebuilt. What need have you of it? You will answer for this, Hardesty. You were there! You were there! What did they pay you, Hardesty? Did it take thirty pieces of silver?"

"Be quiet and listen to the charges," one of the foot soldiers said.

"Put down my tools, you British cur!" Cullah shouted. "I will not be quiet. You have nothing to charge me if you charge not the man beside you. I say, Corporal!"

"Major," the man replied. "You men have witnessed it, he refused to hear the charges. Take him."

"Cullah," I cried.

One of the soldiers aimed his musket at me.

Faster than I realized what was happening, Cullah threw the cleaver. He threw it so straight and true it lodged in the arm of the soldier while the man's finger was still reaching for the flash pan. The other soldiers lunged at Cullah. Cullah fought but briefly, for they pummeled him to the ground in such a way that I was surprised later that he survived, and would not except they did not stab him with their bayonets. I wanted to run to him, but I could not move to him for they enclosed him, using the butts of their weapons on him.

"Get him in the wagon," the officer said.

They dragged him, unconscious, to his feet. Cullah awoke. Raging, screaming curses in English and Scots, my Cullah struggled and fought, his meaty arms soon stripped bare of his linen shirt until bleeding, beaten, they tied him in the wagon bed behind the pile of goods from his shop, all the furniture yet to be delivered, all the tools they could tear from the walls and carry from the racks. The major gave a command. The soldiers got their wounded comrade, tied his arm with a kerchief, and helped him into the cart beside Cullah.

It began to roll away. "Cullah!" I cried. Gwyneth and Roland uttered cries, too. The wagon moved. Cullah roared in anger, blood coursing down his face, smeared with dirt and grit, his body lashed to the sides of the wagon like an animal. Fury filled my soul. Screams filled my mouth. The foot soldiers followed the wagon keeping up their terrible rhythmic tramping. "Cullah!" I screamed. I ran after the wagon, following them.

"Resolute! Stay back. Stay there, Resolute!" Cullah called. "Find Brendan!"

On a command from the officer, three of the foot soldiers stopped, turned, and aimed their muskets at me. I ran straight toward them. They had not loaded the pans. They could not yet shoot. I kept on. But they braced themselves and the bayonets gave them a reach far beyond a man with a knife. I stopped. We stood there while the wagon rumbled away, farther down the road toward Boston.

"Where are you taking him?" I begged. "Tell me where!"

The man who'd given orders said, "To be tried. It will either be a judge at the royal administration or back to London. It's his lordship's choice."

"Who? Whose choice is it?"

"Lord Wallace Spencer. He's who made the charge against him."

"Wallace?" My word drifted away into silence. Then all I could hear was the grinding wheel of the wagon, crushing gravel beneath the iron wheel rims. Cullah's head nodded forward as if he'd lost consciousness again.

The soldiers turned and trotted to catch up with their fellows. I ran behind them. I ran until my breath would not come, crying Cullah's name, screaming my heart out, until I felt something burst in my throat. I tasted blood. I could not keep up. The horses and the men outpaced me and the wagon got smaller and smaller until it rounded a corner and I could see it no longer. I cried out once more and fell on my face in the road. I lay there for many minutes, breathing in the dust, sobbing into the rocks and grass and filth from years of horses. I had no shoes. I had no wrapper on. Blood dripped from my lips.

Gwenny rushed upon me with a cloak and wrapped it around. I watched, dull-witted, as if they would turn round and return. Gwenny brushed grass from my hair. "Ma?" I could hear. Someone called again, "Ma?"

CHAPTER 35

October 1767

On Sunday next, I sat between Alice and Dolly, listening to Reverend Clarke, myself still unable to speak. My throat ruptured and bled anew if I spoke. Rather than Bible texts, he used my husband as an example of our rights being trampled by a Crown that had no feeling for its own people. He read aloud the Declaratory Act, which proclaimed that "in all cases whatsoever, Parliament had taken away the rights of all British Citizens to an open trial by jury." At the end of the reading of the act, the last paragraph said that anyone arrested for any suspicion named upon them would be transported to the Vice-Admiralty Court in Halifax, Nova Scotia, and tried by a single judge in the employ of the Crown. There would be no defense, no witnesses called, only a reading of the charge and judgment by a Crown appointee. No longer were colonists to hire their judges. The Crown owned them, and rewarded them for the fines they levied. Reverend Clarke said, "If we can no longer control the hiring of those whom we see fit to judge us of our wrongs, we have lost the rights of free British citizenry granted by the Magna Charta."

Those around me were enraged on our behalf. They patted my hands, said soothing words. But that did not bring Cullah home. Several of the men who were in the practice of law offered to write letters to Parliament, and to those I agreed. "I will pay you," I offered, though they all declined to accept my money. At home, I wept. I wandered through the house, calling his name, crying out. Dorothy feared I had gone mad, I believed. Perhaps Alice did, too. I cared not. I could not lie down for blood from my throat choked me. I was mad. Mad with fear and anger. Raging, yet mute, for my throat, said Dr. Warren, might never heal.

During those first weeks, visits from Reverend Clarke kept me thinking there was yet hope, but when he left, and I closed the door, though I had tried to smile, as soon as the latch slipped into place, I wept anew. I woke up at night, hearing Goody Carnegie howling in the wind. I tried to cry out, but my muteness felt as if the cleaver Cullah had thrown had landed in my own throat. It hurt as if an egg-sized scar had formed, and I could make nary a whisper. I wept and sobbed so that my inhalations made cawing sounds like a child taken with throat distemper. It pained me so not to be able to hear his name from my own lips, that I cried the harder, and wept myself to sleep. I dreamed of my childhood. Of running across the widow's walk to watch gulls diving in the air. Of Ma and Pa, and Allsy. And of jumping over a candle. I sat up in bed, crying out, "Eadan!" Had I doomed all I loved by that one candle?

October 26, 1767. Cold weather made chills in my feet and ankles as I walked to Boston to see Margaret Gage. I hoped to implore her to seek her husband out on my behalf, though I had not seen her since that terrible day. I had not been able to locate Brendan, who I hoped would help me appeal to some commander or other. Since Margaret's husband was the general and the troops who had taken Cullah were his men they could as easily bring him home. I feared she might not receive me, though her butler showed me in just as always. I sat in her parlor, fidgeting with my bonnet ribbons. When she entered, I stood and cleared my throat, for I was still quite hoarse. I whispered, "Margaret, if you would rather I leave, please say so. We have too much honesty between us for you to act as if nothing were wrong between us."

She lowered her chin and looked at me under her frown. "I would not rather you left, Ressie."

"Let me speak frankly with your husband."

"Thomas is not here to ask, dear friend. They are shipping thousands more soldiers of foot here this month and he is dashing everywhere at once."

I sobbed, saying, "They have taken my Cullah. He will not live through this, Margaret. I know him. His anger will betray him like no accusation could."

"Who has accused him?"

"Wallace Spencer."

"Oh, no."

I waited.

"Did he do the things of which he is accused?"

"Even if I knew, I could not claim it against my husband. I only know he is accused."

"Spencer is making specious claims to torment you?"

I said, "I know he would do anything to hurt me. It has been his life-long passion."

"You hurt him so much?"

"I hurt him? He deserted me, at night, alone in a filthy wharf tavern. He disappointed his mother so much that she left her house to my brother August."

"He resents your happiness, and longs for your love, or he would forget you rather than chase you. Perhaps," she said, taking a long breath, "perhaps you should ask him to withdraw the charges."

I stared at the rug. "I will. I will ask him that. I know not whether he still resides in Boston."

"He does. He has already returned to their house. I am sure it is deliciously ghastly, the two of them alone there. Did you hear one of their sons took a sack and unloaded the silver service and ran off to New York with one of their yellow African slaves? Another one is a cripple for taking opium, and it is told one of their daughters does the same."

"The thought of talking to him sickens me. I would have to find him without Serenity near, for when she is about everything becomes a mere aside to her jealousy. Would you come with me?"

"What would you say to him?"

"That I would do anything to save my Cullah." Tears coursed down my cheeks.

Margaret hugged me, and I her. "Don't tell him that. You know what he'd require. The man's a he-goat and he'd use you under pretext and still not help you. Tell me when, and I will arrange an invitation for Serenity so you'll have him alone."

"Tomorrow?"

"As good as done."

"Thank you so. This may do more to help him than all the lawyers in Boston."

"I daresay. Now, would you have wine?"

At three in the afternoon the following day, I arrived at the Spencers' home in our wagon. Roland drove it. Alice sat in it, waiting. I had dressed to appear, I hoped, appealing. I felt keenly aware of the fine lines under my eyes, and I had rubbed raw apple on them to tighten the skin. I walked up the steps and rapped the knocker. The butler raised his eyes and showed me to the parlor. A few minutes later, he returned and said, "Master Lord Spencer would see you in the study, Mistress. If you will follow me?"

The study was a man's lair. A room of darkened wood and books, two suits of armor on stands, the walls hung about with stuffed creatures such as I had never seen. Wallace stood and bowed with politeness that would have pleased a king. "Mistress MacLammond, I am flattered by your visit. How lovely you look. Time has been good to you, Ressie. One would think you had some witchcraft to keep so beautiful."

Until he had said the last, I had absorbed his statements with good humor, but witchcraft? That was Wallace as I knew him. Poison at the core like the seeds of an apple. I smiled and said, "You are too kind, Lord Spencer. I am humbled by your attention."

"Will you have claret?"

"Thank you." I must save Cullah, spoke my heart. Think of Eadan. Think of him.

He poured two small cut-crystal stemmed glasses, the same type that I had once claimed to have broken. "I am so relieved that you have seen fit to forgive my wife for that unfortunate scene when last you called. I'm sure she was just having a spell. She does now and then. Unfortunately, she is out just now."

"Lord Spencer, oh Wallace, I knew she was out. I wished to speak to you alone."

"Oh? Well, well, Ressie. I am flattered indeed." He sat before me and pulled the chair closer so that his knees touched my own. "How, dear lady, may I serve you?"

I took several deep breaths, remembering everything I meant to say as I had rehearsed it. At last, I looked into his eyes, putting in my heart the feelings I had not for Wallace but for Eadan, so that I could speak with my love upon my face. I knew that he would see it and mistake its meaning. "Wallace? I have ever remembered our earliest friendship with great fondness, and considered the enmity between us as a natural product of jealousy between silly women. I know you are not jealous, but we foolish women, myself especially, I was always—troubled—by Serenity and your love for her." I watched as a flush rose under his collar. Perfect. "I believe, no, I hope, that you do not hold that against me." He smiled. Much, I thought, like the lipless grin of a snake. He leaned toward me and sipped the claret. I continued. "You have heard, have you not, that my husband has been arrested?"

"I have." He stiffened and sat more upright in his chair.

"I know it is too forward of me, Wallace, too assuming upon our past friendship, but I hoped I could prevail upon you to ask his release. He is a very ordinary man, you see. Without your complexities of aristocracy. I was young, and without you, and without you I was heartbroken. He seemed good at heart and honest, and hardworking enough to give me security. Security is important to a woman, for we have no honest means of making it ourselves." Then I made my boldest move yet. With the same movement that I had seen Margaret use to unmask many a farce and loosen many a tongue, I raised my right hand and artlessly let it fall upon Wallace's wrist as if we were long in the habit of touching each other. As I did, I opened my mouth to continue my speech.

Wallace's eyes closed lazily and he cocked his head. "Save your wiles, Resolute MacLammond, for you are not good at it. You think you have come here to seduce me into letting a criminal go? Do you think you are that desirable any longer?"

I pulled my hand back as if I had been stung, but Cullah was at stake. I was determined to continue the flattery until he threw me out. "I meant only friendship, not seduction. Perhaps I misread what I thought was compassion in your eyes."

Wallace lunged at me, tossing aside his glass as he did, and taking my head in both his hands, he kissed me, pressing my lips apart with his so that I felt assaulted by him. When he stopped, he asked, "What would you do, Resolute, to have your man back at your hearth and in your bed?"

I felt the hoarseness overtake me and struggled to speak. "I ask only for your help. Someone has charged him with treason. They've destroyed his shop and carted away his work. Thrown him in prison."

He kissed me again, and clinging more closely, knelt before me, pushing one of his legs between my knees. He stopped, his own face reddened and his lips swollen as mine felt. "You can barely speak. Have I aroused you so? After all these years, tell me, what would you do for Eadan Lamont?" Wallace ran his hand up my back and under my bonnet, loosening it, pulling it down, rummaging with my hair so that it began to fall in wisps. "Eadan Lamont, who should have hung when he was eight years old? Who attacked the royal governor in his home and burned it down? Eadan Lamont, who assists your scourge of a pirate brother in taking down my ships and smuggling stolen cargo, so that I am forced to pay more for cannon to defend them than for the cinnamon and silk they carry? That Eadan Lamont? Pirates, you see, are not a noble lot. One of them recognized the sign the so-called Cullah MacLammond carved into the backs of all his work, crated on their ship, as a clan insignia. Lamonts are pathetically uninventive in passing out names. The only one the blighter could come up with was Eadan, and would you imagine it? There was an Eadan Lamont still wanted on the rolls of the royal sheriff, disappeared into the American colonies. Naturally, I had to do my duty as a citizen and turn in a criminal." Wallace grabbed a handful of my hair and pulled it, jerking it just so that I knew he had me fast. "What would you do to save them both? For August Talbot's rotted corpse will hang in chains at the crossroads before your own house by the end of this year. When the bones fall apart, I will personally wire them together so he will stare at you with his hollow eye sockets for the rest of your life."

He held my hair but of course, he did not hold my heart, and though he tore both out, I would flatter him no longer. "I have friends. Powerful friends." I would ask Margaret's husband to intercede, I thought desperately.

"Who, Revere? That Frenchman?"

Suddenly it occurred to me that Thomas Gage might not listen to his wife any more than Wallace would listen to Serenity. "I am asking you, Lord Spencer, Wallace, begging you for mercy, for lenience. But if you think I would sacrifice my body on the altar of your pride, you are mistaken. If you think I would betray my husband and my children because I am idiotic enough to believe you mean anything you say, you are mistaken. If you think you are worth having at all, you are mistaken." With every word I said, he pulled my hair tighter and tighter. "I feel sorry for you, Wallace. Sorry that you will never know love. I would die for Cullah, and I will not lower myself to you for him."

"I could break your neck, with one"—he tugged—"quick"—he tugged again—"twist."

I stared into his eyes. "But you won't," I said. To my great surprise, there rose a rim of tear in each. I said nothing but kept looking at his eyes. He took his hand from my hair and stood. He walked to his credenza and poured himself another glass of wine, drank it, and poured another before he turned around. I said, "You know the charges could be dropped."

"You know they are true."

"What would you have me do? Beg you on my knees?"

"Good day, Mistress MacLammond. Or should I say Lamont?"

I stood and replaced my cap and bonnet, letting the hair hang as it fell. I walked to the doorway and turned.

He drained the wine again. "We shall see who wins this, Resolute. You came here to make a fool of me. Your brother is trying to destroy me. I would as soon watch you hang with him."

I ran from the house, leaving the front door wide. Roland helped me into the wagon, snapping the reins over the round and patient rumps of our plow horses.

All Saints' Day loomed. I had prepared ribbons and tied them around dried Indian corn in pretty clusters to decorate all the graves. A sudden snowfall melted rapidly and wind dried the ground. The weather warmed, but the golds and crimsons and oranges of the woods gave me no warmth, no joy. My clothes hung on me as if they had been outfitted on a scarecrow. I tried to weave and spin, but my work was not fit for rags.

On a day so warm I needed no shawl, I walked beyond the garden to clear new ground with the hoe while Alice swept the house. I was determined to plant bayberry so that I would not have to go so far into the woods hunting it. The seeds would lie in the ground over the winter and sprout in the spring. I imagined every chop of my hoe coming down upon Wallace Spencer. White stone came up with the dark brown. First two white stones, then a dozen. I bent low and picked up a couple of them. They were not stones. They were bones. I chewed my upper lip with my teeth. I went to find Roland. Gwenny's children played outside in a puddle, merrily painting stripes upon their legs with mud, a few yards from where she had hung a freshly washed blanket to dry in the sun.

Roland and James came with shovels. Together we scraped away soil until we came to a human skull. If it had been a grave, I thought, it was a rude one, no more than a foot at the deepest, and less than six inches of soil covered it at the head. It was tall. The man had been wrapped in a black cloak and buried. In his still awkward English, Roland said, "He seems buried quickly. By someone lazy." James crossed himself.

I added, "Or perhaps someone not strong enough to dig it." I stared at this form, a reminder of what little fiber was a man, what little time our flesh had upon this earth.

Roland turned over another shovelful of soil by its head. The remains of a three-cornered hat came up on the end of the shovel. It was not a fine one of beaver fur, but a roguish felt well tarred, as they wore on the ships. As the hat came up, it tore itself in half by the weight of soil which had collected within its crown.

"Do you suppose he haunts the dell where he would rather lie in peace, next to his child? He is always there, by the little unwritten stone. Should we move him? Is it sacred to leave him here or put him where he would choose to lie?" I asked.

Roland looked at me with fierce determination. "If we disturb his bones, he may change from haunting the graves to haunting the house."

"We must ask *l'pasteur* to move these bones," James added.

I was not happy with leaving this skeleton open to the sun while we went to seek counsel from Reverend Clarke so I said, "Will you fetch him? I will wait here in case the children come this way."

Reverend Clarke arrived in about an hour with three other men. They helped Roland dig a proper new grave, and they lifted the bones onto an old horse blanket to carry them to their new resting place. Roland tipped the skull to set it atop the crossed bones, and something small and heavy slipped from its opening to his feet. He jumped as if he had been stung, but he stooped and picked the thing up and said, "Maybe the disease that killed him was lead in the brains." On his hand, a smashed ball from a musket.

Reverend Clarke prayed a lengthy prayer over the bones before we covered them with the blanket. We tucked in the hat and laid his rotted cloak over him, then fashioned a cross out of red maple leaves over it. Last, they started shoveling in the dirt. I said my own secret prayer, talking to the man himself, asking him if these were his bones that he might rest in peace now, amidst the others buried here, and stop walking the earth.

I went to the graveyard on All Hallows to clean and decorate the graves for All Saints' Day. I stood next to the small, unmarked stone, facing the vine-covered rocks. I turned about. Turned again. The spirit in the black cape did not appear. I said another prayer, hoping for the man, at last, eternal rest. I smiled. I patted the headstone of my darling Barbara. The wind began to blow. A gust flung leaves about me, spinning as if I were caught in a whirlwind. I hurried home and did not look back.

That night, I sat alone at my bedside by a single candle. I had gone through my trunk and pulled out Goody Carnegie's old book of leech-craft and herbs. Much of it I could not read, for it was in an old style of words and lettering, though some was in modern hand toward the last pages. I paged through it, scanning for anything readable, until I found a page that seemed writ not in ink but in some faded brown. The words chilled me so that I pulled my shawl closer about my shoulders and read it again.

Fairies ha tak my husbnd. I teld them to bring him home and say'd many charms for it, tho this one demanded I be mad. No, say I, I shall not be had by fair folk, & I pointed at it a smoking pistol. The fairy left him, then, when the bullet went in, but my husbnd was not returned to me. I buried the old fairy skin out in the pasture and the cows are afraid to eat the grass thereof.

I crossed myself as I might have in the old days, and turned still more pages, filled with receipts for concoctions and cures using herbs with names I knew not. All seemed then to be written in ink, and in English. Until again, a page writ in brown—could it have been blood?—and telling a story that brought me tears.

Abigail be tak by fair folk. I saw them running with her beyond the field where the cows graze, and what was left in her place was an old nasty fairy woman. And I teld it I would burn it to bring back my child, yet it did naught but whimper. I say'd to it, leave her be, And then it called up a storm. & so I burned it and buried it in the dell below the house. Water cress and a salmon's tail I put therein, and walked around it three times three.

I flipped to the last page. Near the end of the book was another writing in the old script that I could not read. I expected it was the final entry she had made, and turned back a few pages. There I read:

Abigail has grown up in the fairyland & escaped after all the leaves I have burnt for her. She came home and knew me but for the sake of townfolk pretended not. I have made her to stay in the old house. If she stay in this house where fairies live in the shadows, she will be tak again and I will have to put her in the fire again. Abigail asked me to stay home from the storm but for her sake I ran fast eno to keep her safe & not burn her.

I tore the page from the book. The paper was yellowed with age though the ink bright. Leafing backward, I found again the other pages where she had confessed to murders of her husband and child. I tried to tear them out. I creased them with my scissor and worked them out, stirred up the coals in my fireplace, and laid the three papers upon them. I said a prayer, then sat watching the smoke rise to the chimney, remembering Goody

Carnegie's kindness to me, and yet feeling sure that the brown ink had once been red blood, and that some darkness had filled the old stone house where she had lived, now home to James. I looked down at the book in my hand. I had always known books, could not remember not being able to read. For me, to destroy a book was a crime. Was this volume I held a book of spells, or the ramblings of a madwoman? Was it a priceless volume of antiquity, or the habitation of Satan, able to unleash charms and spells from a time long past that should never see daylight again? I said another prayer, this time Memorare, and in English, Our Father. Feeling as if I knew not the right thing to do, I opened the tragic old book and made ready to lay it in the ashes.

It burst into flame, ripples of color dancing above the thing. I dropped it into the fire as I said, "If, just if, there is magic in this book of a kind I know not, if there is power beyond this earth, send this fire to keep Eadan warm. Take this smoke to keep him full. Bind away all pain from him and bring him home to me." Then I was filled with fear and dread that I had brought Satan himself into my life by my own selfish longing. I prayed on my knees through a Rosary, and sat up the night through, begging forgiveness.

Though I wrote letter after letter to the magistrate in Nova Scotia, I heard nothing. I sent a cloak to "the prisoner, Eadan Lamont," though feeling uncertain to use his real name even as I did so. I sent a coat, too, made from his pattern. I stayed at my loom until my back felt as if it were growing a crook in it.

At times, I could sell nothing, for the searches and the soldiers questioning everyone who went down the roads either to Lexington or to Concord. Boston was all but emptied of commerce. Battleships were said to be anchored in the harbors to ward off smugglers and to keep the peace by intimidating any colonists who remained. The Crown passed new duties on paper, paint, lead, glass, and tea. They sent soldiers to count our trees and handed me a tax bill for every one of them that still had apples or pears clinging to it. I put the bill into the fireplace and warmed our cider with it. I told Alice I was not flaunting the king's authority, as much as I was in need of kindling. She gave me a look that frightened me, for I knew not whether she mutely approved of it.

Our friends began to organize groups and meet in the woods, in houses. I let them use our barn for meetings and even drilling in formations like soldiers, but I allowed no firing of muskets.

At the end of January 1769, on a bitterly cold day, Alice sat sewing while I spun fine linen I meant to weave into a cloth of silk tracing, and Dolly read aloud to us from a sermon at one of the Boston churches. It was another leaflet that had been smuggled in and out of that town, for Boston was by then completely occupied by the army. The fire in the grate crackled while snow drifted down in light flurries that moved about as if they were living things, dancing across the fields.

The sound of wheels of a light carriage interrupted our talk and I stood from my work, pressing my hand against the wheel to slow it. I stopped at the door. No one had knocked from outside but the carriage had stopped. I waited. The others watched me. I inclined my head toward the door and felt an agony awaited the opening of it. At last, a hand rapped upon the wood and caused me to start.

Dolly said, "Ma? Will you open it? Do you want me to do it?"

"I will open it." I raised the latch and let it swing open. The tall, imposing figure of Reverend Clarke filled the gray, misty day. He removed his hat upon seeing me. I said, "Please come in, sir. Are there others?"

"I came alone, Mistress MacLammond. Good day, ladies. Miss MacLammond. May I sit at your fire?" I sat on the settle where Cullah and I had shared so many, many chilly nights. Reverend Clarke took my hands in his and petted them the way you might stroke a piece of leather or cloth, to note the strength of it. He took a deep breath, and said, "Mistress MacLammond, your husband is dead. It came in word to me, a written letter, that is. One of our men carries the post and thought it best if I bring it and tell you, so that you are not informed as if it were nothing of consequence. I am deeply sorry. We knew Cullah to be a fine, upright man. If he did wrong, he did it in the name of the freedoms we all seek to maintain—"

I raised my hand to stop his deluge of words. The pastor was a kind and loving man, but he did like to talk. And talk was not what I wanted right then. Cullah answered every conflict with silence. I wanted silence. I stared at the hearth. It could not be true. Dorothy sobbed. Alice comforted her, patting her back. An ash popped just then and tumbled toward me. "Thank you," I whispered. "For coming."

"I am so sorry."

"How? How did he die? Did they shoot him? Hang him?"

He pulled the letter from his coat. "No. He was sentenced to a year. He had already served it and was released." He laid his hand upon mine again. "He was much reduced by then. Starved and beaten. They turned him out before Christmas and he began to walk south. The weather, as you know, was more bitter than here. The letter said he was found by a swamp, frozen to death, one of your letters in his pocket."

"He had no cloak? I sent two." I gulped and stared into the fire, saying, "He had not even a shirt, for they tore it from him. My husband frozen to death in a swamp? After all he risked, to die like a sick animal. It would have been kinder to put him in a noose."

"They write that he was a cooperative and gentle prisoner. He was liked."

How many times had I stopped what I was doing, listened to the air, waiting to hear Cullah whistling, merry, smelling of rosewater, and lifting me in his arms? "Liked? Liked not well enough to give the poor wight a shirt."

His face bore deep sympathy. "I am sorry, Widow MacLammond. I have the church's widow's offering for you." He placed a folded paper in my hand. It was heavy, wrapped within it, a few coins.

I looked down at the paper, afraid my tears would overcome me. I had probably donated the coins now come to me. "I would rather you gave them to someone else."

"I know, but keep it. You might need it for something which you do not yet know."

"I have been without him almost as long as I was when he was sent to war. I know how to be alone."

"For your Dorothy, then."

"For Dorothy." I squeezed the coins to my bosom and bowed my head over them. Then I said, "Will you have food, Reverend? Will you have meat and hot cider?"

"Thank you." He ate with us, sparingly, as befits someone conscious of the meager means of a widow, and then drove his sad curricle away from my door.

I held Dolly and cried. Finally, it grew late and we went to bed. I argued with the darkness. "It was not he. My Cullah is coming home. He will come back to me." When I slept, it seemed the darkness clawed at my ankles while I clambered up a stair of a thousand steps. "Allsy, come with me!" I called. "Come to the widow's walk."

"It is too far to climb. The wind will take you away and dash you to your death."

"Allsy, do not leave me alone! I cannot be here alone. I cannot stand it. I am so afraid. Open that door! Unlock it. Do not leave me here!" I ran from one end of the widow's walk to the other, trapped. There was no way down once Allsy shut the door behind me and locked it, for the door itself vanished. I raised my hands to the sky, to one of the gulls laughing at me. "Take me with you, Cullah. I want to fly."

I jumped toward the gull. I felt the roughness of its toes within my grasp but it darted away before I could close my fingers. I fell, not drifting like a feather on a breeze, but flat, a stone in dead drop to the beach. I tasted sand.

I opened my eyes. Someone held a candle above me and the glare of it hurt my eyes. "What are you doing, Dolly? How long have I been asleep?"

"Two days, Ma."

I said, "I have to get up." I dressed, stunned at how feeble I felt. Little by little that spring, my strength returned.

When March turned to April, one day I was alone in the house. I pushed open the door to the secret room over the loom. I crawled inside the small doorway then backed out again but returned with two large candlesticks that held three lights each and a stob from the fireplace. I lit all six candles.

The room seemed alive with the feeling of Cullah's having been the last person there. The dust motes stirred under the flare of the candles. Hung on the wall, as if he would return any moment, were his claymore, his pipes, a worn leathern shirt, and a length of plaid. Under that was the old chest. I opened it. Inside it held a pair of soot-black leggings, trousers not made by my hands. A ragged and scunging black woolen shirt lay folded atop a black cloak, thin and torn in a multitude of places. It looked useless, and it, too, I could see, was not made by me. There was a folded linen, also black. Someone had gashed it. I clucked my tongue. People could be so unthinking of fine cloth. I raised it to judge whether it were worth cutting for something else. Then I saw that the two gashes were eyeholes. I laid the cloth over my head and peered through the eyes. His hat was still on its peg. How did he keep this upon his face? Another folded cloth lay below this one. It had been knotted in the end so that it made a headscarf. I put it on. This was how my husband had slipped through the woods. I felt a surge of power, a feeling almost as if Cullah had lifted me and swung me like a bell.

"*Tante?*"

I jumped with such violence that one of the candles tumbled, still lit, into the open trunk. I pulled the cloth, blowing out the smoldering cinder. "What do you want, James?"

"What is this place?"

"A room. Just a room."

"A hiding place." He paused, searching for words. "Those are weapons. And there, rolls of cloth you have not paid tax for. It is lawless. God ordains all kings and you and your husband shun the laws of this land. Your brother, my uncle, is an outlaw and now your husband is as well."

"My husband is dead. These rolls of cloth incur no tax sitting here, for I made them and intend to use them. Do you mean to make charges against us, James?" I felt fear and anger welling. I smelled the hatred in my soul, the brimstone of hell, for all that his father had done. I saw Rafe MacAlister in James's face and the memory of Goody Carnegie's book of herbs and stories exploded again before my eyes, as if Lucifer himself stood before me.

He thought again, far too long, so that I felt keenly uncomfortable. Then he said, "It is a Christian's place to bow to the authority given him, but I am a French citizen first, and not a British one. Perhaps I should leave, *tante*."

I could no longer bridle my anger. "For New Orleans? I'm sure there are no godless outlaws there. Perhaps you should have stayed in Montréal," I snapped at him. I would be glad to see the heels of his shoes, I vowed. Then my heart lurched within me. "James, are you willing to join the British army to quell the people of this continent for their love of independence? Would you see us turned out, our farm taken, so King George could buy another cannon to shoot other Frenchmen?"

"No. Not that. It is not as simple a decision as that. I had come to find you to tell you I have been thinking for three days that the time has come for me now to head south, that I had decided to go. I appreciate all you have done for me, but I am really no farmer. I think I will make my way in some kind of trading on the river."

"Then I am sorry for being angry with you just now. I thought you were condemning me. What will you trade?" Even as I spoke, I had to push away thoughts of Satan's beguiling ways.

He smiled, a genuine, honest face, with no guile, I saw. Not Rafe MacAlister, but Patey's abandoned and forgotten son. "I have learned much about the price of woolens."

We laughed together. "I have some, but I will not sell them to you, because then we would have to pay taxes. I will give them to you, to start your trading business, but I will write you a bill that shows you own them. And, James, I wish you the best of fortune. Will you help me sort them? I can tell you much about how to keep moths away."

James nodded and turned away just as someone rapped at the front door, making it rattle in its hinges. I climbed from the room and straightened the panel, then my cap. The gusty air of April seemed to press against the door as it opened.

Margaret Gage swooped at me. "I just heard, Ressie. Oh, poor dear. Oh, dear. Poor Cullah. And your sweet Dolly, I am so fond of her. She must be heartsick. Oh, dear, your heart must be broken. My husband said it was a terrible shame. It was not his doing, I swear it. Please say you will come to Boston for a few days? Please say you will. I so want to be near you at a time like this."

My face went slack. Painful, bitter tears flowed yet again, and I let her clasp me as Patience once did, my arms round her waist. I looked about at my house, my Dorothy standing as still as an ice-covered tree. "That is so kind of you, Margaret, but I could not leave my house." In truth, I cared not what Margaret wanted, for I was numb.

"I meant all of you. Alice, too. Please do come."

Dolly spoke up. "Your horse is wandering, Mistress Gage. I'll get him."

I raised my brows at Margaret. "You rode horseback?"

"What else could I do? I had to come to you the moment I heard."

I marveled at her to have jumped upon a horse to be with me. I smiled, though it felt weak and trembling, even to me, and said, "If you will have the three of us, I shall come, then, Margaret."

"Oh, my sweet friend. You are so kind to me," she said.

"Kind to you?"

"I feared that you somehow placed blame upon me."

Without a knock or waiting for us to open, Gwyneth let herself in. "Ma?"

"Gwenny? You look afright."

"I cannot find Sally. She wandered out the door while I was changing Peter's clouties."

"She cannot have gone far."

"You know that one. She has feet like wings. And the sun is setting."

"Where is Roland?"

"At a meeting in Concord. I sent Nathan to the Parkers' and Dodsils' to ask help."

Margaret fastened her bonnet, too, and followed fast on my heels. We went first toward Gwyneth's house, calling for my next-smallest grandchild. The babe, Peter, cried, so that Gwenny was forced to stop and feed him, but carried him with her, calling Sally.

The sun set. Roland and James joined the search. Before long, everyone was hoarse from calling. We fetched lanterns, and the neighbors came with more lanterns, so that our woods was alive with moving lights. It seemed as if we had just begun when the sky turned such a strange color it seemed lit from some magic within the woods and hills. It was sunrise.

I told Gwenny I had to fetch water for my throat, so weakened since that terrible day that I had nearly lost my voice calling for Sally. I opened the door to the barn to go through it to the house simply to save a few steps. I felt such panic, such rushing of need, as if every step I wasted could cost the life of this wee girl.

Out of the corner of my eye, I saw a flash of gray-green amongst the dry hay where a single needle of sunlight illuminated a bit of cloth. One of the cows, ripe with its own odor, lay there, chewing cud. At the cow's back, a wee form. Whether she slept or had died there, crushed perhaps, or fallen from the loft overhead, I could not tell. Teeth clenched, I let myself in and the cow stood. To my horror, beside the child, half buried in straw, lay the form of a man. His clothing was tattered to shreds, his long hair and beard knotted and greasy, and his skin scaled. I pushed the cow and went to Sally. "Is this Grandma's wee mite?" I crooned as I picked her up, expecting a stiff little corpse.

Sally's eyes opened as if on springs. "I hided, Grandma. No one found me. I found Cap-aw."

"Cap-aw?" I searched my memory. "You found Grandpa? No, child, every old man you see is not your grandpa." I looked down at the man's foul-smelling body, unmoving still, and began backing out of the stall with the child in my arms. "That's not Grandpa, dearie. Oh, little Sally, did he hurt you?"

Sally reached toward the ragged stranger. "Cap-aw!" she cried.

The man moved! His arm swatted at the air as if he fought against awakening.

Sally called again and fought in my arms until I was forced to put her down. She ran to him. "Cap-aw, I keept you warm." She petted his matted hair. I did not move, trying to think what I would do with this vagabond adopted by my grandchild.

He spoke one word. "Wife?"

"Cullah?" So haggard. So shrunken. I knelt in the dirty straw and held him to my bosom. "Cullah. Oh, my husband. They told me you were dead." We wept, our tears washing his face. "My Eadan," I moaned. Sally nestled herself between us and cried, too. I helped him rise and walk to the house. Soon as I gave him bread and fruit, and a cup of ale, I called Gwenny to come.

James was true to his word, and stayed until Cullah had been home a week. Then, with a cloak I had made him rolled around his other clothing, and a pushcart loaded with ten bolts of my best woolens, he walked away from our lives at sunup.

I loved them all, these people in my life, even he, Patience's first child. We were all guilty in our own ways; all had been formed by our lot in life. Was I also the godless outlaw he saw in my husband? It must be, else I could not love Cullah, could not tolerate August. Was it unholy to love a person in spite of their actions? For the first time in years, I wished Ma sat by me.

Alice came to my side. "You sad Master James is gone?"

"Of course."

"Don't be, Mistress. He a man. You can't mother a man fully grown. It isn't natural. Best he leaves. Wasn't good at farming. He t'ink everyt'ing in the world has to come on his terms. World isn't like that. More natural that he find it out somewhere else, then he won't judge you so harsh. That's all I got to say."

CHAPTER 36

May 23, 1769

Cullah's strength grew. Every day I made him oatcakes and beef broth. I washed and cut and treated his hair and made him herb teas. He was so thin and reduced, so unlike the man of old, and his hair had gone straggly, grayed, and rough textured. Sometimes I studied his face, searching for the merry expressions I had known. He smiled wanly at me. He spent hours with his grandchildren upon his knees. He peeled vegetables while I baked bread. At night he clung to me as if I were all that kept him afloat in a stormy sea.

One night when he lay awake, he told me how he'd made his way here. They released prisoners one or two at a time. Another man had died along the way, and Cullah found the fellow by a swamp, lying frozen, wearing both a coat and cloak. He'd taken the fellow's clothes and boots, even cut off the man's pants and shirt and used them to wrap his feet and legs. Because none of the men had been allowed the luxury of bathing or shaving, there was about them all a uniformity, and sometimes only their height and the rags they wore marked their identities. He said, "I left rags there, what little was left of my coat, and when they found him, they probably thought it was I. I took all the clothes he had, poor devil."

"But he was dead, and with them you survived." I waited. It was not the same as Cora taking Patience's shoes, the man had not needed them. "I am so very glad to have you home. Only that. I am thankful you are here and I will make you new clothes."

After June turned to July, I felt secure in leaving him to call upon my friend. Margaret sat in a chair in her grand parlor with tears in her eyes. "Please stay," she whispered, staring at the drapery at a window. "There is nothing but talk of war from every quarter. I am so tired of it. That night spent hunting for your grandbabe made me realize I have so little of what is real in this life. I have made a life of pretense and meddling. It is all for nothing. Everything that matters at all was in the eyes of your granddaughter, lost all night long, the face on that little girl when she saw her mother and father. The joy of finding your man. You have everything, Ressie. I am a hollow shell." She burst into tears.

I sat by her, comforting her in my arms. "You slight yourself. If I thought of you thus, I would never have befriended you. Margaret, I believe you are afraid of war not because you think your husband is right, or because you are loyal to the Crown or sympathetic to the Patriots, but that you are so afraid you will be wearing widow's black yourself the rest of your days, you cannot bear it."

"Whatever shall I do?" Margaret cried.

"The general is not dead. And if something does happen, then you press forward. You find a purpose for your life."

"But my purpose has always been effrontery. What else have I? I have no religion, and nor do I want that. I have no substance, Resolute. Nothing."

"I think you do. I think you wish me to be here because your husband is gone and you are alone in the house. People are not visiting as before the occupation. You keep having parties because you do not wish to be alone and face yourself."

Margaret looked up at me. "Resolute, you are so unkind."

I said, "I am being honest with you, my dear friend. I will tell you what you will see when you do look. A lady. A real lady with courage and cunning and ideas in a mind so rich she should have been allowed to go to Harvard. Made to go. You must have some peace, Margaret, but you will have to find it yourself. I am not unkind. I am honest with the people I love."

"Won't you stay for my party? Dr. Warren will be happy to see you. The Hancocks are coming."

"I will stay for your sake. Margaret, my dear friend, I will say this to you as if you were my child. Please find all the richness I see in you. It will not take you long, for it is not far from the surface. And though you may now be afraid to look at yourself, what you see there will fill you with joy and you will find that you think back and wonder why you were so afraid."

Margaret came to visit me a month later in August, and stayed two days. While we spent our days chattering like ravens over a cornfield, we spent quiet evenings while I worked at my wheel and she read aloud. Cullah seemed to haunt the place, as if he feared her or hated her. He was polite, but claimed to be deeply tired, and would go up to bed soon as the food was done. It troubled me that he cared not for Margaret. I asked him if he preferred she not come, or whether he blamed General Gage for his sentencing, but he insisted he was simply, truly tired.

When she left, I asked him to stroll in the field. The trees were lush with fruit, the grounds smelled of vegetation and yesterday's rain. Swirls of mosquitoes boiled in the dappled sunlight. We held hands and walked the length of the line of apple trees. I asked, "Husband? Are you well, now?"

"More, I suppose. Do not make me eat another oatcake. I will turn into a horse the way you feed me those things."

I smiled. "You need some meat on your bones."

"So, did your friend have something to say to me? There must be some reason you called me here as soon as she left."

"No. Nothing she said was about you. But everything she says reminds me of you in some way. No, she believes I am the lucky one, and I agree with her. I only wanted to tell you that I miss you. I miss the old way you were. I felt as if you were invisible the last three days."

Cullah asked, "Are you ashamed of me?"

"Whatever for?"

"I am a broken man."

"I think your heart is broken but your spirit is alive. My heart was broken for you. Then, when I was told you had died—"

"I am so sorry."

"You need not fear Margaret. She is as true a friend as a person could have."

"General Gage's wife?"

"An American. A continental American. Cullah, you used to stare into the fire or into your memories, and say to me 'war is coming,' do you remember?"

"Well and aye."

"Cullah, war is coming."

And still more British soldiers came from across the sea. Margaret wrote me that by then the streets of Boston smelled of ordure. No woman was safe walking alone even in daylight, and except for her own, colonials' houses and businesses were regularly searched and the latter closed for nonpayment of taxes.

Our men of the local militia from Massachusetts Colony began calling themselves Patriots, and meeting in fields, even my own, for drilling and instruction in musketry and swordplay. I remembered vivid images of Cullah swinging his axe and claymore, a man become a whirling, mighty fighting machine. He tried his best with them, but he had indeed lost vigor. I reminded him to learn the musket, too, very much afraid he would misjudge his strength against an enemy with cannon and musket, and like the Highlanders of old, charge against them with but a sword. I clucked my tongue, wondering how these lads and old men would stand against a regiment of soldiers from an army that controlled much of the world.

One afternoon Cullah met me in the barn as I milked the cow. He held a long-barreled fowling musket, and seemed startled when he saw me, as if he were guilty of something. "Where did you get that, husband?"

"Isaac Davis made it from parts. I carved the stock. He's shot it. It's a true aim."

I stood. The thing was taller than I was. "You have never owned one before now. Have you decided to go fowling, then?"

"I may not have the strength to swing a sword like a young man, but this war will be fought with weapons such as this."

"Yes, I am sure you are right," I said and sighed, trying to hide my relief. He was coming back, then, fully, and did not need a wife to tell him how to fight. Did I want a war? I asked myself. Naturally, surely, I believed, things on this continent would eventually be settled by courts, and justice will be more free. But for my husband, something about preparing for a battle gave him life, gave him courage that simple farming did not. I believed he always anticipated war the way some people always look for bad weather, but the man who was prepared for bad weather always had a snug roof, too. "Do you have shot for it?"

"I do. I took money from our last chest."

"How much is left in there?"

"Ten pounds and seventeen shillings. I'm off now. Isaac is drilling us in shooting, all day. Will you be all right?"

"I will, Cullah." As I watched him saunter away, I thought, Ten pounds? That would not get us through a year. Those who owned farmland as we did at least did not have to fear starvation. A paper of pins that had cost six shillings the year before was twenty, and none to be found. Black pepper to season food was almost nonexistent. Someone put a rhyme in the newspaper about seasoning his eggs with gunpowder and serving them to the royal army. The cinnamon with which I had once enlivened our Christmas pudding was to be had no more. Tea was up three shillings an ounce and coffee could not be found, so that those who preferred it were attempting to create it from burned wood bark and causing themselves illness. Myself, I boiled water and made a toddy of apple cider, and sometimes I boiled pears, too.

Dysentery rampaged through Boston, then started in Lexington, too. Influenza hit that December of 1769, and then smallpox was found on a sailor dead in an alleyway. His body had been eaten by rats, and for two days no one thought unusual a man lying facedown in a gutter after a ship of the line made port. The disease spread to three fourths of Boston, others being already immune, and then through the countryside.

And then with the new year it took my Gwyneth. I had sat by her side and sung to her, old nursery songs of windy days and Maypoles. Baby Peter got the scourge as well. Gwenny held Peter in her arms when she followed him to the next world, for the babe was already gone though she knew it not. We buried them together in the same grave. Gwenny and Roland's oldest son died also; the eldest daughter, Elizabeth, recovered. Though Roland became ill it was short-lived, and little Sally suffered a day of fever and then was up playing. I watched her as she visited my house, fearing that she would return to illness even worse, but she did not. Two weeks later, she continued in good health. Dorothy escaped, too, though I knew not why. All one can do in these times is to be thankful for survival.

My dearest Gwenny. I missed her so. She was both a child and a sister to me. Cullah put down his musket, barely ate, and spent nine evenings sighing, staring into the fire. Alice, like me, had come through smallpox as a child.

I traded a bolt of silk for several bushels of roving, and wove a hundred yards of plain gray wool with no more color than the sheep had bestowed it for dyes were not to be had. I wore black. I did little embroidery for I could not buy silk thread and I could not embroider with my needles worn so small I could not hold them. I found that there was always someone who knew our signals and codes, and who could get me five pounds for a bolt of wool, ten for a bolt of linen. When I was not at my loom I spent days hackling linen in the barn.

On March 5, 1770, in Boston, some drunken young men threw snowballs at a soldier in uniform. They had caught the Redcoat alone and had been having fun at his expense when some of his fellows heard the commotion and rushed to his aid. Taunts and ignored orders came from both sides. The snowballs coming at the soldiers turned to ice chips and rocks, broken bottles, then horseshoes. The soldiers fought back with what they carried. Muskets. In a moment, five young men lay dead, a score more wounded.

Now a craftsman in his own right in Revere's shop, Benjamin told me that he had helped, working well into the night on an etching, so that by March 6, the newspaper published a print of soldiers firing upon an innocent crowd. "They were warned to stop, Ma," Benjamin said as I looked at the drawing. "They were told. Why would a person not take hold of themselves when faced with a musket? Why not simply cease? It was all in fun but they grew violent."

"The human heart is harder to turn from its course than a river," I said.

"Five died, Ma. Five boys. I knew two of them. They were just drunk, Ma. Fools full of drink, throwing snowballs. Redcoats should all die."

"No. Your brother is one of them, too. They are not all cut from the same cloth."

"Few of them have any intelligence at all, then."

"That may be true. Then again, a soldier follows orders and it is his ranking officer we must blame if something is amiss."

As spring drew on we worked our own farm from sun to sun. Cullah's strength seemed to come back to him, though not his size. He seemed thin, but he could still fell a tree and split firewood just as quickly as before.

One afternoon in mid-May, Roland came to the door. He sat at the table before us. He looked into Dorothy's eyes, and asked her to marry him, to take her sister's place. She already knew and loved the children, he said. They needed a mother. He needed a wife. Would she accede to his offer? He promised he would make her a good husband, and provide for her all the days of her life.

"But will you love her?" I asked.

"Fondness grows," he said. "Like a wild rose. She lived with us for years. We are comfortable together. I am old, but I will be a good husband."

Cullah turned to Dolly. "What say you, of this?"

She smiled. "Pa, Ma, I have always loved Roland. I loved Gwenny, too. When I felt my heart growing attached to my sister's husband, I came back to your house so I would neither tempt nor be tempted. I could never marry another. I will go with Roland. I love Gwenny's children."

"Well," Cullah said, "a girl needs a husband. But it seems so soon. I suppose if Reverend Clarke will approve it, I will not stand in your way."

They married just two weeks later in the apple orchard. Reverend Clarke blessed their union under a bower of apple blossoms, their perfume drenching us like mist. It was as if the earth stretched herself at that moment, as if the loss of so many of her children allowed abundance of her other gifts. I looked at Gwenny's poor babes, scars pitting their faces, and knew Dolly would be mother to them as if they were her own, for I saw them take her hands eagerly as only a child could.

Cullah decided not to reopen his shop. Though he had some tools at home and our friends and neighbors sought after his work, his large machinery could not be replaced with the money we had. I believed that in that year of deprivation, his heart was gone out of it. Our passion for each other seemed to wane, too, but our affection grew. I was startled one day to realize that my courses had ceased. There would be no more children for us. Cullah was no longer obsessed with making his lovely furniture, and I missed the sparkle that came into his eyes when he used to tell me about the challenges of it. Making a bead around a drawer front, set so that it had exactly a sixteenth of an inch on all sides when closed, was as exciting to him as a tracing of yellow silk on a gray linen to me.

We planted our fields, side by side, and spent our summer evenings hand in hand, walking the orchards and the fields, lingering by the stream when the wild geese led their goslings about, or settled on a bench he had built by the stream's edge. If the weather was rainy, we stayed by the fire and read aloud. Cullah was quite proud of his ability at last to read, and though it went slowly, we had many a good evening's entertainment that way. I found myself smiling at him as he worked at a word, thinking how humble and good he was, how earnest. How I loved him.

Alice kept the house, tending it until things sparkled in ways I never had managed before. Our house seemed so empty, to me, yet in every corner, I heard the echo of children laughing or squabbling over some slight by one of the others. I saw their little noses pressed against the window glass looking out at the snow, or remembered tending them and the endless days of illness.

When next I went to visit Margaret, intending to do some errands on the way, September's first hint of frost was in the morning air as I set out to drive through barricades and questioning soldiers to brave Boston's streets searching for needles and pins. Margaret seemed drawn and she wore a patch upon her face I had not seen before. "I am marked forever by this disease," she said, pulling the patch from her face. "This ridiculous thing is the rage in London. People there wear patches though they have no smallpox scars to cover, did you know that?"

"No, I did not."

"I look like a cur."

I studied my callused fingers. I had spent so many hours at the loom, I felt almost as if I could not walk without repeating in my mind the clickety-tick sounds of the countermarche. It was just as the day we alighted the ship and the sand on dry land seemed to roll like a wave. "I have my scars, too. You look like a woman. The reason we love to see a babe is to be reminded what immortal beauty will be. We cannot walk this earth without our marks. Will you and George come for Thanksgiving in November?"

"Did you not hear? Governor Hutchinson has outlawed it. He said it was too frivolous, and that the colonists ought to be thankful they are not all hanged, rather than celebrating."

"*He* is a cur."

"Resolute? When did you grow so old?"

"Why, what a terrible thing to say."

"I told you I was rude. I did not wish to imply your mien was unattractive. But, as you said to me, we are only as good friends as we are honest ones. I meant that you have such a motherly way about you. It is wisdom as if you were a hundred years old. I never noticed it when we used to sit and gossip. When did that change?"

I did not want to repeat the obvious to her that it often came with motherhood. I valued Margaret. I loved her spunk and vitality. I wanted to see myself in her, I suppose. "It comes with the scars, sweet Margaret." As I picked up the reins—for I had learned to drive my own wagon—I said, "Margaret? If I have need of you? If ever I cannot get into Boston and want you, what can I do?"

She smiled as if she, too, knew we needed this. She reached into her skirt and into her pocket, and pulled out a silver shilling. "Send me this," she said, placing it in my hand and closing my fingers with hers. "Send me a shilling and I will come. Only keep it in your hat, and let no one spend it."

"Send a shilling," I said. "It will only happen, of course, if I may trust any messenger with a shilling in these times."

"True. Sixpence will do as well. Farewell, friend. I know not whether we will meet again soon. There's talk they will close the town completely."

"Let us plan, then. Come to my house next Tuesday for tea. I will spend my last lump of sugar making cakes."

"I will, then. As long as it is your last," she said with a grin. "I relish that sort of extravagance." We both laughed, knowing, I suspect, that it was no doubt true, and that it would be bittersweet in any event. "If I can find a needle I shall bring it, also." We kissed each other's cheeks and bade farewell.

Tuesday morning arrived and I gathered eggs earlier than usual, intending to begin whipping the whites for a light cake. Alice sat sewing, making herself a quilted petticoat in the fashion I had showed her, one with secret pockets sewn in. Cullah was in the field with Roland. I worked happily, expecting my friend, and sifted flour, then set to beating the eggs. My arms grew weary before I got the egg whites to rise up in stiff mountains, like snow in a bowl.

A heavy hand rapped at my door and a voice called, "Open up in the name of His Majesty King George."

"Just a moment," I called in reply, knitting my brows as I stared at Alice. I went to the door just as it came flying inward at me. "La!"

There stood a gaggle of soldiers, seven or eight of them. "Outside, woman. Who else is in here? Everyone outside, now. Look lively. Out the door!"

"What do you mean?" I asked. "You have but to ask and I will provide you food such as I have."

"Our orders is to search this house and premises."

"For what, sir?"

"For anything that seems amiss. Now out with you."

I turned my head this way and that, looking at my bowl of beaten egg whites, mounded up for a cake sitting beside a crushed cone of sugar and a pile of whitest flour, sifted nine times. I took my cloak from its peg by the door, and Alice did likewise. We stood in the yard while seven soldiers ran indoors. From the yard, I heard all manner of banging and crashing, quiet periods, and then more knocking about. After a while, one of them held the door ajar while the others joined and carried out chests, dumping the contents upon the damp ground. They brought out the mahogany highboy, Cullah's last creation for our house, pulled drawers from their places, tossing them here and there.

One of them said, "See if that has got a false bottom on it," and kicked his foot through the back of the cabinet. "Anything suspicious, that can't be opened, bring out here and we'll open it that way," he said to the others, laughing.

"I'll be glad to open anything for you," I called. "Please do not break my furniture."

He pointed his finger at me and said, "Quiet."

I heard glass breaking from inside.

"Do you not know what a window costs?" I asked. "Tell them to stop, sir, and I will open all to you."

"I said quiet, Goody. If you impede His Majesty's search, you will be arrested."

"Pray tell me what His Majesty is searching for?"

"Anything amiss, I told you already. Here, boys, bring that one over here."

He caved in the top of a small cloverleaf table with one thrust of his boot. They emptied every drawer onto the floor, opened every cupboard, and even upended the crocks of flour upon the table. One of them opened a tin where I kept precious black pepper.

"Here we go," he said to his fellows with a grin.

"You leave that be," I said. "It is pepper that cost me dear."

He sneered. "It's black powder, eh? And look at this, a silver sixpence."

"That is to keep it fresh," I said. Cullah came running and stood beside me.

"So you're hiding money and black powder. We could shoot you on the spot, but as we are gentle chaps, we won't. Long as you close your yap. Word is that you're hiding wool and soft cloth. Where is it?"

As he said that last, one of them pitched my flax wheel into the yard where it landed with a crushing sound.

Cullah put his arms protectively about me. I shook with fury. After a while I was even more angry because I sensed he was protecting them from me. Of course, I would have suffered, but the storm raging in my ribs was the size of a hurricane.

By the time they had dragged half of the household outside to the front yard, one of them decided to search the barn. He returned, leading one of our three cows. Another man came from the house with the bowl of egg whites. He stuck in a finger and licked it, made a face, and tossed the bowl into the flowerbed where the crockery broke in three pieces and the eggs lay like a tiny snowdrift against a stand of summer daisies past their season. Alice stayed close to Cullah and me. One of them poked a dagger at her chin, which she raised defiantly, and he asked her, "We seen that spinner's wheel. Where's the wool from it, wench?"

"It is a flaxen wheel," Alice said. "It does not make wool; it spins flaxen thread. It's the stuff your underwear is made of, if you are so gentle as to wear it."

The man's mouth opened and his face reddened, saying, "I'll show you, wench, who needs underwear and who don't." Then he laughed and ticked at the ruffle of her cap with his dagger, laughing again before he walked away.

Finally, the soldiers assembled themselves at my front door, and began to walk away, leading my cow. Two of them held folded woolen blankets, our best quilted ones, the warmest for winter. Off they marched, as much as they could with a cow in step.

I took a breath, ready to protest again, but Cullah nudged me. I ran to the highboy chest, now stoved in at the back of it, splintered wood everywhere. I threw my arms about it and cried. Every inch of it had been touched by Cullah. With tender fingers I pressed the splinters in at the poor broken side.

In the parlor, a blanket smoked at one corner where it lay too near the fire. I pulled it back, and as I did my mind spun to the parlor on Meager Bay, the night of devastation caused by cannonballs falling through the roof. Not one thing had escaped their search. I ran to the stairs down to the loom. Slid open the panel. They had not found the secret room. Upstairs in my bedroom, I sighed with relief. They had not pushed the wall and found the other stairway.

In the barn, August's crates lay untouched in the room above the loft. Cullah joined me there. I asked, "Did they find your new musket?"

"No. I hid it in the last place anyone would look. Plain sight." He stood upon a barrel and reached above the door where, standing, its length almost invisible in the shadows, stood the fowling piece. "It is my best guess," he said, "that men hunting something or someone almost never look up, and certainly never look back after they've gone through a door."

It took all three of us, Cullah, Alice, and I, with Roland's help, to get the highboy back up the stairs and set in place and it took weeks to restore a semblance of order. Even so, the drawers would not close in their tracks.

January 1771

The new year found us thankful that the last year had been a mast year for acorns—for the bulk of them fell every other fall—and that I had gathered acorns to hoard against the worst of winter. By February, we grew weary of boiled acorns, but we stayed full on them, and ground them, adding them to hasty pudding and bread, too.

The last week of February, we got word that our poor Rosalyn died in childbed. Brendan brought his boy Bertram to my door shortly after the letter had arrived. I asked him, "Why do you not leave the army, then? Is it possible? You could care for your boy and live here if you like."

"Ma, I am a proud soldier of the Realm."

"Well and aye. I am a proud mother of a soldier. But son, the Realm is sapping the life out of her people like a canker. We are poor farmers now. The Realm has taken your father's shop and all his tools, and others of those proud soldiers have come to this house too many times to despoil it."

"Will you not welcome my son, then?" he said, sadly.

"Of course I will. Bertram may stay with me as long as he likes; as long as I live, he has a place. Just know, my bonny Brendan, that I—"

"I will send you money for his support."

"If you do I shall put it by for his education. Brendan—"

"Mother, please speak no more of this. I must trust you to raise my son to be a loyal British subject. Promise me you shall?"

"I promise to raise him in truth and honor, seeking ever the high ground. I will take him to church. I will feed him. He will have everything I can give him, Brendan, but loyalty? As he grows to be a man, just as you did, he will choose."

"Very well, then." He turned to the lad. "Son, you know I have no choice. Mind your granny, and be helpful. I'll come for you when I can."

"Pa, take me with you."

"I cannot. You know that, boy. Straighten up, now. Let's see my little soldier. Take it with pride and hold your chin up. That's the lad. Your mother would be proud."

The boy Bertram, deprived of his mother, now lost his home, too. I knew well the taste of that abandon, but when I tried to speak to him, he turned away.

"Brendan," Cullah said. "There is something I must tell you."

"Pa, there is something I must tell you. The rebels are all but shaking pitchforks in the streets. They throw rocks at His Majesty's men. That is why I want Bertie here, away from Boston town. You must be very careful. Uncle August has long been suspected of smuggling goods to the colonies, and I'm told his path leads often to your door. The suspicion may fall upon you as well."

"It has already," Cullah said. "At least you were not among those sent to search and destroy our property."

I chewed my lip, weighing words. "Brendan, you brought a French man home from the war, the way some men brought home a string of wampum or a necklace of bear claws taken after a battle."

Brendan smiled. "My sister was so homely I had to capture her a husband."

I looked to the sky and shook my head. "I should box your ears for such an insult to your beautiful sister. May she not hear you from heaven. Think, son, why you did such a thing. Because you looked about you and saw more than orders. You saw the small thing, a single man, who, once you knew him, was not your enemy. You saw the large thing, too. A war fought over greed, a thing that was inherently wrong. From where I live, the crushing of Britain's subjects to use their blood to grease the wheels of world conquest is equally wrong. Every pulpit in Massachusetts rings every week with talk against such by the king. We are a churchgoing family. Do you hear what I am saying?"

His face held firm but his eyes would give away his thoughts even in the dark. "Be safe, Ma. Keep my son safe."

"I will." Brendan shook hands with his son and his father, settled his hat upon his head, and walked away, that tall son of mine, that man who spoke with Cullah MacLammond's voice and strode with his father's stride. I said, "Well, Bertie, let us see if you have need of clothing."

Bertie was a good lad but easily bored. It was my thought that he was too intelligent to be satisfied without schooling. I dug through my hidden troves and came up with six pounds in total. I felt such an odd dismay, for on the one hand it was not enough to ensure Bertie an education, and on the other, it was more than enough to have provided better food and shoes for all of us in the present. Should I put it away in keeping for that future day or spend it now upon keeping us alive and in warm shoes? I raised my hem. A couple of yards of twine held my shoes together even now. Perhaps something now must be spent on the boy. Perhaps I should not face another year in these old shoes for the sake of my own health.

One evening Cullah called him to sit beside him on the settle. "Have you any yearning, Bertie, for education? Medicine? Law? The clergy?"

"I do, sir. I should like to be a minister."

"You will have to go to Harvard for it. It will mean a great deal of work for you and me both. Do you feel as if you are called by God to do this?"

"I want to be able to move people with words like Reverend Clarke does. I want to have people weep, or cheer, or shake in their boots. I wish to speak so that happens."

I thought that was what I had wanted as a child, to speak and be heard. I asked him, "Are you good at writing, then? Have you read any books or poetry?"

"I cannot read at all, mum."

"Then we will start there. You will soon read." Cullah listened and smiled to himself as we began that very night by the fire.

CHAPTER 37

December 1773

That winter snow flew early. Cold seeped into every crevice of the house. In mid-December the navy set up a blockade of the coastline from Long Island to Maine until the East India Company should be repaid for the shipload of tea broken and soaked in brine at the bottom of Boston Harbor. What were we to do? The ones who had spilled it would not pay, and the rest of us could not pay. I knew Benjamin had taken part in it, and I held a very real terror that one day my sons would find themselves aiming at each other. On every street corner men preached day and night against the burdens upon us, but rarely did they get their second page of notes from their pockets before they and their listeners were dispersed at the end of a bayonet.

The long winter days seemed to give Bertram dark moods. I asked him, "Next year, do you want to apprentice? Would you like a trade rather than a profession? What about going after your uncle Benjamin?"

"I should like to be a woodcarver like Grandfather, but he says he won't teach me. He's always minding cows, now. Maybe I should go to sea."

"They say the difference between being a British sailor and being a prisoner in Newgate is the added possibility of drowning, but if that is what you want I shall ask Uncle August—"

"No, mum. I should want to be in His Majesty's navy. Uncle is a pirate."

"He is not a pirate, Bertie. Child, I cannot make you happy. I believe you are troubled, wanting a man around, a father. I am but your grandmother and none too exciting. Try to take some interest in your schoolbooks."

He made a face.

"Well and aye, boy. It is high time you were apprenticed, if you are not going to study. And if you do not appreciate what I have done for you it is also high time you learned to keep that face under control. A lad who wears his every thought upon his face is asking for someone to change his opinions. You could help your uncle Roland more on the farm. No? Then we shall have to ask around. I cannot give you happiness, but I can at least give you a chance to find it." I felt vexed with the lad. He was never satisfied, never settled, and only half accomplished chores given him.

"I am sorry, mum. I know Pa tossed me off on you."

"He did no such thing. Brendan is my son, Bertie, and you my grandson. As long as I am able, I will help you both but you have to do your part. Boys go out at fourteen and you are almost that age." I sat. "Your father is doing the best he can for you. He cannot disobey his orders."

"He could become a Patriot, then he would not be a soldier. He would be a rebel."

I sent him to bring in extra wood one day and opened the secret room above the loom. On a passing fancy, I took Brendan's drum from its place, found the drumsticks, and closed up the wall before Bertie returned. On Hogmanay morning, I served up cakes of Indian flour with a slice of cured pork and treacle. "Look," I said. "This was your father's. It shall be yours now. Remember, make no face, young man, other than one of polite curiosity. I will not order you to play it, but it would be something to do. Take it, if you want, to Meeting on Sunday and we will see if there are any men who can teach you to make some music from the thing. I will not harp at you about it. Do it or not, as you please. We shall also ask if there is one who would apprentice you. You may try out five or six trades before you find your task. A man must make a living, and you will see what suits you."

"Mum? I would rather join the Sons of Liberty and learn to drill with a musket."

Cullah was, at that moment, doing exactly that. The Tories expected the colonists to be at their hearth sides on such a wintry day, and so it was deemed the perfect day for drilling and firing. "They need boys who can drum. Your father was fair at it. You might have the talent."

"I wish to be a soldier for the colonies, not a drummer."

"I have got work to do. I shall be down at the loom," I said. When he stared ahead in silence, I asked, "Would you like me to teach you that? Most weavers are men."

"No."

"Go out and help Grandpa. Clean the stalls for him."

"I hate cows."

"Do you miss your pa?"

"I hate him."

"Ah. He will come for you. He will."

"No he won't. He will die. Some Patriot will put a ball through his eye."

"You are afraid the Patriot will be you." Bertie's face reddened and he turned away from me. La. I knew so well that mixture of anger and longing for a child missing parents. My heart yearned with love for him, but the boy was old enough he would not do well if smothered by a grandmother's kisses when what he longed for was a father. "Did you know they pay drummers more than they pay soldiers? Anyone with a finger may shoot a musket, but not everyone can play a drum."

Later that day, as I sat at the loom I heard an extra thump. I stopped, fearing my loom was coming apart, and I could ill afford to have it repaired. I began again and a definite thump-bump followed the normal sound of the pedals. I got off the bench and inspected everything on the machine, and nothing was loose. I began again. Thump-bump, thump-bump. "It is I, mum," called Bertie. He stood, holding Brendan's drum and descending from where he had sat upon a stair just out of my sight.

We laughed together. Then he sat again, and as I started, he tried to follow with drumsticks. "There," I said. "I cannot tell you how to do it well, but you might start keeping time with me." By the time the snow melted and the days of muddy roads began, he had learned from one of our deacon's sons how to get a smart pattern out of the drum.

In the summer of 1774, Margaret's husband, Thomas, was made governor. Great celebrations were held across the colonies, for people hoped that he would relieve the state of siege we felt under Governor Hutchinson. I read about it in a paper I brought from Lexington the following week. But Margaret herself sent me the notice along with a folded and wax-sealed packet full of pins, needles, an ell of small lace, and a thimble. I felt hurt that she did not invite me to the celebration, but I knew I would be so foreign to other people there as to be looked upon as an oddity, a token American. After I read it, I walked to our stream and sat by a still small hollow in the streambed where the water's surface rarely moved. I set the letter from Margaret adrift there. It swirled in an eddy and the ink washed from it. Too late, I remembered how dear the paper itself was, and I reached for it but it was gone from my grasp, moving downstream. Moving toward the ocean, a letter with no words, heading out to sea.

I leaned over enough to see my reflection there. When had I stopped being Allan Talbot's daughter? When had I stopped being fit to sit with duchesses and peers and become a colonist? An American. We were rabble from England's crofts and gutters, Scotland's Highlands, Dutch outcasts, Irish and African slaves, and though some came here given grants of land, in our way we were prisoners all.

A leaf touched the water. A butterfly wobbled down to look at it and flew away. There I was, a wee girl in a torn and bedraggled blue silk gown, sitting crouched in the bottom of a pirate's snow, that longboat rowed by my brother and some strange men who would plant me here on this continent. When had I taken root? When had I become part of this cold, savage land and its people? When had I grown old? I was fifty-five, an age rare among women. If I did not see my faded hair in the reflection, however, I felt no more than twenty from the inside. I still yearned to wear a silken gown to a ball. I wanted to dance with Cullah wearing his beeswax-smelling boots. When had I gone from wearing embroidered silk to drab gray wool? The image that looked back at me looked more like an Ursuline *soeur* than a landed freewoman. I had not chosen the drab things that remained to me, I had come down to them as an earl might come down to being an inn-keeper when his family lands were escheated by the Crown. My plain clothes now reflected not a smug choice, but our reduced circumstances.

In the house, I leaned over a basin of water to wash my face. The ravages of the constant searches of our home showed. Everywhere I looked, a scar of invasion caught my sight. My linen wheel was wearing out and did not work well, but my dear woodsman had no tools to fix it. I looked at that wheel, so much a part of my life, and thought that my heart was in the wheel, and that it, too, was wearing out. It did not work well. A tear left my chin and stirred the water.

Margaret, now the wife of the governor, moved from her gentle but nice home into the large mansion opposite August's home, a house known to be the abode of a noted privateer and smuggler who had never so much as re-placed the Spencer *S* above the portico with a *T* for Talbot. I sighed. It had brought me much pleasure to have a friend in Margaret Gage. I supposed I must resign myself to the change in her life now, and that she as wife of the governor must be more careful about her acquaintances, meaning I was no longer acceptable.

As if she had heard my lament, Margaret sent a handwritten invitation for me to take tea at her home the following week. All Massachusetts was in merry conduct, for we believed that Governor Gage would put an end to the burdens of our lives. I went to see Margaret in part hoping I would hear some gossip about what provisions he would enact soonest. Take the man-o'-war out of the harbor? Remove the four thousand soldiers from Boston town? Stop the searching of our homes, the stealing and rifling of property? My friends at First Church continued their secret messages as the Committee of Safety. Minutemen and militia drilled in my farm fields when there were no crops. "Please, Margaret, tell me some good news I may spread abroad?"

"My dear," she said, "I trust Thomas to act wisely. He is a man of the king, but he is more sensible than Hutchinson. We are all thankful for the change of leadership."

"That sounds too guarded for my friend of old. I know you may not feel we can be as close as before, but tell me it will be different."

"Of course it will be different. His first priority, he told me, is to remedy the seditious talk of war."

"Will he lift the embargo? Reduce the taxes? Return my cow?"

"He must quell the rebellious spirit of the colonies."

I bristled. "That sounds ominous." I sipped tea. "Margaret?"

"Do not ask me more, Ressie. I asked you here for a purpose. If you are my friend, if you have been my friend, please let us say farewell for a time."

I set the teacup in its saucer and straightened my back. "For a time? What sort of time? Until you deign to speak to me again? Have I grown less entertaining? Are my clothes too drab to grace your parlor?"

"You know it isn't that."

"You are always welcome at *my* house," I said, though I had a difficult time keeping my lips from turning down and weeping like a child. "I shall not trouble you any longer." I stood.

"Ressie, please. My husband's position makes your coming here suspect to your *own* people. Surely you can see that."

"I think it makes you suspect to your people."

"It does. Can I lie to you? No. Of all the people I know, you are the one for whom my lips cannot be forced to lie. Ressie. Everything is wrong now. Please let me explain."

I looked at the fine velvet draperies hanging at her windows. I remembered how proud I had once been of the linens I had made that once filled our home, how they filled my heart with pride in my own labor and joy that my children were warm. How the soldiers had slashed at their rings with swords and carted them all away. "You are correct. It is not only your husband's occupation. Everything *is* wrong, Margaret. Good day."

Margaret followed me to the door, leaned her cheek against the jamb, and whispered, "Good day," as I walked down the promenade to the street. I stilled my expression, even managed to smile warmly at a lady and gentleman, though I wept inside the entire way home. It was only after I got there and removed my bonnet that I found tucked in its brim a silver sixpence. I spent two days just staring at the sky. It seemed as if it might just fall, I thought, and I wanted to be forewarned.

Cullah left the house at midnight a few days later, and did not return for a week. He brought August with him, along with a cart full of barrels of black powder. They stored it in the barn and ate as if they were growing boys, then both slept almost around the clock. Soon as he could leave, August slipped away in the small hours before dawn. I did not ask where they acquired the powder nor where it would go from here. It was enough for me that Cullah had become himself again, and right or wrong, pirate or Patriot, my brother was part of that transformation.

Almost a year later, in March of 1775, I received yet another invitation to visit Margaret. This time the lettering was printed on expensive paper. *"The Lady Margaret Gage begs the honor of your presence at tea, Tuesday next at three in the afternoon."* I told the messenger, a young man Bertie's age and dressed in livery, riding a fine horse, that my answer was simply, "No, thank you."

Alice stood at my side as the fellow rode away. "Why did you say no, Mistress? You have been more than one time in tears for lack of your friend."

"Alice."

"I am sorry, Mistress. I know it not my place to say this t'ing."

"I was not going to chastise you, Alice. I meant to say that you are my friend. I do not wish to have a friend whose love for me moves upon the rise and fall of the waves of fortune."

"Am I your friend, Mistress?"

"I consider you as much."

"I may speak free?"

I turned to her, seeing Alice's familiar face as if anew. "I presumed, because you have long ago earned enough to leave my employ, that you have chosen to stay. You never again asked me about returning to Jamaica. Of course you may speak within the bounds of friendship."

"Then I t'ink Mistress Gage love you, Mistress. I t'ink she caught in her husband state. He get closer to the king with every move. It hard for her to claim a friend except women that step in that same place."

"Six weeks ago Gage's men rifled my barn and house yet again, claiming I had stores of black powder."

"I remember." A slow smile brightened her features and her eyes twinkled with mischief. "They didn't find any, did they, Mistress?"

I returned her smile. "No, they did not." August had come and removed the wares the very next day. Still, Gage's men had ransacked our house five other times before that.

"Mistress, I know most men will not be governed by they wives. Mistress Gage does not guide her husband here or there. He does what he want. She goes to tea with his friend. She has to make his friend her own because of him. What woman has her own way? Not many I can name."

"I know, Alice."

"I say, she was once your friend, see if she is still."

"You are right. I should have sent the young man away with an invitation for her to come here."

"I will carry your word to her. It only decent."

In the morning, Alice left with my message in her head and a shilling in her pocket, and for this I had to trust to her loyalty, for one word amiss could alter everything. Yet, what was I to do, for I had not so much as a strip of paper?

"She's right," Cullah added. He held a brace of grouse by the feet and flopped them onto the table. "You should go. Take the invitation, for that's why she sent it, you will need it to get through the barricade. If she will come here, so much the better, but if she calls for you again, you should go. Take Alice with you."

"Cullah, do you think Margaret means this as a signal?"

"You said yourself, she is an American."

On the following Tuesday, Margaret came to my house, escorted by our old friend Dr. Warren. I served them tea such as I had, for it was not real tea but stewed of herbs and mint though they were gracious and took it. Dr. Warren asked about my health and I replied it was fair. "Samuel Prescott asked after Miss Dorothy," he added.

"She has married," I replied, without telling him more. I cast my eyes back and forth between them. Bertram sat in a corner pretending to be reading a book, but I looked in his direction, for I felt sure he was listening. I said, "Bertram, would you come here, please? I want you to take that satchel of candle wicking to your aunt Dorothy."

"May I take my drum?"

"Of course, but ask her if there are babes asleep before you play it in the house." In a few minutes, the boy left, whistling and trotting out a complicated rhythm on the drum as if it were as natural as breathing to him.

Margaret seemed preoccupied and spoke little. I tried to smile and be gracious but inside I felt put out with her again, and wondered why she came if she had naught to say to me, for indeed, including Dr. Warren was congenial but it hindered any freedom of our conversation. At last I said to her, "Margaret? I have missed you so, all these months. Well, then. I know not where to begin. Who made your gown?"

"A new seamstress; it matters not. You know I have missed you, too. You must accompany us back to Boston today. And please come to tea next week. Ressie, I had to come here because I could not speak to you at my house. I know not which of the servants is to be trusted. There are ears in every wall."

"And that is why I never hear from my old friend? We could have spoken of music, or hats," I offered. Uneasy silence filled the room. I touched my cap nervously, suddenly aware there was no reason to signal either of them. "Dr. Warren? I hope you have not too many patients ill?"

He looked to Margaret, and then to me. "No. Actually. Your brother—is— quite ill. He asked me to beg your presence. Today."

I said, "I shall tell Cullah to be ready."

"You alone, dear, but the house is watched," Margaret added. "Wallace Spencer has again pressed charges against Captain Talbot for piracy. You don't want Cullah anywhere near him, for he's too often been said to be at his side. My husband has, has—oh, Resolute, he has men watching your brother's house night and day for any activity."

I said sharply, "Your husband has been tormenting everyone I know. My own house has been searched half a dozen times since he became governor. If August is so ill, what activity could there be?"

"Doctors coming and going," Margaret said. "Only doctors. It would not seem amiss for his sister to arrive. Or to stay a bit."

Dr. Warren added, "Captain Talbot asked that I should come to tell you."

We left Alice to cook for Cullah and Bertie, and mind the house, which, I was glad to think, at last left both of them feeling quite safe with one another.

After we stopped under the grand porte cochere and left Margaret across the street, Dr. Warren took me to August's house. I learned that my brother was still pretending to be sick, though since I had last been there, he had dismissed his entire staff but for Rupert. When August left at night, he left Rupert, a man about his same size and hair color, to wear his dressing gown and walk before the upper windows so the spies would think it was he. After greeting the doctor and me, he pushed a leather sack of coins into my hand and said, "Tomorrow, I will be leaving for a week. If you need anything, any more money, contact Rupert. If you can get word to your son Benjamin, tell him it is a matter of a horse, and I will know to come to your aid at once."

August led me to his library, where, though lack of a regular cook should have made things meager, Rupert had laid a nice supper of mutton stew with barley and potatoes. He poured us Madeira wine, and served us at a small table before a nice fire.

"Ressie? I have something to ask of you. I know you tried to volunteer to carry messages, but there are plenty of men to do that. We have a net of spies and committees that can do what we need to do but this is something few could do, and no one could execute it the way you could." He opened the battered trunk, the one Cullah had once criticized as not belonging in the room with the other fine furnishings, and lifted up a rolled blue cloth which he unfurled to reveal a coat. "This came from France, and a few of us have ordered scores of them. We don't have them yet, of course, because no one can pay for a quarter of what they want delivered, plus we want the Continental uniform somewhat different. Wider here, narrower there. Less of a collar. We want our men to see. The British soldier is not meant to see or think, and his foolish collar will not allow him to turn his head. So, less of this thing." He pointed to the undercollar. "To do this, you will have to take it home unseen. You cannot leave this house with it, because everyone who goes in and out is searched. They even stop the doctors, search their satchels and verify their credentials to make sure they are real doctors, as if a doctor cannot be a Patriot. The blighted Tories actually did me a favor, doing that. Found one of the kitchen wenches helping herself to the silver and pewter like a thieving tinker."

I examined the coat, inside and out, adding, "Where will I get these buttons and braid?"

"I have a few. There is a bag here somewhere. Oh, yes." He took the lid off a Chinese vase and pulled out a ratty linen sack. "Benjamin will get you more. Revere is procuring them as we speak. Benjamin will visit his mother more than he has in the past, and each time he will bring you something. Here is the thing, sister. I need to get this coat out of this house and into yours. I'll go with you to protect you. As many uniforms as you can make, take them to Hancock's house in Lexington as soon as you can. I will send blue wool and dye but don't wait for it; use what you can. Two weeks, I'd like a half dozen or so. It's not far for you to go, is it, to Hancock's? Some of their woolens are being shipped from France. If you can use wool you already have, and dye it, so much the better. Tell me if you can do this. I had to have you here to show you. Can you make this coat?"

"I think this might be a shade of indigo mixed with crimson or rouge. I will have to experiment. If you can get your hands on it, send me vinegar. I will need gallons of it, but send all you can. What about trousers? Will you need linen trousers with each coat?"

"Yes, make pants. Wool and linen. Different sizes. Plenty of our men are wearing rags. Two men showed up naked. You never saw the like. Determined as a Trojan but with not a stitch of clothing. Some cut up saddle blankets and sewed themselves some short pants. For that matter, while I'd like to have uniforms, if you have aught to make pants of any sort, rough and homespun, as long as they have buttons I'll take them. We've got Indians, too, but you can't tell me any man doesn't get cold in the winter. Summer is coming, but I don't think, as some of the fools say, that this will be over in a month. We'll be having this same conversation next year at this time.

"We will leave tonight under cover and take it to your house, return, and you will be able to rest tomorrow. You then leave whenever you feel it is proper. I would not take you but for the woman at your house who might fear me. You have to accompany me. Will you join us, then?"

"I will. But Cullah is there. He would have let you in."

"No he's not. The Sons of Liberty have business in Braintree tonight, and I fear your Alice knows too well how to fire a pistol." He gave me a quick kiss on the cheek, then called, "Anne?"

"*Oui?*" came a woman's voice.

"Come in, please."

A young woman, mahogany colored and strikingly beautiful, entered the room and glanced at me before turning her eyes to August. He said, "Anne, this is my sister, Resolute MacLammond. Ressie, Anne." He held not the slightest hesitancy that I both knew and could overlook his introductions, for in it he left nothing to be imagined of their relationship in not adding either a last name, "miss," or "mistress." August looked me up and down as if he had not seen me before, made a face of near derision, and continued. "I much prefer you in satins, Ressie. I had not expected you in black but more's the better. Anne, find anything you have as close to the shape of my sister's gown. Just make it black, it matters not about the details. And fetch that black gauze. Resolute, take this," he said, holding the filmy cloth to me. "Your hair is too fair and a white cap will shine like a beacon. It is my experience that one can see quite well through this stuff, and it hides the glow of skin. Wear it under your bonnet so it doesn't blow off. Give Anne your cap. She will wear it, and keep your back to the windows at all times," he said to her. "We will be back before daybreak. See that you both bar the doors at seven and retire by ten, since that is when I put out the lights."

"August, it is nearly twelve miles to my house. Another twelve back here. I doubt I can walk that in a night."

"We'll take a boat across the river. A man I know keeps two horses always at the ready for me. Tonight I shall take them both."

"I cannot ride a horse, brother. I have never done it. Can your horse take two?"

The sun lowered and the evening's mist arose, adding gloom to my fears as I pulled the veil across my eyes. I felt some courage in that I could see quite well through it. How I wished I had stayed in bed and nestled next to Cullah, wished all of us were not part of this terrifying world around us. August and I crept through the lower window, dressed in blackest black, wearing gauze upon our faces.

August was adept at slipping through shadows and alleyways I would never have dared to breach had he not been there. At the river's edge, we stepped into a shallow boat well hidden in the reeds. The boat was a leaky hull with a shallow draft and August's oars had been wrapped in sacking and tarred so that they made little noise. At the center of the river, he believed he heard something and we bent low in the hull. I remembered my ride in such a craft, a much larger boat, remembered the haughty slave girl upon my knees, and I remembered my blue silk gown and how little I had valued such things, thinking only that it must be replaced. The boat rocked and I was ten years old for a moment. Then we were at the other shore, and I stepped into the water and mud, soaking myself to the knees.

In one hand, I carried the wrapped bundle of blue cloth. I held August's hand with my other, holding it with all the strength I bore as I pulled my feet from the mud. "August, please stop a moment."

"What's the matter?"

I reached for his neck and hugged him. "I never said before now that I love you."

His broad shoulders and strong arms held me for a moment, in a way Cullah could never have done. He held me without desire, but in a loving way that gave courage in his touch. "Let's go."

We reached the stable. He leaped onto the horse and pulled me up behind him, and we made it to Menotomy in less than an hour, and made my home before midnight. I pulled at the string that knocked a hammer against the jamb inside, then gave three taps followed by two, and Alice opened the door.

"Mistress? Sir?"

I said, "Alice, please hide this in the inglenook next to the fire. The nails in it are loose and all we must do is raise the lid."

August and I ate some bread and had a small ale. Then we mounted and left Alice, heading for town. About halfway through the swamp, he stopped and reined his horse to one side so abruptly I nearly fell. "What—" I began.

"Quiet."

Men ambled past us. They talked among themselves, we guessed about five of them. After a while, we followed them at a good distance for a time so that we would not overtake them. My heart bumped. I closed my eyes. From somewhere in the distance I believed I heard drumming and smelled smoke. It was so like hiding from the dangerous Indians when I was a child. I wondered what ghosts wandered these woods. The path narrowed in a few places. All felt familiar, yet terrifying. The deeper into the forest we went, the more fear gripped me. The horse shifted its weight and I nearly fell off again. August told me to "toe a line" and stop my foolishness.

How had Cullah done this, and on foot? He, who was more afraid of a fairy than a soldier with a musket trained upon him? My brother, I believed, had no such goblins to fight. His whole person seemed to bristle with excitement at the notion of a confrontation. An owl wooed overhead and glided above me on silent, silver wings. Crickets sang. Night thrushes warbled, their spooky song part of the mystery of darkness that kept good people in their homes at night with the doors barred. In the distance, the howl of a wolf made the hair rise on the backs of my hands. I remembered Massapoquot and the other Indians leading us through the north woods, carrying us at times, ever moving, never afraid of the dark. The Indians had seemed one with the forest, to embrace it as a familiar place, a hearth side populated with its own furniture. I straightened my frame and took several deep breaths. My skirt was soaked with water over my knees, and the weight and cold of it made it seem as if I were pulling anchors on my feet when we finally left the horse and crossed the river. Slinking through the shadowed alleyways, I nearly fainted when a dog barked. A cat yowled and I heard voices overhead from a window left open.

The greening sky and the smoky heaviness of morning fires added urgency to my feet, though by then August had my hand in his again, and pulled me along. We reached the courtyard of his home and got through the window before the watchman called five.

We joined Anne at breakfast. I sat at table in August's dressing coat. August said Anne would give me the clothes she had worn, but that he wished I would sleep and spend another night. "I will," I said. "But I have much to do when I get home. How do you have horses always at the ready?"

He smiled. "It's a web like that of a spider, Ressie. One must simply tug at the right connection, and things fall into place. I leave the boat where it was, too. No one has found it though it be used every night. Revere and Dawes run across the river at least once a week. Prescott had it yesterday. It's all a silken, invisible web. You know the strength of a single strand of silk."

"I do."

When I arrived home the next noon in Margaret's gilded chaise, Alice sat at the fire tatting lace, her feet upon a hassock.

"What are you making?" I asked.

"House cap for the lady of this house."

"That looks beautiful. Most extravagant. It is lovely. Thank you."

"I t'ink you wear this, and you t'ink of my affection with it."

Warmth flowed up my face from my bosom. "How kind. I shall. Is Master Cullah home?"

"He is, Mistress. Sleeping upstairs from the sound of his snoring," she said with a grin. She blushed.

I said, "Now, we have work to do, rather, I have work. I am going to mix dye and see if I can replicate that blue with indigo and whiting. I will not insist you help me. This is treason against the Crown. I alone will hang for it if I must."

"I have already made a pattern of it for you. I took apart the sides real gentle, and pressed it, and laid it on muslin. Marked all the places of it. I didn't cut any of it, so it can be put back together in no time."

I straightened. "You did in so few hours?"

"I didn't want to cut it, so I took some time holding it and pinning it. Missy Dolly helped. She going to have baby, you know? She and I cut the pattern. All we need is cloth."

"I have cloth. All we need is the dye. A baby? La. Another grandchild. Wonderful!"

"Mistress? I have somet'ing to tell you."

"Yes, Alice?" I busied myself with clearing off the table to begin work.

"Mistress, it was me dropped that crystal glass."

"I have no crystal glass."

"Long time ago, at Master Spencer's ball. It was me."

I searched my memories. "Why did you say it was not you?"

"Because I already owed you for too much. You buy me from Mistress Spencer, her throwing a fit. Then you say I am free. You saved me from a beating that night. I didn't want to have you t'ink I owed you so I must stay, must do as you say, must be somebody's slave. I wanted to see how it would be if you had not'ing more to hold me."

"Why tell me now?"

"Just want you to know, I see you now."

"I do not understand."

"It took a long time to trust. Now I know."

I nodded. "It does. That is good of you to tell me. I will love my new cap."

Outside, I stirred and boiled and dried dye mixtures on differing weaves and thread. I could not get the blue of the coat exactly, but what I had was within five shades of it. I bleached whites and creams, and we pressed and shrunk, stretched and dyed yard after yard of cloth. Then we began to cut them. I worked until my fingers bled.

Two weeks later we had ten coats made, and as many pairs of breeches and waistcoats in contrasting white linen. It was fine work, with small stitches, and not a pucker would I allow. Even Bertie helped, becoming quite a hand at sewing on buttons. This was a small thing, I knew. There was no way a single small family could clothe an army. What I wanted to do was to just make a few soldiers warm.

During those two weeks, five different sets of travelers came to my door begging food. One group consisted of four young men and one old one. We had already finished our meal, but I invited them inside, and said, "Sirs, I have some hasty pudding in the pot. I will share it with you, but I have nothing else."

"Give us money, then, that we can buy something in town."

"We have no money."

"You have money. This is a big house. There is always money."

Cullah said, "This house was built big because it housed a large family, and once there was money to build it. It is not so now."

One of the men sidled past Alice and toward the stairway. He stopped and backed from it, feeling with his hands behind him. Down the stairs came Bertie, the pistol in hand, aimed right at the man's head. Bertie's voice had not yet deepened, but when he said, "You leave this house," they listened to him. "I am but the smallest, and my five brothers wait up the stairs, each bigger than the other, and each one carries a pistol and a musket and sword bigger than the last. If you make it past me you must fight the next man, six of us in total, and that man there is my grandfather who is Cullah MacLammond, the heartiest Highlander who ever lived. Waiting by the door is my uncle, a vicious pirate who scuttled seventeen ships on the high seas and never was caught. He will put a dagger through your liver and pin you to a maple tree so the sap will run across your middle forever."

The men left my kitchen fast as they could. I barred the door. Alice looked at me, at Bertie, and I stared from him to her, too. Cullah laughed, saying, "The lad has your gift of a sharp tongue and a quick story, my love." Bertie glowed with pride in himself.

I stared hard at Bertie. "Best mind that tongue. It will cause you trouble, too, if you are not careful."

Cullah said, "Put the pistol away and come with me. We have rows to hoe and a ditch to dig. Nothing like hard work to build up a boy and still his tongue."

Bertie's face fell. I arched my brows. "Go on and dig, Bertie. When you are grown you will thank us for it."

"That is what old people say when it is most miserable," he said. I smiled.

"Come on, lad. Blisters and a sore back," Cullah added, "will make a man hungry for an education." As they left, Alice and I laughed as we went back to work sewing, and now and then, we laughed again.

Two days later I answered another knock on my door to find Emma Dodsil again standing there, holding a bushel basket topped with boiled eggs. I heard Alice rushing the blue cloth from the room even as I greeted her. "Emma? How nice to see you. Would you come in for some pie?" I dared to glance over my shoulder before I opened the door wider.

"Yes, thank you. I mean, yes, I will come in. But I won't ask you to share food today. I have come to share other things." She stopped talking, sat down, faced me, and deliberately touched her bonnet twice. I was not convinced. She said, "Virtue and I have been long married, and all our lives have tried to live above any contempt, above reproach, above rebellion."

"Very admirable of you, I am sure," I said.

"Your husband has helped us often, when he can."

"Cullah is a good neighbor." I felt hairs on the back of my neck rise. She was leading to something, and I felt I could easily be trapped if I were not circumspect with my words.

"As am I," she said. "Oh, Mistress Resolute, we feel we must support our neighbors who have done so much for us. Will you not take these things for the rebel militia? I know they might help someone." She raised the sack with its eggs again, dumping it none too gently on the floor, and this time revealing a stack of shirts and pairs of stockings.

I watched closely as her gaze charted the room. "Take those things to the rebels? Mistress, I am not in the business of outfitting a militia that stands against King George."

"Neither am I," she said, with a touch of anger in her tone. "I am in the business of outfitting a militia that stands for my family and lands against a tyrant of a governor. I—I have no use for these stockings and shirts. Do with them what you will. Only know, please, that I am no less a Patriot, and no more a criminal, than any of the other wives who make stockings for people they care about." Emma dropped the stockings and shirts at her feet, scooped up the sack of eggs, and dropped it into the basket again, then headed for the door. "You'll see someone gets them?" When I said nothing, she went rather angrily out the door and down the path.

Alice came from the stairs and said, "Mistress?"

"We will see if we can know their sympathies from a source other than her words. Cullah said Virtue is never at the meetings. If he is one of us, we have to find out before I say anything to his wife that will put all of us on a gibbet." I could imagine a certain number of shirts and stockings, being found in my possession, and placed in the hands of another of our friends, could be enough to hang us all if she were to be plotting.

The next morning I wrapped the coats in layers of old rags. I took Emma's stockings and shirts, too, but wrapped separately, so that if this were a trap, they were not mixed with my work. I set them into the bottom of the wagon and put a blanket across them and my feet upon them. Bertie drove and Alice sat beside me. Soldiers walked up and down the road in groups of five or six. They were not armed, and paid us no attention, so that when we arrived at John Hancock's house, I felt confident that all would go well. A butler answered the door, and when I asked to see John, he showed me to a fitted parlor.

"Mistress MacLammond, oh, how good to see you," John said. "Do you know my friend here? Quite an irascible lawyer. I am forced to entertain him, for I think no one else can stand to do it. Please let me make you acquainted with Mr. John Adams of Braintree."

A man no taller than I, but stout, stood and bowed. "Good morning, madam," he said grandly. "Will you have refreshments with us?"

I had heard of him, and it was none too flattering, so I simply smiled. "Good morning, sir. Thank you but I cannot stay. I have people waiting for me. I only came to deliver some goods ordered by August Talbot to be sent here."

John scratched his head. "Adams, lend a hand here. We shall both prosper by some physical labor, eh?"

So my parcels were carried by the twine around them, one in each hand, by John and John, Alice, Bertie, and myself. As I said farewell, John Hancock kissed my hand and, leaning his head, said, "Mistress MacLammond, your work will serve a mighty purpose. Keep an eye on this fellow here. Mine are the pockets. His are the brains. My regards to your friend Talbot."

"Mr. Hancock? Are you familiar with all the families who provide supplies for the Patriots?"

"Not really, no."

"Would you be so kind as to let me know anything you discover about a man and wife, Virtue and Emma Dodsil?"

"Where did you hear those names?"

"They are my neighbors."

The two men tried to maintain their composure, but I saw John Adams's eyes flick nervously to John Hancock's, and he turned as if his attention were caught by a robin whose russet fluttering crossed the window. Hancock smiled and said softly to me, "Dodsil and wife are Tories to the bone."

"Ah," I said. "I feared it was a trap. She brought stockings for the militia. I have them hidden in the wagon."

"Deliver them to the first British soldier you come across, Mistress. No doubt they have something in them of the nature of itching powder or poison."

Adams pursed his lips and added, "Or a length of rope."

Alice and I removed our bonnets in my parlor. It had been that simple. This gave me a joyous feeling of being part of something wonderful, and the great relief of having escaped a trap by such a sweet-voiced neighbor.

Late the following night, the sounds of a horse in full gallop stopped just outside our door. A hand rapped. Cullah opened the door. August darted in. "Ressie, put out the candle."

"Yes, but why?" Without answering, he pulled his horse right into my parlor, straight through the kitchen, and down the narrow passage to the barn. I followed him and yelled, "Take it all the way to the far stall. There are two cows on either side, and the smell will mask a run horse."

Cullah ran after him, calling over his shoulder, "I'll tether it. Ressie, you go in the house and sit by the fire as if nothing happened. I'll watch from the doorway. Tell Alice to hide Bertram."

August turned, saying, "I'm going into the hidden room. Sweep your floor. Trust no one except my man Nathaniel—do you remember he came with the messages?—or Rupert, unless they give you the word *gumboo*." Before I could say another word, he crawled behind the stairway panel.

In the kitchen, Alice already had the floor swept and leaned the broom against the chimney just as we heard more horses at a gallop headed this way. I blew out all but one candle, took off my apron and house cap, pulling my hair loose about my shoulders as if I had been ready for bed. Bertie hid at the staircase with Alice. I sat in the settle with a book close to my nose, as if I were too poor to light another candle.

Their words came through the door, "This way. In here." One of them put his hands around his eyes against the window in the kitchen. I was sure he could see me but I did not look up. A few moments later, they opened the door. "We're chasing an outlaw, Goodwife. Did anyone come by here? Did you hear a horse? Anyone enter this house?"

I closed the book. I cupped my hand behind my ear and asked, "I am gone deaf, young man, you will have to speak up. Did you say you were raising dust? I should say. Look at this floor!" I looked beyond him to the soldier behind him. "What did he say? Can you not understand English? Now, do not mumble. Is he speaking to me?"

With frustration upon their faces, they left. I waited until I heard horses' hooves striking the stones in the road before I dropped the bar inside the door.

CHAPTER 38

April 17, 1775

That Monday afternoon, Cullah, Bertie, Alice, and I were sitting in the shade of the flowering apple trees, petals so delicately scented as a whisper drifted about the shadows like lights falling at twilight, when a messenger arrived. He was sent from the governor's house, with another invitation from Margaret for me to come to tea on Tuesday at four. It was handwritten, folded and sealed with her husband's seal and a very large glob of wax holding her own. When I opened it and the wax came off, a shilling was pressed under the red wax. In truth, I felt so busy, so exhausted, and so weary of the soldiers in Boston, that I wished to tell her my regrets. But her last line said, "Make me no excuses, dear friend. I shall have no greater joy in my life than the sight of you that day. As a candle warms the night."

"Terribly dramatic of her to write such a thing, is it not?" I said.

Cullah said, "That's odd."

Suddenly, without explanation to them, I ran with the message to the house. I pulled a stob from the fire and lit a candle, holding the paper across the flame. After a couple of minutes of warming the whole thing and worried it would burst alight, writing appeared at the side margin. "The tide turns tomorrow. Come."

Cullah stood behind me. I watched the mysterious lettering disappear as it cooled. "I must go."

He said, "I'll drive. Take the note with you. If soldiers stop us, we will need it."

We left in the morning after sending Bertie and Alice to Dorothy's house. While Lexington had been busy with troops, commerce had not stopped. Boston, however, was closed down, a city under siege. So many streets were blocked, so many soldiers crowded the way, that getting to the governor's mansion was an hour from the Neck, where it had used to be but a few minutes.

"Will you come inside with me?" I asked him. "I may be an hour or more."

"To a lady's tea? No, my love. I have suffered my share of torments. No, I will sit here. I will be your patient lackey. An hour's quiet thinking will do me no harm."

Margaret's parlor fluttered with the silks and voices of many ladies. Most of them were well-dressed Tory wives making the best of their husbands' dreary assignments when they had rather be in a drawing room in London. Margaret rushed to kiss my cheek and pet my hands. She was too flawy in her words, too demonstrative of affection, her fan waving about my head as she kissed me. When she drew away at last, I saw in my palm another silver shilling. Quickly as a butterfly in flight, she murmured, "Find a reason to go to the library and I shall meet you there."

In the library, Margaret closed the doors. She all but scurried through the room, checking every nook for the presence of another. Then she came to me. "We must make a ruse that we are discussing books I should donate to a dame school you may plan to run."

I paused. "Very well," I said.

"Tonight. It is tonight. You must get home before sundown."

"What is tonight?"

"Ressie, do not ask me to speak more plainly. Do what you have to do to get word to the committee as quickly as possible. Do not wait so much as an hour."

"You know about the committee?"

"Everyone does. We don't know who they are but we know that they exist. Thomas invited all these women here as a diversion for me. He thinks I have paid no attention. I can do no more than this, my friend, except to pray for your safety. They plan to break the rebellion starting tomorrow morning. Soldiers are mustering tonight."

"How shall I make my exit from you?"

"Headaches are always convenient." There was a rattle at the door. She raised her voice a bit. "And I should like you to mark every book that it was donated from my generous collection. I think that is nice, do you not?"

"I will not forget your generosity, my dear friend. The schoolchildren will always know it was you they should thank. May I send my maid for the volumes later, after you have chosen them?"

"Please do. Next week will be soon enough."

"I find I have a dreadful headache and travel is preposterous with the conditions on the road. Would you feel slighted if I am excused, then?"

I turned to find there was indeed a woman standing at the door, listening to us. She said, "Margaret, dear? We wondered if you could tell us which of your cooks made the apple pudding. I should like her to teach it to my cook before Friday."

Margaret tittered and flapped her fan before her face. The woman wanting pudding preceded us, I followed, and Margaret in the rear. I stopped at the front door where a butler held it ajar and bowed. I looked into Margaret's eyes and saw there a flicker of emotion that stunned me. Her lips smiled but tears filled her eyes. She kissed my cheeks. "Fare well, my friend. Godspeed." As soon as that, she smiled her winning smile and swept her gown up with her hands to join the other women. Violins played a duet somewhere in that grand room. As I slipped out the door the chatter of careless women nearly drowned out the music.

I told Cullah what Margaret had said as I stared at the bright shilling in my palm. He turned the wagon and drove down a side street to a wooden building with no sign out front. As he pulled to a stop, he leaned against my bonnet and whispered, "This is the back of the silversmith's shop."

Cullah went inside and I followed him. I could barely see for the darkness. He tapped his head twice. I made as if to adjust my bonnet, and touched the brim twice, also. At last the man said, "This is a private house. Looking for someone?"

Cullah said, "A friend of liberty."

"Have you any news?"

"A little that needs telling, tonight."

"Aye?"

"Tonight."

"Who declares this?" It was Dr. Warren!

Cullah looked at me. He said, "Wife, tell him where you heard this."

I gulped. "From a Patriot in the governor's mansion." I handed him the silver coin.

Dr. Warren took a breath and held it. "God preserve you on your way," he said, and ran from the room.

Cullah inclined his head toward the door, took my elbow, and escorted me to it. Then, rather more loudly, he asked, "Will you give our regards to Benjamin? Tell him his father needs him."

Getting home to our house, beyond Lexington on the road to Concord, was never as difficult as it was that night. Everywhere, I saw women with their maids and children shopping, craftsmen at work at bellows and wood lathe, yet scores of soldiers walked the streets and it seemed as if one or more of them would stop us at every corner. They wore pistols in their belts, some carried muskets with bayonets affixed. After no less than seven times when we were bade to stop and alight while they looked fore and aft in the little wagon, the sun was down and mist rolling in from the bay made every step of the road treacherous.

At the last search, I laughed in the soldier's face. "It is not enough room to hide a dog or a boy, this small wagon. You can see the back is empty. What do you think we are doing? Smuggling?"

Cullah sat like a statue. He seemed half asleep, but I saw the flicker of a muscle in his jaw.

"It is orders, Mistress. We have word traitors are hiding under women's skirts to get in and out of town, and that some pockets are full of lead. Move along."

As we drove along, I asked, "Margaret said tonight. What if it is not?"

"The minutemen would rather be called out falsely than be called not at all."

I remembered so many years back when I had offered to carry a message, and had been soundly rebuffed by the men in Lexington, including my own husband. "A woman? It's terrible. It's ungodly. It's brilliant. It's heresy." This night, I had done just that, in a way no man could ever have done. I wondered how many of men's bold plans throughout history had actually turned on the passing of a shilling between two women? It was past midnight when we got to the house. Bertie and Alice came downstairs. Cullah went to the barn to fetch his musket. I heard church bells. Any joy I felt at having stayed on our mission was soon lost with the face of this boy before me, so eager to see battle.

"What is that sound, mum?" Bertie asked.

Cullah answered for me when I hesitated. "Church bells from Lexington and Concord." He reached for his fowling piece, a pouch of shot, and a powder horn.

Bertie jumped from his seat. "Is it the call to arms?"

I took a deep breath and said, "Yes."

Bertie jumped to his feet. "I'll get Pa's drum."

I blinked back tears. "Very well, Bertie. Go with Grandpa."

Before long, Dolly and her children came to the door. They hid downstairs by the loom. Roland fetched a musket and a lantern while Alice and I climbed the stairs to watch that dim light cross the road and descend the slight hill toward the green of town. Bells rang across the countryside. Drums sounded from every direction.

We made tea. We sat in the parlor and tried to rest, but there was no rest. Surely, surely, until there was bloodshed, there could still be peace. The answer came to me as drums echoed across the hills. I opened the window and leaned out. The night was clear, though the moon rose late, and every echo of every bell seemed to make the stars move.

And then I heard it. Dozens, perhaps, or hundreds most likely, of boots, marching in step. British soldiers marched up the road, among them, cavalrymen and officers.

"I am going," I said to Alice. "I stayed behind before. Always waiting, wondering. Benjamin is no doubt there, Cullah and Bertie are, too. I am going." I pulled on my bonnet and tied it under my chin.

"Mistress, you can't go up there. Them men are going to start a war."

"I have spent too much of my life waiting for Cullah to come home. I can be there to bring him home if such is the end."

"I will come with you."

We took a lantern and made for the road then into the woods until I found the old trail Cullah had shown me. We hurried to the edge of the swamp, across a stream, and over a small meadow, then on through thick maples, birch, walnut, and hemlock. I stopped at the edge of the woods where we could see the village green, for to move forward would have put us in the ranks of the British army. There looked to be hundreds of them. Our fellows gathered on the green, bonfires and torches still alight, adding heavy smoke to the scene. The regular soldiers bristled in their ranks, so precise, so practiced. Our men looked as they were, men who had just stumbled out of bed and off a farm. In the distance, horses rode at full gallop. Men called to one another.

Alice warned, "Find a big tree. Any balls come this way going to kill us, standing here."

One of the British officers shouted at our men to disperse. Cullah, I saw, stood right out in front. I had just slipped behind a wide tree to get my footing betwixt the roots. My head was down, my sight in shadow. Clearer than the beat of my own heart I heard the hiss of a flash in a pan. A chorus of sound filled the air, the clash of metal and clatter of musket fire. I could see nothing for the smoke. I knew not whether our Bertie lived or died. Alice and I held each other in the shadow of that tree, and in a few minutes, British Regulars began to stream through the woods.

I took her hand and screamed, "Run!" I ran, pulling Alice as fast as we could move, though she and I both stumbled. We splashed through the swamp. Men ran behind us. Someone came closer and closer. I could hear him breathing, running, and then he seemed to have fallen back. I crossed the stream. Musket fire rattled behind us, and shot riddled the trees beside us.

Alice fell. "My knee," she said.

"Are you hit?"

"I tripped."

I pushed her and followed her into the shelter of a holly. We wrapped our arms about each other. The prickling leaves tore at my face and hands. "Be still," I mouthed. Feet thundered past us, first one man, then a dozen. We caught our breath. I counted twenty men passing us. "Can you stand, now?"

"I will wait here. You run."

"I cannot leave you, Alice."

"No one will t'ink anything. I'll tell them I am hunting berries."

"Come on, lean on me."

"Go, Missy. You run."

"Not without you."

Alice began to weep but she came when I took her hand. In a few more minutes, we were almost home. Through the trees I could see the open soil of the road, and flashes of red coats as soldiers moved upon it. "Run for the house now, and bar the door. I will come the long way around, through the barn."

She nodded and hobbled across the road, reaching the oak on the other side just as another Regular soldier came down the road. I waited, then stepped from the shadows just after five mounted officers went barreling by. I dropped into the grass at the side of the road until the thunder of hooves passed me. I raised my head. They did not look back.

I thought of Cullah's words about soldiers in pursuit not looking back. I ran up the road, across the field, toward the barn. Someone followed me. I heard feet, the heavier tramping of a man. A man in boots. More steps! There were two at least, I was sure. I felt I would choke, my throat so dry I could not swallow; I needed to cough. The men wore metal. Perhaps a sword. A musket or pistol or both. I ran until, breathless, I fell against the barn door and then got inside the barn. The cows and geese made a racket. Rather than going for the kitchen, which was well seen and obvious, I headed for the narrow opening hidden behind the farm implements, crept between them and a useless shock of dried cornstalks, and slid through the door. Alice went to the basement to hide with Dolly and the children.

I made my way up the steps, trying with every footfall to make no noise. When I reached the top and stepped into Gwenny's bedroom, I tripped and fell to the floor. A chair stood by the opening where I had used it to stand upon to ring the bell. I heard a loud knock below me on the front door then another anxious knock and a voice called out, "Open the door, Ma. It's I, Brendan. I've brought Bertie and a couple other ragged boys you should feed."

I came down the stairs. Alice was panting, sitting at the table with a huge carving knife in her hand. I asked, "Are you going to open it?"

She answered, "Do you know it's him?"

I flung wide the door, to see Bertie, hung by his collar and grinning, held by his father in full Redcoat uniform. He pulled off his hat and rushed inside.

"Brendan! What is the meaning of this?" I asked, though I was barely able to speak. On Bertie's heels followed Benjamin and Cullah. "You are safe!" I cried.

Brendan said, "Roland went home to get his kit. Ma, Pa, don't think me a coward. I saw what happened. I've turned 'cat-in-pan' against them. I could not fire upon my own friends, my own son, my pa and brother. The Lexington boys made good show of it, but they seemed hopeless. Unkempt, untrained, and most of them unarmed. It was meant by the Regulars to be a massacre. In the end, it was the pathetic Patriot who gave us a rout. Perhaps some of the Regulars were loath to fire, I cannot speak for them. I have fought for my country and my sovereign but I cannot go on if we are to war against our brothers. I think I scared poor Ben out of three years' growth when I caught up to him, him thinking he was a prisoner of war." Brendan stripped off his coat and buckler and untied his neckerchief as he spoke. "Have you a plain coat, Ma?"

Benjamin looked at his brother then and gave Brendan's neckerchief a tug before he had it removed. "It's the gallows for you, now." They nudged each other then put their arms across each other's shoulders and clasped Bertie to them.

I gasped at the word "gallows."

"Boy!" Cullah roared. "Don't upset your mother."

Benjamin was a good two inches taller than his older, brawnier brother. "It is all right, husband," I said. "I knew he was teasing. They are brothers." I cupped my hand across my lips, fighting the urge to weep for joy. This was a bold and terrifying comradeship I saw before me.

Alice went to fetch the latest coat we had finished, made of undyed wool.

"But, Pa, where are you going?" Bertie asked.

"We're going, the five of us. Come with me, son, and we'll find Roland." He picked up his musket. "Bring your drum."

And then all of them were gone. I sat, my mouth open, my heart aching, my mind spinning in the smoke of war that filled the house. "Godspeed," I whispered.

Alice said, "We have to get rid of that red coat he left."

CHAPTER 39

April 19, 1775

The Tories marched on Concord. Dozens of Patriots and perhaps hundreds of Tories died, though my men were not among them. I did not know when I would see them again. Two days later, I asked Alice to return with me to Boston. I wanted to see how August was faring, though I felt confident he was away. I also wanted to see Margaret, to thank her. The houses were straight across the street from each other. I asked Alice to find out if Margaret was home while I headed for August's house, where armed British Regulars stood at attention. The door stood ajar, and I saw that what had happened at my home—a search that felt more like an invasion—was in full force. Troops rumbled here and there, carrying boxes, crates, trunks overflowing with silks. They made a pile in the yard and another in the entry hall, where other soldiers rifled each box. Being small and dressed in black, it seemed I faded into the walls, for I moved about without question. In the parlor, a man in a uniform well decorated with gold braid fished through August's aged and battered chest. Maps had been scattered across the table upon which he laid another stack of papers and rolls, causing many of those already there to fall on the floor. I heard voices overhead in loud argument that grew more so. I ran to the stair.

A man's voice—it sounded like August—said, "You will not!"

Another swore, "I have you at last. They will not stop until every candlestick is turned over, every door opened, every pocket emptied. This house belongs to the king."

I made my way up the staircase. Soldiers busied themselves in the library. Several of them came across the gallery with boxes and drawers from chests, their arms stacked high. I hurried until I reached the bedroom where Cullah and I had slept. A man blocked my view. His elbows stuck outward and his silk cloak draped across it. I heard the first slick sound of steel upon steel. August drew a cutlass in one hand and a curved Turkish sword in the other.

"Guard me," shouted Wallace Spencer, as he swung to my left. His cloak fell to the floor. August was squared against three Regulars with swords drawn; he saw me but looked to his accusers. Wallace continued, "There is proof in this house. I know it. This blackguard has deviled me across the seven seas for years. Hancock has delivered to me my own goods, taken off my ships and resold them to me at ten times the price. He's charged with smuggling even now. You will be arrested and hung next to him on the same gallows. Don't stand there, men. Take him."

As I watched, August looked from man to man, at the eyes of the soldiers. A sly smile spread across his face. He squinted then, as if he enjoyed the sport, and said, "Yes, fellows. 'Take him.' How will you have it? Decapitation? Gutting? Shall I let you live but unman you and run the giblets up a gibbet? Come for me. Here's your chance to die like men. Is that not why you joined the army? Are you cowards to the last?" None moved.

Wallace said, "You will not leave this place alive if you murder one of His Majesty's men. As a traitor you will hang anyway. If you make a move against these men, I will have you tortured first. Get him, you cowards."

I opened my mouth to speak. August's head moved side to side, warning me against it. Another soldier came brusquely through the door and all but bumped me out of his way. "Lord Spencer? The colonel wishes to speak to you downstairs. *Immediately,* your lordship." Wallace turned, and as if no others remained in the room, he suddenly locked his eyes into mine. I could hear him breathing as he moved past me and out the door.

August used the diversion Wallace's movements made to strike the sword of one of the three soldiers, sending it flying across the room. I held my hands to my mouth to keep from screaming. Another man crossed him, and with two quick strokes, my brother slashed his face and ran him through. The third put up a brave attempt as the first man regained his weapon and they both worked their swords, but even two at a time could not overcome the man they knew as the Pirate Talbot. When the men lay upon the floor, August wiped his blades on the bed linen, and as he came to me, put them back into scabbards.

He took my face in his hands and kissed my forehead, whispering, "Rupert will bring the old trunk to you. Do not look for me; I will come to you."

"Old trunk?" I asked.

"The trunk in the parlor? You remember? It was in our father's study. It has a false bottom."

I did not. But when he said the words they made me treasure the old trunk. "What about Anne?"

"She's already on her way to New York to wait for me. Good-bye, Ressie. And I love you, too." He clutched my hand and shook my wrist, as if he could think of no other embrace.

"Farewell, August." I kissed him, barely a brush from my lips to his.

He pushed his way through the stumbling soldiers in the gallery, straight up to the last door, the one to the east room where I had once slept. With one great kick he sent the door splintering into the room, entered it, and vanished. I ran after him. There was a window open. A rope hung from it. I watched as in the courtyard below Rupert held a horse. August's black cloak and black tricorn hat gave him the look of a phantom though the day was clear and bright.

I turned to leave just as soldiers entered. I knew I had to act a part if I were to survive this day, too. I pointed to the window. August was away. I knew he was safe. I shouted, "Look! He went down the rope. Follow him, you! He is escaping!" I continued as if I were a child watching a play, calling, "That man is getting away. After him. Go, go!" I urged them on, amazed at how my words stirred them to act. They ran from me and down the stairs.

More was astir in the grand bedroom. The dead guards had been found. I reached in, crouching low at the door, and pulled Wallace's cloak from the floor where he had left it. As I did, I raised my hand and bent my elbow. It crinkled with the sound of paper. August had tucked into my sleeve some sort of message. I pulled it forth.

Honorable Sir, everything is arriv'd. Seventy-five kegs of raven eggs and two hundred h.k. blk powder, deliv'd to store, half that more deliv'd your Res this night under cov. dkness. Our honor'd friend W. will X for his service. J.H.

This letter had been meant for August. Raven eggs were cannonballs and "your Res" meant Resolute, not residence. More powder was on its way to my house! The signature, a work of artistic frills and ruffles, was unmistakably that of John Hancock. I liked John a great deal, yet I smiled, knowing those who scoffed at his penchant for showmanship led them to call him "Jonathan Peacock." Thank God for such a worthy peacock, and thanks also to Margaret, that he, Dr. Warren, and John Adams had escaped the night before the battle at Lexington. I knew one small thing I could do.

I refolded Wallace's cloak, searching for and finding a slit pocket in the inside right-hand seam. I slid the note into it so that one end of the paper was exposed. Then, as if I had actually come to participate in the search of my brother's house, I carried the cloak across my arms as I descended the stair. In the main parlor, I approached Wallace Spencer and the colonel as they shuffled through papers, hunting, perhaps, for this very note. "Lord Spencer?" I called. "Your prisoner has escaped. You should have taken him yourself."

Wallace shouted. He cursed. He ran up the stairs.

I faced the colonel. I said to him, "Sir, do you know subterfuge when you see it? Have you ever been in the presence of an actor so cunning at lies that not a word from such a one can be trusted? I hear the Patriots have such in their employ."

The officer said, "I have not time for you, woman. Get out of this house. We are trying to conduct business here."

"Lord Spencer is *such* a gentleman, is he not?"

"Yes, yes, I suppose so." He stacked some papers, straightening the edges.

Wallace returned to the room in full run, grasping at the doorjamb as he came. "The villain is away! Why did your men fail? We had him! Blast your eyes, man."

"I *am* sorry, your lordship," the colonel said.

I held Wallace's cloak, gesturing. "Here, Wallace. Lord Spencer, I brought your cloak so it would not be soiled by the villainy afoot."

He shook his head, his teeth gritting together so that I heard the squeak. "There it is. I thought the man had taken it, too. Give me that." He whipped it from my arms and the note whisked out of the pocket, flew through the air, and spiraled to the floor at the feet of the colonel as Wallace stormed toward the front door.

The colonel looked at the note for a count of three before he knelt and picked it up. He read it. I counted three ticks, like the circling of a spinning wheel. Tick. Tick. Tick. The colonel shouted, with a voice I expect had been trained on a battlefield, "Stop! Arrest that man! Arrest Lord Spencer!"

In the ensuing chaos, I slipped from the house and ran for the wagon. Alice helped me in. She said, "Mistress, the servants at Mistress Gage's home would not let me in the door. I went to the back and say some words with the cook. Mistress Gage is gone. Her husband shipped her to London this morning. The ship sailed before dawn."

I was breathing hard. I hung my head. "Poor Margaret, but I may write to her?"

"The cook told me to ask you not to do that. She said, Mistress Margaret give you her last, best gift. Best way to accept it, is to leave it all be."

I would weep for her later. I would not weep in the street. "You are right. Let us get home immediately."

"What of your brother, Mistress? It look like there are soldiers there."

"There *are* soldiers there but my brother is escaped. I saw him go."

Two days later, a man with black gauze over his face knocked on my door at midnight. He did not give me a signal I could trust. I did not open the door. When the sun arose I saw at the doorway my father's old trunk.

It took me three days to discover the secret to getting the hidden panel open in the trunk's bottom. It held the deed to August's house in Boston. It held the license granted to him by the Crown to privateer Dutch, Spanish, and French ships and commandeer them for the British navy, and it held a single peacock feather, long and slender, shimmering with blue-green and light; at the top the colors formed into an eye shape, as if the bird could see from it. This was the one thing August had taken to remind himself of our childhood, our beginnings. I saw him anew; that gruff, perhaps hard man had indeed once been a boy who played, carelessly gamboling as I had done. He had gone back to Jamaica and fetched this chest after the place was ransacked. Had walked among the ruins and found a trace of the peacocks. The feather brought to mind the cry—almost a woman's scream—of the peafowl wandering the grounds at Two Crowns Plantation. I took it to my bedroom and placed it upon two nails above my bed. Every night when I put out the light, I would see the eye of it, and look into that, to my first home.

Alice and I lugged the chest up to my bedroom. I put the secret things in their secret place, and I put on top of them, as if all were innocent and calm, old and ragged winter bed linens for the upstairs. All the good ones, I hid beneath the beds themselves in case a search party should seize my linens, again.

Brendan, August, Benjamin, and Bertie had set out with their officers, to fetch the cannons left at Fort Ticonderoga. On their return, Benjamin had promised they would also take the two their uncle had sent, from my barn. They returned by the first of June, moving at night through dismal rain over the roughest of ground. I packed them food in knapsacks, and I covered their shoulders with shirts and their legs with new britches. The cannons rolled away just two days before my house was searched again. It was so full of bolts and bolts of cloth I had woven, baskets of tow and spun wool, there was barely room for them, and the Redcoats found little to confiscate. So they took a rug August had sent me from the Orient. It was battered and threadbare, I said, to console myself.

Many nights, I could not sleep. Every night I thought I heard a distant drumming, a distant firing of guns, like distant thunder, so much so that rain surprised me when it actually fell. I heard Goody Carnegie wailing with sorrow, and I heard Cullah's voice saying, "War is coming. War is coming."

And then it came. June seventeenth.

Breed's Hill, they called the place. Later the name would be forgotten and the taller mound, Bunker Hill, remembered.

My Cullah fell there and I will never forget that place. It was said by a man who had stood shoulder to shoulder with him that when he'd fired five shots that old fowling piece jammed. After that, he fought with claymore in hand like a vicious fighting machine, boldly fending off soldiers three and four at a time, while behind him, Dr. Warren loaded and primed a musket. The ball that felled Dr. Warren pierced Cullah through the heart first.

Something told me, as I washed him, lying naked on my kitchen table, that he had always been meant to die this way. That there were indeed better and worse ways to die, and that he deserved a death both valiant and quick rather than the slow torment of disease or aging's loss of mind. I pictured him standing there, reloading that fowling piece, finally giving up and resorting to fighting the way the Scots at Culloden had done and died, swinging that claymore against an overpowering enemy bearing powder and shot. "My

Cullah, my Eadan. My Scottish Highlander. Your mind always hearing the echoing drums of war from centuries past, in which you might have been a valiant hero. You were not meant for this time, were you?"

Alice helped me dress him. The hardest part was putting onto his feet the old boots that used to smell of beeswax. It took us an hour but I could not bring myself to bury him barefooted. We laid him beside Jacob, next to Gwyneth. As Reverend Clarke read the words, my heart, so often hollowed by loss, had always known Eadan Lamont was alive even when he was not with me. Now the emptiness I felt was a vast ocean. I closed my eyes. A stiff gust of wind moved my hair and bonnet, and I felt myself holding to the swaying gunwale of a great ship moving through stormy seas. I inhaled and held my breath. Then I knelt at the grave as men I knew not filled the earth in upon my love.

"Widow?" one of them called. "I say, Widow MacLammond?"

"Do you mean me, sir?"

"Yes, Mistress. Have you a sixpence for us?"

In my pocket, Margaret's shilling. I placed it in his hand. "Take this."

"La, *thank* you, Mistress. 'At's generous of you."

I walked home, pushing my feet to a hard rhythm so that Alice, whose knee still pained her, had no choice but to lag behind me.

My sons and grandson survived Breed's Hill and cheered their rout of the British army, though Bertie was sent back to me for a rest, and for two weeks could not keep his food down. He fretted until I gave him permission to return to the fight once he was well. In the meantime, he practiced, inventing new drum patterns, so that no one would mistake his beating for that of a British drummer boy.

July 21, 1775

No one moved through Boston. It was besieged. We worked our farm as we could then, we women, always with Cullah's pistol nearby. We hid from any travelers on the road.

On a night in July, a birdcall and a tap at my window made me open the door. My brother August stood before me, dressed in huntsman's leathers.

He motioned behind his back, and a cadre of men in fine blue coats entered. One of them was taller than the rest. He would have towered over Cullah, and I saw he was seconded and attended by my son Brendan, who also wore a blue coat. Brendan looked neither right nor left, nor at me. I held my breath for a moment, sensing that this was not the time for motherly kisses.

"Madam," began the tall man. "I beg your indulgence. May we spend a couple of hours before your hearth?"

"If August Talbot brings you to my door, you are welcome. I have a piece of mutton warmed, with parsnip roots and celery. I have cider."

August jerked his head from Brendan's direction to the kitchen table, then he addressed the tall man. "General Washington? You will do the Continental army a good service by letting this lady inspect your coat."

By the end of summer, an epidemic of bloody dysentery hit Massachusetts and devastated the British army. There were by then more of them in the country than of us. I stayed away from the city but I heard Serenity Spencer died of it, as did Daniel Charlesworth. America Roberts Charlesworth moved to Pennsylvania to live with her sister Portia.

In September, as it began to rain, Reverend Clarke called upon his congregation, now almost all women, to mind how judgment could come upon the earth when her inhabitants displeased their Creator.

We did not get dysentery or suffer for food, though Dolly, Alice, and I worked long days at harvesting and drying. We had no salt for curing so we butchered nothing larger than a hen. I missed things like salt and sugar, spices and wheat flour. I sent and spent the gold August left with me for food for our army. When Alice and I managed to shear a sheep—poor animal looked as if it had been caught by some wool-eating animal, so rough was our job of it—I made a man's coat and gave it to the first one who came to our door.

During the long rains of autumn, I filled my secret room above the loom with cloth, stockpiling it in the barn, too, searching twice a week for moths and weevils. I traded bolts of it for precious indigo and whiting. Once, on a street in Lexington in broad daylight, my skirt heavy with vials of indigo, my wheelbarrow light and empty, I glared at some young British conscript until he turned from my eyes.

I worried much about my sons, but not my brother, for I held great faith that because I heard nothing from him, August was somewhere doing what he could in the name of the Continental army. I moved some boxes and crates and came upon the first chests he had once hidden with me. Neither was locked.

I turned the latch of one and raised the lid. It held a few papers. They seemed to be letters, from August to a woman. Love letters. I smiled and held them to my bosom. I hoped he was happy at least for a while, as I had been. I set them down reverently. Under the letters sat a boxed set of dueling pistols and a box of shot and powder. I lifted them out. We might need them. Beneath that was a small casket, about the size of two loaves of bread. Its latch was closed and no key sat in the lock. I set it on the floor, and took out some clothes. They looked to be a boy's clothes, with stains and holes. Ripped keepsakes of his past, I supposed. In the pocket of the waistcoat, I found a small key. It opened the casket. The casket held doubloons. Dozens of them. We would be able to eat, I thought, and buy more wool. I could make more coats. No American who crossed my path or my doorway would leave without a coat if he needed one.

The second chest was lighter than the first. It was loaded with ships' maps. A captain's logbook, and another. Four of them. A sextant. A long glass. At the bottom lay five cutlasses. One of them was battered, dented, its tip broken off. I feared to touch it, though I supposed if the thing were haunted with the blood, we would have seen the spirits by now. I closed the lid and held my hand against it, thinking of my brother's hand having lain upon this very wood, and I wished him health and life.

In the mornings oak leaves captured the slanted sunlight, fooling the eye, as if they held the last golden rays of summer suspended for a few more days. The nights turned cold. One day, just before noon, a hand knocked at my door. A winter wind was howling. Before me stood a boy dressed in rags, thin as Roland's poor frame had been so long ago. "M-m-mistress? Have you got a spare crust? Anything?"

"What are you doing abroad in this weather, young man?"

"Going to join the rebels, Mistress."

"Where is your musket? Your cartridge bag?" He ducked his head in a clumsy bow and pulled his weapon, an ancient blunderbuss, from where it leaned against the wall. "Come in this house." I fed him bread, such as I had, and meat, both of them meant for our noon.

He drank every drop of the broth in the pot. "Thank you so, Mistress. I hain't et in two days."

When he rose to leave, I pulled at his sleeve. "Wait," I said. "Take this." I draped my cloak across his shoulders. It was too small, for though he was all bones and angles, he was tall. "This will not do you. Wait, boy, would you please? I have something else." I hurried up the stairs to my room. There behind the door hung a new cloak I had made for Cullah. I pulled it from the hook. I held it against my cheek.

When I put it across the boy's shoulders, he took hold of it with reverence. "Oh, Mistress, this is so very fine. It must belong to the master of this house."

"It did. Now stand there while I bless it upon you," I said. I chanted the old Gaelic words, circling the boy, my hand upon the wool of the cloak. It began, *"Nar a gonar fe-ahr an eididh. Nar a reubar e gue- brath,"* and the words settled oddly, going from asking protection for the man who wore the garment, to describing the leg bone of a deer piercing the tail of a salmon. I believed the meaning was long lost, for even Goody Boyne, who had taught it me, knew them not, but I imagined, too, since the words had survived all this time, that they had strength, and perhaps the leg shank referred to the sharpness of a spear tip, so that the wearer of my goods would be swift in battle and safe from all piercing. Perhaps I was wrong to say the words, but they were said, and I patted his shoulder.

"Wait," he exclaimed, stepping back. "Do you cast a spell upon me for having asked food?"

I smiled. "It is not witchcraft. It is a prayer older than this time. We must not question what has stood since before King Richard's day."

"Oh. It's a Christian prayer, then? What language?"

I almost said Scottish, but the tongue was outlawed in its own land and I dared not. "The tongue of angels. When you wear this cloak, you will embody courage and cunning skill in battle, clear thinking, and bravery. Yours will be the mind of a general at arms, a strategist. Keep it always with you, even on warm days when you cannot wear it. Never forget the power of it."

"Mistress, your words give me fear."

"Let them give you comfort instead." I questioned him with my expression and changed my tone to be more motherly. "Would you rather not have the cloak? You may leave it here if you wish. It is not a spell, I promise you on the Holy Cross." He took one look at the snow piling against the glass over the kitchen table, shook his head no. I said, "Then see that you wear it well and proudly. This belonged to a great man, a Patriot. A gentleman and an American Patriot."

"Yes, Mistress."

When I closed the door after him, I said, "Alice? Let us make another cloak. Another man will come along soon enough. They will all be hungry and cold."

"Mistress, you give away Master Cullah's cloak."

Tears dripped from my chin, already rushing the moment his name crossed her lips. "Yes."

"Why you do that?"

"The boy needed it. He will fight for freedom."

"How you know that?"

"Well, I do not know it. He said it, and I believed him."

"Not every man comes to the door going to tell the truth."

"Alice, did you suspect him of something?"

"No, Mistress. He was honest enough. Just hungry enough to tell you what you want to hear. Any boy might be hungry. Can't feed 'em all."

I smiled. "Then I have done him no harm. If it keeps him alive, it is given gladly."

Alice stared at the fire, then without turning her head, she glanced in my direction and asked, "Mistress, would you give me a cloak?"

"Is something amiss with your own?"

"I gave it to a slave woman I know."

I held out my hand. Somewhat reluctantly, she reached out with her own. I held her hand in mine. We both welled up with tears, and her face darkened as did mine.

Alice asked, "I suppose we making another cloak?"

"Probably better make two."

"Yes, Mistress. We have to sew all night or wear blankets to Meeting tomorrow."

The next week two fellows came, cold and hungry. One of them was smaller, and so I gave one of Brendan's old coats to him. I had nothing finished yet for the larger man, except Cullah's old and tattered cloak. "I am sorry it is so poor," I said.

"Mistress, it is marvelous warm. Thank you kindly."

January 2, 1776

Christmas and Hogmanay we celebrated in Dolly's kitchen. I made a pudding the size of her new babe's head. His name was John Paul. By Epiphany, Roland returned home to tell us of a place called Valley Forge, and that our own Congress had left the men naked and starving after promising food and uniforms. Smallpox, he said, killed scores every day. Men deserted whose enlistments were up because to stay meant starvation. I had little money left. I rummaged through trunks and every hidey-hole in the house for coins or clothing to send. He offered to return to the field with anything I could find.

On a shelf in the attic, a little crate held some old clothes I had never meant to part with. I pulled out my quilted petticoat made by Ma. Almost nothing remained of the original, though I expected it still lay inside the other layers. In a sort of desperate hope that I had overlooked some odd ha'penny, I carried it downstairs. By the fireplace, I took up scissors and began to cut it apart, carefully opening every wide place where anything might be hidden. I found a lump that was not tow or lint. I cut into the place and pried it open. A length of gold chain fell out, and when I pulled it, it was a ruby necklace. Three large stones set in pure gold hung from the chain. I saw by the familiar design that they had been meant as a set with the ruby ring, the only thing of value I yet owned. Ma had given one of her daughters part of the set, one another, as sisters should be two parts of something that went together. I put it in my pocket and returned to Dolly and Roland's house. A great lump stilled my voice, as I tried not to weep, and held it up so that the fire showed through the stones. "Roland," I said, "take this. Take my wagon, too. We will use yours. Take everything we can spare, and use this to buy whatever it will buy."

March 21, 1776

It was a blustery, muddy spring. With Bertie driving the wagon, Alice sat next to me as we made our way to Boston, for now women could trade a little there, and the soldiers did allow us to buy flour though it was costly. She seemed oblivious to the uniformed army all about us, busy at her tatting. I remarked to her that in a moving coach that was no small feat, for I could do aught but stare at the trees when I rode else I suffered motion sickness. I asked her to look about, just to appear more natural, but she said, "Mistress, you admire all the pretty gentlemen's red clothes for me, as I have got a knot here I am trying to fix and I am vexed out of my eternal life over it." Then she winked at me, slyly, and wrinkled her lips in disgust. Bertie was filled with a fervor that I reckon could be accounted for by his being so great a part of the events that had called us all to arms. It was all I could do to remind him not to thrash the horses into a run, and that decorum and a straight face would serve us both. We passed line after line of British soldiers, fusiliers, and marines, ranks of artillery and wagons full of ammunition pulled by mules.

Tied under my petticoat by their stocking straps and overlapping like great pleats hung four pairs of men's buff breeches. Two more were rolled into each side of my small farthingale. Under our feet in the false bottom were seven blue coats of differing size, all cut to resemble General Washington's fine habit. I had not attached braids of rank, for I knew not to whom the coats would go, but I had sewed on gold buttons, rows of them, and turned up the cuffs so elegantly. I had prayed the chant over every one of them, that the man wearing it would never be wounded, that blood would not touch the work of my loom and my needle.

We reached the woods beyond Menotomy, and Bertie began to sing "O Waly, Waly." A man walking past wearing plain clothes and a flat parson's hat looked up at us as we passed. He nodded, touching his hat brim. I smiled. In a few minutes, after crossing and heading up the road, toward the Neck, three plain-clothed minutemen appeared from the woods and walked ahead of our horse. One more came from behind, carrying a pack as if he were a craftsman on his way to sell his wares though I knew him from the Committee of Safety.

At the green in Boston, we turned right and made for the lower end of town, at last into the yard behind Boston's First Church, traversed the gravel between the walls, and made for a shabby mercantile and warehouse district centered behind Faneuil Hall. Our aim was an old house, which had been converted into a storefront, though the door of it was battened and nailed shut. In the alley next to it sat a hogshead seeping with tar and treacle, printed with MOLLASS on the side.

Checking for eyes upon us, I stepped down from the wagon, opened the back where the concealed drawer lay, and pulled out my bundles, stacking them against the wall. By reaching into my skirt where a pocket might have hung, I could untie the first pant leg and all the others slithered to the ground. Alice took the two from the farthingale then got quickly back aboard the wagon. I pulled the lid from the molasses keg. It was so tall the top was even with my elbows. First came a four-inch trough filled with reeking, soured molasses. Under it was another trough, also marked molasses, but this one I knew was filled with clay and bore a top drilled full of holes to sop up any leaking of the real molasses. Under that, the opening was lined with tarred cloth and paper and I packed the buff breeches and blue coats with great care into it. As I laid in the sixth coat, pressing it down, Alice began to hum, "Gloomy Winter's Now Awa'," and as we had planned, Bertie flicked the reins and the wagon moved forward, carrying them away, leaving me behind. The committeemen vanished between buildings and into shadows. A boy driving a black-skinned nurse or maid on an errand seemed as normal a sight as any could be.

Peering around the corner of the building, I saw three armed Redcoats across the street, talking to each other. One of them looked to be no more than a boy, a lad like my Bertie. He pointed my direction with a finger, then looking at the other men, nodded.

I laid the clay trough into the hogshead, on top of the coats. I put the molasses trough upon it, but it was full; the lid would almost not shut. On the ground were two broken bricks, so I laid them atop the lid. If I had put in the seventh coat it would not have shut, and we would have been found out.

I saw Redcoats halfway across the street so I turned my back to the soldiers, pulled the string from the wrapping of the last coat, and as if it were my own garment laid it over my arm, pulling my cloak over it. As I strolled from the alley and turned to the left, one of the Redcoats pointed at me.

"Ho, there, granny!" a voice called behind me. I quickened my steps. "I say, stop there, old woman!" He had a decided lisp that was hard to understand.

I stopped before the road that led to the front of the hall. I turned. I searched their faces, and decided upon a tactic of indignity combined with innocence and silliness. "Were you addressing me, young man?"

"Yeth! You, granny. We ordered you to th-top." It was the youngest. He not only had a lisp but had a vile accent, as far removed from nobility as could get. One of the many pressed into service with no other hope of employment, one of the many who just as well made up our rebel army here.

"It is a great thing I am not your grandmother, young man, for if I were I should box your ears. How despicably rude. Good day, gentlemen." I wheeled around, keeping my cloak about my form with my hands, and stepped off the walking stones, moving around a large, fresh pile left by horses.

One of the older Redcoats quick-stepped in front of me and placed his musket across my path at an angle. "Where are you going, Goodwife? What have you got there? We have orders to question all passers-by."

"I am not 'Goodwife.' I am 'Widow.' I have *naught* to do with *you* or your questions. Now be off with the three of you before I report you to General Howe. Yes, I see you know him. I have—" At that moment, the youngest man took my shoulder. I could control my face but not my body, and at his touch I wrested myself away from him with a turn that opened my cloak.

"Ho! Wha' 'ave you there? Why, thith granny ith one of them *bath-tardth!*" he said. He reached into my cloak and tore the coat from my hands. "We've caught a rebel thpy, a traitor against Hith Thovereign Majeth-ty."

"Give me that," I said, reverting to a whining tone. "I *found* it fair and true. It is not yours and I can make many a good covering for my babes with it. Now let it go. You shall get it filthy before I have had a chance to sell the buttons. I found it."

The third man, who until then had yet to speak, asked, "Where did you find it?"

"It was rolled up natty and squashed into the center of a bush, as if the man who wanted it was coming back but could not carry it into town. You would not want such a thing left there for the use of rebels, would you? No. I thought to myself, I thought, what others have lost is mine to gain, is it not? I am a poor old widow with seven mouths to feed, and I can sell these buttons and cut the rest to clouties for my grandbaby's bottom."

He watched my face as I spoke and I saw that he was a little too wise. Perhaps his quietude meant he had better judgment than the others, and he was not believing my tale. He said, "Let's take her to the colonel. See what he says to do."

I stood before his colonel in the parlor of Lady Spencer's house where once I had danced a reel, where I had made Wallace a traitor with us, where I had helped August escape. The brigand did not so much as ask me to sit or offer tea. He did not recognize me from the day August escaped, either. He talked with the soldiers for a moment and then came toward me, adjusted his powdered wig, and leaned forward. "You know, do you not, what this coat is, Mistress?"

"I do, sir." I leaned toward him and crooked my finger at him, then cupped my hand across my mouth as if to tell a secret to a child. "It is nearly new. I found it in a bush."

He snarled. "Since you had to walk past breastworks and artillery to come here, I warrant you know that this color of coat, this blue, is the one chosen by the outlaw Washington and his men—soon to be hung, mind you—as a uniform of their treason against the King, His Royal Majesty George Third, do you not?"

I smiled and nodded. "I do know that, sir."

"And here, in broad daylight, you are caught carrying just such a coat."

"Yes, your lordship, that is true."

"I am not a lord."

"No, sir."

"Have I met you before? You look familiar."

I knew the colonel from his raid on August's house. I smiled. "Perhaps it was last market day. Did you buy my hog foot stew?"

He made a face of disgust. "Did you make that coat?"

"Why, everyone knows the rebels get these from France. See this weft? Only French mills make such. The color is—"

"Where were you taking it? And to whom? I suppose you would not confess to treason, but would rather some poor fool hang in your place? You tell me who was to receive the coat and who made it, and then I will let you go, grandmother."

I winced at him calling me that. "I may be convicted of being foolish, your lordship, but as I see so much of it around me, I am sure it is not a hanging offense. I saw this bright color and found the coat in a bush, rolled up. I knew at once it was either hidden for someone's return or placed as a trap by your men. I have mouths to feed and those buttons are sure to bring some beef tongue or a bit of hog back."

"What is your name?"

"Widow MacLammond." Those words felt like a firebrand upon my heart.

"Where do you live?"

"Me, sir? Why, down the main road and take the second path past where there was once a tree but it was taken down in a storm in seventeen and fifty-one. Then go as far as it takes to sing three verses of the Doxology and turn right on a path where there was a mill some years back but now it has become a grain house—"

"Enough. What do you do in this town, madam?"

I smiled when he interrupted me, as if I wished to appear helpful. "I do a little tatting and toting, you know. Selling odd bits I find. Cleaning shoes."

"Let me see your hands."

I held them forth. The tar-soaked hogshead had left my fingers blacked and the calluses were real. They trembled, but I exaggerated it to make it seem more of an old woman's palsy than fearful trembling. My heart jumped and bucked like a spring colt.

"I think you are lying."

"Lying? Sir, I am a woman of good repute. Honest as a *fairy*. Your accusation cuts me to the bone. I never, *ever*, lie." I saw from the corner of my eye

Bertram driving past, with Alice facing this way. I said, "Ask any soul in this town. Ask that woman there, or the boy driving. Everyone knows me, sir."

The British colonel returned to the far side of Lady Spencer's buffet he was using for his desk. He moved some papers and uncovered a pair of clippers. "Here," he said, tossing them toward the edge of the table closest to me. "Cut it up for clouts."

I put the thought of all those hours of work, the strain on my eyes, the tortured fingers, out of my head and as far from my face as the moon was from the land. "Are you going to let me keep the buttons?" I asked, as I began snipping them from the sleeves and coat front. My fingers trembled so violently the metal blades gave a little drum roll against the button's metal shank.

"Cut it," he said with a voice that sent a chill into the room.

I slashed into the sleeves, folding them out as I cut them from the jacket. I cut the front from the back and frowned to hide my lip quivering.

"Why do you stop?"

"If I cut it this way it will be too small, and if I cut it that way," I said, turning the remainder as I spoke, creating havoc amongst the papers on the desk, "it is long and narrow. Look, it has padding inside. That will hold a wet bottom, will it not? Thank you, sir, for the use of your scissor. I would have had to take a knife to it on the kitchen table, and you know how clumsy that might be." I shoved papers, strewing them to the floor. I stacked the scraps of blue wool, leaving shredded bits across his desk and whisking the papers about again; I reached for the buttons. He brushed them from my hand. I could not hide the dismay on my face. I said, "Those might be gold on top. I could feed my family with 'em, sir. Would you not give me a few?"

He poured them from one hand to the other, then into my outstretched hand, saving one last button. He took the last gold button and tossed it twice, catching it as he stared at my face. "I could have you searched, madam, to see if you are hiding blue coats elsewhere on your person."

I stilled the rather silly smile I wore and stared. I unhooked the frog on my cloak and dropped it behind me. I unwrapped my shawl and let it fall before me, and took my apron by the strings, holding it loosely while never letting his eyes free of my stare, and made as if to drop it, too.

A harried soldier came in a far door. The colonel shifted his gaze. "All right. You are a simple old woman who found a rebel coat. Take your foul-smelling rags and be off with you, and for heaven's sake wash yourself when you get home. All you rebels reek of rancid treacle."

That very afternoon in the stone room below the house, where no sound penetrated outside, I sat upon the bench and put my feet on the pedals of the loom. Bertie lifted the strap over his shoulder and pulled his sticks from his back pocket. Back and forth on the pedals, click with the right foot, clock with the left, my hands pushed the shuttle loaded with blue across the warps of pure, good wool warping of rebel blue. I determined I would make five more in place of the one ruined coat. I had told a pack of lies to keep it yet no blood of any Son of Liberty had stained it. It was not ruined. It would become patching, buttonhole binding, facing, and pockets. It was the cost of war. I rubbed my sore hands with sheepskin. These hands are given, too, I thought. My soreness was nothing compared to what others suffered and gave.

I knew what I believed and I knew at last, not what I would die for, but for what I would live. I was caught up in this land, and its time. I no longer wished to go home, for this was home. And I believed in what I had heard all my years on these shores. First of all, the right of free people to live without tyranny.

Liberty.

The very word tattooed a cannonade across my soul as Bertie trotted the sticks on the drum to the rhythm of the loom. Faster and faster we went, Bertram's eyes locked into mine, the drum and the loom beating out the words to a song. He added flourishes that would do any commander proud. We dared to raise our voices above the rattle and rhythm, singing "Yankee Doodle Dandy."

I watched closely this boy, whose skin was so like my own. His eyes had my color and spark, his hair more like Cullah's than mine. He had come home yesterday for food and clothes and he would leave with the Massachusetts men in two days more. The battle was not done. The boy's feet stepped with lively art, his dark hair, tied with a white ribbon, lifting against his back. I closed my eyes and felt my hands and feet moving quick-step, brandishing the only weapon of war I could use, my whole being doing the dance of freedom, as a man with a claymore and an axe once told me to fight, wielding my loom.

EPILOGUE

November 11, 1781

I am past sixty, now. The British have surrendered, and in just a few weeks, there were no Redcoats left on this shore, and if there are, they wear brown and mind their manners. I have not seen August since that night in July of '75, when he showed up at my door with no less than General Washington himself. I like to think that somewhere, on some vast ocean, he and beautiful, exotic Anne are standing side by side, watching seagulls swirl above the mainmast as their ship crosses the waves. As Lady Spencer advised, I make believe all my dear ones are not gone, just out of my line of sight beyond some curtain or cluster of people, or tree. I tell no one, of course, though I am of an age when I might be allowed my oddities and still not be considered as frighteningly mad as Goody Carnegie had been. The ruse is most difficult on moonlit nights when I used to wake and behold the outline of Cullah's profile next to me.

Benjamin and Brendan both came home and make their living together as brothers in trade goods. Roland came home after taking the food to Washington's army, and though unwounded, he promptly died. We believe his heart gave way. Bertie married and I have given him and his fifteen-year-old wife a section of this land for their own farm. Dolly is a grandmother and that makes me a great-grandmother. Gwenny's daughter Elizabeth died last year of milk sickness. Alice is still with me. She helps me carry on, though I have continued to encourage her to find a life of her own if she wishes.

Now, too, that my children's children are grown and I become more useless by the day, I think sometimes of going to Jamaica. There is nothing to stop me. I have a little money. I have time. I have no one to care for who cannot fend for themselves. I think of the house on Meager Bay and when the wind freshens through the upper windows here sometimes I lean out, imagining myself on a ship cresting a wave, headed to the West Indies. My grandchildren cannot imagine that I came from a place with wide white buildings and warm breezes, a place never touched by ice and snow.

I know that I would never return from such a voyage. Whether death found me on the ship or on the shores I remember so well, it would find me, so I choose now to not go. My life is too interwoven here to survive pulling its strings asunder. While I spent my whole being longing, aching for freedom and a chance at leaving this place, I see that I am also free to stay. Free to choose my ties. I will not go because to stay and live here, to die here, will give my children what I never had. Certainty. A headstone to polish. A mother who stayed.

My fingers ache so that I often dream of carrying a heavy iron kettle through the woods, and I wake afraid of bears and Indians, and I rub mutton fat on the swollen knuckles. My hands no longer slide a shuttle as if it were a smooth stone, rippling the warp as if it were water; my back is bent and will not straighten. My fabric has irregularities for which I take full blame. For a long time, I thought that my days mattered little beyond the children I bore and the labors I accomplished, that invisibility was virtue.

Any woman's life has its heartbreaks and raptures, its evils, its blessings. My life has not been one of pure and even weft, smooth and strong, a warp of courage spanning the loom of my heritage. Out of ignorance or spite, hunger or anger, I have at times done what I must to survive, not thinking of the cost. There were also those times when I hid my tears and faced my enemies, when I won by guile and inner strength, and when I believe I touched, in my mind and heart, the highest capacity in a human for the divine.

I have been swept along by life's storms, made to choose my life's path on the wing, often with few options. As I look back I see that even when I thought I was choosing, often I elected merely to survive. I have struggled with a natural tendency to anger and to fabricate tales, but my heart was ever watchful for rightness and goodness, and love. There are those like my Cullah, who stand stalwart without lies, without anger, against the gale of life, and I honor them. I was placed on this shore in a time that has changed, I think, the world—at least if I am to believe what I heard and read when at last our Declaration was read from an upper window in Boston. Perhaps, along with hundreds of other women in this place during this momentous time, I have made a difference. Perhaps I kept some from freezing or starving. The hidden room and unseen stairs in this house have been a respite place for one runaway slave and her babe on their way north.

I am my own tapestry, then, made as I could for myself. Some holes in my fabric have been made by others, some torn by chance. Missing threads in the weave represent all those I have loved who died so long before me. Sunshine and apple blossoms tint it, along with sea foam and stars. Dark places mark where tears dyed the cloth, darker still, the stains of blood, all of it laced with the crystal blue of Meager Bay on a bright day and a single strand of ruby the color of the ring of my mother's that I still have. The strong, even places consecrate moments where love outmatched loss, and where great good came from sacrifice. When it was finished, it was not what I expected it to be. I had once imagined to live as a delicately fashioned bolt of fine silk of high and gentle quality, perfect but for a minor slub or two. The life I have lived was not a lady's silk but a colorful, natty tapestry of embroidery, wincyette, lace, and motley. Many men I have known in my life will be written about and remembered for the deeds they have done these many years since the colonies loosed their bonds. My story is the story of other women like me, women who left no name, who will not be remembered or their deeds written, every one of them a restless stalk of flax who lent fiber to the making of a whole cloth, every one of them a thread, be it gold, dapple, crimson, or tarred. Let this tapestry be a record, then, that once there lived a woman, and that her name was Resolute.

GLOSSARY AND PRONUNCIATION GUIDE

Bewend (bee-WEND)—to berate

Blithest (BLEYE-thest)—loveliest

Eadan (AEH-dan)

Flawy (FLAH-wee)—flowery

Gamock (GAMM-ock)—fool, silly person

Gree-a-tuch (GREE-ah-touch)—a female child before baptism and be-
stowal of a name

Gumboo (gum-BOO)—transliterated from Scots *giumbhu: Bless me!*

Hack-slaver (HACK-slah-ver)—a rogue

Hasken (HAH-skuhn)

Hogshead (HOGS-head)—a barrel

Johansen (yo-HAHN-sehn)

Lamont (Scots LAMB-int)—a Highland clan

MacPherson (Mack-FAIR-sn)

MacLammond (Mack-LAMB-int)

Massapoquot (Mass-ah-POE-kwaht)

Meager Bay, Jamaica—later changed to Montego Bay

Mistick—old spelling of the town of Mystik, Massachusetts

Mummers (MUM-ehrs)—traveling theatrical band of poets, musicians,
and mimes

Pasties (PASS-tees)—double-crusted pastries filled with meat and vegetable

Patois (pah-TWAH)—combination of French, English, and one or more native tongues

Sally—to commerce with, to venture, or to ambush

Sclarty-paps (SLAHR-tee-paps)—slovenly housekeeper, lazy

Scunging (SKUHN-jing)—dirty and unkempt

Williwaw (WILL-ee-WAH)—a turbulent storm

Wincyette (win-see-ETT)—cotton fabric with a raised nap on both sides

GAELIC CHARMS

FROM *Carmina Gadelica* (ca 1870)

Blessing the Loom

. . . Consecrate the four posts of my loom, Till I begin on Monday.

Her pedals, her sleay, and her shuttle, Her reeds, her warp, and her cogs,

Her cloth-beam, and her thread-beam, Thrums and the thread of the plies.

Every web, black, white, and fair, Roan, dun, checked, and red,

Give Thy blessing everywhere, On every shuttle passing under the thread.

Thus will my loom be unharmed, Till I shall arise on Monday . . .

Blessing the Cloth

The shank of the deer in the head of the herring, in the tail of the speckled salmon.

May the man of this clothing never be wounded, may torn he never be;

What time he goes into battle or combat, May the sanctuary shield of the Lord be his.

This is not second clothing and it is not thigged, nor is it the right of sacristan or of priest.

Cresses green culled beneath a stone, and given to a woman in secret.

The shank of the deer in the head of the herring, in the tail of the speckled salmon.

BIBLIOGRAPHY

Anderson, Fred. *Crucible of War.* New York: Vintage Books, Random House, 2000.

Belknap, Jeremy. *The History of New Hampshire.* Boston: Stephens, Ela & Wadleigh, 1784.

Bisset, Robert. *The History of the Reign of George III to the Termination of the Late War.* Philadelphia: Levis and Weaver, 1810.

Bourke, Angela. *The Burning of Bridget Cleary.* Middlesex, Harmondsworth: Penguin; New York: Viking, 2000.

Campbell, J. F. *Popular Tales of the West Highlands, Orally Collected.* Edinburgh: Edmonston and Douglas, 1858 to 1877.

Carmichael, Alexander. *Carmina Gadelica.* Edinburgh: T. and A. Constable, 1900.

Evans, Elizabeth. *Weathering the Storm: Women of the American Revolution.* New York: Charles Scribner's Sons, 1975.

Fischer, David Hackett. *Albion's Seed: Four British Folkways in America.* New York: Oxford University Press, 1989.

Foster, William Henry. *The Captors' Narrative: Catholic Women and Their Puritan Men on the Early American Frontier.* Ithaca and London: Cornell University Press, 2003.

French, Allen. *The Day of Concord and Lexington.* Concord, Massachusetts, 1925.

Halliwell, James Orchard, Esq, F.R.S. *A Dictionary of Archaic and Provincial Words,* vol. I, vol. II. London, 1852.

Hart, Avril, and Susan North. *Seventeenth- and Eighteenth-Century Fashion in Detail.* London: V&A Press, Victoria and Albert Museum, 2009.

Herbert, Kathleen. *Looking for the Lost Gods of England.* Norfolk, England, 1994.

Hudson, Charles. *History of the Town of Lexington, Middlesex County, Massachusetts, from Its First Settlement to 1868.* (Revised). Boston and New York: Houghton Mifflin, 1913.

Jolly, Karen Louise. *Popular Religion in Late Saxon England: Elf Charms in Context.* Chapel Hill: University of North Carolina Press, 1996.

Lawrence, Bill. *The Early American Wilderness as the Explorers Saw It.* New York: Paragon House, 1991.

Lillback, Peter A. *George Washington's Sacred Fire.* Bryn Mawr, Pennsylvania: Providence Forum Press, 2006.

Little, Benerson. *The Sea Rover's Practice: Pirate Tactics and Techniques, 1630–1730.* Washington, D.C.: Potomac Books, Inc., 2005.

McCullough, David. *1776.* New York: Simon & Schuster, 2005.

———. *John Adams.* New York: Simon & Schuster, 2001.

Meltzer, Milton. *The American Revolutionaries: A History in Their Own Words, 1750–1800.* New York: HarperCollins, Inc., 1987.

Nutting, Wallace. *Furniture of the Pilgrim Century, 1620 to 1720.* New York: Bonanza Books, 1921.

Paine, Thomas. *Common Sense.* Philadelphia: Rush, Bell, 1776.

Pollington, Stephen. *Leechcraft.* London: Anglo-Saxon Books, 2000.

Rogers, Woodes. *A Cruising Voyage Around the World: First to the South Seas Thence to the East-Indies and Homeward by the Cape of Good Hope.* London, 1712.

Schultz, Eric B., and Michael J. Tougias. *King Philip's War.* New York: W. W. Norton & Co., Inc., 1999.

Shattuck, Lemuel. *A History of the Town of Concord.* Boston: Russell, Odiorne and Co., 1835.

Smith, Captain John. *A Description of New England.* London: Humphrey Lownes, 1616.

Tyler, Moses Coit. *American Statesmen—Patrick Henry.* Boston and New York: Houghton Mifflin, 1887.

Ulrich, Laurel Thatcher. *Good Wives: Image and Reality in the Lives of Women in Northern New England, 1650–1750.* New York: Vintage Books, Random House, 1980.

Woodard, Colin. *The Republic of Pirates: Being the True and Surprising Story of the Caribbean Pirates and the Man Who Brought Them Down.* New York: Harcourt, 2007.

Yeats, W. B. *The Celtic Twilight.* Mineola, New York: Dover Edition, 2004 (London, 1902).